CW00496378

TUTANKHAMUN UNCOVERED

The Adventure Behind the Curse

Michael J. Marfleet

APEX PUBLISHING LTD

First published in Hardback in 2009 by

Apex Publishing Ltd

PO Box 7086, Clacton on Sea, Essex, CO15 5WN

www.apexpublishing.co.uk

Copyright © 2009 by Michael J. Marfleet
The author has asserted his moral rights

British Library Cataloguing-in-Publication Data
A catalogue record for this book
is available from the British Library

ISBN 1-906358-73-7
978-1-906358-73-0

All rights reserved. This book is sold subject to the condition, that no part of this book is to be reproduced, in any shape or form. Or by way of trade, stored in a retrieval system or transmitted in any form or by any means, electronic, mechanical, photocopying, recording, be lent, re-sold, hired out or otherwise circulated in any form of binding or cover other than that in which it is published and without a similar condition, including this condition being imposed on the subsequent purchaser, without prior permission of the copyright holder.

Typeset in 10pt Baskerville Win95BT

Production Manager: Chris Cowlin

Cover Design: Siobhan Smith

Printed in Great Britain by the
MPG Books Group, Bodmin and King's Lynn

This book is a work of fiction based on historical facts.
Names, characters, dialogue and incidents either
are products of the author's imagination, or are real and
interpreted through the author's imagination.
Any resemblance in detail to actual events and dialogue
of the time is entirely coincidental.

*To the family Marfleet,
past and present.*

Acknowledgements

Thanks are owed to my late father, who inspired me to write this novel; my wife, Elaine, for her persistent help and encouragement; my closest friends, for their helpful opinions and advice; Mr. Bankes of 'Bankes Books' in Bath, Avon, who was kind enough to permit me to include a short vignette on a late friend who had met Carter; Mr. R. Partridge, editor of 'Ancient Egypt' magazine, for his technical guidance; to those scholars who through their studies and writings provided the research material that made this novel possible, (all are listed in the bibliography); and to Howard Carter - had the discovery fallen to a lesser man I have no doubt the peoples of the world would not now be enjoying riches so complete.

Introduction

Perhaps more than any other in history Howard Carter was personally responsible for accelerating the reality of an ancient, lost civilization into worldwide public centre stage. But the traditions of his time limited any meaningful degree of official recognition for his achievements and, in the traditions of his time, the man quietly and modestly accepted this fact.

At his work, however, he was never 'quiet', nor was he 'modest'. He was brave, committed, focused, patient, disciplined, accomplished, unyielding, unforgiving, confident, methodical, meticulous, arrogant, out-spoken and stubbornly tactless. During his lifetime these last three 'qualities', along with his humble origins, were more than any other responsible for the lack of official acknowledgment from his home country. Happily there has been much acknowledgment since. Let us hope he can hear it.

This is Howard Carter's story and the story of him whom he tenaciously sought and ultimately found. There is drama, humour and tragedy in the pages that follow, but above all, for those who seek it, there is knowledge.

Three final points:
* This is a work of fiction based upon fact. I have tried to honour the reported facts and the scholarly conjectures.
* Largely because the Egyptian hieroglyphs transliterate only to consonants there is no right way to spell any Egyptian word much less correctly pronounce it. The selection of the interceding vowels is the privilege of modern interpreters. In all cases the order of the consonants, transliterated from the original ancient Egyptian, is identical. The boy king's nomen is a case in point. There are several variants in the literature, probably the most extravagant of which is 'Touatankhamanou', by Gaston Maspero, Director General of the Egyptian Antiquities Service from 1881 to 1886 and 1899 to 1914. In this narrative the nomen is spelled two ways: In the chapters

following the life and times of Howard Carter it is spelled as Carter had spelled it in his popular work, 'Tutankhamen'; in the chapters concerning the boy king it is spelled in its other most common western form, 'Tutankhamun'.

* Terms/names used in the text are explained in the Glossary.

Michael J. Marfleet
Carmel Valley, California
February, 2005

Putney Vale Cemetery, 6th March, 1939...

The end of winter and the beech trees remain leafless, their dark, bony arms silhouetted against a featureless grey sky. The grass lies uncut, brown, damp, thickly matted. The drab gravestones, lined up in serried ranks, are scabbed with lychen and variously tilt with age - some ornately extravagant and hung with old, dew-heavy cobwebs; others plain, careful memorials, inscribed with deeply familial but quietly simple remembrances. All about, announcing regeneration, the daffodils are in glorious full bloom. Resplendent bunches of them grace the spaces between the roots of the old trees.

As the small party of mourners leaves the cemetery, one of the ladies trailing somewhat behind turns to look back at the grave site. The rude mound does not stand out amongst the profusion of others around it. Were it not for the few colourful floral tributes laid upon the rise of freshly dug earth it would be totally indistinguishable from any other.

"A common departure for so uncommon a man," she whispers.

Yet, other than his commonplace appearance, there had been little of the ordinary in this man. And, although the lady admirer herself is unable to observe it, his departure had been no less unusual than his extraordinary life...

The First Chapter
An Ending

The general chose his time in the ninth year of Pharaoh Tutankhamun's reign. Events seemed to be falling into what might be recognised, by those inside the royal circle at least, as a natural order. The Pharaoh had fallen ill, to all appearances with 'the sickness' - the same lethal pestilence that had struck the royal family and the people a dozen or so years earlier. Shortly following his return from the forbidden city he had complained of headaches and nausea. And there was some bleeding from the nose. Ever since he had come of age the young king, from time to time, had suffered from nosebleeds, occasionally prolonged. The form of assassination the general had designed should, with care, go undetected.

Tutankhamun was attended at his sickbed by those closest to him: his wife, his bedservants, his principal advisers - Parannefer, the high priest; Maya, who as treasurer held the purse strings of the kingdom; Ay, uncle of Akhenaten, the now long dead heretic pharaoh and father to Tutankhamun's queen; the vizier, Nakht, administrator to the Pharaoh's household and of Thebes; and General Horemheb, his military chief.

The priest was close to four cubits in height; a tall, spare, ageing man still with much of his own hair; a strict, inflexible man, controlled by his office and his beliefs, unyielding and often unkind in his discipline. Parannefer was so locked within his faith - as all would expect him to be - that were his sickly king not to recover, his most pressing need, in this land so familiar with the cruel hand of premature death, would be to ensure the survival and safe passage of his regent's spirit through the treacherous labyrinth of the afterlife and into the eternal embrace of Osiris.

The treasurer was a sage man, somewhat shorter than the priest but well built, and younger looking. Maya was Tutankhamun's father figure, deeply trusted, the man from whom the boy king actively sought advice - the king's mentor and instructor - and he truly loved this king for himself, not just his majesty.

Pharaoh Akhenaten's uncle was diminutive; he was old and he was frail, but also he was revered, for, although it was unlikely that his age would permit him, in the absence of issue from the royal pair, Ay was closest in blood line to the throne.

The vizier was a somewhat sheepish man, subserviently agreeable to his master but unsympathetically direct with his underlings. He was more under the control of the general than the young Pharaoh. This little man

1

was most noted for the high standard of his personal stable. The general had always admired and hungrily envied the invariable quality of his harem. How this tiny, inconsequential piece of humanity could command such a beautiful retinue was beyond understanding. To keep this affectionate herd so close about him hidden within him somewhere he must have something far greater than his looks or personality.

And so we come to General Horemheb. He was - most who knew him would agree - an ugly man: short, squat, fat, remarkably repulsive in appearance and in nature, a man short on endearment, long on avarice. His fat lips curled slightly upward on one side of his face giving him a persistent leer; his nose was small and flat, the nostrils broad and prominent; his cheeks were puffy and oblate; his trumpet-like ears so large they protruded from beneath his wig; his eyes barely opened - they were black, just distinguishable from within the slits of his eyelids which themselves appeared to open from the bottom as well as the top, rather like those of a crocodile. The general's personal appearance reflected the obscenity of his ambition. What he lacked of the elegantly slim, tall stature of Parannefer and the physically robust form of Maya, he doubly made up for in the energy of his malevolence. Holding no illusions about his physical appearance the general set himself to things he could more easily control. Things that would bring him the power to transcend his physical inelegance. In life he was already powerful enough to obtain for himself all that he wished. But there were more important things in death - the guarantee of a richly blissful eternity that could only accompany the burial of the Pharaoh.

The general had long held personal aspirations for the throne, but by publicly visible natural accession, not by force of arms. Up to this point his scheming had succeeded. He had succesfully conspired to ensure there were no living offspring from his regents' union. Just a few weeks ago he had, through another, tried unsuccessfully to dispatch the king by a contrived accident. Now, to his great good fortune, the stage seemed set for a further attempt. This time he would see to it himself.

And he was preparing ground far beyond these ugly acts. He had been slowly but steadily maturing the matrimonial connection that, through the female blood line, should ultimately confirm his ascendancy. He had even thought beyond the coronation. To cement his pharaonic security and seal the inevitability of his eternal afterlife he would appease the people and the gods by razing the forbidden city built by the dead heretic. He would extinguish all visible evidence of that reign and wipe out any memory of the new religion that had, in the event, served only to destabilise the kingdom and confuse its people. Outwardly, to the people and the priesthood, the boy king's death would become a natural physical manifestation of the gods' displeasure at his clandestine return to that place. His passing should be fitting exorcism for their anger. But first the general must play villain again.

2

Isolated in a nearby valley in the desert not far beyond the belt of abundant vegetation and cultivation on the other side of the great river lay the tiny, closely enclosed village of Pademi. At the northern end of the single alleyway that ran the length of the stone-built village the pale orange light of oil lamps flickered in the open windows of Hammad's bar.

Parneb, the village scribe, basked in the uniqueness of his exalted educated position - not only a writer for the illiterate hundreds but also the accounting controller of the tomb builders. He was to all the residents of Pademi, if not the most respected, the most important and powerful man in the village. For all that, however, he was still one of the boys, well known for his appetite for the ladies and a regular fixture at the local drinking hole.

Desire kindled by lotus scent fought the heaviness of alcohol. With his elbows firmly planted on the table before him, and his chin supported in his cupped hands, he gazed languidly over a cup of date wine at the Nubian seated opposite.

"A beer... A beer for your thoughts, Ugele," he stammered.

Ugele, master mason, a tall, lanky black man from the southern regions and settled in the village these last several years, had three empty jars in front of him. "Oh... Nothing. The beer thinks, not me. But yes, I'll take another. You have been here some time, scribe. You have yet more for barter?"

"I have bread... Plenty of it. My wife has been industrious - as plentiful as she is in the begetting of my children - may the gods bless her. Hammad is in need of bread."

The scribe eyed up one of the washer women who was being more than usually attentive to the landlord behind the bar. In close embrace with Hammad she glanced over the landlord's shoulder and caught Parneb's eye.

"In the grip of thighs," he moaned whistfully.

"Mmmm?" murmured Ugele, not really listening.

"Women," mumbled the scribe, dismissing the wanton female with a turn of his head. He thought a moment and, staring intently at his friend eye to eye, he continued, "Ugele... You know me. I have been around - to places and amongst women you would not dream of..."

'Nor, perhaps, wish to', thought the black man.

"...I have some advice for you. Advice you should heed..." Parneb nodded as if to drive the point home with his forehead. He leaned closer to his comrade. "...Love your wife in the house - wholly and rightly. Fill her belly and clothe her back. Oil for annointing is the medicine for her limbs. Make her heart rejoice as long as you live - she is a field profitable to her lord. Enter not into disputes with her - she will withdraw herself before violence and sulk. Make her to prosper permanently in your house. If you are hostile to her she will become objectionable. Attempt not to direct her in her own house when you know she is an excellent housewife. Say not to her 'Where is that thing? Bring it to me' when she has set it in its proper place. Watch her with your eye and hold your tongue - then you will be able to appreciate her wise and prudent management. How happy you will be if you go forth hand in hand with her. Many are the men who do not understand this. The man who interferes in his house only stirs up confusion and never finds himself real master - in any matter!"

Ugele could hardly believe his ears. 'His wife has caught him philandering again. Such hypocrisy! The man must be drunk!' The black man returned, "Scribe, I know not what brought on this bout of philosophy, but it seems poorly chosen. You preach but you do not practise what you preach. So I have some words for you...

"Firstly, if you wish to maintain a permanent friendship in the house to which you are in the habit of going, whether as master, brother or friend or, in fact, to any place to which you have entry, strive against associating with the women there. The place that they frequent is not good for you. Only an imprudent man would follow them.

"Secondly, remember, a thousand men have been destroyed in the quest for what is beautiful. A man is made a fool of by their dazzling limbs. The pleasure lasts but for a brief moment - even as a dream - and when it is ended a man finds death through having experienced it.

"Thirdly, guard well against the strange woman who is not known in your quarter of the town. Do not cast longing glances at her. Have no intercourse with her, of any sort or kind whatsoever - you know what I mean - she is deep trouble, and where her currents may lead no man knows.

"And lastly, remember, in particular, when a woman whose husband is absent from her reveals her charms and beckons you to her every day and says there is no one present to bear witness and so arranges her net to snare you, you must resist. For a married man to harken to her is a most abominable deed which surely merits the penalty of death - even if she does not succeed in her objective!" (*Quotations of Ptah-hetep, the sage, and the scribe, Ani. See Budge, 1926.*)

The scribe was dumb struck. He had not faced so direct and eloquent a lecture before; least of all from an artisan, a man who worked stone. Speechless to respond in any meaningful way, he shrugged his shoulders and promptly changed the subject.

"We are rekhit, you and I, and should behave accordingy."

"Rekhit. Hrrmph. Rekhit in caste, but little more than aperu in deed. Most of us are forever grubbing around in the dust and heat. You less so because of your learning - clean, fresh papyrus and good inks - there is much honour in the knowledge and application of writing. I envy you, Parneb... And your ability to irritate the competent artisan at your every whim!"

"I cannot help it if you and your men keep losing your tools. I have my masters, too. The priesthood is unforgiving. You should have my problems. It is I who must satisfactorily explain the misdemeanours of your team. I have to deal with the likes of Parranefer. I'd like to see you try that just once!

We each have a job to do. Mine just happens to be, among other things, one of control. It's no fun being the perpetual bad guy."

"We do not make you so. You should take your job less seriously... Where's that beer you promised me?" The black man banged his fist down on the table between them.

Parneb signalled to Hammad.

"...And how about one for me?" The new arrival was a short, spare man - all sinew and bones it seemed, but not at all weak for all that. The apparent frailty of his body belied the strength of his character and the power of his will.

"Dashir! The gods be with you. We thought you were working the foundry this night."

"No, not this night. Mentu has taken my place at the foundry. Tonight I am to work my wife. She has summoned me. She feels the fertile time. I fear she will have me work very hard this night. I am, therefore, in need of drink!"

"Count your blessings. Would that my wife were so inclined! I fear she has closed that particular avenue off to me for ever. I fear her tunnel is as dry as an old brick!"

"Count my blessings? Aye... perhaps," Dashir sighed. "But there is no sport in it any more. The mechanics of it have made it a mundane pastime. Hours of anticipation - days sometimes - all over in a few brief seconds. But, I admit, the tunnel of my sister is not dry! At least, tonight it will not be so!"

The three men laughed together, as the beers arrived.

"Tell me," enquired the lecherous Parneb, eager to get the details, "what will she wear tonight to excite your loins?"

"Not a lot!" Dashir answered, grinning. "But I hope she doesn't scent herself up as she is sometimes wont to do. In my passion I am likely to grab her hair and the cursed stuff gets all over you. Uncomfortable afterwards. Difficult to get to sleep with wax hardening in your creases. Know what I mean?"

Experienced nods from the other two.

Dashir's tale of anticipation had taken a firm hold on the attentions of his colleagues. Parneb leaned forward. As he was about to press for more information he felt a strong hand take a grip on his shoulder. He turned to look up into the face of his close neighbour, the master carpenter in the village, standing over him with a jar of beer in his other hand.

"Meneg! Didn't see you here. What kept you?"

"The gods be with you all. Been talking outside with the spirits of my parents. It is a lovely night. Osiris is bright within the glittering firmament."

"Ah. The gods protect them. Come, sit. Dashir entertains us with personal secrets! Haven't had this much fun for months! Be seated and hush!"

"Neither has Dashir!" acknowledged Ugele. "We wouldn't be being treated to this insight were he not in such an extreme state of excitement in expectation of what - he assures us - lies in wait for him later this night!"

The fat carpenter winked at the goldsmith.

Dashir blinked back. By this time he had consumed several beers and was having trouble focusing.

"Where...? Where am...? Where was I?"

"The wax was drying in your creases," said Parneb.

"Ah," Dashir acknowledged. "Most uncomfortable. Quite takes the edge off the passion."

"Softens the complexion, though," followed Ugele, grinning.

"Ah. That it does... That it does. Devilish crisp, however, and a devil of a job to remove when you get it on the member..."

The group laughed.

"...Especially when it dries before you lose your hardness," observed Dashir.

Their laughter became louder.

"What's going on over there?" Hammad yelled from behind the bar. "Quieten it down will you? We'll have the priests among us."

Parneb ignored the landlord. "You, Dashir? Are you trying to tell us you do not lose your hardness easily? Come on, man... You are but a frail thing, not the likes of myself or Ugele - we have real trouble losing our hardness!"

"Speak for yourself," said the black man. "My hardness is my affair. As should it be for every man. You talk about it like the washer women! An end to this nonsense. An end to the beer. I am to my bed."

"Me too," said the goldsmith with renewed urgency.

"Don't over extend yourself now," said Parneb. "But, if in the event you do not rise to the occasion, remember, I am just two doors down - be glad to help."

Dashir raised his fist as if to strike the scribe but Meneg's large right hand closed around his wrist. "Indeed, master goldsmith, it is time for bed. We all wish you the strength to create."

He and Ugele bundled the drunken Dashir out into the street and guided him to his front door.

Back at Hammad's, Parneb tilted back on his stool and rested his back against the wall. That washer woman was looking at him again.

The death of Pharaoh Akhenaten, the great builder and heretic, had occurred eleven years earlier. Akhenaten had reigned for eighteen years, some of them in co-regency with his father, Amenophis III, whose steadily declining health had rendered him not incapable of reliably carrying out his kingly duties, just less interested in doing so. The old Pharaoh preferred the duties of the bedroom. In his later years, successful unions brought him two further sons, the first through his chief wife. They named him Smenkhkare. The second came some twelve years later, through one of his younger wives. This latter issue came to be called Tutankhaten.

Not long after taking power, Akhenaten set about accelerating the religious changes his father had initiated. By order of their primary physical deity - Pharaoh - the fundamental basis for religious belief that had held the Egyptian people together for as long as they could remember was about to be torn from them.

For time immemorial there had been a multitude of gods, each with its own specialisation - a god for every need. The father, Amenophis III, revered by the people for his heroic deeds in foreign lands and believed to have single-handedly engineered the consistency of maat in Upper and Lower Egypt, had skilfully manipulated the introduction of the sun disc, the Aten, already deified in a number of different guises. Publicly the Pharaoh had gone no further than this. Within the confines of the palace, however, worship of the Aten had become a daily ritual. Preparation for ultimate succession and education in affairs of state were the responsibility of the next in line, Prince Thutmosis. The mind of the Pharaoh's second son, Akhenaten, shy, slight in build, sensitive and impressionable, was not occupied with these matters. Akhenaten had the opportunity, the time and the inclination to become totally absorbed in the new cult. He devoted every moment of his otherwise idle immature life to its study and received fulfilment through worship.

However, the unexpectedly premature death of his elder brother flung him headlong into kingship - an office for which by design he was totally unprepared. But his infatuation with his sole deity shielded him from fear of this new position. Within just a short time of becoming Pharaoh, Akhenaten proclaimed to his people that from now on there would be just one all-powerful god, the god of the sun disc, the Aten, who blessed and protected his people with his gentle, warming rays. He became represented in the stone reliefs of temples everywhere as a disc, its rays of light falling on the royal family and ending in open hands to caress them with warmth and profer them gifts of health and long life. Akhenaten was consumed by his faith. Administration of the great Egyptian state and empire was subordinate to worship and, surely, better left to lesser mortals.

Nowhere would the god be more exalted than at Aten's birthplace, Akhetaten, 'the city without equal', which the Pharaoh conceived, designed and had built for him and where the Pharaoh, his family and his entourage could live out their lives in the sun god's blissful care. The site the heretic chose to build this crucible of the one faith lay on the Nile about half way between Thebes and Memphis. It was three or more days' good sailing downstream from Thebes. The new city rose up from the dust of the virgin desert. It was built on a broad plain held close in the embrace of a bow-shaped arc of cliffs and hills on the east bank, at the doorstep of the sunrise. It became a land in itself - beautiful, colourful, verdant and self-contained within its natural borders; a sacred, land-locked island unlike any other in Egypt; a city literally planned from the ground up on a grid dictated by the daily passage of the solar disc; a city of unmatchable beauty, with massive buildings and exceptional, lively art.

Akhenaten's creation became a magnificent tribute to his faith, but the Aten heresy, as it came to be known, did little to protect the people of Egypt. The Pharaoh gave no attention to the stewardship of his kingdom. There were insurrections, border problems, failed military campaigns, corruption in government, chaos in the bureaucracy and worse - towards the end of Akhenaten's reign a great plague had descended on the land; 'the sickness' everyone called it.

The royal family were not immune, nor the Pharaoh himself. Akhenaten's wives had died one by one. His queen, the beautiful Nefertiti, mother to most of his children, was the second of the royal family to succumb to the illness. All but one of his remaining daughters had died, almost year on year. And, after just three years in power, his brother, Smenkhkare, who had succeeded Akhenaten on his death, was himself lost to the same vile hand.

Through this unhappy litany the much younger half-brother, Tutankhaten, ascended the throne at the tender age of eight. He was betrothed to Akhenaten's sole surviving daughter, Ankhesenpaaten. And she, of pure royal blood but yet a child, became his chief wife, cementing the succession.

Too young to rule without a guardian, the child Pharaoh was easily manipulated into returning to the old religious order. Thereby his elders could restore a sense of foundation and normality to the country, appease the gods, and lift the deadly veil of fever from the land. His old and trusted uncle, Ay, previously Master of the Horse for Akhenaten, had helped and guided Tutankhaten through this religious metamorphosis. To signal rejection of the sun god and properly reflect the old ways, he had the young king's name changed to Tutankhamun and that of his queen to Ankhesenamun.

But Ay himself had been manipulated. Through his earlier campaigns General Horemheb had become a man of some influence. His well-publicised exploits had made him popular with the people. A powerful and strong-charactered man he had made sure he had more public visiblity than any of his contemporaries at court. He anticipated a profitable return from these vignettes.

For some time Horemheb had sensed conditions were developing that could ultimately see him placed on the pharaonic throne. The people were anxious for a complete break from the past - to return fully to their old, traditional ways of worship. While this was slowly being achieved through the boy king and under the guidance of Ay, it was clear to Horemheb that until the entire Akhenaten blood line had been wiped out the people's fearful memory of the great heretic would remain. Reminders were everywhere - the physical presence of the dynasty was all too clearly represented in the monuments, the most blatant statement of which lay in the now deserted forbidden city. And then there was the boy king himself... his queen... and Ay, come to that. They were all more or less related. Only the general could claim to be totally and cleanly separated by blood. With any of the others in place, a sense of return to the old ways would be in name but not in substance. The end of the family would bring an end to 'the sickness' and would leave an expectant and leaderless populace willing and eager to accept a new line of authority so long as it appeared totally unconnected with the former. He saw the opportunity and would grab it with both hands. This he must do before too long, lest the new king managed to endear himself to his people. Time is a great healer and might permit such acceptance. The boy king had been on the throne eight years already. The general would have to act soon.

Successful longevity of pharaonic power comes with ordered ascendancy, not force of arms. The general knew that. He had no wish to risk destabilising the empire. He was too advanced in years himself to cope with controlling the inevitable patchy uprisings that such a move might generate; too much work; too much distraction from the pleasures of being a god. To accomplish a visibly natural flow towards his ultimate coronation Horemheb would have to design and execute a sequence of events that on their outcome would, in the eyes of the people and particularly the priestly household, naturally place him in the accession. The young king must die at some point before he came of age, certainly before he became able and assertive enough to govern effectively alone.

These evil conspiracies notwithstanding, the general would see to it that the king had the noblest of burials. After all his brother, Smenkhkare, Pharaoh for only a brief time, had had a lavish funeral, although expediency had dictated a severely understated tomb. To appease the people's inevitable grief and distance himself from suspicion in the forthcoming conspiracy, the general would see to it that no expense would be spared. Appearances were everything, and he would act out the charade to the very end.

The general did not plan to take the throne immediately upon the boy king's passing. Ay, the natural successor to a king with no issue, was ageing and surely would expire within a short time of his coronation. And with the succession of Ay, any suspicion that Horemheb had anything to do with the boy king's death would appear farcical. With a judicious marriage the general would then become the only choice. So first he must woo and secure to himself the 'correct' chief wife.

There was, however, at least one unpredictable element in this design - the queen, Ankhesenamun. Young, exquisitely beautiful and ambitious, she would not willingly yield her regal status. Doubtless craving for confirmation of permanency, she would swiftly seek to remarry. But to whom? Who would have the stature to assume the dead Pharaoh's place? Horemheb himself, perhaps? But no such marriage could be contemplated. Ankhesenamun had hated him ever since she first set eyes on him. His manner, deceitful and condescending, betrayed his cause and belied trust. Besides, for the general, marriage to her was unthinkable - she was of the blood line of the heretic.

Horemheb was well aware of the queen's feelings towards him. She had made no secret of them. He would bide his time and remain vigilant to her every mood.

Above all, he had to be sure that during the young king's lifetime there would be no issue from their union. In the fifth year of the king's reign the general had become uncomfortably anxious when Ankhesenamun first became pregnant.

As was the custom and belief, to ward off the evil spirits that may do harm to her unborn child, the queen had festooned herself with lucky amulets of all kinds. But to no avail. To his relief she had miscarried having sustained a fall while descending the steps of the temple during the harvest religious festivities. The tiny foetus of just five months' gestation was now mummified and lay within a diminutive plain wooden box laid to rest in the palace in a secret place known only to the queen and king themselves.

The second time she found herself with child, the pregnancy lasted longer and the general grew anxious. She appeared far too healthy for his liking. Horemheb was not about to risk waiting for what this time could well turn out to be a normal birth and an unquestioned heir.

A plague had infested Pademi, the village of the tomb-workers, situated across the river from the palace. The artisans, most of whom lived in this village and many of whom were painters, had become reduced so much in ranks that a great deal of commissioned work, both in tomb preparation and palace decoration, was running behind schedule. The illness appeared to be easily passed on through casual contact with those infected but not yet showing outward signs of ill health. For those living in Thebes it was fortunate that the affected population was contained on the west side of the river. They had little choice in the matter. The general had posted guards along the river bank to police the normal crossing points.

But now he saw opportunity in the pestilence and decided to take a major gamble. Although he would have to trust to chance taking a fateful turn, the plan he had contrived would, if successful, provide a cleaner outcome than the more drastic and, for him, necessarily more dangerous measures he would be forced to take should the coincidences he was hoping to assemble not transpire as planned.

At this time Ankhesenamun was having the chambers that would house the new baby painted with inscriptions and amuletic illustrations intended to embolden the gods in protection of the child and guarantee its health, wealth and happiness throughout its forthcoming privileged life. Gilding was to follow completion of the painting and for this an artist expert in his trade would have to be summoned from the west bank.

When the queen asked Horemheb to send for the man, the general went as far as he dared in his apparent attempt to dissuade her from placing herself, the king and her unborn child in danger of falling ill from the affliction that was by now well established throughout the workforce. Happily for him, the queen was adamant that the work be completed in time for the royal birth. If the inscriptions were not in place in their full glory by the time she came into labour, she stated, the gods would not be present to protect the child at its earliest and most fragile time. She explained the obvious. She could not slow down the pregnancy. She was quite evidently very large with child. Horemheb was gratified that she had delivered so compelling an argument. He could find no reasonable further course but to agree reluctantly to her demands. It would allow the fateful events that should follow to take their course sadly but naturally and with no apparent thread of evil.

The general had the artisan smuggled across the river late that night. The man looked gaunt, as did nearly all the villagers, but he appeared fit nevertheless and Horemheb could only hope the maleficent parasite was already within him, dormant but about to waken.

Dashir was over awed by his first meeting with the queen. It was most unusual for a commoner such as he to be introduced to anyone in a position of power, let alone a member of the royal family.

When he was brought into her presence the queen was sitting on a golden, throne-like chair, her feet resting on a low stool. She had two hand maidens on either side, one fanning her with an ostrich-plumed staff, the other holding a tray of fruit and a vessel of water. She was wearing a perfume cone upon her wig. The wax had congealed in the hair from the heat of the day and the scent of it was thick in the air. It was secured by a golden and blue glass inlaid diadem which surrounded her head, the uraes, the regal cobra, reaching up from it in the middle of her forehead. The densely plaited black wig framed her face. Large golden earlobe pendants hung either side of her cheeks. Around her neck she wore a collar of hollow gold and coloured glass beads. Her dress was of fine pleated white linen, which fell almost in a single piece to her ankles. On her feet she wore rush sandals embroidered with delicate gold thread and embellished with more coloured glass beads. Her arms, resting on the arms of her chair, were naked but for two large gold bracelets. On the fingers of her slender hands were four gold rings - two with the cartouche of her husband; two with her own name.

The entire picture was so different from anything that Dashir had previously beheld that he felt compelled to fall to his knees and bow to the floor.

The queen acknowledged his salute by calling for him to raise his head but remain on his knees. She sat bolt upright, her head held high, and looked directly at him as she spoke. "You have been selected for your special skills, goldsmith. You have been selected to create beauty. Beauty which it will please the gods to behold. Please them so that they may grant long life and good health to this, my son." She placed her right hand on her swollen belly.

"It is you who will do this according to my instruction. Should you fail in my bidding, should your work not please the gods, should my son become sick and die, likewise you will suffer his pain."

Dashir worked hard. The queen watched him closely. She would touch his work, and complain that the gold leaf was not adhering well to the wooden frame of the texts, tear it off and throw it at him. He would fall to his knees before her and with his arms outstretched beg her forgiveness.

"I am nervous in your ever present eye, oh Great One," he would say. "My hand, though skilful, is not steady in the light you throw upon me. Some sleep tonight will strengthen me."

The queen let Dashir leave early that evening. While the power of her status could inflict anything on him and his family that she might wish, she knew his skills well and did not want to extinguish the creative flame within him. It was he who had gilded the magnificent statues now erected in her father's tomb.

That night when she and her king had retired to their chambers early, Dashir, not at all confident that the queen, during her waking hours, would ever leave him alone long enough to complete his work successfully, stole back into the palace with the help of his servant friends and, by the light of candles, set to his work with renewed vigour.

The following morning, to Ankhesenamun's astonishment and consummate delight, the gilding had been completed. The painted texts were framed in a glitter of bright gold. The gods surely would be compelled to visit the newborn and protect him from all dangers.

To Horemheb's disappointment, Dashir had left in seemingly jubilant mood and excellent good health. The queen was equally enthralled with the completed work and, in the general's eyes, all who shouldn't be feeling so good were in reality in far better spirits than they had been before they had met.

As things turned out, it was Horemheb himself who felt off colour. That night a feeling of nausea overcame him and, unusually for him, he took neither food nor drink nor woman. He did not sleep, notwithstanding. No sooner had he rested back upon his couch than an uncontrollable energy sprang up within his bowels. The malevolent organism had such power that, although he tried to hold it back ultimately he was forced to deliver the rising issue into an alabaster fruit bowl lying adjacent to the bed. There was little relief from this evacuation. The movement was repeated quickly and, as his servants busied themselves frantically with collecting up the mess left by his first outburst, he propelled himself towards his toilet chambers with a speed and strength of purpose the like of which he had never before exhibited, even on the battlefield. The repetitive retching stayed with him all night and into the following day and night and the day after that. Although there was nothing to bring up but the water he tried to drink, the body continued to pump itself dry until finally there was no strength left within his aching frame to respond to the demands of the tormenting creature that lay within him.

Horemheb lay exhausted and mindless on his stinking bed. He ached for the blessed relief of oblivion. But the creature inside him was restless and the general once again found himself urgently attempting to respond to its demands by evacuating the remainder of his rapidly shrinking organs. Unfortunately for all present, this would invariably occur while he was in flight towards his toilet. There were few in the room that a piece of him did not touch.

Later in Horemheb's life, when he himself would be king, those who had shared the dreadful experience would feel themselves blessed with the intimacy of his foul touch - but not this day.

It was ten days before the general had recovered strength sufficient to show an interest in the normal affairs of state. His first and most important news brought an imperceptibly wry smile. The queen had given premature birth three days earlier. The baby was weakly and was not expected to survive the ordeal, but the mother was recovering well. He asked that his thanks for her survival be given to the gods that evening in a special ceremony and, with anticipation, smugly eased his aching body back into the cushions of his couch.

All but Ankhesenamun were appeased. Another tiny wooden box would become secreted away into a dark place within the palace.

On the night that Horemheb had chosen to deliver Tutankhamun, a rare but not unusually severe belt of electrical storms was moving over the Theban vicinity. The accompanying rains were torrential. Where the soil was unvegetated, the sand and rocks were quickly loosened and fell from the bare cliffs, driving down the ravines in a thick, red, boiling holocaust of boulders and mud. That night Pharaoh Ahmose's tomb was lost beneath the sediment blanket left by the flood waters and three luckless tomb robbers in the act of plundering it became entrapped and suffocated - by nature itself condemned, sentenced and summarily executed for their crimes.

The sickly king parted from his queen early that evening. She had lain with him a while and tried to stimulate him with lotus blossoms, her hands and her mouth, but he complained he was completely spent and had no energy to linger with her.

In the din of the thunder and the rain lashing against the walls of the palace, Horemheb walked to the king's quarters and, saying that he wished to leave an amulet with the Pharaoh to assure the king a good night's rest, commanded the Nubian sentinels to let him in. He paused on the threshold for a moment. It occurred to him that Seth in his wisdom was his protector this night. The general strode purposefully into the room. The noise of the large cedar doors closing behind him was drowned out by the thunder above.

The king had been given an additional sleep potion that evening to ensure he rested fully through to the morning. Horemheb had seen to that. Although all the halls were open to the sky, the king would not be disturbed by the cacophony of thunder and the rattle of the continuous downpour splattering on the floors. Should the Pharaoh awaken during the act of murder, the noise of the storm would be sufficient to extinguish his cries.

Since his design was to appear to have discovered the king in death, the general could avoid suspicion only by being brief. He hurried over to the king's bedside and drew a long, narrow, copper rod from his tunic.

Tutankhamun was asleep on his stomach with his face towards the left. Horemheb bent close and carefully positioned the palm of his left hand with the rod lying on it such that one end was aligned with the entrance to the king's right nostril. He knew he could not introduce it slowly; there was too much risk that the sensation would rouse the king, even from his induced stupor. Worse still, any slight movement of the king's head might cause the rod to penetrate the cartilage. Were there any visible perforation of the skin, the entire conspiracy would be exposed. Horemheb had to be quick and he had to be accurate. He clenched the opposite end of the rod tightly with his left fist, checked that the shaft was still in line with the right nostril, and struck firmly with his right hand.

In one immediate movement, the rod drove up through the nasal tissue and perforated the thin skull wall, embedding itself in the brain mass. The young king's head jerked back violently, but he remained unconscious. The general gave the rod a quick twist and withdrew it. An urgent, sanguine flood issued onto the bed linen, turning it a sodden crimson in just a few seconds. Horemheb quickly wiped the rod on the bloody bed clothing, returned it under the material of his tunic, and ran to the chamber door shrieking for the guards as he went.

That infamous night all who observed the rapidly paling body in the bed chamber were quick to come to the same conclusion. The king's death was quite naturally attributed to his known malady - this time a massive haemorrhaging, probably precipitated by his fever. No one, outwardly at least, suspected any wrong doing, let alone any thought that the general could have been instrumental in this horror. After all, he had been in the chamber only moments enough to discover the ailing king's predicament.

The shock at the sudden death of the young king spread rapidly about the halls of the palace. The wailing began. Horemheb realised he must take control of the situation.

"Look to your emotions!" he bellowed. "Our early departed lord would have no wish for hysteria. Give thanks that his ka still sleeps and may not hear you. We must set ourselves to the task of awakening him in eternal life. Summon Parannefer for the preparation. We must turn to Ay for leadership. Awaken the Pharaoh! Our new lord must be present at the cleansing."

14

"The queen, Excellency," said a maidservant timidly. "Who will tell the queen?"

"The queen?" The general turned and glared down at her.

She saw the anger in his face and a cold fear overcame her. The girl fell to her knees. Horemheb realised his error and took a deep breath. He smiled one of those forced, insincere grins that were so characteristic of him.

"Permit Queen Ankhesenamun the dignity of peaceful sleep until sunrise," he said obsequiously. "She shall grieve enough presently. No need to deny her rest as well. We must prepare the king such that she does not see the horror of his bloody state. Be about your business with haste!"

The girl bowed low to the ground and ran off with the others to get clean bedclothes.

Nakht, in charge of many things but above all the security of the king's quarters, was probably more worried than any. "There is no doubt it was the humour, right, General?"

"No doubt at all, Vizier. There can be no thought of foul play. Besides, the security forces under your command are beyond reproach, are they not?"

"Indeed, General, indeed. Trusty servants, indeed." Nakht gave one of his sheepish grins.

A scuffle at the entrance to the chamber caused both Horemheb and the vizier to turn their heads.

The old Ay, dragged hastily from the shallow sleep of the aged, was escorted into the king's private suite by two chambermaids. After briefly examining the body of the boy king he turned to those assembled about him, drew a deep breath and gravely pronounced his ascendancy. "My friends," he announced, "we have unhappily lost a sapling king and, deprived of his issue, gained an aged tree. All here know that as father of the great queen Nefertiti - the gods protect her - my blood is the purest of the regnal line. While my energies fail me in these, the shadowed years of my life - and, I fear, I will be no match for your expectations of our dear departed Tutankhamun - I shall nevertheless give of my best as you know me to have done in the recent past. In so doing I shall claim of you your strongest allegiance."

With the exception of Horemheb and his guards everyone present prostrated themselves before the Pharaoh designate. The 'protectors' never compromised their state of readiness.

"Rise people!" commanded Ay. "There is work to do. Our first and most immediate task is to assure our dear departed king safe embarkation on the ark that will bear him on his blissful, eternal voyage!"

The village of Pademi lay cradled in a shallow depression under the shadow of the pyramidal mountain. This great rock overlooked both the villagers and their place of work - The Valley. There, on the west side of the ridge, lay the resting place of kings long past. With the help of the villagers it was from here that the Pharaoh would begin his eternal journey through the paradise of afterlife.

This evening, as every evening, The Valley drank in the dying sun, and the spirits of those few who had survived uncorrupted danced on. For those who lived in the village, sunset always took on a deep significance. It was a time to pay tribute to their own dead. The modest tombs of their forebears lay clustered on the eastern side of the ridge, just above the village boundary wall.

Stooping like a man bearing a great weight on his shoulders, Meneg eased himself down onto his knees and positioned the small offering in the centre of the colourfully decorated alcove within the small pyramidal chapel. Every day near sunset he came from his house close by in Pademi. Every day near sunset he would leave a little something to aid his parents' survival in the underworld. Every day when he arrived at the spot he would find that the previous offering had gone, scavanged by the jackals and the vermine that infested the place. But he comforted himself in the belief that the kas of his parents first would have eaten and drunk their fill.

The old wood-worker whispered a short prayer and touched his lips with the fingers of both hands. Using his walking stick for support, he pulled himself back to a standing position, turned and walked down the slope towards the village.

He sat once more on the doorstep of his house and returned to his work. The evening shadows extended towards him across the narrow street. Old man that he was, it was with some difficulty that he crossed his legs to address more comfortably the inanimate object before him.

He was a man of slight build, but one of his more evident physical features included an incongruous oblate paunch that hung like a water bag over his loin cloth. The fingers of his large hands were artistically narrow, the skin toughened through years of woodworking. The toll of responsibility that accompanies a lifetime as master wood carver of the village showed in the lines cut deep within his thin face. Written in the creases about his eyes was the history of thousands of hours of squinting in bright sunlight and straining to pick out detail in the dimness of evening. Yet his eye for form and the dexterity of his hands were as true as ever.

The alleyway that ran by his door divided the enclosed village along its centre. Diminutive 'dolls' houses' of dwellings lay huddled so closely together on either side that they seemed to embrace one another, with just three or four rooms and a single door, each home sharing its boundary walls with its neighbours. The cobbles, polished smooth by the foot traffic of ages, glinted violet in the twilight. The evening air was thick with the pungent smell of kitchen ovens and the satisfying odour of freshly baked bread. At the darker end of the street Dashir and his gang, once again returned from their labours, were breaking the otherwise peaceful setting with the noise of their carousing amongst the ever energetic washer women in Hammad's bar.

Meneg looked down at the unfinished wooden figure in front of him and sighed. He had always strived to make his art of a quality that would match its celebration. Usually he had been filled with such inspirational strength that execution of the work was almost easy. But this time it was different. Since returning from his parents' chapel his lack of concentration had sent him back into the house for beer three times already, and this had done little to improve his demeanour or his sensibility. He felt tired, listless. Inspiration would have to come from somewhere and quickly, or ultimately he would answer to the general.

Ugele was on his way to join the evening action. He had had a hard and unsatisfactory day completing excavation of the new tomb in The Valley. Master mason he may have been, but it had been his turn these last few days to take his place in the long line of bodies passing baskets of debris from one to the other towards the tip on the valley flank. The supply of rock chippings seemed endless. There could be no indication of how near the tomb was to completion until the baskets stopped coming. He much preferred being within the bowels of the earth hacking at the limestone bedrock himself, watching the cavity take form and slowly grow before him. There he could sense progress.

His tired, long legs hung down loosely either side of the donkey's spare belly, almost reaching to the ground. They swung from side to side together following the animal's rolling gait. The donkey and its rider drew level with the figure squatting in the doorway.

The man stared with an expression of hopelessness at the freshly cut wooden object before him.

"The gods protect you, Meneg," Ugele greeted as man and beast ambled past.

"And you, Ugele," Meneg gestured back with a dispassionate wave of his hand.

"As I descended from The Valley I saw you praying at the remembrance shrine of Kha and Merit. You care for them well. Yours is a good family. They were good parents. They will be proud to have such a son."

"Aye. But no more than my sacred duty. They cared for me well. My sons will do so for me."

"Praise be to the gods," they both said.

"But enough of duty talk. How about a few beers with Dashir and the lads, Meneg? Parneb was on good form last night, was he not? Perhaps he will force a report from Dashir! Looks like you need the amusement as much as I."

"That is part of my problem," the old man replied. "I have drunk sufficient already this evening. I am far behind in my work. I cannot afford to waste what little light remains."

While the two had been conversing the donkey, with a full fodder bag and a night's rest ahead of it, and therefore being in no mood to dally, had continued on its way homeward. Ugele was already well past Meneg's doorway. The black man signalled back an acknowledgement with his hand, the donkey loped purposefully onward, and the two disappeared into the shadows.

Meneg continued his reflections. This dead king deserved only his very best work. The Pharaoh had achieved much in his short life. He had returned the order of life to godly sensibility. It was true to say that much of this had been dictated and controlled by the elders who had advised and instructed him in the ways of kingship during his most formative years, but the boy king nevertheless had willingly supported their recommendations. He had personally given orders for the work to be carried out. On the rare occasions that he had appeared in public he had pronounced his plans before all with lucidity, never once showng malice to Akhenaten, yet always looking to the future. A sense of optimism returned to the rank and file. Sadly his death came too quickly to establish any lasting memory. The people had not come to know him as a warrior. By the time of his passing he was barely a man. The coming celebration of his deliverance into the afterlife would be mixed with a pervasive lack of substance. Meneg and his colleagues would be guests at a funeral for a pharaoh they had hardly come to know. But the community would make sure that the burial and its associated ceremonies would be none the less for all that. Meneg's art, his skills, all he had learned and become accomplished in execution, all this was in service of the community, this monarch, past monarchs and, perhaps, monarchs yet to come. He must fulfil all expectations.

Meneg drew a long, heavier sigh and turned his eyes once again to the unfinished wood carving before him. Anubis the jackal, this great, wise animal god, would be guardian to the king's tomb. The old wood carver had executed such a piece many times before and ordinarily it presented no difficulty to him, but on this occasion he was without the passion he had felt in times past. As he steeled himself to continue his work, he looked towards the darkened pyramid of natural rock that dominated his skyline, its silhouette crisply cut against a backdrop of violet evening light.

Meneg blinked. He was tired and his eyes were having difficulty accommodating themselves to the closeness of the work, especially in the subdued twilight. Glancing up to absorb the remaining drops of sunlight he caught sight of a dark, slim figure moving with some determination across the entrance to the alleyway.

The jackal stopped and scratched itself. It stood still with ears erect, listening for any sound that might betray the ubiquitous rodent. At the same time it sniffed the air, searching the odours of the evening cook-fires. The dog's silhouette was poorly contrasted with the dim background of the closely packed houses, but as his eyes once more became accustomed to the dimness Meneg could clearly make out the familiar shape. Elegant in stature, slender of build - the pickings were slim for a scavanger in the desert - long and bushy of tail, aquinine in snout, large and erect stiletto-like ears - a fitting guardian to any king. Above all he was black, death black as the most moonless of nights. Observing the flowing lines of his live form helped lift Meneg's spirits.

The jackal turned its head to look down the street at the figure crouched behind the partially formed piece of wood. There was something familiar about the shape but no recognisable scent. As the animal turned its head forward once more, the light of an oil lamp in a nearby porch flushed the retina of one eye and, for an instant, a blood-red spot of light flashed back at Meneg.

Impressionable as always, a deep fear conjured within the old wood carver. 'The god speaks! The king on his funeral barque is impatient for his escort to the afterlife. He is angered at my slothfulness, at my carelessness, at my loss of purpose. This is a warning!'

As the dog loped away, the energy of fear welled within Meneg. He turned back to his work and picked up a scoop-shaped copper chisel. He instinctively tested it for sharpness with a stroke of his left thumb. A tiny bead of blood squeezed from the shallow cut. Meneg licked it with his tongue and set to work. The skilled, old hands began working around the chest of the figure, bringing the bones of the ribcage up in high, deliberate relief. A sublime confidence built within him. He felt the familiar inner assurance that, after all, the outcome of this work would be as good as any he had yet created.

This Anubis, black as pitch and elegantly lying on its charge, would watch over the king, protect his body and his disembowelled organs, and stand vigil beside the ark of his voyage through all eternity.

It was early spring. The Upper and Lower Niles would shortly have a new king, new rules and, in its own way in the order of things, a new way of life. The boy king was dead - murdered, some said - taken from his people prematurely after a reign of little more than early promise. Certainly it had been sudden - a terrible bleeding from the nose one night. He never awoke to cry out. And now there was much to be done and very little time.

As was the custom, the site for his tomb had been selected at the time of his coronation. The entrance had been cut at the base of the cliff face within the extreme upper reaches of The West Valley, closer to the sunset. But that had been only nine years ago. Excavation had been progressing without any sense of urgency. As the traditions of the period dictated, the design laid out lengthy corridors and intermittent processional staircases which would extend ever deeper inside the valley flank, joining one palatial chapel to the next and culminating in the burial chamber. Smaller, ancillary store rooms would supplement the larger chambers. But at the time of the king's death the masons had barely started on the well room. Within the time remaining before the funeral there was no way now that this tomb could be completed as originally intended.

An almost finished but much smaller sepulchre, originally selected for a noble who was yet still living, lay in the bottom of The East Valley, close to its centre and almost opposite the similarly small tomb of his brother. This became requisitioned as the boy king's final resting place. Ultimately it would consist of just four rooms clustered together and separated only by the thickness of their shared walls. As the king's body was prepared for mummification the rooms of the tomb were hurriedly enlarged to hold the multitude of grave goods, the walls being dressed by as many masons as the cavity could effectively accommodate.

The artisans had a little over two months before the funerary ceremonies would begin.

Chapter Two
A Beginning

Thousands away in time and space...

Norfolk - a boy in his early teens bicycles through country lanes resplendent with the anxious, frenzied life of spring. The lad's appearance is not remarkable. He is small for his years, rather thin, and his skin tone is pale, but a strength of character and single-mindedness shows in the lean face. His chin juts out strongly, the mouth is full-lipped, the cheekbones are high, and the nose long and prominent. Beneath the thick eyebrows the eyes are a deep brown.

He cycles in his shirtsleeves and waistcoat, his jacket rolled up in the pannier strapped to the handlebars. He wears a tie thickly knotted at the neck and his best trousers, clipped at the ankles. There is determination in his pedalling. Pushing his body forward over the handlebars, he presses purposefully ahead.

With the spring weather so gently sunny it is a pleasant ride. Best of all, he is alone, away from the over indulgent care of his two aunts and the confines of their modest cottage in Swaffham. He is on his way to an environment that could not be more different.

He takes the sweeping single-lane road that bypasses the villages of Cockley Clay and Foulden. Like a verdant corridor it runs between tall hedgerows across almost imperceptibly rolling countryside. The odd cock pheasant, casual and indefinite in his direction, fat from the bounty of spring and unaware he has been luckily spared by the hunter, waits in confusion and at the last moment moves out of his way. Just after Swaffham Gap the boy turns off to the right along a narrow track until he reaches Didlington hamlet. Here the road divides about a tiny triangle of grass. In the centre of the triangle stands a solitary parish noticeboard announcing forthcoming local diocesan events and little else. The lad cycles off to the left.

Almost immediately he spies the old church enclosed within its small graveyard on the far side of the field ahead. The clear, bright morning light reflects off the flint-knapped walls still unsoftened by years of inclement British weather. As if studded with diamonds, the building virtually sparkles. The boy stops and dismounts.

His birthright has endowed him with a sensitive artistic skill and an eye for detail. He has his drawing instruments with him and settles down on the grass verge with his sketchbook open on his knees. Tongue licking lips in the intensity of his concentration, his delicate pencil strokes accurately follow the outlines created by those who had laboured to build the place. He is very precise. He makes no errors. Each of the headstones in the churchyard - leaning, mildewed, many now anonymous from the attrition of time - each is faithfully documented. In twenty minutes a near perfect copy has been transferred to paper. He records at the bottom, 'St Michael and All Angels, Didlington. Howard Carter, 1888'.

He gathers up his things, picks up his bicycle, returns his drawing pad and instruments to the basket on the handlebars and pedals on. The entrance to the grounds of the hall itself is no more than a short walk south of the church. He free wheels up to the massive front door, dismounts and places the bike against the outer wall. The butler had seen him coming and the door opens before he can reach for the bell pull.

"Hullo, George," he says. "Is his lordship in?"

"Yes, sir. And m'lady is on the terrace playing ball games with the children."

"Oh." He has not come to play. But it is customary and polite for him to present himself first to the lady of the house. "Perhaps then I should go and join them. Thereafter maybe they will permit me some time in the library."

"Of course, sir."

"First, though, I have a picture for you." Howard pulls out his sketchpad and tears off the drawing of the church. "I hope you will like it."

"Sir. How kind." The butler regards the drawing for a moment. "His lordship's family church. A very faithful rendition, sir. You are very good, you know. I will get my wife to find a suitable frame for it. Thank you, sir."

"Oh, George, it's nothing. Certainly not worth a frame. A memory... for your scrapbook."

"Thank you all the same, sir."

Howard trots through the house and out through the tall French windows at the rear. Typical of such a home the garden is a designed affair, walled all about. The back of the house is laid out to an immaculately manicured grass terrace. This falls away to a large croquet lawn backed by formal flowerbeds enclosing an ornamental pond. A classical stone arbour, festooned with clematis, overlooks the pond.

Before he casts his eyes on the group playing below the terrace, he looks to his left. Spread evenly along the rear façade are seven elegant, serenely seated stone statues of Egyptian goddesses. They stare fixedly out over the alien estate toward the southeast and a distant land of contrasts, a land of barren sand and luxuriant greenery; their land, the land they had previously inhabited undisturbed for millennia. Their enigmatic expressions, their cold, bland, open eyes, give no hint of personality. But, for the young Howard Carter, the silent conversations he had held with them during previous visits to Didlington held more magic and delight than he could ever get from engaging the very English souls that now surround him.

He is jolted out of his preoccupation by a greeting from the lawn below.

Lady Amherst, the energetic young mother of the house, waves to him from beside the pond. Well aware of her station in life she gives the boy, whom both she and her husband have grown to like very much, a friendly but not overly familiar welcome.

Although his mind is not focused on garden and ball games, he converses in politely trivial pleasantries with the menagerie of ladies and children for as long as he can stand. When the conversation turns to the latest styles in haberdashery he finally spots his moment.

Howard asks if he might be excused and go to the library to talk with his lordship. "If he is not too busy with other things, ma'am."

"Summon Amherst, George, if you would be so kind. And tell him Master Carter has need of his attention in the library."

The boy politely takes his leave of the garden group and purposefully struts back into the house to seek out the library. At every visit he has felt stunned by the sheer multitude of objects it contains. He walks through the double doors directly to the piece he first wishes to examine. The small ushabti lies in its usual place on a table alongside a number of similar objects. He picks the figure up gently and with a light puff, blows off the dust. He regards it closely. The colours are paled by time. As it lies in his right palm he runs his left forefinger over its painted face, along the arms crossed over its chest, over the abdomen and legs covered with hieroglyphs. He tries to picture where it had originally lain, probably little more than twenty feet from the dead king for whom it was supposed to serve - the Pharaoh whose needs it was commanded to satisfy throughout the tortuous labyrinth of the afterlife.

This is the reason he comes to this place - the sight and touch of the Amhersts' collection of Egyptian antiquities; their personal historical commentary and good counsel; their answers to his questions. Both husband and wife were much accomplished in the Egyptology of the time.

Lord Amherst is not long in coming. He is not a large man and is still relatively young. He has fair hair, straight-combed on either side of his face to just over his ears, a well trimmed moustache, deep eyes, and the receding bottom lip attributed so often by commoners as an affliction symptomatic of the aristocracy. But he is a highly educated man with a natural sensitivity, the talent and the pocket for picking out the very best of ancient Egyptian artefacts. He very much enjoys talking with one so young and who takes such an active interest in the subject. Such encounters bring welcome relief to the business and social burdens of the office he holds.

"Howard, m'lad!" he exclaims, as if he has not seen the boy for ages. "I have a new acquisition which I have been anxiously waiting to show you. Put that down and come over here. Tell me first what you think. Then I will fill you in!"

Lord Amherst beckons the boy over to the darker, furthest corner of the room. Being distant from the small windows, the area is poorly illuminated;

the dark-stained, oak-panelled walls absorb what little light falls on them.

"What do you think of that?" Amherst asks expectantly.

As he moves over to the area his lordship is pointing to, the boy's eyes become more accustomed to the gloom. He begins to make out a large object, somewhat larger than life-size and upright, humanoid in shape. As he approaches within an arm's length, the full, imposing majesty, beauty, reverence and sheer size of the wooden, mummiform coffin absorb all his senses. He is dumbstruck. He stares back at Amherst with his mouth agape.

His lordship is full of himself. He begins telling the lad how he came to acquire the piece - from where, from whom, from what time and the name of the mummy it had once contained. Howard examines the painting on the coffin. In the midst of his excitement he barely hears Amherst's lecturing. Nevertheless the grandee's words become firmly fixed in the catalogue of his mind. He will have no trouble recalling them. The immediate registration and clear recollection of such facts are quite natural to the boy.

Now seventeen years of age, Howard Carter continued to spend much of his time at the Amhersts', but, on the few days that he had sufficient money to take the train up to London, he would make his way to the British Museum. There he would squat amongst the Egyptian exhibits with a pad of cartridge paper across his knees, and a palette of watercolour paints on the stone floor beside him. He would pick out a sculpture, mix up a wash of colour similar to the hue of the stone and spread it across the page. Taking a pencil he would sketch the shape, faithfully reproducing the bold, smooth line of the ancient artist. He resisted the temptation to restore the original vividness of the colours. The mixtures of paint he used were subdued, very much on the pale side and true to today.

The public tapped across the paved floors from exhibit to exhibit, pausing now and then but for far too short a time to truly appreciate the presence of the piece before them. Over the years the lad had trained himself to become oblivious to the traffic around him. The work took concentration and a steady hand.

He was so focused on his work that he barely felt the gentle touch of a woman's silk-gloved hand on his shoulder. "Lady Amherst!" he exclaimed, startled and almost embarrassed at the interruption. He scrambled to his feet. "How nice to see you, m'lady."

He held up the almost finished watercolour in his left hand. "Do you... Do you like it?"

She took it from him and studied it at arm's length, glancing once or twice at the statue he had copied.

"You are so good at this, Howard," she said. "You bring life to dead things. Look," she continued hastily, "now I have interrupted you I must tell you why I am here. This meeting is no accident. Your brother William told me you would be here all day, so I came quickly up to town to bring you what I hope will be most agreeable news.... Howard, how would you like to go to Egypt... to the excavations taking place there... all expenses paid, plus a little - very little I'm afraid - pocket money besides?"

In his surprise Carter dropped his paintbrush on the floor. He quickly bent down to pick it up and replace it in his palette. He closed the lid carefully and pulled himself back up to his feet. "What...? What for? I mean... to do what, Lady Amhurst?"

"Why, just what you are doing here, of course. Doing what you do best. Mr Newberry is someone who needs a fellow to help him copy the wall paintings at Beni Hasan and I have told him of you and your skills and he has agreed to take you - providing your work meets with the approval of Mr Griffith, of course..."

"Mr... Mr Griffith?"

"...And there are other projects there, besides, at least two of which his lordship is supporting. What do you think of that, now?"

The teenager couldn't believe his ears. He was in shock and unable to grasp the sense of purpose in her words. All he could summon in response was, "When?"

"We start right now," Lady Amherst said, "right here. I am to take you downstairs to Mr Griffith's rooms. He is not expecting us but he will receive us. The BM has much to thank the Amhersts for."

"But I... I don't think I am ready for this..."

"Nonsense!" Lady Amherst tugged at his sleeve so hard he almost dropped his sketchpad. Stumbling to recover his composure, he kicked his watercolour paintbox across the floor.

"Pick it up and follow me, Howard. No time to lose. I have come a long way just for this. I am not of a mind to return to the Hall without the satisfaction of knowing that you have been accepted."

"But my parents... My aunts..." he wittered on.

With the single-minded determination and self-centredness that accompanies wealth, she ignored his pleading and led him down the marble staircase to a solid door emblazoned with gold lettering: 'EGYPTOLOGY ARCHIVE'.

Francis Griffith, just twenty-eight years old, was a curator of the museum and a senior officer of the Egypt Exploration Fund, not unimportant in his field and well known to Howard Carter even though hitherto they had not met.

The curator was just inside the door and apparently in the act of leaving. Lady Amherst, being in the act of entering, came upon him face to face. Startled by their close encounter they each retreated a short distance. Her ladyship announced herself, quickly related her contact with Newberry, and introduced the stunned young man who was still hugging the unfinished illustration closely to his chest.

"That so, Lady Amherst? That so?" Griffith's first words were said in a rather disinterested tone and reflected a preoccupation with other matters. However, the presence of aristocracy - aristocracy well respected for her support of the Fund and, for the time, aristocracy in possession of the most important private collection of Egyptian antiquities outside of the museum itself - caused the curator smartly to compose himself.

"I am greatly indebted to you, ma'am, to have come all this way and to bring this young man to my attention. What you got there, sir? Something relevant to the future task at hand? May I see it?"

Howard was surprised to see such a young man in so important a position. But the way the gentleman carried himself reflected a maturity beyond his years. This, along with the seniority of the position held Carter in awe.

"May I?" Griffith reached for Carter's sketchbook.

He had not meant to hold on to the book quite so firmly but his arms were folded tight about it in an almost terrified embrace and the curator had to let go for fear of tearing the pages.

"Show Mr Griffith, Howard, what you have just this minute been painting."

Carter turned the pad around and faced the unfinished painting towards the curator. Griffith took it from him gently and held it more directly under the globe of a hanging paraffin lamp. With his forefinger he pushed his wire-rimmed spectacles further up the bridge of his nose. "One can tell this is freehand... but most accurate in its detail. You are very good, sir."

"Thank you, sir."

"Could you work here with me for a few weeks doing a bit more of this stuff, but on things that need copying, so I can get a better look at your abilities? If you turn out the way it looks you might, I'd like to send you to Egypt to work under Mr Newberry. What do you say to that?"

His answer was a silent nod, a smiling glance of gratitude to the lady who had brought him this good fortune, a feeling of trepidation and an almost uncontainable rush of excitement. Howard felt himself tremble.

Howard Carter began work at the museum the following week and took to his assignment with absolute commitment. He greatly appreciated the faith the Amhersts had placed in him and would do his utmost to build on that trust.

The aunts, and above all his parents, were very happy to see him get this work. For himself, although he would barely be able to make ends meet, so long as he could afford to eat and have a place to lay his head he would have no complaints. He would be working alongside published scientists. The work was truly creditable; honourable even. This kind of experience had no price.

Griffith was quick to bless the lad's abilities. The curator, from their first meeting, had not doubted he would. Within three months of Howard Carter's tenure at the British Museum, the young man had been summarily despatched to Egypt. He took the ferry across the English Channel to France and, after a lengthy rail trip, found himself aboard a sailing steamer bound from Marseilles to Alexandria. For the first time in his short life he was beyond familiar territory and on the initial leg of a journey that, unpredictable to the boy at this time, was before too long to become one of the lengthiest annual commutes in history.

As the ship eased out of port, the fresh sea breeze caught him full in the face and he turned to look back at the slowly receding coast. He reflected on his father who had accompanied him to Victoria Station. He had taken leave of Samuel Carter with a light and expectant heart. The moment of goodbye had been poignant - parental confirmation of the graduate. Howard loved his father dearly and acknowledged that, like his brothers, he owed his talents to this man and this man alone.

Howard leaned out of the carriage door window. His father spoke loudly to make himself heard above the noise of hissing steam. "Take the greatest care of yourself, my boy. You are precious to us all." As if in a sublime ceremony of coming of age, he pressed a small tin of tobacco and some packets of cigarette papers into his son's hand. His father told Howard he was now permitted to smoke.

"Thank you, sir."

"Take care, my boy. Watch y'self over there. Gordon is dead these six years. The Sudan is lost. Yet the papers say the Mahdi is vanquished. Be careful. The infidel was well on his way to extinguishing the foreigner in Egypt. He is not beaten yet. You watch them fuzzy-wuzzies! A treacherous breed of untrustworthy ragamuffins. Make your mark and stay close with the occupying forces. Like 'em or not you know you understand 'em - not so the darkies. Cut your throat soon as look at you. Mark my words."

"Father." Howard acknowledged with a condescending nod. The 'fuzzy-wuzzie', be he corrupt or compassionate, could await his personal assessment when he finally arrived. He knew full well that his father's cautions were based on nothing more than unsubstantiated reports in the British press and recycled, embellished pub banter. The boy held no fears, just anticipation.

The train shuddered and slowly began to move out of the platform. Their hands parted. It was only a moment or two before the smoke and steam from the engine descended in thickening white billows over the carriages. The image of his father, arm raised in farewell, became at last extinguished in the pungent, tumbling fog. He would never see him again.

So now he was embarked on the broad, blue Mediterranean. Howard was not physically accustomed to sailing. Worse for him, the ship's galley lay adjacent to his cabin and the thick, oily scent of cooking issued liberally through the louvres of his cabin door. This was quick to cause a revolting discomfort within his belly that, as it turned out, could only be relieved by an unfamiliar potion administered by a cloaked, priestly Irish gentleman answering to the name of Seamus. They had befriended each other at embarkation. Hitherto unused to more than the odd small glass of beer the continuous draughts of champagne Howard consumed rendered him blessedly insensible for the duration of the trip.

On his arrival at Alexandria, Newberry was there to greet him. In the milling crowd of waving arms, dusty suits and swaying smocks, a sorely hung-over Carter had been barely able to focus sufficiently to pick out his new guardian. Even if the teenager had been feeling one hundred per cent, he would have had difficulty recognising the man.

Like Carter himself, Newberry was not of the build to stand out in a crowd. He was thin and had a small face with a prolific, bushy moustache, from the centre of which protruded a bent cigarette. He wore spectacles and a pith helmet, the brim of which sat uncomfortably upon his ears.

With the help of a contemporary photograph sent to him earlier by Lady Amherst, Newberry picked Carter out from the line of disembarking passengers relatively easily. Carter had, after all, only one suit. He advanced and shook the young man's hand warmly and a little too vigorously for Carter's fragile state of mind. As Newberry spoke his few words of welcome, the cigarette end remained adhered to his lower lip. The teenager hardly noticed. He smiled back as best he could and submissively followed the lead of his new master to a waiting carriage and horse.

Greatly fatigued after his journey and his drinking, Carter took to his bed early that evening and slept peacefully through the night. He awoke the following morning clear-headed, recharged and very much looking forward to the railway trip to Cairo. Every moment provided a new sight and a new experience and generated more than enough adrenalin for the energy to continue looking forward - never a thought back from whence he came.

First impressions had left Percy Newberry not so enamoured with his new charge as Griffith had led him to expect. He was but a boy for his years and clearly unused to anything outside of a typical English village. He noted in his diary: 'Looks spoiled to me. For his age he seems overly drawn to the bottle. He will have trouble accepting the hardships of field camp. He had better have a good eye, a steady hand and a lust for work - for work is all he is going to get, all the daylight hours available. There will be no personal money of significance. I dearly hope his exalted friends have acquainted him thus.'

Newberry need not have worried. The morning trip in the train did much to help settle the Egyptologist's mind. Carter spent the entire time asking questions about Beni Hasan. What were the rock-cut tombs really like? The state of preservation of the reliefs? Did he have an understanding of the texts? What stories did they tell? What matters of life did they depict? Who had been buried there? Are the colours discernible? What techniques did he use to copy the paintings? How large a piece did he copy at one time?

The questions continued. Newberry's chain-smoking didn't bother the young man - the windows in the carriage were all open. Carter, his curiosity unconstrained, hopped from one thought to another. Newberry responded willingly - such hunger deserved his full attention. By the time they had reached the Hotel Royal in Cairo, Newberry was as encouraged with the prospect of his charge's talents, dedication and enthusiasm as he had been discouraged at that initial meeting on the dockside.

During those first few days in Cairo, Newberry was occupied with the provisioning. This task included the purchase of a long list of excavation supplies and the essentials for survival. For Newberry these included his visiting a number of tobacco shops to ensure supplies of cigarettes adequate to keep him 'lit up' for the anticipated duration of their forthcoming stay in the desert. Carter, meantime, was able to acclimatise.

Back at their hotel at the end of the day, Newberry ushered Carter into the smoking room. He removed the cigarette from his mouth. "There is someone here you must meet, Howard." He led him over to a gentleman sitting alone and absorbed in his newspaper. Newberry announced himself and then said, "Mr William Matthew Flinders Petrie, I would like to introduce to you my new assistant Mr Howard Carter who is about to begin his first assignment in Egypt."

The teenager was dumbstruck - the great man of Egyptology was actually seated before him.

The words "M' pleasure, Mr Carter," came from behind the raised newspaper. That would be all he would hear from Petrie for the rest of the evening.

But there was better to come. Before their trip south, Carter had had the opportunity to meet with Petrie a number of times. In the course of their encounters the boy discovered that he and Petrie held a common interest - their individual love of fine art - sufficient in common that the famous man would spontaneously talk to him; that is to say, more exactly, at him. Petrie was accustomed to controlling all situations and particularly conversations about, among other things, his propensity to collect scarab seals and his consequent expertise and knowledge of this prolific form of ancient Egyptian art. Carter would listen in silence for as long as Petrie was happy to speak, but, as soon as he had finished, the Egyptologist lapsed back into thoughts of the more immediate puzzles he was trying to solve elsewhere. Carter respected this and would leave immediately it became obvious that Petrie had finished his dialogue. The young man's display of early maturity did not go unnoticed.

For the few days that Newberry busily scurried about town continuing with his provisioning, Carter, at the time thinking that his trip to Egypt might be the one and only opportunity of a lifetime, was determined to see as much of Cairo as he could. One morning he took advantage of a horse-drawn taxi waiting outside the hotel and was driven to the Cairo Museum.

He studied the poorly displayed treasures for at least six hours. All the time he was there he felt neither thirst nor hunger.

At three in the afternoon he took time for a cold lemonade at the entrance to the museum and then left for the pyramids at Gizeh. Initially he did not grasp the immensity of the three pricipal structures. But the closer he came, the huger they became. The great stone paws of the partially excavated sphinx emerged from slopes of sand and gravel. Behind the deeply scarred and eroded head the greater portion of its body still lay buried. Behind this, the two largest pyramids filled his field of vision. As he walked on, the great structures continued to rise in height before him. The clear, sandy horizon provided no scale. It wasn't until he could make out the diminutive figures of one or two tourists and the odd Arab walking about the base of the largest pyramid that he could grasp any sense of perspective and appreciate the immensity of the massive stone structures planted firmly four-square on the limestone plateau ahead.

He paid the entry fee and went inside. It struck him that the interior was not unlike the labyrinth within a natural limestone cavern. Though in part confining, after a while it opened up like the aisle of a colossal, inclined cathedral. That all this could have been built by the hand of man - the enormity, complexity and magnificence of the building - a mere tomb, a grave for one soul - quite overwhelmed him.

Right now, just like the rest of them, he too was enjoying himself as a tourist. Tomorrow he would not be - not ever again.

Even though it was nearly nightfall when they arrived, Carter eagerly scrambled up the slope ahead of Newberry. He was desperate to look inside one of the tombs. When he got there he found the interior was almost totally dark and stood for a minute hoping his eyes would become accustomed to the blackness. Faint images gradually materialised from the gloom - the simple, elegant shapes he had become so familiar with at the British Museum here in place where they had always been. He breathed an atmosphere thick with the presence of long dead peoples.

These open, naked, rock-cut tombs, high up on a terrace above a limestone escarpment in the desert, provided shelter for his body and much to absorb his mind. The shelter part, however, took a bit of getting used to - the bedstead made of the branches of a palm tree; at night the bats wheeling noisily in and out of the tomb; the deep cold of the night following the scorching heat of the day.

But he quickly adjusted to his surroundings. He became infatuated with the gentle dignity and clarity of the art form and buried himself in the work as if he were one with the original artists.

His greatest discomfort was not physical, however, it was the method by which he had been instructed to copy the friezes. Newberry and copyists before him reproduced the works by tracing the scenes on paper with a soft pencil. Carter despised the technique. It was quick; it was accurate; but it lacked the life and personality of the original. On occasion he experimented with freehand copying, as he had done with the still lifes in the British Museum, a technique in which he was particularly talented. The watercolours were more lively and satisfying to his eye but he would show no one. He kept them hidden between the boards that supported his makeshift desk at camp. There would be a right time to reveal the pictures but for now Newberry's emphasis was on speed and quantity and the young apprentice had to toe the line.

Their work at Beni Hasan was completed too quickly, it seemed to Howard, but he had enjoyed it immensely. It was to the yet greater satisfaction of Newberry, who wrote many letters to Griffith lauding the praises of his younger colleague and themselves as a team.

Carter, too, did some writing. He began what was to become a relatively regular accounting of his experiences in Egypt in epistles to Lady Amherst. Without her personal interest and help he could not have come this far and he felt he owed an enormous debt of gratitude. At the time he could have no conception of the melancholy circumstances that would lead to his final payment some twenty years later.

The night before they journeyed south to Deir el Bersha, their next assignment, it was with some considerable emotion that Carter packed his things. He consoled himself with thoughts of expectation and the new wonders awaiting him. This seemed the appropriate moment to show Newberry examples of his freehand work. The demonstration was successful and he obtained his supervisor's approval to try the technique at el Bersha.

During his time at their second site, Carter met two more of Newberry's colleagues, Messrs Blackden and Fraser. Newberry introduced them as 'MW' and 'GW' and thereafter never referred to the pair in any other way. For himself, Carter didn't bother to pursue a familiarity that would get them all on proper first-name terms. The two seemed far too relaxed and undisciplined for his tastes. After a drink or two - a sufficiency for the likes of Carter - they would drink some more and talk much and loudly of the young lady tourists they had seen lately in Minya. To Carter their minds were too preoccupied with thoughts of future liaisons, and less so with the work. Neither was he impressed with their professional handiwork. His unforgiving, over-critical eye observed that Blackden's artwork was barely fair, almost cartoonish in style. On Fraser's skills as a surveyor he held no opinion. It was already Carter's view that this particular component of the profession of Egyptology was little more than blue-collar. Together the pair seemed to develop a thirst every hour or so and would disappear into the tomb the party used as a mess hall long enough to put away a beer or two before returning to their work. Carter tried to ignore them, immersing himself in the task at hand.

A giant frieze in one of the tombs at el Bersha captured the young man's attention. Rows of identical half-clad men, one above the other in four ranks, ahead of and dwarfed by the colossal statue of a seated monarch as, in regiments, they pulled it slowly out of the quarry from which it had been cut. Standing awkwardly on a ladder, he copied it with precision. The discomfort never bothered him.

The day after he had finished work on this relief happened to be Christmas Eve. Carter hardly gave the occasion a second thought. The cooler days of winter provided precious time for comfortable daytime working conditions, and besides it was hardly pleasurable celebrating Christmas in the sand.

Fraser and Blackden, however, were more inclined to play out the holiday season and that morning they took off for Minya, the prospects of a Christmas cuddle or two uppermost in their minds.

Carter and Newberry returned to the reliefs and continued their work.

On the evening of Christmas Day, Carter relaxed with Percy Newberry. They sat in the mouth of the tomb in which they were encamped, gazing out at the paling orange light. The two shared interpretations of what they had seen during the course of the day's work. As their conversation began, the leader of their Arab helpers ran over from his camp. Panting somewhat from exertion and somewhat from fear of interrupting his masters during their private evening discussions, the reis respectfully asked to be heard.

Current small talk in the nearby village reported the discovery of a new tomb, apparently nearby. Any newly discovered tomb was of great interest but the Pharaoh's name associated with this one captured Newberry's attention the second it was admitted - Akhenaten, the heretic.

"We shall leave for the site at first light, Howard," said Newberry. "Do you ride?"

"Oh, yes, sir. On occasion I used to exercise the Amhersts' horses."

"Don't mean horses, sir, camels. You will need some instruction in navigation and seat. No stirrups, y' see. Mustafah, bring... Let me see... Hannibal. Bring Hannibal."

Carter looked about as eager as a schoolboy about to receive his first caning.

Hannibal groaned as he was pulled over to Carter's side. The animal was enormous, grotesque and had an odour to match. The reis yanked at his halter. He groaned again and gradually sank down, bending at the knees until he became supported by his broad belly. The apprentice Egyptologist mounted the saddle and pinched his knees and thighs as tightly as he could lest he lose his seat when the great beast rose up. Carter did not know which end would come up first but guessed it would be the front and tensed his body forward in the hope that this effort would help maintain his balance.

As Carter had expected, the front legs extended first but only so far as to get the beast up onto its front knees. The back legs quickly followed, extending fully so that the buttocks were momentarily raised above the head. Carter, now totally overcompensated forward, was propelled onto the creature's neck. As the front quickly followed and the ground fell away from him, he desperately grabbed for the neck with his arms and legs, holding on as tightly as he could.

Hannibal groaned. The audience laughed. Carter found it difficult to see the funny side. He called to Mustafah to help him down.

"The back always comes up first, Effendi. Try again."

"Mounting the damn thing is the easy part, Howard. Wait until he begins to walk..." Newberry had settled back comfortably in his canvas chair. He was enjoying himself.

The second time Carter did a lot better. As Hannibal got to his feet, Carter was relieved to find himself sitting straight up in the saddle. But he was horrified at the distance to the ground.

The reis showed him how to hook his right leg around the pommel and lock it beneath his left. "Take the cane, Effendi. You will need it to get him to move."

The last thing Carter wanted was for the creature to move, let alone whack at its buttocks to encourage it to do so. Hannibal had the look of an animal that could inflict a good deal of pain on his rider should he choose to take revenge.

"Do I really have to hit him?"

"Yes, Effendi. He will not take one step unless you do. Not one step."

Carter tensed his muscles, tapped the animal's side and said, "W... walk on."

Hannibal groaned but he did not move. Carter tapped a little harder - another groan; no movement. He tapped again.

"You'll have to do a lot better than that, my boy. Give him a good whack!"

The young man mouthed a silent prayer and slapped the creature smartly across its hindquarters. That did the trick. Hannibal groaned loudly and took off down the hill at a canter. Carter, startled by the sudden acceleration, immediately lost his grip on the reins and grabbed for the pommel, holding on to it with all his strength. The camel, legs flailing, and its human load, legs also flailing, disappeared around a rocky abutment in a cloud of dust.

Suddenly all was silent.

Newberry turned to the reis. "D' you think he's got it under control?"

The reis solemnly shook his head. He pointed down the hill. Hannibal was on his way back. There was no sign of his rider.

The two found Carter spread-eagled on his back, looking up at the evening sky.

"You hurt, sir?" asked Newberry.

Carter turned to him. "Pride only." He got to his feet. "Bring the beast back to me. I refuse to be beaten by a lesser intellect."

"That's the way, Howard!" encouraged Newberry. "Thought for a moment you'd given up and the evening's sport was over!"

Carter smiled, dusted himself off, and walked back to his reluctant mount.

Early the following morning, Newberry and his young assistant took off on camelback with their Egyptian guides in search of the new-found tomb. Hannibal, owing to his own special kind of perfume, had been ordered to maintain a rearguard position downwind of the others.

The journey took them along the east bank of the Nile south and east from el Bersha, across the desolate plain that cradled the ruins of Akhetaten, and into the enclosing cliffs.

Notwithstanding the discomfort of his ride, the excitement for Carter was electric. Nearly every Egyptologist with a right to search in Egypt was hoping to be the first to encounter the final resting place of this most different of kings. For Howard Carter, at this junior stage in his career, any discovery would have done. The chance of being present at a find of such importance was quite beyond his wildest aspirations.

After many hours the party latterly found themselves on a rock-strewn plateau. Carter's anticipation heightened as the camel trail merged with a trackway, obviously ancient, polished smooth by hundreds of years of traffic. The track continued into the relatively flat yonder without any suggestion of an end. The painful camel riding continued.

After about another two hours the character of the landscape clearly changed to a topography fashioned by the hand of man. There were piles of debris everywhere. Carter's eye was by now trained enough to recognise that the heaps of rubble were ancient, from some large excavation. As they rounded one of the mounds the ground opened up ahead of them and they quickly realised this was too big to be the entrance to any tomb. Clearly it was an ancient quarry and, once down beneath the man-cut cliffs emblazoned all about with ancient graffiti, Newberry was able to identify the place as the hitherto lost quarries of Hatnub. These quarries dated from the time of the great pyramids at Gizeh and had been in use throughout much of ancient Egypt's history.

There was little disappointment in not finding what they had expected. This encounter was equally exiting. They would receive considerable recognition for their discovery. For the young apprentice to become associated with such a remarkable find was a great stroke of good fortune.

The two made a brief investigative tour of the place, took some quick notes, and then started back. As they returned along the rocky track, Carter reflected on the wall painting of the colossal alabaster statue that he had copied recently in Deir el Bersha. They must have just trod the very path along which it had been dragged to its final resting place.

For once, Carter was impatient to relieve himself of the news of their discovery. The 'testosterone two', who had been carousing elsewhere over the last couple of days, finally returned at about nine that evening and Newberry and Carter were quick and explicit in acquainting them with the results of the previous day's exploration. The two showed little sign of sharing in their colleagues' elation. They took the news quietly with no expression of surprise. After a short silence, they bade their colleagues 'good night' and retired to their quarters.

Carter and Newberry watched them disappear and then looked back at each other, their feelings somewhat dampened by Fraser and Blackden's lacklustre reactions.

Once out of earshot, Fraser turned to Blackden. There was evident anger and frustration in his face. He clenched his fists. "Damn!... Damn, damn, damn! A blasted discovery while we were out of camp. It wouldn't surprise me if the bastards knew about it ahead of time and waited for us to leave so they could take the glory for themselves. What d' y' think, Blackden?"

His colleague reflected for a moment. "You could be right. I wouldn't have given young Carter the credit for that much cunning, though."

"But what about Newberry? That bastard's as cunning as they come. Never liked us. I can tell. Always complaining about my work. Tore up one of your drawings, didn't he?"

"That he did. That he did. But I had been hurrying that day. I was not happy with it myself."

"Don't make excuses for the man. He's been looking for an opportunity to put one over on us ever since he heard you were to be seconded to Petrie's camp."

Blackden gazed thoughtfully into the night.

"Any thoughts?"

Blackden continued his reflections. Finally he turned to his colleague. The expression on his face said it all. "It wouldn't hurt so much..." he began.

"Mmm...? Yes... Yes?" urged Fraser expectantly.

"It wouldn't hurt so damn much if we'd managed to get ourselves a little bit of the other these last two days!"

Reminding Fraser of compounded defeat was more than the man could stand. He smacked his fists against his thighs again and again. As he circled for the third time Blackden caught him by the shoulders and looked him right in the eyes. "Stop your ranting, man, and listen. I have an idea."

Fraser folded his arms in a tight personal embrace, sat back into a canvas folding chair and stared at his friend.

"They were there only for a day, right?"

"R-right."

"They have discovered the place and are going back to document it later. They are too busy here right now and probably will not be able to return to Hatnub for some weeks. Why don't we relieve them of the task - take off for Hatnub tout suite and complete the work for ourselves?"

A broad smile opened up on Fraser's face. "Brilliant! Let's grab some fellahs and a guide in the morning and get after it."

"It would be foolish to be too hasty. If we take it easy here for a couple of days first there won't appear to be any connection."

Fraser took a deep, relaxing breath. "I feel so much better. A defeat turned into a success. As satisfying as the orgasms we failed to achieve in Minya. I'm off to m' bed."

It was three mornings later at daybreak when the two took off for Hatnub on camelback. They were gone almost a week.

Carter thought little of it. They had gone, he felt, in curiosity to see for themselves what he and Newberry had discovered. Newberry, who had never been drawn to endear himself to the two, was less complacent.

"I am uneasy over their absence, Howard," he admitted one evening after work. "Had they been away just a day or two I could have put it down to professional curiosity. But five days. They are up to something, m' lad. Mark my words. This business has a rotten smell about it. Though at present, I confess, I cannot identify the carcass."

The two reprobates and the 'carcass' returned the following evening. As the camels loped into camp, it was clear from the expressions on the faces of their riders that 'MW' and 'GW' were a lot happier than they had been a week earlier. The camels lowered themselves to their knees and Fraser and Blackden eased a little painfully from their saddles. They greeted their colleagues with unashamed glee.

"We have completed documentation of the enscriptions at Hatnub!" Blackden announced in a matter-of-fact way. "Knew you guys wouldn't have the time. Some of my best work, if I say it myself. Should be a book to be proud of, do you not think?"

To start with, Carter did not comprehend the significance of Blackden's words. The experienced Newberry, however, was quite set back on his heels. It was a sledgehammer blow. Newberry looked at Carter. The Egyptologist's blank expression communicated shock, disbelief and distrust.

But Fraser quickly defused the situation. "Your find, of course. You will wish to add a text, perhaps some plates of your own. But you will, naturally, credit us with the majority of the illustrations, will you not?"

Although his mind was a soup of suspicion, after a short pause Newberry reluctantly nodded his approval. Carter, taking his cue from his senior colleague, followed with a restrained nod of his own.

The other two smiled. "Bit tired after the trip and all. Lot of work in a short time. Sorry we won't be able to stay up for a drink with you tonight. Better get some rest. Good night." And they took themselves off to bed.

Newberry and Carter went on about their business notwithstanding.

Despite the clear felony, Fraser and Blackden's efforts paid off. Carter and Newberry were indeed robbed of the recognition they should rightfully have received had they published their discovery first. The young Carter had learned that Egyptology was a competitive discipline, sometimes unfairly dispatched. *(Preliminary translations of some of the graffiti at Hatnub by Blackden and a couple of his illustrations were included latterly with Part II of Newberry's El Bersha publication and, in the honourable tradition of the day, acknowledged in the text. However, no such protocol was followed by Blackden and Fraser in their publication on Hatnub. They had never intended the book to appear under any other authorship than their own and the document was published without a single reference to those who had made the discovery.)*

But there was a silver lining to these clouds of silent resentment. The unwritten laws of gentlemen were, in the course of time, fairly enforced. In return for their unsporting behaviour, Blackden and Fraser would find themselves disgraced, if only temporarily. Theirs had been a conduct not befitting the profession. So tainted, they would, for a time at least, no longer be listed as prime candidates for future assignments.

This, as it turned out, was to Carter's personal good fortune. The scandal was still fresh in the mind of the upright Petrie when he was looking for a new assistant to help him with his forthcoming excavations at El Amarna, the contemporary name for the devastated city complex of the heretic king. Petrie summarily struck Blackden off his list. Howard Carter got the job.

This was not without some trepidation on Carter's part, and not much less so on the part of Petrie himself. Under normal circumstances the great man was not at all inclined to suffer youth, trained or not, in his exclusive team.

Arriving at Petrie's camp while the Egyptologist was still at work in the field, Carter took a few moments to acquaint himself with his new surroundings. A substantial mud-brick building stood in front of him and this, he supposed, must be his and Petrie's quarters. Beside it was a large sack evidently holding more mud bricks and adjacent to this some mud mortar. Clearly the fellahs were about to build a storehouse of some kind.

Before Carter had time to take in any more, Petrie himself returned, sweating and grimy from his labours. The most famous Egyptologist of the time marched into the field camp with a bouncing step. With hand outstretched, Carter walked forward to greet him like an old friend.

Petrie was a tall, powerfully built man with dark hair, a full beard and moustache, and a penetrating stare. But this softened as he came upon his new colleague. One of the man's many talents was his ability to assess character from a person's looks. He had expected one day he would like working with the young man. The brief meetings in Cairo had been enough.

"Good to see you again, Howard," he greeted encouragingly. "Let's get something to eat and drink and I'll explain your duties for the next few days. We have much to accomplish."

Carter was led over to a rude table made of a flat piece of wood supported on either side by two Crawford's biscuit tins. Carter and Petrie sat opposite one another on empty wooden boxes. Youthfully hungry, Carter ate as Petrie talked.

"Y'don't know how lucky y'are, m'boy. When I came first to Egypt I thought I could gain good training from those in the Fund. Instead I found the techniques of the excavators needful and knowledge of what was being dug up limited. I was continually breaking new ground. I learned from things, not from people. However, lucky for you, y'have me. For the first week or so, and until I am satisfied you are absorbing what I will be showing you, you will do nothing but watch me at work and listen to what I have to say. Take note of how I organise the fellahs, what the reis does, how I go about digging, the tools I use and the way I use them, what I do with the pieces as I find them, recording and such. Y' follow?"

Carter was, at the time, in the middle of a mouthful of bread. He swallowed it whole.

Too late. Petrie continued, "Amherst's a good man. Heart in the right place. And the money, thank God. Hope his faith in you is well founded for both our sakes. I don't want to find you needful. I do not tolerate mistakes. Send you home far quicker than you got here. Have another piece of lamb. I have to get back. Oh, by the way. Do y' have any cash upon y' person?"

"About twenty five-pounds, sir." Carter feared he had come to his new assignment insufficiently endowed.

"Do not keep it near you," Petrie whispered. "When it is dark tonight and you know yourself to be alone bury it somewhere away from your sleeping quarters. Mark you, hide it well. The Arab is light-fingered and damned good at it!"

He got up and left.

When Petrie returned in the early evening, Carter, having remained pretty much alone in the meantime, was keen to engage him in conversation about the place they were to excavate. He made the mistake of asking questions that could be answered with a simple 'yes' or 'no', which Petrie was glad to give before quickly lapsing back into his thoughts on the day's revelations. By the time Carter had thought of a question that could not be dismissed so quickly, Petrie was rising to leave the dinner table and turn to his journals.

"You can bed with me tonight. Take my advice and get to bed as soon as you can. I shall be rooting you out before daybreak, so that you may build a room for yourself."

Then he was gone, leaving Carter to reflect on that sack and the mortar.

There is nothing that so fulfils a man as accomplishment. The little, almost square, mud-brick one-room stood there proudly before him. It was all of his own making. He admired his handiwork - the clean, vertical lines of the walls and the pitched roof, the palm leaves held down with stones. Carter pushed the raffia mat that hung over the doorway to one side and walked into the darkened interior. While the walls looked a good deal rougher and uneven from the inside, they nevertheless appeared substantial enough to carry the light weight of the roof. Above all, inside it was cool.

Awakening after his first night in his home-made shelter, he found he had company. Tenants were already present. He disliked the scorpions most, largely because they were as belligerent as they looked. Every piece of clothing, particularly his shoes, had to be shaken vigorously before dressing. All this was tolerable. But Carter could never understand why Petrie insisted on doing without menservants. In a country such as this, at a time such as this, the man had to be a masochist, happy in his self-inflicted discomfort.

On this first working morning, Carter in his thoroughness took too long clearing out his unwanted residents and getting himself ready. By the time he had emerged from his little hut, Petrie was returning from his first trip to the dig.

"Morning, m' boy," he greeted. He was pleased to have English-speaking company for a change and was looking forward to lecturing the young man in the secrets of his practice. "Just been organising the fellahs. Ready for breakfast now."

They sat opposite each other at the rude table and Carter began to pick at the unpalatable-looking bread. Petrie had hardly swallowed his first draught of tea before he began his instruction. "First, a few tips on assembling your troops...

"Selection... We are fortunate that the Arabs have one facial attribute that enables us to assess their character at a glance. Because of their common and lengthy exposure to sun and wind their skin wrinkles at a young age. The wrinkles reflect a person's most frequently used expression. It is through expression that we read character. The record is cemented in their faces for all to see and as a result they either look clearly honest or, more frequently, absolutely dishonest. I have made mistakes, however. I would be the first to admit it. But no fellah can do harm so long as the power of engagement, dismissal and the money bag are all maintained safely within our own hands.

"You will find those who are not used to our kind of work difficult to train as trenchers. When commanded to dig, their natural inclination is to sink a circular pit, like digging a well, and then flail about with the pick, advancing hither and thither in a disorganised fashion. Straight and narrow is not in their natural vocabulary.

"I train three classes - trenchers, shaft sinkers, and stone cleaners - those who can be trusted to be gentle and not light-fingered - and sort them into small gangs, usually two men each, accompanied by three or four women and children, all of whom do the carrying. I never have a party greater than three men and six others, otherwise I cannot see exactly what each one does and thus I become unable to catch the lazy ones. The whole group has at times totalled as many as one hundred and seventy. Requires a great deal of individual attention when it gets to that size. Don't advise you to attempt anything like it until you feel comfortable you can keep an eye on every single one of them.

"It's incredible how much care is required to prevent the fellahs from coming a cropper. They seem to have a reckless regard for their personal safety. Between their stupidity in the fundamental points of mechanics and their unreasoning fear, in order to prevent accidents anything that may require care in engineering or some precision you will have to do with your own hands.

"Then there's Ramadan. Damned Ramadan. Allah's great excuse for doing bugger all and a damned frustrating time for the likes of us. My solution here - while the men are fasting - is to employ the bigger girls to do the pick work. And believe me, there are some big girls!"

Petrie took another long pull at his enamelled tea mug.

"The working day... We take advantage of the cooler parts of the day... Normal start is five thirty."

Carter now realised he had missed Petrie that morning by a very long margin.

"Get the reis and his fellahs working in the right direction. Once they're moving along smoothly, return for breakfast around eight or nine. I sit here and watch the pits with my telescope." He pulled the instrument out of his satchel and gestured with it.

"When it gets hot, around eleven, I whistle the men off work for a rest, usually for a good three hours. Then back to the site until dark. Dinner around six thirty. After that the paperwork - recording, marking, stowing and writing up the journal. Usually quit before eleven. I've found by experience that, no matter how absorbed you are in your work, if you try to exist on too little sleep you weaken, imperceptibly so to yourself, but weaken nevertheless sufficiently for the endemic bugs to bring you down with some nasty malady. Worse, one tends to make mistakes, damage things and the like. Keep your health. It is more than unusually unpleasant to become sick in this remote place, so don't risk it."

Petrie dunked a biscuit in his tea and gobbled the thing down whole.

"During the summer..."

The mention of the word alone got Carter's attention. He had never contemplated working during the summer months. 'This man works during the summer?!'

"...we begin work by moonlight at about four - ten for breakfast - rest from eleven to three - then work again until moonlight at eight. It is hard. Tolerable if you wear little as I do. Bare-foot but not bare-headed."

'Barefoot? Has he no nerve endings in the soles of his feet?' Carter mused.

"Compensation... You are aware there are all kinds of denominations and types of currencies in circulation - some more readily acceptable than others. The fellahs don't like to take grubby or damaged coins. I've got two ways of getting rid of these. The least time-consuming is to clean them with ammonia. Pickle them in it all night. They look as good as new in the morning. More normally I keep a stash of them in my purse. When the fellah rejects one, I give him a worse one. When he says 'no' to this, I select one yet more disgusting. Invariably it takes two tries and he will ask for the first again and exhibit some relief when he gets it. On occasion I have made up salaries in a mixture of coinage - francs, pesos, lire, English shillings; sometimes Swiss and Turkish; even Indian coins.

"You must be firm. If any complains about his pay fire him immediately and pay him off. Don't hesitate for a second. Your action is observed by the others and the word soon gets around. You won't find anyone bitching after that.

"Bargaining... This is an inevitable requirement and an acquired talent. Apart from those on the general antika market - which, by the way, are come by with equal deceit - the fellahs will sequester some objects that you have not observed them find and approach you later to bargain. This is my technique... If the vendor won't accept my offer - and, I hasten to add, this is always a fair one - I hand back the piece at once. If it is offered to me again, I offer less the second time, always, without exception. Mind now - this is a very important detail. Thereby, one gains a reputation for invariable process - defeats the fellahs' innate sense of barter. Remember, the sight of money is irresistible. The vendor cannot bear to see it taken back.

"Always give the value of silver by weight. I weigh silver artefacts against modern coins. You'll find Australian dollars the cheapest to use for this purpose.

"Trans-shipment... This is a crucial piece of advice, Mr Carter. If you have listened to nothing else, hear this." The dark eyes fixed on Carter's. "There is value in the satisfaction of discovery. There is greater value in showing the finds to others. There is yet greater value to Great Britain in receipt. But there is no greater value than publication and recognition..." The rising sun flashed from his retinas as he stared more deeply into Carter's eyes. "...And there is precious little of this if you bring little home.

"Know this... Maspero will be advantageously discretionary with your best pieces if, and only if, you show them to him before you get to Cairo. There his hands are tied. There he has no flexibility. Have it all settled before you get there.

"Now... shipping permits... a timing problem. The bureaucracy in this country has a complexity far beyond the comprehension of even the most collegiate English. In order to have the export permit in place at the time you have booked to leave for England you must apply mid-season. The permit must cover the exact number of packing cases you will be shipping. Problem: at mid-season how the hell do we know how many crates we will have for export by the season's end? I ask you. An insane system. But Flinders Petrie has a solution... simple but artful! If, after you receive the permit, you have too many crates, have some larger ones made and place several cases in each until the number is right. If too few, have smaller crates made, or add empties."

Petrie drew a smug grin.

"Questions?"

Carter, quite exhausted after the monologue, had no questions.

Petrie put down his empty mug. "Let's be off, then."

Following the first week of tuition, Carter was eager to get his hands on the substance of the excavation. Petrie gave him a sector of the dig to himself, along with three of his most experienced men and six carriers. After a slow start, the apprentice began turning up evidence of workshops of various kinds and houses. Fragments of pottery were in abundance, but pieces of statues or more attractive artefacts were nowhere to be found. Carter nevertheless was absorbed in what he was uncovering and in the dimly lit evenings back at camp he would relate to Petrie tentative interpretations of what he had found that day. The great man was quick to depress any feelings of elation in the teenager. These ideas were born of inexperience and an immature imagination, not calculated scientific deduction. He must appreciate that there was much yet to learn.

Notwithstanding his deflating comments, Petrie inwardly liked the lad's consummate focus and deliberate approach to the work. Had he not, in short order Carter would have found himself languishing in Cairo. To be tolerated by Petrie was a mark of considerable esteem.

Some days later Carter was working in a corner of the badly ruined Aten temple when he came upon a large torso fragment of a statue of the heretic Pharaoh. He could recognise it for what it was because of the cartouches carved on the chest and abdomen. It was the first find of substance that the young man had encountered. Petrie credited him for its quality and importance.

In time he would become personally responsible for finding several other pieces at El Amarna, but to Howard everything else paled in comparison to the first. The piece stood propped up in the corner of his hut surrounded by less identifiable fragments of similar stone that could have come from the same figure - all products of the frenetic destruction that had taken place in antiquity. In the late evening he would sit on the edge of his bed writing up his notes on the day's efforts and contemplate the magnificence of the statue as it might have appeared in its entirety.

As things turned out, neither Petrie nor Carter was responsible for the discovery of the El Amarna tomb of Pharaoh Akhenaten. News of the find reached them quickly. Carter armed himself with pencils and paper and they took off eastward, inland to visit the site.

The tomb lay some considerable distance up a steep ravine, set apart from the ruined city and the other tombs excavated in the surrounding escarpment. The interior, like the Pharaoh's city ravaged by those who had tried to erase all memory of the heretic, still retained sufficient detail to attest to its original beauty. There was a strange warmth to the art. The place had real atmosphere.

Among the wall carvings that Carter sketched was a tender scene wherein the king and queen mourned the death of one of their children. To the apprentice Egyptologist's astonishment and intense gratification, his drawing was published in The Daily Graphic in London the following month as an illustration to one of Petrie's articles. Of course, there was no acknowledgement of Carter's contribution. After all, the young man was but an apprentice. Granted he was sponsored by Lord and Lady Amherst, but these unusually lofty connections were overshadowed by the lack of appropriate educational background and an absence of breeding.

Carter took a clipping for his scrapbook. The honour had been deeply felt nonetheless.

Chapter Three
The Forbidden City

On his accession Smenkhkare, Tutankhamun's elder brother, had delivered the royal family and his people from the pestilent city, the palaces and temples of Akhetaten. The seat of regency and of religious order was happily returned, initially to Memphis and latterly to Thebes. This had been decided and enforced entirely on the advice and counsel of Smenkhkare's elders. But this Pharaoh, bringing 'the sickness' with him from Akhetaten, barely survived three years.

Tutankhamun himself, not yet a teenager and untouched by 'the sickness', found himself unexpectedly decorated with the double crown of Upper and Lower Egypt. Very young, but at the same time endowed with enormous power, it did not take the royal juvenile long to understand that every word he uttered would be taken with unquestioned literality. What he said, what he wished, what he commanded would be acted on without a second thought. As he matured into manhood, he came to realise that he must first carefully consider what he was about to say. Second, he must be absolutely deliberate and resolute in whatever he said.

So it was one day that he decided to return to the place of his early childhood. A place of the fondest memories - of a loving father- and mother-in-law; of their six children, all daughters, one now his queen; of his brother. There had been much laughing and playing of games. It had been a care-free time - no responsibilities; security; beautiful buildings with vibrant frescos on the walls; a freshness and newness about everything. He recalled the abundant flowers, the shrubs, the trees, the ponds of clear water populated with lotus blossom and waving stands of papyrus; the birds - in every garden there had been birdsong.

Tutankhamun called for Nakht.

"The Pharaoh and his Queen wish to travel to Akhetaten, the place of our childhood, the burial place of Pharaoh's mother and of the family of his Queen, the place of our birth."

The vizier didn't like the order but understood the young couple's wish to return to their origins. When they had left they had been little more than children. But also he remembered 'the sickness'. He was concerned for the royal family's health, and worse, the possibility of reinfestation at Thebes. In such a visit there was political danger, too.

"Great One, it is well over two, more likely three full days and nights of sailing, even with a strong crew. More than thrice that on the return journey.

And Akhetaten is forbidden. 'The sickness' abides there. There are no people there. It is an empty place. It is a dead place. You should not wish to venture to such a place."

The young Pharaoh was not listening. "Great Vizier, nothing is forbidden to Pharaoh. Do not insult my intelligence. Have I not lived in Akhetaten? Do I not well comprehend the distances? I am quite aware of the logistics. After all these years 'the sickness' will have died away itself. There have been no days of darkness since that which spawned it. There are happy memories - many happy memories - that the Pharaoh and his Queen wish to rekindle. The Queen and Pharaoh shall travel to Akhetaten. Tomorrow you will have assembled for me three ships well provisioned for the journey. We will need horse and chariot plus the usual retinue. You will not accompany us. See to it. That is all."

His personal concerns for the Pharaoh's safety, the politics and superstitions of the time notwithstanding, Nakht wanted the king to have his wish. But first some subtle arrangements would have to be made and for these he would need a little time.

That evening the vizier consulted with the general. "It is a ticklish situation. The gods will be displeased. There is risk of infestation at Thebes - 'the sickness' - although his Highness believes it to be gone. And the people... There is sensitivity... The people must not become aware."

"Pharaoh has ordered that it be so?"

"Pharaoh has ordered it."

The general rubbed his nose. "Can we not explain to him the delicacy of the matter... so that he will understand?"

"He understands 'the delicacy of the matter', General. It is up to us to see to it that the entire visit goes ahead, as it were, 'delicately'... that is, un-noticed."

"Then it must be." Horemheb cursed himself for not dispatching the king sooner. But then he had a thought. What if the king's ship should founder on its journey north? An unfortunate accident. An opportunity altogether simpler than his personal plan. He could not constrain a grin of inner contentment.

Nakht noticed the general's relaxed expression. "You have a plan?"

"Mmm?... Ah... Well... I see it thus... We must arrange it that the royal couple depart at midnight, when the populace is abed... Also, on the return journey it should be so arranged that they arrive in the dead of night. Before he leaves I will send ahead of him a contingent of my most trusted troops to ensure the capital of the heretic is clear of squatters and nomads. He will not be seen."

The vizier knew exactly what Horemheb meant by 'clear'. Those unlucky enough to be present when the troops arrived would be dead and buried without trace long before the king's flotilla berthed. The few who camped in the desert outside but close to the perimeter of the town, hearing the screams from within, would hide themselves or run off into the hills. No living thing would remain to welcome the Pharaoh but for the guards themselves, the birds, the reptiles, the vermin and the insects.

If Horemheb had anything to do with it there might be no welcome necessary. To his knowledge the boy king had never taken the time to learn to swim. If it could be engineered that his barque would run aground on the rocks at some point during the journey and quickly sink, there would be a strong probability he would become entangled in the powerful and wayward currents of the river and be lost for ever.

Staging the accident would not be easy, however. The captain would have to be paid off. And there must be no chance of discovery. In the past the general had been exposed to a blackmail attempt. That particular infidel had come to mortally regret his indiscretion. Horemheb would have the captain killed later, regardless of the outcome. That would be the easy part.

The king and the queen, understanding the need for secrecy, showed no discomfort with their midnight embarkation. The boat would not normally be expected to arrive before sunrise three days hence. They would sleep late in their cabin and enjoy the daylight hours viewing the passing monuments of their kingdom.

Their plans to retire as soon as they were on board, and the moonless night, suited the general's purposes. As he saw the captain off, the general signalled with a wave and looked up at the stars. His meaning was perfectly clear.

The captain did not see his task as all that difficult. The steersman of the royal barque could not see the way ahead and relied on the pilot, positioned high in the bow, to shout direction to him. Being the man in charge, the captain had ably confused messages between pilot and steersman on several previous occasions.

However, in the event, the captain had a good deal of trouble steering the disaster course. The oarsmen did not operate in the downstream direction at night because the noise might disturb the royal couple. There was no wind and the boat would not manoeuvre. The river currents naturally took the deeper channel and the momentum of the boat was with that of the river. He tried hard to force the steersman to guide the boat to the left but soon realised that had he persevered he would have accomplished nothing more than to turn the bow in the upstream direction and then, as the boat drifted backwards, only to stand embarrassed as his crew looked on. So he held course and missed the only opportunity he would have to hole the ship mid-river.

He would make another attempt on the return. The general was not generous over failure. Rather he was known to be gratuitous in his punishment.

The royal flotilla made good downstream headway and secured for the third night at Asyut on the west bank.

The captain cast off in the early hours of the following day. By the time the sun was at its highest, they had turned the last bend of the Nile before Akhetaten. The king and queen were sitting in the royal kiosk in front of their cabin expectantly awaiting their first sight of the deserted city. It was approaching a dozen years since the two of them had been taken from the place.

As the first buildings came into view, the memories started flooding back. But for the obvious lack of people and the absence of colourful banners, the site appeared much the same as they had remembered it. Lying within a natural bowl of lowland rimmed by rugged hills, a phalanx of great temples, palaces and buildings of state fronted a sweeping arc of the river.

The small flotilla pulled alongside the Great Palace wharf and the royal couple disembarked. The Pharaoh ordered the majority of his entourage to remain at the docking area.

The king and the queen with her handmaiden, two attendants to keep them shaded from the sun, four carrying two chairs on stretchers, four to carry refreshment, and four guards, walked through the main palace doors and into the first courtyard.

This enormous building held no memories for them. As minors they had never been permitted to enter the place. As they walked on, the echoes of their footsteps rang between the massive columns. Emerging from a second courtyard they reached the bridge that spanned the great processional way. Halfway across, at 'the Window of Appearances', Tutankhamun stopped. He turned to look along the wide avenue. Slowly the images returned - Pharaoh Akhenaten, his queen Nefertiti and their daughters drawn in their chariots along the great road; a multitude of their subjects flanking either side, cheering and waving colourful banners of all types and sizes; court officials observing from the bridge; loud trumpeting echoes about the city walls; a thousand troops or more in several columns following behind the royal carriages.

A breath of wind drew up dust just as if a moment earlier they had galloped into the distance towards the Great Temple. Now there was nothing - just an empty silence.

The squatters, and there were many, had been warned of the arrival. The fortunate had managed to conceal themselves from the general's purging troops. Consumed by the immediate need for daily survival, they cared little about heresy or the lack of it. They remained huddled in various places of hiding, hoping they would never be discovered, and that the visit would be brief.

The royal party continued across the bridge and into the king's estate. The great doors, flanked by massive walls deeply engraved and painted all over in brilliant green, white, red, blue, yellow and black, opened onto a large forecourt. The royal family's quarters fronted the south side of this forecourt. The group of attendants followed the royal couple as they moved quickly through the reception hall in the direction of the king's suite. Tutankhamun's sandals crunched on the sand that had drifted in on the wind and settled inside the deserted halls. He walked into a room that held intimate memories. In this particular chamber he had sat on his ageing mother's knee watching the Pharaoh and his queen and their daughters playing a board game. They sat on mats spread about the floor, the walls around them covered with all manner of bright, colourful, lively murals - the verdant swamps, the animals, the birds, the people - all alive with activity. All just memories now.

Suddenly Tutankhamun let out a curse. He had stepped on something hard - sharp enough to break through the sole of one of his sandals. He bent down and picked it up. He turned the piece over in his hands. It was a broken piece of polished limestone in the shape of a nose. Holding the fragment in his palm, he walked into the adjoining hall and looked up at the great row of giant replicated statues lining the walls. Three were without noses; two with no arms; one had no face. The spoil of liberal vandalism littered the floor of the hallway.

The boy king turned angrily to his guards. "Gather this up. It must be restored. I will not see Pharaoh's image defaced. Nothing must be lost. Secure it somewhere safe. Gather it up!"

The king had expected to see decline; he had not expected violation. The shock of such discriminate abuse almost reduced him to tears. He turned to the guards once again. "Bring my architect to this place. I order a full restoration that is to be completed before my next visit - within the year. Mark that you remember!"

Ankhesenamun herself had the greater cause for anger. These desecrated statues were the images of her father - he who had cherished her and her sisters as infants. It was true that he had not been a handsome man, but the other qualities he possessed far outweighed his physical shortcomings. The family had been extremely close. He had never allowed his duties as regent to interfere with the normal activities of the family unit.

Ankhesenamun's personal beauty and her strength of will she owed to her mother - a woman of outstanding beauty herself, with perfect physical endowments and a great mind, she carried a presence with her that gained the dutiful respect of all who knew her, and many of those who did not. For the first time in living memory, the people's queen had become a virtual deity in parallel with her husband.

Fond memories, happy times, until steadily, one by one, 'the sickness' had taken them.

She recalled a foreboding darkness. In an instant at midday the sun, the life-giver, had become extinguished. For a few chilling moments the entire population of the city fearfully contemplated the premature night. Then, equally as suddenly, the sun's light had returned, just as brilliant and comfortably warming as before.

But the damage was done. A pervasive sense of panic took hold of the people. For some reason Aten was displeased. He had given them a demonstration of his power to return the land to darkness and cold at his will. The hitherto accepted philanthropy of this god was not so dependable after all. The people's confidence in the Aten had become irrevocably breached.

There was worse to come. It came swiftly on the heels of one of the greatest inundations for years. All knew the Nile to be bountiful. In living memory she had never failed them. This year the people were rejoicing at the sight of a flood greater than any previously witnessed. The larger the area flooded, the more extensive and prolific the future harvest. But the water bore within it a hidden, sinister bounty, the like of which they had not before encountered. An unrelenting, evil humour pervaded the land. It visited every household. Almost every family was touched by it in some way - the royal family as much, perhaps more, than any other. It was as if the Nile herself, in fear of his power, had conspired with the gods against Aten to render his city lifeless.

It was a sign. This was a bad place. With so many dead and, ultimately, the deaths of the king and queen themselves, complete and permanent evacuation of the city, and abandonment of worship of the Aten, became an inevitability. To those people who remained alive and their new Pharaoh, Smenkhkare - himself stricken with 'the sickness' but, although very weak, apparently surviving it - it was the only way to appease the old gods.

By the time the dead king's tomb had been sealed, Akhetaten had become quite literally a monumental ghost town. The new Pharaoh and his entourage, all present at the tomb sealing, left the area by the northern route, skirting the perimeter of the city until they reached the royal flotilla waiting to take them downstream to Memphis.

Smenkhkare would never return alive.

Tutankhamun led his queen on, out and away from the palace and into one of the streets that took them south, parallel with the river, past the tall pylons of the family chapel. After a while they reached the compound that enclosed the house and grounds that had belonged to the governor of the southern region - Tutankhamun's vizier. The guards pushed open the great cedar gates to allow the royal couple to enter.

Here Tutankhamun had played as a boy. The garden was now dead and replaced by dried scrub, but the layout was still evident. The outdoor shrine where the icon of the Aten had been sheltered was now pretty much destroyed by vandals of the restoration, but he was pleased to observe that elsewhere, and more particularly within the house itself, there was little evidence of wilful damage. The painted walls had some stains on them and the colours had faded somewhat, but the pigments still retained much of their original body. There was no furniture - Vizier Nakht had taken that with him during the exodus - but the rubbish of recent, alien habitation was everywhere.

The two stopped in the principal reception room. They looked at each other. The king turned to his followers. "Pharaoh and his queen shall take refreshment here."

Two of the guards quickly assembled a couple of gilded folding chairs they had been carrying and the royal couple took their seats. The queen's elder maidservant, Tia, presented her with a tray of fruit.

"What does this remind you of, my Queen? Imagine these columns are palm trees, there are flowers all about us, ducks are singing from within the papyrus. Over there..." The king pointed to a corner of the room. "Look beyond the walls..."

Ankhesenamun chewed on a date and thought a moment. "The great oasis, my lord. Our family would sometimes picnic there. We would play games - all of us - together. My father would tell stories. Mother would sing to the music of the servants. Sometimes father would hunt. His kill would be prepared then and there. It would be roasted and we would feast on it. But fresh food and fresh water are not always good. To our eternal cost we learned that - here, in this place." She looked around the chamber. Tia bent close to pour the queen a cup of water. The king placed his hand over the mouth of the vessel. "We shall drink wine."

The two took some wine and a little more fruit and were soon finished.

"I wish to make an offering at the cenotaph of my family," said the queen.

"Of course," acknowledged Tutankhamun. He instructed the carriers to bear them to the place.

As the party walked on to the threshold of the short ornamental avenue that led to the front portico of Akhenaten's mortuary temple, the queen suddenly stopped, raised her hand to her mouth, and gasped in horror. The entire building had been razed to the ground. In their frenzy, the vandals had seen to it that not a single piece of masonry, not one fragment of statuary had been left whole, let alone standing. All images of the royal family had been excised from the massive columns, chipped out completely by the vandals' chisels, or smashed beyond recognition. Snakes and scorpions infested the rubble.

Ankhesenamun broke down in tears.

The king realised immediately there could be much worse to come. "My Queen," he consoled, "you must be strong. The infidels who did these things may not have stopped here."

He turned at once to the guards and ordered, "We shall go to the tomb of Pharaoh Akhenaten. Bring me horse and chariot! I know the way. Towards where Amun riseth." He pointed eastward towards a steep wadi emerging like a gash in the hillside beyond the city wall. "Two guards will accompany us. We need no other."

With only a rough track to the 'Royal Wadi', it took the party almost an hour to reach the site of the lonely tomb. It was befittingly solitary, cut low into the side of the valley. As they had dreaded, but expected, the giant doorway lay open, a gaping black portal at the base of the white limestone cliff that towered above it. Evidence of vandalism and looting was spread all about the threshold. Pieces of broken pottery, splinters of furnishings, linen rags and beads spilled from roughly handled jewellery littered the valley floor.

"Light the torches!" ordered the king. "We will enter."

Tutankhamun held his wife's hand firmly as they stepped into the mouth of the tomb. The guards followed closely behind, carrying the torches. The lively flames threw the shadows of the royal couple dancing forward down the staircase of the steep entrance corridor. As they descended the steps, but for the occasional crackle from the torches and the crunch of feet on the sandy floor, they felt a close, foreboding silence within the place. Then, quite suddenly, they were startled by the sounds of a multitude of rodents scurrying between their legs as they made for the light at the top of the stairway. A second later a cloud of frantically flapping bats beat past them as the chaotic creatures made for the tomb entrance.

Ankhesenamun cried out and hid her face in her husband's chest.

Equally suddenly, all became quiet once more. With some temerity the royal couple moved deeper into the tomb.

At the bottom of the stairs they passed through a doorway and entered a gently sloping corridor. With the faint light of their firebrands, they were unable to see how long the passage was. The king moved forward cautiously, keeping his eyes on the floor, looking out for objects, more stairs, a well, anything that could cause them to stumble and fall. The careless rubbish left by those who had violated the sepulchre was scattered everywhere, and the thick stench of dried defecation pervaded the atmosphere.

"Fear not, my King," reassured Ankhesenamun. "As a child I took the funerary feast in this holy place many times - the last for my father. I know its contours well. I shall lead you." Her hand closed over his and she led him ahead into the darkness. About eighteen cubits further on, another door appeared opening into a second corridor that ran off to the right.

The queen pointed into the blackness. "My two youngest sisters, Neferneferure and Setepenre, they sleep within. Beyond them, my mother."

She tried to go right but her husband held her back. "My Queen, are you prepared for what you might see?"

Ankhesenamun looked directly into his eyes. In the flickering lights the determination in her expression was all too clear. Prepared or not, it was obvious she would not leave before she had explored every room. He relaxed his grip and allowed her to lead him through the doorway.

But neither of them had seen a plundered tomb before. Neither of them was fully ready for what might await them in the depths.

"My baby sisters lie together in the first room. Mother lies in the second. This way."

After walking through a second door, the roughly finished passage turned right and then gradually curved to the left. Where this corridor ended another doorway appeared, cut into the left wall. This led immediately into a square room. The guards following close behind held the torches high to help illuminate the area before the royal couple. A scene of absolute devastation met their eyes. Of man-made articles there was little remaining that was in any way recognisable. But the bodies were still there: in the far corner of the room, two small, pathetic mummiform bundles of oil-stained rags thrown one upon the other.

Ankhesenamun shrieked. It was an awful scream. It echoed about the corridors and chambers of the tomb, out of its mouth and reverberated along the narrow valley walls. The cry carried in the still desert air to the royal entourage on the riverside awaiting the king and queen's return. There was much concern that something dreadful had befallen them. The remaining guards were at once dispatched to secure their safety.

The burial chamber of Queen Nefertiti, a crudely cut affair at the end of the corridor, was in yet worse condition. The queen's body, naked but for some linen wrappings remaining about the lower shins, lay face down amongst the rubble that had been her sarcophagus. She had been stripped of every piece of her jewellery.

Ankhesenamun, Nefertiti's only surviving daughter, knelt down beside the body and cradled the dead queen's shrivelled head in her lap. The obscenity of it all was too much for her. She began to sob uncontrollably. She looked up at Tutankhamun. Strings of black paint from her eyelids followed the tears as they fell in torrents down her cheeks.

The king tried to comfort her. "There will be payment in kind for this deed. I will have Maya arrange for their rewrapping. We shall have them transferred to Thebes and re-interred in a secret place with full funerary ceremony. The gods will bless them once more as they recommence their journeys. Osiris yet awaits them. Come..." He gently encouraged her to rise and leave. "For now leave them where they lie. I will post a guard until Maya can get here."

They returned to the main corridor and prepared to investigate deeper into the tomb. At the same time, the relief guard arrived at the outside entrance and called to them.

The king shouted back. "Await Pharaoh and his Queen where you stand. We will return presently." He paused. "No... return to the wharfside. Take one of the boats and go back to Thebes. Tell Maya, Pharaoh's treasurer, that you have Pharaoh's instructions for him to make haste to this place. Tell him to come with the court's embalmers and be prepared to transport the bodies of the family of Pharaoh Akhenaten to Thebes for re-interment. Tell him... Tell him their mummy cases have been violated. Tell him to travel at night only. The journey is to be held most secret. Acknowledge the substance of your understanding..."

The king listened for the guards' response. They took a few moments to gather themselves.

"Acknowledge!" the king yelled impatiently.

"Aye, my lord. Maya, treasurer to Pharaoh. We hear your orders. We will make haste. May the gods protect Pharaoh. Fare thee well."

The king drew some sense of comfort from the sounds of receding horses, and once more took the queen's hand.

The royal couple descended further along the sloping corridor until they reached the threshold of another steep flight of steps. To their right was another doorway.

"It leads to the burial chambers of my other three sisters." The queen's voice quivered as she held back her tears. She pointed. Her hand was trembling.

"It will be as bad as before, my Queen."

"Now I am prepared," she answered defiantly and the king followed her into the first room.

The frescos on the walls had been desecrated by the vandals but they were still recognisable - a picture of the king and queen and their household mourning over their dead first-born.

On the floor were three jumbled bodies irreverently thrown together in a corner. They were still secure in their original mummy linens. Ankhesenamun fell to her knees again. She lent over and gently kissed each dirty package. Through her tears, in a whisper, she called out her sisters' names. "Meritaten... Meketaten... Neferneferuaten... In Heaven the gods will protect thee."

She turned and looked up at Tutankhamun. He had gone. A solitary guard stood above her holding a torch. "Pharaoh is within the king's sepulchre, my lady," said the guard.

She quickly got up and followed the guard back to the main corridor and down the steep staircase. She stopped short at the edge of the well. She need not have worried. The earlier robbers had seen to it that the well was almost completely bridged by a pile of stacked limestone blocks that had once been used to wall up the doorway to the king's burial chamber. Through the entrance she could see Tutankhamun standing under the torch held by the other guard.

As she advanced towards him she stumbled on a loose block, but, with a steadying hand from her guard, she quickly regained her balance.

Tutankhamun heard the noise and turned to face her. "No! No, my Queen. Do not enter this place. I forbid it!"

Ankhesenamun stopped. "You cannot mean that, Pharaoh. It is the queen to whom you speak - Ankhesenamun, daughter of Pharaoh Akhenaten. At the time of his interment it is I who worshipped in this sepulchre. It is I who retain the right to worship here once more."

"No! You will obey me! Do not enter this room. You must do as I say. It is for your own protection that I speak these words."

"My protection? From what do you contrive to protect me, my lord?"

"From that which you do not need to know, my Queen. That which you must not know."

"If those are the orders of Pharaoh, I must obey."

The queen turned to the guard standing behind her. "Give me your firebrand. Now, leave us!" She turned to the other. "Both of you!"

The guards looked at the king. He nodded. The guards disappeared back up the staircase towards the glimmer of light at the tomb entrance.

As soon as the sound of their footsteps had faded away Ankhesenamun spoke. "Now there is no one to hear or see, I will ask you, my lord, once more in this the sepulchre of my father, what is it here that you wish to protect me from?"

So far as Ankhesenamun could see in the light thrown by her single torch, the king was standing in the middle of the burial chamber amongst a thick scatter of rubble. Akhenaten's sarcophagus, like that of Nefertiti, had been smashed to pieces. The queen knew they would have stripped her father for his jewellery, just as they had done her mother. She would be distressed by the sight of him but had to see for herself.

"I await your answer, my lord."

"Ankhesenamun. Beloved of Pharaoh. I pray you let us leave this place."

The queen was quick to recognise that what had previously been an outright order had now moderated to a simple request. She walked forward tentatively and into the huge chamber.

She looked around but couldn't see anything that resembled a body. With her torch held out ahead of her she walked around in a circle examining the floor. All she could make out were slivers of torn bandaging, pieces of broken grave goods and what appeared to be fragments of mutilated mummified animal parts.

Then she recognised the decapitated head.

This morning the sky was clear but for a low mist that hung like gossamer over the sacred lake. The sun was just up, illuminating the surrounding gardens of the temple complex. Shadows thrown by the massive structures cut the mist - dense black, long and blade-like.

Accompanied by his familiar entourage, Maya strode purposefully into the temple compound looking for Parannefer. He walked through the gardens and came upon the high priest sitting on his haunches at the water's edge. Attended by some temple maidens he was cleansing himself before beginning his day's duties. Maya hastened over to the steps where the priest was squatting and signalled to the girls to withdraw.

"Parannefer! Oh, Holy One. Terrible news is brought to me this day... I have been summoned by Pharaoh to Akhetaten, to recover and re-inter Pharaoh Akhenaten and his family at Thebes. I am told there is much despoliation!" Maya raised his arms in a gesture of disgust. "I had no alternative but to come to you. You must know before I depart."

Parannefer stood up. "And what, may I ask, is Pharaoh doing in the forbidden city?"

"I know not. The royal couple did not consult with me before leaving. They knew I would advise otherwise. The vizier and the general assisted them in their wishes. Neither of them would dare question Pharaoh's judgement."

"Royal couple? The queen has travelled thence, too?"

"Aye. It was she who wished to visit the tomb of her family."

"The gods protect us! Pray they will not become angered. I must make haste to give offerings. This is a black day indeed. A black day." The priest knelt and bowed his head.

"I was hopeful of some advice, High Priest. That is why I have hastened to your presence. Our lord is good. We both know that, do we not?"

The priest, still kneeling, nodded his agreement.

"It was the queen who discovered the penetration."

In an instant Parannefer got up again. "Penetration? The royal sepulchre is violated?"

"Aye. Ransacked. Looted. Even the bodies."

The high priest covered his face with his hands. "A black, black day indeed."

"The Pharaoh would not have gone to placate the Aten. He would have gone solely to satisfy the wishes of his loved one. And the Queen must have travelled there for one reason and one reason only - to give offerings to her family, so cruelly abandoned by her subjects following 'the sickness'.

"Help me, Parannefer. I need your good counsel regarding the proper reverent practices that should accompany such a re-interment. I must do nothing to anger the gods. Otherwise the kas of the royal family will meet many dangers, ultimately even, Seth. They will all be killed - forever! They will be but as the dust beneath our feet. Such thoughts are inconceivable. High Priest, help me! Help the royal couple in their time of need!"

Parannefer opened his fingers and looked at Maya. "You will go to the forbidden city as your monarch has commanded. Before entering the tomb you will cleanse the threshold with holy water. Only then may you enter the royal sepulchre and penetrate to the royal household. Go prepared with new coffins - theirs certainly will have been destroyed..."

"I have them already," the treasurer interjected.

"...And the bodies, I have no doubt, will be in various states of dismemberment. Prepare yourself for these abhorrent sights. Most of all, be sure you follow the correct religious procedures or their kas will surely die - for eternity. The responsibility is wholly yours."

With this comforting thought, Maya began to back away from the priest. His boat was waiting at the harbour entrance to the great temple.

Parannefer saluted him. The priest turned and pointed in the direction of the long rows of giant, brightly coloured columns that extended towards the dark inner recesses of the enormous temple. "I, in the meantime, will every day go to the shrine and pray for the forgiveness of the king. Pray the gods will believe in me, Maya. Pray hard!"

Maya was not at all convinced that he had received any helpful advice. He left the temple precinct with a heavy burden on his shoulders and embarked for the forbidden city. For his own personal safety, he had not one thought. His mind was consumed entirely with his concerns for the eternal security of the royal family. That depended on the wills of the gods and their prevailing pleasure. Should they choose to damn the family of Akhenaten, so damned would be Ankhesenamun and Tutankhamun, and thereby the royal couple's accompanying entourage, and thereby the Egyptian people. Maat would become but a memory. It was a terrifying prospect - a responsibility of far-reaching consequences.

The high priest was watching as Maya's flotilla disappeared downstream. "The gods shall support you in your endeavours, Treasurer. I shall see to it. Should it not be so, I, too, will be done for."

The royal party's journey back to Thebes took longer than expected. The wind had got up and was against them. The captain was not displeased. His task had never been to get the royal couple back to Thebes in one piece. Delay was the least of his concerns. He used the winds skilfully. Tacking allowed him to steer towards anything with considerable accuracy. When he reached the appointed place, he felt confident he would have no trouble at all manoeuvring the boat towards its doom.

The king, however, was becoming impatient at their slow progress. He shouted to one of the guards. "Summon the captain!"

The captain appeared before the kiosk and prostrated himself.

"Get up, man. Why is our progress slothful?"

"My lord. It is the current and... and the headwind. They combine against us."

"Ah. The vagaries of the current and of the winds, is it? I thought you were knowledgeable in these things and therefore could use them to advantage."

"Aye, my lord. I am as you say. I have applied my skills. But the elements are unusually against us. Had I not been skilful as you describe, we would not yet have made as much progress as my lord has witnessed."

"These words do not please me. You will make haste or I shall find another."

The captain, given the reward he was expecting from the general, did not fear for his job. He feared, however, for his life. The Pharaoh could take that away with a wave of his hand. The fact was that he had been making as much speed as he could. That the Pharaoh was not satisfied meant he would have to take more risks. Given the objective, that might not be so bad. Should the boat capsize because he let his sails out too early, the king could be lost and he would accomplish his task and receive his reward. But, try as he might, the captain was unable to get the craft to capsize.

Further upriver lay the rocky shallows of his failed downstream attempt. He realised that with the progress they were making he would come upon them during daylight hours. He was not prepared to take the risk while the royal couple were awake and alert. He had to come upon the spot under cover of darkness. He ordered the steersman to pull over to the river bank and tie up.

"Why are we stopping?"

"My lord," the captain answered, "this is our normal reprovisioning stop. And, as my lord has remarked, the journey has taken longer than expected. We are running short of food for the crew. From this point onwards there will be no further opportunity to take on fresh provisions until we reach our destination. I do not want to risk..."

"Enough! Risk it! We most urgently desire to be in Thebes. Use the oarsmen throughout the night if needs be. Cast off! We must make haste!"

"Aye, my lord."

After receiving such an order it would have been unthinkable, not to mention suicidal, for the captain to have attempted to reason further with the king. So the boat continued on its way and, because in broad daylight there could be no opportunity, the flotilla passed the area of rocks without incident. The dreadful deed undone, the ship sailed safely on to Thebes.

Inevitably the captain's fate would be decided by the secret he had held with the general. In the event, his failure to carry out his assignment made little difference to his future. Shortly after disembarkation he had disappeared without trace.

Chapter Four
Appointment

"Akhenaten, as I live and breathe!" Bellowed Petrie.

"How can you tell, sir?" asked Howard.

"Bloody ugly! The only ugly Pharaoh portrayed as ugly - though many must have been. Fat body. Fat lips. My boy, you have come across a truly rare treasure!"

Digging alongside Petrie at El Amarna, Carter had come across a large fragment of what had once been an oblong, flat tablet of limestone delicately inscribed with a family portrait of the Pharaoh along with his wife and his two daughters of that time. In common with most relics of Akhenaten, what he had found was but a piece of a much larger carving smashed during the frenetic purging that had followed the accession of Pharaoh Horemheb.

Petrie closely inspected the object. "Systematic destruction has all but eliminated evidence of this Pharaoh's reign. A rarity. A true treasure," he repeated.

Petrie likened the time to the period of the Restoration - a destruction complete in its scope but not so thorough as to reduce to dust all evidence of the heretic's existence. It was as if the mobs had executed their task with great urgency in fear that the god Aten might catch them in the act and wreak some dreadful retribution on them. The vandals' attack was quick; their withdrawal all the quicker. In a frenzy of industry, the city Akhenaten had built had been sytematically dismantled and the site abandoned. Razed to the ground, ignored and forgotten for centuries, it had been allowed to sink inexorably beneath the eternally moving sands.

The tablet Carter now held in his hands was part of a gentle portrayal of the king sitting on his throne with his wife upon his knee. Her two children were on her lap. The poignancy of the scene impressed him immensely and it became the principal subject of conversation with Petrie that evening at their camp.

But their discussion was interrupted. The camp boy brought a telegram from Cairo.

Howard's father, Samuel Carter, had died of a stroke. The man who had given him the gifts and taught him the skills that he had been using to such advantage these past months he would never see again. The tin of tobacco and cigarette papers he had been given at their parting still lay amongst his things inside the rude brick shelter Petrie had made him build for himself. Impulsively he got up and went to look for them. The gold-coloured tin lid flashed in the candlelight. He held it for a few moments, imagining his father's fingers about it as it had been pressed into the teenager's hands at the station; that anxious look on his heavily bearded face as he waved at the departing train; the following smoky fog that had descended over him and extinguished his father's image for ever.

Carter felt a heavy sense of guilt. He had become so engrossed in his work at Amarna that he had not given his family perhaps one single thought for weeks. Certainly he had not written. He consoled himself privately that any letter he might have sent from the desert in the last weeks would still be languishing in the postal bins of Alexandria awaiting the next ship. It probably would have arrived after the funeral as a not so pleasant reminder for a widow and mother trying to adjust to the finality of a fundamentally changed existence.

He had never held a strong attachment to his mother but from now on he would happily write to her periodically. He was not so preoccupied with his work that he did not realise she would now become more focused on the adventures and prosperity of her remaining family, especially those far away. He hastily scribbled a short return cable to acknowledge he had received the sad news.

Within a few days of this, downcast temporarily in spirit and tired in any case from the hard work he had so willingly endured, Carter fell sick. He begged leave of his instructor and took to his bed to try to throw off the fever.

Never before had Carter experienced a fever this strong. Every bone in his body seemed to ache. So extreme was the discomfort that he longed to be numbed by sleep. But, when this finally came, he found the relief only temporary. Within seconds of falling asleep it seemed he was wide awake again. He was hallucinating.

He could tell these were dreams. He felt no part of the illness. He was at once in Swaffham.

His mother, Martha, sat by the fire, balls of knitting wool in her lap. Amy, Vernet and William sat with her. They were talking about Howard.

"He has not written. I wonder if he knows."

"We will receive a letter soon, Mama. You know it takes a long time. Our post is bad enough, goodness knows. Whatever can it be like in Egypt?" Amy's conciliatory attitude was meant to comfort but it did little to ease her mother's anxiety.

"This, of all times, is no time to be away from one's family," Martha responded.

Vernet moved nervously in his chair. "I... I think, Mama, that in his remote solitude he perhaps grieves more than the rest of us. Please don't misunderstand me in this. We all grieve deeply, but at least we were able to see Father in recent days. Howard's last memory of him is far more distant. Being so far away that can be of little comfort to him. Not that we do not have similar memories, but he more than any of us must regret the things he did not take the time to do with Father when he was alive - the things that he might have wanted to say now forever left unsaid."

Martha began to cry. She clutched the balls of wool and raised them to her face to hide her tears.

Howard reached out to touch his mother, but, as he approached, the group seemed to drift further from him. He realised he was only an observer and drew back into the shadows.

"Do not do this to yourself, Mama," consoled Amy. "Howard is thinking of us as we speak. I feel it."

It occurred to the delirious Carter that he had in fact managed to make contact with his sister. She had heard him after all. The inner contentment this brought him allowed the images to fade, and within moments he fell into a deep, oblivious, healing sleep.

Earlier Petrie had invited his well-endowed friends Lord and Lady Waterford to the excavations and was providing them with food of a quality much improved from that which he habitually consumed himself and had up until now forced on his young assistant. It nevertheless fell some degree short of the Waterfords' expectations. Little matter, however - what Petrie lacked in the finer points of desert cuisine the Waterfords generously supplemented from their private supplies.

It had been obvious to Carter, even in the discomfort of the malaise that kept him in bed, that Petrie was decidedly uncomfortable force-fitting, as it were, his normally austere habitat to that of the wealthy. He recalled being confronted by Petrie's prescription for a happy life during one of their solitary suppers together:

"I have a little money, but want less, therefore I am rich. When I want money to dig with, I have no scruples in asking for it. If I had my way, the college would provide no fees. That is impossible by their custom. Hence I ask the minimum allowed, and make that include whatever I can do. Money and knowledge do not seem to have any common measure, any more than money and affection. A money-making professor seems to my feelings about as indecent a spectacle as a toadying heir or venal beauty. I regard the saving of a sixpence as a sacred duty, when there is no good reason for spending it; and the spending of it as a still more imperative affair when there is a reason."

Small wonder, then, that the extravagances of his guests were not shared and were little more than tolerated by the stoically thrifty scientist.

Carter's earlier background, however, his familiarity with the Amhersts, had permitted him freely and willingly to accept these comforts when they were accessible. The Waterfords had heard good reports of the young Carter and were keen to help him get back on his feet so that they might observe him at work. On the orders of their accompanying doctor came 'Valentine's Meat Juice', oranges and medicinal champagne from the

Waterfords' private reserve. Exorcised by the alcohol, it is doubtful if the feverish Carter felt a thing.

The prescription worked. In three days he was on his feet again; no temperature, just an excruciating headache. Most important of all, however, all sense of grief and remorse had left him.

As Carter had anticipated, it was not all that long before Newberry sent word that he required the young man's help back at Beni Hasan.

Carter's technical experiences with Petrie had been well worth the frustrations of working under the scholar's unrelenting control and thrift. But it had been none too soon when they finally parted company and Carter, now with a well-established basis in pharaonic history, art, language and the skills of excavation, was well prepared to take on new responsibilities.

Unknown to Carter at the time, these would not be all that long in coming. But first Newberry needed the young man's assistance to complete the work they had begun together. Images of the beautiful reliefs had filled Howard's every waking moment during his time at Amarna. He was eager to return, not least because he had had sufficient of Petrie's meagre camp and personal intensity. The two, though far apart in years and experience, were similar in their singular determination and predilection for solitude. Inherent in both of them was an intolerance of their would-be contemporaries, Carter's junior status notwithstanding. In their own minds they had none.

Once returned to Beni Hasan, sitting in the evenings with Newberry at the mouth of the tomb in which they were encamped, Carter would watch the birds on the water of the Nile below. The species were the same as those he saw portrayed on the tombs' walls. In his spare time he painted some of them true to life and in poses characteristic of the ancient, stylised art he had been copying the day before.

The French, Carter's least favourite nationality, were everywhere in Egypt. The invasion begun by Napoleon one hundred years previously had never really ceased. Marching his forces southward along the banks of the Nile, the general had wondered at the enormity of statues celebrating great men like himself. He would be remembered for all time but not in such a way, even though he might have wished it.

Like the British, some of the French were good, even conscientious in their work, and some were bad. But they shared one common faith - they were all bounty hunters at heart. One such 'bounty hunter' sounded French by name but in fact was a French Swiss. It was this particular gentleman who, following the completion of Carter's assignment with Newberry and at Petrie's recommendation, now took Carter under his wing.

Edouard Naville was an accomplished Egyptologist in his own right. With the backing of the Egypt Exploration Fund, he arrived at Luxor intent on excavating and restoring the great mortuary temple of Queen Hatshepsut at Deir el Bahri just across the river. He was nearly fifty. He was a man of some considerable stature who, besides the very necessary pith helmet, always insisted on dressing as if he were going to business in Paris on a summer's day rather than into the field to grub about amongst the sand and rocks. But there was no naivety in this approach. He had no intention of 'grubbing about'. Being thus attired he did little more than recline within his 'director's' chair. The labour was for others.

Naville's unwillingness to dirty his hands never bothered the industrious Howard Carter. The work was his fascination. He could never have sat still and issued orders. He had to handle the artefacts himself, feel the texts with his fingers, transmit what he saw to paper. It was a labour of love. In any case, he was not partial to the company of a colleague, be he lesser or senior.

"Teach the adventurer how it should be done, my boy." Petrie's parting words rang in young Carter's ears. For years Petrie had harboured a strong distaste for Naville's excavation practices. He considered the professor's approach undisciplined and wasteful and had made every effort to have Naville's concession at Deir el Bahri denied by the Service, but without success. So, to do his best to mitigate any future damage, he now had a loyal and well-trained emissary on the inside.

Carter soon learned why Naville's trim dress code was so meticulously maintained. Back at their camp, about a mile from the ruins, the man was in the domain and under the control of one Madame M. Naville, a tyrannical harridan. However, considering the conditions they were forced to live under she was also an accomplished cook of the first order. At the end of the working day, when the party returned to camp, she would tolerate Carter's sweaty and dusty state but, before his master was permitted to sit with them at dinner, she would send him off to clean himself and change into an identical suit of clothes, clean and neatly pressed.

To Howard the most amusing moments were in the mornings. Taking his breakfast - he had been well trained by Petrie and was invariably up long before any other - he would wait for Naville to appear. Having dressed and preened himself close to perfection, the Egyptologist would emerge for his inspection. It was not unlike being in the military. Madame would leave what she was doing in the kitchen area and march stiffly towards him. After closely examining the crispness of his starched trousers and linen jacket she would spend some time arranging the pith helmet correctly on his head. Howard likened the ritual to a daily crowning. If not king and queen, clearly these two were the aristocracy of the Egypt Exploration Fund.

Thankfully he was on the outside of this performance looking in. Untouched by it himself he was not embarrassed and could take relief in the comical daily procedure. It was a far cry from the practical drudgery to which he had become accustomed while in the company of Petrie.

1894. A year on at Thebes and approaching twenty years old, Carter awaited the arrival of his elder brother. He was full of expectation. Like all the others in the family, Vernet Carter also was an accomplished artist and as such the virtual double of his brother. Howard was enthusiastically looking forward to showing Vernet the beauty of the work. He felt confident he would at last have a companion who would have a full appreciation of Howard's attachment to the art form. He dearly hoped he would be able to infect his brother with a like affinity for the place, the people and, above all, the things. More than that, he expected little. He had his doubts but nevertheless hoped that, if everything went just right during this first trip, Vernet might seek to stay and accompany his brother on his future assignments along the Nile.

The elder brother arrived in Egypt in his overcoat - it was the middle of winter, after all. By the time he disembarked at Luxor station he had packed his coat away, removed his tie, opened his shirt to his navel, and rolled up his sleeves. Vernet set foot on the sand of the Upper Nile in total disbelief that such pervasive heat could exist in the Northern Hemisphere in February.

Howard was waiting for him. "You will not notice it once you've set eyes on what it is I have to show you," he said reassuringly.

That first evening, when the air had mercifully cooled, Howard took Vernet across the river to show him the mortuary temple of Queen Hatshepsut - Deir el Bahri, 'The Convent of the North'.

The cooling breeze off the water made the crossing a most pleasing experience. But, once he had set foot on the west bank, Vernet again felt the oppressive heat. Stored within the rocks during the day, it radiated off the stones and sand all about him. Mules were waiting to take them up a well-worn track that ran almost directly west between the rice fields and towards the towering cliffs ahead. In the distance, on the north side of the road, Vernet could make out two colossal statues of seated figures apparently identical in proportion, standing apart from each other and, but for each other's company, quite alone on the flood plain. All he could see were silhouettes. The sun now almost touched the ridge line of the hills ahead and threw crisp, linear shadows of the two great figures towards the river. As the brothers approached, Vernet realised the enormity of the statues. They had to be well over fifty feet high. Pitted, scarred, chipped and cracked by the ravages of time, wind, water and extremes of temperature, their facial features now were virtually unrecognisable.

Howard had been watching for his brother's reactions and, energised by the opportunity to become the instructor for a change, he pulled his mule to a halt and launched himself into a tutorial. "They are the processional entrance figures to the temple of Amenhotep III, each hewn from a single block of quartzite. The temple lay directly behind them. Nothing there now, as you can see. Impressive it must have been, but it was made largely of unfired mud bricks at the mercy of the severe storms that infrequently occur here. The great building has been dissolved by thousands of years of such rains. It has sunk into the mud of the flood plain, been totally looted by scavangers, and ploughed over so many times by the local farmers that it might never appear to have existed. Were it not for the colossi, which the king clearly made sure were too massive to be destroyed, there would be nothing. Amenhotep reigned in the thirteen hundreds BC."

"That's over three thousand years ago, Howard," Vernet calculated. The elder brother was impressed. There was plenty in England that was much older, but nothing its equal in sophistication.

Howard kicked his mule and the party moved on. As they passed by the huge statues, the emptiness of the fields around them served only to accentuate their enormity.

The mules loped onward and turned right, out of the fields and along the lower reaches of the desert's edge past a number of notably large, ancient, pillared buildings in various stages of decay. As they ascended the gentle incline towards the cliffs Howard pointed out the mortuary temple of Rameses II. He promised Vernet that they would investigate the 'Ramesium' in detail at some future date.

The façade of the craggy escarpment grew above them. In the deepening shadow Vernet could make out what appeared to be an incongruous, crude, red tower standing on a desolate ruin of quite considerable size. The structure, whatever it was, or had been, was largely buried. Debris lay all around and over it. Piles of rubble were everywhere. Most of this appeared man-made. Great piles of white and yellow limestone detritus were heaped together much like the coal tips back home.

Howard saw Vernet looking at the rubble and commented, "Many previous explorers." He pulled his mule to a stop some way from the threshold. "This is far enough for tonight. What do you see, brother?"

The sun had now dropped below the cliff line. Vernet strained his eyes. Stretching before him was a dead straight avenue - the like of those bordered by two precisely parallel lines of evenly spaced mature beech trees running to the great front doors of so many English stately homes. Sand-covered plinths - they could have been tree stumps - lined the track with geometric precision and extended onward to the threshold of the first ramp.

"What are those, Howard?"

"What's left of a processional avenue of sphinxes, Vernet, reaching all the way to the foot of her temple. Sadly, but for the pedestals on which they stood, mostly gone now. The Frogs nicked 'em."

Vernet looked towards the top of the first ramp. This upper step appeared to break up into a partially rubble-filled colonnade of stone pillars supporting a wide, flat roof. The building clearly had been assembled on a platform levelled out after extensive excavation of the scree apron that at one time had cloaked the lower reaches of the cliffs. Backing the structure where it joined the cliff face, itself chiselled away in part to more suitably accommodate the architecture, vertical clefts gave the appearance of folds in a colossal grey curtain. Vernet could make out two such platforms, one above the other, each disappearing in its lower reaches into aprons of talus that over the centuries had fallen from above and in more recent times had been added to by the spoils of the haphazard burrowings of the treasure-seeker. The colonnade that supported the upper platform was also filled with rock debris, almost to the roof line.

"Behind those piles of rubble, inside there," said Howard pointing, "are painted reliefs so beautiful in their simplicity and so vibrant in their preserved colour you will wonder which to choose to paint first. Now, unfortunately, it is too dark to go in. We shall return tomorrow to give you a tour of the interior. Then we can begin our work in earnest.

"The anticipation... Gives you butterflies, does it not?"

Although in a comfortable hotel bed, Vernet did not sleep well that night; less because of the sense of expectation and excitement, more on account of the discomforts that awaited him in the Naville camp on the opposite side of the river and of the heat he would have to endure.

The following morning his late-night fears were purged by the beauty of the sunrise. The early light was in stark contrast to the crisp silhouettes and shadows of the previous evening. Once above the horizon, the sun shone directly into the cliffs across the river and the cliffs blazed back. Hardly a shadow was to be seen and the walls of the escarpment melded into a monochromatic yellow. The only exception was that rust-coloured mud-brick tower standing totally out of character with the desolate symmetry surrounding it.

When the brothers reached the excavation field camp the Navilles were already in place. Vernet deposited his things beside the folding bed that would become his sanctuary for the next few months.

Madame Naville caught sight of the new arrival. "Monsieur Carter is it not? The brother of Howard? Why, I am most pleased to meet you." She extended her hand, palm down.

Vernet didn't hesitate. He took the limp fingers gently in his cupped hand and, bowing slightly, raised madame's hand to his lips.

"Most gallant. A true gentleman. Just like your brother."

Before she could ask his name, Howard, realising that in his haste to ready materials for the day's work he had neglected the formalities, shouted from the storage tent, "My big brother, Vernet, madame!" He threw the tent flap aside and emerged. "He is a most talented artist. Along with our father he helped teach me many artistic techniques."

Madame Naville smiled approvingly at Vernet. He smiled back. He felt her hand attempt to pull away from his and loosened his grip immediately. He hadn't been aware he had been holding on to her for so long. He felt embarrassed, but her smile put him at ease and he grinned back sheepishly.

'Butter wouldn't melt', thought Howard.

"We must be off to work, madame, before the professor realises we have not yet left camp. Please excuse us."

In the morning sunlight the form of the temple was much clearer to Vernet. As the two walked up the slight incline of desert at the foot of the rock-strewn apron that fronted the site, the desolation transformed to sheer spectacle. For the time being at least, he had forgotten his anxiety.

They moved ahead up the ramp and onto the middle platform. Naville came into view, standing on a great pile of rubble looking down at his fellahs who were dashing all about in a flurry of work below him. The mêlée virtually boiled within a tumbling pall of dust. A continuous stream of filthy bodies emerged from it carrying baskets full of rocks, which they dumped into a waiting Decauville railway truck. Then they turned and disappeared again into the dust cloud.

Standing erect with one foot forward, somewhat reminiscent of a Napoleonic pose, Naville waved his stick and clicked his fingers at his men. A fellah immediately scampered towards him carrying a canvas chair and umbrella. The Egyptologist eased himself into the seat, adjusted the umbrella for shade, and continued his direction.

The brothers rode up.

"Bonjour, Howard. Votre frère?"

"Oui, Monsieur. Mon frère."

"Je m'appelle Vernet, monsieur," Vernet announced himself.

"Mon plasir." That was the end of the pleasantries. "You know where to go. Take your brother and begin as I had previously instructed. I will remain outside today to ensure the fellahs clear this place in reasonable time. There are but five seasons left on our permit, as you know. Vitement, s'il vous plait."

They walked on.

"Vernet. Before we go up there," Howard gestured towards the upper platform, "I want to give you a flavour of what you will later get to down here once 'Monsieur le Docteur' has completed his clearance... First, however, something for mother..."

Howard had his six shilling 'Brownie' box camera with him. He had become an accomplished photographer of late and was trying his best to keep a visual record of the excavation's progress.

"Give me some scale to this picture. Sit on top of that pile of debris."

Vernet scrambled up the rubble slope and sat uncomfortably upon a rock pile between the tops of two columns in the colonnade. His panama provided some relief from the already hot sun. He crossed his legs, forced a smile, and wished his brother to be quick. The sooner he was out of the sun and within the coolness of the building, the better.

"That's it. Just a minute now... Good."

Howard wound the film on and climbed up after him. He placed his hand on his brother's shoulder and announced with a note of ceremony, "Let us go in."

Crouching to avoid the stone lintel, they scrambled into the darkness and slid down the rubble face until they felt the solid stone floor beneath their feet. They remained in a sitting position for a moment, allowing their eyes to become accustomed to the poor light. The tall corridor of the colonnade fell away from them into the gloom, but the walls nearest to the rubble-filled entrance had sufficient natural light on them to make out the artwork clearly. Howard tugged at Vernet's sleeve and pulled him over to a frieze of hieroglyphs and figures. The expanse was an ordered sequence of verticals and horizontals, texts and pictures. It extended into the darkness, seemingly never-ending.

"Vernet. Observe the fundamental laws of Egyptian art; how it eliminates the non-essential. Copy that art accurately and intelligently, with honest work, a free hand, a good pencil and suitable paper - the Carter creed!" He grinned and patted his brother encouragingly on the shoulder.

They climbed back out of the colonnade and made their way up the second ramp to the upper platform. Howard had been hard at work here for some weeks prior to Vernet's arrival. He guided his brother through the maze of doorways and rooms that led to the Chapel of Tuthmosis I, the father of Hatshepsut. The brilliantly painted arched end wall, though much damaged, was a picture of perfect symmetry. Its beauty was overwhelming.

"We start here."

Vernet applied himself well, but at the end of each work period he absolutely dreaded emerging into the sunlight. Fatigued at the end of a hard day, all he was looking for were immediate rest and comfort. But the amphitheatre of vertical rock that held the temple close focused the sun's rays and baked the desert rocks so that, once outside, radiant heat hit the body from above, from the sides and from beneath. It truly was like walking into a giant oven.

He would lie awake in his bed with a glass of Scotch long into the night. He would drink himself to sleep. Over and over in his mind he would relive the experiences of the previous day. He enjoyed the artwork. His product, though more laboured and less timely in its execution, was clearly the equal of his brother's. But the place, the environment, the interminable heat - it was all too much for him. It did not take long for Vernet to realise that he would not be able to stomach another season. How would he tell Howard he was not up to staying the course? Such thoughts became the stuff of his dreams.

A few weeks later Vernet left his brother to work alone in the small, complexly decorated chapel. The decision to move was not of his own making. The simple fact was that Howard had had enough of his brother's company - for long periods and at close quarters, that is. Vernet liked to chat as he worked. Active conversation kept his mind off his discomforts. Howard found this all too distracting and in the confined space the noise was intolerable to him. He sent Vernet down to the middle platform, which by now had been cleared sufficiently to gain access to the hypostyle hall and the Shrine of Anubis.

"It is a great opportunity, Vernet," comforted his brother obsequiously. "You will be the first to attempt to copy the illustrations on the opposing flanks of the doorway that leads to the shrine."

Despite his imposed solitude and the prospect of now being at the mercy of his own thoughts, Vernet was pleased to be granted this singular responsibility. Under a blue ceiling studded with yellow stars, the door to the shrine was framed on each side by a vibrantly painted base relief. The scenes were complex but exactingly proportioned, that on the left perfectly complementing, but not repeating, the one on the right. On the left side of the doorway, in the top left corner, was the 'vulture of the south'. She overlooked the somewhat larger than life-size engravings of Hatshepsut, in antiquity almost completely excised, and of Amun. They both held the Was sceptre. Engraved between them was a large, neatly stacked pile of sumptuous offerings. On the opposite side of the door similarly opposing but somewhat different figures were carved - the 'hawk of the north' in the top right corner and, in the centre, the female Pharaoh, again frantically grubbed out by the chisels of her successor; facing her the god Anubis, also brandishing the Was sceptre; and, once again, neatly serried ranks of offerings placed in stacks between the figures.

The short commute to and from work each day was pure torture for Vernet and, as time wore on, it became barely worth the pleasure of reproducing the art. Carter and Naville, apparently insensitive to the heat, would exacerbate his discomfort by insisting that the party dismount and leave their mules before they entered the avenue of sphinxes. From there, Vernet would have to walk the length of the sandy avenue, ascend the ramp to the lower platform, walk up the second ramp to the middle platform, and walk all the way across the middle platform to its northern corner. All this under the unyielding sun before he reached the shaded sanctuary of the covered hall where he could begin his work. And it was worse going home in the evening.

On this particular night, however, he lay back in his bed with a smile on his face. He was truly pleased with himself. The art he had accomplished that day had been most satisfying. The subjects themselves had helped, of course, but it had been the gratuitous praise of his brother that had been most pleasing. And, to top it all, Naville had instructed him to make a colour copy of the vulture and of the hawk in opposing corners. He would recommend to the Exploration Fund that it make use of this pair of colour reproductions in a forthcoming memoir. *(Naville acknowledged the contributions of the brothers in the preface to volume one of his report. Vernet's colour plate of the vulture was published in volume two, documenting the second season's work at which he was not present. In the event, his brother was responsible for completing the second colour plate of the hawk. It is not possible to detect any difference in style between these faithful freehand copies. The sixth and final volume of Naville's epic Deir el Bahri report was finally published in 1908. Much of this monograph had been the product of Howard Carter's work. In Egyptological circles it is acknowledged to hold some of the finest examples of reproduced ancient Egyptian art on record; see Naville, 1894 - 1908.)*

The red mud-brick tower that Vernet had noticed at the start of their first day's work, although built in antiquity, post-dated the Pharaohs by hundreds of years. When the brothers emerged from the temple at the end of their fifth day of copying they found it had disappeared. Naville, aspiring to uniformity in the architecture of the buildings he was restoring, had had his men dismantle it. He justified his actions by pointing out that some of the stone incorporated in the brickwork had come from the temple complex itself and therefore was required to assist in its restoration. The original mud bricks were not wasted either. Naville reused them in the construction of a house for the excavation party close to the bottom of the first ramp.

As the season progressed, Naville continued his clearance of the rubble that choked the length of the middle platform colonnade. Howard was not happy with the manner in which he did this, but, without risking total alienation from the more experienced archaeologist, not to mention the possible loss of an assignment that he relished and a note of recognition in the annual publications of the excavations, protocol would not permit him the temerity of any suggestion to take a more careful and systematic approach. In this he failed his mentor, William Flinders Petrie, totally. As he matured, however, consideration of 'protocol' in the face of practicality would fast become a lesser virtue.

During rest periods at the entrance to the halls, Howard would watch Naville directing the fellahs to clear rubble like a human dredge with no care for what fragment of artefact may lie buried in each basketful of sand and stones, tossing the debris in growing heaps into a pit far away from the temple threshold. The professor was himself impatient to get to the business of restoring the structure to something like its original grandeur. There were only a few months each year in which he could execute his task and he was not about to leave unfulfilled.

Finally, the colonnade was completely cleared. Naville announced the end of the excavations for that season, and paid off his labourers. That night the professor broke out champagne at dinner to celebrate the successful completion of the excavations. Vernet, exceedingly relieved and thankful that his discomforts of the past weeks shortly would lie behind him, entered fully into the spirit of the evening and drank heavily. There was considerable joking and laughing at the dinner table that night and Howard joined in the stories, recounting some of his earlier experiences with Newberry and the distasteful antics of Messrs Fraser and Blackden. Vernet himself did not say much, but what little he did say became all the less coherent as the evening wore on.

Eventually, on madame's instructions, Naville retired to bed.

"A fine evening, Sir, madame," said Vernet, as the Navilles took their leave. Vernet tried to stand.

"Oh, please remain seated. The pleasure and gratitude is all ours, Messieurs. We return to Cairo tomorrow. We wish you luck in the completion of the hypostyle frieze. Enjoy yourselves."

"Completion?" Vernet was not so far gone that he did not recognise the significance of the professor's parting remark. He looked at his brother in bewilderment.

Howard touched his arm and turned to Madame Naville. "Good night, madame. Pleasant dreams."

"Bon nuit, Messieurs. À bientôt." And they left the room.

Vernet pulled at Howard's sleeve. "What did he mean, Howard, wishing us luck like that?"

"We are expected to finish what we have begun before we leave. I don't think it's going to take us, together, more than one more month."

Matter of fact words from Howard - he had never contemplated leaving with the Navilles and was completely insensitive to his brother's expectations - to Vernet a sledgehammer blow.

"Another month? Can you be serious? Howard, I don't think I can take another month in this heat... Dammit, it's getting hotter every day!"

"You'll get used to it. Everybody gets used to it. We all acclimatise eventually. Have patience." A virtue the younger brother extolled but had precious little of himself.

"'You'll get used to it.' That's what you said when I arrived last February. Not yet I ain't!"

Vernet took an almost full bottle of champagne back with him to his room that night. Howard did not expect him to appear for work the following day and he didn't. But he was there the day after, and the day after that. And so he continued, forcing himself to rise each morning, the only encouragement being the pleasant artwork ahead and a day nearer to the end.

It had been tolerable working in the shade provided in the depths of the hypostyle hall. So much so that, with the Navilles now departed, the brothers would bed there and so avoid the daily torture of commuting back and forth to the camp. But this would do little to ameliorate Vernet's continuing discomfort. He would see this season through and that in itself would be an end to it. In this decision he was resolute. He would never return. But how would he break the news to his brother?

As spring advanced and it grew steadily and inexorably warmer each day, Howard finally recognised the agony of toleration in his brother's face. One night he saw an opportunity to ease his brother's torment. All it took was a casual suggestion at dinner - the opportunity to leave without fear of return placed before him for the taking. Vernet jumped at the chance. He was greatly relieved that his brother had taken the initiative.

They completed the work in the hypostyle hall together. They shared the copying of the decoration to the doorway of the Shrine of Anubis, Howard taking the north frieze, Vernet the south. But for their signatures, the authorship was virtually indistinguishable.

At the close of that first season's work, Vernet Carter bade farewell to Egypt. It was, as both of them recognised, to be for ever. Howard accepted it more willingly than his brother realised. While Vernet had been a helpful and skilled asset in the execution of the tasks before them, outside of the work they accomplished, his incessant chatter and lack of discipline were to his younger brother at times intensely irritating.

Vernet was to be the only one of the Carter family ever to visit Egypt. The thought did not vex Howard unduly.

Four seasons after his brother's departure there was a break in the routine. A late afternoon downpour caused Naville and his entourage of helpers to leave for the expedition house early. Carter was now copying decorations deep inside the rock-cut shrines. He knew nothing of the deluge until he emerged at the end of his working day. Everyone but his bedraggled horse had left. He pulled himself into the soaking saddle and began the slow amble home.

Years in the desert had conditioned Carter to the perpetual heat and dryness. Nevertheless the downpour was pleasantly cooling and a welcome relief. He relaxed. As they descended the long ramp, Carter's body lolled about in loose harmony with his horse.

The late evening light was poor and the torrential rain made the ground virtually invisible. A few steps from a second causeway that led from the adjacent temple of Mentuhotep, Carter's horse caught a front hoof in a depression in the ground and faltered. Carter cartwheeled off its back and slid for a short distance in the mud. The startled animal quickly regained its footing and sprinted into the darkness. Carter, tired from the day's labours, was slower to recover. He sat for a moment breathing heavily, his heart racing from the shock of the fall. After a while he gathered himself and wiped the wet mud from his jacket. He walked back to the site of the accident to see what had caused the horse to stumble.

The run-off had found a small hole to drain into and this had gradually become enlarged by the continued torrent. A flat slab of rock was exposed in the hole. It was difficult to see clearly, but Carter was sure the hand of man had shaped this stone - it was a step hewn from the solid bedrock.

He quickly regained his composure and his sensibilities. The possibility of kneeling at the threshold of the stairway to an undiscovered tomb filled him with excitement and he totally forgot his fall. It dawned on him that he was alone and there was a unique opportunity to keep this to himself. The notion was irresistible, providing he could also resist the natural and urgent need to investigate. That would be easy, however; discipline was one of Carter's more fundamental characteristics. He would 'bank' this discovery for another day. He quickly obscured the area with rubble. He wiped the rain from his eyes. So he could be sure of recognising the spot again, he took mental bearings on the nearby landmarks, then he collected his horse and continued on foot to the expedition house.

Howard Carter had laboured with the Navilles for five years. He had never become bored with the routine. He had gained great personal satisfaction from the work, and there had been a bonus - publication.

Naville's respect for Carter's talents, the young man's dedication to his artwork, plus his advancing skills at restoration, grew season on season. Toleration of his stubborn streak was a small price to pay for the product. At the conclusion of their work at Deir el Bahri, intent on providing a just reward for Carter's services, Naville was quick to secure for his assistant a position with more permanent prospects. The persistent Madame Naville suggested that the professor talk with Gaston Maspero when he next returned to Cairo.

An old friend of the Navilles and Director General of the Egyptian Antiquities Service, Maspero was an important, powerful and influential man. He was short, plump and habitually dressed in a three-piece suit and bow tie. His bushy, grey moustache was stained at the tips from chain-drinking thick, black Egyptian coffee. During their conversation that day in Maspero's museum office, Naville mused to himself that it was a little like talking with a French-speaking St Bernard - the slight movement of his chin was the only visible evidence of a response; one never glimpsed his lips. There might not have been a barrel hanging from his neck but the brandy was never far from reach.

As head of the Service, Maspero was deeply committed to his responsibilities. He took meticulous care in the selection of those to whom he would entrust supervison of the archaeological licences permitting work on the various sites.

Naville recounted his recent experiences with Carter. The stories did much to endorse those Maspero had heard from other respected sources - Petrie for one - and his own more piecemeal observations. It all helped to confirm his earlier intention to seriously consider Carter for one of the two senior regional posts.

"He is a young man yet, but displays a maturity of approach that belies his years. His art is exemplary," continued Naville. "I have seen the like only in his brother's work, but sadly he did not stay. Madame Naville agrees."

"Hmm. Then I, too, must agree, monsieur," Maspero observed with some conviction. "His youth gives him the considerable energy he will need to cover the territory he will oversee. And he exhibits a tolerance for the heat which permits him to continue working when all but the Arab labourers have retired to the shade. In many ways the Service will realise much value for their money."

"His Arabic, also, is now fluent, Monsieur le Directeur. And he has matured a special relationship with the reis's and their gangs. They return him some considerable respect - also in the conscientiousness of their work, and their particular abilities to pick out small artefacts within the spoil of excavation is quite remarkable. All of this they owe to his instruction."

Maspero reflected for a moment and took another sip of coffee. Wiping his moustache with his forefinger in a sawing motion, he said, "I have but one concern, monsieur - how he may endure his relationships with the many visitors and licensees. I daresay these relationships will not be as symbiotic. I fear he suffers their company as a necessary evil. He certainly does not welcome it. When dealing with the layman visitor there is irritation in his voice - I have witnessed it - and he exhibits much impatience when interrupted in the course of his work. In his personality I see precious little bent towards pragmatism."

Naville chuckled. "You are so very correct, Monsieur le Directeur," he said. "He suffers the company of contemporaries poorly - and fools not at all."

"But," rejoined Maspero with a smile, "no one is perfect, eh, Monsieur Naville?"

Naville laughed, "And he gets on with Madame Naville very well!"

"An unquestionably sound endorsement, Monsieur!" commented Maspero. "So, given a choice between stubborn discipline and loose pragmatism, I would choose the former every time. This job is too important for the conciliatory." He made an extravagant arching gesture with his arm. "To 'Inspector Carter', monsieur!" And the brandy bottle appeared from under Maspero's desk. The two used it well, long into the night.

The Director would not come to regret the decision he made that day. However, in the course of time his fears over the inflexibility of Carter's character would be confirmed, and on occasion his patience sorely tried.

Edouard Naville himself was sorely tried that night. As he entered his hotel room and attempted to remove his shoes Madame heard him stumble...

As the nineteenth century drew to a close, on Boxing Day, the 26th of December 1899, Gaston Maspero summoned Howard Carter to Cairo. He advised him of his new appointment: 'Inspector of Antiquities to the Egyptian Government', responsible for all areas of the Upper Nile, including The Valley of the Tombs of the Kings.

There had been rumours to this effect prior to his trip north but this did not reduce his immense feeling of elation once he heard the confirmation. With a broad smile and with both hands vigorously shaking Maspero's, he made his acceptance and his feelings quite clear.

He took up his position on New Year's Day, 1900. At the dawn of a new century Carter could not have wished for more.

Chapter Five
Mummy

As the general had ordered, Ankhesenamun was not told of her husband's death until she awoke the following morning. She threw on a robe and ran directly to his bedchamber. The queen stopped dead in the doorway.

Now freshly washed, the dead Pharaoh lay on his back on clean white sheets. He was fully clothed in the customary trappings of kingship.

The queen remained still for a moment, staring at the body. She did not see those who stood in the shadows. There was total stillness, absolute silence. The white gown she wore covered her slim body to her slippers. As the queen started to walk over to the bedside, the material barely rippled. She seemed to drift across the room.

The queen sat carefully on the bed of the husband she had said 'good night' to just a few hours earlier. She touched his cold forehead, held his pale hand. Then, in an urgent physical movement of emotion, she fell on him and consumed his motionless body in an embrace so complete that those who looked on became uneasy being present at so private a union.

After some moments she drew back and fell to her knees on the stone floor. She wept. She began tearing at her hair. She wailed - a moaning that rose and fell, penetrating the depths of the palace hallways. Slowly it faded to a low whimper.

No one in the chamber dared move. Rather they wished they were not there. This was the queen's time.

After several minutes she became silent. She inclined her head in prayer.

By now this private communion had lasted so long that old Ay's legs finally failed him and he collapsed to the floor. The commotion brought her back from her holy conversations with the gods. She raised her hand and slowly turned to those who stood in the shadows. With the help of the guards, Ay had regained his sensibilities and had drawn himself up into a seated position on the floor. The queen could make out his frail form in the poor light and, recognising him as the most senior person present, addressed him directly. Her interrogation was calculated, her tone controlled, almost without emotion.

"Who found the King?"

The guards helped Ay to his feet. "General Horemheb, Excellency."

"At what time?"

"About the middle of the night, Excellency."

"Why was I not informed?"

Ay looked around the chamber for Horemheb. He was nowhere to be seen. "Excellency. The king was dead. There was nothing that could be done. Pharaoh was lost to us. Your Grace was asleep. There seemed no reason to disturb you. The general ordered it so."

"'The general ordered it so'? Are you mad? Since when has the general's word been law in this household? And why was he visiting my husband at so late an hour?"

"I know not, Excellency. Pharaoh Tutankhamun was sick. Perhaps he wished to be assured that the king slept soundly. That he had no needs."

"That he certainly made sure of," the queen whispered under her breath. "Old seer, your innocent speculation does you no credit. How long was he in the room before he raised the alarm?"

"Excellency! So many questions. Pharaoh died of an affliction. General Horemheb's only misadventure was that he did not visit Pharaoh earlier to catch the affliction before its fatal outcome. Indeed, that is a misadventure we all share."

Ay fell to his knees once more.

The queen hesitated. "Honourable Ay. You who have guided and supported Tutankhamun through his early years. You who have educated him to kingship. Do not chide my inquisition. It is born of the most immediate grief for the loss of my husband and a desperate need to exorcise this grief through identification of cause. Do you not seek this likewise?"

Ay, standing again, continued, "My gracious lady. To relieve the torment that inhabits you, you must accept my counsel. The cause was affliction, a humour within - perhaps 'the sickness'."

The queen looked down at the floor. "We should never have gone there. In that the vizier gave good counsel. For many reasons, we should never have gone there." She continued to gaze downward.

Of Ay's integrity Ankhesenamun had no personal doubts. He had been wise and correct in his advice of the past and there was no need to suspect a change at this point. He had nothing to gain. He was old and ailing and she could clearly see in his eyes an evident envy of her husband's passage to the rejuvenation of the afterlife. He was now too tired to face the responsibilities of his present, unexpected incarnation and rather longed for his own transition.

The queen dismissed the old man with words of kind gratitude for his attendant concern.

She turned back to look at her still husband. Holding his limp hand to her lips once more, tears began to bead in her eyes, and like so many tiny, shining pearls they softly ran down her cheeks to soak into the linen of the bedclothes. She did not sob as she lamented. Her grief was expressed in silent tears. Those in the shadows, including Ay, silently slipped away.

Her face was expressionless - her anger reserved to the depths of her mind. Those who had watched her kneel beside the Pharaoh's body witnessed nothing of the torment building within her. Her mind filled with visions - Horemheb, the ambitious general, poisoning the king's food with some libation that encourages the body's sap to issue forth; Horemheb raising up spells from the evil god, Seth. It was he. She knew it was he. But how might she expose his conspiracy? As she went down on her knees she felt her fingernails bite into the king's cold palm. Her whole body tightened into a cowed ball. She agonised about how she might discover some semblance of proof, something the general had done that could visibly be demonstrated to the officialdom of the palace and the priesthood and, latterly, to the people. His skill in assassinating her husband without apparent trace of unnatural cause heightened the intensity of her frustration. The tension in her muscles tightened until a cramp developed in her legs and she had to stand up and walk about the room to ease the pain.

As she paced, she regarded the body on the bed. Suddenly it was as if she were on the outside of the situation looking in. There was another realism. For now, proving the culpability of the general was of lesser importance. There was a more urgent need. Ay was not yet confirmed in his ascendancy to Pharaoh. This could not happen until the most holy of the ceremonies on the day of the funeral itself. The seventy days that by religious law must pass before the funeral would provide time to engineer change. The queen would have to move quickly if she were successfully to avoid losing the supremacy of her position. The way forward was clear. Since from their short marriage there had been no living issue, she must marry again - into a royal line - and quickly, within the next two months.

For many days Ankhesenamun remained in her quarters at the palace accepting only water and a little fruit. She would talk with no one. According to custom, and to those outside she would grieve in solitude for the entire period remaining to the day of the funeral ceremonies. But for herself, with the passage of very little time, the shock had taken second place. As her sensibilities returned, she dwelled on a single thought: how could she ensure retention of her royal line? It could be done with a new consort, regal in his own right and as such visible to the people and the gods. But there was no one in Upper or Lower Egypt to fill this position. Those who might be appropriate to kingship were either virtual enemies to her house, already had a principal wife, or were too grotesquely old, fragile and impermanent to inhabit her bed. She would have to look to other states - foreign statesmen.

Horemheb was determined to demonstrate his consummate allegiance to the dead regent. So the general quickly assumed responsibility for coordinating plans for the funeral. He was presently busy preparing the inventory of grave goods for the king's burial. The body itself was now in the care of the high priest and would remain so until the day it would travel to

The Valley.

Tutankhamun had died too young for preparations to have begun on his coffin set. He was barely full grown. Now there would not be time to complete sufficiently elaborate coffins by the appointed day. This notwithstanding, the general would ensure that the funeral was most richly endowed - as richly provided as any other in living memory. To achieve this successfully he had decided to cut a few corners. In physical appearance the boy king was not unlike his dead and buried brother. It was not an uncommon practice to usurp the belongings and memorials of entombed kings. The deed was not dishonourable. It was expedient. And there were many precedents.

Horemheb called his guards. "Close to the place where our noble prince is to be laid to rest lies the burial place of his brother, Pharaoh Smenkhkare, he who also died of 'the sickness'. You know the place?"

The guards nodded.

"It remains inviolate, does it not?"

The guards nodded.

"You will open it. Take from there Smenkhkare's sarcophagus, the shrine that covers it, the outer coffin set, his canopic shrine, and some of the jewellery caskets. I shall give you a list from the royal inventory records. Bring all this to me. Mind you do not disturb Pharaoh in his eternal slumber. Leave him at peace within his inner coffin and reseal the tomb. To ensure the continued sanctity of the burial, the priests will be present at every stage of the opening, evacuation and resealing. This secret must be kept close.

"Obtain for me a troop of strong labourers to execute this task. Watch them, mind, lest they recognise this as a heaven-sent opportunity and turn their minds to robbery. Keep them camped at the site until their job is completed. Search them thoroughly each night before they retire. When the job is done dispatch them, every one, quietly, in a distant place.

"Be about your task at once! Be gone!"

The guards bowed and withdrew.

Horemheb turned to his bare-chested maidservant. "Wine."

She brought him a filled cup.

"More."

She unfastened the slender rope at her waist.

Ankhesenamun had decided upon a way forward. The queen instructed Tia to bring her papyrus, a writing instrument and ink. Hurriedly she wrote to the King of the Hittites, Suppiluliumas I, whom she knew had unmarried sons, requesting he send her one of them so that she might take him as husband and make him King of Egypt. The Hittites had been enemies of Egypt for lifetimes. Each lusted for conquest of the other. A regal marriage of this type could enable a bloodless coup for both sides and greatly enlarge and enrich their individual empires. The opportunity, surely, would be too much for the Hittite leader to resist.

She called Ipay, one of her trusted servants, and asked him to take and deliver the letter, with all haste, to Suppiluliumas in Hattusas, Anatolia.

She was well aware it would be at least three weeks before she could expect a reply. The waiting would be long and anxious. But there would be little time for tedium. She had many responsibilities and duties concerning the reverend and successful transmission of her late king's soul to the afterlife. Her preoccupation with this vigil would not be wholly selfless.

Ipay was not at all enamoured with the mission he had been given. To leave your home for any length of time, especially on a journey of this scale, was considered by all Egyptians as a sentence to purgatory. But this was by royal decree. He had no choice but to obey. He said goodbye to his wife and children and began his perilous trip northward.

The queen impatiently awaited word.

When the letter arrived, Suppiluliumas's response was incredulous. Yet he was sufficiently intrigued to return his chamberlain along with Ipay to obtain some clarification. In a secret meeting with the queen, the chamberlain unabashedly explained that the Hittite king had been necessarily blunt in his reply. He frankly did not believe her story and thought it more likely a murderous plot to rob him of his first-born son, more than to provide him a new kingdom through marriage.

The queen was greatly offended by Suppiluliumas's reaction, but time and circumstances did not permit her the luxury of argument and, assuming all the dignity and reserve that family and position had bequeathed her, she calmly, patiently and thoughtfully settled herself to constructing a more acceptable response...

Great Lord of the North Lands,

For you, for your household, for your wives, for your sons, for your daughters, for your magnates, for your troops, for your chariots, for your horses, and for your country, may all go very well.

You do not believe my request. Your messenger says, "You conspire to kill my son and heir - to cut the bloodline of this great empire." These are your words. What you say is untrue. You must believe my request. You do not understand my position. You must understand my position. By my first marriage I bore two daughters, both stillborn. I am without issue to continue the royal bloodline. No alternative is imaginable. Should you permit it with your distrust of my true intent, an aged uncle will take the line. But there is only a short time remaining to him. Much worse than this, a menace waits in the wings - Horemheb - the hateful one. You know of him. He who has threatened your lands before. He who has proven himself avaricious, untrustworthy, brutal, unmerciful. He who seeks only that which will secure his personal omnipotence. He who must be stopped.

The union I propose will avoid the unimaginable. The commingling of our two bloods will double our two empires at a single stroke, and peacefully, as within the crucible of our marriage bed.

It is from the very depths of my heart that I ask you to grant this behest. I long to unite our two great empires with this marriage.

But there is very little time. I am to take a husband before the next fullness of the moon. Otherwise the kingdom will be lost to the bloodline of an evil usurper. At the funeral that waits upon the rising of Osiris - the rising that waits upon no king - he who is present to open the mouth of my dear departed Tutankhamun - it will be he who takes the crown of Egypt. Send my husband to me.

This is what I long for, day and night.

Ankhesenamun, Queen of Upper Egyptian Heliopolis

To the Hittites, and no less to Ankhesenamun, there would be great appeal to the elimination of the warmonger, Horemheb. For the gods the royal couple were omnipotent, the incarnations of gods on earth. They could exact retribution on any in the court but the priests, and none would question the reason. There would be peace between their great nations. Better still, to his people Suppiluliumas, through his son, could claim peaceful victory and control over the Egyptians. It was too good a fit, too irresistible.

Nevertheless, another three weeks had passed since the chamberlain of the King of the Hittites had left with her letter. She waited anxiously for what, in the time left to her, would be the final response - her destiny.

To the people, whatever the circumstances of King Tutankhamun's death - disease, madness or contrived - his double, his spirit, his soul, his ka must now be released to thrive in the afterlife. The artisans' most present and immediate responsibility was to ensure the dead king's smooth and correct passage and his continuing sustenance. Their workshops were a hive of activity. The death mask had been taken and was already with the goldsmiths. Meneg assembled the finished body, legs, tail and head of the wooden figure of Anubis.

On the other side of the river, in a private, dimly lit chamber deep within the temple complex, the punctual and ordered business of preparing the king's body for its ultimate interment was under way. The body had been cleansed and lay on a bed of sculpted alabaster. Throughout the forthcoming process, in the presence of the king's wife and many others, the high priest, standing in the background and draped in a complete leopard skin, would read from the scriptures at prescribed intervals.

Moving slowly across the walls like black flames, limpid, flickering, pointed shadows were thrown by the stilettoed ears of the head of Anubis borne upon a man's body. His name was Meneptah and it was he who was privileged to perform the act of disembowelment. He was a high official of the dead king's court. Masked with the head of the black jackal and clothed with a thin ceremonial white apron about his loins, a bodice of stitched lapis about his torso and a collar of beads of assorted colours, he moved to address the pale, stiffening body.

He began by placing a small piece of inscribed papyrus on the dead king's face. The priest behind him sprinkled incense over a bowl of flaming oil. There was a brief crackling and the heavy vapour with its thick odour quickly filled the chamber. Meneptah unrolled the papyrus text of Tutankhamun's 'Chapters of Coming Forth by Day', the complex and lengthy multitude of spells that would protect the dead king against all dangers and adversity during his forthcoming journeys.

He read, "My heart is with me and it shall never come to pass that it shall be carried away. I, Nebkhprerure, am the Lord of Hearts, the slayer of the heart. I live in right and truth and I have my being therein. I am Horus, the dweller in hearts, who is within the dweller in the body. I live in my word and my heart hath being. Let not my heart be taken away from me, let it not be wounded, and may neither wounds nor gashes be dealt upon me because it hath been taken away from me. Let me have my being in the body of my father, Seth, and in the body of my mother, Nut. I have not done that which is held in abomination by the gods; let me not suffer defeat there but let me be triumphant."

He passed the papyrus back to the priest and turned. With his arms outstretched he addressed the body. Firmly drawing his spread palms over the torso, he felt for a softness. With the third and fourth fingers of his left hand pressing on the spot, he picked up a scribing instrument and painted a diagonal line on the left side of the abdomen.

A third priest drew close by the body. He was named Asmat. With some ceremony he raised a crescent-shaped flint blade from the table beside the bed and, after performing an exaggerated looping motion with his hand, brought the knife close to one end of the inscribed line.

There was a gasp of anticipation from the queen.

The blade had a somewhat dull edge and it was with some difficulty that Asmat finally penetrated the skin and cut, almost tearing, a gash the length of an index finger from the centre of the belly down to the hip. Abdominal fluid and some blood ran over the stomach and collected in the king's navel. Ankhesenamun winced but continued to watch. She had not witnessed the like before, but stopped herself from showing further signs of emotion. The whole process was as entirely necessary and as normal as the ritual that had attended their marriage.

A brief pause and silence followed the cutting. Asmat laid down the cutting instrument and looked about in nervous anticipation. Without command and all at once, those officials who were present rose and began shouting abuse and throwing handfulls of crushed gypsum at he who had with such grace and reverence just defiled the king's body.

Asmat turned and, as fast as his legs could carry him, ran from the scene along the long colonnade of the ceremonial parade and into the bright sunlight. Those in the chamber did not cease their ranting until the echoes of his footsteps had died away to a whisper. The ritualistic scolding was customery.

Silence descended on the chamber once more.

Meneptah reached to the floor, picked up the discarded knife and replaced it on the table. Offering up a short, reverend prayer to Osiris, he turned back to the body. Slowly he slid his left hand through the opening in the skin until only the upper half of his forearm remained exposed. He drew out the king's viscera, organ by organ, placing them separate from one another upon the table at his side. As the priest's head was totally enclosed in the clay mask, those about him could not see the strain in his expression. The perspiration ran down his cheeks and neck and appeared, in the light of the oil lamps, as glistening rivulets coursing down the centre of his chest and between his shoulder blades.

The other priest acting as Meneptah's assistant brought a bowl of palm wine to wash the embalmer's thickly bloodied arms and hands. Tutankhamun's intestines, his liver, stomach and lungs also were washed. Each cleansed organ was placed to one side in a small bed of natron salts. Much later, when sufficiently dried, they would be stuffed with spices and gum, smeared with unguent and bandaged with strips of linen. As was the custom, each strip would be penned with the names of the four sons of the god, Horus - the faces of a jackal, a hawk, a man and an ape.

Smenkhkare's canopic chest, now emptied of its original contents, stood on the floor to Meneptah's right. The four cavities in the sepulchral container would house the organs of the king for posterity. The chest had been carved from a single block of delicately veined calcite, in the form of a cube, slightly elongate vertically and tapering towards the top. On each of its outer corners in relief were almost identical depictions of the four tutelary goddesses who, as order prescribed, would take the king's viscera under their special supervision. Their forearms stretched horizontally along each panel as if to hold the hallowed contents in close protection. Once entire, the object would be housed close by the king's corpse. As it stood today, the chest was anonymous. The texts that had identified its original owner had been excised and those that would ultimately identify it with Tutankhamun were yet to be carved.

After washing his hands, Meneptah turned back to the prone body. The lower thorax was now collapsed - the abdomen evacuated of the stomach and entrails. He took some linen rags and soaked them with wet salts. He introduced them into the body cavity along with the heart - the heart to restore the body's soul; the salty rags to restore its natural shape and help cleanse and leach its bloody tissues.

The man in the Anubis mask looked down at the face of Tutankhamun. The eyes of the dead king stared straight up at the lofted ceiling. Painted angels borne upon the brightly coloured wings of vultures looked down on him. Meneptah gently drew the body back so that the head fell over the end of the bed.

Ankhesenamun stiffened. She knew what was going to happen next. Pre-ordained process or not, the forthcoming mutilation of her young husband's face would be more than she could bear to witness. She extended her arm with the flat of her hand vertical in a symbolic gesture and turned her head away. Meneptah understood the queen's action and turned his body to block her view.

Religious incantations were recited by those standing motionless in the shadows.

Meneptah once more asked for the blessing of Osiris and carefully closed the dead eyelids. Now came the final evacuation. He introduced a copper needle into the king's right nostril. He then gave it a sharp, firm tap and, with no apparent resistance, it broke into the cranial cavity. Withdrawing the needle quickly, he passed a long, hook-shaped instrument up the nasal passage and pushed it into the brain case. He rotated it back and forth within the cavity, slowly puréeing the grey matter into a jelly.

With the help of two attendants, the body was turned on its side and the head raised back to allow the pulp to drain from the nose into an alabaster bowl. This offal was of no importance to the ritual and would be summarily discarded. Warm rinsing fluids were poured into the cranial cavity to remove all remaining tissue and liquids. When Meneptah was sure that all residue within the cavity had been cleared, the body was rested back to its former position.

Ankhesenamun lowered her arm and turned to face the body. Her husband looked little changed. The expression remained peaceful. But there were clear indications that the drying fluids were beginning to take effect. The skin was discolouring and starting to wrinkle. A rancid odour began to fill the chamber.

Meneptah sensed it himself and hurriedly performed the final cleansing. He cleaned out the unfilled portion of the body cavity thoroughly with a brine solution and, wrapping his right hand in rags, dabbed all about inside until the interior of the cadaver's torso felt relatively dry to the touch. He scooped up more salts and introduced them into the slit in the stomach. This completed, and the abdomen more or less the shape it had been in life, he pinched the sides of the wound together with his knuckles until the opening had fully closed. He placed a single half disc of pure gold sheet on it, hiding the gash from view.

Taking hold of the body under the armpits, he pulled it towards him until the head was drawn back over the end of the bed again. With the nose now inverted, he poured hot resin through the open nostril and into the cranial cavity until the resin vessel was empty. An assistant at the foot of the bed dragged the body back by the ankles, replacing it in its original position. Meneptah held the head so that the closed eyes remained fixed on the ceiling.

Finally, all the priests helped to heap the entire body from the neck downwards in piles of natron. The body's shape became totally obscured beneath a long mound of salt.

Ankhesenamun leaned forward and delicately touched her dead husband's forehead with hers, the last time she would feel the touch of his skin now strangely warm from the fresh resins within. Pulling herself slowly erect, she turned and with measured steps walked out of the chamber. She did not look back. To those who watched her leave there had been a strength of purpose in the queen's stride that they had not observed before.

Meneptah's duties ended with a final sprinkling of natron to conceal the head. He cleaned up the remaining pink fluid residue from the drainage bowl at the bottom of the alabaster bed and packaged up the embalming instruments and soiled cloths. Moaning a last solemn prayer, he and the remaining priestly officials and attendants turned away from the corpse and followed the queen through the single doorway.

The room was left in the twilight of the dying oil lamps. As prescribed in the scriptures, as practised for centuries, the king's body would lie pickled within its pile of salts for almost ten weeks, allowing the minerals to draw the last of the body fluids and complete the drying process prior to the final dressing and wrapping of the mummy and the funerary ceremonies.

More than two months would pass before Ankhesenamun would see her husband's mummy; two months before the sealing of his tomb; two months in which she would have to make haste to complete her private wishes - two months with much to do and much anxious waiting.

Time passed. Soon it was weeks, not months, that remained before the state funeral.

The queen had inspected the new tomb where Tutankhamun was to be laid to rest. It certainly lacked grandeur - too small and not deep enough - but the queen was realistic. The tomb in The West Valley was barely half excavated and there was no time to complete it. She had but one concern - the location. The requisitioned tomb was cut in the bottom of the valley in a main, dried-up watercourse. The risk was high that it could become flooded during the infrequent but violent storms that tore down the valley tributaries - and there was no well to catch the flood water.

The queen was aware of the priorities. To effect a trouble-free transition of the king's spirit to the afterlife it was far more important to complete all preparations within the allotted time than await excavation of an underground 'palace'. The body must not be allowed to overstay its time in the land of the mortal. The king must be set upon his barque to cross the river of life and enter into the necropolis at the time appointed, and no other.

Great piles of stone chippings had accumulated around the stepped entrance to the mouth of the tomb. To ensure it would have the capacity to store the quantity of grave goods that would normally accompany the body of a king on his eternal journey, the general had had the cavity slightly enlarged from the original. Much of this debris would ultimately be used to fill the entrance-way after the tomb doors had been sealed and, in an effort to mask the position of this holy place, be spread all about the immediate area to merge with the natural flood debris of the valley floor.

The stonemasons were completing the final dressing of the walls. They had already finished the chamber in which the king's sarcophagus was to be placed and the plasterers were at work preparing the walls for decoration. The relative coolness of early spring allowed them to work throughout the day and night in shifts.

The inscribers were first into the burial chamber. Along the shorter wall they were drafting small figures of baboons in three rows. Larger figures would cover the longer wall of the chamber. The painters would follow later to fill in their drawings.

At his workshop in the village, Meneg had now completed the bier on which the dog carving would rest. He had varnished the assembled jackal in black - black as the messenger who had called on him weeks earlier. His neighbour, a worker of semi-precious stones, had crafted and set eyes of obsidian and alabaster. The entire piece was now with the gilders. His artwork completed, he now had to turn to more mundane tasks. He supervised the carpenters who were constructing the additional panels of the wooden shrine that would be assembled over and around the sarcophagus.

Meneg also had to supervise the manufacture of the various panels making up the shrine that would surround the king's viscera - lesser in size than that over the sarcophagus but no less grand. Statuettes of the four tutelary goddesses of the compass were to be carved to embrace the canopic shrine. Meneg had selected his two best young carpenters for the job, each with a proven reputation for a steady hand and a reverent eye.

The outer wooden coffin also was being crafted by specialists. All woods had to be selected with care - for grain, dryness, hardness, and weight. Meneg recalled the horror of an error during the preparations for the interment of a local noble. Just last year he had all but completed the detailed carving on the upper surface of the coffin when, without warning, the huge lid had split right down the centre. The entire piece had to be started again with a new piece of wood. On this occasion there would be no time for such errors. The greatest care was taken in assuring that the woods were free of imperfections.

Two life-size statues that would guard the entrance to the burial chamber would come from existing furnishings in the king's quarters. At least that was one difficult task that would not have to be repeated.

The goldsmiths were the busiest artisans of all. The scavanging of Smenkhkare's tomb notwithstanding, there was considerable bullion to be melted down, moulded, engraved, polished and inlaid with coloured glass.

All this work was accomplished in the royal foundry under a prolific, powerful and omnipresent guard. This is where the king's death mask lay in waiting for the likeness it would shortly be used to create. There were no less than thirty goldsmiths working together in that room at any one time.

The most formidable task of all was the casting, dressing and engraving of the king's principal coffin. No mistakes could be made in its internal and external proportions. The wrapped body of the boy king must fit snuggly within it. The coffin itself must fit comfortably within the second of his brother's coffin set. The engraving must be perfectly balanced. Above all, there must be no errors in the fit of the upper and lower halves. At the appointed time they would have to come together like hand in glove.

The weight of responsibility would have overpowered the most articulate of artisans had it not been for the divine faith they held in the inevitability of their departed king's forthcoming passage. The process was ordered; mechanical almost. In their execution of the work, they were carried by a belief in themselves and in the journey they would help to initiate for their dead king. Without this inherent trust and allegiance he would not reach the afterlife. Worse still, ultimately they may not be permitted to follow.

Meneg was resolute. He had toiled long and hard to complete his charge. It had turned out as good a carving as he had ever accomplished. All the better for the depths of apathy from which he had dragged himself. The god had spoken to him, he told the goldsmiths, and the same would happen to them. They, too, would create their best work for Tutankhamun, the young king to whom they had grown so attached after the religious depredations of his father-in-law. The king would rejoice in the eloquent artistry of his people.

Meneg visited the goldsmiths on a number of occasions during the process. He enjoyed drinking with them, relishing the inside stories about palace life. He liked to be kept up to date on the latest regal news. Even if it were largely speculation, it always made good listening. And, all this besides, he intensely admired their work. Their expertise, handed down and matured for centuries, was second to none.

On the occasion of this visit he had heard it rumoured that Ankhesenamun had sent word to the Hittites, but for what?

"Could it be for a new husband?" speculated Dashir.

"A new king?" asked Meneg.

"And a great army to take power from the king's consort, Ay." added the master goldsmith.

"I heard the queen had received a messenger into her chambers last night," said Meneg.

"Not inside?" queried several almost together. Then voices came from everywhere. "'Tis not proper." "It'd be 'proper' for me! She's got to be frustrated by now. That queen needs a real man." "Tuck in your stupid tongue, fool, before I pull it out with my bare hands." "Nut is watching. She will protect us." "She'd watch you die and no mistake. And enjoy it. Stupid man." "The gods' mercy on your tongue, or cut it out."

The people's growing affection for the young king during his short life did not go unnoticed by Horemheb. It had veritably gnawed at him. How could he be so likeable connected as he was with the heretic? Ay and he had manipulated the king into changing his name and in so doing they had likewise manipulated religious practice back to what it had been before his father-in-law had taken power. Clearly the general had done a very good job - too good for his own benefit. His personal influence was not visible to the people - the king's was. And, with such evident public affection for the boy, his mentor now had to ensure that the dead king's burial would be, if only in the smallest of king's tombs, a grand affair, accompanied by the most treasured of grave goods. In the eyes of the people the young god king would be transported to the afterlife with as complete an entourage as any past Pharaoh in living memory - so long as it would all fit.

Ankhesenamun at last had received welcome news from the Hittite chamberlain. Suppiluliumas finally had become convinced by her second appeal and was sending his first-born son, Zennanza, to wed her and join their two empires. The young prince had been dispatched with all haste and should be in Thebes within one week of the time the message had been received. Assurance of her longevity as queen was within reach.

To intercept him and provide some additional protection and guidance, she had sent her unwilling messenger back up the road along which the Hittite would travel.

By this time Ipay was really disinclined to take the trip. After all, it was not long since he had returned. He had not been with his wife much of late and the girls of the north had not been to his liking - a grubby lot. He decided to dally at home for a couple of days more - with his family, with his wife, in his own bed. 'The Hittite will be that much closer to home by the time I catch up with him - less distance to travel - less time away,' he thought.

Horemheb had become somewhat confused by an excess of date wine the previous evening. By morning he was both mentally and physically impaired. Despite his heavy head, he forced himself to rise and inspect the night's progress in construction of the funeral barque that was to carry the king's body to the west bank.

As he rode uncomfortably to the boatyard he happened to catch sight of Ipay leaving the city by the north route. The coming and going was far too coincidental for his liking.

Chapter Six
A Man of Some Importance

Howard Carter took to his new responsibilities with considerable energy and determination. First, however, he needed somewhere to live - quarters suitable to his official position. Happily this was provided by the authorities. It was a stucco-faced building of mud-brick construction with shuttered and louvred windows and a simple but attractively functional three-arched veranda. He gathered about him a couple of servants and a number of pets, most of which, unfortunately for them, were to have foreshortened lifespans. He already had his horse, 'Sultan', with whom over time he had developed a close and devoted relationship. He now added two gazelles and 'San-Toy', a slothful and curious donkey, two characteristics that would soon prove sadly fatal.

He held a special attachment for the dumb and selflessly affectionate - qualities rarely seen in humans, of whom he tolerated the illiterate, who he could dominate without question, more than the literate, who would invariably answer back, usually in ignorance. However, he was all too aware that without the help of the aristocracy and the otherwise wealthy in all practicality there would have been no financial support for the work he wished to accomplish. Therefore, so far as he could maintain control of his feelings, he suffered in silence the inevitable company of his benefactors, most of them inarticulate in Egyptology, and took comfort in the discoveries and restorations achieved through their aid and in spite of their naivety.

Now that he was 'omnipotent' in all areas within the Luxor Protectorate, Carter's most immediate desire was to return to the spot where his horse had thrown him two years earlier and fully investigate that which he had quite literally stumbled upon. As soon as he felt comfortable with the rules of engagement and the arrangement of his office and had acquainted himself with his colleagues in the Service, he gathered a small party of labourers and rode out to rediscover the location of his former fortuitous accident.

He departed his quarters dressed in a three-piece tweed, bow tie, Homburg and light-coloured suede shoes. With his cleanly cut, short moustache he looked every bit the rank he now held. He would look just the same for many years to come.

The landmarks remained quite clear in his memory and he had no difficulty locating the site. He put his men to work immediately. The upper steps were revealed quickly. Carter beamed with delight. But the new inspector was about to receive a lesson on how to contain the urgency of his expectations.

It took his men two months of hard digging to reach, at last, what was clearly the top of a doorway. They were, by then, some fifty feet down. As the door became exposed, Carter saw that it was sealed with mud bricks. Excitement built within him as he sensed that this tomb, as tomb it surely was, could well have survived the ravages of robbers in antiquity. In just the first few months of his inspectorship already he could be about to open a tomb that had not seen a living soul since the Pharaoh had been laid to rest.

As the hole grew larger so did the wall of bricks. All the way to the bottom of the walled-up door they were untouched! Carter could hardly believe his good fortune.

Unable to contain himself any longer he got the fellahs at the surface to lower him into the hole in a basket. On reaching the bottom he scrambled to his feet and immediately began removing the bricks from the top of the door. He opened a hole beneath the lintel large enough to look through and peered inside. He could make out nothing but blackness.

He turned to the reis. "A paraffin lamp. Bring me a lamp... and... and some rope. Quickly... Please!"

With the hurricane lamp suspended inside the cavity, he pulled himself up to the lintel and looked in. Directly in front of him was an inclined ceiling. He looked down and observed that the floor of the passage descended steeply into the darkness beyond. There was nothing apparently in the passage itself but indeterminate rubbish. This was not unexpected. The burial chamber and the rooms adjacent to it would lie some distance away in the depths.

Carter pulled away enough bricks to allow him to squeeze through, then eased himself down to the floor carefully. In dropping the last foot or two he landed awkwardly and almost lost his balance. The passage was very steep and as he scrambled for a steady footing he inadvertently kicked something that bounced and rattled deeper into the blackness.

His heart was pounding. His hands were shaking. His whole body began to tremble. He felt such intensity to be standing for the first time alone in an unidentified tomb and, above all, to be the first to set foot there in perhaps several thousands of years. He drew a long, deep breath. The air had an acrid, stale odour to it.

Regaining his composure, he took the lamp from the rope and examined the floor. Nothing but dust and rock fragments littered the area around him. He turned to look further into the corridor. His eyes were becoming accustomed to the gloom and he thought he could make out some irregular shapes lying on the floor some distance ahead. He carefully edged his way deeper. As he drew closer, the strengthening shadows accented the shapes in front of him. Carter stared hard. As his eyes focused, the picture became less interesting. The ragged objects were animal parts; the desiccated head of a bovine - it did not appear large enough to be more than a calf - and pieces of one of its legs.

'The remains of the funerary feast,' speculated Carter, and with this reassuring thought he pressed on. As he descended further, the quality of the air rapidly worsened. He covered his nose and mouth with his handkerchief but didn't stop moving forward. About one hundred yards further down, his hurricane lamp illuminated an open doorway at the bottom of the inclined corridor. Rarely was this first room the burial chamber, but Carter's senses were on such an edge that any new doorway formed a portal to discovery. As he approached the entrance, the shadows of the doorjambs gradually moved apart and the entire room and its contents were revealed.

Briefly conscious that in his excitement he had come far without considering the rules that were now very much a part of his office, he stopped on the threshold. If he turned back now, the private sense of presence - to be the first to set foot in this place after so many millennia - could never be repeated. 'Damn protocol,' he thought. 'First I will see for myself.' He raised the lamp and looked around the room.

Back at the entrance to the tomb the reis's men were themselves becoming concerned with protocol. They were well aware that any fresh opening of an apparently undisturbed burial had to be in the presence of district officials of a much higher rank than the Chief Inspector of Antiquities of the Upper Nile.

"What is Mr Carter doing, do you think, Mustafah?" said the reis.

"He has spent much time in there. I fear he is either hurt or he investigates deeper - and before the Consul!"

"I will go to see," said the reis. He slid himself through the aperture in the doorway and fell to the floor.

The thudding sound back up at the entrance and the blink in the shaft of sunlight that lit up the floor of the passage startled Carter. He all at once felt like a boy caught in the act of stealing apples in the orchard of a neighbour. He stared at the silhouette advancing towards him.

The reis slithered to Carter's feet. "What are you doing, sir?" he asked.

"Ahmed, my old friend. We have discovered a most curious tomb. Come, look at this."

Carter took the man by the left arm and pointed. A large wedge-shaped object wrapped in white linen lay in the far left corner of the room. Alongside it was a wooden coffin with hieroglyphs inscribed all over it. Elsewhere lay red pottery, pots and dishes all over the place, more remains of the calf Carter had come across along the entrance passageway and a couple of skeletons of birds, possibly ducks or geese, entirely picked clean by the ancient participants of the funerary feast.

The lid of the coffin was not fastened shut. Together, gingerly, they raised it. Carter craned his neck to get the first sight of the contents. To his dismay it was totally empty.

He replaced the coffin lid and attempted to pull back a portion of the shroud covering the large object that lay beside it. He could tell from the shape of the closely fitting shroud that this was a statue of some kind. A black top-knot poked out of the narrow end where the ancient, perished thread was beginning to tear under its own weight. The entire cloaked object resembled the shape of a seated figure. But who?

"Despair not, Ahmed. These have to be the trappings of a funerary feast within an antechamber of the tomb. There has to be more to this place!"

The walls of the room in which they were standing were solid, but this did not deter Carter. He knew that if there were any additional passages more than likely they led further downward. They would begin with a stairway or sheer shaft cut somewhere in the floor of the room. He was standing on debris from the partially collapsed roof so any opening was likely hidden from them.

"Go and get me a rod, Ahmed. We must probe the floor for additional cavities."

Carter bubbled inside with anticipation. Indeed there was no evidence that this tomb had previously been plundered. The remains of the funerary festivities appeared undisturbed. The innermost sepulchre had to lie somewhere beneath him.

He heard the reis drop back down into the entrance, stumble on the slope and in so doing drop the steel probe with a cacophonous clatter.

"Quiet!" Carter hissed incredulously, as if the sound would wake the dead. It felt to him as if noise itself could violate this holy place.

"Sorry, sir. Very sorry, sir," whimpered the reis as he slid backward into the chamber.

Carter grabbed the probing rod and began a methodical search of the floor. He started in the near left corner, probing every three feet in parallel lines each about a yard apart, back and forth. The debris that littered the place lay up to about a foot deep. Carter, on his knees now and with both fists on the probe, stabbed downward, hitting bedrock, the true floor of the room, within a few inches every time. He finished the second row, turned and began stabbing at the ground again. Three penetrations later Carter fell unceremoniously on his face. The probe had encountered no resistance to the full extent of its length. He had found the opening.

Carter wiped the soil from his lips. "I knew it. I knew it," he whispered excitedly. Turning his dirty face towards the reis, he smiled broadly.

Ahmed beamed back. He could have laughed outright at the sight of his ecstatic, dirty master, but respect of position and the peremptory need of a steady job permitted only a knowing grin.

"We shall return to the surface." Carter could see there was evidently too much labour ahead to continue the illicit exploration. "I shall advise the Consul General that we are at the threshold. We shall first clear this room completely. Then the men will begin digging here where I have marked."

Carter pulled the probe out and stuck it gently back into the gravel close to where he had found the cavity.

The two scrambled back up the passage and, with the aid of a rope which the reis had attached for the purpose, clambered up the inside of the mud-brick doorway and back out into the blinding sunlight.

Carter told the men to complete clearing the doorway and then place a guard there for the night. He must return to his house and send a message to Viscount Cromer, the British Consul General in Egypt.

"Ahmed, bring Sultan to me."

That evening in his small study he scribbled on a notepad...

Sir, I have the consumate pleasure to advise I have come upon an inviolate tomb. I have excavated to the antechamber in which I have discovered the remains of a Pharaoh's funerary feast and a magnificent, painted, greater than life-size sandstone statue, probably in the likeness of the king himself. Once I have cleared this chamber I will set the men to excavating the continuance of the passageway which in this particular tomb appears to take the form of a vertical shaft - at this point I know not how deep. It is clear to me that the burial chamber will lie somewhere off this shaft and once I have come upon the doorway it is my intention to advise your Excellency and request your presence at the opening. While it is true to say that to this juncture I have come across no sign that could lead me to identify the Pharaoh within, I am most assuredly convinced that he is here and, once discovered, all will be revealed to us.

It is with the greatest excitement and anticipation that I send you this good news, and I hope it will not be long before I call upon you to visit the site, and that you are able to come.

Your obedient servant,

H.C.

Carter folded it up and placed it in an envelope. He addressed the envelope: 'URGENT. PRIVATE & CONFIDENTIAL. For the attention of His Excellency The British Consul General, Cairo', and passed it to his houseboy, charging him to ensure its delivery.

As the boy left, one of Carter's two pet gazelles came into the room through the opened door and began sniffing about for scraps of food.

Carter addressed the animal as if it were a colleague. "A drink is called for. Do you not think so, my little one?"

The delicate creature put its forelegs on the seat of the chair in which Carter was sitting and nuzzled the palms of his hands.

"This will be a fine find, my beauty." He looked into the two large, black, heavily eyelashed eyes. "I cannot believe my luck. And so soon after starting. Oh, what a story this will make!"

The last glimmers of evening sunlight twinkled on the empty gin bottle standing on Carter's desk. The light faded and was gone. Carter slept deeply and dreamed sweetly that night.

Nearly three hundred evenings would pass before Carter got to the threshold he sought - one for every foot dug! There was time aplenty for his enthusiasm to dull, but many matters to occupy him in other parts of his protectorate. Some were not at all to Carter's liking.

Possibly the most unfortunate affair concerned the arrival at Luxor of one Mrs Charlotte Avery-Oliphant. She announced herself as a close friend and confidante of Lady Amherst. Her husband had recently passed away after contracting diphtheria. He had left her well provided and Lady Amherst suggested that she travel to Egypt for the sights and the clean air, and to overcome her grief - not that that would take long. Lady Amherst told her to make use of her ladyship's protégé as a guide and report back on the progress of his career. His principal benefactor had no conception that her idea could be so badly misplaced. But the die was cast.

This particular lady had a strong propensity for exercising her vocal cords. When she spoke, it was commonly on subjects about which she knew absolutely nothing. Nevertheless, on these occasions she would speak with a strong sense of authority and confidence, a trait that would become all the more acute when she had had a drink or two - she had a fierce liking for the spirits.

At the same time, the protégé in question had a strong preference for solitude and quiet. He spoke little and then only on subjects in which he was well versed. When it came to alcohol he had both capacity and control, unlike the new and unwelcome visitor.

The only areas in which their characters converged were in the degree of authority and confidence in their oral deliveries and their fondness for a little tipple.

Mrs A-O, therefore, was in most respects not a bit like Howard Carter. Consequently, the occasion of their first meeting was a calamity looking for somewhere to happen. In view of their similar tastes, it was natural that the arena for their first altercation would be within the sublime atmosphere of the bar at the Winter Palace Hotel.

"Tot-knees the Fird, I said. You 'eard me quite correctly, sir, the first time - Tot-knees the Fird. 'E was the one wot begat Cleopatra, don't y' know."

Carter had been in the bar just five minutes and had been listening to Mrs A-O expound on her copious 'knowledge' of Egyptian history to an unfortunate gentleman stranger who had made no more untimely an error than to have been readily encountered sitting alone when she had come in. By now he was completely overwhelmed by her unsolicited oratory. Carter could not help coming to the man's aid and see to it that the woman's obvious inaccuracies were publicly corrected. This benevolent initiative he would come to regret.

"Ma'am" he interjected, "I think the Pharaoh of whom you speak is more correctly named 'Tuthmosis III'. That particular Pharaoh lived around 1450

BC. That's over one thousand years before the Romans - not at all contemporary with them." This correction was clinical, and meant to be final. Carter misjudged.

Mrs A-O did not take kindly to the interruption and even less so to the correction. In any case, she didn't understand the word 'contemporary'. "You are mistaken, sir. Tot-knees. I visited 'is tomb only yesterday. And it was 'is daughter Cleopatra wot married that Seezer chappie. It's all in Shakespeare for anyone to see."

In the face of such abject ignorance, Carter lost all patience and discretion at once. "Ma'am, the answer to that is spherical and in the plural!"

The lady did not miss a beat. At first she pretended to ignore Carter's obscenity and lashed back. "You should do a bit more readin' before yer makes statements of that nature, sir. And anuver fing, I takes unkindly to interruptions from ignoramuses like yerself. I'd be obliged if you'd return to yer seat and mind yer own business and enjoy yer drink and not spoil this nice gen'leman's pleasure... An', by the way, yer language doesn't compare wiv that uv a gen'leman. We'd awl be 'bliged if yer'd keep it fer the bord'los in which I'm sure yer feel a good deal more comf'table than in these surroundin's."

Carter was not accustomed to a full-frontal attack of this nature, particularly from a female of the species, a perfect stranger, and more especially when the battle was joined on his personal stamping ground. He was sufficiently in shock that his mind went totally blank for a moment, leaving him at a loss for words. He dutifully returned to his chair at the bar and, rolling his eyes in disgust, downed the remainder of his glass.

Mrs A-O, a large, one might say corpulent woman, copiously endowed with large lungs to match her plentiful chest, returned her attentions to the unfortunate, previously-solitary-and-enjoying-it gentleman in the corner sofa and continued her flawed history at a level of voice quite loud enough to be heard by everyone in the room.

"I am a close friend o' Lord an' Lady Amherst, y' knows. Yer knows oo they are, de yer not?" The gentleman did not get the time to respond. "They are the foremost egyptologists uv England, and in their 'ome at Didlin'ton 'all in Norfolk they 'ouse the greatest c'lection uv ancient Egyptian artefac's in the 'ole of Europe. It is from bein' close t' them all these years that I 'as come to be somewhat of an orfority on fings in these parts, y' see."

'Now she's got the gall to name-drop,' thought Carter. 'I can't stand by and let her use their name in association with this flagrant dissertation of lies.'

His composure was restored but now he was quite angry. He shouted to her from his seat at the bar. "Ma'am! Ma'am! You would do well to consider in whose name you speak such balderdash. You persist in misleading this gentleman in every way and now you have the affrontery to do so citing the friendship, counsel and experience of the Amhersts. It is quite clear to me that you must know nothing of them but their good name, for they would have ensured you came to Egypt with a good deal more basic grounding in its history than you clearly have - a fiction you have dreamed up in your own mind for the purposes, no doubt, of appearing authoritative well beyond the means of your personal level of intellect."

Lightning struck.

"Just 'oo the 'ell do you fink you are, mister? 'Ow dare you address a total LADY stranger wiv such familiarity and contempt! I shall 'ave you ejected from this establishment at once! Boy! Boy! Get the manager! I want the manager... An' I wants 'im now!"

Carter, again taken aback by the energy, arrogant confidence and directness of the fat lady's tirade, did not comment further. Instead he decided to await the arrival of the manager who, of course, he knew very well and who, of course, would quickly settle the matter in Carter's favour.

On his arrival, the poor man was subjected to a full-frontal volley of Mrs A-O's version of the events. He was not permitted the option to reply but ordered to eject the offending gentleman in the three-piece tweed. He took a little time to consider his options, however, and waited long enough for the woman to repeat her demands, Carter all the time regarding him with a knowing smirk on his face. Then, without saying anything to her and with an almost imperceptible nod of his head, he turned and walked over to where Carter was sitting.

"Sir," he began in a whisper, "this is most embarrassing for me. You see this lady is a close friend of her ladyship. Upon her return to England which, Allah promise us, must occur within the week," he rolled his eyes, "I would not care to have her displeasure with the hotel related to her ladyship. Her ladyship's type of clientele, you understand, is most desirable, most generous and, quite frankly, the essential lifeblood of this establishment. Consequently, and begging your understanding, on this occasion I am forced to ask you to leave."

Carter couldn't believe his ears.

"Anton," he returned patiently, "she wouldn't know Lord and Lady Amherst from a hole in the ground. She's a fake, man. Can't you see?"

The manager responded quietly and matter of fact. "The room she occupies was reserved for her by a recent letter in the hand of her ladyship herself. I fear, Mr Carter, that on this occasion it is you that is - how do you say - barking up the wrong tree. In this case a veritable cactus!" He grinned condescendingly.

Carter's eyes were wide open in anger and shock. He whispered back once more, "Show me the letter. I demand to see the letter!"

The manager was quick to recognise this opportunity to remove Carter from the battlefield without embarrassment, much less force. "Of course, sir. Please follow me to my office."

They left the bar together. Carter, to avoid eye contact with the woman, looked doggedly ahead.

To the manager this was a most satisfactory end to what could have been a publicly nasty affair; to Carter, once he had seen the letter and realised the situation was indeed genuine, a most hurtful experience. He returned to his house on the west bank and drank alone until the clock struck one.

The following morning Carter decided he would stay on the west bank. He had been told that Mrs A-O was in the area for another week. This was Monday, so for fear of accidentally crossing her path he would stay on the other side of the river for the entire week. The excavation at the tomb he had stumbled upon was proceeding slowly and seemingly without end, so he decided to take his painting materials to Deir el Bahri.

For a December day it was blisteringly hot and he was only too happy to get into the relative coolness of the shaded colonnades. He settled into his folding stool and began to lose himself in his work. He had been there about an hour, his sketchbook on his knee, the watercolour beginning to take form, when he heard it: the faint but unmistakable echo of a female voice reverberating from pillar to pillar, column to column.

"Mr Carter! Mr Carter! This is Mrs Avery-Oliphant. I am told you are in 'ere somewhere. I 'ave a message from Lady Amherst for you. Could you please make yerself known to me?"

Carter quickly replaced his brush, closed up his palette, folded up his stool, quietly turned and scurried for the nearest niche, pressing himself against the wall.

As she searched betwixt and between the columns, he could hear the woman's footsteps on the sand-strewn stone floors crunching nearer, then further from him, then closer again. He remained motionless, hoping she would not come near enough to spot him.

"Mr Carter! 'E is in 'ere somewhere, isn't 'e?"

"Oh, most assuredly, madame. I believe he is painting one of the friezes over there."

'Dammit. Abdel. He's guiding her right to the spot. What the hell can the woman want? Not content with yesterday's victories, to cement her achievement she is up for a second engagement - tell more trumped-up tales to the misguided in the bar this evening, no doubt.' Then it dawned on him - they had not been introduced; she did not know what he looked like - she had no idea the person she had confronted the previous night was he. The letter was proof enough that she did know the Amhersts. Perhaps she was seeking him out on their behalf after all. He must avoid meeting with her again at all costs.

"You are mistaken, man." A welcome remark of irritation from Mrs A-O.

"But it was I who saw Mr Carter enter, madame. And I have not seen him leave."

"Stupid Arab! Stupid Arab... Waste of time... Grubbing about in this dark and dusty place... Waste of my time..."

To Carter's relief her words faded into glorious silence as she bustled out of the temple and into the sunlight. 'Go burn in hell, ma'am,' he thought as he reopened his stool and prepared to resume his painting.

Abdel had remained in the colonnade as Mrs A-O had left, and he immediately spotted his master. He tried to hail Mrs A-O but she was already beyond earshot.

His slippers scuffed on the stone floor as he hurried over to Carter's side. "That lady, Mr Carter. That lady..."

"I know. I know. I was hiding. I do not wish to meet her."

"But she is very insistent, sir. Very persuasive."

"Yes, Abdel. I understand. Now you understand this... From now on, whenever she asks you where I am, you have no idea. NO idea."

"Sir? But I always know where you are."

"I am asking you to lie to her, Abdel. Have you never lied before?"

"No, sir!" Abdel was emphatic. With a shocked expression on his face he shook his head and waved his arms to underline the statement. "Never."

"Do you wish to remain in my employ?"

This particular option had not occurred to the reis. "But of course, sir."

"Then, you will lie when I tell you to."

"Sir."

The truth was, of course, as Carter well knew, that lying was all but second nature to the likes of Abdel. He just didn't wish to admit to the attribute. Allah may overhear. However, being ordered to do so, and to take on the responsibility with such evident reluctance, purged his conscience most satisfactorily.

But, as things were to turn out, this simple conspiracy was all in vain.

Carter looked up from his painting and out into the temple forecourt. The sun was already dipping behind the Theban hills and the light was going fast. The Valley and the great rock amphitheatre of Deir el Bahri were now in shadow. It was time to leave. He gathered up his things and walked out across the middle platform and down the ramps, dodging a few late tourists on the way. Before leaving the area he visited the site under excavation. As expected, the reis reported little progress for the day's efforts.

Carter sighed. 'Count your blessings, Howard, my boy. You had a close shave today.'

Abdel was waiting for him with his horse. He packed his stuff in the saddlebag and the reis helped him up. They ambled home slowly down the processional way, Abdel leading Sultan by the halter. By the time the inspector's residence came into view, the entire Nile basin was bathed in twilight.

As they approached, it became obvious to Carter that he had visitors. There was a motor car in the forecourt guarded by two uniformed fellahs. He dismounted and went in. It had never occurred to him who might be awaiting him inside. He blundered into his sitting room without a single thought for caution.

There she was.

"You? What effrontery is this? What the 'ell are you doin' 'ere? Abdel! Ask this man to leave immediately!"

Shocked, Carter nevertheless had the composure to respond. He was brief. "This is my house, ma'am. I ask you to state your business or leave now."

The boot at last was on the other foot. It was now Mrs A-O who was shocked sufficiently to be placed on the defensive. She almost whimpered, "You are... You are then..."

"Howard Carter, Inspector of Antiquities in the Upper Nile. Not exactly at your service, ma'am, but eager to assist you to leave."

Once the identity had been confirmed, Mrs A-O was quick to regain her composure.

"Young man, I am prepared to overlook your rudeness of last night if you can bring yourself to speak civily with me for one moment and permit me to pass on the message I 'ave brought to you from 'er ladyship - all this way, I may add."

Carter wasn't about to apologise but he could hardly refuse to listen.

"As you wish." He sat down.

"Aren't you goin' to offer me some refreshment?"

'God, I have to pay the piper, too?' Carter thought. He signalled to Hosein to bring in the drinks tray.

He badly needed one himself.

Mrs A-O sat in silence until the tray arrived. All the time she avoided eye contact with Carter, self-consciously patting at her skirt and looking all about the room.

Carter's gin and tonic was already prepared. "What'll you have, ma'am?"

"That will do just nicely," she said, and made a grab for Carter's glass.

Carter sighed and turned to the smiling Hosein. "What's so amusing, Hosein? Get me another one. At once, if you please. Now, ma'am. The message..."

"My Lady Amherst asked me to enquire of yer 'ealth."

"I am in fine health, as you can plainly see. Will there be anything else before you leave?" asked Carter, rising from his chair.

"I 'ave not finished. Sit down. You are givin' me neck ache. Be seated."

Carter silently obeyed.

"'Er ladyship wishes to convey 'er best wishes to you... An' to Abdel and Hosein." She turned and smiled condescendingly at the reis whom she had abused just a few hours earlier. "'Er ladyship would like you to visit when you next return to England. 'Er ladyship told me of yer expertise in Egyptology and commended you to me saying that you would be only too glad to escort me around some of the less well-known antiquities in these parts."

This was anathema to Carter's ears.

"That is somewhat academic now, in view of the circumstances, do you not think, ma'am? Besides, I am a very busy man. The responsibilities of my position weigh heavily. You will appreciate that, although you are an acquaintance of Lady Amherst..."

"A very, very good and intimate friend, Mr Carter - NOT an 'acquaintance'."

Carter continued as if the interruption had not occurred. "...Although you are an acquaintance of her ladyship's, I have neither the time nor the inclination to assist you in your endeavours. It became clear to me from our brief encounter last night that you already are most well endowed with knowledge of Egyptian history and have no need of one such as I to enrich you further. Indeed, I recall that at the time you had the temerity to correct me. Therefore, ma'am, I regret that I will be unavailable to you during your brief stay in Luxor."

Mrs A-O downed her gin in one and slapped the tumbler back on the tray.

"That bein' yer attitude, I feel there is nothin' more that can be said between us. I bid you a very 'goodnight', Mr. Carter." She raised her hand to him, indicating she wished assistance in rising from her chair.

Carter reluctantly took her fingertips.

"Abdel. Show this lady out, if you please. Goodnight, ma'am. As you drive to the riverside watch out for the bats. The local variety is quite venomous. A quality shared by some such as I have the misfortune to meet from time to time."

Carter's last statement was quite unnecessary but the opportunity to have the last word before losing sight of her altogether was irresistible.

As she was helped into the car she turned to Abdel to issue one last word of abuse.

But before she could say anything the reis stammered, "Madame, please do n-n-n-not ask me where the master is ever again. I do n-n-n-not know where the master is. I n-n-n-never know where the master is."

For once at a loss for words, she sat herself down in the back seat of the car and looked directly ahead.

The dwindling sound of the motor chugging away down the hill was music to Carter's ears. He eased back in his chair and attended his second gin.

The lady with largesse settled herself down and gestured with her third sherry glass. "Well, Lady Amherst, what can I say? I don't fink that boy of yours can come to any good. 'E was most rude to me, an' doesn't appear to 'ave learned much in 'is time out there. Told me Tot-knees is 'Allitosis, or some such. 'Owever did 'e get an important job like that?"

When the reis finally told Carter that a doorway had been discovered in the shaft, he had almost forgotten that the workings were still in progress. Practically a year had elapsed since they had uncovered the entrance to the tomb. He immediately sent word to Viscount Cromer. The great man's arrival was set for New Year's Day, 1901, and Carter prepared for the opening.

A plumply rounded Mrs Maspero was the viscount's escort, along with the usual and considerable entourage of 'qualified' hangers-on, many of them befezzed and suited Egyptian representatives and associates of the government and the Antiquities Service.

For the occasion, Carter had had constructed within the shaft a wooden platform on which, depending on their sizes, five or six men could comfortably stand. Two of them, Carter and one of his fellahs, would perform the physical labour of removing the slabs of limestone that sealed the doorway. Seniority decided who would be lucky enough to descend to the platform and witness the proceedings as they unfolded.

"Your servant, sir," bowed Carter, lending Viscount Cromer a hand as he reached the platform.

"And I yours, Mr Carter. It is with great respect and admiration for your reputation that I come here. I am truly honoured to be present at this the opening of your first discovery. You certainly have a nose for these things - but one year on from your confirmation as inspector - quite remarkable, sir. Quite remarkable!"

The inspector smiled in appreciation. These comments meant much to one such as Howard Carter, of relatively mean and common British descent but extremely proud of himself and his station in Egypt.

The viscount was stocky and well-built with all the stature one would expect in a man of his position. He was square-headed with full cheeks, a prominent, chubby nose, a strong, jutting chin, and thin, determined lips framed by a bleached, bushy moustache. His dark eyes penetrated from beneath overhanging lids that slanted downwards to either side his face - barely half of the iris peaked from under the grey lashes. They betrayed the arrogant self-confidence of the supreme leader of the occupying power. His personality was overbearing, his expression serious, determined and uncompromising.

In full dress regalia that included the ostrich-feathered, longbow-shaped hat, Cromer was glad to descend into the shade and relative coolness of the deep shaft. Once set on his feet, he waved his right arm at Carter in a flourishing signal to begin the opening.

By now visibly sweating - a mixture of physical effort and some not inconsiderable mental stress - Carter, with the help of the reis, removed the heavy limestone slabs. As they eased each one out they would secure a strong rope around it and the labourers standing at the top of the shaft would slowly raise each to the room above and out of the way of the spectators on the platform below. The opportunity for lethal accident was considerable and Cromer spent rather more time nervously watching each block find its way safely out of the shaft above him than gazing expectantly into the widening opening in the doorway.

It took about an hour to completely free the door blocking. With the removed blocks all safely out of the way, the viscount, Maspero and Carter leaned forward almost in unison to look inside the room which now lay open before them. The remainder of the small group craned to look over their shoulders. As their eyes became more accustomed to the darkness, an intense, expectant silence fell upon the place.

At a time like this, expression of one's feelings, when the heartbeat of anticipation is strong and rapid and the hands all a-tremble, is difficult enough for any who has the good fortune to experience the moment and toughest for the man whose business it is to seek out these discoveries. Never tougher, however, than in the face of immediate disappointment.

Carter was dumbstruck. There was little more than rubbish in the small room that faced them - a few pots, some crudely made model boats and rock debris.

An anticlimax of the profoundest proportions. The outcome was so much less than grand that Carter found it desperately hard to find words to break the silence of astonishment that was so pregnant it was fit to burst.

"Sir," he began in a faltering voice, "rather than find a dead Pharaoh languishing in his finery, I fear we have come upon little more than a dead end." He had nothing else to say.

The consul was clinically emotionless in his comments. "I share your disappointment, Mr Inspector." And after a brief pause, "Perhaps next time."

"Sir." Carter remained virtually speechless.

"Unfortunately I must return forthwith to Cairo to continue my appointments, already delayed. The Khedive wilts and pines for my counsel. My transport awaits. I am sure I speak on behalf of all who have accompanied me on this trip. We thank you for your kind advice and good efforts to bring this find to our attention. Better luck next time, perhaps." He signalled the boys at the top of the shaft to take him up again.

Carter looked back into the chamber in disbelief. He felt Maspero's hand on his shoulder and turned to face his globular little friend.

"Let us clear this chamber together quickly, Howard, and then descend further into the shaft to examine the walls closely for other openings. This surely cannot be all there is. This tomb has no evidence of ancient robbery. All this is most peculiar. Most peculiar."

More work was just the remedy Carter needed to help him forget what had just happened. They took little time to clear and examine the small room. There was nothing more than they had seen on first inspection and there were no more passageways leading from this chamber. Together they descended to the bottom of the deep shaft, examining the walls as they went. They found no evidence of any concealed openings all the way to the bottom. The shaft led nowhere - no more than a catchment well for flood debris, it seemed.

When the two finally returned to the surface, Carter ordered the reis to continue the search for openings in the upper portion of the shaft and the passageway itself. Then they left for his house. Maspero was as dejected as his protégé. That evening they consoled each other over a sufficiency of brandies.

Carter lay awake for some hours after Maspero had gone. 'The curse of Mrs A-O, I'll be bound', he thought. In the activity of mind he was unable to fall asleep. He went over the day's proceedings repeatedly, each time becoming crosser with himself. If, and it was a big 'if', he was ever to be so lucky as to discover a sealed tomb again there would be no mistaken identity. There would be no invitations to those who must, by law, preside over the expected spectacular openings of such discoveries. No invitations, that is, until he was absolutely sure he had a find that warranted such ceremony.

The following evening San-Toy, solitary in the yard of Carter's lodgings, nibbled absent-mindedly at his bale of hay. Inside, Carter reclined with a glass of Scotch. He was still nursing his acute embarrassment. Meanwhile, a cobra, energised by the warm sand as it gave back the radiant heat of the afternoon, glided towards the house in search of some small rodent.

The fortification of a light snack within him combined with the cool of the evening caused San-Toy to feel a little frisky. He had, as usual, done nothing all day and the sight of the legless creature sliding across the sand perked his curiosity. He plodded over to the reptile until he blocked its path.

The snake regarded the stone-like hoofs for a moment and then raised its head. The hoofs extended to a pair of hairy and bony legs that reached up above the cobra and terminated in an enormous expanse of chest, neck and head towering over it. It must have appeared by far the largest rat the cobra had ever set eyes on and quite beyond its expectations for a fulfilling supper.

The creature would have harmlessly avoided the obstruction had the beast not lowered its head until its two massive dark eyes came level with those alert beads staring intensely from just behind the flicking tongue. For a moment or two they regarded each other silently. San-Toy bared his brown teeth as if to better taste the scent of the reptile. That did it. With a barely audible hiss the cobra, its jaws agape, lunged at the huge head in front of it. The donkey reacted too slowly to avoid the great teeth that closed firmly through its soft lips.

Startled and in considerable pain, the donkey immediately raised its head pulling the cobra up with it, its mouth clamped like a vice over San-Toy's lips. The donkey reared, tossing its head back and forth and lashing the snake like a whip from side to side until finally its grip broke and the creature fell to the ground in a tangled heap.

Hearing all the commotion outside, Carter emerged onto the veranda to take a look. It was easy to conclude what had happened. By this time San-Toy had stopped bucking and was standing almost motionless about ten feet from the coiled snake. The venom had begun to dull his senses.

Carter ran back into the house for his gun. By the time he had re-emerged the donkey had begun to sway slowly in an almost circular motion. Carter pointed his pistol at the cobra and emptied the entire chamber into the creature. Dust, skin, blood and guts flew everywhere. When he turned back to look at San-Toy, the animal had fallen on its side, its eyes open, breathing heavily. Carter dropped the gun and ran over to it. As the head rested its full weight in his arms, he felt the breathing become steadily fainter. Within a minute or so the eyes closed.

Carter laid the head gently in the sand, ordered the houseboy to have the body buried in a corner of the yard, and returned to his room. He refilled his tumbler to the brim, sat back in the wicker chair and swallowed a long, burning draught.

He could be forgiven for reflecting... 'The curse of Mrs A-O.'

In the 1901/02 season, Howard Carter walked luckily into the financial embrace of one Theodore M. Davis - a millionaire lawyer-cum-philanthropist. The American was inexperienced in Egyptology but totally besotted with it and eager to get someone digging on his behalf.

Davis was not a big man, but what he lacked in stature he made up for in the flamboyance of his dress and the arrogance of his style. He had a lady friend who would accompany him on all his Egyptian excursions - a certain Emma B. Andrews. They cohabited on his own private Nile houseboat, or dahabeeyah, which would languish in the cool, rippling waters just offshore of his current concession. He sported a bushy handlebar moustache that extended to closely cropped 'mutton chops' over his cheeks and all the way up to his ears. He was as comfortable on a horse as he was on his feet and usually took to the road suitably dressed for the saddle, even if he did not expect to ride that day. An ambitious man who had during his career accumulated a substantial fortune, he now sought a new form of wealth - the timelessness of public recognition that would accompany a discoverer of long dead kings and of the treasures encountered along with them. His goal was to return as much of this wealth as possible to the Metropolitan Museum of Art in New York where his achievements, duly recorded, published and advertised, would become evident to all. His fame and his name would live for ever.

It was an interesting match. Two equally determined characters whose backgrounds could not have been more different. One with the power of money, the other with total authority, the power of discretion and all the expertise. But Davis was not one to be 'permitted' to do things. He was more used to the role of permitting others. Old habits die hard, and before too long they were bound to butt heads.

The association had begun quietly enough. Carter had been commissioned by Emma to paint watercolours of the wall decorations in

Queen Hatshepsut's temple - copies he had accomplished before in the official work he had completed for Naville and many times over since. He never tired of returning to the place and repeating the paintings. Each time he looked upon those walls it seemed as fresh as at the start, the work itself a consumate pleasure. And the sight of Miss Andrews' evident delight at receiving the finished watercolours was a personal reward, to him considerably greater than payment.

Davis, extravagantly moustached and gaitered, was hungry for Howard Carter's instruction in excavating techniques and Egyptological sleuthing. And, during the second work season of Carter's new post, he got more than he bargained for.

The inspector was supervising work for Davis in the clearance of what ultimately turned out to be the tomb of Queen Hatshepsut herself. The entrance to the tomb had been located almost at the very end of The Valley of the Tombs of the Kings. It was choked hard with sand and rubble from ancient floods. Ever hopeful it had not been plundered in antiquity, Davis was anxious for Carter to get started.

"Inspector," he said, "there cannot be that much to excavate. There surely will be a well a little way in and this will have caught the debris of earlier floods. Then the way will be clear for us. With luck this debris will have dissuaded any heretofore philanderers."

Carter, the memory of the lengthy and disappointing excavation of 'the tomb of the horse' still fresh in his mind, cautioned his new patron. "You are well informed, sir, on the usual architecture of these tombs. Indeed your speculations may be right. However, I do not believe this will be easy work. The ground is cemented hard. Steel yourself to be patient. You could avoid the boredom of being a mere spectator by helping sift the debris for artefacts. You never know what will turn up, and it is so much more satisfying to find it yourself."

Carter was pushing the envelope with Davis whom he knew would not be at all taken with this idea. He shook his head. "Get that fellah to bring me some champagne. And an umbrella. The sun is up."

'Do it yourself!' mused Carter to himself, then thought better of it and waved to Abdel. Better without him, he concluded. 'He can rest in the shade in passive benevolence and keep the hell out of my way!'

The digging went on for ages just as Carter had warned. To begin with Davis came to the site every day, but when he realised that all he was seeing was nothing but bag on bag of rubble and sand emerging from the orifice before him he came less and less. After a week or so, Carter didn't set eyes on his patron from dawn to dusk - there were more pleasant surroundings and things to do on the dahabeeyah.

As Carter's men dug, the crudely cut, low and narrow stone corridor reached onward and downward extremely steeply, further and further into the bedrock. There was no apparent end.

Davis, fed up with the same old view of Thebes, had taken to journeying on the water more or less permanently. He sent messages to Carter at the site asking him to advise if there was anything worth seeing that day, in which case he would immediately make his way upriver to see.

Carter never gave his patron's disinterest a second thought. It was a blessed relief to be without him. He was much happier left to his own devices. The excavation was sheer hard work and he had no time for casual banter with the rich and idle. There was a job to do.

The tomb corridor was so steep that each time he descended Carter found it difficult to maintain a secure footing. The air was foul, too, and it was, for a subterranean cavity of this depth and penetration, most unusually and oppressively warm. There could be considerably deeper yet to go. He was tired and, with the absence of any encouraging finds, he was disinclined to attempt to complete clearance in this season.

When Carter got back to his residence that evening, to his surprise and dissatisfaction he found Davis reclining on his porch sipping a regulation martini from Carter's stock.

"I can tell by your expression, young man, that you have found nothing today. Damn glad I didn't attempt the ride up that infernal valley. It's gettin' hotter 'n' hell here, even on the river, and I'm considering returning to New York early this year. That is... unless you have something to excite my senses."

"Not today, I am sorry to report," said Carter tiredly. "I am fatigued, Mr Davis. I am sure you will understand. I must go and wash off the accumulated sweat and grime. Then I may join you for a drink. Perhaps we shall have a breakthrough tomorrow - one never knows in this business."

Davis was not a patient man and he'd just about made up his mind to pack it in for the summer. "I tell you, Carter, if not tomorrow, I'm off home."

Carter waved dispassionately and disappeared through the bead curtain into the house. He cared less.

When he re-emerged washed and refreshed, in his hand a tonic water heartily stiffened with Gordon's gin, he was in more receptive mood. Davis was still on the porch, now on his third.

"Mr Davis, my apologies for appearing brief. The work has been harder and taken longer than I had expected and, I am sure for the both of us, thus far depressingly without reward. But I have thought of something that might just catch your attention."

"Really? Tell me quickly. I am all ears." Davis was physically active at last. He leaned forward, eager for something of interest. He hadn't done a thing all day but write business letters home, and, if Carter had something to show him after all, he wanted to see it now.

"It is getting dark. No time to lose. Let's get going. Mustafah, fetch me my horse at once!"

Carter raised his free hand as he drank a long draught with the other. He swallowed quickly. "No, no, Mr Davis. Just a minute. It's too late to do anything today. Tomorrow morning, first thing. And while we're on our little sojourn the fellahs can keep on digging. I don't think either of us'll miss much for the next day or two. Anyway, we can look in on their progress on the way back... May I offer you a share of my dinner tonight? It will be a modest affair. Not what you are used to, I am sure, but you are most welcome to share it so long as you promise not to mind if I do not care to change."

Davis's mind was on other things. "Dammit, Carter, you just remember whose money is paying for all this. If you've got something to damn well show me I want to see it now!"

"Sir, with respect," Carter softly responded, "I frankly do not think I can find it in torchlight. Too dangerous. You will enjoy it much more in the morning. I am tired. I am hungry. And, to be quite truthful, I could do without conversation this evening. If you'd rather pass on dinner that's just fine. I'd be indebted to you if you would leave me alone as you have done thus far."

"You damn British are a boring lot of bastards. Unsociable, stubborn, and damnedly ungrateful!"

As Davis mouthed expletives at Carter the houseboy brought in another martini.

"Ice, dammit, I want more ice!"

Davis' attentions now on the houseboy and the imperfect cocktail, Carter took the opportunity to disappear into his room and prepare himself for bed. But no sooner had he pulled on his nightshirt than he heard Davis creating an awful commotion out on the porch.

"Goddam fuzzy-wuzzy! What the hell do you think this is? A goddam fruit punch? Bring the ice. I'll mix the goddam thing myself. The ice, dammit!" He grabbed for the bucket himself. "Watch me, now, so you will get it right the next time." He snatched the bottle of gin from the Arab's hand and glugged it into his glass. "See that? Four fingers. Four!" He thrust four hairy digits at the unfortunate servant boy. "Four - like that. Then..." He poured a dash or two of vermouth into the glass. "This much. See? Son-of-a-bitchin' camel dung's got more brains." And he drank the glassful down in one gulp, much of the ice falling about his waistcoat and onto the floor.

"Another!" he ordered, thrusting his empty glass at the boy.

Carter, astounded by Davis's outburst and anxious to stop the onslaught before things got too ugly, emerged from his room in his dressing gown. He had worked long and hard to endear the Arabs to him and he wasn't about to let an egotistical American destroy all the trust and respect he had built up over the seasons. He spoke to the boy softly in Arabic and sent him away. Alone with Davis, he walked around his chair until he faced him straight on. He made no allowances for his patron's irrational state of mind.

"Mr Davis," he announced firmly, "I think it better you leave my house at once. The Antiquities Service has no need for disrespectful bigots. Please be good enough to retire peacefully while I am inclined to believe it is the drink that is doing the talking. I hope you will be feeling better in the morning. If you do not, I may be forced to reconsider my options regarding this partnership."

Davis, although somewhat sleepy with booze, was alert enough to comprehend fully the implications of Carter's words. Much as he despised authority in others, he well recognised that this young man indeed held the power to revoke his licence to dig. Davis's consuming passion to find an intact royal tomb, to return to the United States bedecked with trophies, and to receive the public honours attributed to those who donated such artefacts to the Metropolitan Museum transcended all other considerations. More than anything else, he wanted to publish and to have his name as a donor engraved on the description plate of a rare and beautiful display piece, there for all to see in perpetuity in the grand halls of the Met. He had better tread carefully from here.

Presented with what amounted to an ultimatum, therefore, Davis's response to Carter was most thoughtful and, a first for Davis, totally submissive. "Howard, my apologies. I have been too long drinking on the porch. This will not happen again. Let us go tomorrow to this interesting place you mentioned, as you suggest. I am indeed most sorry for the rudeness of my outburst."

"I understand," said Carter. "I will bring the houseboy in and you will apologise to him as well. Then all will be put to rights."

"Mmm? That really necessary?"

Carter nodded.

Davis did as he was told. They took dinner together after all, Carter in his nightshirt, Davis in his waistcoat, buttoned jodhpurs, boots and spats. They each had a final brandy and a cigar. By 10 p.m. Davis was on his way to his houseboat and Carter was in bed.

The late evening's dose of humility took much out of Davis. Perhaps for the first time in his life he had failed to get what he wanted through sheer force of will. He chose not to share the evening's events with Emma. His sense of failure allowed him little sleep that night. So it was the following morning that he was already at breakfast on Carter's veranda before Carter was out of bed. As the sun broke the horizon and threw a reflective glare across the river, Carter emerged, still in his nightshirt.

"Mornin', Howard. Not like you to sleep in, especially when we have work to do. You do remember your promise, don't you? What is it we are going to see today?"

Carter breathed in the cool morning air, stretched and sat at the table opposite his patron. "Good morning to you, Mr Davis. What a super sunrise. Invariably remarkable from here. Best location on the west bank. Fair sets one up for the day.

"Abdel! Coffee, if you please."

Davis wasn't interested in pleasantries. "What's in store for me today, Howard?" he repeated.

"Not sure you deserve anything after that exhibition last evening, sir." Carter couldn't resist the jab.

"But I apologised. Can't ask for more than that."

Carter had had his fun and decided to leave it. "Recognising your mood when I returned last night, I felt you needed something to spice up your senses, sir, but the martini issue got in the way. What I had in mind for you was a little pornography."

Davis's face lit up. "Glad you didn't tell me, man. Had little enough sleep last night. With the extra anticipation, I may have had none!"

Following breakfast, Carter got dressed and they left the inspectorate house at about 7.30 - Carter on Sultan; Davis on a mule; and the usual entourage of fellahs on foot and carrying supplies for their refreshment.

Carter led Davis southwest along the clearly defined margin that separates the fertile, green fields stretching to the riverside from the golden, lifeless desert. Then they cut inland towards the great amphitheatre of cliffs in which the mortuary temple of Queen Hatshepsut stood, itself almost an extension of the rocks themselves. The excavation and restoration of the structure were now pretty much complete. Davis had visited the temple many times. He had marvelled at its architecture and the art on its walls, but since its discovery could never be attributed to him it bore less attraction than the mysteries that still lay hidden beneath it and, of course, inside the walls of The Valley of the Tombs of the Kings.

"Pornography, Howard? I have been here many times. I have studied the reliefs and the paintings. They are beautiful. There is no pornography."

"We are not going to the temple, sir," said Carter. "We shall have to dismount shortly and climb the scree slope that leads up to the cliff over there. D' you see that cavity - there, to the right and to the rear of the amphitheatre?"

Davis, who was by now feeling considerable discomfort from his overindulgence the night before, could barely squint tightly enough to bear the punch of the sun off the blazing yellow cliff face. But he could make out a black spot in the brightness.

"All the way up there? Son-of-a-bitch! Have y' no mercy?"

Carter was unyielding. The trials Davis had put the poor fellahs through the previous night were still fresh in his mind.

"We begin our walk from here, sir," he said in a matter-of-fact way.

The two men dismounted and Carter led Davis up the rubble slope. As they walked, their feet sank in the loose debris. The going was so soft it felt almost as if they were making no progress at all. But when Carter paused for a moment to look back at the temple below and the river beyond, it was clear to both of them just how far they had already climbed. To Davis the cave, the tomb entrance, or whatever it was, did not look so very far away after all.

They scrambled their way to the cliff face and then along the top of the scree slope to the left until they stood beneath the opening. It was about fifty vertical feet away. The climbing was now firm footing and Carter had no trouble reaching the mouth of the cavity. Davis, under the weather as he was, lost his footing a couple of times, but made it in the end. When, panting, he reached Carter's side, it became clear that this was no cave. It was another rock-cut tomb - unfinished; uninhabited. No royal body had ever lain here.

Carter, stooping, led Davis into the crudely cut passage. The increasing darkness temporarily blinded them. Gradually their eyes became accustomed to the feeble light. All Davis could make out were the unfinished walls.

"There's nothing here," panted Davis. "Why have we climbed all this way?"

"Are your eyes not open, Mr Davis?" taunted Carter.

"Damn right they are. I see nothing. Not a damned thing. Just rock." And then he paused for a moment. "Wait a minute..." He laughed. "Son-of-a-bitch! It's Hatshepsut being rogered by a serf, is it not?"

"In so many words, sir. At least, that is one interpretation," said Carter. He continued clinically, "There is some controversy, however. The apparent lack of breasts - a cartoon of a homosexual act? But the figure has the headdress typical in portraits known to be of Hatshepsut. She is often depicted as a man and, and..."

"Yes, yes?" urged Davis, now totally fascinated.

"Well... The triangle between the legs - surely intended as a female representation."

"And would y' look at this guy waving his weener around!" Davis burst into laughter, then pulled out his sketchpad and penned a few lines for posterity.

On the way back, descending the scree slope and looking down on the magnificent spectacle of the queen's temple below them, a thought struck Carter. To Davis' surprise the inspector suddenly turned back and began to climb up the cliff again.

"Where the devil are you going now, man?" asked the aching millionaire.

"I just want to check something," Carter shouted back. "Back in a minute." And he disappeared over a ledge.

Five minutes in the unrelenting sun was far too long to expect Theodore Davis to wait. He made his way back to Carter's house and took a light and unusually booze-free lunch by himself. By late afternoon he was at the excavation site, his energies recharged by the food and the morning's excitement. On occasion, he was to be seen down amongst the fellahs scrabbling about pulling rocks from the gradually lengthening corridor. It was by now quite deep and he found it so hot at the debris face that he could spend no more than five or ten minutes there at any one time. Even the candles were softening and bending on their holders. On his third trip out of the mouth of the tomb he met Carter coming down the valley side directly above the tomb entrance.

"Where the hell have you been all this time?" Davis asked. "I've been working m' guts out down in the bowels of this thing and you've been gallavantin' wherever y' please. Found somethin' up there, have you?"

"No. Found nothing, Mr Davis. But I have exercised a theory of mine. And when we have completed clearance of this tomb I shall perform a survey to see whether my theory has foundation. Until I climbed that cliff with you this morning I did not realise that the burial chamber, when we eventually encounter it, could be located beneath the innermost bowels of Hatshepsut's mortuary temple on the other side of this divide - intentionally so - leading us to conclude that this must be the queen's tomb. It might explain the tortuous path we are now excavating. I believe the tomb-makers started at the valley head and the point closest to the queen's temple in an unfinished and abandoned tomb that for its first few feet ran entirely in the wrong direction. So, using this initial drop, they continued at the same angle of descent but gradually turned the corridor towards and beneath the temple's innermost shrine. That would make it unique among the tombs in The Valley."

The young archaeologist's speculations appealed to Davis' appetite for mystery and he decided to stay with the tomb clearance operations until they had been completed. But, with the air rapidly becoming too foul to breathe he first had to spend some additional money bringing an air pump to the excavation. Thankfully this was readily obtainable in Luxor and they had it at the site within twenty-four hours.

The season ended as expected, still tunnelling and with no end in sight.

With Davis back in the United States for the summer, Carter took off for Dendera with his palette and brushes, a sketchpad of heavy cartridge paper, and a folding canvas seat, for what he looked forward to as a pleasant, peaceful, uneventful, artistic interlude unencumbered with pampered, pestering hangers-on the like of TMD. He was to be sorely disappointed. The very first day turned out to be extremely uncomfortable, even horrific.

Seeking a shaded spot inside the halls of the great temple, Carter placed his chair at the base of one of the massive columns in front of an enormous frieze, a section of which he planned to paint. He looked up at the great ceiling high above him. Row upon row of vultures and serpents, their wings spread wide and painted in vivid reds, blues and gold, guided the eye towards the ceremonial entrance. The sunlight momentarily blinded him and he jerked his head back into the shade. As his eyes focused once more, the early light crisply picked out the engravings in the wall before him. The moment was too precious to miss. He pulled the pencil from his jacket pocket, licked the sharp lead point and leaned forward. Just about to make the first pencil stroke, he was disturbed by a commotion coming from outside the temple walls. The noise became louder as an Arab ran into the temple, his white robe fluttering all about him.

"Effendi! Effendi! Mr Carter, sir! Come at once! A body has been discovered! A body! Not two minutes from here." The excited Arab gestured behind him.

Carter knew the man. He had from time to time been a senior helper in his excavation gangs. 'A mummy?' he thought. The adrenalin flowed. The heartbeat increased. All at once he forgot his painting. He rose to follow the man who was beckoning him hastily and already running back but looking at Carter to see if he was coming.

"I am coming, Sama. Be calm, I beg of you. And look where you are going or you may run into something!"

Outside the temple boundary, about one hundred yards ahead, Carter could see a dozen or so Arabs clustered about a small pit. Sama shouted to the group of bystanders as he approached and they moved apart to allow the inspector through. When Carter got to the edge of the shallow pit and looked down, his feelings of excitement were wiped out at a stroke. Lying in the pit was no two, three-or four-thousand-year-old mummy, rather a dead Egyptian and, judging from the lack of bloating, an Egyptian probably not more than twelve hours dead.

"God almighty!" exclaimed Carter. "Who could have done this? Summon the police, Sama, at once. Ghastly!"

Stunned and appalled by the sight at his feet, Carter took a little time to recover his composure. While he awaited the arrival of the local gendarmerie he examined the body. The corpse was grotesquely contorted. The unfortunate man had clearly suffered the most horrific torture that ultimately must have led to his death. His hands were manacled tightly behind his back by a pair of crude wooden rowlocks secured together by large nails that skewered his wrists. The arms were bent over and tied to a wooden halter which had been used to drag him along the ground behind a vehicle of some sort - probably a horse. His torso was deeply incised from the dragging, sand and gravel virtually cemented within the dried blood and flesh of the open wounds. The legs were wide apart as if dislocated at the hips from the terrible physical punishment his body must have endured as he had been towed over the rough terraine. His tongue protruded from between his clenched teeth in a grimace of agonising death.

"Savages!" Carter swore under his breath. 'No value to human life; no feelings; the like of wild beasts.' The sight turned his stomach. He looked away and breathed deeply, filling his lungs with fresh, tepid air.

Presently two policemen arrived. "Who found the body?" asked one.

"Me, Effendi," said Sama, coming forward from the crowd of onlookers.

"How?"

"There was a square depression in the ground. I thought it might be an opening to a shaft. I got down on my knees and scraped away at the sand with my hands and very soon came upon the man's toes. I ran at once for Monsieur l'Inspecteur here," he gestured towards Carter, "who was working in the temple over there. By the time we got back here the body had been exposed - as you see it now."

"By who?"

"By them." Sama waved his arm at the surrounding rabble.

"The evidence is corrupted, then," stated the policeman authoritatively. "The site is despoiled. There is nothing more we can do here. We will remove the body to the morgue. There is a tarpaulin on my horse. Fetch it."

On the policeman's directions the Arabs wrapped the body in the tarpaulin and secured it with some rope. An idle donkey was selected to carry the load. The policemen took the names of all those present and then set off back to their hut to do whatever they chose to do. 'Surely as little as possible,' thought Carter.

Carter made no attempt to interfere. He was not at all surprised at the lack of interest in the discovery and the absence of normal police procedure. Procedure meant responsibility and work, and the Arabs always looked for ways to avoid both. Besides, Carter had already recognised this horror as the handiwork of a former Moudir of the area. He was well known for his merciless treatment of the fellaheen. This barbarism had been a message to the rank and file that it was far less painful to yield to conscription.

Carter returned to his equipment in the great hall of the temple of Dendera. Try as he might, he could not summon the energy to draw. A long, frustrating and fractious winter season with Davis, the heat of summer, and now this gross obscenity. 'Is there no hope for these people?' It was as if the waters of the Nile itself had contrived to sap the last of his energy. He gave a long sigh, picked up his things, and left to return to Luxor - to sleep; hopefully not to dream; and to forget. In the morning he would telegraph his personal report with his own thoughts on culpability to the Viceroy's office.

The following season's work revealed that the tomb entrance corridor just kept on getting deeper and deeper, and weirder. As it continued to descend, it curved in a lengthening sweep to the right until coming around to a westward direction, a full 180 degrees from where it had started at the surface.

Carter sensed they were nearing their goal - west was the setting sun, west was death - and indeed at this point they at last broke into the burial chamber. Clearing of the rubble fill was followed by the usual anticlimax - devastation, fragments, rubbish, amongst which were the remains of a rifled wooden sarcophagus.

Carter pursued clearance of the chamber with his usual attention to detail until every scrap of evidence had been sifted from the dirt and faithfully catalogued. Little more was found until one day, while Carter and Davis were taking a lunch break outside the tomb entrance, the reis summoned them back into the tomb. With difficulty, they once more made their way down the long, narrow and precipitous corridor until they reached the burial chamber. Barely half of the floor had been cleared, but in the far right-hand corner of the squarish room the top step of another staircase had been uncovered. Carter and Davis's excitement regenerated, but the two did not wait around while their men cleared the staircase. The atmosphere was stifling and only partly relieved by the air pump. They were compelled to climb back out for some fresh air.

The new and last room to be discovered in this strange tomb yielded a pair of open but complete and relatively undamaged yellow quartzite sarcophagi. One was oblong, the other fashioned in the shape of a cartouche. Carter lowered his oil lamp into one of them and a glow of yellow lit up the translucent hull. As he withdrew it, the lamp accidentally struck the inner wall. The sarcophagus rang like a great cathedral bell, startling everyone within earshot.

A quick inspection of the names on the two sarcophagi confirmed that they had been intended for, and probably originally had received, the mummies and nested coffins of Hatshepsut and her father. The evidence that may have appeared coincidence at first was now beginning to make sense - to Carter, at least. This last tomb not only had contained the body of the female Pharaoh, and not only was its location close to that of the inner sanctuary of Hatshepsut's temple outside The Valley, but also its architecture was based on the same geometric system used to construct that temple. Her father was buried with her - this was reflected in the reliefs that memorialise the two of them together in life on the massive walls of her temple complex. The fit was as complete as Carter could have hoped. He was well satisfied with his conclusion, particularly after all the miserably hard work and the odious fights with his patron.

Davis was ecstatic with the outcome of the project and he pressed Carter into publishing an account of the discovery. Edouard Naville himself supplied an historical narrative on Hatshepsut. The publication would be put together abroad during the summer recess.

For Davis, there were many years and considerable money left to search out more treasures in the Egyptian dust and he was keen to get on with it; but he would not work with Carter again. The inspector of modest means had had quite enough of the wealthy lawyer. Their parting was mutually and willingly agreed with no embarrassment on either side. There were others available to help Davis accomplish his goals. For him the best was yet to come.

For Carter, there would be years yet, too. For him, alike, the best was yet to come - and the worst. With his tenacious regard for principle, his respect for his Egyptian employees and his personal pride, he was developing a stubborn complacency that would, in times of crisis, cause him to forget that to successfully achieve his ends he was and always would be entirely dependent on the goodwill of others considerably more well-to-do than he. That was a fact. Alas, he would blind himself to it.

Chapter Seven
Misadventures

Ipay reached a vantage point from which he could survey the length and breadth of the wadi. He looked back to check for telltale signs of dust that might indicate he was being followed. There was a haze but for all he could make out, squinting southward with the sunlight across his face, no dust. He rode on a little further to take advantage of the shade provided by some large boulders. This was far enough. He could wait here until he spotted the approach of the Hittite prince and then take off towards him to arrive sweating as if he had galloped all the way from Thebes without stopping. There could be little danger to travellers this far from habitation. Ipay sat down to rest.

The ground surface was uneven and he had to push a few of the larger stones out of the way before he could lie down without too much discomfort. He pulled off his goatskin water bag and laid it down as a headrest on the shaded rocky surface. He eased back until his head and neck made contact with the cool surface of the water bag. A soothing sensation ran through his senses. He had another bag - date wine - and settled down to drink a little.

Ipay awoke to the sawing cries of buzzards. The shadows had gone and the full force of the late afternoon sun shone down directly and reflected off every facet of rock about him. The gaunt birds' dark forms wheeled overhead and flashed occasional menacing shadows across his eyes. By now the temperature of the water in the goatskin was the same as that of his body. He felt the sweat curling down his cheeks. Discomfort compelled Ipay to get up.

He drew himself back to the shaded side of the boulder he had used for shelter and searched the northern horizon for some sign of movement. It took his sleepy and still somewhat drugged eyes a moment or two to accustom to the light. There was nothing - no sign of motion. He turned to look south. There was some haze, or was it dust? In the distance there was just a suggestion of a shimmer. Could he have missed him? By the angle of the sun he estimated he could have been asleep for at least half the day. The Hittite prince could have passed well by in that time. An intensity began to build within his head, soon maturing to a sense of panic.

'The queen will have me put to death! The gods will execute my spirit! There will be no afterlife!' The visions and his pounding heart compounded within his mind until the pressure on his temples felt like it would cause him to go blind.

The dust that he had seen to the south might have been nothing more than another traveller. Nevertheless, he had to check, just in case. Pulling his horse behind him he stumbled down from his vantage point and made chase. Ipay galloped as fast as his horse would allow him. The dust was so far away, he might never catch up in time. And if it were not the prince, then he would have to turn once again and go back. His panic grew all the greater. His mind wheeling, Ipay jabbed his heels into the horse's flanks. Then, all of a sudden the animal faltered, pitched headlong, and fell to the ground. Ipay was thrown forward and came to an inelegant stop face down, spread-eagled across the desert gravel. The startled horse leapt up, cantered off a short distance, then stopped and began grazing on the spare desert scrub.

Ipay looked up. He was sore. He turned over and examined himself. What a sorry sight. His palms, his forearms and his chin were grazed and bleeding where he had connected so unceremoniously with the coarse gravel. He removed the cloth that he used to shield his head from the sun and dabbed at the bloody scores on his arms. The grit partly came off with the congealing blood but not all of it. He lamented his disfigurement and began to worry about possible infection - he had always had a personal tendency towards hypochondria. He yielded up a quick prayer to Isis.

Ipay drew himself up to a seated position and, for the first time, looked back at what had caused his headlong tumble. It was a broken spear - a freshly broken spear. His preoccupation with his personal well-being was immediately extinguished. The icy chill of deep fear descended on him. He looked all around. To his horror, there were the bodies of soldiers, three of them, scattered about in the dust. To the left lay a dying camel, a pike through its neck, still struggling for breath. Its decorative saddleware lay crushed under the weight of its own body.

Ipay stood up and limped over to the animal. He was no longer conscious of the pain from his injuries. In his worst fears he knew what he would find inside the broken canopy. He raised one of the decorated curtains. A dark-skinned youth - half of him trapped under the beast, his upper body only showing from beneath the belly of the camel, a virtual mat of congealed blood covering his neck and chest, the fear still showing in his open eyes - lay frozen in death. By his clothing the young man was clearly a person of some importance and definitely not Egyptian. Ipay at once knew he had failed. His future was sealed in the drying blood of the young, dead Hittite. So was Ankhesenamun's.

Unable to return to the palace with this dreadful news and unwilling to face his family, for one final moment of pleasure Ipay took a northern village prostitute for the evening. Following that moment he rolled onto his back. Holding an effigy of Min close to his chest he asked the girl to hand him the beer he had poisoned.

When he was discovered, his penis was still erect. A poison of passion no doubt. His wife thought he had died coupling with the gods - no better end for any man. Feeling a curious mixture of joy and sadness, she hurried to prepare for his embalming.

General Horemheb received the news with characteristically suppressed gratification. He had had the assassins jailed and beheaded that same evening for sundry crimes against the community, most of which they had indeed committed. That night he slept a deep and most satisfactory sleep.

The following morning he remained in bed until late, reflecting on his future. Reclining in the cushions, he gazed up at the ceiling. He had goals: he would be Pharaoh. He would have a long, peaceful and comfortable reign. He would die while on the throne and would be entombed in the largest and finest tomb yet created within the holy bowels of The Valley of the Kings. Eternity as Pharaoh then would be assured. He did not seek the people's adoration. He just did not want to be disliked so much that every waking hour he might fear for his life.

Establishing himself on the throne should not be hard, his lack of royal blood notwithstanding. He would marry it. That, and his historical achievements which had flawlessly ensured the personal security of his three previous kings throughout their individual reigns, should be endorsement enough.

But keeping himself securely established on the throne would be another matter. The legacy left by Akhenaten, still in living memory of the people, was one of negligent stewardship and bold blasphemy. The dead heretic's energies had been wholly dedicated to the new religious order. He had all but ignored his duties as administrator of the State. These he had left entirely in the hands of Nakht.

The subsequent tenures of Smenkhkare and Tutankhamun were too brief to achieve much visible change. And the forthcoming reign of the aging Ay - surely this would be little more than ephemeral? These were not hard acts to follow so long as he prepared himself well and was careful to avoid any glaring errors.

The longevity he sought he would secure for himself through force of arms only if absolutely necessary. Brutality was such hard work and he was experienced enough to realise that the factions that might rise against him would be difficult to eliminate completely. In one part of the empire or another the fighting would continue. It would be costly and he would perpetually fear for his personal security. He was not getting any younger. It would be all too troublesome a sovereignty - all just too hard.

No. In the land of Egypt, blessed as it was with such bountiful resources - those for subsistence, for trade, and for art, and all this combined with the intellectual and artistic capital of the people themselves - there were far easier and less painful ways to mature a contented populace. He would redouble efforts to re-establish the old religious order at Thebes. He would make these projects highly visible. There would be new construction on a grand scale. There would be no idle hands with time for thoughts of mischief. Labour would be adequately compensated. The workers' families would have full bellies. He would wipe the forbidden city off the face of the earth and let the desert reclaim it. He would use stone from the dismantled buildings as foundation and filling for the enormous new façades he would have commissioned in the old holy city, hiding the heretic's art form from public view for ever. What he could not make or usurp he would destroy and bury. He would eradicate the corruption that presently infested officialdom. This he would achieve by ensuring that those highest in the pecking order maintained the standard of living to which they had by then become accustomed. He would ensure that these men, including his most senior military leaders and their large families, were well paid and provided with the best of creature comforts. For the plethora of lesser officials, including the walking militia, all those of no influential consequence to him, he would sign into law the severest penalties for any caught over-zealously practising their official mandates and likewise reward those who identified such persons. And he would be ruthless in his execution of the law, making public examples of all those convicted and exacting punishment where he was assured the largest audience.

In this manner, he had no doubt, the people would observe real signs of prosperity and change for the better. The old religious order would renew their confidence in an afterlife. They would warm to him. And he would achieve that which he desired most - maat on earth followed seamlessly by paradise in heaven and for all eternity.

Many commented on the general's uncommon good spirits that day.

Ankhesenamun waited. Ipay did not return. No one came. There had been rumours - heard mostly from her maidservants, and by now much embellished, who had heard them from those who brought supplies to the palace, who had heard them from tradesmen and tax collectors, who had heard them from nomads - that the Hittite boy had set out on his journey but had expired in transit. The exact manner of his disappearance became the subject of many different interpretations. No one story prevailed.

The queen resigned herself to the finality of this setback. 'Whatever is written', she thought. But she could write history, too. In the weeks of waiting for her unfortunate suitor she had constructed a parallel plan - much simpler, less dangerous and considerably less visible than that perpetrated by Horemheb. Its execution could attach no blame to her and, so far as Egyptian beliefs were concerned, it would be far more finally fatal to the general than the untimely death of her husband.

The Egyptian people fervently believed that tomb robbery and elimination of the inhabitant's name shortly after burial, though common enough in practice, if not rectified through early reburial and accompanied by all the traditional ceremony, would bring eternal oblivion. The 'journey' could not be completed. If, once Horemheb himself had died and become entombed, Ankhesenamun could contrive to ensure the total loss of every piece of the grave equipment so judiciously placed to help speed the general's spirit to the afterlife, including the complete destruction of his mummy, his death would become absolute.

She need take no active part in accelerating Horemheb's mortality. She had trusted servants to whom she could discharge that duty. Even if she died before him, they would willingly and most assuredly execute her instructions.

But much time would have to pass before she achieved this final revenge. For now she must put her recent disappointment behind her and busy herself with her husband's transition, the preparations for which had to be completed on time and without fault. As it was with the people, she also must ensure that Tutankhamun lived on so that she may join him later, ultimately blissfully in a world without end, and without the general.

In the midst of these thoughts she was interrupted by Tia, her oldest and most trusted maidservant. The woman announced that Ay was at the door to her chambers and wished an audience. The queen knew why he was here. She had considered the option herself - now that it was certain the Hittite prince would never arrive. The thought had rested distastefully in her mind for some days, but she had never dismissed it entirely.

However, the sight of Ay at the door to her rooms - his thin, lined face, his pale, almost opalescent eyes, his narrow lips, wet with the drool of advancing senility, his missing and blackened teeth, his wheezing, his arched back, his bony, gnarled hands, the rings hanging loosely around his fingers, the support of the guards on each arm - did not endear him to her, and she knew he was about to ask for her hand in marriage.

He needed her to cement the line fully and, hopefully, to provide an heir. She needed him to be certain of acceptance at court through the next few vital years during which she would seek to complete her plan for reunion with her departed husband. Without endorsement through royal marriage she could be exiled. To contemplate the additional requirement - that of the provision of an heir - was, however, unthinkable.

Before Ay could take a breath and open his mouth to speak, the queen raised her hand. "I know why you have come. I accept your invitation. Legitimacy - it is necessary for us both. However, there is a condition to our union. I will not share your bed. I will not bear your children. It is to be understood that this is a marriage of convenience for the two of us. I bring to it the substance of bloodline. You bring to it..." she paused, "...authority." Her last word almost faded away to a whisper. "It is done," she continued. "Summon the priests. We shall be married in the morrow. You may leave."

The old man smiled ingratiatingly and withdrew.

It was with some considerable surprise and great pleasure that Ankhesenamun observed Horemheb demonstrate detailed, even devoted attention to the preparations for Tutankhamun's funeral. He visited each grave goods workshop every day to check on progress with assembly and collection of the funerary paraphernalia. He had compiled the inventory himself. Some items were being manufactured especially for the burial, and some would be brought from the king's quarters at the palace - the dead king's most personal things, those he used most frequently, those he loved to use, the trappings of everyday life that would provide him with comfort and security in their familiarity. Other items would be brought from available stock; some, originally meant for others, would be usurped and altered to personalise them to the boy king, particularly some of the larger objects, those more difficult to manufacture in the time remaining - these were to come from the tomb of his brother.

The general had anticipated delay and had prepared for it. From Smenkhkare's tomb the sarcophagus already had been removed for alteration. The outer coffin had been found to fit within that of the boy king almost pefectly and its interior was large enough to accept Tutankhamun's inner coffin currently being manufactured in the goldsmiths' foundry. Smenkhkare's canopic chest had been usurped also and would be re-inscribed with the names of its new owner.

The stoppers to this chest were another matter. To establish a true likeness of Tutankhamun, Horemheb had ordered that they be remade. But the mason fashioning the heads had broken or chipped many pieces and had begun again so many times that he was falling well behind schedule.

"With respect, sire," the unfortunate artisan complained to the general, "I am not used to repetitive work. Each piece I create is unique and unrepeatable. I cannot stop my hands from adjusting the pattern. Worse still, this type of work stifles my creativity. I cannot excel at it."

The artisan felt well satisfied with this statement and mentally congratulated himself on the eloquence of its delivery.

Horemheb was not so impressed. He stared earnestly at the man. "At the discretion and generosity of the royal family you are granted supplies of food and drink more than sufficient for the sustenance of your wife, your children and the elders in your family. Are you not?"

The artisan gave a hesitant nod.

"What we ask in return is nothing more than the perfect product of your skills. If you are unable to perform this requirement, then return to the fields. I shall find another who can."

The artisan opened his mouth as if to respond but became fearful that if he kept talking things could become a whole lot worse than working in the fields. Without a murmur he turned back to the work at hand.

Horemheb knew it was far too late. The sculptor was young and indeed most skilful. At some future date he could be assigned to the crafting of grave goods for the tomb of the general himself. This was particularly important to Horemheb. He did not want to turn the man against him. He would much prefer him a willing ally. 'Mine shall be the finest. He shall help see to it,' he thought.

"Artisan!" he bellowed. "Go to the stores and seek out the four original stoppers to this chest. The faces are not that dissimilar from Pharaoh. Bring them to me. We shall see if some small adjustment can be made to improve their likeness to our dead king. With this done to my satisfaction, you may return to your creative business. Away with you before more precious time is lost!"

The sculptor was only too glad of the change in orders and departed without hesitation.

Activity in the tomb-workers' community was now at fever pitch. A celebration of immense proportions was but weeks away. Each man who had a part to play in the preparations had committed himself to the task. Horemheb, on his rounds of inspection, did not have to chide any artisan for slack workmanship or tardiness. If there were errors, and there were many, the artisan responsible felt it more personally than the wrath or discipline of his master and set himself to begin again with greater energy than before.

The general also spent considerable time at the goldsmiths'. He went there in large part to view progress on the gold coffin that would enclose the king's mummy. The immense mummiform casket had not been started until the time of the king's death because up to that point Tutankhamun had barely reached adulthood and the correct size could not be determined. The job had to be completed from scratch in two months. So far, one half had been beaten to shape from sheet gold and was being burnished prior to engraving and inlay. The other still awaited the artisan's hammer.

The carpenters had completed some adjustments to the facial features of the mask at the head of the lid to the second coffin - that usurped from Smenkhkare - and Horemheb stood back examining it closely to determine its likeness to the boy king. There was something distinctly dissimilar about it, however. The general regarded the face once more. It bore a more severe look than the expression on the outer coffin but its proportions - the cheeks, the nose and mouth, and the forehead - were roughly in balance and a reasonably correct likeness.

'It is the ears that are wrong,' he concluded. 'Far too low on the head. No matter. Garlands of flowers in profusion will cover all the coffins at the time of sealing. No one will notice.'

The much larger outer wooden coffin was practically ready. The delicate carving had been completed, and it was being prepared for gilding.

The general moved on to find the object that, other than the mummy itself, was to become the most important symbol in the tomb. The elegant, solid gold statuette of a standing figure lay on a bed of straw on a small table in the corner of the foundry. Again in the likeness of the king, this glistening work of art was to represent the spirit of Tutankhamun himself. This particular piece had been originally cast a year ago and until the king's death had stood in a dark sanctuary deep within the temple complex. Since it was already finished, all that remained was to put the final touches to its shrine, give it a last polish, and ensure its security until the funeral proceedings commenced.

Horemheb, notwithstanding his basic disdain for the boy king, felt moved by the figure. It elicited regal godliness and glowed with life. It stood less than a cubit high. An effigy of the king - in sandalled feet, a corselet about his waist, his arms straight down by his sides with fists clenched, a broad necklace about his shoulders, the typically striped nemes headdress and the uraeus, the striking cobra, at his forehead, the raised arms symbolising ka on his wig. The eyes stared through all who gazed on them.

A feeling of fatigue came over the general. Was it the staring golden eyes or the heat of the foundry? Or both of them? He ordered his entourage to escort him back to his chambers.

The foundry fires burned throughout that night as they had done since orders had been placed for the grave goods. The flickering orange glow brought the eyes alive to all who looked at them and, when the time came to break their labours, nothing but disturbed sleep.

Horemheb's sleep was no less disturbed that night. When he finally lost consciousness it was not for long. An hour past midnight and he was rudely awakened by a shrill wailing from outside the chamber. He rose up on one elbow. The noise clearly came from within the palace halls.

'A time for mourning, yes, but not every day! Gods save us! Why is she doing this to me?' He believed it to be Ankhesenamun but it was not she. The wailing continued and he was compelled to get out of bed. Emerging into the great hall in some disarray, without his headdress, which was still on its pedestal, and his loincloth, unsecured, hanging about his waist and swinging inelegantly between his legs, he called out for the unfortunate mourner.

"Oh, Queen who grieves! Show yourself!"

He stumbled into a hallway and came upon his guards. They were in the act of wrestling an old woman from a prone position on the stone floor. Reacting to the general's bellowing, they raised their heads and came to attention. The sight of their immodest master would be food for some stories in the barracks later, but for now the guards' faces were expressionless.

The woman, continuing to moan, hung limp between them. She looked very old but in those times women aged quickly. She might have been little more than forty years of age. Horemheb could not see her face but he could tell that this was not the queen. The hair of her wig was plaited in multiple ropes and well shaped. Her clothing was in disarray but only because she had prostrated herself. Clearly her clothing was of some quality. She had several gold bracelets on her skinny arms, earrings, and rings about her bony fingers. She was not of low caste.

"Who is she? What is her business here?" scowled the fatigued general.

"She burst in, sir, before we could stop her. We did not want to strike her. She is old and frail. She carries no weapons."

The woman continued to wail.

"What can she want?" yelled the insomniac, irritated almost to the point of insanity. "Speak your business, old woman. No one enters here without specific business with his Excellency. Your business. Speak! Quickly, speak!"

She carried on wailing.

Frustrated with this untimely interruption, Horemheb lost all patience. He grabbed at one of the guards' daggers and pulled it from its sheath. He brought the blade up under the thin, arching body with a single turning motion that gathered speed in the upswing. As he did so the old hag's head raised itself and a pair of large, yellowed eyes looked directly and fixedly into his.

His arm was still moving as his fingers relaxed their grip. The knife fell to the floor and clattered to one side. He knew this woman. He regained his composure and shouted at the guards. "Loose her and leave!"

The two curious soldiers ensured the old lady had found her feet, then let go of her and left the hall, closing the great cedar doors behind them.

The woman continued to stare the general directly in the eyes.

"Please sit, mother of Mutnodjme. How can I be forgiven for the welcome I have given you?"

To achieve his ultimate ambition, Horemheb needed this woman's daughter as his principal wife. The line was most suitable - like his, it had no blood connection with the family of the heretic. To become king by ascendency and not by force of arms, the marriage match had to be absolutely correct - and visible to the people as such. He had had designs on this daughter several years since. He could not afford in any way to alienate her family.

Horemheb took the old lady's arm and guided her gently to a couch. As she sat down she jerked her arm away from him in a gesture of repugnance. She did not take her eyes from him for a moment.

Once seated she spoke. Her voice was hoarse. "Oh, Horemheb," she began, "what have you done? How you have disgraced the name of this family."

"I know not of that which you speak, mother of Mutnodjme."

"Indeed, General? Indeed? Then tell this 'ageing old hag' - for I believe you have called me such in other company many a time or two before..."

"My lady, please..."

"...Tell me why you killed our king."

Horemheb was struck dumb with so direct an accusation. How could she possibly know? The adrenalin of fear now filled his mind with panic. Had she been witness to the act? He searched for a convincing reply.

"My lady, you cannot be serious in this. For, if you are, you hurt me deeply and I know that cannot be your intent. Our families have grown so close of late. You well appreciate my feelings for your living daughter - that I seek her hand in marriage when she comes of age."

The old woman's eyes grew wider and, her brow creasing deeply down its centre, she blazed back at him. "You have not answered me, General Horemheb! Answer my accusation!"

The general took a few seconds to think.

"I underestimate you, mother of Mutnodjme. The depth of your grief has brought out the years of aggression you have hitherto been able to suppress. Am I to become the target of this release? If so, let it be. Whatever I am able to contribute to satisfy your needs, I am only too willing to provide. But I cannot satisfy you through admission of such a heinous crime. Better I kill myself than admit to that which I did not do."

So saying, he dramatically bowed to the floor, picked up the fallen dagger and offered it to her. As it lay cradled in his open hands he nervously contemplated her physical abilities. He need not have worried. She did not reach for the instrument.

"Better you kill me as you did the king - and now!" she gestured, raising her chin to expose her narrow throat. "But you will be found out, my General, regardless of my demise. My daughter knows my mind on this matter. As you lie with her in your marriage bed and for years thereafter you will be forever affeared that she might raise her hand against you in the night, while you slumber, to avenge the death that you so cruelly contrived to satisfy your avarice for the throne of the two lands. Live in fear, Horemheb. Live and die in fear."

She slowly got up, turned and quietly left the hall through a side entrance.

Horemheb did not go after her. She might talk more to others but she would not be believed by enough to make a difference. After all, there was no proof, and she was old. The old have visions. They imagine things. Few would believe her rantings. The publicity would be confined to the family circle and he could weather that. He might have to think more about how he might deal with his most intimate personal security - with Mutnodjme - but that was yet some years away. There was much wooing still to be done.

The general secured his loincloth and shuffled back into his bedchamber. The apparent zeal with which he was directing the preparations for the king's embarkation to the afterlife would be proof enough of his love for Tutankhamun. His grief at the loss would be visible to all. No one could suspect him of any crime. This thought satisfied him immensly and he slept well and soundly for what remained of that night.

Chapter Eight
The Trouble with the French

Howard Carter's successes as overseer in the Upper Nile made him a prime candidate for reassignment as Inspector of Antiquities to sites in the north. He didn't exactly feel he was getting stale in his work on the Upper Nile, but a change of scenery would be quite acceptable. The opportunity to put the stamp of his style of doing things on the only other district of importance in Egypt was irresistible.

As things turned out, the move was to cement a bridgehead in his career. What was about to happen during his tenureship of the Lower Nile would earn him a reputation for immovable stubbornness that would stay with him throughout his life. At the same time it would set him irretrievably apart from the class to which he most aspired, and he would attach to himself a stigma that would ensure that however remarkable any future achievement there would never be one hint of professional recognition from those who under normal circumstances might be considered his peers.

So, some serious misfortune lay just around the corner, and it was his nemesis, the French, who visited it upon him - just a few arrogant, wealthy, well-connected and inebriated Europeans - nothing more, nothing less.

Georges hadn't wanted to come to Egypt in the first place. He was idle at home and his mother had insisted he needed the education. "Travel in Napoleon's footsteps," she had encouraged romantically.

"The place is full of wogs and big, broken buildings, Mama."

"You spend too much time around the house. It will do you good to get away. It will do me good. I need some time to myself. If you covet your allowance, you had better travel!"

He knew she didn't want to be alone, she just wanted privacy. He wanted to keep his allowance. "I will only go if you allow me to take my friends. They may need this education, too."

And five young Frenchmen arrived in Cairo. Within a few days, their early familiarity with the more affluent bars in the city had added nine more of their countrymen. After eighteen society parties, a couple of dozen various ladies, and a string of bar hops, it was time to take a short trip to see what new delights might lie in store upriver.

Georges was becoming accustomed to the place. He knew he had little to look forward to when he went home. Life would fall back into a predictable routine. The sexual favours of a proliferation of debutantes were always gratefully received, but he felt like a stallion in a field - walled in, unable to do anything else but eat, sleep and service the chosen. There would be no purpose in his life but to wait on his father's death.

Here in Egypt things were different - the atmosphere, the people and, above all, the surroundings. When he returned to France he would have something that few others had, experiences the like of which his friends could never comprehend. Now, all of a sudden, he found he had the desire to feel the essence of a place that was truly different.

Jacques, however, did not. One more chance to get pissed and have a bloody good time at someone else's expense.

That particular morning they all carelessly and indulgently imbibed a late champagne breakfast at the Continental Savoy Hotel. For their forthcoming excursion, Jacques ordered a case of red wine, a dozen sticks of fresh bread from the hotel bakery, and drew from his own personal cache a large tin of finely matured Brie. With these materials gathered up in a small, open-topped tea chest, and with a single Arab bearer in tow, the party of youngsters took a horse-drawn carriage to the wharfside.

The river trip was quiet and uneventful. Georges sat on the side of the boat with his sandals cutting a slice through the water. Jacques, seeking the shade of the sail, sat uncomfortably on his case of wine and watched the river traffic.

At the end of the short trip, the party of Frenchmen rolled off the sailboat in some disarray, each of them taking a different and evidently aimless route from the riverside. Georges, yelling at the top of his voice to overpower the rantings of the profusion of Arab salesmen buzzing around each of the visitors, directed his friends towards a line of tethered donkeys. The sad looking animals were standing next to the mud-brick wall of a small shelter, their heads down and their ears mechanically twitching amidst a cloud of teeming flies.

It was as well there was a step to assist each of them in mounting. Jacques nevertheless somehow managed to get onto his donkey facing to the rear. Grabbing the whisking tail of the unfortunate beast, he made a gesture as if he were holding reins and about to take off at a gallop, albeit in reverse. Evolutionary progress has blessed the nether regions of a donkey with the flexible muscle tone of a flautist's lips. Jacques pulled on the tail hairs. The flatulent animal responded by evacuating itself with a timpanous roar executed with considerable force and a resonance that only this animal's capacious intenstines were capable of. Those in his audience were in the right humour to appreciate the orchestration and applauded the young man's efforts by swirling their hats about in the air and cheering loudly.

Georges kicked his donkey forward and signalled his group to follow.

Sensibility returned to Jacques as he realised his donkey was now untethered and free to move and take its position in the line of animals now forming up behind their leader. This was too late, too casual, and too inefficiently connected with his musculature to permit him to quickly correct his position on the donkey's back. Worse still, the donkey's decision to take its place in line was immediate and irrevocable and most effectively connected to its actions, and before he could summon the presence of mind to jump off with dignity, Jacques found himself propelled from the backside of the animal head-over-heels to the ground. Happily for his pride, the donkey had not left a deposit to break his fall, and the remainder of the group did not turn to look, each concentrating hard on maintaining a secure seat and the way ahead.

The donkey-master grabbed the animal's halter and guided it back to the upset rider. Jacques picked himself up, dusted himself off, remounted in the correct direction this time, and urged his shabby steed to follow his thirteen colleagues. The animal advanced side-step up the incline and onto a dry bank raised between two irrigated fields.

When he caught up with his friends, they were still talking about his donkey's posterior vocal cords and commenting about Jacques' ability to play the instrument with such professional vulgarity. As time and distance passed, however, merriment gave away to uncomfortable silence. The rolling gait of the animals began to tear at the Frenchmen's untrained thighs, and the consciousness of physical discomfort rudely replaced their earlier amusement.

The necropolis at Saqqara is dominated by an eroded, sand-draped, but still visibly stepped and colossal pyramid. Twenty pyramids of varying sizes and frequency dot this desert skyline. All are situated within a mile or so of the west bank of an old watercourse of the Nile and, to the enthusiast, provide an overwhelming resource for study. The ragged group now descending on this holy place of the dead, however, was not remotely connected with this prestigious class.

The tomb and temple complex of the step pyramid is surrounded by a great wall outside of which at this time stood a rest house for the use of personnel engaged in the business of the Antiquities Service. While it was only a relatively short trail from the flood plain of the river across the sand to Saqqara, the effects of the alcohol taken at breakfast, the bright midday sun, and the uncomfortable barrel backs of the donkeys sorely tried the young Frenchmen's endurance. They reached the door to the rest house and dismounted. They quickly surrounded the bearer who had walked all the way carrying the tea chest on his bent back. They pushed him before them through the open front door.

The ticket inspector sitting inside watched aghast as they wrestled the box to the floor and drew out four bottles of wine. Mohammed plucked up the courage to speak. "Sirs," he began, "you cannot stay here. This is not a public place."

"Nonsense," reacted Jacques. "We are 'antiquaries', not 'public'!"

"Do you have the wherewithal, Jacques?" asked one of the group as he pinned a bottle between his knees.

"Indeed I have it!" He produced a silver corkscrew from the pocket of his dusty jacket.

The bottles were opened and the bread was placed on the ticket collector's table. Jacques dove deeply once more into the tea chest and with a flourish produced the tin of Brie. From another pocket, to the cheers of his watching colleagues, he brandished a can opener.

Two minutes and the feast was all before them. Jacques cut the Brie into cake-like slices with the tin lid, broke the bread, and took a first swig of wine from one of the bottles.

Overcome by numbers, Mohammed sat and watched as the men sat round on the floor passing the bread, cheese and wine between them. The 'pop' of another cork was heard every fifteen minutes or so, and with each of these the conversation grew louder. After about half a dozen bottles had been consumed the noise perceptibly softened.

Georges picked his moment to speak. "Gentlemen. If I may call you such!" Much laughter. "We came here not to picnic in the desert, I believe." More laughter. "We came here to see things. Great things. Sights most Frenchmen may not even dream of witnessing. And," he raised his voice, "in the footsteps of Napoleon!"

"Bor-ring!" Shouted one member of the group.

"Vive l'Emperor!" yelled Jacques as he leapt to his feet.

Bedlam broke out. Jacques led the group in a stylised march about the tiny room, loudly clomping his boots on the wooden floor. Someone carelessly kicked over an open bottle of wine and the mock parade came to an abrupt halt. Jacques whisked the bottle up before too much had spilled and gurgled a long draught before sitting himself down again and setting it upright on the floor beside him.

Georges took advantage of a break in the general clamour to address himself to the ticket collector. "Monsieur le Ticket Collector," he began, "we are antiquaries and we wish to see the Serapeum. At once, if you please."

"Sirs," said Mohammed, not a little nervous at coming to the attention of fourteen young, strong, rowdy and obviously careless European trespassers. "You... You must first purchase tickets." And he raised an example high for all to see.

"How much, my friend?" asked Jacques.

Mohammed's answer was almost inaudible above the cries of the others.

"You've got to be kidding!"

"That much to see a pile of rubble?"

Georges tried to quiet his colleagues, but Jacques pulled himself to his feet and turned to face him. "Georges, the man is just trying it on. These Arabs love to bargain. We shall have some fun." He looked at Mohammed. "I will offer you, for all of us..."

Mohammed broke in at the top of his voice. "Fixed price, sir. The money goes to the Antiquities Service, sir. I have no control over it. Everyone pays the same price. No one enters the monuments without paying the fee."

There was further shouting and much waving of arms. Finally, Georges advanced out of the crowd towards the ticket collector and paid over the money.

"This is sufficient only for eleven tickets, sir." said Mohammed quietly.

"This is all the money we have, Monsieur. Surely it is enough for all of us?"

"I am sorry, sir. You have paid for eleven and eleven may see the monuments. Three will have to wait outside."

"Come on. We're going." Jacques grabbed Georges's arm and pulled him from the room and into the sunlight. The remainder followed, some carrying a bottle or two of wine.

"You got the tickets?"

"Yes."

"Then let's go. No one's going to care about a few extra once we get there."

The group moved off along the gravel track that led to the Serapeum. The key-master took off running ahead of them, his white robe gathered up between his flailing legs to help him in his frantic scramble to reach the doorway first and execute his official duties. It was almost a kilometre to the subterranean mausoleum and he had to stop frequently to catch his breath. But the donkeys were in no hurry.

The Frenchmen, uninitiated in the archaeology of the area, variously expressed their impatience at being traipsed around a ruined wall and into an apparently empty desert wasteland beyond and away from what they could clearly see were antiquities of massive proportions.

"Where the hell are we going, Georges?" cried Ferdinand, a tall, skinny youth without a perceptible chin. "It's all back there!" He vigorously gestured over his shoulder. His weight suddenly and carelessly redistributed on the top of a rolling barrel and his reactions dulled by the wine, Ferdinand immediately lost his balance and fell unceremoniously to the ground. Amid uncompromising laughter from his colleagues, he picked himself up and struggled back onto his donkey.

The gaffir, in the meantime, had reached the Serapeum and positioned himself at the threshold, panting heavily. The following Frenchmen arrived presently, dismounted and clustered closely about him. Impatiently they thrust their tickets into his hand, some being momentarily withdrawn and then resubmitted. In the confusion, his ability to count the number who passed was impaired, let alone check the number of tickets he was receiving.

Mohammed was left frantically counting the tickets he had received as Jacques propelled himself down the steps of the entrance to the Serapeum. He forced open the door, tearing the padlock from its loosely secured bolts. All could now enter freely and, like swarming bees entering a new hive, they charged down the stairs. By the time the gaffir had reconciled the numbers, the tourists had disappeared into the darkness below.

Jacques, in the lead, sprinted down the entrance corridor. He could not see his footing, nor anything ahead of him and, weaving somewhat from his self-induced lack of balance, he soon tripped over some masonry that had long since fallen from the vaulted ceiling and fell headlong. His foolishly precipitous dash came to an abrupt end as his head smartly connected with a wall. The shock of the impact half dazed him, but at least for the moment the alcohol mercifully suppressed the pain. Then the noise of the others dashing in behind him added to his temporary confusion. It was not until all of them had caught up with him that his senses began to return.

A still silence followed, all the quieter it seemed for the lack of pandemonium that had preceded it. Each of the Frenchmen stared into the noiseless blackness. They waited for their eyes to become accustomed to the gloom. Nothing appeared - not the faintest change of contrast, not the slightest definition of the walls, the ceiling, or the floor. They hung there, it seemed, in black space.

Jacques, now sitting up on the rock floor of the corridor, was first to break the silence. "My God! I can't see. I am blind! I am cursed! My God!"

"Be quiet, Jacques," yelled Ferdinand. "Don't be so damned hysterical. None of us can see anything."

"My God!!" screamed Jacques. "We're all blind!"

"Stupid bastard. Turn around and look back," said Georges.

Back up the long, straight passage a thin shaft of light extended along one wall towards them, gradually dimming as it neared. The dust that had been thrown up by their dash into the cavity continued to tumble in the stale atmosphere and sparkled in the sunlight.

"Thanks be to God!" exclaimed Jacques. "What a moment I have lived through!"

"The gaffir will have candles. In our hurry to escape him we forgot to pick them up," said Georges. "We must return to the entrance."

They didn't have to go far. As they filed out of the passage the worried gaffir bustled towards them carrying a torch.

"Meusieurs. Meusieurs!" he shouted. "Three of you have not given me tickets. Everyone who enters must have a ticket. I am responsible to see to this. Please. Your tickets, please!"

Jacques, now quite recovered, shouted back. "What's the use in paying for tickets if there is no light to see by, fool? Bring us lamps, candles - whatever 'le Service' provides. At once! You can give us your torch for starters." And he made a grab for it.

The gaffir had the presence of mind to extinguish the firebrand before the Frenchman got a grip. "Messieurs, we do not have these things. You must provide your own lighting. There are notices. Now, I need the money from the three people who have not paid."

Jacques took the man by the shoulders, pushed him backwards up the steps and into the sunlight and pinned him against the wall. "If you do not provide lighting, my friend, it will be the worse for you, and there will be no money for any tickets. We want our money back!"

A fairly severe shaking began. As his head thumped against the stones a third time, the gaffir yelled for help.

His colleague had been watching not far distant. He could see that things appeared to be getting a little rough for his friend and he scurried over to the entrance to the Serapeum as fast as his legs could carry him. Jacques continued to thrust the gaffir back and forth against the wall. After some fearful hesitation, Mohammed's colleague plucked up the courage to reach out and grasp the elbow of the agitated Frenchman. With little control left - a combination of alcohol and a not insufficient dose of French guile - Jacques wheeled round and elbowed the unfortunate rescuer in the face, dislodging his head cloth and knocking it to the ground. Singing a strident but unintelligible French battle song, he proceeded to stamp disrespectfully all over the fallen headgear until it became little more than a tattered, sweat-soaked, sandy rag.

Although the gaffir was his kith and kin, his friend, hurting from the blow to his face, wished he had not tried to intervene. For better or for worse - likely worse - he was in the thick of it now, and greatly outnumbered - by foreigners; by nonsense; and by social position. But he was the head man of the keepers at Saqqara and must attempt to bring some authority to the occasion. He rejoined the mêlée and jumped onto the upturned tea chest. From this makeshift pulpit he addressed the group. "Gentlemen, please listen to me."

The noise died. The faces of fourteen young Frenchmen in various stages of inebriation turned to look up at the gaunt, cloaked figure perched precariously above them. With the sun at the reis's back, his thin body stood out jet black against the fine, flowing white linen of his clothing. Standing assertively astride the tea chest, the reis prepared to address the multitude below. The fragile wooden frame wobbled uneasily beneath him and he adjusted his footing to steady himself. He began to speak.

To all who gazed up at him, back-lit as he was by the setting sun, it was clear that the reis wore no underwear - as was the custom in these parts. The dangling appendage and the adjoining ragged cluster were crisply picked out in silhouette and without dignity hanging there for all to see.

There was a short almost reverent silence. Mohammed, observing the situation for himself, frantically gestured to the reis to get down. Then, shrieks of laughter. The poor reis could only conclude that the Frenchmen were so drunk they were unable to comprehend the gravity of the situation. He raised his hands in the air, shouting to them to be silent.

As the reis maintained this evangelical posture, Jacques fell to his knees in the dust and raised his arms towards him in mock worship. "I see the light!" he exclaimed. "The prophet has balls!"

Mohammed leapt up and elbowed the reis behind the knees. The Arab lost his balance and jumped to the ground. Wishing desperately to defuse the situation Mohammed pressed the foreign multitude to return to the Service house so the entire matter could be discussed and hopefully settled in a calmer environment and, better still, under the authority of 'Monsieur l'Inspecteur'.

The amusement finally over, the giggling group followed the gaffir back to the house. As they chattered their way on donkey-back, the reis ran off to find the Inspector.

Howard Carter was at the time explaining the finer points of Egyptian irrigation methods to two young, unmarried ladies attended by Arthur Weigall. One of the two, it appeared to his company but not to Carter himself, had taken rather a shine to the stoic and starchy little man.

As he described the irrigation network in the fields and gestured towards the river, the reis came into view panting down the track towards them, robe flowing, legs flailing.

"Monsieur l'Inspecteur! Monsieur l'Inspecteur!" he gasped. "There is much trouble at the rest house. Mohammed has been struck by a Frenchman, and some have not paid, and others are demanding their money back, and there is much noise, and they are drinking, and they are saying very bad words to us, and we have done only our duty, and..."

"Ali! Ali!" Carter broke in. "Calm yourself. Be still. Explain this to me slowly, please."

"You must come. You must come at once!" Ali tugged at Carter's sleeve.

Seeing that the man was far too agitated to calm down, Carter turned to Weigall and the ladies. "Ladies... Weigall, old man. Sorry about this but it looks like this little matter requires my immediate attention. Forgive me for having to cut short our chat. I will join you for a drink later tonight at your hotel." And, doffing his hat, he took his leave and walked briskly after the reis.

By the time Carter arrived at the rest house, the Frenchmen had barricaded themselves inside and were applying all their energies to berating the gaffir in pursuit of their money. Not that it was, when all said and done, really about money at all, but more about a bunch of belligerent Europeans having a smashing good time.

Carter got his shoulder to the door and pushed it open. The first sight - their obviously excited state of inebriation, their rowdiness and generally irresponsible behaviour, their appearance as lay tourists with no real regard for the heritage of the monuments around them, their clearly disdainful attitude towards his Arab employees, and their Frenchness - quickly filled Carter with unmitigated anger. He applied the full authority of his position clinically and forcefully.

"Gentlemen! Gentlemen!" he shouted. "Messieurs! Silence!" he bellowed in Norfolk French. "You must settle down before we can progress this matter. Who will speak for you?"

Above the din of 'Franco-slang' issuing, it seemed, from every corner of the small room, Carter could hear one Frenchman threatening the terrified ticket collector with a list of unspeakable forms of retribution, not less than being diced by the guillotine, beginning at the feet, should he not refund their money in full and at once.

Carter was not of a mind to negotiate. Furious at the disrespect shown to his men, he took the unruly throng on full face and with both barrels. "You have no right to be in this place. You have no right to behave so despicably towards my men in the execution of their duty. Leave at once!"

The loudly exercised French word shouted back at him could have been loosely translated as 'bollocks'.

Like a schoolmaster who has just entered a classroom full of rowdy teenagers, Carter roared, "I want all of your names! This nonsense shall be urgently and explicitly reported to the authorities. If you do not leave immediately I shall have you forcibly ejected."

The mocking laughter continued.

Carter turned to the gaffirs close behind him and told them to manhandle the Frenchmen out one by one. But the Arabs were no match for the excited French who were not pulling their punches. The first Frenchman to be touched by the two gaffirs took the opportunity to display his boxing skills and planted a brick-hard fist squarely on one gaffir's nose. With a yelp of pain, the unfortunate Arab grabbed his nose and fell to the floor. Carter leapt over him to challenge the youth who immediately took up a classic boxing stance with both arms bent and his clenched fists jabbing within a whisker of Carter's face.

"Come on. Come on," he taunted. "Have a go if you've a mind to. Let me rearrange your features for you, Englishman!" But the young man was not wholly in control of his balance. Carter, dead sober, caught a flailing arm with his hand and easily pushed him off his feet and back into the crowd behind him.

It was clear that there were too few of the Service's men present to control the situation. Carter called to his reis to run for help. He continued to shout above the noise of the swaying group. After a time it seemed that things were beginning to quieten. The churlish bunch appeared to be tiring.

Then the 'cavalry' arrived - a dozen or so gaffirs ran in through the door opposite. All hell broke loose. As if ordered by Napoleon himself, each of the Frenchmen grabbed an item of furniture close at hand and laid into the unfortunate Arabs. Seeing his men accepting the blows without defending themselves, the inspector yelled at the gaffirs to fight back with all their might and force the offenders out. So authorised, the Arabs attacked with relish, wresting some of the weapons from their aggressors and hitting back with more than equal ferocity. They accomplished their task within two or three minutes.

The Frenchmen scrambled out of the house as fast as they could, picking up stones as they went and hurling them back towards the building. One of the group, more bruised by his beating than the others, stumbled at the doorway and fell, striking his head on the doorjamb and collapsing in a heap. Carter went over to take stock of his condition. Another Frenchman turned back to see what had happened.

It was Georges who had taken the fall. By the time Carter leaned down to touch him, he was showing signs of movement. Looking up, Georges saw his friend, Ferdinand, at the door.

"Georges! You all right?"

"Of course. I tripped. We showed them, didn't we?" He turned his face towards Carter. "You, Monsieur, have not heard the last of this."

'The audacity!' thought Carter. "Neither you, sir," he spat back. "You and your friends have attempted fraud. You have viciously attacked the Service's men in the course of their duty. You have trespassed. You have damaged government property. Not to mention your insulting behaviour towards me. All this shall be recorded and reported to the appropriate authorities. Your names, if you would do me that much courtesy?"

"Georges Fabre and Ferdinand Estienne, Monsieur. And your name and official capacity, if you please, is...?"

"Howard Carter, Chief Inspector of Antiquities for the Lower Nile. You people disgust me. Be gone before I do something I might later come to regret." Carter was shaking with rage and close to losing what little was left of his customary self-control.

The two Frenchmen were not so insensible that they could fail to recognise the seriousness of Carter's mood. They had indulged themselves enough for one day and felt not a little physically uncomfortable to boot. Helped up by his friend and silently suffering his pain, Georges limped away towards his group who had reassembled beside their donkeys. Without another word, the party quietly beat a respectable retreat. As their dust tumbled in the distance, a relative peace once more settled on the desert.

That evening, Carter kept his appointment with Weigall and the ladies at the Hotel Royal in Cairo. He marched out to the terrace and plopped himself down in the soft cushions of a wicker sofa. His earlier angry confrontation had left him physically tired and mentally exhausted. No sooner was he seated than a neatly waistcoated and befezzed waiter appeared beside him. Carter spoke in Arabic. "Gin and tonic, Effendi. Big one!" The man nodded and left.

Carter gazed out through the palm trees in the hotel gardens towards the silhouetted pyramids on the skyline. He contemplated the future. He sighed. He didn't relish the thought of the list of unpleasant duties now facing him, but he must ensure that those careless Frenchmen were adequately punished for their disrespectful misdemeanours.

He was jerked out of his preoccupation by the arrival of Arthur Weigall.

"Good evening, Howard. How'd it go today after you left us?"

"A most unpleasant experience, Weigall. And one I hope never to be repeated. Alas, it's not over yet."

Weigall took the seat opposite.

"Ah, ladies. Good evening to you." The two men rose.

"Good evening, Mr Carter. Such a pleasant temperature at this time of the evening."

Weigall pulled up another chair. One of the ladies positioned herself quickly on Carter's couch and the other sat in the chair, and the two men retook their seats. The waiter reappeared.

"May I offer you some refreshment, ladies?" asked Carter - lemonade for one; champagne for the other, whisky soda for Weigall; a second 'G and T' for Carter.

All settled themselves cosily on the terrace. Carter broke the silence. "My apologies for leaving all of you so abruptly this afternoon. As things turned out, I should have stayed with you! I am sure the remainder of your day was far more pleasant than mine."

"As you arrived, ladies, Mr Carter was about to relate the goings-on of this afternoon," said Weigall.

"Oh, please continue, Mr Carter," said the smaller and younger lady sitting beside him. "We are intrigued."

Carter recounted and relived the afternoon's activity in clinical detail as if dictating his report. For the ladies' sake he moderated some of the abusive language he had heard, but did not hold back in painting a vivid picture of his disgust for the French. At the conclusion of his story he felt suddenly lightened - almost exorcised.

"You were lucky you were not hurt, Mr Carter," observed the lady at his side.

"Yes," agreed the other. "You were extremely brave to stand up to such a rowdy crowd single-handed."

"I had the assistance of my gaffirs, ladies. Without their loyalty, strength and bravery we would not have won the day."

'That day is not won yet; not the last we shall hear of this.' Weigall kept his thoughts to himself. "Yes, well done, Howard. A man to be confronted at one's peril, I'll be bound! To y' health."

All raised their glasses in acknowledgement.

Carter's embarrassment was eased when the younger lady turned the conversation to the pleasures of what they had seen on the west bank to this point in their trip. She enquired of Carter what he would recommend she and her sister should see henceforward. He was only too happy to oblige and, reinvigorated dually by her charm and curiosity, along with the influence of his second gin now busily coursing through his veins, he launched himself into a lengthy description of a suggested itinerary. As the two ladies became, more apparently than really, absorbed in this monologue, Carter responded alike with yet more enthusiasm, embellishing his talk with sketches and maps quickly executed in pencil on the pages of his notebook.

The second lady could easily recognise where all this was leading and as the discourse continued, she turned nervously to Weigall and made a brief, quivering smile.

Weigall was quick to pick up on the signal and, speaking more softly than Carter for fear of interrupting his intensity, he said, "Miss Dalgliesh, have you enjoyed your trip thus far as much as your sister?" And so these two began their own conversation.

Carter was by now in full cry and oblivious of the sideshow. "Miss Dalgliesh..." he continued.

She held up her hand. "Dot, Mr Carter. Please call me Dot. Otherwise we will not know which of us you are addressing."

"In that case... Howard," returned Carter.

"Howard," she repeated softly.

"Dot, it is then!" acknowledged Carter with a smile. He noticed that the other two were engaged in their own dialogue and asked, "Would you like to take a turn with me in the gardens, Dot? We can continue our discussion on the wing, so to speak."

"I'd be delighted, Howard." She turned to her sister. "Sorry to interrupt, Sally, but Howard and I are going for a quick perambulatory. We'll join you in the dining room, say, in fifteen minutes?"

"Fine, Dorothy. See you then."

Carter took the girl's arm in his and the two left the terrace.

Sally turned to Weigall, a broad smile on her face. " 'Howard and I' is it?" And they both chuckled.

The drinks, the talk, the walk and this sweetly interesting young lady, not necessarily in that order, were entirely therapeutic for Carter. By dinnertime he'd lost his earlier seriousness and was freely joking in the relaxed company of Weigall and the two sisters.

When he retired to his quarters that night he reflected that he had not enjoyed himself so much in others' company since the early days with his brother at Deir el Bahri. And it's not over yet, he thought. I do believe I was forward enough to offer my services as guide tomorrow.

His usual uneasiness in the presence of ladies, particularly young and pretty ones, was totally absent in the company of the sisters. Dorothy made him feel relaxed - perhaps too relaxed for what was normally a tightly controlled and ordered personality. He grinned contentedly. He was on the rebound from a severely taxing experience and he relished the moment.

The following day he was up before the sun broke the horizon. He had had a totally restful, dreamless sleep. The Frenchmen had gone from his mind and were replaced by a figure in flowing gossamer. He had nothing but expectation for a day filled with lecture in the delightful company of

Miss Dorothy Dalgliesh.

Miss Dalgliesh herself had also risen early and was busy within the bowels of her travelling trunk, attempting to find appropriate attire for the day's forthcoming activities. She held a striped shirt up to her bosom and turned. "What do you think, Sally?"

Her sister was sitting up in bed reading. She looked up from her book and glanced over her spectacles. "It looks fine, Dorothy, but then so did the other two blouses. I don't know why you are dithering so much over your appearance. Why all this trouble for a boring little man? You amaze me sometimes, you really do."

"I don't find him boring. He has a passion for his trade, that is all. I find his singular preoccupation fascinating. And he's lonely. He needs our company."

"Your company, you mean. You're not expecting me to come, surely?"

"No. I'd rather be by myself," she smiled. "I fancy it may be I who holds the key that will unlock..."

Sally broke in. "You'd better be careful. If you are right you could end up with more than you can cope with. At best a bruised back! The floors in those tombs don't compare with the bluebell woods of your last adventure."

"That's unkind," Dorothy chided. "I have no other intention than to enjoy his conversation and get to know him a little better. Besides, you do him a great disservice. He is too much a gentleman, and too shy, to venture to make inappropriate advances. And you know very well there has been no previous 'adventure'. That is a jealous accusation. In any case, you liked the man in question more than I. I am glad you are not coming. Stay in this stuffy hotel with your book and that nice Mr Weigall. We'll soon see who will have had the most boring day."

Dorothy pulled on the shirt, quickly buttoned it down the front and tucked it into her skirt. She took a tie from the pile of clothing she had by now accumulated on the floor and hurried into the bathroom to preen. Neither sister spoke again that morning but for the courtesy of bidding each other farewell.

Carter was waiting for Dorothy at the front steps of the hotel. As she emerged from the doorway flanked by two doormen he smiled, removed his Homburg and, with a swashbuckling gesture, bowed in greeting.

Standing at the top of the steps, she took a moment to absorb the picture. He was dressed in a loosely fitting, light brown, striped, single-breasted three-piece suit. The cuffs of a crisply starched white shirt extended some distance from beneath the sleeves of the jacket and the collar was attached at the neck by a crookedly knotted bow tie. His straight hair, slicked back over his head, had now been partially displaced by removal of his hat. His face was long and sun burned with a strong chin and a pronounced nose. His smile was reflected in his sensitive eyes and beamed under the carefully manicured moustache. His light suede shoes, although they'd been cleaned that morning, were already dusty from the few steps he had taken in the street. To Dorothy Dalgliesh he looked every bit the archaeologist.

"Good morning, Howard," she greeted. "I am sorry if I am a little late. I was trying to encourage Sally to join us, but she is still in bed, I am embarrassed to admit."

Carter took her by the hand and helped her into his carriage. "She does not have the appetite for antiquities as you do, I fear. Never mind, when you return you can educate her with what you will have learned today. Perhaps you will be able to convert her and she will want to come another time ... May I say how lovely you look this morning, Dot? Very smart, but practically dressed as well. That hat will provide excellent protection from the sun - I would that mine were as broad."

He got in beside her and gestured to the driver to take off.

When they came close by the Saqqara complex they transferred to donkey-back. Carter described each site explicitly, all the time checking for any suggestion of loss of interest on the part of his partner. But she seemed intent on learning all she could, from time to time asking questions and making observations of her own. It was a joy to him to be able to give back some of what he had gained in these last fourteen years in Egypt - especially to one so enthusiastic to receive the information.

But her appeal was more than this - he felt an inner warmth that he had not previously experienced. That he liked her very much was clear in his attentions. He was completely relaxed in her company and she in his. 'She does enjoy my company,' he reflected. Up to this point he had not consciously thought this of anyone - he had cared less; it had not mattered to him until now. All of a sudden it was important. There was an unfamiliar current developing within him. But the feeling was enjoyable and he did not want to suppress it.

'This slight, dusty gentleman's heart is totally devoted to his work,' she thought. 'Is there room for anything else - anyone else, I wonder?'

Carter looked at his pocket watch. It was already two o'clock in the afternoon and his companion admitted she was flagging. Even Carter was tired from the heat and the walking and the bending in confined spaces. They would have to find shade and take the picnic he had had prepared.

"We need refreshment and we need cooler surroundings. I know just the place." He took the reins of his ward's donkey and edged ahead towards the Service's rest house.

He knew it to be deserted after the goings-on of the day before. Following the incident, the place had been cleaned up and his ticket collector was at home recovering from his bruises. Carter helped his companion from her mount, unlocked the door and waved her in. The cooler air from inside brushed her face as she entered.

"Chez nous, mademoiselle. Chez nous."

"Howard, this is a most unfortunate and distasteful business. I must say quite candidly that while you acted clearly within your authority, you exercised no discretion in the matter - a blatant by-the-book approach - dealing with these well-connected young Frenchmen as you would have a bunch of guttersnipes from the back streets of London. I really do wish you had moderated your actions... But that is all history now. The case against these men will not be taken any further. There will be no prosecutions. On the contrary, there has to be some form of modest - modest, now - reparation of the past... some form of apology - from you."

"Gaston! You are my superior and also my friend. I do value your counsel. But please stop there. I have acted quite properly - within my authority, as you say - even with some restraint, which the situation did not deserve. Those damn Frogs behaved atrociously. They were violent and abusive, not to mention wholly disrespectful to my employees and myself. They attempted fraudulent entry to one of the Service's premier monuments, trespassed, damaged the Service's property, abused the Service's staff, and then had the gall to ask for their money back! So, if you are about to ask me to make a formal apology to the French Consulate, stop now. Please do me that much courtesy."

"Howard, please! I implore you on this occasion to relax your personal code and fall into line with the protocol of conventional international diplomacy. For me - for all of us who have held the highest respect for the good performance of your office over these many past years - please! Just a gesture." Carter's doggedness was frustrating Maspero to the point of anger.

"Monsieur, with respect, you were not there. They were nothing more than spoiled hoodlums. Should I do as you ask of me I would undermine the respect and due diligence of my poor employees, with whom I must continue to work, and from whom I expect only the best quality of work. Worse, I would endorse the French louts' behaviour. These..." He faltered on the word, and after a short pause almost spat it out, "...tourists will not be back. I have no doubt of that. It is they who should swallow their pride and take a lesson from the affair. I wish only for justice - and then to forget it ever happened."

"If you insist on taking this position it will not end here, Howard. They will not forget the affair. It is already highly visible in the halls of the British and French Consulates in Cairo. It is - yes - a trivial matter, now blown out of all proportion..."

Maspero hardly got the last part of his statement out before Carter snapped back at him, now so incensed that he had no thought for his friend's efforts, nor his feelings.

"Trivial? Trivial? How can you trivialise this event? These Frenchmen represent the worst kind of vandal - the careless rich. They dishonour the Egyptians. They defile the Egyptians' heritage. They trivialise the monuments with their drunkenness. They have no interest in this place. To them it's just another playground... I will have none of it. My last word, monsieur. Positively my last word."

There was silence. Maspero sat staring incredulously into Carter's stern eyes. He knew the man well. Carter had taken his position. He had dug himself in. There would be no going back. 'He is deadly serious,' thought Maspero. 'Quite, quite determined.'

"I must take my leave," said Carter at last. "I am falling behind in my work. Au revoir, monsieur." He picked up his hat and strutted rapidly out the door.

Maspero, exasperated and exhausted, had no further words for him anyway.

Some days later Carter received a letter from his old patron, Theodore Davis. The millionaire had heard of the affair and, being well versed in the bigotry of the rich and famous, felt compelled to counsel his old colleague. It was, unusually for Davis, a sensitively written missive, exploring the facts of the affair, laying out the options and proffering advice on the steps that Carter should now take. In addition, it addressed the hitherto unthinkable - leaving the Service.

This was all too much for Carter. He needed time to relax and think. He decided to contact Maspero the following morning and request leave.

He was back in England within the month.

Carter returned to Cairo in the height of summer, 1905. After a couple of days provisioning in the city and a brief visit with Monsieur le Directeur he took off for his house in the delta. The place was just as he had left it, perhaps a little dustier than usual, indicating that his houseboy had not been overly diligent in his duties whilst his master had been away, and a lot hotter. Otherwise things were much the same. While the gaffirs carried the boxes of provisions into the small kitchen, he dumped his bags on the bed and began to unpack.

He had been away one hundred days. It felt like years. He was totally refreshed and keen to return to work. His veins tingled with new enthusiasm - the anticipation of new discoveries. He drew back the top drawer of his bedside chest and pulled out the old newspaper lining to dust it off. An envelope fell to the floor. He picked it up. A drop of perspiration fell from his brow and the ink began to run.

It was the Davis letter. It all came flooding back. All that his holiday had erased returned as fresh as if he had never left. He sagged back onto the bed and read the letter again.

Carter remembered how he had felt when he first read the words. Though he had done little more than put up with Davis's rantings and physical laziness in their past associations in the field, the fact that this impersonal, totally selfish man, a man with little regard for those about him, and foremost regard for his own aggrandisement, had taken the time, let alone the thought, to put these words to paper, became of the utmost importance to Carter. He read the letter twice more, took a brandy, rested back in his easy chair and reflected, not on the incident now months past, but upon the American.

'They have not our history, our traditions, our stoic principles', he thought. 'Theirs is a selfish lust for riches regardless of class. And when they achieve riches they take leisure pursuits to fulfil themselves. So why make any effort to turn me from my conviction? Why take the time? Why care?' It was this, more than Davis's words, that peeked Carter's curiosity. 'The man has either been got at by his politically minded associates or he really cares - perhaps a bit of both. Funny bloke. Well meaning, but Americans will never understand the history and traditions that underpin the principles of an Englishman.'

Carter contented himself with this final thought, arrogant as it was. He knocked back a mouthful of brandy and dozed off in his veranda chair. The evening sunlight soon faded to indigo and then moonless blackness and, as the stars twinkled above him and the blessed coolness of the evening comforted him, he fell into a deep sleep.

Suddenly there was a cacophony of foreign voices all about him. Those blasted Frogs. They were everywhere, taunting him with obscenities and offending in their stylised Napoleonic marching. One of them was urinating on a nearby obelisk, calling for all to see how far up he could reach. Another presented Carter with a diminutive wooden ushabti, then withdrew it before he could reach for it, placed its head in a cigar cutter in the shape of a miniature guillotene, and with a quick snap, and the roaring applause of his parading comrades, chopped off the head. Carter tried to stop them, but his body felt unusually slothful. He moved, it seemed, in slow motion, never getting any closer to them. As if to complete the insult, Jacques advanced from the crowd broadly smiling with a bottle of red wine in his hand and chanting, "Amun Re - oh, holiest of inspectors - we annoint ye with the blood of Napoleon!", and shook the bottle at him, the wine spurting all about his head and clothing.

Startled by the cool liquid on his face, Carter leapt to his feet. But he stood alone on the veranda. The wind whipped the rain into his face. With his hands he dragged at his clothes in an effort to wipe the imaginary wine from his dampened clothing. After a moment or two, his senses returned. He went back into his house, dropped his suit on the bathroom floor, closed the bedroom door behind him, fell on the bed, and once more gave himself up to sleep.

It was personally embarrassing for the inspector to be woken by the reis at ten in the morning. The brightness of daylight blinded him and for a moment he couldn't think of an appropriate excuse for the situation in which he had been discovered. Worse still, he quickly realised he was not in his bed attire, rather a horribly creased shirt and tie, underpants, socks and suspenders, and lay in sheets damp with his own sweat.

"Ah... Er... Ali. Thank you for waking me. Long trip. Rather a late night. Very tired. Too tired to undress. Just collapsed."

"Tea, sir?"

"Please. Just what I need. What... What time is it?"

"Two hours before midday, sir."

"My goodness. My duties. What have I not been doing that I should have?"

"Nothing, sir. You were expected to take rest this day after your journey. Miss Dorothy is visiting you, sir. She awaits you in the office."

"Oh, my goodness," Carter repeated. "Oh, goodness me. Tell her I will be with her presently. Give her some tea while I shave."

Carter emerged about thirty minutes later, now appropriately dressed. He walked over to the lady who sat at his desk examining a small alabaster oil lamp, a find he had made some years earlier.

"Dot," he began, "I must apologise for my late rising... Working into the wee hours on my notes. How nice of you to visit a man in such public isolation, and at such an inclement time of year."

"Howard," she acknowledged, smiling. "It is good to see you. We were distressed when we heard the news. Sally and I have been most concerned for you. Are you to resign from the Service? The talk in Cairo is that it would be for the best. You have not been truly happy working the Lower Nile - not as you had been in The Valley. That unsatisfactory affair with the young Froggies surely provides a more than adequate opportunity for you to resign with honour?"

Carter reflected on her candid words for a moment. "Well, if that isn't what's called coming right to the point, I don't know what is! You don't believe in pulling your punches, do you, Dot?" The shoe fit, however. "You read my mind. I do believe you do. I have been giving the subject much thought these past few months."

He lied. But Dot's endorsement of Davis's suggestion was just what he needed.

"I am gratified you agree with the course I think I must now take. Your sensitive support provides me with some considerable inner peace."

He looked relieved.

"And what will you do with yourself once you become a free man?"

"I have been giving that some thought as well, Dot," he lied again. After a pause he said, "There seems little course but for me to become the proverbial starving artist."

They laughed together.

Chapter Nine
Tomb

Horemheb awoke to the piercing monotones of the early morning trumpets. His bedservants brought him a warm libation to help lift him from his drowsiness. As he sat on his bed and contemplated another day of inspections, he reflected upon the goings-on of the night before. Despite the soundness of his sleep, the old woman was not a faint memory to him. Her accusing words still rang in his ears. He shivered as a draught of cool morning air swept from the open ceiling. 'No matter,' he thought. His only real concern was ultimately how he might engineer her approval to take the hand of her daughter, the fair Mutnodjme. But then she may not care - had he not heard her give tacit approval last night? 'Anyway, with any luck the old witch will die before I need to marry.'

Be that as it may, right now he had more pressing problems. He would visit the goldsmiths and the sculptors again today.

At the time of the boy king's death, the block of quartzite that was to become his sarcophagus was barely rough-cut from the quarries at Hatnub and it was quite clear there would be no time for its completion prior to entombment. General Horemheb was prepared for this kind of crisis. He had earlier ordered that the yellow quartzite sarcophagus enclosing the body of his brother be brought up from Smenkhkare's tomb and re-engraved with texts applauding Tutankhamun. However, the lid to that sarcophagus had been hastily made from a local granite and was known to be flawed. It had a clear crack across the middle. The general had a solution for that, too.

"It is but a single fissure." he told the masons. "Fix it!"

Horemheb's arrival at the foundry was not welcomed at the best of times. Today, as it happened, things were going particularly badly. Mentu, using a hammer, had been delicately raising the contours of the king's facial features from two sheets of gold. These had earlier been partially beaten to fit the casting of the king's plaster death mask. Form slowly materialised from Mentu's light, rapid, repetitive blows, the point of hammer contact moving imperceptibly over the surface between each strike. But soon came disaster. Probably due to a slight thinning in the metal, the gold sheet had stretched and drawn a tiny crack. The aperture was on the outer skin and little more than a hair's width, but this was cause enough for Mentu to die a thousand deaths. The plaster mask was now smashed and discarded. There was no way the die could be recast. There had been no room for error; the piece had to be flawless; any mistake was critical.

The accident stopped work. Artisans from the entire foundry gathered around Mentu to share in his crisis. After all, it was to be through the mask that the gods would recognise the king and defend and support him in his journey - of all things, this treasure had to be perfect.

Dashir, chief goldsmith, stepped forward to see if he could help. He examined the piece closely, then put a reassuring hand on Mentu's shoulder. "Mentu, fear not. I can attempt a weld. The scar can be removed with burnishing. No one will notice. Not even Tutankhamun himself - long may he live."

Cradling the complete piece between the two of them, they took it over to the glowing hot-box. Mentu worked the bellows until the fire was almost too hot to bear. With a glowing copper rod Dashir applied heat to the inside of the mask under the spot where the lesion had occurred. As soon as he saw the glow shine through on the facial side he took a small, preheated hammer and lightly tapped the crack in the cheek. As he worked, the small, dark line in the fiery metal shrank and within moments, as if by magic, it was gone. His helpers lifted the mask away from the heat. As the metal cooled, Dashir brushed lightly over the affected area with a soft linen rag. With all the workers about him and Mentu eagerly looking over his shoulder, Dashir withdrew the rag to reveal the aperture successfully closed. There was a slight scar in the metal where the repair had taken place, but Mentu knew he could easily work this into the contours of the face. Ultimately the blemish would become imperceptible.

But not to Horemheb. He arrived later that day and, after approving the engraver's design work on the gold coffin, he came over to Mentu to inspect progress on the mask. "The king's cheeks are out of balance, Mentu!" he grumbled immediately. "He looks as if he has the toothache! You have erred, I fear."

"Yes, my lord," responded the submissive artisan. "But you can see I am working to remove the offending inaccuracy."

"Be precise in your artistry, Mentu. The gods see all things. Pharaoh sees all things. It must be right."

"I will, my lord. The king's face will be perfect. The gods will guide my skills in the execution of this task."

"Mark that they do. Pray. Make offerings at the shrine of your parents."

Horemheb chose to underline his statement with a solemn scold to all about him. "Men!" He swung about and bellowed gruffly, "Before you reach the afterlife - whether there is to be one for you or not - you must first live out this life. That can be in comfort, or it can be in hell. It can be prolonged, or it can be foreshortened. All these things are within the power of Pharaoh. Remember this."

With these final words of comfort, he left the foundry to pay a visit to the sculptors, surely bent on delivering the same fearful message to them.

As the foundry doors closed behind the departing general and his entourage, the metalworkers stood for a moment in silence. They looked about guiltily, the one to the other.

Mentu was the first to speak. "Well? Which of us is to tell him? There is more. It is inevitable he will discover it. The general must be told before he discovers it for himself. Who is to tell him? We must decide, and quickly. There is little time for reparations. His Excellency must be told," Mentu repeated.

"Let the general find out for himself," said Dashir. "We have had sufficient excitement for one day."

The artisans shrugged their shoulders in agreement and got back to busying themselves with their respective tasks. In the end, what happened to them in this life mattered little. For the guarantee of eternity, and nothing else, they would work to ensure as much as possible was perfect and complete by the appointed day.

They need not have worried. Horemheb had anticipated that construction of the golden shrine would take longer than the time available. Three of the planned total of four nested shrines were far from completion. He knew this and had prepared accordingly.

Some weeks before the funeral was to take place, the general ordered his guards back to Smenkhkare's tomb, since resealed following its earlier breaching. Its previous priestly violators had dismantled the shrine-set in order to get to the sarcophagus. On Horemheb's orders they had left the panels and doors stacked against the back wall of the burial chamber.

In their haste, the guards did not completely clear the refilled entrance corridor and did no more than burrow a shallow channel the width of the passageway. While the inner pieces of the shrine were manhandled outside with relative ease, when they attempted to remove the sides of the outer shrine they found the panels too wide to get past the doorjambs at the entrance. Realising it would take some considerable time to clear the remaining rubble that choked the corridor, they left the first of the panels where it was and rushed off to report to the general.

To their surprise, Horemheb showed no concern. He had kept the artisans working on the outer panels of Tutankhamun's shrine and their progress had been much better than expected. These would be ready in time after all. As the general moved about the workrooms just a week before the funeral, his sense of relief was manifest in his unusually agreeable disposition.

He was not the only one feeling relieved. The faces of Mentu, Dashir and the others, those who had kept their secret, were positively beaming.

In the days leading up to the funeral celebrations, Ankhenesamun would work around her daily duties to find time for personal mourning and reflection. Each evening she visited the temple which housed the slowly desiccating corpse of her husband. She would sit with him alone in a simple wooden chair at the head of the stone embalming bed, facing away from it. Behind her lay the long, even pile of slowly discolouring salts, busy at their passive work on the body beneath. She sat erect, looking out at the stars glinting between the pillars of the temple colonnade. For an hour each night she would create Tutankhamun's afterlife in her mind and live within it, then retire to her chambers, hoping to dream on in his company.

Occasionally, this nightly preoccupation worked. Shortly after subsiding into sleep she might find herself walking with him, hand in hand, along the verdant banks of the Nile...

Anubis is close beside them, the other gods all about them, the scene fills with a golden light.

Birds start from the cover of the papyrus reeds and flutter into the sky. The drops of water spilling from their wings catch the rays of the sun in brilliant flashes. Tutankhamun sinks to one knee and pulls his bow. Ankhesenamun takes an arrow from the quiver on his back and hands it to him. He steadies his aim ahead of the arc of the bird's flight, draws the bowstring tight and looses the arrow into the air.

A barely audible cry is heard and the bird falls gently earthward. There is some swift movement in the tall grass. The court cat emerges with the bird in its jaws. The king takes the bird and turns to show it to his queen. He cradles its head in one hand. Thin rivulets of blood issue from its beak and nostrils...

The queen awoke with a start. The vigilant Tia lit the oil lamp beside her bed couch. The queen sat up. The dreams were now occurring so often that she wished for the day of the funeral feast to be past. Perhaps then the all too real images would cease. She would no longer have to relive her tragedy. In reality, however, there were yet twenty nights before all would be behind her. But strength of character would not permit her to dwell on the prospect. Rather, her mind would turn to plans for Horemheb's eternal damnation.

This day she was to visit the foundry on the pretext of examining progress for herself. Later, in the evening, she would arrange to meet with Dashir by the riverside before he took the ferry to the west bank.

Dashir, a man with an appetite for drink and the ladies to match, was well known nevertheless for his strong sense of loyalty towards the boy king. He had been one of few of the king's subjects who had become deeply touched by Tutankhamun's early reversal of Akhenaten's religious order. Dashir did not credit the king's consorts with these reparations. They had, after all, demonstrated in the past regency that they were mere followers of Pharaoh's will, and they had reacted in the same way to the orders of Akhenaten's young cousin. All the more remarkable, then, was this boy king who had judgemental skills and strength of character developed well beyond his years. All the more remarkable were his achievements. All the more promise had he held. All the greater the loss for the community now that his consorts must inherit.

Ankhesenamun knew Dashir felt this strongly. She was well aware of his dedication. The spies planted in the village across the Nile had reported to court everything that was material to the ongoing health of the community. Many an evening she and her husband had listened with gratification to Dashir's reported conversations with his friends at the bar in Pademi. The queen had no doubts as to the strength of loyalty this man possessed. If there was anyone who would carry out her wishes faithfully it would be he. There could be no other.

The guards opened the doors wide to allow the queen and her entourage free passage inside. The vision of Queen Ankhesenamun standing in the open doorway with the morning sunlight shining brightly through the skirt of her white linen dress brought work to a standstill in an instant. The artisans fell to their knees. The Nubian who held the parasol which shaded her waited outside while a guard and Tia, as lady-in-waiting, accompanied the queen into the foundry.

"Please rise. I wish to inspect your work. Who will act as guide?" she asked, looking directly at the man by the blazing fire.

"I would be most honoured, my lady," said Dashir, bowing low.

He took her first to the two engravers who were embellishing the inside of the golden coffin with written texts. They had not yet started decoration of the outer skin. Beside the two inverted open halves lay the two larger, wooden coffins, the outer one now complete and temporarily closed. Its gilding sparkled in the light from the foundry fire. The brilliance was almost overpowering. Smenkhkare's coffin lay open beneath a linen pall. The cartouches in the texts were yet to be altered to those of Tutankhamun.

Mentu was not at all happy that Dashir had singled him out to show his progress on the mask. Although his earlier error was now virtually invisible, the features of the king's face were still in the making and the proportions, to the artist's eye at least, still somewhat unbalanced in places. While he could visualise the completed product, he did not expect the queen to do so, and he was most embarrassed to be forced to show the piece in its current state to one who would find the experience so personal. He need not have worried; the queen did not appear disappointed with what she saw.

"Mentu, you bring life out of dumb gold. I honour your skills. I can see that which is familiar emerging from your hammer strokes. You will finish it in time?"

"I must, therefore I shall, Excellency," said Mentu with conviction. "The gods guide these hands. I merely hold the instruments that work the metal. The gold mask shall be completed - it shall be bejewelled - it will be true to the likeness of our dear, departed lord."

Inwardly, the queen was much relieved that the likeness was not too obvious at this time. Life-size and bright as it was, the sight of it would generate an emotional rush more than she cared to bear. Ankhesenamun turned away from the unfinshed mask lest she dwell too long and break down notwithstanding.

On her signal, Dashir, bending submissively low, ushered her over to the darker corner of the room.

"Let me show you that which we have completed to perfection some time ago, my lady."

And there it lay, reclining on a bed of straw, like a newborn awaiting its first cleansing. On setting her eyes on the figure, a warmth filled her body from her heart to her cheeks. Her skin prickled with excitement.

"My eternal lord," she whispered, leaning over to touch its forehead, her words inaudible to Dashir. "I shall lie with you for all eternity."

"It is good, is it not, my lady?" asked Dashir with a broad, expectant smile on his face.

"A true likeness. Most handsomely executed. The gods truly took a hand in this."

Her words fell on the eagerly receptive ears of the artisans now closely gathered about her. They could be paid no better compliment. There would be much to tell their wives and others in Pademi this night. Truly a day to be remembered. Tomorrow each of them would return to work, their energies recharged aplenty.

The queen drew back. "Dashir, I wish to speak with you in private."

"Aye, my lady."

Dashir's colleagues moved away and resumed their various duties.

"It is my wish that we meet - alone, mark you - on the east bank at sunset near the place where you embark the ferry. I have some serious business to discuss with you."

"Oh, my lady, what have I done?"

"Be not afraid. You have done nothing of harm. It is that which you should yet do that will be the subject of our meeting. Tell no one of your appointment, and do not fail me."

She signalled to the guard. In a moment she was gone.

For the remainder of that day Dashir was so preoccupied with speculation that he sat alone in a corner of the foundry and did little of substance other than issue a few instructions to his apprentices.

As the sun disappeared behind the mountain on the west bank, the men stopped their frenetic labours, cleared up their work areas, and left for the ferry. Mentu, himself late in tidying up his tools, noticed Dashir still working at the fire box. With the prospect of beer ahead, it was most unusual for Dashir to be the last to leave.

"Dashir, you laggard. We shall be late for the ferry. I need you. I cannot pay for a boat tonight. I have nothing to barter for my carriage."

"Go ahead, Mentu. I must finish this." Dashir was still sweating over the fire and apparently holding some small piece within the blazing coals. "I have spent the whole afternoon in supervision of other work and neglected my own." He handed his friend some bread. "Do not worry. I have sufficient barter with me. I will join you all presently at Hammad's."

Mentu knew there was no time left to continue the discussion and took off in haste towards the river bank. As soon as his colleague had left the foundry, Dashir removed the empty tongs from the fire and stopped pumping the bellows. After waiting a while for the fire to die down, he closed up the foundry, gave the same instructions he'd always given to the guards posted outside for that night's vigil, and trotted off towards the river and his appointed rendezvous.

The queen, her senior maidservant and her guards were quite obvious as a group. They were assembled on a small rise above and set back from the river bank. She was sitting on a small folding chair. Tia knelt beside her with a flask of date wine and a bowl of fruit. The guards stood equidistant and erect on either side and about six feet from her. Ankhesenamun was gazing out at the faint blue reflections rippling on the waters. Her expression was almost whimsical.

Dashir was careful not to come upon the group too suddenly. He announced his arrival with a low cry from about thirty feet distant.

"Approach, Dashir. You are welcome," greeted the queen. At the same time she gestured to the guards to move out of earshot.

The master goldsmith came close by her feet and went down on his knees.

"Dashir," she began. "These are grave times, and I must speak grave business with you this night."

Dashir became troubled. He had been this close to the Pharaoh's wife just the one time before. He had never expected to be summoned into the presence of the royal family a second time. Now he was here, he could not begin to imagine the business of which she spoke.

"I have heard many good things about you, Dashir. You were loyal to the Pharaoh during his short reign, were you not?"

"Aye, my lady, loyal. But no less and no more than any other. Most loyal."

"Your loyalty persists in his death, does it not, Dashir?"

"It does, my lady. It most certainly does."

"Then you will do my bidding, Dashir, if it be for the welfare of Pharaoh, will you not?"

"That I shall, my lady. That I shall. Say it and it will be done." Dashir was relaxing a little. He felt less convinced that the queen was going to accuse him of being the cause of her last miscarriage, and more so that she might be preparing to ask him to create some unique and beautiful object to be added to the king's grave goods.

"Pharaoh lives through his ka. I wish Pharaoh to continue his life with me. I wish his ka to lie with me as Tutankhamun did..."

This was all getting a bit much for poor old Dashir. The queen's innermost bedtime wishes were hardly something he wished to share. But then came the surprise...

"...You will bring him to me. When Pharaoh is laid to rest and the tomb sealed, you will enter, seek out his ka, and bring him to me!"

Shocked and stunned as he was by this totally unanticipated directive, Dashir nevertheless comprehended exactly what his queen had instructed him to do. The gold ka figure, that which had been completed in the king's likeness and, as they spoke, still lay on a bed of straw in the foundry, was what she expected him to remove from the tomb.

Dashir bowed his head. "Oh, my lady," he whispered, "you ask too much of me. Much as I love Pharaoh, I am not able to do this thing."

Rather than raise her voice in the anger of command, the queen counselled her servant. "Master goldsmith, do you not agree that all Pharaohs' tombs have been robbed shortly after burial?"

"Aye, my lady. It is a tragically common affair."

"Do you not think it possible that our Lord Tutankhamun's is no less likely to be desecrated? Everything lost for ever?"

"Possible? Aye, my lady. It is possible. But we... we faithful, will try hard to protect it from these irreligious vandals."

Dashir knew of many examples of the nighttime business of several of his colleagues, particularly the tomb builders themselves, who knew exactly the tombs' whereabouts and their architecture. To some degree, violation was almost inevitable.

"In this light, then, do you not think that through our conspiracy, should we succeed in securing the safekeeping of Tutankhamun's ka, this is a responsible act? Our duty, even?"

"Aye, my lady. Duty." Dashir could think of nothing more to say. He trembled at the reality of her words but continued to listen.

"Then you will do it. We need have no more words on the matter."

"B-but what if I be caught?"

"You shall not. I shall engineer the circumstances such that you have the freedom to execute your business in my name. This thing that you will do shall be a good thing for Tutankhamun, for Ankhesenamun, for Pharaoh's subjects. Through your deeds - your deeds - eternal life for his spirit will be assured, as it will for all of us."

When Dashir finally met up with his carousing friends that night, he carried a weighty secret.

The Anubis dog was complete, painted, gilded and already lying on the large wooden casket from which, with its black obsidian eyes, it would overlook the king's body.

Meneg had new problems. This time they were more practical than psychological. He had been instructed to carve a likeness of the king in his late boyhood. His ageing memory was failing him - he was unable to picture the king in his youth; he had no recollection of any early piece of artwork that could act as a guide, and the reliefs and frescos of the temples were too stylised for his liking, and in any event, these were two-dimensional.

He was pondering this dilemma as he walked home that evening. It was one of those rare close evenings when storms were gathering to deluge the dry valley in which he lived. He quickened his step in case he got caught before he reached shelter. He entered the narrow street which formed the spine of the village and began to trot - no more than this - being careful not to lose his footing. As he neared the doorway to his little house, he came to be in the path of some children running at full pelt in the opposite direction. Clumsily, they tried to overtake him. There were many of them and, the street being so confining, it was unavoidable that one of them would connect bodily with the older man. He was sent tumbling, finally coming to rest on his back and, as it happened, on his doorstep.

The children all skidded to a halt. Recognising him to be an elder of the village and as such greatly respected, the boys became fearful of their carelessness. "Sir, are you all right?" asked one of the boys anxiously.

Meneg was by now sitting up with his back against the wall of his house. He looked thoughtfully at the group of boys. The first raindrops fell on his face. He smiled.

This concerned the boys greatly - perhaps he had taken a severe blow on the head; perhaps they had caused him some permanent damage. They stood in stunned silence staring at the old man, not knowing what to say or do next.

It was the old man who broke the silence. "No harm done." He gestured towards one who stood to the right of the group. "You. Yes you, boy. You are the third born of Dashir, are you not?"

"Y-yes, sir," replied the child nervously, puzzled as to why he had been singled out.

Meneg stared at him for a moment. The boy had large eyes and well-formed ears; the top of his partly shaved head was elongate, his cheeks chubby with youth. The boy was as close a likeness to Tutankhamun as a child as Meneg could remember.

"What a piece of luck," Meneg said spontaneously.

The boys regarded the old man quizzically.

"You will model for me, boy. Go tell your father. We begin tomorrow. Now be off with you - with you all!"

The boys stood there, stunned, motionless.

"I said, be gone! If the ears on your heads do not hear me they will feel the sting of my whip!"

By now the skies had opened up and everyone was becoming rapidly soaked to the skin. In an instant they scattered to their various doorways. Meneg picked himself up and turned into his own. He felt an internal, satisfying warmth that insulated him from the biting cold of his sodden clothing.

He could see it already... A small statuette portrait of the king appearing as if made when he was just nine years old, as if made at the time of the royal couple's coronation. Just a head, the neck implanted on a lotus-flower base, the earlobes deeply pierced and supporting earrings of gold with lapis inlay. He would see if he could get Dashir, who, he was quite certain, was on close enough speaking terms with the queen, to obtain the appropriate jewellery.

He entered his house and closed the door on the weather.

This day Ugele felt doubly blessed. He took the greatest satisfaction in being the last worker to emerge from the completed tomb. After all those weeks of what had seemed such meagre progress - along with the added irritation of the ever-present Parneb who, persistent in his duties, insisted on noting down the issue of every consumable tool and demanding visible evidence of wear before releasing another - the chippings were now finally cleared and the walls dressed.

In the burial chamber he examined the surfaces for defects. The light of his oil lamp illuminated the smooth, white limestone. It practically glowed.

The king's treasurer, Maya, had confirmed that the four rooms were now large enough to store all the grave goods. It would take some creative organisation, but he had no doubt that the king's funerary paraphernalia would be adequately accommodated and sequestered safely below ground level. It had been an exacting task to complete this space to the demands of the architect. Maya had been explicit and unyielding in his instructions. The largest room, presently a single, L-shaped cavity with a three-foot step down between the two parts of the L, ultimately would become divided; the lower portion was to be the burial chamber. This part was a totally new creation, not conceived of in the original design for the usurped tomb of the noble. The assembled shrine-set would fill the room floor to ceiling and cover full five times the area of the sarcophagus itself, leaving space within the chamber barely sufficient for a man to negotiate his way around the stucture.

An additional two store-chambers led off both arms of the L-shaped room through smaller apertures, that one off what was to become the burial chamber so small that a short man could not walk through it without stooping. The entrance to the one off the upper part of the L was considerably smaller, not much larger than a crawl space. It provided access to the smallest room, the floor of which once again had been excavated below the level of the entrance. This chamber would serve as overflow storage space for the more mundane articles - food and drink and such like.

Unlike the tomb of Smenkhkare, which lay almost opposite on the other side of The Valley, this small crypt now had sufficient space to accommodate, packed tight, every bit of the trappings necessary to sustain Pharaoh in his celestial flight. The elder brother's reign had been yet more foreshortened than that of Tutankhamun, and there had been no time to extend the tomb beyond a single chamber. It had been necessarily light in all but the most essential of grave goods - by now a good deal lighter following the intrusions of the general.

Ugele took one last look around. He recalled the great corridors of the tomb of Pharaoh Akhenaten, extending seemingly forever into the bowels of the earth: the furnishings, the food, the clothing, the jewellery, all arranged comfortably about the many chambers, corridors and ancillary rooms, as they had been in life - a virtual household for the dead. Nevertheless, for Tutankhamun, one way or another it would all be there, crowding the three chambers surrounding the royal remains. With everything to hand, the king would be able to rearrange it to his liking in the halls of his heavenly Osiride palace.

The master mason was the last to leave the empty tomb and the first to introduce an object - the usurped sarcophagus. The great stone casket lay at the top of the stairs, its engravings altered to identify it with its new owner. As he emerged into the midday sunlight, the Nubian's team of labourers stood in a crescent at the top of the stairwell awaiting his orders.

Ugele shielded his eyes, temporarily blinded by the sun's reflection from the barely translucent quartzite box. It was as if a celestial fire had been kindled inside the sarcophagus. The bodies of the goddesses, delicately carved at each corner, glowed golden with warmth.

"All is ready, my friends," announced Ugele to his nine associates. "Let us get about our business."

He marshalled the men around the sarcophagus. One stood at the head to ensure that the wooden rollers, placed on each step, would not dislodge as the heavy box descended. The others took the strain.

Before anything moved, Ugele raised his arm, signalling the men to hold.

"Just a minute." He thought for a moment, miming the entry of the great stone box with his hands, turning his body this way and that. "Ah! I thought as much. The sarcophagus is the wrong way around. Once it is placed within the burial chamber, the goddesses will end up in the wrong positions. If we take it from here as it is, I am not sure there will be sufficient room to turn it about. To be on the safe side, we will have to turn it here first."

With some difficulty the men managed to rotate the sarcophagus so that it was correctly repositioned above the stairway. Those above ground, including the Nubian, took their places on the ropes that surrounded the quartzite box. Their job would be to restrain the sarcophagus from sliding unrestricted down the stairway.

As the sarcophagus was levered up at one end, they took the strain and the great stone block crept over the lip of the first stair to begin its short journey into the darkness below. The operation went smoothly all the way down to the smooth floor of the entrance corridor. Then, suddenly, the upper rim became wedged against the lintel of the entrance door. The sarcophagus was too tall and too long to make the turn to the more gentle slope of the corridor.

Ugele yelled to the man at the far end, "Mose! Mose! What is the trouble?"

"It is almost within, Ugele," replied the man trapped on the other side of the jammed sarcophagus. "Very little will have to be excavated to permit access. However, first you must withdraw it. There is no other way."

This was not good news to the nine sweating men who now had to pull the great weight back up the stairs again.

"The casket is too heavy for us to pull it back up. We are going for help, Mose," Ugele shouted. "We shall be some little time. Hopefully you are not in need of water, my friend. The water bag will not pass between the sarcophagus and the wall."

This was not good news for Mose. In his impressionable mind, thoughts of his own personal entombment - alive - were quick to realise themselves. Shafts of light shone either side the gods-faced façade which now stood between him and home, but there was no space to slide by. He heard the voices recede, then silence - an awful silence. Although he had light enough to see by, it was ever so quiet there, in the depths, alone.

Buried alive! In Pharaoh's tomb. There could be worse places. The thought was not comforting.

Mose began to fidget. He could feel his heart beating heavily and more rapidly. It was audible, echoing about the stark, flat walls around him. He felt like screaming. He held his head in an effort to suppress his feelings. The perspiration was running from him. If he remained in this place he would drive himself mad. In panic, he took hold of the lip of the sarcophagus and in a futile effort tried to pull the thing towards him.

Then a thought finally dawned. He could see there was sufficient room between the top of the sarcophagus and the roof of the corridor for him to climb in. Presumably likewise there was room at the other end also for him to climb out.

When Ugele and his men at last returned with reinforcements, Mose was sitting at the top of the stairs in the shade, much rested and relaxed after his ordeal.

"Mose!" Ugele cried on seeing him and with some relief. "Is this a miracle?"

"No more than my own ingenuity, Ugele. You give me up for lost too easily, I fear."

"You do us wrong, Mose. You knew we would get you out. Just a matter of time."

"A matter of time? Time enough for me to go mad! Thoughts of entombment before my time. A living hell. You could not understand this if you had not experienced lying within, like me, walled up and all alone in the darkness."

"Enough drama," said Ugele. "Let us to our task with some urgency now, before the light fades."

There were now at least twenty hands on the ropes. It took some considerable effort to dislodge the box from its three-point grip but ultimately muscle triumphed over dead weight.

With the massive object once more at the top of the stairway, Ugele and three others ran down to the bottom and cut away all the offending steps. To ensure that the next attempt would be successful, Ugele also instructed the men to remove the upper door lintel and cut away the doorjambs. All could be replaced later.

Once more Mose descended to the entrance of the corridor and the rest of the team manoeuvred the great quartzite box towards and over the lip of the stairway. They took the strain of its weight on the ropes and let the sarcophagus creep slowly towards the darkness. This time it slid into and down the corridor without mishap, finally tilting onto the floor of the first room.

As it slid into the room, Mose placed wooden rollers on the floor beneath it. The team waited a moment to allow their eyes to become accustomed to the dim light and then Ugele instructed them to turn the great box to the right towards the lower part of the room - that which was to become the burial chamber. The manoeuvre was more difficult than expected. Without leverage of some kind it proved impossible. Ugele sent for a stout pole. While this was being fetched, he took out his copper chisel and cut a small cavity at the base of the wall opposite the entrance. When the pole arrived, he stuck one end of it into the hole in the wall, brought the side of it against the corner of the sarcophagus and, with the help of four other men, levered the box towards the elbow of the L-shaped room. It was carefully manoeuvred down into the burial chamber, the goddesses facing in the directions set for them by religious law, and set upon four calcite blocks - one at each corner. The great quartzite sarcophagus at last was in its final resting place.

Their last act was to bring in the broken sarcophagus lid, now repaired with a copper dovetail, and place the reconstituted piece against the wall at the head end of the stone casket.

When Ugele left the tomb that night he felt relief and, at the same time, loss. He had completed his assigned tasks successfully and on time. The inside of that holy place now awaited Pharaoh. Ugele himself would not set eyes on it again.

Horemheb, dressed in his official regalia, stood in the embalming room. He was there to preside over the wrapping of the mummy. By this time he had had quite enough. He looked forward to when all the formalities were behind him. To add to the general's discomfort, Ay, who was to oversee the funeral ceremonies, had waited until this late stage in the proceedings to deliver a long list of disparaging comments. He grumbled about the size of the tomb. He criticised the unlikely second coffin. He pointed out the mismatched sarcophagus lid - its obvious repair. He complained of the poor likeness in the canopic stoppers. Few details escaped his critical eye. The criticisms had been very public - this, no doubt, to appease Ay's new queen - and the old man proffered no solutions.

It was all most irritating. After all, the general had toiled long and hard to ensure that everything was in readiness and on time. Perfection had been an impossible goal from the start and he had never promised it. Now this practically senile old man, shortly to be confirmed as Pharaoh, who had made no effort to help in the preparations, had the audacity to decry the general's achievements in public.

Horemheb seethed to himself, 'I'll be glad when the dry, salty bastard is finally put away. Then, perhaps, this silly old man will turn what remains of his fragile mind to thoughts of his own passing, and I with securing the kingship for myself.'

The old man's rantings had generated an impatience within the general that he knew he would have to take steps to control. If his involved conspiracy was to succeed, he may not indulge himself in this kind of emotion. He must avoid drawing attention to himself. He shrugged his shoulders and concentrated on the scene before him.

The salts had been removed from the king's body. The cadaver lay between the two priests. It was totally naked but for a frail golden diadem encircling the dead king's temple. The skin had taken on a bluish-grey colour. As it had shrunk, it had wrinkled. The originally youthful features had taken on the appearance of old age.

Behind the priests, running parallel with the king's stone embalming bed, there were two long tables. On one lay neatly arranged piles of papyrus and rolls of bandages of differing linens and widths. On the other lay a host of jewellery and golden decorations of various shapes and colours, large and small, from the complex to the simple, placed in rows, all arranged in the prescribed order in which they were to be applied to the body.

One of the priests cradled the boy king's head in his hands. The other removed the diadem and placed it on the jewellery table. He picked up a linen skullcap of beads sewn together to form a frame of cobras and carefully fitted this over the shaven cranium. He secured it in place with a broad, flexible gold temple band which, with his fingers, he locked in place by gently but firmly bending it to the contours of the king's head. A padded wig was placed over this and secured at the back of the head using perforations in the temple band to tie it in position. On the wig were attached the symbols of royal dominion - the uraeus of the Lower Nile, with its long, snaking body and cobra head, and nekhbet, the vulture of the Upper Nile. A thin wrapping of bandage was placed over these and the diadem was replaced.

Horemheb shifted uneasily from one foot to the other. The process was interminably slow. But he was responsible for ensuring absolute adherence to custom and the security of the dead king's grave goods. He whispered a sigh. This was but one of several distasteful duties he must fully endure.

The priests turned to the feet. A wrapping of linen was applied to each toe and then golden toe stalls, engraved to the likeness of the toes themselves, were placed on each and gently squeezed to grip the linen. The feet themselves were then wrapped and gold sandals carefully placed on them, the front of the pointed soles bent upwards to help keep the toe stalls in place.

The two priests moved to the hips. One took hold of the shrivelled penis. He extended it forwards while the other took care to bandage it delicately but sufficiently robustly to ensure it supported itself erect. (*Ithyphallic symbolism is an essential element of deification. The Pharaoh is, after all, a creator of gods.*)

The process continued in ordered stages - decoration for a limb, a bandage enclosing it, a bangle and a dagger laid on the bandage, another strip of linen to enclose the pieces, another gold plate on this, and another bandage.

As the work proceeded, the lesser priests, standing in the background, read incantations and spells from the texts of the great papyrus, 'The Chapters of Coming Forth by Day'. These lessons would help lead the king through the long and dangerous road to his eternal paradise.

The general tensed the muscles in his back and shifted his position once again.

The two priests by the bed continued the ritual. In part intended to suppress the king's lifetime indiscretions, in part adding to the strength of the spells, each additional piece placed within the mummy wrappings became symbolic protection for the king's trials during his forthcoming journey through the underworld.

Horemheb, resigned to his duty, moved his feet further apart, folded his arms across his chest, closed his eyes, and bowed his head.

Picture it...

Eight amulets in chased sheet gold are laid on the chest, these fastened by strings about the neck: two human-headed, winged serpents, one uraeus, one double-uraeus, and five vultures.

A wrapping of linen. More amulets in the form of holy symbols: two in green feldspar, one in blood-red carnelian, one in sky-blue lapis lazuli. A wrapping. Three amulets: two golden palm leaf symbols placed either side of the neck, and a serpent of chased gold. A wrapping. Four amulets: one of red jasper, one of gold, one of green feldspar, another of gold inlaid with coloured glass. A wrapping. A double-headed falcon collar is placed so as to enclose entirely the chest and the shoulders: The collar of Horus in chased sheet gold. A wrapping. Three pectorals: a scarab, an eye and a falcon, gold, enamelled and inlaid with coloured glass. On the chest, an elaborate collarette of tiny blue glass and gold beads. A wrapping. Three pectorals: ornately crafted in gold and glass inlay and arranged across the chest, to the right, one of the falcon, to the left, the scarab in the name of the king with

157

the wings of a falcon, and in the centre, hung on a bead necklace, an eye pendant.

Horemheb adjusted his stance once more, pressing his hands into the small of his back. The readings from the great papyrus paused for a moment. He nodded at the priest to continue.

A wrapping. Another pendant: three large, brilliant blue, gold-backed scarabs, marguerites and lotus blossoms in glass hanging beneath, the entire creation hanging from a necklace of five rows of coloured beads secured by an elaborate gold clasp. A wrapping. A gold pendant: Nekhbet with her wings at rest suspended from an intricate gold and lapis chain-link neckband, the pendant inlaid with green glass, lapis and carnelian, orbs of carnelian clasped in her gold talons. A wrapping. Two great collars: one with the bodies of the vulture and the serpent and, laid on this, another of the vulture, both of these backed with a multitude of engraved gold tiles, each infilled with coloured glass. A sheet of papyrus. A large chased gold pectoral: a serpent with huge enclosing wings which are bent by the priest to enfold the neck of the king and fix the massive breastplate in place. Several wrappings. Three gold bangles: decorated in semiprecious stones, these are laid on the stomach and on the chest, again secured from the neck. A large pectoral of a hawk: this in chased sheet gold with two gold amuletic knots laid either side. A wrapping. A golden pectoral of Horus: this positioned in the centre, entirely embracing the chest with its wings and inlaid with hundreds of tiles of coloured glass. A papyrus sheet. Another pectoral: a falcon in chased sheet gold.

Horemheb moved once again, standing more to attention this time. Once again the general folded his arms across the rise of his belly.

A wrapping. A large scarab: made of black resin with a gold base and coloured glass inlay, suspended from the neck to the navel on a long gold wire. A wrapping. Covering the entire chest of the king's body, an arrangement of four large gold collar shields, each individually secured about the king's neck with gold thread: a vulture, another with the heads of a vulture and a serpent, another serpent, and a collar with two identical falcon heads facing away from each other. On the arms, gold bracelets and broad, colourful bangles over each wrist: six to the left arm, seven to the right. They cover each dry, shrunken forearm to the elbow. On the fingers of each hand, long gold finger stalls, like thimbles: the priests slide rings of solid gold over each but only two on the left hand will stay in place. They put the remaining rings to one side. A wrapping for each hand, each finger, each arm, then both arms are folded across the chest, the eight remaining rings placed between them: three near the left wrist to complete symbolically the decoration of the hand, five adjacent to the right. On the hips, first a girdle: of gold and glass beadwork, drawn up around the king's legs and laid about his waist. On this a pectoral: an eye in bright blue glass suspended on a necklace of gold beads. A wrapping. A chased gold girdle: suspended from it an articulated gold apron of glass beads with, tucked carefully beneath the girdle and to one side, a gold dagger in its gold sheath. More wrappings. An anklet of gold, inlaid with coloured glass. A wrapping. A gold collar of dark blue glass. A wrapping. A second girdle of chased gold. A wrapping.

The general placed his hands on his hips and moved his feet further apart.

Three plain sheet-gold symbols: one ellipsoid and placed coincident with the position of the embalming scar, another in the form of the letter T, the third a Y. On the legs, four gold bangles placed along and between them. A wrapping. A bangle and collarette: of gold and coloured glass, with golden falcon heads at the shoulders. A wrapping. Two more bangles and two more collarettes. A wrapping. Another collarette. A wrapping. The headpieces from the king's diadem along with a gold anklet. A wrapping. An iron dagger with a gold haft, inlaid with coloured glass, and a gold sheath, these laid alongside a ceremonial apron of large gold plates, inlaid with coloured glass. A final wrapping.

The jewellery table was empty.

A long and very audible sigh from Horemheb ensued. The general quickly remedied this momentary display of disrespect by drawing himself smartly to attention, bowing his head once again and closing his eyes.

The ritual continued. Without pausing, the two priests finished the padding and outer wrapping of the body. The direction and order of each binding followed a set procedure and they worked together from the feet upwards, one taking the bandage and one moving the body alternately until it became fully cocooned.

The mummy now was bound so tightly it was as rigid as a log. It also was heavy. With some effort the priests lifted it up by the shoulders and slid it off the foot of the funeral bed until the feet rested on the stone floor. Leaving it temporarily leaning against the bed, they turned to face the general.

Horemheb opened his eyes.

At his feet, standing in a specially made wooden cradle, stood the magnificent mask of heavy gold. On the priests' signal he bent down and, with the help of the two guards standing by his side, raised the object. The priests took the mask from the general and approached the mummy from the front. As if performing the coronation itself, they solemnly lifted the mask above the mummy's head and slowly lowered it on its shoulders. The long beard of gold and inlaid blue glass was attached to the chin. With the help of the guards they carefully lifted the mummy back onto the bier.

Parannefer's final holy act was to place a golden ba bird on the mummy's abdomen. A last prayer was recited and solemnly he led the party from the chamber.

The great cedar doors closed behind them and the royal guards took their places either side. There they would stay, standing vigil until it was time for the funeral celebrations.

The general remained behind, alone in the chamber.

Numerous articles of inestimable value had passed him in a blur. He hadn't been counting. There could be no reason to suspect indiscretion. From now until the final sealing of the tomb the entire event was too solemn and the process too ordered and prescribed. Any errors or falsehoods would disturb the smooth passage of the king to the afterlife and all would suffer when their time came. There would be no exceptions. Of this he was certain.

The general moved over to the head of the bed. As he looked down the high-eyebrowed forehead, the face glowed eerily blue-grey in the light of the oil lamps, and the great black orbs of its eyes burned back into his. He drew a sharp breath and stepped back in alarm. 'He lives! Truly, he lives!' The reality would haunt him the remainder of his days.

Later that night, Horemheb walked over to the foundry one last time and checked the line-up of grave goods set ready for shipment the following morning. The huge gold coffin glowed in the light of the dying furnace. He smiled gratuitously. Its magnificence set the standard for his own casket.

'Yet more grand,' contemplated the general. 'This one shall become so much tomb-robbers' booty. That much is certain.' The thought pleased him so much he almost spoke it aloud, but checked himself - a human shadow flickered across the foundry floor to his left. He turned to confront it, his hand resting on the hilt of his dagger. He was about to draw the blade when he recognised the crouching figure.

Ankhesenamun had not heard the general enter the foundry and remained totally oblivious to his presence. She was kneeling before the standing gold ka statue of her husband which was now positioned on its plinth within a small golden shrine, its doors wide open. As Horemheb drew closer he could hear her whisper.

"Eternal, with me, thou shalt be. We shall never be apart."

'Very touching,' thought the general. 'Touching. I, too, pray you will not be apart for long. Pray I help you to your goal.' And he stole out of the foundry without closing the door.

Ankhesenamun kissed her fingers, leant towards the open shrine, and gently touched the tiny gold feet.

"We shall be together once again, Tutankhamun... within but a few nights hence."

Had he been present, the words would have given the general some food for thought.

Chapter Ten
Lordship

Emma Andrews took her time inspecting the watercolour. Carter, a Scotch and soda in his hand, made himself comfortable while he awaited the verdict. They sat in the main room of Davis's temporary house which sat close to the entrance of The West Valley. Although it was early afternoon, all the windows and all the doors were open, allowing a refreshing breeze to flow freely through the room.

"Magnificent - as always! Howard, bless you, you always excel. Is the usual okay?"

"Oh, of course, Miss Andrews. Whatever."

"A trifle more on this occasion, perhaps? It is, after all, slightly larger than the last one you painted for us."

"You are too kind. But, to tell the truth, my bank balance is looking somewhat lean this month."

"Twenty pounds, then. And we'll hear no more of it. Theo won't mind a bit!"

"You are too kind." Secretly he'd hoped for more. This winter there were fewer tourists than usual and very few of these were inclined towards his artwork. But beggars can't be choosers and he should be content with the appreciative market he held so secure.

As he took another mouthful of his Scotch, the houseboy came into the room with a note. Mrs Andrews opened it.

"It's from Theo, Howard. He has reached the inner sanctum and would like to show it to us."

"The 'inner sanctum', Miss Andrews? Of Horemheb's tomb which Edward found just a few days ago?"

"The very one, Howard. But Maspero calls it 'the tomb of Harmhabi'. I cannot for the life of me fathom why it is that you archaeologists cannot agree on a common spelling. "Horemheb, Harmhabi, Humbabumba - I do declare! Well, enough of that. We should go up there directly. His automobile is waiting."

Carter resisted the temptation to lecture Davis's companion. He quickly downed the remainder of his drink, put on his Homburg and followed the woman outside. It took them no time at all to drive to the site.

Theodore Davis and Edward Ayrton, both covered in dust, were there to greet them.

"My dear!" exclaimed Davis. "We have such delights to show you! And it is so fortunate you were visiting us, Howard. You can perhaps help us decipher the texts. The place is full of grafitti of the most excellent workmanship! It's a big one, this one. Unfinished, but big all the same. Totally robbed, of course. Hardly a thing worth salvaging but for the sarcophagus. Never mind that. Plenty to write home about, that's for sure! *(In the event, Davis' publication, prolifically and precisely illustrated with photographs by his good friend Harry Burton, was journalistic in its text. Ironically it acknowledged the contributions of all his collaborators except that of Burton himself; See Davis, 1912.)* Let us go in."

Carter looked at the entrance to the excavation. A pit dug by Davis's men into the accumulated rubble had revealed a man-made rectangular hole cut into the very floor of the valley itself. It descended steeply via a rock-cut staircase which penetrated the limestone as far as the eye could see.

Davis was eager to show off his discovery. Despite his age, he ran down the steps almost two at a time. Ayrton extended his hand to Emma and, going ahead down the staircase, led her carefully into the depths. Carter followed.

After the first cleared stairway there was nothing but rock refuse to walk on - rubble from ancient floods; debris from the collapse of the ceilings. With little to see but plain walls, the party hastily scrambled over the slabs of rock and piles of rubble, descending along three inclines of varying slope, until Davis stopped them at the first decorated room. Here there was no debris. There was no floor. This was the well room. Ayrton had bridged it with a double ladder which they all had to negotiate.

Immediately beyond the well was a double-pillared room with a staircase let into the floor. After three more inclines of varying angles of descent, they reached a small room which clearly led into a much larger hall beyond. The debris of earlier flooding appeared to have penetrated this far and fanned out into the room at the base of the incline. A great chunk of the small room's ceiling had fallen away. Limestone shards of considerable size littered the floor. Like the well room, the walls were brilliantly decorated with life-size figures of Horemheb paired with various deities.

Davis waved his arms about the room as if wishing his guests to relish the sight.

He led the party onward. They picked their way carefully from boulder to boulder across the decorated room into the larger, pillared hall beyond. The chamber was huge. It appeared all the larger because it opened directly into the room holding the sarcophagus. There were six pillars in the room, all undecorated. One had broken from the ceiling and lay at a crazy angle within a pile of ceiling debris. Centuries of earthquakes were responsible for the structural damage and cracks were everywhere - in the plaster, the pillars, the ceiling and the walls. The place looked like it was about to fall in on itself at any moment.

It was clear that the decorating of this holy place had been cut short. In places the original draughtsman's grids were in evidence. On one wall, the first rough but elaborately sketched drawings were in red, over-drawn more precisely in black. Along one or two registers these were partially sculpted. But none was painted.

Davis proudly pointed out the only painted effigy in this area. It stood solitary in the centre of an otherwise blank wall in one of the flanking storerooms. It was a large, colourfully but not brightly painted figure of Osiris standing on a plinth in front of a large djed pillar, the whole contained within a representation of a multicoloured shrine. The face was green, the body was white, the remainder painted variously in yellow, shades of grey, blue, green and red ochre. Carter had not set eyes on its like before. He was captivated by the painting and stared at it for some time.

The floor of this little room was littered with tomb debris cast aside by the robbers in antiquity - everything disassembled, stripped of its gold. Most had been removed altogether.

The excited Davis tugged at Carter's shoulder. "Howard, my old friend, come and examine the magnificent sarcophagus!"

The carved, red granite box stood in its original place near the rear wall of the lower of the two large rooms - the burial chamber proper. It was indeed magnificent. Carter looked inside. It was empty - just a few fragments of bone scattered about the base.

"This place has been very well cleansed, Mr Davis," he said. "Doubt you'll find much beneath all this rubble."

There was a small doorway in the left rear wall of the burial chamber. Davis led his party through into another relatively large room. In the back wall of this room another opening led to a small chamber, but the doorway was almost filled with a pile of mason's cuttings.

"This place really has a story to tell," observed Carter. "These fellahs walked off the job before it was completed, did not bother to clean anything up, moved his lordship in, stacked his wares, sealed him up, broke in, took everything of value, busted up everything else, including his mummy, and left what remained of him in pieces." he chuckled.

"What's so funny?" asked Emma Andrews.

"Oh, nothing, Miss Andrews"... "Wonderful, wonderful find, Mr Davis. Congratulations, Ayrton. I wish you luck in completing the excavations."

Although the exploration had been brief, it had felt good to be back, if only for a moment.

The sun now directly overhead, Howard Carter sat in the shade of a palm tree sketching the bustling composition in the entrance to the long corridor of the bazaar that stretched before him. He had painted the scene several times before albeit from slightly different angles and in differing lights. For over two years now Carter had been painting watercolours of Egyptian life and artefacts for profit, and through this and the odd trip to the sites acting as an authoritative guide, he had made sufficient in commissions to keep himself from starving, but little more than that. Had Gaston Maspero, his earlier boss, not helped by latterly loaning him the use of his previous quarters on the west bank, he might not even have achieved this much. Since it had come from Maspero, it was not below Carter to accept this charitable gesture. He rationalised it as a clearly well-earned response to ensure his continued support and well-being; a gesture demonstrating appreciation for his talents and efforts during the execution of his earlier duties as Chief Inspector. With no rent to pay, he managed to survive and still had time to study the antiquities about him and visit the excavations of others. But he wasn't doing what he wanted. The lack of a steady salary brought with it a sense of insecurity and loneliness. A feeling of almost total solitude consumed him at times. He hadn't seen Dorothy since he'd resigned. Some evenings he had felt compelled to relate his personal anguish to his diary. There was no one else to talk to. Bereft of funds, he had no prospect of re-establishing himself in the field.

But that was yesterday.

As the quick, deliberate strokes of his pencil continued, he glanced up from the sketchpad momentarily to pick out another character from the busily trading crowd. What took his eye in the indifferently lit shade of the market was the sight of two Europeans, one short and plump, the other tall and lanky, both properly suited and hatted, talking vigorously to each other as they advanced from the shadows within the bazaar and out into the bright sunlight. When the light caught them, he could clearly see that the shorter man was none other than Gaston Maspero. He did not recognise his companion. The other, despite walking with a pronounced limp, exhibited the carriage and dress of a man of some breeding.

The two were making their way purposefully towards where Carter was sitting. There was no doubt he was their target. As they neared, Carter examined the taller man more closely. He was dressed in a grey, finely checked three-piece suit open at the jacket. He had a shooting stick for support, and from the same hand he swung a feather fly-whisk. In his breast pocket flopped a large white handkerchief and, between the two pockets in his waistcoat, a long, gold pocket-watch chain bounced in tune with his uneven step. His white shirt was roll-necked so he wore no tie. On his head perched a large-brimmed panama sporting a wide white headband. His fair moustache was bushier than Carter's, his face leaner and longer, and his eyelids had that slightly half-closed downward look - that which comes with years of looking down on lesser mortals.

'I am not going to enjoy this,' thought Howard, breathing in deeply. As the pair of them neared he pulled himself up to a standing position and dusted off his pants.

"Knew we'd find you here," Maspero began and then with a wave of each hand added, "Mr Howard Carter. His lordship, George Edward Stanhope Molyneux Herbert, Lord Porchester, the fifth Earl of Carnarvon of

Highclere."

'Mother went overboard naming this one,' thought Carter uncharitably. 'If the number of characters in his name and title are anything to go by, he must be very well-heeled indeed!'

"Mr. Carter! Delighted to meet you," pronounced Carnarvon as he shook him vigorously by the hand. "I fear I have been delinquent to this point in not ensuring I made your acquaintance much earlier during my stay in Egypt. The growth of your reputation in recent years seemingly approaches eclipsing that of the great Flinders Petrie!"

"Your lordship, the honour is all mine. I have heard much of your keen archaeological efforts in these parts."

"Will you be good enough to take some coffee with us, Howard?" asked Maspero, hastily. "His lordship has a proposition he wishes to put before you."

Maspero led them quickly back to the entrance of the sukh. On the corner stood a small outdoor bar boasting five or six tables with crimson-chequered tablecloths, all shaded by a canopy extended between four tethered poles. Each of them drew up a chair and sat down. Maspero gestured to the owner of the rude establishment to bring three coffees.

As he exchanged pleasantries with Carnarvon, Carter looked almost disinterested. He fully expected the proposition, when Carnarvon was ready to make it, would be some form of commission for paintings of artefacts or wall decorations; work he might be glad of, nonetheless, but not likely to get his heart pounding. The arrival of the coffees was the signal to switch gears from introductory small talk to the business at hand.

"Mr Carter," Carnarvon began directly. "You have been kind in your comments about the results of my recent excavations. The truth of the matter is, however, that my proudest possession from these digs has been the full mummy case of a cat. Of interest, of course, and most gratifying, but it goes only a small way towards fulfilling my ambitions - and compensating my costs. I have come to Egypt primarily on my doctor's orders. My health, you see, is sufficiently fragile that I am greatly vulnerable to the ill humours of the British winter..."

"Aren't we all, sir?"

"Hmm. Perhaps some more so than others, Mr Carter..." The earl quickly returned to the subject of his forthcoming proposition. "...So I come to Egypt for its health-giving sunshine, warmth and clean air. While I am here I do not wish to be idle. I have maintained an interest in Egyptology since I was a child and have been a modest collector to this point, but this is my first opportunity to touch provenance, so to speak. Touch it is all I can do, I fear. I am not knowledgeable in the craft of excavation, nor where to look. The concessions I have held to this point have been bestowed on the advice of Mr Weigall, your successor in the Antiquities Service. I am sure he has advised as wisely as he could, but equally I am sure that being sensitive to my inexperience he has tempered his choice of site to that likely to be of lesser importance, lest I do some irreparable harm. Kept me out of harm's way, so to speak, with grace!"

As Carnarvon continued this monologue, Maspero regarded Carter's expression. It was clear that the Egyptologist's attention was growing stronger by the minute. Carter had realised that this man was not leading up to a commissioned painting or two. The director's face broke to a wry smile, discreetly concealed under the herbage of his matted moustache.

"So this is my frustration," the earl continued. "I have sufficient fortune to adequately fund excavations of some importance for the Service, but I am restricted to almost squandering these funds on trivial sites with little opportunity for any discovery of importance. I believe it to be a considerable waste. And I fear my sense of dedication to the task has suffered. Without some new incentive it may perish altogether."

Carnarvon turned to look Carter directly in the eyes.

"This brings me to my proposition. And for this idea I have to thank Monsieur Maspero for his good counsel."

Maspero, grinning, nodded in recognition of the honour so bestowed.

Carnarvon smiled back in acknowledgement and continued. "Monsieur Maspero made an observation that hitherto had not occurred to me. Without an experienced Egyptologist working with me, how could I expect to gain a concession of sufficient potential? Simple as that."

He clapped his hands as if in recognition of this revelation, and then turned his eyes towards Carter again. "Will y' be that man, Mr Carter?"

By this time Carter was quite prepared for the climax. "Your lordship, I am quite overcome. You could do me no greater honour. When shall we start?"

"Splendid! Splendid!" Carnarvon and Maspero exchanged gratified glances. "We shall negotiate a new concession at once - this time with your advice as to its location."

"It is too bad that Mr Theodore Davis still pillages in The Valley," Carter responded. "Until he releases that concession we shall have to content ourselves with lesser prospects. But I promise you better than a cat!"

Carter pulled his notebook from his coat pocket, turned to a clean page and began sketching a rough map.

"That is where we should apply for a concession, sir," he said, jabbing a finger at his hasty scribblings. "The foothills of Dra Abu el-Naga, at the mouth of The Valley of the Kings - right on Davis's doorstep, awaiting our turn to enter!"

Carter turned to smile at Maspero. "Please accept my thanks, monsieur, for I have little else. You will not regret this referral, I promise you. Your thoughtfulness will be repaid many fold in kind."

Though Maspero would not live to see it, it was quite beyond Carter's wildest dreams how great his repayment ultimately would be.

From their first week of working together, Carnarvon was himself convinced he had as symbiotic a marriage of connoisseurship and talent as he could have hoped. The two of them even enjoyed each other's company and conversation in the evenings.

Carnarvon, most refreshingly after Carter's experiences with Davis, held a sense of responsibility that, to Carter at least, men of his station in life rarely exhibited. The earl took most seriously the gift of stewardship bequeathed through his concession in the west Theban foothills. Despite his earlier lack of success he had no wish for Carter to accelerate things but, along with him, persevered in a diligent manner, sifting all debris to ensure no small fragment of artefact was lost. Neither did he habitually retire to his riverboat or hotel suite in Luxor while the superficial work was being carried out and appear only when some discovery of significance was anticipated. More often than not he was personally present during excavation activity. The man was serious. He had substance. And there was more - a real friendship was developing between them.

Over the following years there were a great many discoveries, all of them significantly improved in quality and quantity relative to Carnarvon's previous excavations. By the time the first decade of the new century was over, Carter's methodical 'scratching about' within the great amphitheatre of stone that cradled Hatshepsut's magnificent mortuary temple had yielded much to them.

The treasures had included a virtual multitude of coffins and mummies, many untouched, and a good deal else besides. His lordship was much pleased and considered in his mind how he might make a gesture appropriate to his degree of satisfaction at the fruitful efforts of his colleague. He wanted to give Carter a gift that could be taken as an expression of genuine gratitude for the relentless hard work, patience and exacting practice that had brought them their successes thus far. In addition, he wanted it to stand as an enduring statement of his confidence in Carter's stewardship and the grandee's wish to continue financial support for many a year to come.

One evening while taking a drink alone on the porch of Carter's loaned house at Medinet Habu, Carnarvon watched the shadow of the roof line extend slowly towards the river. He had an idea. 'I will build him a new house. His house. He will no longer have to concern himself with how long the Service might tolerate his lease; no longer have to rely on the goodwill of others. It will provide him a permanent base from which to continue his work. A most pleasing thought. I quite excel myself!' He grinned contentedly.

When Carter joined him a moment later, Carnarvon came out with the proposal immediately. "Been thinking, old boy. This place is comfortable but somewhat insecure as digs. You need a more permanent establishment, do you not think?"

"That would be most desirable, m'lord. But it will be some time yet before I am sufficiently flushed to fund such a project. We have profited some from trading in the antiquities markets back in Luxor and Cairo, but I still have very little spare to put away."

"Understood, Howard. Understood. But what if I provide the wherewithal - as a token of my appreciation these past years, and as a basis from which we can step to even greater achievements."

This last statement was music to Carter's ears and Carnarvon well knew it. He would bite. He was sure of it.

Without hesitation Carter took him at his word. "If I had a choice, sir, I would build at the entrance to The Valley, overlooking the river, as we are here. Just a simple place. Enough for my own needs, plus a little room for guests. I may call it 'Castle Carter'! You are serious, m' lord, are y' not?"

"Absolutely, Howard. Let us see to surveying an appropriate site tomorrow morning. It is time we did something different for a day or so. Capital idea if I say so myself!"

The two laughed together and shook hands.

Carter looked north. In his eyes, to be paid a living wage for what was nothing more than pursuing his life's ambition, was entirely sufficient. The affection and generosity so openly displayed by his lordship was so unlike the clinical, businesslike approach of his erstwhile benefactor that it reminded him of a yet greater need. He grew more impatient to obtain access to the concession which Davis still administered.

Carnarvon owned, among a great many other things, a brickworks in England. He told Carter he would have a consignment of bricks made of fine British clay and baked in the best of British kilns sent out to Cairo to add strength to the construction, which otherwise would have been built with sun-dried mud bricks, much like those Carter had cut his teeth on in his early employ with Flinders Petrie and, in their inherent vulnerability, would have relatively quickly succumbed to the elements - although perhaps not in Carter's lifetime.

By the time the bricks arrived at the wharfside on the west bank at Luxor, the foundations had been dug. True to his word, Carter had laid out a simple plan: his room to the right; a second bedroom; a central hall for entertaining; a dining room; and the servants' quarters and kitchen added on to the left. Both the dining room and Carter's bedroom were to have covered verandas with the bathroom between.

Carnarvon was at the site watching Carter lead the pack animals up the incline from the flood plain. As Carter neared, Carnarvon leaned forward in his chair and called to him, at the same time gesturing towards the donkeys with his shooting stick.

"Howard, have you checked to see what manner of brick it is we have here?"

"Manner of brick, m' lord? What 'manner of brick'?"

Carter looked towards the first donkey and the piles of bricks in the baskets on either side. He walked over and took one of the bricks in his hand. What he had thought from a distance was the brickworks name stamp was in fact a good deal more than that:

MADE AT BRETBY
ENGLAND
FOR HOWARD CARTER
A.D. THEBES 1910

Carter was dumbfounded and at the same time filled with an immense feeling of pride.

"I feel like the Pharaoh himself, sir!" he exclaimed. "Customised brickwork - whatever next. Most thoughtful of you, m' lord. Nothing but good can come of this!"

"I echo your feelings, Howard. This is the start of something big. I feel it." The feeble aristocrat was brimming with excitement, much like a child anticipating a gift.

"I will not use this brick, m' lord. I shall keep it to remind me of this moment when I lie infirm and in my dotage with little else to do but review the achievements of our association. And great achievements these will be..."

Carter's mind was racing, but before he could connect the next sentence Carnarvon broke in. "Together, I am convinced, we shall do more for Egyptology than anyone thus far. We are a formidable force, Howard, are we not? You and I. A formidable force!" The earl raised his right fist and his eyes to the sky in a gesture of triumph.

It warmed Carter's heart to see such a demonstration of commitment from the aristocrat. A close bond had developed between them. Perhaps it was true after all - they would achieve great things. But slower days lay ahead.

The house built, furnished and occupied, once more the two returned to excavation. They chose to move the site of their investigations to a concession in the Nile delta. Now far distant from Castle Carter and any hotel, of necessity they worked out of a field camp, but not your average field camp.

Carnarvon, despite his persistent ailments, enjoyed 'roughing it', but in his own fashion. He would willingly abandon himself to the discomfort of living in, on and with things that could be carried, provided, of course, there were enough men available to do the carrying. Apart from the usual canvas for tents and cots, folding tables and chairs, also included amongst his travelling paraphernalia was a full wardrobe of suits, shirts, ties, hats and accessories, tablecloths, silver, cut glassware, crested porcelain for the dining table, candelabra, etc, etc. Since her ladyship would be present on this occasion, her maidservant would have to be in attendance. With his manservant already present and his personal doctor also at hand, additional tents were required. One was given over to the storage of claret from the cellars at Highclere and, of course, the provision of separate facilities for bathing and for toilet. It was a temporary, canvas country seat.

However, notwithstanding these extravagant preparations - entirely normal for the likes of his lordship - the excavation team's stay was short-lived.

The pegs had been in the ground just ten days.

Lady Carnarvon was at her toilet in preparation for dining that evening. As she watched her maidservant pick out a relatively plain, long linen evening dress from her trunk, she detected a movement in the clothing beneath as if her dress had come alive.

She cautioned her unaware maid. "Jane, stand away from the chest! I'm sure I saw something move in there."

They both looked intently at the clothing in the trunk.

"There! See? It moved again!"

"Oh, my lady. Whatever do you think it can be?"

The clothes were now in continuous motion, rippling right across the trunk. It was either a number of small creatures or perhaps one large one.

"Summon Ali," ordered Lady Carnarvon. "But help me on with that dress first."

Ali hurried into her ladyship's tent and quickly began prodding about amongst the clothes in the trunk with his walking stick. As the end of his stick pushed into something sausage-like and soft, the clothes sprang up as if unnaturally levitated and flipped backwards over themselves to reveal the diamond-shaped head of a viper. Its head was perched erect on its arched neck, tongue flicking at the air sensitively, poised to strike. The snake's eyes stared directly at Lady Carnarvon. For a moment she froze; she didn't even take a breath, the blood draining from her face as shock overcame her senses. Ali was equally transfixed. It took a second head to emerge from the clothing to move him to action. Ali withdrew his stick, both vipers striking at it as it moved, and slammed the lid of the chest closed. "I will get rid of them, my lady. Do not worry. Your clothes may get a little dirty but I shall wash them straight away. Do not worry."

He was worried even as much as her, though she could not tell it and did not much care. All she was thinking of was her own safety and how close she had come to what might have been an agonising death. She gave little thought to the task that Ali now had before him. She frantically gestured at him with her hands. The action was enough to convey the purpose of her thoughts.

"Get the box out of here and quickly, you silly little man."

Ali manhandled the chest out of the tent and into some nearby reeds. He lay it down on its side. Standing away from it, he poked the catch with his stick so that the lid fell backwards to the ground, and waited for the creatures to emerge. They did not. He moved slowly around to the opening so that he could better see if there was any movement inside. The clothes lay half-spilled onto the sand. Nothing moved. Like snakes in a snake charmer's basket, the docile two lay motionless, entwined in the folds of cloth.

Still in her tent, Lady Carnarvon sat down on a canvas folding chair and looked about her. Hiding places were everywhere. Could there be others in her bed? She began to shake uncontrollably. This was not Highclere. This was not the Elysean fields of England, raining, grey and cold, infested with rabbits and squirrels and foxes and badgers and weasels and stoats and cats and dogs. This was a foreign desert, an eternal beach with no water; dry, golden and blistering hot during the day, freezing cold at night, and infested with venomous lucifers. She had so wanted to share the experience of adventure and discovery with her husband and demonstrate her ability to tolerate the discomforts of this alien environment. She had determined to be strong. She would support him when he, often flagging in energy because of his intermittent ill health, would turn to her for help. But now cold fear and a building sense of panic filled her head. When he returned from the field that night, it would be all she could do to hold herself back from dashing into her husband's arms in tears and relief. She knew she would have to admit her weakness sooner or later before her self-control broke down.

She moved out of the tent backwards, surveying all items for signs of movement as she left. As she emerged, she turned to see Ali holding a snake down with his stick and beating at it with his knife.

"All dead, my lady. Nothing to fear now."

But she could not stop herself shaking and clasped her arms about herself in a vain attempt to still her shivering body.

Preoccupied with her fear, she did not hear the men approach. She continued to stare at the chest until the figure of Lord Carnarvon moved across her line of sight. On recognising him, the sense of relief took the strength from her legs and she almost collapsed to the ground. It was all she could do to maintain her stature and some semblance of dignity. She tried hard to control her expression. Her face displayed a normal welcoming smile which belied her unfathomable relief at his return.

Carnarvon took off his panama. "That's it! Had enough! Ali, get packing. We're moving back to Cairo tonight. Damn place is infested with vipers. Can't abide snakes. Neither can Mr Carter. Damn dig isn't worth the risks. Sorry, my dear. Know you had been looking forward to roughing it a bit but I don't think I've got your grit!"

Lady Carnarvon felt all the tension leave her in an instant and she burst into uncontrollable laughter.

The earl glared at her. "Might sound amusing to you, my dear, but it was damn scary out there for a moment or two. Damn scary. Don't think you have any comprehension." He turned to Carter who was helping one of the fellahs with his load. "Her ladyship finds our experiences amusing, Howard. Damned if I'm not of a mind to take her out there and have her taste it for herself. Would if I wasn't such a coward."

They both began to chuckle.

Ali, all the while, had been surreptitiously kicking sand over the dead serpents' bodies.

Ludwig Borchardt, a name that, second only to the French of Carter's earlier career, was to engender intense dislike within our hero's breast, had arrived in El Amarna during Carnarvon's abortive excavations in the delta. The man himself, distinguished as an Egyptologist for some years had, like so many who attain some populist recognition, built on the natural foundation of arrogance that is so characteristic of that nationality and obtained a reputation for bigotry that transcended even that of Carter. His excavations had met with little success that year and, hungry for the regular publicity to which he had grown accustomed, he looked for something that could make more of a statement. Something that would be lapped up by the German press and, perhaps, others.

He decided to build a reconstruction of an Egyptian villa of the Amarna period - a replica, as he imagined it, of one of the houses that Tutankhamen might have enjoyed as a child. Other than the ground plan he did not know what such a building should look like. But that mattered little. Neither did the public and, after all, it was he who was the Egyptologist. He could construct what he liked. The layman would tacitly accept the personal endorsement of Ludwig Borchardt.

He employed a horde of labourers and set them to constructing his 'villa'. The site he chose for the building was on the tourist route to the two royal necropolis valleys. In such a location it was assured that most who visited the west bank would see it and be impressed with its insightful beauty. In other words, it could hardly be missed.

On the return trip from the delta, Carnarvon had elected to stay in Cairo to placate his wife, by now desperate for some home comforts. Carter continued on to his 'castle'.

When he disembarked on the west bank, Abdel was there to help him onto his donkey. The journey took its usual slow, ambulatory course through the green fields in the flood plain of the river and up the winding, dusty track to the mouth of The Valley of the Kings. Although Carter was tired from his journey, it would be a real pleasure to get back to the house he had built and the location on the threshold of his ultimate quarry. He drank in the familiar scenery as he approached. But, as they turned north, Carter caught sight of a vulgar, red construction.

He rubbed his eyes in disbelief. "Abdel!" he yelled, the sound of his voice echoing for a few seconds. "Abdel. What has happened here? Who built that... that thing?"

"The German master, sir. He who talks much and does little. Many men were employed. Very happy they were. There has been little work in the area this season, so they were glad of the opportunity. It is good, yes?"

"Bloody monstrosity. What the hell's it for? What's it s'posed t' be?"

"It is for the tourists, sir. He said it is a copy of a villa in El Amarna."

"Looks like a bloody tenement block. Bet they build things like that all over Berlin. Who d'you think's seen a villa of the Amarna period, Abdel? No one, that's who. Not even a reasonable illustration of one in any of the texts I have looked at. A combination of poor taste and the man's inept imagination is what we're looking at. Nothing more. It's a bloody disgrace. How could the Director General have allowed it?"

Fact was, Monsieur le Directeur himself was as yet unaware of the building's existence.

It was late April and Carter, in the sole company of his brandy, sat on the terrace of the Hotel Royal. It was early evening and he enjoyed his solitude. He contemplated the events of that day.

He had received and responded to several letters since she had left - sweet letters. He had kept them all, read and reread them from time to time when the mood took him. He rolled the crystal goblet between his palms and looked through it at the shards of glowing light thrown by the sunset.

Will she want to see me this summer? he thought. Will she be there or on her holiday excursions once again to some other country?

He had missed her so many times during his earlier summer visits to England. It had been his own fault. Absent-minded about matters not directly associated with the work at hand, he would never think to write advising her of his return. This time, to ensure that at some point during his leave their paths might cross, he would write sufficiently in advance of his leaving Egypt.

The reappearance of the waiter brought Carter back to the present. Poised delicately on the four fingers of the waiter's right hand was a silver salver, the yellow envelope of a telegram centred on it. Carter picked up the envelope and tipped the waiter. Tapping it on the edge of his wicker chair he tore off one edge, withdrew the slip of paper and unfolded it.

His earlier expression of pleasant contentment fell all at once into one of visible concern. "Waiter!" he shouted in Arabic. "Summon the concierge immediately. I must leave for England as soon as I can obtain a berth."

The spring in England that year was more colourful than he had remembered it. The exceptional precipitation of the winter months had, it seemed, enriched the ground with water sufficient to sustain, as it were, the lush jungles of the Amazon Basin. The rains were now gone and everything about him was growing. After the unyielding starkness of the desert environment to which Carter had become so accustomed, this blazing array of colour was like arc lights turned on in the darkness.

He took the train to Swaffham and secured a horse and carriage for the trip to Didlington Hall. The entire journey was a delight and the sight of the Hall after all these years filled his heart with emotion. The rhododendrons were just beginning to go past their prime, and the lawns were a brilliant, fresh green. But, as he got nearer, he could see that things were not quite as he had remembered them. The grass had not been cut for some time. Much of the shrubbery had remained unpruned that winter. The gardens were much overgrown. There was no evidence of outside activity.

He drew up at the front door, alighted from the carriage and walked up the steps. No one was there to open the door as he arrived. No one had been watching for him. He heard no lilting voices from the garden behind.

He knocked on the door. A stranger answered. A dour man in a black suit. 'Looks like an undertaker,' Carter thought.

"My name is Howard Carter," he announced.

"Ah. You were expected some weeks ago. Where have you been? We had given you up and were looking for another."

"I have come as quickly as I could. I was in Egypt, y' know."

"Better late than never, I am sure her Ladyship would have said, but now you're here you'd better get about your business right quick. The vultures are at the door."

"Are her ladyship or his lordship present?"

"Gone this long since, Mr Carter. Living with friends in Marylebone. You are to report to his lordship when you have finished here. I will give you the address."

Carter couldn't believe it. He was standing in a house that, once vibrant with aristocratic life, was now filled with sheet-draped furniture, insects and little else but Egyptian ghosts. He could still hear the echoes of Lady Amherst's children playing on the terrace, and Amherst's authoritative instruction in the library. Where had it all gone? How had it all gone?

'Nothing is forever', he contemplated sadly.

Carter took out his notebook and walked into the library to begin cataloguing and valuing. He was by now far more knowledgeable than Lord Amherst himself, hence Carter's selection as valuer and adviser to the auctioneers. The experience he had gained in purchasing antiquities on the Cairo market and his total grasp of Egyptian art and period made him eminently suitable to maximise the value of the collection for the forthcoming sale. It was, after all, the very least he could do for them. In the misery of bankruptcy, they needed to have someone they could trust working in their best interests. He attacked the task with energy and not inconsiderable sadness.

For the time being at least, he had forgotten Dorothy Dalgliesh. She knew he was in the country but had no idea where he was or what he was doing. She waited for a letter.

Chapter Eleven
The Seventieth Day

By midnight, all the funerary barques had been assembled inside the processional harbour which lay before the great western pylon of the temple of Karnak. In the moonlight the graceful hooked prows cast dancing pale blue shadows on the water. Tall standards topped by long, narrow flags waved to the slow roll of the boats like a giant forest of papyrus reeds rippling in the wind. Other than the occasional creak of straining wood, the fleet kept its neatly tethered position in silence.

So did the palace guard. Early that morning, before sunrise, a large contingent of brightly tunicked warriors had assembled. They arranged themselves in double ranks, lining four avenues which, nearer the harbour, joined together and thereafter continued as a single corridor to the point of embarkation. The four avenues extended from different buildings, one from the temple of Karnak, a second from the foundry door, another from the structure which housed most of the funerary equipment, and the fourth from the temple of Mut which lay some four hundred cubits to the southwest.

The soldiers stood silent. A long duty lay ahead of them.

A long duty also lay ahead of the royal widow. In the early hours she was awakened by Tia. After refreshing her with incense, cooled water to drink and freshly peeled fruits, she preceded the queen to the bathing chamber where the junior maidservants would wash her and annoint her skin with softening oils and perfumes. Her make-up was simple - just the customery dark outline to the eyes; the blackened eyebrows; and a delicate enhancement of the eyelid. Then her clothing - two pieces of diaphanous white, pleated linen joined at the waist. The dress extended to her ankles, open at the front. The material was gathered tight about her waist with a broad, long, red linen sash tied in a bow and falling to her feet. The upper part fully covered her breasts, her back and her shoulders, draping to her elbows. Her forearms and a small portion of the left and right sides of her midriff remained bare. She wore nothing beneath. On her feet they placed gilded rush sandals. Then the wig - her favourite wig, the black hair, natural, most of it her own and the remainder her mother's, was plaited in narrow braids and gathered so as to fall over her head and hang naturally about it to her shoulders, leaving her ears visible and forming the perfect frame to her pretty face. To ensure the wig was secure, a narrow red sash was tied tightly about her forehead.

Then the jewellery. First, they set the royal diadem firmly on her wig. Large, gold, hooped earrings were threaded into her pierced ears. Slender tassles of varicoloured faience hung from each. The collarette of heavy gold and stones about her neck, normal at formal occasions within the palace confines, was today replaced by a light, broad collar of fresh spring flowers and leaves, delicately stitched together in colourful rows and tied in a knot at the back. Two glittering bangles encircled each of her forearms, two more on each of her wrists, and five gold rings on each hand.

The picture was complete.

Lit by a partial moon, the dark silhouette of the cliffs on the west bank stood out against the violet sky. As the sun neared the eastern horizon, the escarpment began to lighten, almost imperceptibly at first but later accelerating. With the break of dawn, the first long shadows stretched out towards the river in lean fingers, as if pointing the way.

Shattering the sleepy peacefulness of early sunrise, a cacophony of trumpets sounded from the temple pylon. Birds rose from their roosts - it seemed from everywhere - and filled the paling sky with chaotic, swirling, black swarms. The trumpets' single, shrill note sawed through the air and echoed back from the west bank cliffs as if to awaken the innermost reaches of the necropolis itself. The note ceased as suddenly as it had come and, as the echoes faded away, with a loud creaking the huge cedar doors of the temples eased open.

Within the dromos of the great pylon of the temple of Karnak, utterly dwarfed by its colossal proportions, stood the slight figure of Ankhesenamun. Flanking her on one side was Parannefer. The high priest was clothed in a simple linen tunic. Completely covering his head was the black, fired clay, dog-head headdress of Anubis. On her other side, her new husband - the diminutive, bent Ay. He was cloaked in a leopard skin and made up in the likeness of the god, Osiris. Each cradled a small mummy casket in their folded arms - Ankhesenamun's two stillborn children had been retrieved from the dark niche within the palace where they had lain these last few years. They were to take their final resting place close by their father.

Some distance away, within the threshold to the temple of Mut, in full general's ceremonial regalia stood the massive, oblate form of Horemheb.

A second blast from the trumpeters.

Soldiers pulled open the doors to the funerary stores and the foundry. In the dim light of early dawn, the glow of the dying fires still flickered from within.

A third note echoed across the river.

The processions began. The Karnak entourage was the first to move. Behind the chanting priest and the royal couple emerged the mummy bearers, four men in front and four behind, between them the large, open, four-posted, gilded shrine supported on a wooden sled. The canopy above it was surrounded all about its top with repeated, brightly coloured cobra heads. The mummy lay open to view beneath, lying on a low bed. The brilliance of the golden mask on the mummy's head was at first subdued in the shade thrown by the canopy. Its black eyes stared hypnotically skyward. Three necklaces of gold disks and beads of blue glass surrounded the neck. A crimson outer shroud now covered the mummy bandages. Securing the mummy shroud and equally spaced from the ankles to the chest were four bands of inscribed gold, inlaid with coloured glass and semi-precious stones. A broader fifth band extended the length of the body to the feet. Crossed on the chest were false hands of sheet gold enclosing the crook and flail within their clenched fists. Between them lay a large black resin scarab, a heron carved into its carapace. Below the hands lay the human-headed, gold Ba bird with wings outstretched. Colourful garlands and bouquets of spring flowers, large and small, covered every part of the funeral cortège.

The shrine was followed by two lesser priests. They held a stretcher bearing several sealed alabaster jars, each containing holy fluids.

As the temple procession embarked on its journey down the corridor lined by the rigid palace guard, there was a fourth blast from the trumpeters.

Four bearers emerged from the funerary building. They carried a long, low, gilded shrine supported on two long horizontal poles, a bearer at each corner. On the roof of the shrine, lying elegantly with forelegs outstretched and head held erect, and with a crisp, white linen shawl about its neck, reclined the dark and unmistakable profile of the black jackal. As was the custom, Meneg walked in front. The honour was to the maker.

Behind followed the canopic chest borne on two cedar stakes, the brilliant whiteness of the calcite box hidden from view under a linen cloth. Behind this followed six stretchers, the first two with the gilded wood panels that would be used to construct the shrine over the canopic chest; on each of the other four, lying upon beds of linen, exquisite gilded statues of the four protective goddesses that were to surround the king's organs with their embrace - Neith of the north, Nephthys of the east, Isis of the west, and Selket of the south. Following them, a seemingly endless line of bearers carrying a multitude of articles - wooden boxes, small wooden shrines, inlaid caskets, and a host of model boats of various sizes. At the rear of the procession was a large gilded head of the god Hathor, the cow, its long, curved, black horns contrasting starkly with the glittering gold. It, too, had a white linen scarf about its neck.

A fifth blast from the heralds on the temple pylon.

There was a brief sense of movement in the shadows within the foundry and then, as the first bearers emerged from the doorway, the early morning sunlight caught the roof of a diminutive golden shrine as it was carried out to begin its journey to the waiting flotilla. The gold sheeting that covered the tiny shrine had been engraved all over and the facets raised by the artist's hand reflected the sun's rays in starbursts, momentarily blinding any who took the time to steal a look. Within the shrine and, the doors now being sealed, hidden from view, stood that which Ankhesenamun had blessed the night before - the pure gold statuette in the likeness of the boy king - and, alongside it, the rolled papyrus containing 'The Chapters of Coming Forth by Day', the spells that Tutankhamun would need to guarantee his spirit's safe passage through the tortuous labyrinth of the underworld.

Following behind, each preceded by a massive, gilded, bestial bed dragged on a sledge by two men, advanced the three great coffins. The first of these was brilliantly gilded and so large as to appear cast for a giant. The second was encrusted with a complex mosaic of varicoloured glasses inlaid in gold. Then came the last: although the smallest of the three, it took eight strong men to bear it. The massive casket of solid bullion rested on a stout wooden stretcher. Dashir, as master goldsmith the artisan responsible for most of the workmanship, walked in the place of honour at the front.

The engraved and inlaid gold shone bright orange in the morning sun. About the torso two vultures, brightly coloured with glass cloisonné, held the arms and shoulders in a protective embrace. Below the hips, two goddesses held the legs close within their spread wings. A third kneeled at the foot, raising her wings in protection.

These three pieces - their regal beauty, the riches and artistic skill that they embodied - were but a theological normality to the community that fashioned them; splendour beyond all comprehension to those who had not.

The last pieces in this column were the huge dismantled panels that would ultimately form the four protective shrines nested one within the other over the sarcophagus itself. Twelve walls, four sets of doors, and four roofs of gilded wood were supported on individual stretchers, the last of these bearing the parts of a frame that ultimately would support a gold-studded linen pall.

As the foundry doors closed behind the coffin procession, the trumpeters sounded yet again. Once more birds swarmed into the sky in all directions.

The patiently waiting entourage at the temple of Mut at last began its slow walk along the avenue leading to the southern pylons of Karnak. Beside the general walked Vizier Nakht and behind them marched a troupe of nineteen young female dancers, one for each year of Tutankhamun's life, and a smaller group of musicians, each rhythmically shaking a tinkling sistrum. Apart from their dark wigs and colourful necklaces, the dancers were naked to the waist.

Horemheb had picked them out from the palace entertainers himself. He had taken some considerable time to delicately match their heights, slim waists and small, firm breasts. His attention to their beauty in the pageant was secondary. He had promised that, should their artistry please he would honour each of them with a summons to dance privately before him in his chambers, followed no doubt by a night in his bed. This was not necessarily all bad. It had occurred to most that the lustful union could result in their bearing a child, the offspring of a high official no less, perhaps ultimately even Pharaoh himself, thereafter to enjoy the favoured status that came with that lucky outcome.

The girls wore simple, unpleated, white linen skirts, translucent in the twilight of early morning, and brightly coloured, thonged sandals. Each carried a small basket of flowers and garlands. They swayed as they marched, tossing the long tresses of their wigs from side to side in unison, one with the other.

Horemheb glanced back at them and smiled contentedly. Some pleasure awaited at the end of these tedious celebrations, if only he could keep himself from growing too tired.

The rear of the procession was brought up by officials, each bearing gifts for the future life of the departed king: Nakhtmin, Horemheb's second in command; Maya, the court treasurer and highly respected architect of Tutankhamun's funeral; Usermont and Pentu, the prime ministers of the Upper and Lower Nile; a number of other dignitaries; and ten men carrying platters and parcels of vegetables, bread and fruit, with an equal number of older women balancing pitchers of wine, beer and water on their heads.

The procession continued towards Karnak.

With a final blast from the heralds, and another flock of frantic birds, another line of bearers was dispatched from the funerary stores. Leading the column was an upright life-size statue of a sentinel bearing a gilded royal headdress and wearing a gilded tunic. Contrasting starkly with the gold, the unclothed parts had been repainted with a thick black resin symbolising death.

Following this - some on stretchers, some suspended either side of yokes stretched across the strong backs of scantily clad workers - were beds, chariots, more caskets, ornamental objects, games, boxes, bows, boats, pots and jars of alabaster and calcite, baskets, staves, weaponry of many kinds, seats and thrones. Most glittered with gold. The objects were those that would have accompanied the king in his normal daily life, here and now all brought together for him to draw on as his needs required during the life that was to follow. One after another, the stretchers all neatly stacked with the stuff of life came out of the funerary stores and snaked slowly between the columns of soldiers on their way down to the wharfside. At last the final stretcher emerged, bearing a second sentinel in most details identical with the first.

The cedar doors were pulled shut.

As if sucked into a vortex formed by the flow of the processions through the corridors of guards, the last in the double lines flanking the roadway moved in to march at the rear of the procession.

The far end of the entire processional was by now well out of sight, assembling at the bay of embarkation. The boats were already filling, indeed, the first two with the treasures that had led the great parade were already being delicately manoeuvred into the current. With their sails reefed the oarsmen steered the craft directly across the river towards the west bank.

On the opposite side, the white tunics of the reception party could be clearly picked out in the brightening sunlight. Ugele was among them, his muscular black body silhouetted against the phalanx of white surrounding him. He and his stonemason colleagues stood expectantly on the levee. They waited to help tow the arriving barques along the inland irrigation canal that reached through the green fields to the very edge of the desert.

From this point, the processional colonnade moved through manicured gardens towards the magnificent spectacle of the three terraced mortuary temples nestling within the embrace of the golden cliffs, now lit brightly by the early sun. To the south, standing well apart from one another, stood the lesser mortuary temples of Pharaoh's Tuthmose III and IV and, further away still but dominating the skyline, the massive temple of Pharaoh Amenhotep III.

From the mooring at the end of the canal it was about three miles' walk to the tomb. The track to The Valley wound its way north then west and finally southwards in a great arc. It would take the leaders of the processional more than an hour to ascend the incline and reach the threshold.

One by one the fleet drew alongside the west bank wharf and waited their turn to be pulled up the canal. One by one at the unloading point the processions resumed their orderly progress - now a single, sinuous mass of people and goods punctuated only by the gaps created by the time it took for each ship to unload its precious cargo. The guard took up the rear. The grand parade stretched over a mile, the one end unable to see the other.

It was now approaching midday. In The Valley itself there was little in the way of shelter from the unrelenting sun. As Meneg neared the tomb, the crags of the valley sides continued to grow and steepen above him. He felt a desperate fatigue building within his ageing limbs. The dog on the shrine was a lot heavier now than it had seemed at the start of his journey. He was fit to drop where he stood.

Then he caught sight of the smoke. A smile of relief broke across his face. They were close now. Just a few more steps. A freshly slaughtered calf was roasting on a blazing fire close to the tomb. Its burning fat created a thick, black pall that drifted down The Valley on a descending breeze. The rich odour pulled him onwards.

The Pharaoh's entourage arrived at the tomb entrance first. Two oxen had towed the sled from the canal wharf. The great rocking canopy that housed the mummy of the king came to a halt. The mummy was removed and set to one side on its bier beside the queen and beneath a portable cloth canopy supported by four of the palace servant girls. The queen sat down on a folding stool to await the coffin procession. A Nubian boy fanned her lightly with ostrich feathers arranged at the top of a long golden stave. While she rested, the bearers disassembled the mummy canopy and carried the parts into the tomb. The oxen were led away. Out of sight of the funeral party they were slaughtered, dressed, and readied for the spit. Preparations for the forthcoming feast were well under way.

Meneg and his four colleagues at last arrived at the entrance and set their burden down on the gravel. The old wood carver stretched his aching arms and sat down with his friends on a convenient boulder.

The following canopic chest continued past them and was delicately manoeuvred down the steps and into the gently inclined corridor of the tomb. In the furthest chamber, standing against the rear wall, was the reassembled canopy that had protected the mummy on its journey across the river. The bearers gently laid the chest within it, checked its orientation and replaced the linen pall.

More stretcher-bearers brought in the walls of the shrine and busied themselves with its assembly. When it was complete, the four goddesses were carried in and placed gently within their prepared footprints fronting each wall. Their arms outstretched towards the corners, they surrounded their precious cargo in a protective embrace. For the first time, the artisans could view the object that they had spent the last two months fashioning fully assembled - now in its appointed place for eternity. It occurred to more than one of them that, if history were anything to go by, its physical existence in this place likely would be something less than eternal.

Boxes, boats and caskets followed; a multitude of them, carried in one by one and placed in orderly fashion against the walls. The Hathor cow was brought in and set down at the front of the shrine, facing the doorway.

At last it was time for Meneg and his colleagues to carry in the shrine of Anubis. It was not easy to manoeuvre in the confined width of the first chamber. They positioned themselves between the poles that bore the shrine and, tilting it a little, managed to negotiate the turn to the right and gently placed the jackal in position on the threshold of the treasure room, staring outwards at the as yet empty, waiting sarcophagus. As his friends withdrew, Meneg took a solemn moment for a last look at the piece that in its creation had caused him so much grief.

The sharp, erect, gilded ears flickered in the light of the oil lamps and threw dim, waving shadows on the chamber walls. Apart from a little glint from the eyes and a faintest suggestion of a glimmer at the tip of the long snout, the black beast melted into the pervasive gloom. He reached out and touched one of the paws. Although he couldn't see it he could feel what he alone had made and a sense of fulfilment welled within him. For ever now it would gaze on the boy king.

The noise from outside reminded Meneg that he had overstayed his time within the sepulchre. The coffin procession had arrived. The most holy part of the ceremony was about to begin. This was the burial of a king, and to dally more within this holy place and interrupt the orderly flow of the proceedings could be a capital offence. The old man pulled himself up into the antechamber and scrambled for the exit as fast as his tired legs would carry him.

But he was too late. As he emerged from the corridor at the bottom of the entrance stairway he spied the lead bearers of the outer coffin advancing backwards down the stairs. Before anyone could see him, Meneg turned and retreated down the corridor once more. He had to hide, at least for the time being, until he could find the right moment to exit unnoticed. He stumbled across the vacant floor of the antechamber to the small opening which led into the adjacent ancillary store room. Dropping flat to the floor, he hurriedly dragged himself through it. Unfortunately for Meneg his friend and colleague, Ugele, who had directed the fashioning of this place, had never taken the time to explain the architecture of the tomb to him and the old wood carver was quite unaware that the floor to this room was over two cubits below that of the first chamber. In his scrambling urgency he propelled himself into the small room headlong and fell unceremoniously to the floor, striking his head on the limestone and knocking himself out cold.

Unaware of the old artisan, the coffin bearers entered the tomb with the first and largest casket. It was manoeuvred through the entrance to the burial chamber and laid on a slack double sling adjacent to the sarcophagus, its head towards the west.

As soon as the bearers had left, a group of engineers entered the tomb. Using stout beams of wood, substantial ropes and crude pulleys they set about erecting a makeshift gantry. Its purpose was to lift the finally assembled coffins and mummy in their entirety and lower them safely into the sarcophagus. The gantry, built like a housing above the outer coffin, was mounted on two sleds, one at either end, resting on loose, horizontal poles. The poles acted as rollers, allowing the makeshift structure to pass clear of the ends of the sarcophagus as it was moved over it.

While the engineers completed their task, the two remaining coffins were brought into the tomb and laid in sequence beside the first - again each of the bases laid on two slings.

Outside, the sun was about to touch the lip of the escarpment and bathe the bottom of The Valley in afternoon shadow. As it did so, Horemheb's entourage arrived at the tomb entrance.

The royal party now assembled, the musicians arranged themselves in an arc and began to play. The girls ran to the centre of the arc and responded to the music with a slow, melancholy, swaying dance. The solemnity was lost on Horemheb, who instead found their movements sensual and was soon rapt by their performance. He warmed with anticipation.

In the shade provided by the queen's canopy, Parannefer and one other raised the rigid mummy until it stood upright. Now taller than he had been in life, the mummy of Tutankhamun looked down on everyone. It positively towered above Ay. The old Pharaoh raised his head and squinted as he tried to look upon it, but the highly polished metalwork of the mask magnified the brilliance of the sun and at once he had to close his eyes and turn away.

The Anubis-headed priest supported the mummy from behind while Ay, looking downwards, stood before it. In his hand he held a small crook-like instrument. The music suddenly stopped. The dancing stopped. The dancers began to utter a low moan. The moan gradually rose in pitch until it became a high, wavering, shrill and piercingly long note reverberating within the valley walls. Ay, now acting as Horus to Tutankhamun's Osiris and thereby claiming ascendancy, symbolically gestured with the instrument close to the mouth of the mask. The wailing grew all the louder, the mummy 'spoke', the ka of Tutankhamun was released, and the ascendancy was confirmed.

The roasted calf had been dismembered. The butchered oxen were now on the fire. The food bearers moved forwards to the mummy. A great tray of offerings of meat, vegetables, fruit, stuffed duck and goose, bread, beer and date wine was spread at its foot so that the dead king could take sustenance before embarking on his eternal journey.

The silence was punctuated only by the crackle of the nearby spit as the mummy took its meal, and all those present closed their eyes and bowed their heads. After a suitable pause, Parannefer waved the offerings away.

Now it was the widow's moment. Ankhesenamun would hold a last communion with her dead husband. She came slowly forward and knelt before the mummy. Clasping it firmly around the hips, she drew the crimson body to her and pressed her lips hard against the vertical gold strap that ran to the mummy's feet - a gesture symbolic of drawing new life from its reincarnated spirit. The embrace lingered. The high priest gestured. Tia moved forward and touched the queen's shoulder. She slowly, reluctantly, released, and the mummy was laid back to rest once more on its low bed.

Two of the lesser priests took hold of opposite ends of the king's bier and, with some evident difficulty, carried the body carefully down the steps and into the tomb.

It was for the queen to follow, but before she did so Ankhesenamun bent down to open the box containing the two mummified bodies of her stillborn children. She lifted the lid of the tiny, nested coffins of the younger child and regarded the pathetic linen bundle inside. It barely filled half the available space. Carefully removing the small gilded mask, she leant over and tenderly kissed the head of the bundle, then gently covered the head again with the mask and replaced the coffin lids.

She opened the coffin set of the second diminutive body, removed the mask and once again embraced the tightly wrapped bundle. She paused. From the palm of her hand the tiny golden face stared fixedly upwards. It all came flooding back - the feelings of remorse. Through their silent deaths, so much has been lost, she thought.

Tears stained her make-up. She began to shake. Impulsively she covered her face with her hands. In the flood of emotion she didn't feel the mask slip from her fingers. She sobbed out loud. Tia reassembled the coffin lids, replaced both within the box which had held them and secured it. Gently she coaxed the queen to her feet and led her to the entrance of the tomb.

On the threshold of the burial chamber and in the glimmering light of the oil lamps the priests lifted the mummy from its bier and reverently placed it within the lower portion of the gold coffin. The bier itself they laid within the sarcophagus.

Followed by Tia, who carried the box containing the mummified children, the queen walked by the sarcophagus into the entrance to the treasury and, saying a short prayer, directed her senior maidservant to place the small burden before the Anubis shrine so that it would lie under the watchful eye and protection of the jackal. She took one step back, one long last look, and withdrew to the foot of the open gold coffin.

Those who were to witness or assist in the sealing of the coffins filed into the tomb behind the priests. As they descended the steps, the cooling cloak of early evening covered The Valley in twilight. Outside, the dancers continued their swaying. Their wailing was somewhat softer now and the rhythm of tinkling percussion filled the huge amphitheatre of The Valley. As the small party of mourners disappeared below ground level, the sounds gradually faded until they were but a lilting whisper to those within.

The priests appeared at the entrance to the chamber. Each carried two large jars of scented oils. They placed them at the feet of the queen. In this confined space were now gathered the four priests, Ankhesenamun, Ay, Horemheb - each attended by a servant girl - and, carrying linens and flowers of several varieties, ten labourers dressed in pure white tunics along with their supervisor, Rashid.

As Parannefer chanted a prayer, another priest took a scoop of oil from one of the jars and began to pour it slowly over the feet of the mummy shroud. Ladleful after ladleful, he worked his way up the body, stopping at the false hands. The mummy shroud progressively blackened as the unguents soaked into the fibres. The resinous liquid ran thickly over the shroud to find its own level, filling the gap between the mummy and the walls of the coffin. The dark fluid worked its way around and between the mummy mask and the back of the king's head - the body virtually floated in the annointing oils.

On a signal from Parannefer, Rashid gave an order to his men. They looped ropes through the carrying handles on the golden mummiform lid and slowly raised it until it was suspended above the lower portion of the casket and the mummy itself.

After another short prayer, the men lowered the lid into place. The silver tongues that would attach the lid firmly to its mate slotted comfortably into the mortices provided for them. As the lid connected with its base there was an echoing 'clunk', amplified within the confining rock walls. Tutankhamun's mummy had disappeared from from the sight of mortals for ever.

The men hammered small gold pins through the coffin wall and into the silver dovetails now snug within the casing. Then they inserted poles into the loops at the ends of the slings which lay underneath the coffin and carefully took the weight of the massive gold body. Testing one another's balance, they took the strain. The first coffin was slowly laid within the base of the second.

The prayers continued. In the relative stillness of the chamber the sounds of the musicians and dancers outside the tomb were barely audible. The Anubis-headed priest took another ladle of annointing oil and, beginning once more at the feet, ceremoniously poured the glutinous unction over the casket all the way up to the hands. The golden shine that had until then sparkled in the flickering light of the oil lamps gradually dulled. The holy unguent slowly rose within the well of the lower casket until it reached within an inch or two of the lip.

Finally, the jars were empty.

Each royal member of the small congregation then took it in turns to place a floral or fruit remembrance on the chest of the annointed coffin. Ankhesenamun was the last, positioning a wide collar of blue glass beads delicately upon the upper chest. As she withdrew, the priest took a crimson linen sheet, folded so that it would fit the coffin lengthways, and tucked it tightly around the gold casket. As he stabbed his fingers around the edges, he felt the material soak up the fatty oils. He wiped his hands briskly on his tunic and signalled to the labourers' supervisor.

Rashid gestured to his men. Four of them came forward to lift the lid of the second coffin and carefully position it on its base. The men attached the lid with pins just as they had done the first.

The weight of the two coffins together was now considerable. It took all ten labourers to lift it on its slings and lower it into the base of the third coffin. With the second coffin safe within the outer coffin base, the labourers cut the slings that had been supporting it and withdrew the linen from beneath.

The queen came forward and laid a tiny circlet of olive leaves on the uraeus at the coffin's forehead. As she stepped back, the head man of the work team handed a folded cloth to the two priests, then backed away slowly with his head bowed. Unfolding it between them, the two laid it over the colourful coffin lid and, beginning at the feet, set about neatly tucking it in. The shroud ended up so tight that it revealed the contours of the casket, the hands, the tip of the stylised beard, the shape of the nemes headdress, even the nose itself.

It was Horemheb's duty to lay a single necklace of olive leaves about the neck of the enshrouded mummy case. Pharaoh's successor, Ay, followed, steadied by a priest. His arms laden with delicate garlands of spring flowers, he laid them one by one across the shroud, murmuring low, unintelligible incantations. He decorated the body from its neck to below the crossed arms and stepped back.

The final tribute came from the widow. She held a tiny floral wreath in her hands about the size of a bracelet. In the dim light of the chamber, like the others, it had no colour. Like the others it was made of folded olive leaves, sewn together in a circlet, each leaf capturing a tiny spray of spring cornflowers and blue lotus petals. Gently she laid the tiny garland over the lump in the shroud that reflected the uraeus beneath.

The royal entourage stood back and the labourers took up the final coffin lid and laid it exactly on its base. The pins were tamped home and, with no audible command, the queen and her royal party turned together, left the burial chamber and walked silently back to the surface.

The priests, the queen, the Pharaoh and the general went out to take refreshment, food and music. The labourers were left inside to complete the physically demanding task of securing the entirety of the coffin set within the sarcophagus and then constructing the shrine around it.

Ankhesenamun, Ay and Horemheb emerged from the tomb. The sun was gone, the moonless sky an indigo blue. But for the roaring fires of the feast lighting up the valley sides with boiling flashes of red ochre and gold, The Valley would have been in total darkness.

The beat of the music, which had taken a slower turn during their time below ground, now picked up. It was a happy time; a time for celebration. The king had been embarked successfully on his journey. Servant girls rushed forward with trays of food, cooked meat, vegetables, fruit, trays of water, beer and date wine. The general took the wine and gazed leeringly at the assembled dancers. The queen took some fruit and stood beneath her canopy, her eyes cast solemnly downwards. And Pharaoh, assisted by one of his manservants, sat down in a folding chair, took some water and hoped he could fall asleep and that no one would notice.

Within the lowest empty chamber of the tomb a body stirred. Meneg had recovered his senses. Although his head ached his fearful mind was alert and focused on how he might extricate himself from this place without being detected. The ringing in his ears was entirely secondary. He heard voices. He pulled himself close by the entrance to the storeroom into which he had fallen and squinted to the left to see if he could catch sight of what was going on in the burial chamber. He was relieved to see that those of any status had left, at least for the time being. Noticing that the workers were concentrating entirely on their task, he took the risk of pulling himself up sufficiently to obtain a better view. He could clearly hear their conversation.

The coffin set had been successfully laid to rest on the low bier inside the stone sarcophagus. The exhausted workers quickly tucked two linen sheets tightly about the outer coffin and then turned to dismantling the gantry. Their next task was to lift the stone lid and position it securely in its place. The lid was heavy, but less heavy than the coffin set and easier to manage so, notwithstanding their fatigue, they accomplished the task with relative ease.

Taking some considerable trouble to centre the stone lid correctly, they began to lower it so that the carrying poles rested on the head end of the sarcophagus. This done, they slowly slid the poles out from under it, easing the head end into the open lip. Finally they pulled the poles clear.

Rashid saw the problem first. The toe end of the lid was resting on the foot of the outer coffin which was standing just proud of the lip of the sarcophagus. For a moment all froze in stunned alarm. They stared at it, trying to think what to do next.

Rashid whispered sharply, "Get it off! Quick! There is little time! The coffin is too big. We shall have to cut down the foot."

The men reinserted their carrying poles into the open end of the lid and levered it up. In their careless haste, one of the poles slid sideways. The imbalance of weight forced the other to slide out on the opposite side and the lid fell back onto the coffin foot, cracking along the old, repaired fissure. The copper dovetail that had held the two broken halves together popped out and fell onto the shroud beneath. In the confinement of the burial chamber the break sounded like a clap of thunder. Rashid could only hope that the music above ground would drown out the noise.

"May Hathor plug your cow's teats!" Rashid's yelling at his men was suppressed, but yelling nonetheless. He whispered emphatically, "What are we to do now? We shall all be impaled by Pharaoh. An agonising and eternal death awaits! Osiris protect us!"

The tired workers looked one to the other and to their master back and forth for some moments. Then one of them spoke up.

"Master, Pharaoh will not have heard us. The break is still clean and it is dark in this place. We can repaint the crack. No one will notice. Let us be quick."

Rashid accepted the proposal immediately. The alternative was, after all, unthinkable. "Remove this end and the linen quickly and shave the foot of the coffin so that it will fit when replaced. Come on. Come on!" He gestured wildly in the gloom.

Their energy rekindled with the adrenalin of fear, six of them removed the two broken halves of the lid. Another picked up the loosened dovetail and pulled the shroud off the bottom half of the coffin. Two others used an adze on the foot.

"Enough! Enough!" Rashid flapped his arms at the men before they did too much unnecessary damage. "Replace the lid. Quickly! Quickly! You two clean up the mess." Rashid recalled the pots of holy oils in the corner and pointed to them. "Wait! First pour some of that over the foot. Perhaps that will absolve us of the misery of our errors and inculcate the Gods of our innocent intentions."

The broken lid sat perfectly within the rim of the box this time. With some haste, one of the men painted over the clean fracture, giving it some semblance of normality. Truly, in the poorly lit room the repair was not noticeable.

The men gathered up the disassembled wooden members that had made up the gantry and threw them unceremoniously towards the tomb doorway. Assembly of the four shrines was next. These they now had to put together in sequence, one inside the other, to complete the sacred golden structures that would house and protect the sarcophagus.

"Quickly!" urged Rashid in a strong but low voice. "We shall all be punished if we do not leave this place by the time Pharaoh returns."

In his anxiety to make up for lost time Rashid chose not to supervise his men's efforts but rather stand on one side of the sarcophagus and take up a mallet himself. The various panels that would make up the shrines had been stacked against one wall in reverse order, the smallest outward. The four walls of the innermost shrine were quickly passed among the men surrounding the sarcophagus.

Unfortunately, with Rashid helping in the assembly of the shrine rather than supervising the construction, symbols painted on each panel, being in any case illegible to his illiterate team, went unnoticed. It soon became clear that the walls were not fitting together precisely and the chamber became loud with the frantic hammering of mallets as the mismatched corners were bludgeoned together.

The first and second shrines were, in this way, crudely engineered into place. Then the third shrine was quickly assembled and the roof manhandled into place. The canopy frame was constructed over it and, taking a corner each, four of Rashid's men draped the studded linen pall over the fragile framework. The fourth and final shrine was then forcibly assembled and the roof bashed into place by the hammerings of sixteen frantic hands.

The job was done. The entire nest of shrines, awkwardly botched in places but to all but a detailed inspection perfectly constructed, stood firmly in position. All was well. The Pharaoh had not reappeared. Either they had made up some time or Ay had fallen asleep again and the others at the surface were having too good a time to notice.

As Rashid and his team prepared to leave, they stopped short. The dark silhouette of a man stood between the labourers and their exit. Believing the shadow to be that of a royal guard, Rashid broke into a cold sweat and fell to his knees.

The shadow spoke. "Help me out of here, Rashid, I implore you. If discovered I am a dead man."

At the sound of Meneg's voice Rashid was greatly relieved. "My dear friend," he began. "You frightened me. But what have you been doing so long within the tomb?"

Meneg told his embarrassing story.

"This is not good. If they catch you they will assume you to have been plotting robbery. You are in much danger, my friend. But we also are late and must exit with haste. I cannot hide you. They will count us out as they counted us in. There is no way for me to do this."

"We can run out as a group. Chances are by now they will not be of a mind to pay sufficient attention to count us. If I left on my own, however, I would be easily recognised. You must allow me to join with your group."

"If we are discovered with you we could all be put to death. I cannot. I love you Meneg but I cannot."

The old master carpenter stood back so that the light from one of the oil lamps threw deep, menacing shadows across the features of his face.

"You are artisans are you not, Rashid - you and your men?"

"That we are - and very proud of our work. Look, Meneg, I'm sorry about this but time is short and we have to go. Please do not hold us up any longer. We must go. You must take your own chances."

"So you would leave this botched job for me to confess to Pharaoh under torture? Is that what you want?"

Rashid, in the act of pushing past Meneg, stopped in his tracks. "You would never betray us, Meneg. You would not... would you?"

"Would I? How do I know what I might say in the agony of torture?"

Rashid didn't give the matter a second's thought. The party picked up their equipment and, with Meneg partially hidden in the centre of the pack, left in a hurry. In the confusion and disarray of their departure, the tired soldiers - who had in any case found more interest in watching the dancing - gave the scrambling group no more than a cursory look.

Rashid and his gang pushed through the cordon and ran down the valley track back towards the river. Meneg, once satisfied he was out of sight, stopped. He sat upon a rock and watched the illuminated festivities from a safe distance. He waited his turn. His ordeal was not yet over.

In the light of the dying fire that had roasted the calf and oxen, the priests signalled to all that the final rituals in the burial procedure must now begin. They led the queen, the Pharaoh and the general down into the tomb one last time. As they entered the empty room that opened onto the burial chamber, the masons were just completing the wall which, but for a remaining doorway, now separated the first chamber from that containing the king's remains.

The queen, carrying a bouquet of olive leaves, was assisted down into the sepulchre, the priests following close behind. Each of them held a small magical object. The room was for all practical purposes completely filled with the outermost golden shrine. Just a narrow passageway remained around its perimeter. Working her way around the chamber clockwise, she stopped beside a small cavity cut into the wall near the first corner. She placed the bouquet on the floor in the corner and turned to take the first object, a djed pillar, from the priest behind her. Carefully she placed it in the tiny niche.

189

A second cavity was positioned about halfway along the next wall opposite the head of the sarcophagus. She placed a small model of Anubis here.

The third cavity was positioned in the wall opposite the first. Here she placed an ushabti effigy of her husband.

The fourth was cut into the east wall about halfway between the door to the treasury and the south wall. The queen stopped momentarily to take a last look at the diminutive casket that lay on the floor below the outstretched forelegs of the black jackal. The proud head stared directly back at her. She pressed her fingers to her lips and bent down, touching the box gently.

Turning her back on it for the last time, she was helped out of the chamber, placing the last magical object, a small figure of Osiris, in its niche as she departed.

Each of those who followed, including the priests who continued their recitals of incantations, had some burden to deposit in a preordained place of significance on the floor of the burial chamber - golden sticks, jars, bundles of reeds and, most important of all, the paddles, ten of them, carefully placed in a row along the north wall, all there to help the king safely navigate his journey along the waters of the celestial Nile presently spread across the night sky high above them.

The Anubis-headed priest was the last to leave the sepulchre. Watched by the jackal himself, he squatted at the east end of the shrines and looked through the open doors of each at the sarcophagus inside. In solemn, slow actions he closed, bolted, tied and sealed each door in turn and, rubbing the remaining wet mud from his hands, departed this Pharaoh's presence for ever.

By the time the royal entourage had returned to the antechamber, the servant girls had laid out more food and drink on a cloth in the central part of the floor and everyone - the priests, the treasurer, the commander of the army under Horemheb, the general himself, the queen and the Pharaoh - seated themselves upon the folding stools provided. Having already eaten and drunk their fill above ground, their attention to the tomb feast at this time was little more than symbolic. And, while they nibbled, the painters put the finishing touches to the wall decoration inside the burial chamber.

Ankhesenamun wistfully watched the shadows thrown by the flickering oil lamps. Her mind drifted to the adjacent room and the huge golden canopy that surrounded the instrument of her husband's eternal journey. As the workers bricked up the doorway, she could make out the occasional flash of gold as the faint light caught a facet in the engraved surface of the huge shrine wall. But soon there was nothing. The last brick was in place, sealing off the burial chamber for ever.

A secondary priest summoned four men waiting at the top of the stairs. The plasterers filed into the chamber carrying broad, shallow baskets of wet mud. They at once took to plastering the doorway, smoothing the surface with their hands, then left as quickly as they had appeared.

Together the priests all rose from the feast. Each took a large seal stamp from the satchel secured about his waist. Beginning at the top of the walled - up doorway they took it in turns to make impressions. Every bit of the wet surface was covered. They made one last inspection to ensure that no portion of the wall had been missed and then withdrew to the outside.

This was a signal to the remaining members of the royal party to divest themselves of their funerary regalia. They removed their floral collars and let them drop to the floor amongst the debris of the feast. With some relief Parannefer eased the Anubis mask off his head and let it drop. It smashed into a thousand tiny fragments at his feet. The funeral party followed the high priest up the inclined passage to the steps and to the surface for the last time. The servants stayed behind in the chamber.

Those who remained below ground could hear the lilting music reaching down the corridor from outside. The servants began to dance. It was a stylised, circular dance. With exaggerated steps, they stamped on the dishes and cups left on the floor until everything was broken into tiny pieces.

They stopped their dancing and immediately set about cleaning up the debris. The floral tributes, the fragments of smashed earthenware and remains of the food were gathered into the centre of the large cloth. They brushed the floor of the chamber clean, pushing any additional refuse onto the cloth with their brooms. Then, breaking their brush handles in half across their knees, they tossed them onto the cloth along with the other funerary rubbish. Gathering it all up into one bundle, they carried it out of the tomb.

The two remaining accessible chambers were left clean and empty, ready to receive the last of the grave goods.

On the surface the royal group were re-established in their seats overlooking the dancers. As they moved to the rhythmn of the musicians the dancers were lit from behind by the roaring bonfires which warmed the cold night air and threw long, wildly moving shadows against the valley sides.

By this time each member at the funerary feast had had his or her fair share of alcohol. The dancing and singing became all the livelier and noisier. The Valley of the Dead vibrated with life.

Senefer, a servant at the earlier feast within the tomb, stood mesmerised by the joyful carousing. Standing at the top of the stairs with the clothful of feast remains gathered in his clasped fists, he watched the dancing shadows and brightly highlighted silhouettes bending and swaying to the beat of the music. He longed to become a part of it. As he gazed in wonderment at the spectacle before him, the brightly flickering firelight flashed off an object in the sand before him. He bent down and picked it up. It was a small gilded mask not much larger than a baby's head. For a moment he stared at the tiny golden face. He half thought about pocketing the object, but a sharp prod in the back from his supervisor brought him back to reality. He dropped the mask into his sack and moved on.

Senefer carried his burden along a track leading up a tributary valley and then turned off to the right to climb a short distance up the gravel slope towards a small pit which had been excavated specifically to accept the funerary rubbish. It would have been hard to find in the darkness of late evening had it not been for a colleague of his who had walked to the spot sometime earlier. Calling to his friend, Senefer found the place easily and together they busily set about stuffing the accumulated rubbish into several large, tall jars. Once the jars were full they sealed them as tightly as they could and stacked them neatly in one corner of the excavated cleft.

To conceal the deposit, the two dragged gravel down from above with their fingers until they were satisfied that the natural slope had been restored. The job done, they set off over the cliff for Pademi, wife and bed.

While the burial chamber closing had been taking place, the bearers on the surface, who had done little so far but stand dutifully beside the materials they had carried from the canal, once more took up their stretchers. The palace guard stood shoulder to shoulder the full length of the line, securing it on all sides as it wound back down The Valley.

The constellation of Orion now glittered high above them in the night sky. The filling of the remaining tomb chambers - as complete a supply of grave goods as any dead king might need to sustain him in his forthcoming travels - must be accomplished before dawn, thereby permitting Osiris to witness the entire proceedings.

The first objects to enter the tomb were items of food, drink and aromatic oils. These were placed on the floor at the small, low entrance to the chamber that Meneg had fallen into earlier. Two of the party slid down into the room and began taking the material from the doorway and stacking it against the north wall - jars of wine, of oils and unguents, cosmetics, and baskets of fruit - a storehouse that would have kept the labourers' personal households going for many a month.

The material bric-a-brac of life followed - chairs, model boats, beds, weaponry, boxes, games, musical instruments, items of ritual, tools, writing instruments, clothing - any objects that would fit with relative ease through the confining aperture, all stacked in orderly fashion and progressively filling the small chamber until there was space sufficient only for the two labourers who had been doing the stacking to scramble out through the small doorway.

The aperture was quickly bricked up, plastered with mud and sealed - a priest reluctantly returning from the festivities above for the purpose.

The procession of goods resumed. First to be introduced into the antechamber were the two black sentinels fashioned in the image of Tutankhamun. They were placed facing each other at either side of the sealed doorway to the burial chamber - eternal guards. Between them stood the tiny golden shrine enclosing the king's ka statue. Next followed the parts of the three ritual beds. These were carefully reassembled and placed head to toe in a line along the west wall of the entry chamber - boxed food, caskets and boxes of jewellery and clothing, alabaster and calcite ornaments, chairs, jars, games, lamps, musical instruments, tools, writing equipment, weaponry, disassembled chariot parts, and effigies of the Pharaoh - all neatly stacked in serried rows about the walls, beneath and on the beds. It all fitted to the very last piece.

At the top of the stairway a solitary, cloaked figure stood clutching an object close to his chest. Meneg, his earlier worries now at rest, had this one final honour. He had made one of the first and he had made the last of the grave goods to be placed with Tutankhamun: a small wooden carving of the head of the king as a child. He had fashioned it with the greatest care and love and he was to place this piece in the centre of the central bed facing the doorway. A headdress of gold and lapis enclosed the scalp. Small, pendulous vulture earrings of pure gold dangled from the ear lobes.

Alone he walked down the stone steps and disappeared into the dark corridor. As he approached the doorway to the first chamber, the glimmer of the flickering oil lamps gradually brightened. And when he stood at the threshold he found himself surrounded by the glitter of gold - gold chariots to the left, gold sentinels to the right, gold beds between; everywhere the glint of gold.

He blinked, then kissed the bust softly on the forehead and placed it in the centre of the bed in front of him. Stepping back, he took one last, long look. Truly this king had been buried with all the honours and the grave goods akin to those in the most elaborate of tombs. A tight fit. Not placed in spacious order as within the cavernous halls of Pharaoh Akhenaten but it was all there, just the same. The king had everything. That was what was most important.

Those large, boyish eyes, just as he had known them, stared serenely back into his. He remembered the night in the rain. He remembered the boy. And he thought on his good fortune.

But he was dallying again. He must leave this place. Swallowing hard, he reflected momentarily on his narrow escape just a few hours earlier and broke his solitary communion.

All who were above ground continued to engross themselves in the flowing bodies of the dancing girls. Except for the queen, none of them thought on the time Meneg was taking within the tomb. Ankhesenamun was anxious to complete the closure and be gone. She signalled to a lesser priest.

"The old master carpenter remains within," she said. "Bring him out at once. I wish to seal my husband's tomb."

Reluctantly, the priest turned away from the dancers and stumbled down the steps into the tomb. He slowed as he reached the bottom of the stairway, spying Meneg standing almost in the portal. He bent down so he could see the man's head. The wood carver was motionless, looking directly ahead, his hands at his side.

The priest leaned forward and touched Meneg lightly on the shoulder. The wood carver jumped and then turned. There were tears in his eyes.

"My best work," he whimpered. "My very best."

"Come, artisan. It is time."

The two scurried back up the steps. Meneg ran over to his artisan colleagues who were standing behind the musicians. He accepted the first jar of beer he was offered.

The priest returned to the queen's side. "The sepulchre is complete and no one abides within, your Majesty. We may begin the sealing at your Grace's pleasure." He turned his eyes back to the dancers.

Ankhesenamun slowly rose from her seat. The movement was a sign to all - the closing was at hand. The music died. The dancing stopped. The palace guard came to attention. The priests resumed a saintly posture. Horemheb took his lecherous eyes off the girls. Ay awoke.

The royal group assembled at the top of the steps and looked down into the darkness below. The oil lamps had been removed. There was nothing to see but impenetrable blackness. The bricklayers were already at work at the bottom of the corridor. Within an hour they had completed bricking up the doorway to the antechamber and were busying themselves with plastering the outer surface with a gypsum mud. The priests advanced down the stairs and with much lilting incantation stamped the wet plaster with their seals.

The door completely covered with impressions, a troop of the most trusted royal guard filed down the steps in twos until they reached the bottom of the passageway, filling it completely. The last two stood at the threshold to the stairway. This guard of honour would ensure the security of the tomb until the door had dried hard enough to take the weight of gravel that ultimatelty would fill the corridor.

This protective armament in place and the first glimmers of dawn once more gilding the peaks surrounding them, the royal entourage began the long walk back along the valley track to the canal and the waiting royal barques - sleep and expectation for Ankhesenamun, expectation and sleep for Horemheb, sleep and pray no dreams for Ay. The musicians and dancers followed. The guards remained.

Later on that second day the guards filed back up the stairway to make way for the leader of the work gang. Under the guards' watchful gaze he descended the steps and tested the plaster on the walled-up door for hardness. All was well. He ran back up the stairs and summoned his labourers to start collecting gravel. A line was soon formed on the steps and in the corridor. From one to another each man passed a basket of rubble down into the depths until the corridor was filled. It was midday before enough gravel and tomb chippings had been thrown into the cavity to bring the filling level with the bottom of the stairway.

The bricklayers were summoned from their uncomfortable slumbers on the rough valley track. Fresh mud had been brought from the flooded areas near the river and the workers set about plastering their brickwork, tossing baskets of gravel into the corridor as this last wall rose. Two very tired priests stumbled down the stairway to the newly plastered door to complete their final duty - stamping impressions of the regal and royal necropolis seals into the wet mud.

After the priests had left, the militia reassembled in the stairway and stood guard in the growing heat of the day. By the time the order to fill the stairway finally came, the sun had moved over to the west. The tomb stairway quietly simmered in the irradiating shade of the surrounding cliffs.

The soldiers threw the scraps of refuse that still remained after the night's feasting to the bottom of the steps and filled the cavity with gravel. Having restored the surface of the ground to its original profile, they shouldered their hoes and marched in double file to the boats awaiting them at the head of the canal. Behind, they left a group of fresh sentries standing at attention on the flank of the valley. But for a shapeless stain of slightly darker sand, all evidence of the tomb entrance had been erased. Beneath their feet and to their left a monarch in the eternal cycle of slumber and reincarnation lay amidst a treasure trove beyond all comprehension.

At least one of them had to wonder...

Chapter Twelve
Conscription

It was 1914, and the war to end all wars was about to start. Theodore Davis was no longer young and was in ill health. He had given all his energy, most of the latter years of his life and a sizeable chunk of his fortune to exhausting the secrets which remained within The Valley. He had explored every inch of it. He had even found the paltry pit tomb of the boy king, 'Touatankhamanou', as he called him - or so he believed. There was nothing left. Too tired to continue and with so little prospect of future discovery, he announced to the press and his colleagues at the Met that his life's work was finished. He declared The Valley empty, relinquished his concession and left Egypt for ever. He died a year later, peacefully complacent in his vindication.

Another distinguished career ended that year. But before Gaston Maspero closed his records at the Antiquities Service for the last time and handed over to his French successor, he had one happy, final duty.

He had felt immense personal satisfaction in bringing the wealthy aristocrat and the tenacious archaeologist together that day in the market. Since then the union had not exactly been without fruit, but, although Carter had worked tirelessly at all the sites they had excavated, until now he and his sponsor had been prevented from entering The Valley - the very target of Carter's ambitions. Now at last Maspero would have the pleasing task of opening up this opportunity to them.

Carnarvon and Carter arrived at Maspero's office on the dot of ten. The director welcomed them warmly, an unmistakably broad smile beneath that stained, tufty moustache. All three were beaming. The normally staid Carter could hardly contain himself and stuffed his hands hard into his pockets to keep himself from fidgeting. Carnarvon was outwardly more relaxed, expressing the controlled appearance that is the legacy of a lifetime of traditional behaviours. But, much as a child, inside he bubbled with anticipation.

They each took a seat across the desk from Maspero. The director passed them the handwritten contract that would permit Carnarvon the exclusive right to excavate in The Valley of the Tombs of the Kings for the next ten years. Carnarvon signed in the appointed space and handed the contract back to Maspero. The business was done.

"This calls for some celebration, does it not, gentlemen?"

The director withdrew three small glasses from his desk drawer, the familiar bottle following quickly from beneath the desk. He filled each glass in turn.

"To your success, gentlemen," Maspero toasted, and each raised his glass.

"To a well-earned, happy and comfortable retirement, sir," responded Carnarvon.

"You will be sorely missed, Monsieur le Directeur," added Carter with feeling. He meant it.

At that particular moment, however, he could have no idea how very much he would miss the old man. The entire environment to which the three of them had become so accustomed over the years was about to change dramatically, and irrevocably. The war to end all wars would be only the start.

The lights burned late at 'Castle Carter' that night. Carter and Carnarvon, with the enthusiasm of two children playing with a new toy, absorbed themselves in the development of a plan of attack. They sat opposite each other poring over a large sketch map.

Carnarvon looked Carter in the eyes, reached out with his right hand and grasped his arm.

"Howard," he began, "our expectations are high, I know, but there are many unknowns. Each holds significant risks of failure. The Valley may indeed be empty. Davis could have been right ... Maspero is soon to leave us. The new director may not share such a generous demeanour. We must work to enjoy his affection ... There are signs, too, that England soon will be at war. It may escalate into world conflict. It may touch this secluded world of ours in some way. It may destroy it."

Carter shook the earl's grip loose. His response was clinical.

"Sir, many 'maybes'. And you may be right. But these things will transpire one way or the other. We personally have no control over them. So why give them a second thought? Let us concentrate on the target we have set ourselves and let the fate of the world take its course. If fate wishes to intervene in our endeavours we can face up to it at the time and review our options accordingly. But if we allow ourselves to become preoccupied with thoughts of 'maybe' we may execute our task with less conviction and, in the end, achieve nothing. God forbid!"

To emphasise this final delivery, he leaned forward and stared directly back at Carnarvon.

"The Valley is not empty, sir. Believe me. Davis's methods were crude, unsystematic, and perfunctory. The tombs of many kings have yet to be discovered - amongst them perhaps one or more may remain undefiled. The odds are long, I admit, but I am convinced we shall make many discoveries - perhaps some of them great - perhaps the likes of Davis's Yuya and Tuya tomb. But to have any chance of success we must be systematic." He stabbed the map in front of them with his forefinger as if to physically underscore his last word. "Systematic, sir. Systematic."

"Oh, Howard. We have so much to look forward to. I hope I can contain my patience."

"That is a virtue we shall both need to cultivate, m'lord. There are three Ps in 'approach': patience, practice and polish! You have the polish, I have the practice, and together we must generate the patience!"

They both chuckled.

Carter dragged his chair around the table to sit adjacent to his patron. "Sir," he began, "I must confess to you now that not only do I expect that we shall find at least one of the several kings yet unaccounted for but that I have one particular Pharaoh in mind, 'Tut.Ankh.Amen'." He penned the name on the map in front of them. "The boy king."

Carnarvon was captivated. "I thought Davis had reported he had found the tomb. Anyway, why he, Howard? From my readings, of all remaining kings he was of little significance in the history of Egypt. A stopgap, if you like, between the heretic Akhenaten and the new order of... er... 'Harmhabi'... I believe Maspero called him."

"Horemheb, sir, is the pronunciation I prefer to use. I might have thought the same myself, m'lord, had it not been for some recent clues."

Carter's obvious seriousness held the earl's attention. He leaned closer to his colleague.

"Consider this," Carter continued, "Davis. Bless his spatted feet. Quite by accident he finds a small alabaster cup under a rock. The cup has the cartouche of Tutankhamen inscribed into it. He found it about here..."

Carter picked up a pencil and drew a small 'X' on the map.

"...Much later he discovers what he believes to be Tutankhamen's 'tomb'. But this is nothing more than a small, shallow pit. Perhaps the abandoned beginnings of a pit tomb in which, among other things, he finds fragments of gold foil bearing the names of Tutankhamen and Ankhesenamen, his queen..."

He drew a second 'X'.

"...About six or seven years ago, on the flank of the valley not far from the tomb of Ramses Ten, he finds what any experienced archaeologist would ascribe to 'foundation deposits' - the buried remains of funerary rubbish. He found that stuff about here."

Another 'X' appears on the map.

"You do not find this kind of material evidence if the very tomb itself is not somewhere close by. It just doesn't happen.

"Now, consider this... Why hasn't the tomb been discovered? Could it be so well hidden that even robbers could not locate it? Nearly all the tombs in The Valley of the Kings have been totally rifled in antiquity - even the cliff tomb of Hatshepsut, well hidden and dangerous to reach. Am I not correct in my assertion?"

"Yes. Yes. But not that of Yuya and Tuya." Carnarvon's observation was directly in line with where Carter had been leading.

"Right!" Carter slammed his fist down. "Right. And why Yuya and Tuya, do y' think, sir?"

Carnarvon shrugged his shoulders. He couldn't think. He was too excited, eager to hear what Carter had to say next.

"I'll tell you," conceded Carter after a pause. "Plenty of scattered evidence but no tomb. That of Yuya and Tuya was discovered in the very bottom of the valley, the area most vulnerable to the catastrophic floods that occur here - infrequently, yes, but they occur all the same - and to devastating effect - often leaving mountains of debris, burying all in their path."

He paused once more.

"Now... Tutankhamen died young - that much we know... So young, perhaps, that no tomb had been constructed for him. And there was no time to construct one from scratch, like that of Smenkhkare - also found by Davis - who died after only three years as regent. Now, what if the tomb of this king was built originally for a noble... like the tomb of Yuya and Tuya? In the bottom of The Valley... not like the kings, high up and potentially protected from the ravages of flooding, but in the bottom... And what if... What if there was a tremendous storm shortly after burial that wiped out all evidence of the tomb's location before robbers had the opportunity to enter... Like Yuya and Tuya?"

"Perhaps too many 'What ifs', Howard. But, I confess, a plausible scenario all the same." The earl grinned. "Damned exciting thought, if nothing else!"

"Now consider this, m' lord," Carter pushed on, answering his own questions. "Where is the greatest accumulation of excavators' tailings? And here I am not referring exclusively to modern excavators. Consider also those in antiquity - those who built the tombs. Where did the stones brought up from within the rock get dumped?"

The earl remained silent.

"I'll tell you - at the lowest point... in the valley bottom. And how long has it been since the bedrock of the valley bottom has seen the light of day?... Centuries, my lord... Nay - millennia!"

Truly, as Carter had just described, were it not for the profusion of geometric apertures in the valley flanks and the whitened, worn tourist paths snaking all about the valley bottom and its sides, The Valley might have resembled a worked out open-pit gold mine. The spoils of excavation were piled high in mountainous heaps all about the valley floor. They littered the entire place, tons and tons of the refuse of contemporary and earlier excavators, of tomb masons' chippings and reworked natural flood debris.

"It is a captivating logic, Howard. But where do we start?"

"A methodical search, m'Lord, beginning here and ending here." Carter planted his finger on the map. "A systematic clearing to bedrock of the area between these three tombs."

He took his pencil and drew a triangle in the heart of The Valley. The lines joined the mouths of the tombs of Merenptah, situated at the head of a tributary valley to the west, Ramses II, in the central valley to the east and Ramses VI, also in the centre of the valley but to the south.

For what Carter had in mind he knew he would have to have a considerable fortune at his personal disposal. The Earl of Carnarvon had the necessary substance and, for now at least, given Carter's enthusiastic story, an eager enthusiasm and strength of purpose, perhaps also the patience to see it through.

With Carter's plan and his conviction firmly in place, the two attacked their first season in The Valley with considerable energy. Although his patron departed early, Carter toiled for a full seven months with hundreds of men removing tons of material. But the effort turned up absolutely nothing of value.

And then the Great War started.

A firm hammering at the front door disturbed Carter in the middle of his breakfast.

Abdel came in and announced, "It is a soldier, sir, of the British Army."

Carter swallowed his mouthful of toast and marmalade. "I will see him, Abdel. Bring another chair."

A ruddy-faced sergeant appeared, cap in hand. He drew himself to attention and saluted. "Mr Carter, sir?"

"Yes. Please be seated. And who am I addressing?"

"H'Adamson, sir. Sarn't Adamson h'at your service, sir. I 'as been sent up 'ere from H'Aich Queue to request your h'attendance at a h'interview wiv Major Dorking, sir. Prefer if I stands, h'if you don't mind, sir."

"Indeed. What did you say your name was?"

"H'Adamson, sir. H'Adamson. H'Ay-Dee-H'Ay-H'Em-H'Ess-H'o-H'En, H'Adamson, sir. Easy to remember, sir. I is assigned to assistance duties h'at Aich Queue. Kinda h'odd-job man. H'assist whereva needed, sir. When you needs me just call 'H'Adamson' and I comes h'at the double, sir."

"Well I'm glad to make your acquaintance, Sergeant Adamson. As you can see I am in the middle of breakfast. Will you not join me for a cup of tea?" Carter was much amused at the man but resisted the temptation to grin.

"Don't mind h'if I do, sir. Fair works h'up a thirst riding a donkey for h'any length of time, don't it?"

Abdel poured the sergeant a cup of hot tea. The soldier leaned across the table, heaped three spoons of sugar into the cup, gave it a quick stir and then poured the contents into the saucer and began slurping. Carter, crunching on his toast, ignored the noise and signalled to Abdel to fetch his hat and coat.

There was a car waiting for them on the other side of the river. It spluttered into Luxor, scattering animals and children before it, and eventually drew up outside the building that the British Army was using as its headquarters.

Sergeant Adamson guided Carter through the entrance hall and down one of the narrow corridors to a small room. The door was open. Inside sat an officer chewing the end of his pencil. Adamson saluted.

"The gen'leman from The Valley, sir."

Seeing the two at the door, the officer stood up and saluted back.

'Typical starchy, vertical, chinless, public school product,' Carter thought to himself. He felt a little uneasy, but he wasn't sure why. He took off his Homburg and clutched it to his chest with both hands.

The officer sat back down, drew out a sheet of paper and sharpened his pencil.

"Name?"

"Howard Carter, sir."

"Cwistian name or surname?"

"Both, sir."

"No. I mean 'Howard'. That yaw surname or yaw cwistian name?"

"Christian name, sir."

"'Carter'. Also sounds like a cwistian name. That yaw middle name or yaw surname?"

"Surname, sir."

"No more names?"

"No, sir."

"How d'you spell it?"

Blimey, thought Carter. 'How long can this inane dialogue continue?

He took a deep breath. "Aich - Oh - Double You - Ay - Are - Dee..."

"No. Surname first."

"See - Ay - Are - Tea - Ee - Are."

"Now the cwistian name."

Carter's raised voice showed irritation. He answered, each letter carefully separated, "AICH - OH - DOUBLE YOU - AY - ARE - DEE, LIEUTENANT."

"'Sir' will do nicely, thank you. Date of birth?"

"May ninth, 1874. EM - AY - WYE..."

"Don't twy to be funny. We don't commend humour in His Majesty's Armed Fawces. Sewious business, war. Wequiwes killing people, blood and whatnot."

Carter rolled his eyes. His fingers tightened their grip on the fabric of his hat. 'Why should I have to put up with this nonsense?'

The questions continued. "Mawwied?"

"No... sir."

"Good. Don't want mowr widows. Nasty job having to tell 'em."

Carter felt himself chill. 'He can't be serious. This - whatever they want me for - this can't be dangerous, surely?'

"Don't think there's any need for a medical. You look pwitty fit to me.

Wight... Sign here."

"What am I signing, sir?"

"Just that you have been interviewed - found fit for duty - weady to serve your countwy - all that sort of fing."

"But what am I to be doing, sir?"

"Can't tell you - hush, hush and all that - need to know basis only. You'll be told what you need to know shawtly. In the meantime go and get yawself a cup of tea." Then, even though there was no one there, he yelled over Carter's shoulder, "Next!"

Carter was happy to leave the presence of this 'commissioned product of our public school system'. But the tone of the officer's earlier remark had disturbed him. 'Surely he wasn't to be sent to the front? He was too old... surely? The only thing he'd be good for would be translation. That was safe duty... surely?'

Boiling hot, copiously sugared tea out of a chipped, white, enamelled mug did little to quell his anxiety but he drank it down all the same. His hat on his lap, he sat at the canteen table looking down at the tea leaves in the bottom of his drained mug.

Then he heard the click of hobnails on the tiled floor outside. The canteen door opened and a military policeman appeared. The policeman drew himself to attention. "Mr Howard? Mr Howard?"

'Blimey,' thought Carter. 'The scholar got my name wrong after all.'

"Here!" He smiled and got up.

"Major Dorking wishes to see you, sir. Please come this way."

The MP led him noisily down a long, marble-floored corridor until they reached a door with a white label pasted on it, which read: 'MILITARY POLICE - U.C.O.'

As the MP reached to knock on the frosted glass panel in the upper half of the door, Carter caught his arm. "What does 'U.C.O.' stand for?"

The MP stared at him for a moment and then furtively glanced both ways along the corridor.

"Under - Cover - Operations," he whispered.

Carter's eyes widened. He released the man's arm and the soldier knocked.

There was a loud, stentorian shout from within. "Come!"

The MP opened the door and entered ahead of Carter. Snapping to attention and saluting he announced, "Mr Howard, sir."

The major was sitting behind a collapsible metal desk covered in a mêlée of dossiers of various thicknesses, some more dog-eared than others. The man had a full beard.

'No doubt hiding a weak chin,' thought Carter. Indeed he was so hairy that Carter couldn't see his teeth even when he spoke, just a ripple of hair.

"Glad to make your acquaintance, Mr Howard. Please take a seat."

"It's Carter, sir. Howard is my first name."

"Me apologies, Mr Carter. Damned irregular filling your name in back to front like that. Sergeant, take this back to Lieutenant Horsell and get a new one - and make sure it's filled out correctly this time."

"Sir!" The MP took the paper and was gone.

"Carter. Heard a lot about you. Understand you're some kind of art dealer. Work in the bazaars a lot - trade in antikas and the like - got a lot of local contacts - speak the language and all that."

"I have done some trading, sir, yes. I am on good terms with most of my contacts. And I am fluent in Arabic - written and spoken."

"Just what the doctor ordered." The major leaned closer as if there were others about who should not hear. He lowered his voice. "Y'see, we need someone to pick up on the local talk. Keep his ear to the ground, you understand. News of the Turks and such like. We believe there are spies in the bazaars working for the Turks - keeping an eye on our movements and reporting back to their masters in Damascus. That's where they're bivouacked at present. We'd like to know who they are. We've got a man assigned to the Arab Bureau out of Cairo. He's in the desert right now - can't remember which one - moving with Faisal. Name's Lawrence, Major Lawrence. Speaks the language like y'self."

Carter had heard much of King Faisal but nothing of Lawrence. The name didn't mean anything to him. 'Rather him eating Arab food, riding camels and sleeping on carpets than I. So they want me to do the same thing. Snoop around the Arab community. I can do that. Safe duty in the bazaars of Luxor and Cairo.'

The major continued, "You will, of course, get some compensation for your trouble. Not much, but I'm sure it will come in handy. Ten shillings a day."

"Most generous, sir," commented Carter, now feeling less irritated and much relieved. "How do I do this reporting? And to whom do I report?"

"You'll pass your information to Sergeant Adamson - preferably by word of mouth - kind of casually - in bars and such like. He will never be in uniform when you meet. It'll look like you're meeting with a trading partner."

Carter smiled. 'Not 'H'Aich Queue' Adamson?' he thought. It all sounded rather farcical. A game of undercover cops and robbers played by a mixed band of commissioned products of the British public school system, a common garden lacky who couldn't speak the King's English and an Arabic-speaking archaeologist, acting as a spy.

"What kinds of information am I to look out for?"

"Any old information. You'll know what's important to us. You'll know it when you hear it. We don't expect you to make enquiries. Make you too obvious. Just keep listening. You'll pick stuff up. Just be alert and report back to us when you have something."

Sergeant Adamson drove Carter back to the ferry.

"Looks like we is goin' t' work togever, sir. A h'absolute pleasure, sir. H'I'm really looking forwud to it. Which, may h'I ask, are your favourite bars?"

Carnarvon had returned to England half way through their first season in The Valley. It had been more like painstaking mining than excavation. The tons of debris they had moved had yielded nothing and there was so much more of the area as yet untouched. It would take years to clear everywhere to bedrock and great patience to see it through. For the time being, however, there were other, more urgent things on the earl's mind. The armed forces were to requisition his home to serve as a convalescent hospital for soldiers recovering from their injuries.

As he rode back through the fields towards his house, Carter thought about his sponsor. 'It is imperative he sticks with this. In his preoccupation with affairs at home perhaps he will forget these early disappointments and return refreshed, invigorated, energetic to do more. When this flap's all over.'

As he neared his house, a dog barked. Gaggia ran out to welcome his returning master.

"How are you doing, you mangy old bastard, eh? Miss me? Abdel feed you, did he?"

Apart from his balding coat, the dog was fit enough, but he stank of the paraffin Carter had been using to treat his condition. The two trotted into the house and Carter went straight to the drinks cabinet and poured himself a gin. He sat back in his wicker chair, took a long draught and smiled.

'So now I'm a spy. The feedstock of thrillers. Doing my bit for England.' "To King and countwy!" he mimicked and took another swig. 'Listening in to the conversations of the Arabs I go around with, I doubt I'll find out a single thing of any use at all to the bloody war effort.'

As the alcohol began to take hold, he felt melancholy creeping over him. And, as he fell asleep, Miss Dorothy moved back into his dreams...

This summer in England had been truly wonderful. Howard had been as happy at other times but not in this way. She had not changed a bit. Always understanding, she had patiently accepted his reasons for not connecting in the previous seasons. Now, after all, the war had intervened and, sadly, no doubt there would be additional cause for extended separations. But this hardship they would share with millions of others. And a hardship shared is a hardship lessened, so they say.

They were reunited appropriately at teatime in the Ritz Hotel on Piccadilly. Dorothy had dressed in her newest outfit and, armed with a pretty flowered parasol, she had come prepared to take a walk in Green Park and enjoy the sunshine.

In the staid lounge of the hotel, over teacakes and crumpets with melted butter and assorted condiments, Carter recounted the adventures of the years they had missed together. He enlightened and amused her with stories of his conscription into the intelligence unit of the British Army in Egypt and his singular failure since to obtain one scrap of useful information on the Turks or their spies from his contacts in the bazaars of Cairo and Luxor. Perhaps there had been none for the taking.

At the same time, he confessed that he should not even have told her this - 'Idle Talk Costs Lives' spoke the posters all about the streets. They both shared the comical irony with subdued giggles.

"Why don't we take a promenade in the park, Howard? The weather is so lovely right now." She leant forward and lowered her voice. "There we can talk without worrying if we are disturbing anyone - or if anyone is eavesdropping!"

There were lots of couples and several families taking a walk in the park that day. A small boy ran past them spinning a hoop, lost control of it on the downward incline and, in his efforts to catch it, tripped and somersaulted on the grass. The hoop careered into a passing baby carriage, alarming the nanny pushing it but doing no real harm. She stood with the hoop in her hand looking all about for the culprit responsible for the incident. But the boy had the presence of mind to remain where he had ended up, sitting on the grass supported with his hands behind him, looking nonchalantly skyward. The baby began to cry. She dropped the hoop by the side of the pathway and pushed the pram on down the hill. The boy quickly recovered his toy and took off in the opposite direction.

Dorothy smiled. She took Carter's arm and gave it a slight tug. "Let's sit in the shade of that tree over there, Howard."

They walked over to the base of the tree. Carter took off his jacket and spread it on the grass. She sat down and he sat next to her, took off his Homburg, unbuttoned his waistcoat and rolled up his shirtsleeves. He pulled a stalk of fresh grass and leant forward. With his arms about his knees he twiddled the stalk thoughtfully between his lips.

"Penny for them, Howard," she said.

Carter sighed. Staring pensively ahead across the park he said, "I am forty. At least halfway through my life. A life so far full of halves. A strange existence is it not, Dot? I spend fully half my life digging up the past in pursuit of an unknown quarry. I don't know what the next find will be - how great, how small - but I know that my goal is discovery, hopefully one day a great discovery and fulfilment. The other half of my life? The other half of my life..." His voice died away momentarily. "...It has no goal. I feel unfulfilled. It seems I am living an existence like a Dr Jekyll and a Mr Hyde. Every winter and spring Dr Howard Jekyll is fulfilling his needs attempting to exhume the Egyptian dead. Each summer and autumn Howard Hyde continues a frustrated search for fulfilment in the land of the living - a so-called 'normal' life."

"You are no Jekyll and Hyde to me, Howard," Dorothy broke in. "It is not an 'average' life you lead, no, but it's what you want. There is nothing 'average' about you, Howard."

"If it were not for the unbearable summers, Dr. Howard Jekyll would be in Egypt the year round. He would need for nothing else. But there the summers are unbearable and so he comes here. And in coming here he finds he needs something else. Not now, though. Not today. Not now he is in good company."

Dorothy smiled. 'That's better,' she thought. 'That wasn't for effect. I do believe he means it.'

Carter ceased his staring into the middle distance and turned to look at her. He spoke quickly. "Dot, I do so enjoy your company. I would like for us to spend some time together. Are you doing anything the next few days? Will you come with me to visit the town where I grew up?" It took all his strength of will to get the words out.

"Oh, that would be such fun. I will have to rearrange some appointments. Nothing important. For next week, right?"

"Right. Next week. I could meet you at King's Cross on Sunday. There is a train at two in the afternoon - if they have not changed the schedule."

His face reflected the pleasure of his anticipation. It was as if a great weight had been removed from his shoulders. Dorothy glowed back at him. They shared the moment. He slapped his thighs with excitement. They got up and walked on down the slope towards Buckingham Palace.

The following Sunday Carter purchased two first-class tickets at the station. They sat opposite each other in window seats. After a few minutes the drabness of the back streets was behind them and views opened up over wide expanses of farmland, hedgerows and copses. Each time he stole a look at her she was looking out the window. She caught him once and he flashed an embarrassed smile back, shifting his gaze to the outside once more. The smoke from the engine fell to the ground and billowed about their side of the carriage, temporarily extinguishing the view. They both instinctively drew back to look at each other. Meeting each other's eyes at the same time, they both smiled. Carter felt compelled to speak.

"I have made two reservations at the White Heart in Swaffham. Small rooms, I'm afraid, but each has a washbasin and the bathroom is on the same floor. I have always found them cosy. And the food's not bad either."

"I'm sure it will be lovely, Howard. I am looking forward to this."

"Please don't raise your expectations too high, Dot. This is a farming community - country folk, country comforts, nothing more and nothing less."

"On the contrary, Howard. My expectations are very high. At the very least, I do not expect to be disappointed." She winked at him.

Carter couldn't really fathom what she might mean by it and it troubled him when he couldn't detect the meaning in things. He took it as sarcasm.

"Well, you might be." It was all he could think of in response.

"I don't think so. You haven't disappointed me ever. This cannot be an exception."

They arrived in the early evening and went straight to the inn. Carter registered for them both and they went up to their rooms to drop off their bags. Dorothy's room was indeed small - a solitary single bed; a dressing table with so little space between it and the bed that there was no room for a chair; she would have to sit on the foot of the bed to attend to her toilet.

It didn't bother Carter. He had been used to so much worse in his various encampments in the desert. This was comparative luxury. Everything is relative.

Dorothy unpacked her things and hung them in the tallboy. She powdered her nose and went downstairs to join Carter in the lounge bar. He was sitting in a 'snug' in the corner halfway through his first gin. His eyes lit up as she arrived and he got up to show her to her seat.

"What'll you have?"

She bit her lip pensively. "Mmm... a sweet sherry, I think. Thanks."

He went over to the bar to order her drink and get himself another gin. She watched him. He was wearing the same creased and baggy grey tweed suit he had worn in London. The Homburg for once was not on his head and the obvious thinning on top was now clearly exposed. Although he was adequately presentable, Dorothy couldn't help herself musing: 'He does not look after himself well. He needs someone to take care of him. But would he allow it? He is not one to take orders or advice from others.' She felt more of a maternal concern than a physical attraction for the man.

He, on the other hand, had metamorphosed at last. He was attracted to and very much enjoyed the company and conversation of this Miss Dorothy Dalgleish.

Carter turned to walk back to the table with the drinks. He allowed himself a few moments to drink in the pretty little vision before him. She had a heavenly round face, pale blue, smiling eyes and a perfect complexion. And, although petite and extremely slim, she had a firm and shapely chest. Whenever he had been with her, as now, she had been dressed to the neck. He had never seen any sign of cleavage. But there was some recognisably distinct fullness there pressing outward against the tight cotton of her print dress.

He placed the drinks on the table between them. The tinkling of the glasses betrayed the trembling in his fingers. He sat down.

A longing was welling within him, but for once he lacked the tools to express himself coherently. Dorothy couldn't suspect how he was feeling. He had always been strongly focused on his profession. Up to this point, they had talked together mostly about his experiences in Egypt. In discussion of his subject he had been amusing as well as serious but they had rarely dwelt long on life outside his work, except perhaps his associations with the aristocracy and the otherwise seriously wealthy, but certainly not his personal, more intimate feelings. She was here to enjoy his company and his stories. There was no anticipation beyond this.

So for a moment she was struck dumb when he clumsily blurted out, "I... I am greatly attracted to you, Dot."

In the intensity of his feelings he translated her momentary silence to indicate she was offended by this forwardness. Perhaps he had ruined the whole trip right at the start through this brief confessional. Perhaps she would want to take the next train back to London. Perhaps she would not speak to him again. In the few seconds that followed, all these thoughts flashed through his confused mind. He hurriedly constructed a follow-up sentence and was just about to fumble a second delivery when she responded.

"Howard!" First a startled admonishment, then, "Oh, Howard," softer, gentler, delivered with a clearly receptive smile. "I don't deserve such words."

Carter, surprised and greatly relieved at the tone of her response, took a grip on himself and collected the presence of mind not to answer 'Oh, Dot', which were the first words to come into his head. If he were not careful, his dialogue could easily become comical and the special moment he had so indelicately created could be lost. All he had to do was keep the theme going and with her willingness to play the other part in the duet his task would be all the easier.

Over dinner they talked about themselves; they talked about Norfolk, they reminisced about their childhoods, their parents, their brothers and sisters, their likes, their dislikes; they talked some self-criticism, their personally perceived idiosyncrasies - those they observed in each other, those they observed in others. They talked about the war. For once Egypt did not figure in the conversation.

And so to bed.

Pecking her nervously on the cheek, Carter said, "Good night, Dot. Pleasant dreams."

"Pleasant dreams, Howard," she repeated, kissing him back. And they parted company.

They each had much to dream about: she with the unexpected realisation that he did, after all, have feelings for her, he with a new and consuming obsession that had in some considerable measure, for the time being at least, displaced his life's work.

They were both awake when the innkeeper's wife brought the tea. He was down to breakfast by eight o'clock and she shortly afterwards. As they laid eyes on each other for the first time that morning, it was with a sense of mutual acceptance. There was no awkwardness in their conversation. A pleasing atmosphere of total comfort existed between them. Even though this was all new to him, Carter nevertheless felt like he'd known her this way for years. Dorothy, on the other hand, had always felt she knew the man. What was different now was that he wanted to know her.

They spent the first day visiting his brothers. They talked about painting. They went through a portfolio of his father's works. They visited his aunts' house. They had dinner with Vernet. And finally, at bedtime back at the inn, they parted company as they had the night before.

At breakfast the next morning, Carter introduced his plan for the day. "I told you, didn't I, Dot, that during my boyhood and early teens I would visit the Amhersts frequently and receive instruction from his lordship on Egyptian antiquities and history. It was like a free tutorial - as often as I wished it. It is he whom you should blame for my infatuation."

'Well, Egypt was bound to creep back into the picture sooner or later,' she thought.

"It's quite a long way."

They set out on bicycles for Didlington Hall. Carter was on his way to revisit the crucible of his career. Riding beside him was a woman who had lit a fire where coals, let alone flames, had not existed before. He felt possessed.

First the old church and then the familiar lines of the house came into view. Carter stopped and dismounted. Dorothy drew up beside him.

"It is much overgrown. Gone to seed. The Amhersts fell on hard times a few years ago and I had to help them sell everything. No one wanted the house. It's been empty ever since I catalogued his collection for auction."

"It must have been lovely in its heyday," observed Dorothy.

"It was. It truly was. I never thought..." he paused.

"What, Howard?"

"Well, when you're there you don't think - when it's alive with people, the family, their belongings, and you visit almost daily - you never give a thought to how it could change - just like that," he snapped his fingers. "Overnight almost. And all you are left with is an overgrown, empty shell - this thing we are looking at now - like a ransacked tomb, left to the elements after the scavangers have taken their pickings; a beautifully crafted palace, constructed at great expense; a home, loved and cared for by its inhabitants - all gone, as they are gone."

They got back on their bikes and cycled on to the gateway just as he had done so many times all those years ago. Even the gates had gone, sold with the rest of the contents. But the carefully crafted brick walls still stood.

The couple rode on up to the house. They left their bikes at the front steps. Carter pulled off his trouser clips and they walked around the building along the overgrown pathway to the rear terrace.

"It wouldn't take too much effort to revitalise this garden," observed Dorothy. "They look a bit dishevelled now, but these are all cultivated trees and bushes. All it would take to bring them back to their former grandeur is a little 'TLC'."

The bright afternoon sunlight bathed the rear portico in leafy shade. The paint had peeled from the frames of the long row of venetian windows that opened onto the terrace. Howard had frequently observed the family at play here. Now weeds reached through the cracks between the pavers. The grass in the lawns which swept down to the ornamental pool was tall, thick enough even for haymaking.

Carter pointed back the way they had come.

"Across the road the Amhersts of the last century are remembered. It was the family church. There is a plaque near the altar erected to the memory of Mary and William George Tyssen Tyssen Amherst. What a name! They died in '54 and '55. In the bell tower there are even more plaques - to Amelia, Francis, Beatrice, Charles and William. All Amhersts. All of them died in the last century. Where my friends rest I have no idea." He looked downward.

"Howard," Dorothy spoke firmly.

He smiled, took a breath and changed the subject. "At one time there were seven statues of seated Egyptian gods positioned all along this back wall," Carter swept his hand in a wide arc. "I can still imagine them staring at us. Such a prize they were. So easily sold. Now sadly scattered. They don't stand together any more. Too many museums wished to share the prize."

The man in the baggy tweed suit and hat walked along the terrace with exaggerated steps, stopping briefly at each place where a statue had once stood, each time taking up a position with his back against the wall looking out across the gardens in stone-like pose, mimicking the fixed gaze of the gods. As he acted the part, he named each one and described its purpose in the ritual of ancient Egyptian religion.

Dorothy was lying on her stomach on the grassy slope that ran from the terrace to the ornamental pool. With her elbows firmly planted in the thick turf and her hands cupped under her chin, she watched Carter's nostalgic theatricals with obvious pleasure. She didn't hear most of the words. Her mind was filled with the picture of this dowdily dressed, moderately attractive but otherwise unnoticeable little man elegantly playing the script and the parts that he knew so well and with a flourish that belied his normal reserve.

But he had a singularly private audience. He felt completely released from the discipline that normally characterised his behaviour. He finished his description of the seven deities and, bowed like a maestro accepting a bouquet. His lady friend clapped. He threw off his jacket and came over to sit down beside her. She rolled over onto her back, rocked her head in the grass to tousle her hair a little and looked up at him.

The picture, perfectly framed in his eyes, gave him the same rush of excitement he had felt when he had sat having dinner with her that first night in the pub.

Howard Carter returned to Egypt a changed man - more inwardly complete and feeling less solitary. Although he was not sure whether she would join him in Egypt again, he knew when he felt cornered by the strains of his work he would have someone he could confide in, someone he could go to for help, perhaps more.

The war was escalating outside Europe. Everyone had thought it would be over within the year, but things were getting worse. Influenced, as all were, by what he read in the newspapers, Carter fast developed an intense dislike for the Germans. They now took first place on his 'most hated' list, displacing even the French.

Determined to make his own contribution to the war effort, he returned to Luxor at the usual time of year. He had selected his target, but before he could take any action he would first need to enlist the help of his erstwhile colleagues in the UCO.

On his journey back up the track to Castle Carter, it loomed large as life - that brutally arrogant statement of German bad taste, the red villa of Borchardt!

As he approached his house, the mangy Gaggia bounded from the porch towards him. Abdel stood in the doorway, a broad grin on his face, always relieved to see his master return. They exchanged greetings. Abdel proffered the obligatory G and T. The welcome drink didn't stop Carter delivering some early criticism. "You have not looked after Gaggia well, Abdel. His mange is worse than when I left. Have you been applying the paraffin daily like I told you?"

Abdel profusely denied any delinquency in the execution of his responsibilities. But Carter knew he had been less than diligent. There was not the slightest scent of paraffin on the dog.

"Go and get me the can right now, Abdel. I shall do it myself."

The dog hated the application and would run for cover as soon as he saw Abdel bring the paraffin can into the room. He had become so clever at hiding that Abdel invariably could not find him and would give up looking.

True to form on this occasion, as soon as Abdel returned with the paraffin can, the dog scampered out of the room, its paws sliding on the tiled floor in its panic to get away.

"Gaggia! Come here, boy!" Carter shouted. "Gaggia!"

Not a sound from the other room.

"Go and get him, Abdel."

"Sir," acknowledged Abdel, and he went looking once more.

He was gone long enough for Carter's mind to drift into the catalogue of pleasant memories he had accumulated during his summer leave. The dry bottom to his glass brought him back from his Elysian dreamings.

"Abdel! Where the hell are you, man? Get the dog and bring him back here at once. And get me another drink, dammit."

Carter's irritability was a complex cocktail - fatigue after his long journey, Abdel's negligence with the dog, the sight of that monstrous red construction a few yards back down the track, and an unaccustomed longing. The heady mixture had been fermenting within him since he had returned. And now there was the alcohol.

"Abdel! Come back in here at once!"

Almost immediately his servant reappeared holding a fresh glass of gin. Abdel's face was a picture of anxiety. When among Arabs, his master had not been prone to irritability - with the general public, yes, but not with his own men. Abdel, fearful of worsening matters was at a loss how to react.

"I... I am sorry, sir. I cannot find him anywhere."

"Nonsense, man!" retorted Carter, almost snatching the glass from Abdel's hand. "I'll get him myself."

He got up and purposefully strode into the other room. Abdel followed him, staying close behind, trying to see over his master's shoulder as Carter looked under and behind the furniture.

It's a fact, thought Carter. He's not in this room. He turned to Abdel. "Where could he have got to?"

Abdel made a pathetic gesture with his hands and face that transcended all language barriers.

"While you have been away, sir, he has become very good at this. I have been having much trouble... much trouble indeed."

Carter didn't like to be beaten, least of all by a poxy mutt like Gaggia. The fact was, however, that the dog had disappeared into a room with no exit, had not been seen to come back out, and was nowhere to be found within.

"Damned peculiar," offered Carter after a moments' reflection. "Damned clever."

But he quickly accepted defeat. There were more palatable things to do after all. He resigned himself to his chair and his gin and tonic.

The following morning Carter awoke greatly refreshed in body and in mind. He finally felt he was back in harness again. As he sat at breakfast, he dwelt on his plans for the upcoming season's work in The Valley.

'But first,' he thought as he bit into a burnt piece of toast, 'a strike for England.'

"Abdel," he called, "get my donkey and make sure there's a ferry at the riverside. I must meet with His Majesty's armed forces this day."

As he got up to leave, the mangy dog emerged from the room into which the previous night he had so mysteriously disappeared. Carter never did work out how the animal had managed to conceal itself. But conceal itself it did and, each time the paraffin can appeared, on several occasions thereafter.

"Sergeant Adamson," greeted Carter as he marched up to the main door of the barracks.

"Sah!" Adamson stamped to attention. "H'I 'aven't seen you fer a while, sir. Wot brings you to th' UCO t'day?"

"The King's business, Sarn't Adamson." Carter winked at him. "The

King's business."

"H'I see, sir. Mum's the word, eh? Major Dorking is down the corridor h'in 'is usual office, sir." Adamson gestured to Carter to follow.

"Thanks, sergeant." Carter strode on down to Dorking's office and knocked on the door.

"Come! Carter! Good to see you, old chap. Been on holiday, eh? Any chuffy? Ha, ha, ha!" Dorking noticed the serious expression on Carter's face and his tasteless chortling quickly faded. "Sorry, old chap. You look like a man with a mission. What's up?"

It was important that Carter pitched his story just right. He could not achieve what he planned without the help of the military. The story had to be compelling. During his boat trip over, he had carefully thought through his approach - something with instant appeal to their quest for recognition, even glory.

"Sir," he began. "I need the UCO's help. I know the war hasn't touched us here yet, sir - I hope it never will - but there is a bad side to that, is there not?"

"Mmm? Y... yes. Oh, yes, of course. Bad side." The major didn't have a clue what Carter was talking about.

"Yes. As you say, sir, a bad side. No publicity. No public recognition. Not on the map and all that."

"Wait a minute, old man," reacted the major. "This is the UCO, y'know. Undercover and all that. Publicity is not a word in our vocabulary."

"Understood, sir. Understood. But hear me out on my proposal, sir. An undercover operation, sir, resulting in negative publicity - for the Germans!"

With this statement he got the major's attention. Dorking listened intently as Carter related his plan. As the story unfolded, the major's eyes brightened and, as Carter concluded, he burst into unrestrained chuckles.

"Capital! Capital! Just what the doctor ordered. Been too damn boring around here for too damn long. Give the men some practice. Oil the gimbals, so to speak."

Carter couldn't fathom what he meant with his last sentence but didn't much care, either. As long as Carter got what he wanted, the major could oil all the gimbals he cared to.

"We'll lay the plans tomorrow morning. Do the deed tomorrow night. No moon. Excellent timing. Speed is of the essence. Element of surprise and all that. The Hun won't have the time to find out, let alone prepare a defence."

Carter hadn't expected such urgent acceptance, but the major was decided. He hadn't faced anything so exciting for months. The rest of his paperwork could wait.

"Sar'nt Adamson!" he called loudly.

The door opened quickly and the sergeant saluted, snapping himself to attention. "Sah!"

"Fetch Horsell at once. Tell him to pick out four of his best men."

The sergeant was almost out of the door when the major called after him. "Oh... and make sure at least one of them knows how to handle explosives!"

"Sah! H'at once, sah."

"I'll be off, then, sir," said Carter.

The major turned to him quickly.

"Oh, no you won't, Mr Carter. Not so fast. This is a UCO mission. Everything we do is, by definition, top secret. Need t' know basis only. Just the eight of us. Noone else. You're in the loop. Like it or not we do not lose sight of one another until the entire operation is successfully completed."

"But, sir, I have work in The Valley tomorrow morning. I have men coming."

"Should have thought of that before you brought this idea of yours to me. Important business is the King's business. Don't you ever forget it." He grinned with self-satisfaction.

"You sleep here tonight. The sar'nt will find you a cot."

There were many things Carter disliked. One of the most distasteful was having to use a communal shaving brush. It seemed an unnecessary insult after an uncomfortable night on a portable canvas bed. The blade wasn't all that sharp either. Getting back into his previous day's clothes was not unusual for him, however. It was an acceptable prerequisite to fieldwork. So he hardly gave that a second thought. But using someone else's comb for his hair, and the same to preen his moustache, that was most disagreeable.

It was breakfast time in the mess room. A severely disenchanted Carter took his appointed place at the table that had been set aside especially for the undercover team in a far corner of the room.

"Bwight and early! That's what we like to see in this King's army, Mr Carter." The chinless Lieutenant Horsell greeted Carter with a wave of his hand.

Carter reluctantly sat down beside him. Horsell leaned over. "Looking faward to heawing your plan, Mr Carter. Sounds like a weal cwacker. One in the eye for the Hun, eh?"

"As you say, sir. One in the eye." Carter was short but cordial.

The breakfast was less than palatable. Undercooked eggs swimming in fat, greasy bacon, burnt toast.

If only Abdel was here, thought Carter.

When they had finished their meal the major called them all into a nearby room. They sat down on steel chairs in a circle. The major stepped into the centre and held stage.

"Right, men," he began. "Kept you in the dark to this point to minimise risk. 'An idle word can cost lives,' and all that. Now it's time to give it to you straight. Mr Carter here, one of our civilian plain-clothes operatives, has come up with a plan to give the Hun a poke in the eye and provide this backwater in the desert some notoriety in the tabloid press back home. There could be a decoration or two in this for some of you. By the looks of you, you could do with a bit of decoration!"

From the troops came clear murmurings of mixed feelings. Decoration was usually connected with danger.

"The good news is the Germans aren't expecting us, so surprise is on our side. Bad news is we're not sure if the place is guarded. However, if it is, it will be guarded by Arabs. So it'll be ineffective. I don't want any killing. Sensitive immobilisation is all that is required. We will have to black up. Which of you is the explosives expert?"

"Me, sir." A diminutive subaltern with a piping voice drew himself up to sitting attention. "Trained at Sandhurst, sir. Bridge demolition mostly. Know exactly where to put it on a bridge, sir."

The major was startled by the boy's high voice.

"What's your name, boy?" he asked.

"Watson, sir."

"How old are you, boy?"

"Eighteen, sir," came the shrill reply.

"Not dropped yet? Or blow your gonads off in the lab, did you?"

All those around the boy burst into laughter.

The lad lowered his eyes.

"Well... Whatever... Balls or no balls it's you who's going to have to do it. But it ain't no bridge." The major paused as if for effect. "It's a building. Constructed by the Germans without the permission of the Egyptians, purportedly as a base for their archaeological expeditions, but actually, no doubt, as an HQ for subversive ops."

To emphasise the gravity of this last statement, he glared steadily around the circle of the assembled group. Carter was bubbling with amusement. It was all he could do to maintain a serious expression.

"Mr Carter here will explain." The major beckoned to Carter to enter the circle.

Carter was startled. He hadn't expected to have to say anything. The levity he was feeling would make it all the more difficult for him to deliver any speech that held a sense of gravity anything like that of the major. He tried to pull himself together.

"This building is situated on the other side of the river near the Ramesseum. It is quite obvious. It is red. Blow it up. Wipe it from the face of the earth. Simple as that."

The major wasn't very satisfied with Carter's matter-of-fact response but there was little he could say. He took over again.

"'Simple', yes. Simple to the experts, eh, Watson?"

The teenager gave a nervous smile. "But I haven't been trained to blow up houses, sir. Don't know the first thing about where to place the charge, what type of charge, how much charge..."

The major ignored him.

"At zero-one-hundred hours tonight we shall push off for the west bank in two of our small dinghies. At precisely zero-two-hundred hours we shall rendezvous under cover of the columns in the Ramesseum. At zero-two-fifteen hours Watson here will creep over to the building and place his charges. Horsell, Johnson, Smith and Davis will stay with him to keep a lookout and immobilise any intruders. Do y' need a hand setting the charges, boy?"

"Sir?" Watson, contemplating his forthcoming challenge, had not been paying attention.

"Stay alert, boy. Do you need help setting the charges?"

"Someone... Someone to tell me where, sir, and how much," was the trembling reply.

The major glared at the boy. "Trying to be funny, boy?"

"Someone to help play out the firing wires, sir."

"Adamson. Your job."

"Sah!" The sergeant stood to attention.

Carter was quietly beside himself with the theatrics.

"Right. Now comes the dangerous bit. Once the charges are laid and primed and the firing box is in position..."

"Where, sir?" It was that piping voice again.

"What, Watson?"

"Where do you want to place the firing box, sir?"

"Er..." He had to think. "How far is safe, Watson."

"It depends on the charge, sir. And the enemy."

"What d'you mean, 'the enemy'?"

"Well... If they're in the vicinity..."

"There's no one in the vicinity, Watson. How far away do we have to be to be safe?"

"It depends on the size of the charge, sir."

"You said that. Well...?"

"I won't know what size of charge to place until I see the structure, sir."

This could go on for ever, thought Carter.

He broke in before the dialogue continued. "Major, we will need cover in any case, will we not, so why don't we set the firing box in the Ramesseum? It is quite far enough from the villa - providing you have enough firing wire, that is."

"Good thinking, Carter. Ramesseum. Excellent cover. We set the bombs off from there." The major looked well satisfied. "Good show. But we need to look beyond success. The escape. Hardest part of all, the escape. Often bungled. Many a successful mission lost its heroes due to a lack of escape planning."

'Oh, my God,' thought Carter, rolling his eyes.

The major was in full flow. "Following the attack, Watson reels in the firing wire and we regroup at the east entrance to the Ramesseum." He waited for indications of recognition from each in the circle. Satisfied he had their attention he continued. "It's a longish walk to the boat, but it's important we make it in as short a time as possible. Means we shall have to double-time it. While we're in the boats everyone gets their face-black off. Don't want to turn up in Luxor looking like a bunch of darkies. Then, back to your bunks. Nothing ever happened. You know the drill. Any questions?"

A single hand was raised. It was Lieutenant Horsell.

"Sir. Permission to speak?"

"Go ahead, Horsell."

"This black stuff, sir. I suffer fwom washes."

"'Washes?'"

"No, sir - washes, sir. This stuff hurts my skin. May I wear something dark over my face instead - a gas mask, for instance?"

"Very well. Very well. Now, men, synchronise watches! At the count of three it will be zero-nine-fifteen hours pwe... precisely - one, two, three!"

Everyone but Carter, who was preoccupied with subduing his giggling, clicked their watches into action together.

"Remember now, we all stay within sight of one another until the raid is over. Watson, take us to the armoury."

Carter tolerated the company of the soldiers all day and all evening. They played cards together most of the time, but only one of them played bridge. Unable to make a four, he soon became bored. It seemed an age before midnight finally came around. They began to ready themselves to go down to the river bank. They each took a dollop of boot black and rubbed it into their faces, oily with perspiration. All, that is, except for Horsell, who sat beside them with his gas mask on, quietly perspiring. He was visually oblivious to all that was going on around him. The glass apertures for his eyes had misted up.

Carter helped paddle one of the boats to the other side of the river. They disembarked, dragged the dinghies up on the sand and set off across the fields towards the Ramesseum. Carter led the way.

In another twenty minutes or so they were at the threshold of the temple. The soldiers moved between the columns, darting from the cover of one to the other as if they were stealing up on some dangerous quarry. Carter, totally unaware of his colleagues' cautionary tactics, walked straight through the centre. Reaching the rear of the Ramesseum, they looked out into the darkness to try to pick out the shape of their target.

They had no trouble seeing it. There was a small log fire burning just outside the entrance, and right beside it two Arab guards asleep on blankets.

"Damn!" hissed the major.

"Looks like we're in for a bit of 'sensitive immobilisation', eh, major?" whispered Carter, unable to resist the opportunity to add some flavour to their adventure.

"Horsell!" the major hissed.

"Sir!"

The 'creature from beyond' scurried over to the major's side. Dorking started at the sight of the masked lieutenant.

"God, you look ugly, Horsell! Now. Pay attention. Take Adamson and nobble those two fellahs. Make sure neither of you is recognised. Bind and gag 'em, then drag 'em away somewhere where they'll be safe from the blast. Ensure they're left somewhere where they'll be easily spotted when daylight breaks. Don't want 'em frying before they get found. Not good for local relations." Dorking needn't have worried.

Both crouching low as they moved across the rocks and sand, Horsell led the sergeant around in a wide arc so that they came on the men from the side and, so far as was possible, out of the light thrown by the fire. With all the stealth they had been taught during training, the two reached the corner of the building and eased themselves along the wall towards the sleeping, unarmed custodians. Close by now, Horsell positioned himself to leap on one of the Arabs. He rose up before the unsuspecting unfortunate with his arms held high and prepared to jump.

The two guards opened their eyes almost simultaneously. The flickering light of the fire blazed from the orbs of glass in Horsell's gas mask. What a sight they must have beheld. The devil himself, his eyes afire, had come to claim them! Together the two let out a terrible, primeval scream and took off into the darkness at a speed that would have challenged any sprinter. Adamson attempted to fall on one of them as they ran past, but he was slow to react. He missed the man completely, fell to the ground and hit his head on a rock, knocking himself senseless.

"Fine mess," was all the major could think to say as he watched the charade. "Fine, bloody mess."

"Not that bad, sir," reassured Carter. "Looks like you achieved your objective - guards gone, effectively immobilised, unharmed, their attackers unrecognised - for what they were, at least - and the house now safely secured to us. Not at all bad."

"Don't like to say it, Carter, but more by luck than judgement, I'm afraid. More by luck than judgement."

He turned to Watson. "Well, don't just stand there, boy, get over there and do what you're trained to do."

He turned to the remainder of the attack force. "You help him. You others keep a lookout."

As Horsell tried to bring Adamson around, Watson went into the building and began to lay out his charges. He knew he had to lay the gun cotton at the base of load-bearing pillars, but he hadn't a clue what size of charge would be sufficient to bring the place down. That it would have to be less per charge than that which he would use for the steel members of a bridge he was certain, but how much less? After all their trouble he couldn't afford to have the mission fail in its objective. He decided to err on the safe side and place a little more than he judged might be necessary.

His charges laid and primed, he drew the cables out through the front door and walked backwards to the Ramesseum, laying the wires out before him.

"All set and ready, sir."

"Good man," said the major. "Everyone back behind me!" he shouted.

"Horsell! If you can't wake him up, carry him, dammit!"

The lieutenant by this time had finally managed to slap some life back into the dazed sergeant and was able to help him back onto his feet and guide him slowly back to cover.

Once safely within the temple walls, they all crouched down and waited for the order. This would be Carter's moment of triumph. A real poke in the eye for the Hun - one particular Hun to be exact - Doktor Ludwig Borchardt.

Watson charged up the firing box and poised himself above it with his hands on the firing stick. The major looked about one more time and then dropped his hand. With all his weight Watson fell on the firing stick.

There was a tremendous flash and one almighty crack, lengthened by a split second as the several charges ignited in rapid succession. Each of the conspirers felt the draught of the shock wave. Heavy objects rushed through the air about them. In the stony confinement of the pillared hall of the Ramesseum the amplification was almost unbearably loud. Worse still, as the noise died and the perpetrators took their hands from their ears, echoes reflected from the walls of the cliffs about them almost as loud and from multiple directions, as if they were being bombarded themselves.

For a moment or two the troops stared from one to the other in startled amazement, not yet daring to look at the results of their work. Falling about them, the dust of many thousands of disintegrated mud bricks settled on their shoulders. The echoes finally trailed away into the darkness of night and peace returned.

The pillars of the Ramesseum reflected a glow from the fires which now quietly crackled on the remains of fallen wooden lintels.

Dorking switched on his torch and shone it into Carter's face. He winced. The major laughed. "You're all bloody red, Carter! What a sight! Hey, men, look. He's all bloody red!"

The light from the torch reflected off the pillars about them. Horsell looked around quickly and, pulling off his mask, announced, "Evwyone's wed, sir. The whole bloody lot of us!" And he began to laugh.

A moment later pretty much everybody in the group was laughing. The bright, white elipse of face left by Horsell's mask shone like a ghost in the dim light thrown by Dorking's torch.

"They're all laughing at you, Horsell. You're the only white man in the 'twoop'!"

An embarrassed Horsell quickly replaced his gas mask and Carter turned to look towards the villa. The dust was finally settling. At the positions where Watson had laid the charges, glowing embers flashed and sputtered momentarily. For all that anyone could see in the faint light, there was literally nothing left. Even the sand on the bedrock had been blown away. All that remained was a polished rocky outcrop with broad scorch marks in eight places.

The major was the first to speak. "Back to bridges for you, Watson. You nearly killed us all, boy."

"I... I told you I had never been trained on buildings, sir. I just guessed."

Carter leant over and patted Watson on the shoulder. "You did well, boy. We got rid of it. Wiped it. Completely. Nothing remains. As if it had never existed. And no one the worse for wear... apart from 'Sarn't Adamson', that is, who only has himself to blame."

The major grunted. "Let's get out of here. Gather up the stuff. Follow me."

That night the devil had made an awful appearance, wrought his wicked work and left. Two frightened fellahs with an horrific tale to tell would never be the same again. Howard Carter would sleep soundly.

Chapter Thirteen
The Hundredth Day

Tutankhamun was not dead - not to Ankhesenamun, not to Ay, not to the people, not to any who believed.

To Horemheb, however, the thought of meeting in the afterlife he whom he had murdered was unthinkable. Who knows what manner of retribution his spirit could fashion? It would have plenty of time to prepare. However long it might take, one way or another the general would have to see to it that the king's body never completed its journey.

Ankhesenamun was equally resolute. She would rejoin her husband in the everlasting. She would assure him a peaceful and safe journey. They would live, once and for all, in eternal harmony. It would be Horemheb who would not survive the afterlife.

What Horemheb had not bargained for was the depth and complexity of the queen's creative subterfuge. It would not occur to him that she might attempt to pre-empt his plan. Interfere perhaps, but it was beyond comprehension that she could reason against him, let alone ultimately defeat him.

It had seemed to Dashir over these last three months that the queen had gone over her plans in explicit detail more than one hundred times. But, on the night he was to do the deed, the queen once more had summoned him to her chambers.

He entered, flanked by two palace guards, and prostrated himself before her.

"Leave us!"

The guards dutifully departed and reassumed their positions outside the doors to her rooms.

"Dashir, rise. Welcome. Tonight we shall taste victory over evil. Tonight you will bring me the soul of my husband. Tonight you will be rewarded beyond your greatest expectations."

Dashir raised his eyes. There was a puzzled expression on his face. He had not thought of payment. He had just hoped to complete the job and get away with his life. That would be gift enough. If she wished to give him something besides, so be it, but he would have to be alive to receive it.

She continued. "Dashir. You will cross the Nile tonight - alone."

He couldn't believe it. She was going to go through the whole thing again. There was so much to do before dawn. She was wasting valuable time. He forgot himself for a moment and interrupted, "My... my lady... permit me, please... to speak."

She was taken aback by his forwardness, but her regard for this servant was so great that she did not take offence at it.

"You are free to speak."

Dashir paused. His fear returned.

"Well then... If you have something to say, speak your mind."

"My lady," he nervously began again, "we have been over this plan many, many times these past weeks. I know it like the skills in my hands. I can do this thing. But I do need time. Please let me go now so that I may have the fullness of the night."

She understood. "Very well then. Be gone. I will not expect you until tomorrow's sun falls into the Royal Necropolis. Be off with you!"

Much relieved, he smiled and at once departed.

Dashir met his son on the other side of the river. Together they walked as quickly as they could to The Valley and the site of the entrance to the tomb. As the queen had indicated, there were no guards. The gravel covering the stairway looked exactly like the rest of the debris in this part of The Valley - invisible to all but those who remembered precisely where it had been.

"We start to dig here," he ordered his son. "You will dig the tunnel. I will remove the debris. It will be easy. It is still soft. Start here. In this way you will excavate to the top of the first door. The roof of the tomb will protect you. Mind you make a hole big enough for me to crawl through!"

His son smiled. "Yes, father." And he began scraping at the area his father had pointed out to him.

It seemed to take for ever. The boy eventually reached the first door and began chiselling away at the bricks, dragging them out one by one. As soon as he'd cleared a space large enough for each of them to pass through he began shovelling at the fill in the corridor, pushing the debris behind him with his hands and feet. Dashir gathered it up in a basket and dragged it outside.

Every time he emerged at the surface, Dashir would stand motionless for a moment, listening for any sign of movement within The Valley. There was nothing, thankfully, but for the intermittent whirring of a cricket or two.

He pulled himself back down the narrow tunnel until he reached the pile of rubble at his son's feet. He called ahead to him.

"Are you at the second door yet?"

"Yes, father," answered the panting boy. "I'm pulling out the bricks now."

"Clear a space for me and then come out."

Dashir filled his basket with the remaining debris and backed out of the tunnel. The boy emerged a few moments later dragging the remaining bricks with him.

"This is it!" pronounced Dashir. "Light me that oil lamp."

Taking the lamp, he wriggled his way along the tunnel. The bed of the cavity was uneven and occasionally he scraped his back on the roof of the corridor but he didn't let the pain distract him. He pushed the lamp ahead until he reached the door to the antechamber. Gripping the edges of the hole in the doorway he pulled his head through. Flashes of reflected gold were suddenly all about him and in the flickering lamplight, amidst the aura of golden reflections, weird shadows danced randomly on the walls like so many cavorting lucifers.

He took a moment to gather himself and then rested the lamp on the gravel filling of the corridor next to his right shoulder. With some effort he managed to pull himself into the room head first. Because of the gloom it seemed a long drop but he forced his heels against the roof of the corridor to slow his fall and by the time he felt himself losing his grip his fingers had touched the floor of the chamber. He slid down the inner wall of the door and picked himself up. He recovered his lamp from the entrance to the tunnel and placed it on the floor.

Once again he paused a while to take in the flickering glitter that surrounded him, but only for a moment. There was no time to indulge in the extravagance of it all. He turned to the golden shrine standing between the feet of the two great gilded statues. Sinking to his knees before the doors of the shrine, he quickly crushed the dried mud seal in his hands and untied the rope securing the bolt. He pulled the bolt clear and opened the doors. The light from his lamp shone on the feet of the diminutive gold effigy standing inside. The remainder of the figure was obscured by the roll of papyrus that had been pushed in beside it.

He was deeply troubled at being within the tomb. The sight of the statue added to his anxiety. It was, after all, the representation of the king's spirit in the afterlife. The very life force of the king himself may already lie within it.

He became conscious of his hesitation and pulled himself together. He removed the papyrus and stuffed it inside his tunic, grabbed the statuette firmly in his fist, wrapped it hurriedly in a linen rag and turned around to face the breached doorway.

His son's head protruded from the hole. Dashir passed the figure to his son and they joined hands. The boy backed into the tunnel and helped to pull his father up. A few moments later they had managed to wriggle their way back out and into the night air. They refilled the stairwell, taking care to smooth off the surface to obscure evidence of their illicit entry.

The two of them ran out of The Valley as fast as their tired limbs could carry them.

The next night, with the effigy secure in her possession, the queen went to bed in such royally good mood that all in her company had observed and remarked on her improved demeanour.

"You heard the general yourself," reaffirmed Nefer. "There is no danger. He will see to it that no one comes. We can take all that we can carry. Untold riches await us, Senet. Riches beyond our dreams."

Senet was anxious. He knew the penalties should they be discovered. He had never trusted the general. He knew full well that if they were caught in the act the general would deny all knowledge of them. They took all the risk. They would take all the punishment. But, then again, should they succeed, they would have all the rewards. It was, after all said and done, far too tempting an opportunity. If they didn't take it, someone else would. And many had plundered before them and got away with it successfully.

"Let us be quick, Nefer. Before I change my mind."

They stole into The Valley at midnight, leading a small donkey with two large baskets slung across its back. When they reached the spot, in the darkness the discoloration in the sand left after Dashir's recently disguised penetration went unnoticed. But, as they excavated down to the lintel of the doorway, they found the digging easier to the left, and when they reached the top of the door they realised why. The hole left by Dashir lay open before them. They looked at each other in gaunt surprise. Could the risks they were now taking be all in vain?

Senet was trembling and clearly ready to leave.

"No," ordered Nefer, restraining his colleague by the arm. "We must first go in to see the extent of this robbery. Perhaps it is no more than superficial. The tunnel is not large."

Without waiting for a comment from his friend, Nefer got down on his stomach and pulled himself in, pushing an oil lamp ahead of him. As his bare feet disappeared into the blackness, Senet felt compelled to follow but held back to listen for others. Presently he heard Nefer's voice whispering from the depths.

"There is much here, my friend. Many caskets. Come, I need your help."

Senet dove into the entrance but soon found that the fullness of his girth did not allow him to penetrate further than his shoulders. He backed himself out again and began scrabbling at the edges of the tunnel with his hands, enlarging it until it was big enough for him to get the full length of his body inside and provide sufficient elbow room to push the debris he was excavating back to his feet. He manoeuvred backwards up the slope, kicking the rubble behind him until it had cleared the tunnel, then scrambled back in and repeated the process, gradually getting himself closer to the top of the door to the antechamber.

While he awaited the appearance of his friend, Nefer looked around. The child's face on the centre bed stared directly towards him. Without hesitation he grabbed it, plucked the jewellery from the ears and the scalp and carelessly tossed the carving back on the bed. He stuffed the baubles into his tunic.

When Senet finally poked his head into the dimly lit room, for a moment he became still. The sight of the three great golden bedsteads flanking the opposite wall made him catch his breath.

Nefer reached up to him. "Here, take this." He passed him two handfuls of jewellery bundled in his head cloth. "Be gone! And return quickly for more."

Senet edged his way painfully backwards to the entrance.

The gold in his hands glinted in the moonlight. He dropped it into one of the baskets on the donkey, listened for a moment to reassure himself that The Valley remained silent, and then returned to the tunnel with the cloth. When he arrived at the hole in the top of the antechamber door, his partner was ready with another bundle. They exchanged cloths and Senet scrambled backwards once again. When he got back to the chamber the third time, Nefer had disappeared.

"Nefer!" he called in a muted shout. "Where are you?"

He could hear a considerable noise coming from beneath the bed to the left - much crashing about, some snapping wood, some obscenities.

"I'm in here," Nefer shouted at last. "A lot of stuff but not much of value. Found some wine. I'm coming out."

A clay wine vessel emerged from beneath the bed; then a head appeared; then an arm with a bundle in its fist; then the rest of him.

"Here. Take this. All I could find in a hurry. The place is packed but there isn't much jewellery. It was difficult to move around in there. The burial chamber will have more. Let's have a quick drink." Nefer waved the wine jar in front of his friend's face.

"Not me," said Senet, and he retreated up the tunnel once again.

Nefer broke the seal on the vessel, grabbed a small, light turquoise-coloured glass cup standing on one of the beds, wiped it out with his head cloth and filled it to the brim. He took a long draught.

By the time Senet returned, his friend was knocking back his fourth cupful.

"Nefer!" he shouted, then quickly brought his hands to his lips and whispered. "Put it down! Plenty of time for celebration when we're safely out of here." He grabbed the jar and placed it behind him. "Get on with it." He pointed to the plastered wall.

Murmuring under his breath, Nefer pushed the little golden shrine out of the way and set about smashing at the base of the plastered doorway to the burial chamber. He made a hole large enough to crawl through and dragged himself in.

The black sentinels either side the door looked on dispassionately.

Nefer was nowhere to be seen when Senet arrived back at the mouth of the tunnel. At least the wine jar had not moved from where he had left it. Senet cocked his head to the right and saw light flickering dimly from behind the hole his friend had made in the walled-up doorway. He could hear him opening caskets and tossing the lids aside, emptying the contents onto the stone floor and rummaging through them.

After a while, Nefer emerged from the hole with another bundle. Senet took it from him and withdrew to the donkey once more.

When he had scrambled back to the antechamber again, Nefer was waiting for him with another head cloth full of jewellery. But, as Senet stretched out a hand to receive it, he felt something touch the sole of his right foot. Instinctively he propelled himself headlong onto his colleague, the bundle all at once flying into the air and the two of them collapsing in a heap on the floor and extinguishing the oil lamp.

Nefer sat up. "What possesses you, my friend?"

"There is a scorpion in the passage, Nefer. I felt it pinch the sole of my foot."

"This is serious indeed," reacted his friend. "Finding it in the dark will be difficult. It will make our escape doubly hazardous!"

"We are leaving already?" asked Senet, somewhat relieved but at the same time surprised at Nefer's apparent haste.

"No! There is much jewellery yet to be retrieved from the treasury. But we shall need help to get at the mummy. For that we will have to return another night."

The prospect of a second risky venture into The Valley was more than Senet could bare.

"If you come back again, you come back without me. We're not yet out of this predicament."

"Senet, you worry too much. Remember, those who do not participate do not share in the reward."

"What we have here is sufficient for my needs - for ever."

"You were never a man of ambition, my friend. Do as you wish tomorrow. Tonight we have more urgent matters. How do...?"

Senet slapped his hand over Nefer's mouth and signalled him to listen.

There was the faint but unmistakable sound of voices issuing from the mouth of the entrance tunnel. The air in the tomb suddenly felt chilled. They listened, trembling, straining to make out the words.

Someone outside said, "There is no light. No one can be within. We may be too late. Did you notice anyone as you came over the track from Pademi?"

"No. Nobody. Nothing," answered another.

"Can you hear that? An ass running! They have gone already. That way! Towards the mouth of the valley. Come! We must make haste. They are getting away. Come quickly!"

There were sounds of some scuffling and suddenly there was silence again.

"I think they've gone." Nefer had his head in the tunnel.

"Can't have. They'd have seen the donkey. They'll know for sure we're still inside." Senet's heart was in his mouth.

"Nonsense," said Nefer. "The ass has bolted. They believe they're chasing us down the valley. We'd better leave at once. Follow me."

Eagerly Senet followed his partner back into the tunnel. Nefer's feet scrabbled forward just ahead of Senet's face and stopped every now and then as he listened for evidence of activity above. Reassured by the silence, he would move on once more, just for a few inches, then stop again. He didn't give the scorpion a second thought.

When they finally emerged at the surface, after what seemed like an eternity, in the limpid moonlight all was silent - no one, no donkey, no people, not a sound.

Nefer whispered to his friend, "We won't take the hill track. We'll go the other way - to the valley head. If they return they will never think of looking for us there. We shall hide 'til daybreak, then climb to the ridge."

Senet was beside himself with worry. In his blind panic he was unable to think and was only too happy to follow his partner's lead.

"Can you hear anything?"

Senet listened for a moment and then shook his head.

"I'm going back for the jewellery and, since we're going to have to stay out here all night, I'll get the wine as well."

Before Senet could stop him, Nefer's feet were once more disappearing into the hole in the ground. Alone on the surface in the dark, Senet imagined all manner of sounds about him.

Nefer finally dragged himself out of the tunnel, pulled the wine vessel after him by the heels, and stood up.

"Couldn't find the bundle anywhere. Dark as hell in there. Managed to stumble into these, however." Smiling he held up the wine jar and the drinking cup.

There was no answer. Nefer looked about him. Senet was nowhere to be seen.

"Senet!" he called, in a half whisper. "Senet! Where in the name of Seth are you?"

Nothing - not a sound, not so much as a stirring cricket. It was eerily silent. He listened. The breeze blew up for a moment, rustling his robe. There was a low rumble from up the valley as some rocks tumbled down from the cliff, then silence again.

Nefer decided to go his own way. 'Maybe Senet is up there already,' he thought. But, as he turned to go, he heard it. The sounds were unmistakable. The officials were on their way back up The Valley.

He took off up the nearest ravine until he reached the valley head. The open entrance to a disturbed tomb lay before him. He stopped and listened. The voices were still there but it appeared they were not getting any closer.

'They will investigate the tomb now,' he thought. 'Then, hopefully, they will leave once more.'

He settled back on his haunches behind a large boulder and filled his cup with more wine. But no sooner had he swallowed the first draught than he heard voices again. They were coming closer. 'Unbelievable!'

The sound was unmistakable. Senet's voice was among them.

'He is leading them to me!' Nefer panicked. He dropped his cup and let go of the wine vessel. It eased over onto its side and, spilling the remainder of its contents, slowly rolled to the floor of the ravine. Frantically he tried to scramble his way up the steep valley flank. He couldn't see what was ahead of him and grabbed hold of a loose boulder. As the rock pulled free, he lost his footing and skated down the scree slope on his rear end. With his flailing hands he searched desperately for something to hold on to but found nothing and continued sliding downwards until finally coming to rest at the feet of his pursuers.

They had made their protestations. They had said that they had discovered a tomb-robber's tunnel and had gone inside to apprehend the criminals in the act. They had denied the existence of the lost donkey. In final desperation they had accused Horemheb. But this only served to seal their fate.

Now they felt little. They had been imprisoned without food for three weeks and the lightness of the impoverished blood now supplying their minds did not give them the energy for anxiety. Their only emotion was a desire for eternal sleep.

It was Horemheb himself who gave the final order - Horemheb, the general who had publicly damned their indiscretions; Horemheb, who had condemned their violation of the late king's tomb; Horemheb, who had slept little since their discovery, bemoaning in the privacy of his chambers that the tomb remained essentially intact. He did not even know what his conscripts had managed to take. The donkey had galloped away as the priests had arrived. It was never found - not by any officials of the court, at least.

They were brought to the place of execution. They gave no outward expression of fear or any resistance. They were each placed on their backs on a mat of reeds, their arms tied behind them at the elbows. Nefer and Senet did not hear the words the priests chanted to the assembled public. Four large soldiers appeared above them. Each pair carried a stout wooden stake, crudely sharpened at both ends. On the priests' commands, the soldiers raised the stakes vertically above the two prone bodies. The weakened muscles tensed. In a single stroke the soldiers plunged the stakes deep into the unfortunates' bellies. Then, in a wheeling motion, the guards inverted and elevated the two bodies until they hung upside down, the stakes within them but not piercing them all the way through, and planted the stakes firmly into prepared holes in the ground.

Senet and Nefer made no sound. They had lost consciousness. Their sad forms hung there, bent over the pikes. Rivulets of blood spiralled swiftly down the stakes and matted the sand. Their wives wailed and rent their hair.

In the immediacy of the moment the assembled crowd took heed of the lesson. But memories are short.

The general was not a compulsive man. He would let some time pass before trying again. He knew very well that first there should be reparations - a demonstrable effort to make amends. He gathered the most skilful artisans who had been involved in the creation of the funerary objects and took them to The Valley. They entered the tomb by the passageway created by the robbers and set about reorganising those grave goods that had been disturbed.

Of those repacking the caskets, few but the scribes were literate and most could not read the inscriptions on the dockets. Things got stuffed back into any old box. Meneg did his best to ensure they stacked all the objects where they had been placed originally, but he couldn't answer for the caskets. There was so much to do and with such urgency mishandling was inevitable. Some of the objects were damaged. Many were misplaced.

"We have not the time to bother with the storeroom," shouted Meneg. "It's too much of a mess. Leave it - the ka is gone, so there is no more need for the provisions."

He urged his men out and was about to follow them himself when the tiny carving of the boy king's head once more caught his eye. It was lying on its side on the bed. The jewellery had gone but the beauty of his work looked directly back at him. The temptation was too great. They will believe it to have been taken by the robbers, he thought, and he grabbed it at once, stuffed it under his clothing and climbed back into the tunnel. He scrambled back towards the sounds of his colleagues, but halfway along the tunnel he became wedged fast. It was the head. He looked forward into the daylight thrown from the entrance and realised that the tunnel became no wider as it rose. There was no time. He had to dump his possession. He backed down slightly until he had room to loosen his robe, allowed the head to drop out beneath him, and pulled himself reluctantly onward until he reached his friends.

No sooner had he emerged than the men at the entrance began the process of refilling the tunnel. A plasterer wriggled in with a few mud bricks to reseal the antechamber door. When he reappeared, another labourer set about repacking the tunnel with rocks. Finally the plasterer resealed the outer doorway. The stairwell was refilled quickly and the labourers left The Valley in peace.

The priestly guard re-established their positions high up on the ridge above the tomb entrance, out of sight but within earshot, and resumed their vigil.

Some months later the general decided that the time was right for another attempt. He carefully selected a second troop of tomb robbers - by reputation most successful. He would be able to improve their chances of success if he could devise a way to divert the attentions of the queen's priests for long enough to allow his men to complete their task.

It was the date wine that night that gave him the idea. He had drunk plenty and become so inebriated that he could not get up from his couch. The room was moving about him. The dancing girls, who were dancing, seemed to him to be in a state of suspended animation - a blur of colour and shape that his mind could not lock down sufficiently to focus. As he struggled in his stupor to make some sense of the images before him, a strange feeling of benevolence began to absorb him. To the normal, sober, sane Horemheb this would have been totally out of character, but in his bath of alcohol it felt warmly comforting. The images in his mind turned to celebration - a great celebration, a royal celebration in which the royal priests would be honoured for their good worship and appeasement of the gods all these years. An event that would be looked on by all the deities as a celebration of themselves - a great demonstration of appreciation for their years of protection from bad harvest and pestilence, a great appeasement that would ensure that the new Pharaoh would live long and rule a fruitful reign - maat would prevail. No priest could refuse the invitation. Ay would accede to the general's request with enthusiasm - while the aged Pharaoh contemplated death, he was at the same time fearful of it.

The images stayed with Horemheb all night and in the morning he awoke with his head thumping. Nevertheless, spirited to act on the concept seeded in his dreams, he rolled off his bed and struggled to find his footing.

"Dress me at once! I wish to be taken to the High Priest!" he shouted. "I wish to have counsel with Parannefer before the sun is overhead."

Dressed in the regalia of his official office and imposing enough to deliver an impressive soliloquy, the general was brought to the high priest's place of reception.

"Holy one, you, the priesthood and your guard are summoned to Pharaoh's presence to receive his gratitude for the years of bountiful crops and good fortune which have been bestowed on our land since the passing of the heretic and for your assistance to Pharaoh in assuring the return of maat. This has come to pass only through the integrity of your linkage with the gods. We thank you..." The general bowed. "...And remember, it is Pharaoh's pleasure to entertain all the priesthood and all the temple guard this night at the palace. There will be two days and nights of revelry to celebrate your good works."

The high priest backed away with a few appropriate words of gratitude and Horemheb turned and hastily disappeared through the chamber doors.

He returned to the palace. "Guard!" spat Horemheb, immediately he entered the great hall. "Get Minuit and his men to come to the foundry at midday. I have an assignment for them. Quick! Be about your business!"

When the three arrived, the foundry was closed and the furnaces were cold. The general was waiting for them. As the clandestine group gathered, thunderclouds were appearing on the horizon. It occurred to the general that Seth appeared pleased - the inundation could be early this year.

"You have two nights and one day to complete the task of which we have already spoken. Do you understand that which I wish you to do?"

"Yes, sir," answered Minuit.

He was a diminutive little man but he had stout arms. A little like a mole, thought the general. Built just right for tunnelling.

"This night is the first. All the guardian priests of The Valley will be at the palace receiving gifts from Pharaoh. Be gone, then. Do not return to me, ever. I shall know if your task has been completed successfully. You shall reap the reward."

As the general left, it began to rain.

They waited until late evening to begin their assignment. They waited also to ensure that what Horemheb had said would actually transpire. The fates of their colleagues, Nefer and Senet, were still fresh in their minds. Their poor bodies, now picked clean by the buzzards of the desert, had become a pile of bleached, disaggregated bones lying on the ground beneath the pikes that had impaled them - a lingering, awful testament to their crime.

True to the general's word, there was a great feast that night. So far as they could tell from their vantage point far off, there were indeed many priests present; hopefully, as the general had promised, all of the priesthood. The infidels chose to embark on their task without further delay. Thirty-six hours was not long to complete a tomb robbery of this importance.

They stole across the river in their own boat, the continuing rain allowing them to row without fear of being heard, and moored at the head of the canal which lay closest to the entrance to the king's necropolis.

As Minuit tied up the boat, there was a crash of thunder. One of the others grabbed his arm. "I do not have a good feeling about this. Seth travels the firmament this night! Who knows what he is planning!"

Minuit jerked the knot tight and shrugged his shoulders. "He troubles not over the likes of us. He prepares to dampen the general's feast. On your way!"

They had walked some considerable distance into the throat of the valley, trudging through the slurrying mud, before they heard it. Beyond the noise of the rain lashing at their faces, there was indeed a perceptible sound of running water. But they saw nothing and did not fear it. As they walked on, the track narrowed and the valley sides steepened above them. Then, as they rounded the corner, in a flash of lightning they caught sight of the spot where the ground had been freshly disturbed, the rain already excavating a cavity in the softer soil. They increased their pace, keen to begin their work.

A split second before the tumbling water and bouncing debris hit them, Minuit heard the roar and realised what was happening. He gestured to his men to run in any direction to gain some elevation. But, as they turned, the wall of water rose up before them. The suspended rocks within its boiling froth immediately rendered them senseless. They tumbled before the torrent, their bodies torn apart by the boulders, their blood so diluted by the volume of the flood that it left no trace.

Unaware of the catastrophe in The Valley, Horemheb, just as he had promised, kept the festivities going the following day and into the following night. The Valley was left unpatrolled.

It mattered not. The gods had taken it under their own guardianship. As the sun broke over the cliffs and bathed the bottom of the damp valley in its midday light, a new carpet of rocks and mud had been laid along its length. Tutankhamun had been re-interred. This time for good.

Chapter Fourteen
Pause For a War

November was approaching and the days at Karnak were becoming noticeably cooler. The Great War was in its third year and with excavations still suspended Carter found the drafting sessions in the shade of the massive colonnade a wholly pleasing pastime. One afternoon, while well established at his easel with a thick, black coffee at his side and deeply engrossed in his tenth drawing, a cloaked Arab of obviously senior quality advanced on him in some haste. Carter recognised the man immediately.

"Sheikh Mansour!" he greeted, putting down his instruments and rising to shake the panting man by the hand. "Allah be praised. It is good to see you."

"Mr Carter, sir.... Mr Carter..." The Arab gulped for breath before continuing. "I am so happy to have found you.... We need your help.... Now.... Tomb robbers have been discovered at work in the hills behind The Valley.... They are active as we speak.... Please say you will come."

The thought of a new tomb discovery was music to Carter's ears. "Of course. At once."

"I have a boat waiting, sir. We can pick up your men when we get to the other side of the river."

Carter lost no time packing his things. They both walked briskly to the river and embarked.

Once on the west bank, Carter ran up to his house and dropped off his drawing materials.

"Abdel!" he shouted. "Assemble my fellahs. I need them now!"

Sheikh Mansour called from the doorway, "Sir, you will need much rope. The tomb lies beneath a cliff and the only access is from above."

A party of six, a donkey and mangy Gaggia left the house that evening and began the slow climb to the place where the tomb robbers had been spotted. Sheikh Mansour pointed it out as they walked up the path. Carter couldn't see too well in the failing light, but what he thought he could make out was almost unbelievable. The cliff wall looked sheer. In the middle of the valley head towards which Sheikh Mansour was pointing there appeared to be a vertical gash running about halfway down the cliff from the top. Vertical scars such as this were common in these hills. They were lines of weakness in the rocks that had been exploited by flood waters during the infrequent downpours. They became the focus for short-lived waterfalls - giant vertical tears gouged out in a geologic instant.

"You mean it's at the bottom of that cleft?" he asked the sheikh, hoping he was mistaken.

"Yes, sir. At the bottom. They climbed down on a rope. Very brave rascals. But rascals nonetheless."

The path took them by a circuitous route around the more gently sloping back of the hills and thence to the top of the cliff. Carter was quiet the rest of the journey - he spent the time contemplating what might await him at the top and below. He had no congenital fear of heights, but the very thought of climbing down a rope in the darkness onto a den of iniquitous pirates was beginning to chill him to the bone. From this point on, their trudge up the track seemed unhelpfully short.

By the time Carter arrived at the place, it was midnight. As he moved carefully towards the cliff edge, he saw where the robbers' rope was fastened. He used it to guide him to the cleft and gingerly looked down. In the darkness he could see very little. There was a faint glimmer below - perhaps the robbers' lamp shining from within the cavity - and in the stillness of the desert he could hear voices. They were down there all right. He couldn't make out their conversation. There were several voices talking at once and the sounds were far off and faint. It sounded like there were at least as many of them as there were in Carter's party.

He sat back on his haunches for a moment and gathered his thoughts. Was his party sufficient in number to successfully see off the intruders? If he went down there it would be just him against all of them. In the hysteria of discovery and the surprise of being caught in the act they could get violent. Once at the mouth of the tomb, a small push and he would be sent tumbling to his death on the rocks below. Should he wait until the robbers themselves climbed back out of the tomb so he could confront them with lesser odds? But then the damage would have been done. Then again, it was almost impossible to believe that this could be a tomb at all. His brave efforts could all be in vain.

Sheikh Mansour whispered in his ear, "You must stop them, Mr Carter, sir. They will be damaging priceless objects. Better you get down there quickly before it is too late. I shall stay at the top to ensure your safety," he said, and nodded a reassuring smile.

Carter was little comforted by the sheikh's words and less so at his offer of help. But it was clear he had to steel himself to go down there before they did too much harm to whatever lay inside the tomb. From the sounds of their excited chattering, it seemed they could already be in amongst the booty.

"Abdel, bring me the rope we carried up here." Carter took up the robbers' rope, severed it with his penknife and allowed it to fall towards the cavity below. Abdel tied the new rope around a firm enough looking outcrop. Carter checked the security of the knot and took a tight hold on the rope as he slid over the edge. As he felt his footing give way, the change in balance caused the rope to twist and swing to the left and he bounced uncomfortably against the rock on the other side of the cleft, bruising his left shoulder and scraping his tightened knuckles against the sandstone. He now hung free, suspended from his grip on the rope, his feet flailing about trying to pinch the rope between them. Feeling the rope wind around his right leg he finally brought his feet together, one over the other, and felt in control enough that he could once more allow himself to slip downwards.

As he slid towards the ledge below, the sounds of the robbers' voices became louder and rang with echoes from the confined space in which they were busy at their mischief. It took a few minutes before he felt his right foot touch the ledge. In the darkness he was unsure of the size of his precarious perch and chose immediately to sit down and gather his composure. As he did so, Gaggia barked anxiously from the cliff. The voices all at once stopped. The brief silence that ensued was overpowering.

With the passage of time, one by one the Arabs within the tunnel began talking to one another again. This time Carter could plainly make out what they were saying.

"Did you hear something?"

"I thought so, yes."

"Listen..."

Through the light of the robbers' lamp flickering dimly from the other end of the tunnel Carter could now make out the shape of the cavity. He decided to address them while they were still inside. His words would surely be amplified within the corridor and, since they couldn't see who was speaking, the impact, particularly the English accent, would be all the stronger.

"You there! Come out immediately!"

Arabic with a country English flavour did the trick. Anything from an Englishman represented authority. They knew at once they were discovered and their retribution would be merciless. After a minute or two, and in silence, they began to crawl towards him one at a time.

Carter, on the other hand, did not feel quite as confident as his voice may have sounded. Had it not been so dark, his expression would quickly have given away that he was truly frightened. But, as the first man approached the entrance to the tunnel, Carter switched on his torch. The temporarily blinding light successfully added to the leading robber's anxiety. Instantly the man stopped moving and tried to back up, stabbing the calloused soles of his feet into the face of his following colleague.

"We are dead men!" whispered the man.

Carter's fear all at once left him and the arrogant authority that found its roots in Victorian England - Empire, 'Ruling the Waves' and such like - blossomed within his bosom. "Come! You are discovered! Out with you!"

The first man resigned himself to his fate and nervously emerged. Carter raised the torch from the man's face and, now able to see his captor clearly, he instantly recognised Carter as the former keeper of antiquities in this area. The fact that Carter had lost that station some time ago did not lessen the robber's respect. The man fell to his knees and bowed to the ground. This cemented Carter's resolve and he let into the men as they emerged one by one - eight in all - reading them a litany of Egyptian profanities and promising them the severest of punishments through due process of law should he discover that they had damaged anything.

The rabble was suitably impressed. Without argument, they began the difficult climb back up the rope to the cliff top, Carter checking each man for contraband before he handed him the rope. He found none.

About thirty minutes later, Carter sat alone on the edge. He turned his face upward and shouted toward his colleagues at the top.

"Sheikh Mansour! I am going inside! Hold the rascals until I return!"

Gaggia barked an acknowledgement.

Carter got down on all fours and dragged himself into the small aperture the robbers had excavated in the tomb entrance. It was an arduous and uncomfortable journey down the narrow, rubble-filled tunnel. Because of the tomb's situation at the bottom of a cleft, the tunnel had completely filled with flood debris and was almost totally choked. After about fifty feet the robbers had reached a wall of limestone. At this point they had excavated in many directions, searching for a way onward, eventually discovering that the way ahead was to the right. This far into the tomb, the amount of debris lessened and there had been no need for further tunnelling. Carter scrambled down the pile of rocks choking the passageway until he reached the chamber floor. Here his torchlight caught the yellow translucence of a quartzite sarcophagus lying open at the edge of another passage which itself descended yet further into the darkness. The sarcophagus was impressive but empty, and there seemed to be little else about. He crawled on down the passage in the hope of finding more below. But he was to be disappointed. Water filled the cavity ahead and he was unable to penetrate any further. So far as he could see the robbers had gone to considerable effort, not to mention risking their lives, to find nothing of value that was in any way portable.

Gaggia barked with anticipation as Carter pulled himself back up the rope and re-established himself safely with his colleagues at the top of the cliff.

He turned to the anxious sheikh. "Search them once more and, if you find nothing, let them go. They can have found little, if anything, of value. The tomb is almost completely filled with rocks from the flooding. It requires careful excavation. We shall begin tomorrow. I am tired and I hurt, it seems, everywhere! Post a guard. Let's get back."

The journey back down to Castle Carter seemed to be over almost as soon as it had begun. Carter had fallen asleep the instant he'd sat himself on the donkey. The combined effects of mental stress, physical exhaustion and lack of sleep had at last caught up with him. How he managed to stay upright during the rocking, rolling and sometimes stumbling descent was a mystery - a kind of narcoleptic balancing act. He fell into bed as the sun was rising.

There was something familiar about the banging on the door that dragged him unwillingly out of his slumber and into the daylight.

"Sar'nt Adamson, sir, h'at your service. H'I 'ave been sent by the Colonel to h'ask you to front h'up at 'is quarters h'as soon as you are h'able, sir. H'if you please, sir."

"What is it this time, sergeant? I thought the army had no more need of my services."

"H'on the contrary, sir. You h'are a h'integrool part h'ov the war effit. H'England cannot do wivout you, sir. So h'I am led to believe."

"Indeed, sergeant. Indeed. Well, what is it this time?" Carter knew what the answer would be.

"'Ush, 'ush, sir. H'as you is aware. H'in the Intelligence Service no one knows wot h'anyone does."

"Surprise, surprise," muttered Carter under his breath.

"Beggin' yer pardon, sir?"

"Nothing, sergeant. Just trying to shake the sleep out of my eyes. I have been up all night."

"H'oh, sorry, sir. H'Abdel didn't say. H'I wouldn't 'ave burst in like this 'ad I known."

"Abdel didn't answer the door?"

Adamson paused. "Well... no. Not now you mention it, sir. No, maybe 'e didn't. H'I do believe h'I burst in 'ere h'unannounced, as it were. Me apologies, sir." And with a continuing lack of feeling, "Can you please get dressed quickly, sir? The colonel's waiting."

Carter took his time. The army could wait. "Abdel! Abdel! Wake up, man. I need you at once!"

Abdel appeared at the door in a state of partial consciousness.

"Ah. Good man. I have to go to the UCO over the river. While I'm away I want you to get the fellahs organised with a reis. Hosein will do if he's available. Get back to the tomb and begin clearing the entrance passage. It will not be easy. Get them to construct a gantry of some kind so that the men can access the place more easily and in greater safety. Be sure they sift everything for broken stuff. I want a full accounting when I return. Well... Get on with it!"

The servant left the room. It would be some hours before he had regained his senses sufficiently to begin doing what his master had asked of him. In the meantime Carter accompanied Adamson to UCO HQ. He hadn't met the colonel before.

'This has to be important,' he thought. Colonels have no time for civilians unless they really need them.

His conviction that the matter had to be so important was reinforced when he found himself admitted to the colonel's presence immediately he arrived at HQ.

"Carter! Al-ham-d'Allah!" The colonel stood up as soon as he saw Carter enter the room. "Name's Lawrence. Damned pleased to meet you at last. Please sit down." He waved towards the only chair on the opposite side of his desk.

Carter took his seat and looked the colonel up and down. He was not a big man by any means and was extremely thin, thin to the point that his linen uniform hung off him so loosely that he almost assumed the form of a tube. An incongruously large wristwatch was strapped around the outside of his left sleeve. He wore an Arabic headdress, as many did in these parts, it being the most practical for relief from the heat. This one was unusual in that it was far more extravagant in both the design and the quality of material than any Carter had seen before. The colonel had it draped, it seemed purposefully, about his shoulders. The head cloth framed a large, elongate face, somewhat out of proportion with the rest of the body. Carter looked into the deep blue of his eyes. They seemed strangely sad. There were no smile lines radiating from them. There was an intensity in his gaze. The colonel stared directly at him.

"Mr Carter," he began. "I know a bit about you. But this is the Intelligence Service, is it not? So you would expect that, would you not?" he smiled. "Actually I know a bit about you not through the IS but through reputation. You are very well known in these parts. I am sure you are aware. Well respected - as an artist; as a trader; as an Egyptologist; as an Arabist; as a linguist. I have long wanted to make your acquaintance. I think we have much in common. Hopefully we can be friends."

Carter was puzzled by the man. He was different from those he had previously met in the UCO. There was an educated, even scholarly feel about him - an academic, surely. He had an aura of confidence and sophistication that came only from a solid education at a very good school. At the same time, however, he seemed one who had endured experiences in the extreme. One who had been touched by horror more than once. It was in the face. Carter was greatly intrigued. His personal curiosity and his empathy for the man compelled him to listen.

The colonel continued. "But you will be anxious to know why I have summoned you here. The fact is, I need your specific skills to help me with the problem which now faces me. And I mean me, not the king's army."

'That's a relief!' thought Carter.

"I am temporarily in Cairo. Spend most of my time in the desert. But right now I'm having to put up with Allenby and his entourage. Career army - you know the type - not good for anything else. Not much of a gift for fighting either, if you ask me. Anyway, Allenby's in the process of mustering a large force to support Faisal against the Turks. It's going to require a lot of artillery - big bang stuff. While he's engaged at that, my job is to cut the

Turkish lines of supply. The Turks are using the railway infrastructure which bridges the deserts. We ambush the trains. Sounds dangerous but actually it isn't. It's pretty easy really. The Turks aren't that well prepared - think that when they're out in the middle of nowhere no one in their right mind would bother to come all that way through all that nothingness to clobber their train. They forget that the desert is the Arab's backyard. We fall on them wherever we wish."

"We?" asked Carter.

"Well, me really, and my Arab militia. Guerrillas if you like."

Carter's earlier uneasiness was creeping back. What is he leading up to? Could this mean they at last have come to summon me to the front?

"Never mind that. The subject of our meeting has nothing to do with the war."

The Egyptologist's sigh of relief was almost audible.

"Mr Carter, my travels through many deserts have taken me to and through places that no Englishman has ever seen - very few living men of any race for that matter. In the course of my work I come across objects left by the ancestors of the desert's present landlords. Ancestors, I believe, who in fact did not live in deserts but were, during their lives, surrounded by lush vegetation and fertile fields - all this now turned to barren sand and bare rocks. I have been fortunate enough to have been schooled in the literary arts and in language but, although I have read archaeology, my schooling has lacked any depth of teaching in the ageing of antiquities. Please enlighten me about these..."

So saying, the colonel bent down and picked up a large and clearly weighty sack and placed it on the desk between them.

Carter helped the colonel untie the cord about the neck of the sack and they opened the mouth fully, rolling the hessian down until the top of the pile of objects, each wrapped rather awkwardly in newspaper, was revealed. As he unwrapped the first, Carter couldn't believe his eyes. This man truly had an eye for quality. It was a neolithic hand axe of beautifully polished, frosted quartzite.

The colonel looked at him expectantly. "It's neolithic," said Carter. "Perhaps six thousand years old - maybe older."

"My word!"

As they progressed through the hoard, Carter realised the importance of this meeting. The man could recall the provenance of most of the objects he had collected over the past two years. Their quality and variety were sufficient to stock a small museum. He wondered if he dare ask the key question.

Carter picked up a piece of pottery and examined it closely.

"Picked that up in the Rub-al-Khali - at Ubar - at least I think it's the site of Ubar. Ruined walls, buried in sand. What isn't around here? Been looking for the place for a year. Camel train route. Can't really miss it if you keep your eyes open. Plan to go back there one day. Satisfy my curiosity... And this. Roman. From Um el Jamal, some way northeast of the Dead Sea. But then you probably know that."

All Carter could do was repetitively nod his head. He was virtually speechless.

As another rare piece appeared, he could contain himself no longer. "Colonel," he started, "would it be presumptuous of me to enquire whether you might consider donating these to the British Museum?"

Lawrence looked up at Carter in surprise. He had not once suspected any of the objects to be of any real value. He had merely appreciated the thrill of finding them and wished to learn more about them.

"You cannot be serious, Mr Carter. You mean to tell me these pieces are significant?"

"Indeed I do, Colonel. Most are of considerable historical value, let alone their artistic merit. It would be a sin for them to be enjoyed by just one person. They need to be shared with others."

"I'll be damned!"

"You have a good eye, Colonel."

Lawrence reflected for a moment. Carter became anxious - now hearing of the value of his discoveries, the colonel might wish to keep them for himself. He struggled for something additional to say that might help convince him to release the objects. He was just about to speak when the colonel said, "Damned nuisance carrying them around with me all over the desert. The bag just keeps getting heavier. Can you find a suitable address for them, Mr Carter?"

A relieved Carter quickly responded. "Most assuredly, Colonel. Leave them with me and I will see to it that they get the very best of homes. If you would be good enough to give me an address where I can always make contact with you, once I have finalised the arrangements for placement I would be glad to write to you and tell you where they are situated."

"Just write to me at HQ, Cairo. It'll find me - wherever I am - eventually."

The colonel looked at his watch. He stood up.

"Excellent! That's settled then. A load off my mind, I'll tell you. Well met, Mr Carter. I hope it will not be too long before we meet again."

Carter drew himself up and half bowed in respect. "Colonel. And perhaps you will have more finds to share!"

"Perhaps." The colonel appeared a little crestfallen. "Perhaps. But I fear the engagements which face me next will leave precious little time for idle rock-hunting." He regarded his watch again. "Got to dash... Sergeant Adamson! Carry the sack for Mr Carter, there's a good fellow. Your servant, Mr Carter. Goodbye."

"Your servant, Colonel Lawrence," Carter responded.

They shook hands and Carter left the room.

"Bet you fawt you wuz for h'anuva assignment, Mr Carter, sir." Adamson chimed in with a grin as they walked back to the ferry.

"Must admit the thought had occurred to me, Sergeant. But in the event a most gratifying encounter. Fine man that colonel."

"'E's not a real colonel, sir. 'E's a Lieutenant colonel."

"What's the difference?"

"Nufink much, I 'spose. But this one's a loner. 'E doesn't 'ave no command - h'at least not a British command. 'e looks after the bleedin' fuzzy wuzzys - h'organises 'em, like, tries to make fightin' men of 'em! Bloody h'undisciplined lot. 'E ain't got no chance in 'ell. Ha, ha, ha!"

"I wish him well, notwithstanding. And so should you."

"Oh, I does, sir. Don't get me wrong. 'E's a good man an' no mistake. But 'e's got a 'opeless task. Sad fing is 'e finks 'e can do it."

"That's half the battle, sergeant. A fighting man like you should know that. Believing in one's self and what one could achieve given the will and the effort... It makes men of us all."

The sergeant went silent and looked ahead in disinterest. The draft had got him into this man's army. The end of the war or injury would get him out. He wanted nothing more. In the meantime he'd do his best to stay out of harm's way. He had nothing more to say to men of conviction.

The allies were winning the war. At great cost in men, it was true, but the war was being won nonetheless and at long last. The battle for Arabia was over and this resulted in Howard Carter being officially relieved of his duties at the UCO.

His patron, also, leaving hospital after a painful illness, had finally been permitted to repossess his country seat. He was feeling fitter and in better spirits than he had for many months and, buoyed up by his expectation of new and greater discoveries alongside the Norfolk man in the three-piece tweed. He was itching to get back to work in Egypt.

Carter, however, did not feel at all anxious to receive him just yet. Before Carnarvon returned to Luxor Carter very much wanted to be able to demonstrate that he had made some progress. He had reviewed his remaining bank balance and decided he had sufficient funds of his own to muster a gang of labourers to work during the period that Carnarvon was on his way from Southampton if, indeed, he should come this year at all. There was little time to lose and much to do. The more of the grunt work he could get done before the earl arrived, the longer he might maintain his lordship's interest.

The aristocrat had come a long way with the Egyptologist and he was keen to move forward to greater things. He fervently believed that Carter would deliver. As for Carter, he knew in his heart that the tomb was down there somewhere - somewhere within the boundaries of the area he had outlined when they had made their plans together. It had to be, plundered already no doubt, but there notwithstanding. He knew also that it could take years yet to find it.

He planned to work his men in shifts, around the clock. The object was to remove as much debris as he could before his patron arrived, always hoping that the earl would see another season out before visiting Egypt.

And there was another to please - the new Monsieur le Directeur of Antiquities.

Pierre Lacau was easily distinguishable in a crowd and particularly in the desert. He was a broad man of commanding height. He almost always wore a dark suit. On his large head, and contrasting starkly with the suit, he supported a mass of thick, grey hair which extended to a full beard and copious moustache. The eyebrows were black. Because of his size, the man held absolute presence in any gathering. As director he had position and authority and he knew it. Worse for Carter, however, Lacau was French.

But to his great relief the new director's first visit to the site of Carter's excavations went off extremely well. Lacau even commended him personally on his approach. "Removing all loose rubble to bedrock - a most excellent practice, Mr Carter. It has not been attempted in so systematic and responsible a manner before. We shall finally learn what lies beneath the rubbish of ages of indiscriminate and irresponsible digging. I am sure we shall all be most handsomely rewarded by your thoroughness. Bon chance, monsieur!"

And he left.

Carter was pleased. Their first meeting had gone well. At the same time, he hoped that the director's last words - 'WE shall ALL be rewarded' - were not all they appeared to be. He had already shown that his approach to 'division' was far more strictly biased in favour of the Cairo Museum than had been the practice of his predecessor. He had taken the beautiful, almond-coloured quartzite sarcophagus. It was the only thing of value that had come out of the tomb that Carter had risked his life to save from the robbers. Carter felt the action entirely inconsiderate, but he was powerless to influence the decision. Should he now be fortunate enough to come upon something truly exceptional, he feared that, but for a few of the more miserable artefacts, all would be retained in Egypt. His patron's reward would be the fame accompanying discovery, not the proportionate share of antiquities to which he had hitherto become accustomed as a right.

'There is a temptation to steal'. Carter silently castigated himself for the thought.

But they had to find something first. That night, his mind restless with worry, Carter lay awake thinking. 'What if the excavation to bedrock comes up with nothing? What then? In any case, it could be years before I know even that for sure. How am I to maintain his lordship's interest and keep the money flowing in the meantime?'

The task seemed daunting. 'Perhaps if the earl had more than one excavation to focus on - another licence running in parallel with that in The

Valley - this would improve the odds of finding something of significance - break the monotony'. Finally overcome by his tiredness, he fell asleep.

Within no more than a minute, it seemed, he was awakened by a familiar voice...

"Mr Carter! Mr Carter, if you please, sir! Wake up man! There is work to do and dawn is almost upon us!"

Startled by the suddenness of the noise, he opened his eyes. A huge, bearded man stood at the foot of his bed. 'Dammit. It's Petrie again!' he observed to himself.

It was a sign. Amarna was an obvious choice. Why hadn't it occurred to him before? Personally he had always had strong ties to the place. Not just because he took his first real lessons there and had his first successes of note, but because he knew the site was still greatly underexplored and the odds of making new and wonderful discoveries were a good deal more favourable than most concessions. The Valley of the Kings had been picked over for decades.

The Director of Antiquities was always punctual. As Carter arrived at the door to his office, Lacau was ready for him. Carter knocked.

"Entre!" Lacau's voice boomed from inside.

Carter opened the door and removed his Homburg. "Monsieur le Directeur. Comment allez vous?"

"Bien, merci, Monsieur Carter. Asseyez vous, s'il vous plait." And, as with one hand he gestured to Carter to sit, he pulled up a flagon of rough Bourdeaux with the other and invited him to drink.

"Non, merci, monsieur. Seulement dans l'après-midi."

Lacau laughed. "You English, you will never learn how to enjoy yourselves. Such principles. Such standards. All contrived to make your lives miserable. We French, we have standards. We have principles. All geared to making our lives as enjoyable as possible. Ha, ha, ha!"

Carter, as sarcastic as he was, especially with foreigners and most especially with the French, had considerable difficulty accepting sarcasm from others. He had to call on the deepest of his disciplinary rules of thumb to hold himself back. He was, after all, here to ask permission to do something. A wrong step now, for nothing more than the purpose of satisfying his ego, would render his journey wasted and damage a relationship he had to nurture rather than blight.

"Un verre, peut'être. Merci, monsieur," he softened and accepted the glass that was offered.

Thus settled opposite each other and divided by Lacau's large library desk the Director asked, "And what may I do for you, monsieur?"

"Monsieur le Directeur," Carter began politely but directly. "You are aware that in my early years in Egypt, and under the direction and guidance of Sir William Flinders Petrie, I excavated at Tel el Amarna?"

"Of course, Mr Carter. The study of the history of great excavators in these parts has always been of great interest to me. One learns from their mistakes, does one not?"

That was not a good start. Carter did not seek to lead from behind, as it were.

"Yes, sir," he agreed submissively. He continued, "And for this and many other reasons I have always had a longing to return to that place. There is much yet to be revealed, I believe. My sponsor, his lordship the Earl of Porchester, is of the same mind and harbours much enthusiasm for the area, sir."

"Indeed..." Lacau reflected for a moment. "Indeed it is a premium concession - one to be held for those who can execute their tasks in the most professional manner - scholars of the most prestigious universities, and of the most upright of museums with well-established collections of Egyptian antiquities. Do you not agree, Mr Carter?"

'No, not necessarily,' thought Carter. His lips tightened as he silently suppressed his irritation at Lacau's veiled personal attack. Their conversation, having already begun poorly, was taking a turn for the worse.

"Monsieur le Directeur," Carter began again with polite reserve. "I agree with everything you are saying. But does not experience - twenty-five years of experience - have a place in qualification?"

"Quite so, Mr Carter. Quite so," answered Lacau half-heartedly. "But you and your sponsor already have the premier site of all - The Valley of the Tombs of the Kings. You have just begun on your admirably thorough plan there. Surely you do not wish to give it up already? Such an apparent lack of perseverance would not augur well in the Minister's consideration for any future concessions."

"You know me better than that, monsieur. I meant, of course..."

Lacau smiled a wry and powerful smile and cut in, "...I do indeed, and that is why I wish you most earnestly to focus your efforts on your present concession in The Valley and forget any aspirations elsewhere while you do so." For some time now the Director had been decided on how he would administer future concessions. This uneducated but admittedly talented Englishman with his overprivileged English aristocratic consort was not about to influence him now.

Carter was not a man to be beaten easily, least of all by a Frenchman, but he saw the future only too vividly and Lacau figured boldly within it. When and if he made his great discovery in The Valley, Lacau would preside over his every action. So it was essential that Carter did everything he could for the director - within the limits of his pride (and there were limits) - to maintain himself and his patron in a favourable light.

Quite against his inner feelings he softly replied, "I understand, sir. Perhaps later, then."

"Perhaps," conceded the massive Frenchman. And they parted company.

Now it was all or nothing. The Valley would just have to turn up something soon - anything. Carnarvon, the philanthropist who had invested so much faith in Howard Carter to this point, would have a limit to his unrewarded endurance. Worse still, The Valley itself truly may have nothing left to yield. Carter strongly believed otherwise but could not know for sure. His analysis of the evidence, his design for exploration - in the light of his undying passion for the place and discovery - were they all so unrealistic? There was absolutely no question in Carter's mind. There were lost kings to be discovered. It was just a matter of time. And which would come first - discovery, loss of financial support, failing health? He was realistic. There was a very real logic to King Tutankhamen being buried in The Valley. There was a very real logic to the Pharaoh being buried within the area Carter was now investigating. Perhaps more importantly, there was no counter logic to these theories. He was convinced he was on the right track. The only doubts that he held in his mind were the doubts that any risk taker would have when the outcome was not a virtual certainty. He could not be certain. He had an unknown period of time in which to prove his conviction. He couldn't know how long Carnarvon would hold out in the face of disappointment. He did know, however, that if the earl was considering pulling out, his lordship would give him fair warning.

At his house that night, filled with these thoughts, Carter decided that a short letter of encouragement would do no harm. He settled down at his desk with a Scotch and put pen to paper:

Dear Carnarvon,

I have to tell you, I am afraid, that Director Lacau - that staid Frenchman who, in place of our dear old friend Maspero, now controls our actions - has denied us any additional concession. On your behalf I had attempted to gain access to Tel el Amarna. Though very different from The Valley, it is a site of great promise, much that will be new to you, and the opportunity, while so many excavators were absent, seemed too good to miss. However, he has, as I said, denied it to us. No matter. Our strength of will towards our endeavours in The Valley will be redoubled. It is on this matter that I wish now to dwell.

As you are aware we have begun to clear the area we spoke of - now years ago, what with the war and all, it seems - down to bedrock. The going is slow and I do not want to get your hopes up too early, but I remain positive that we are on the right track.

Unless your doctor directs otherwise, I would respectfully suggest that you postpone your next trip and make plans to return to Egypt in the autumn of next year. In addition to the travel risk (they are still clearing mines in the Med., don't forget), too much unexciting work awaits us this season. I see little opportunity for discoveries of significance. But if we are fortunate enough to chance upon something, be assured I shall telegraph your lordship directly.

Also, you will, when you come again, find Egypt a greatly changed place. Not for the better, I fear. The people are much angered by the deprivations of this war. There is trouble in the streets of Cairo from time to time. This is put down quickly and with little sympathy by the militia. I am sorry to report that the British are more foreign to this place now than they have ever been. Sadly we alienate ourselves further almost daily.

In any event I shall, as soon as I have it in mind, advise you as to the best timing of your visit in 1918. By then, God willing, this terrible conflict will be behind us all and I shall have more for you to see.

My regards to Lady Evelyn.
Your most obedient servant,

Howard Carter

He replaced his pen thoughtfully. He had, over the years, built a bonding relationship with the frail aristocrat. The man respected him tremendously. He knew that. But when you are paying for everything and there is little or no reward year after year, can you not reasonably be expected to lose some of that faith?

Carter drew a deep breath and stared up at the ceiling. Excavation itself was not enough. A strategy of investigation was required. 'There may be other opportunities in that place which I have not yet thought of and might overlook should I not investigate the entire area,' he thought.

The most likely area in which Tutankhamen's tomb could have been overlooked had to be where Carter had come across some ancient workers' huts. These had existed from the later dynasties and were built on the tailings of earlier tomb excavations. Quite clearly the area had not been disturbed since ancient times. It was the most obvious logic to Howard Carter that he should leave this place until last, for if it were dug out first and found to be barren his patron might choose that moment to up and quit. The remainder of the area, to all appearances much less attractive, would be left unexplored. The tomb, or something else of importance, could well exist elsewhere in the triangle of his excavations. If he had no success in his clearance of the area all about but kept this particular place untouched until his lordship began to berate his lack of success he would have something in reserve to whet his lordship's appetite one final time. He decided to leave the area around the worker's huts until the end, unless his lordship should dictate otherwise.

He folded the letter precisely, running his finger along the crease, and slotted it into an envelope. As he dabbed the glue with a damp sponge and sealed the envelope, he felt some sense of comfort that the letter was as good an attempt as any at preparing his patron for a lengthy and not too ambitiously expectant wait.

The following morning Carter was in The Valley early. He instructed his fellahs how to lay the first short length of portable railway that would help them remove the cleared debris to a point far distant from the area in which they were excavating and deposit it where the valley had already been cleared to bedrock. This helpful equipment had arrived as a direct result of his past good services and relationship with the British Army. Sergeant Adamson who, eager to distance himself from military responsibilities had taken a real interest in Carter's archaeological efforts, had played a leading role in its procurement and, in return, was in hope of being asked to take a more direct part in the excavations at some future point in time. The same thought, however, had not occurred to Carter. His opinion of the militia remained as disrespectfully low as it had been in the chaotic days of the bombing of that tasteless Germano-dynastic villa. But they had their good points and their prolific and comprehensive ordinance was one of these.

The dusty days and lonely nights came and went slowly that season. It got to a point where Carter almost dreaded the next day's unrewarded drudgery before it had begun. It was a blessing that his patron had heeded his advice and stayed at Highclere.

But his men didn't seem to lose their energy. Every morning as he entered The Valley on his donkey and rounded the slight bend where the tributary valley branched off to the site at which Davis had found the complete tomb of the royal parents, Yuya and Tuya, he would see the head of the tip and behind it the long snake of men winding out of a pit in the distance and dumping their rubble-filled baskets one by one into the small steel buckets of the mining trolleys.

Despite the tedious hours, with the earl absent Carter was far more content at this work. He had not the pressure he would feel from having his lordship close by. The sense of expectation that he must find something was not there. Neither were there all those special arrangements and preparations necessary to keep his lordship and his entourage as comfortable as possible in a desert environment - none of the formality in the meals he would take; no ensuring that there was a clean room in one of the opened tombs in which to shelter from the sun and in which to eat and take rest; no ensuring there was a table of sufficient size, as well as clean tablecloths, appropriate food, and adequately temperate storage for the wine brought from Carnarvon's personal cellars; no dressing for dinner; none of those long, almost intolerable evenings answering the naive questions of the unimpressive persons that Carnarvon may on occasion invite to share dinner with them; no real need for a privy, even. These were chores that Carter always had preferred to do without. He found them a totally unnecessary distraction.

So, regardless of the lack of discoveries, his job was eased by this solitude. He could eat when he wished, eat how he wished, begin work when he wished, cease work when he wished, sleep when he wished, drink his own Scotch, think his own thoughts, and enjoy his own company.

As Carter watched the men working, Gaggia stood at his feet and sniffed the dust-laden air. There was hardly a breeze, but what little there was bore on it the scent of something attractive to the mangy hound and the dog sprinted off into the pit where the men were digging. Carter watched Gaggia disappear amongst the mass of heaving bodies and dust. Within a few minutes he noticed the animal re-emerge, jumping at the legs of a fellah who was carrying in his basket what appeared to be a pot. The man came straight towards Carter. Clearly he had found something.

As the man neared, Carter could see he had a large, open urn cradled in his basket. The piece appeared complete. The man called to him. It had been some time since they had found anything and there was the pitch of excitement in his voice. "Sir! I found this! I found this!"

Carter took the vessel from the basket. It was a plain enough artefact, but it was something. He looked inside. Gaggia was barking at his feet. Now he understood why the dog had shown so much interest.

'What a fine set of barrels that mongrel must have,' he thought. He put his hand inside the pot and pulled out the stiff, dry coil of a long dead snake. A very long dead snake, thought Carter. Perhaps three thousand years dead. A fine set of barrels, indeed. "Okay, Gaggia. Good boy." He patted the dog's head. "You will be rewarded when we get home tonight." He turned to the workman. "Show me exactly where you found this."

The man led Carter towards the excavation. The other men, busy scraping debris into their baskets, stopped as Carter approached. He waited for the dust to settle. As it cleared, the fellah pointed to the spot. Two partly eroded slabs of limestone stood on end before him and met at about a ninety-degree angle. They clearly formed the corner of an ancient hut, perhaps one of the huts that had been constructed for the men who had built the tomb of Ramses VI, the great doorway to which now yawned above them.

Carter, somewhat alarmed at the progress his men had made in the area that he had intentionally reserved for last, called to the reis.

"Ahmed. I want you to cease work in this area. We are too close to the tomb of Ramses VI. These stones which you are uncovering are those of the houses of ancient workmen. They will need careful excavation. I want you to bring your men to dig further south of this place. Tell them to move now, if you would be so good."

Carter turned to examine the pot more closely. Unfortunately there were no distinguishing marks on it. He was unable to tell from what exact period it had come. All this would have to be conjectured from inference - from its situation relative to earlier finds.

'Poor old bugger,' he thought. 'Left in his pot by his master and forgotten, I'll be bound - and for ever.'

He picked up the desiccated snake and reverently replaced it in the urn.

At home one evening, late in the 1917-18 season, Carter was surprised by a knock on the door. He had been busy at his notes and was not used or inclined to visitors at any time, particularly those who had the rudeness to arrive unannounced.

A second knock indicated that Abdel had not attended the door.

"Abdel!" he snapped. "Get the door!"

Nothing.

'The man must be out fetching something. Maybe he's shopping for food,' Carter concluded.

He reluctantly got up from his desk. As he opened the door his irritation metamorphosed instantly to warmth. "Colonel Lawrence!" he exclaimed. "What a surprise."

"Hope you don't mind the intrusion, Mr Carter. I was in Cairo for a couple of days and took the opportunity to come and visit you on site, as it were. It's good to see you again, sir."

"Well... A most pleasant surprise, Colonel. Please come in. Sit down. May I get you a drink?"

"A lemonade would be just wonderful, sir."

"Abdel!" No answer. "Oh. Forgot. Me man's out. I'll be but a moment."

Carter disappeared, then quickly returned with his guest's lemonade and a Scotch for himself. He passed Lawrence the glass and then settled himself in a chair opposite.

"Tell me now, what brings you all the way out here?"

"To tell you the truth, sir, idle curiosity!"

"You don't appear the idle type to me, Colonel. Surely you have some plan in mind?"

"No, truly. Enjoyed our first meeting very much. Glad to get away from the action. Opportunity to get away from the army for a while. Always wanted to see what it is you do."

"You'll be disappointed, Colonel. Very boring excavations going on here at present. Bit like mining but no money to be made from the spoil. And just a big hole in the ground to show for our effort."

Lawrence pressed Carter on what he was trying to achieve and the Egyptologist willingly described his plan. The man appeared fascinated and this encouraged Carter to explain every detail of his search. Eventually he reached a suitable point in his soliloquy to pause and take the opportunity to ask Lawrence what he had been doing since they had last met.

He got a lot more than he had bargained for. The colonel had been desperate to unload on someone and Carter became the priest for his confession. It began with descriptions of the Arabs, their way of life in the desert, their hopeless feudalism. Then came the stories of the raids on the Turkish railways. There was some considerable excitement in the words of the colonel's tale and Carter became wholly absorbed in the adventures. But then it moved on. The hardships - the incredible journeys, the lack of sleep, flirting with death through starvation, thirst, inhuman heat, enduring wounds, enduring the bloodshed, the deaths of friends and his two servants, enduring the killing until he practically relished it, even against the helpless, the unpalatable imbalance between his allegiance to the crown and his loyalty to Faisal.

There was probably no British soldier who could begin to comprehend his feelings - certainly no Arab. It fell to Carter to listen. Carter at least could understand the man's need to release his torment to someone. And now Carter felt the need to do so himself. This night the lonely two would share their inner thoughts in the security of uncommitted confidence.

"That's quite a story, Colonel," said Carter. "And I daresay there is more to come for you before this war is over. There is no shame in it. Great, unique adventures. You should write about them some day."

Lawrence looked into Carter's eyes. "Perhaps. If I live through it and my brain and my writing hand remain articulate! You, too, when you find your dead prince."

"I will find him. I will write about his discovery and I will send you a copy."

"Likewise. That's a promise. A pact between us."

Both smiled broadly and they shook hands.

After the colonel had left, Carter felt greatly uplifted by their exchange. At the same time he felt very alone again.

At the end of that summer's break, Carter had planned to return, as usual, in the autumn, but the war dragged on until November and he ended up staying away from Egypt for a full twelve months.

The drudgery continued in 1919. The blessing was that Carnarvon stayed away. Carter kept him satisfied and at bay by sending him the odd quality piece which he had purchased on the open market. The clearing continued its monotonous pace without result. But this season Carter was not bored. He had brought his lady friend with him. She would accompany him to The Valley most days and watch him direct the work. And her company in the evenings was a considerable boost to his state of mind.

As the season wore on, the embankment of tailings and the railway on it grew ever longer. It now reached to the corner of the valley where the tributary extended off towards the tomb of Yuya and Tuya. The area cleared to bedrock within Carter's triangle steadily became larger but still nothing of importance turned up.

He closed the season early in May, secured his equipment, gave his usual instructions to Abdel on maintaining Castle Carter and how to manage the dog, and paid off his men. Saying goodbye to Abdel, he took the ferry to the east bank and joined Dorothy, who had been staying at the Winter Palace, for one last night at the hotel.

Dorothy was down to dinner first that evening and selected a corner table.

She saw Carter appear in the doorway and beckoned him over. Apart from the severely slicked back hair and the manicured moustache, he looked almost unrecognisable. He had on a white linen suit that was more a shade of yellow from the washing, a white, high-collared shirt, and a yellow bow tie. There was no hat. The only part of his apparel that could normally be associated with the man was the suede shoes.

"My goodness," commented Dorothy. "A man of the tropics, I presume."

"Don't you like it?" Carter, naturally, had been out to please and was sensitive to criticism.

Dorothy smiled. "A joke, Howard. I think you look most distinguished. Turn around so I may see all of you."

The suit, although neatly pressed, had shrunk a little. The sleeves were short and the jacket was somewhat tight across his back. The trouser cuffs showed a little too much of his yellow socks. But he had made the effort and she was certainly not going to spoil the effect by drawing attention to these imperfections.

"You look positively dashing!" She waved her hand at the chair across from her and he sat down.

The waiter came immediately, handed him a menu, and waited for their drinks order.

"Dot?"

"A sweet sherry, please."

"And a Scotch and soda for me."

The waiter left.

"I have stayed in this hotel too long, Howard. I have been through every item on this menu several times. Why do they never change it?"

"It's the war, Dot. They have only rarely been able to import anything exotic. Most of the time it's Nile perch and like it, I'm afraid."

"Well tonight, since it's a special occasion and all, I asked Anton if he could pull out all the stops and find something a little more racy than fish. And he did, bless his heart, especially for us."

Carter searched the short, typewritten menu he'd just been handed.

"You won't find it there, Howard. Pheasant! Roast pheasant, with roast potatoes, peas, spinach and redcurrant jelly! How about that?"

"Well done Anton! Well done Dot! Food fit for kings. After such a bloody miserable season we need to be spoilt. I don't know how you stood it, Dot. But I'm bloody glad you did. Would have gone nuts without you."

"I must admit I am glad to be going back to civilisation at last."

"Me too. I hope the pheasant was up to the journey from England!"

"Anton didn't do it for a send-off, Howard. He did it because it's your birthday."

"Happy birthday, Mr Carter!"

He hadn't noticed the manager who had come in as he sat down and was now standing right behind him holding an ice bucket with a half bottle of champagne.

"All I had left in the store, I'm afraid. The shipment is late again."

"Birthday?"

"Yes, Howard," chimed Dorothy. "May the ninth. That is your birthday isn't it?"

Carter grinned in acknowledgement. In all these years this was the first time anyone had remembered his birthday. It had been so long since he had last celebrated it that the anniversary had been forgotten.

"I do believe it is. Anton, how nice of you to do this for us. I must come more often!"

"Can't promise this treatment all the time, sir. But I will always do my best for you, you can be assured of that."

"And now you must tell us, Howard, how old you really are." Dorothy had speculated on his age but thought she must be wrong. He was probably one of those types who looked older than he really was.

"Oh, goodness. I don't know. Late twenties going on fifty perhaps."

They all laughed.

"I will go and check the state of progress in the kitchen." Anton poured champagne for each of them and left.

"I have a little something for you, Howard." Dorothy produced a small package from her purse and placed it on the dinner table in front of him. "Happy birthday."

They clinked glasses. Never before a birthday, and now a present. Carter was beside himself with embarrassment.

"Please. Open it. I am so concerned whether you will like it."

Carter drew the bow and unfolded the wrapping paper. It was a small book - a children's book about Belzoni's adventures in Egypt.

"I found it in a second-hand bookshop in Mayfair just before I left England. I thought it appropriate for one such as you. He blazed a trail before you, Howard. You are birds of a feather, don't you think? They will write books about you one day. I am sure of it. 'Carter, Sand, Sun, and Solitude'!" she smiled.

Howard wasn't listening. He was totally absorbed by the gift. His eyes lit up as he fingered through the pages. He paused at the tiny engravings. He didn't know what to say. "It's a beautiful little book, Dot." He waved the book at her. "This man... You know about this man?"

"He was a circus strongman, wasn't he? I don't know how he ended up in Egypt but I do know that he found the pretty tomb of Seti I, the tomb you have shown me at least three times."

"Well, it is the most magnificent. Worth seeing more than once. And yes, he was the first to find it in modern times. And he was in the circus, yes. He was personally responsible for returning some enormous treasures to the British Museum. Have you seen them there?"

"No, Howard. I have to confess I have never been. I remember in my youth that my mother took us up to London one time intent on taking us there but we couldn't find it."

"Not surprised. It's not signposted and is very much off the beaten track for a museum of its importance."

Carter regarded the book again. "Poor chap died in Nigeria of dysentery. But before he left Egypt he procured considerable booty for the Empire - bit of a cavalier, but God bless him! Those were the good old days for Britain. We could take what we liked. The French were the only competition. Bloody Frogs got away with more than they deserved."

Carter took a quick sip of champagne and continued.

"Now our skills, our scholarship and our money are all taken for granted. Our discoveries are 'looted' for their own museum. We count ourselves fortunate if we end up with one-tenth of the least important finds." He paused to take another mouthful of champagne. "But, no, I wouldn't call us 'birds of a feather'. Belzoni was an unskilled trophy hunter like all the rest of that time. Perhaps more of an exhibitionist than the others, however - no doubt due to his background under the 'big top'. A man with an ego large enough to match his size. Did you see his outrageous graffito in the pyramid at Gizeh?"

"Yes. But don't you think he had a right to be proud of himself? The first to find the way inside since the robbers. You, Howard, you have traded trophies for fragments and a search through every grain of sand. It takes for ever."

"But think of the benefits, Dot. People like Belzoni in their avarice overlooked and damaged so much that is now lost to us for ever. We have saved so much more for future generations to enjoy. And we will find trophies, real treasure, one day. I know our patience will pay off. Just have to stick with it, my girl. Good things take time."

As did the roast pheasant. It was a full hour before it appeared. But the time had passed quickly for them. Their conversation had crossed time and geography. It had been largely humourless and instructional but she didn't mind that a bit.

When the meal was over, when the last of the champagne had been enjoyed, when Carter's brandy glass was empty, when their cigarettes had died in the ashtray - they parted company with the customary peck on the cheek and each slept long and deeply through that night.

The two of them left for England together. It proved to be one of the most pleasantly relaxing boat trips he had ever made. She had provided enormous support to him during the weeks of monotonously unrewarding toil.

When he arrived at his London lodgings, the concierge followed him up the stairs carrying a soft, sausage-shaped brown paper parcel, rather grubby from the trials of travel but well bound up with heavy cord and covered with dozens of franked Egyptian stamps. Carter unwrapped it directly and found it to contain a small, colourful Baluchi carpet. When he unrolled it on the floor of his drawing room, an envelope fell open in the centre. He pulled out the one-page note inside and read...

In memory of our first meeting. Hoping this finds you in good health. No more ancient artefacts, I am afraid - there has been no time. But here is a small token I received from an old lady of Medina following our efforts in a campaign against the Hejaz railway.

Be sure to walk on it and remember.

Belated happy birthday.

Lawrence, T. E.

Alexandria, June 16, 1918

The gift had been languishing in the basement storeroom for over a year.

He now had two seasons of unsuccessful digging behind him - and who knows how many before him. He could put it off no longer. He was obliged to pay a visit to his patient patron and make his report.

It was always a pleasure to ride into the grounds at Highclere. As he approached, the massive, square house stood out proudly in a clearing at the top of the rise. The car drew up outside the main door and Carter got out just as Carnarvon, with outstretched arms, emerged to greet him.

"My good friend! It does my heart good to see you!"

They embraced like reunited brothers and Carnarvon stood back, examining his colleague up and down.

"You are not as slim a man as you were when last I saw you, Howard. Surely you have not been idle these last two years?"

"It is good to see you, too, your lordship. Your presence has been sorely missed in Luxor." Carter lied for himself but not for others. "I confess my portliness. My largeness is indeed a sorry fact. I have had to let out my trousers and provide more fullness in my jackets. I have grown larger in every direction, it seems. But I do not confess to idleness. I put it down to age and metabolism - both of which are changing inexorably, and over which we have no control. So depressing." He smiled.

Carnarvon laughed. "Don't we both know it. Come, let us go inside and quench our miseries in a brandy."

He led Carter to the library where Lady Evelyn was resting on a Knole sofa taking tea.

"Howard!" she greeted him with a refreshing smile. "I had thought you were coming tomorrow. Such a nice surprise to see you. My, you are looking well."

Carter bent down to kiss her hand. "You are the radiant flower I have always known, Lady Evelyn. When are you coming again to see me at Luxor?"

"Next year, Howard. The earl will bring me with him when he visits - I believe in February. Is that not the month, Father?"

"Yes, my dear. That's the plan at least. We already have the steamer reservations. Howard, what would you like to drink?"

"A brandy would be fine, if you please, sir."

"And you, my dear?"

"I am fine with my tea, thank you, Father."

Carnarvon gave orders to the butler and, waving Carter to the sofa beside Lady Evelyn, settled himself in a chair.

Knowing already that Carnarvon had been most pleased with his acquisitions Carter began by enquiring as to the degree of his lordship's appreciation of the pieces he had procured for him in Cairo and Luxor over the past months. This successfully established a favourable tone to the conversation and from this platform he then launched into the more melancholy report on his progress at the excavations in The Valley. He made it as up beat as he could, cautiously raising expectations wherever possible. He finished with, "So you see, sir, we have to date cleared barely a third of the area of interest. There is much yet to do before we achieve our goal. I remain convinced we are following a procedure which will ultimately prove fruitful."

"Thank God I have a man of such great conviction and patience. You know very well my faith in you, Howard. It is as unshakeable as ever - as unshakeable as your own tenacity."

'Thank God for his mercy,' thought Carter. "I believe you are the one to be applauded for patience, sir. One thing is certain, without your continued support there can be no achievement. And I am sure the achievement will be all the more remarkable for it."

"My daughter and I look forward to our visit next year. I miss the place... But let us turn to the moment. Tomorrow I have arranged a shoot. Will you join us?"

Chapter Fifteen
The Thousandth Day

Ay was buried with a finality the like of which had not been seen since the passing of Akhenaten. There was no issue, and Horemheb, now secure in marriage to Mutnodjme in spite of her mother's efforts to stop the union, had sealed his bloodline connection with the royal family. Akhenaten was dead. Smenkhkare was dead. Tutankhamun was dead. Ay was dead. The mother was dead. Horemheb was Pharaoh.

Ankhesenamun, now totally disinherited of the kingdom, nevertheless rejoiced in her widowhood. She had withdrawn to quarters in the rear of the palace with her most trusted retinue. Already she had taken steps to reacquaint herself with the Hittite ruler.

She summoned her faithful servant to her side for one more important assignment. Greeting Dashir with all the charity her position would allow, she said, "My friend, it is with great rejoicing that I welcome you once more."

"My lady."

As for Dashir, he was less than enthusiastic. He half-expected what it was that she would now ask him to do - another tomb robbery. And the only reward was the ex-queen's continued confidence or a painful death for him and his helpers including, perhaps, his only son.

As if to anticipate his thoughts, Ankhesenamun launched into the matter immediately. "You will need help this time, my friend. Do you have friends whom you would trust with your life?"

"I do, my lady, as most men do."

"That is good. I, for my part, just have you. My ladies I can trust, yes. But the men about me, since the passing of my beloved Tutankhamun, have become, if they were not so already, totally self-serving. Thank the gods for Dashir!"

She was absolutely sincere in her plaudit. Without his faithfulness she could never have the means to execute her plan - murder most absolute.

"You are to sack Pharaoh Ay's tomb. Completely. Destroy even the mummy in your frenzy to find the jewellery. I want nothing left - NOTHING! Do you hear me?"

"My lady," Dashir acknowledged. This was no surprise - he feared her demands, but it was no surprise.

"As before there will be no guard. You and your men, and your son..." she had not forgotten. "...will return safely."

"On what nights must we do this thing, my lady?"

"On the fifth night from tonight, Dashir, there will be no moon. And the sixth and the seventh. No more. All must be accomplished within three nights."

"It will be so, my lady. What we cannot take we shall destroy."

"Bring me Pharaoh's ka, that I may destroy it myself."

The light from the oil lamps glowed pink in Ankhesenamun's eyes.

"Now leave, before the guards begin to talk."

Dashir had men he could trust all right, but nevertheless he had to be selective, very selective. If a breath of this got out after the fact, all of them would be killed, perhaps also the ex-queen. He understood how important his task was. Ay must be stopped from entering the afterlife. Having shared the ex-queen's bed, he could not be allowed to inhabit the same world as her consort. It was unthinkable.

Later that evening, Dashir made his way pensively towards Hammad's bar at the end of the narrow, cobbled street. As he approached, echoing between the confining walls of the stone buildings he could hear the uninhibited noise of those who had been there some time already. There would be little chance of a discreet entrance. Sure enough, as he entered nearly everyone in the bar shouted, "Dashir!"

He took some wine and sat with a few friends. Some of these he would trust with his life, but a few of the others he found wanting.

As the evening wore into the early morning hours, people at last began drifting away to their beds. Dashir signalled to his closer friends to stay. By the time all but Dashir's most trusted friends had left, the goldsmith had so much wine inside him that he had forgotten the purpose that had taken him to the bar in the first place.

Mechanically he began, "Now, my friends..." and stopped.

"Yes, Dashir..." they all answered, and stared at him expectantly.

There was a long pause. "I... I have something important to relate to you..."

"In secret?" asked one.

"Aye... Aye... In secret," mumbled Dashir slowly, not at all sure what he was going to say next. "This is something..." He looked furtively about the room.

"Yes... Yes..." his men spoke with anticipation, almost in unison.

"This is something..." Dashir repeated. "Something..." His words faded to a whisper and died.

"Dashir!" Ugele shouted and prodded him in the chest at the same time. "Wake up, man. We wait on your message."

"Mmmm?" Dashir was hardly able to talk. He was close to sleep. "Some... thing..."

Ugele realised that Dashir indeed had something of importance to share with them but equally he realised the hopelessness of the messenger's condition and he decided it was time to close the evening.

"Come on, lads. He's had enough. Let's take him home. Besides, we are all in need of our beds. We can reassemble tomorrow - my house - at sunset."

His colleagues expressed their relief. Beside his profligate drinking Dashir's solemn behaviour had been seriously out of place with the evening's otherwise lightheartedness. Everyone was pleased he had all but expired. They each happily played their part in helping to bear him homeward. It was not that far. They left him propped up in his doorway and took care to evacuate the area immediately lest they expose themselves to the venom of his wife.

Awoken by the commotion outside, she was not long in coming. Dashir felt no pain. Her instant wrath was quite wasted. With considerable effort she dragged him inside and left him, totally unconscious, on the cool stone floor. She went back up to the roof and settled back to sleep, dreaming irritable dreams.

It was very, very late that morning when Dashir finally opened his eyes. He was conscious but in indescribable distress. His wife, cooking bread at the time, noticed his body stir and launched herself mercilessly at him. There was not a family in Pademi that did not hear her that day. The ringing in Dashir's ears lasted until evening.

When Meneg came for him - for he knew Dashir would not be able to leave of his own accord and might not even remember to do so - Dashir's wife answered the door. This was not an event Meneg felt strongly inclined to deal with. To Dashir's wife this was evening, this was a friend coming for her husband and there was only one reason for the visit - they were off to Hammad's again. As she began her incomprehensible tirade, Meneg closed his eyes tightly as if he were about to be smitten.

"Do not strike me, madam," he implored. "I am come but to summon your husband to a meeting of the Council."

It was quite evident she did not believe him. He had not heard such obscenities issue from the mouth of a woman before - a married woman at that. He stood his ground until she had finished, whereupon, by this time fully vented, she slammed the door in his face. With relief he turned to leave.

"Meneg!"

An urgent whisper came from the rooftop. Meneg looked up.

"Help me down, man, before she finds us! Be quick!"

Dashir shinned down the wall onto Meneg's shoulders and in a twinkling they were absorbed into the shadows and hurrying toward's Ugele's house.

"Feeling better, Dashir?" enquired Meneg as, now out of sight and out of earshot, they slowed to a walk.

"Oh, Meneg. What made me do it? Never again. Never again. Never again. Never again."

"I understand, Dashir." At one time or another they had all said it as many times.

Ugele welcomed them at the door and ushered them into the small room. All Dashir's most trusted friends were assembled before him, some sitting on chairs, some on the floor, some standing. All had wine.

"A drink, Dashir, before we begin?"

Meneg grabbed the wine flask and a cup and presented them to his friend. Dashir thrust out the flat of his hand.

"Thank you, no. But I will surely need a drink once we have finished the task set us by her Royal Majesty."

That got everyone's attention. It was clear from his remark that there would be something distasteful in what he was about to tell them.

"First you must all be clear on one thing. Not a breath of what I am about to say to you must leave this room - not today, not before, and not after this thing is done - NEVER."

He looked at each of their faces one by one, searching for a sign of acknowledgement in their eyes. Satisfied he had their silent vows, he continued. "We are commanded to sack the tomb of our recently departed Pharaoh Ay and..." Before any could react he added, "...there will be no guards for three nights. This should be sufficient time to complete the deed."

There was little apparent outward reaction - as if his colleagues had expected something like this, as if it was a relief to know at last.

"What about our wives?" asked one of them astutely after a pause. "They will have to know. Three nights away from home. It is more than my life is worth to allow her to speculate."

"And you know how women talk!" chimed another.

Dashir was quite matter-of-fact. "Tell them the truth and tell them you will be killed if they talk."

"In my wife's current mood, I'm not so sure she wouldn't happily spread the word!" claimed one.

"Mine, too," said another.

It was easy for him to tell the others how it should be done. How he himself was to accomplish this same task with his wife, still fuming and unforgiving from last night's nonsense, only the gods knew. Of all in this band of reluctant thieves, he probably had the hardest task of all.

"It is decided then. Three days from now we shall assemble at the head of the west bank canal one hour after nightfall. We shall each make our own way across the river. Groups of people attract unnecessary attention. I will have my son with me so there will be eight of us in all. If we are not all accounted for, we will not do the deed. And he who is absent shall be cursed in the name of Seth."

Dashir hadn't needed to add this last warning.

"We are friends, are we not?" said Meneg. "We always stick together or there would be no friendship. I remember the burial of Tutankhamun." He smiled. "All of us shall be there, Dashir. All or none. Have no fear."

But, unlike Dashir himself, none of these men had robbed a tomb before. On the contrary, like he they were the artisans who had helped craft and fill the tombs with great works of art. Indeed, much of what they would plunder would have the mark of their personal skill on it. They did not give a second thought to how they might dispose of their booty for gain or even where they might hide it.

When they finally collected together on the west bank, it was absolutely pitch black. They dared not use their lamps until they were inside Ay's tomb, so the walk into The West Valley was long and difficult. It was located at the distant head of a ravine, close to the unused tomb of Ay's original master, the heretic, Pharaoh Akhenaten. They walked in single file, close enough that they could touch each other's robes for reassurance.

Dashir's instructions were explicit - they must remove everything. They could take all they wanted for themselves, but not the ka statue, not the spells, nor the mummy itself. The statue and the spells were to be delivered into the hands of Ankhesenamun; the mummy must be totally destroyed. Not a single identifiable fragment must be left - not any recognisable image of the dead Pharaoh within the tomb or on its walls. The ex-queen's anger was not so much at Ay for his own sake - much as she reviled the very thought of her nights within his bed - it was more to appease her Tutankhamun. The tomb in which Ay now lay had been intended for the boy king and had lain but half-completed at the time of his untimely death. If her young husband could not enjoy it, neither should any other. She wished it to remain empty and anonymous for eternity.

The party moved around the valley flank to the place where the freshly sealed tomb was situated. Dashir, who was in the lead, suddenly stopped. He thought he could hear voices up ahead. Something was moving in the darkness right about where the tomb entrance was situated.

He turned to his men and, raising a finger to his lips, whispered, "We have company."

A stunning cold coursed through their veins.

"Donkeys," whispered Dashir to his men. "I can make out heavily laden baskets on their backs."

They were not the first.

Dashir drew back to his men. "The tomb is being plundered as we speak," he whispered. "This is an incredible piece of luck!"

The men looked puzzled.

"Don't you see, my friends? We can let them do our work for us. We will not need the three nights. We will be able to accomplish the queen's wishes with almost no effort and in far less time. Best of all, others will be culpable of this crime. This truly is a gift from the gods."

"But we shall have no booty," spoke up one.

"We did not come here for booty! We came here at the queen's behest. Any booty would have been incidental and should not have been expected."

"You mean we risk our lives and the livelihood of our families for nothing more than... than duty?"

In the darkness it was difficult to make out the expressions on the faces of the eight who huddled close to hear one another's words. Without expressions and delivered in whispers the words carried little impact. To emphasise his meaning, Dashir caught his friend by the nose and twisted it in his fingers until he let out a subdued yelp.

"Yes," he said. "Duty. Let that be an end to our discussion." He took a breath and continued. "It is well we did not bring donkeys tonight. Our position would have been revealed. We must withdraw to watch these infidels and descend only when they have finished their business and departed this place."

Since there was no lookout, Dashir's party scrambled up the scree face to a rock ledge and settled themselves there, looking down on the access hole dug by the robbers. The band of brothers sat cross-legged and stared into the darkness, searching for some sign of movement. The entrance was faintly visible in the glimmering light of the robbers' lamps coming deep from within the tunnel. Clearly it had been dug large enough to accommodate two men in an almost standing position and side by side, thereby allowing the passage of objects of some size. The light extinguished for a time as four robbers scrambled out of the tunnel and emerged at the surface. As they came out into the open, the light once more glimmered from behind, framing them in silhouette and picking out golden reflections from the large coffin lid they were carrying.

"They're in the burial chamber," whispered Meneg. "They can't have that much more to do."

They saw the men place the coffin on a sledge made of poles slung behind one of the donkeys. As the robbers disappeared once again into the mouth of the tomb, Meneg turned to Dashir. "They will surely finish tonight. Why don't we go home and return tomorrow night to examine what is left? Then we can ensure that the queen's wishes are fulfilled."

Each nodded eagerly and the party quickly scrambled back down the slope and made their way back to the river.

Despite the apparent good fortune of being relieved of all the hard labour and much of the risk, Dashir did not sleep soundly. He was troubled. He had already failed one of his queen's orders. The tomb already robbed, likely he would not be able to bring her the gold effigy she had so vehemently demanded. The hopelessness of this failure would have kept him awake longer had his wife not awoken at his tossing and, gratified that he had returned late but sober this night, in her restlessness turned over and placed her hand directly between his thighs.

Afterwards he slumbered in peace.

The following evening, the small band of eight wound their way back into The Valley hoping that this time all would be quiet. Knowing now what they might come upon, they crept to the spot more carefully than they had done the night before, stopping every few steps to listen for voices. They heard nothing and arrived at the tomb entrance in total darkness - no donkeys, not a sound issuing from the throat of the tunnel, and not the slightest glimmer of a light. They carefully filed down the entrance corridor and, considering themselves far enough inside, they lit their lamps. Emptiness glowed back at them. As they penetrated into the bowels of the tomb, they found only pieces of broken pottery, of wood, fragments of gold sheet, a few beads, and a smashed alabaster vase. Everything was gone but for the sarcophagus and the mummy.

The mummy, naked but for a few ragged bandages still clinging to its wrists and legs, lay inelegantly on its face in the corner of the burial chamber. The broken lid of the sarcophagus was lying upside down on the floor. They peeked inside. Even the coffin bed had gone. The entire tomb had been most effectively emptied.

Dashir was the first to speak. "Come, there is no time to lose. We are to destroy the sarcophagus and the mummy, and the name and any images of Pharaoh. Eternal death - as the queen has ordered."

"How do we do this, Dashir? The sarcophagus is massive and we have no tools," said Meneg.

"There are eight of us. It should not be too difficult. Each of you take hold of the upper lip on this side. We shall push it over. The impact will break it."

"No!" The voice was Enet's, a relatively junior stonemason.

"You said we were to plunder. You never said we were to work havoc in this place. I made this thing with my own hands. I toiled on it for months. Perfect, is it not? Beautiful. A glorious and enduring statement to the gods. Do you realise how hard it is to carve a piece like this and avoid breaking it? And now all you wish to accomplish is its destruction. I will not let you do this." He rushed around to the opposite side. "You must stop this foolishness."

"Ignore him!"

The others pushed, it toppled, and a great echo resounded within the chamber as it fell on its side. The huge stone casket broke into three pieces over Enet's toes. The mason let out an ear-splitting scream.

Enet fell, crying, to the floor, unable to move. Dashir asked his son to see to the bleeding and then turned to the others. He instructed them to continue pushing the pieces over and onto the fragments already scattered about until they were small enough for a single man to lift and smash them down on the floor. Soon, all was rubble.

As his colleagues laboured, Dashir picked up a piece of the broken wall of the quartzite sarcophagus that was small enough to use as a hand adze and set to chiselling at the paintings on the wall of the tomb wherever he saw the name or image of Ay. The soft limestone yielded to the quartzite easily and within a few minutes he had successfully removed all trace of the late

Pharaoh from every text and panel. Meneg dealt the last blow to the sarcophagus, dropping one last large piece to the floor. The rubble scattered in all directions and the dust billowed around them, glowing eerily in the light of the lamps. A strange quiet descended on the emptied place. It was a solemn moment. They each felt it. A gnawing guilt for the desecration they had accomplished. They were this day, each of them, for the first time destroyers, not creators.

"Well," started Dashir, aware of his colleagues' feelings, "who has the most right to destroy? I ask you. Surely of all it is he who first creates."

They stood in silence exchanging anxious glances. Enet's whimpering brought them back from their thoughts.

"Quick," said Dashir. "Meneg and Ugele, take Enet by the shoulders and ankles and carry him out of here. You two bring the mummy. You others bring some scraps of wood."

He was determined not to carry the mummy himself. It was still greasy with the unguents that had only recently been poured over it. The sickly sweet odour turned his stomach.

Dashir carried the oil lamps outside and gestured to his men to dump the body on some rocks. Using the shards of wood they had brought from the tomb, they built a fire base under it. Dashir touched the oil lamps to the bandaging. The cloth ignited immediately and within seconds the wood was crackling. A strong glow burst beneath the pathetic remains of the king. It lit up the valley sides around them, throwing their wavering shadows grossly long against the rocks.

Now the men's dilemma was to incinerate the body without producing so bright a fire that the glow could be seen from the far side of the river. As the flames took serious hold and grew higher, Dashir took off his robe and handed one side of it to Meneg. The two brought it down over the fire with the edges to the ground, briefly smothering the flames.

"Up!" shouted Dashir as he saw his robe begin to char, and they drew the cloth away allowing the fire to breathe again.

The fire quickly grew intense once more. They had to repeat their manoeuvre many times. By the time the body was in ashes, three of their party, including Dashir, had lost their robes to the inferno. As the dying embers signalled the final success of their mission Dashir observed an expectant look on the faces of the two who, like he, were now without night clothing.

"Fear not, my friends," he chuckled, "our queen will compensate us for the loss."

And so she did. Indeed, when they returned in the early hours of the third morning her plaudits were unconstrained, notwithstanding the absence of the trophy. The men departed relieved and content.

Once the crime had been discovered, Ankhesenamun eagerly took part in the royal visit to the site. She publicly demonstrated her shock at what had transpired to so noble an old man - her late departed second husband. And for the benefit of all those around her, including Horemheb, she damned those infidels who had perpetrated this horrific act.

Her final official function as the departing queen was to preside at the coronation celebrations of the new pharaoh. The very thought of Horemheb taking the title that her Tutankhamun had so briefly held enraged her to such an extent that she knew she would be unable to disguise her distaste in public. On the night immediately preceding the ceremonies, at the stroke of midnight, accompanied by Tia and what remained of her faithful palace entourage, she silently stole away towards the lands of the Hittites, her boy king's effigy safely secreted within her quarters in the barque.

Queen Ankhesenamun as a mortal disappeared from her Egypt for ever.

Firmly established on the throne of the Upper and Lower Nile Horemheb's objective was to rid his country once and for all of the memory of the Aten cult and firmly re-establish the old ways. The act would be well received by his subjects and would doubly reinforce his position as Pharaoh.

He had the great avenue of sphinxes that flanked the processional way to the Temple of Amun in Karnak, which at the time of his coronation alternated with the heads of the heretic and his principal wife, resculpted to anonimity with the heads of rams. He ordered the razing of Akhetaten and the removal of all references to Akhenaten, Smenkhkare, Tutankhamun, Ay and their families from the great temples and obelisks of Thebes and from the king list. He began an ambitious and complex building programme. He ordered the construction of new pylons at Karnak, liberally sculptured in reliefs attesting to his grandeur, and he had the bodies of the pylons ballasted with dismantled stonework from the temples at Akhetaten, the beauty of their sculpture and the vivaciously painted friezes becoming sealed for ever as disembodied fragments within the cores of these massive, processional gateways.

His was to become a long and glorious reign. Although he lived barely long enough to celebrate his first Sed Festival, wealth and stability nevertheless returned to the great land that straddled the beneficent Nile. The people would rejoice in the new-found harmony of their old ways. There would at last be true maat. Horemheb would be worshipped by the faithful. The general was a very happy man.

Chapter Sixteen
Finally

The earl arrived in the middle of winter, 1920. Long before the visit, Carter had been busy in The Valley. He was keen to have the operation looking as practised and as neat as possible for the arrival of his patron, and had hoped to come across a small discovery or two to add some lustre to the forthcoming visit.

Luck was on his side. Shortly before Carnarvon and his daughter arrived in Luxor, Carter's men came across the remains of some artefacts used in the burial of Ramses IV. These included some tools, a few blue glass plaques, several beads and one or two models of animal parts; not a great deal to write home about, but nevertheless a timely find of some archaeological importance. Practically any find of interest, if not of value, would favourably punctuate the tedium of what otherwise had been fruitless excavation.

When Carnarvon and Lady Evelyn first entered The Valley, it occurred to the earl that it was like walking into the midst of a full-scale mining operation. Their usual first sight of the necropolis proper was obscured by a wall of rubble standing high above them and blocking their way forward. The sheer size of the tip caused them to stand and gaze at it open-mouthed. As they regarded the crude pile, a trolley appeared at the top edge and tipped, cascading its load down the slope, the rubble bouncing down the incline. A few rocks rolled close to their feet.

Carter appeared at the top and signalled to them to go to the left. There they found a prepared gravel ramp which took them gradually up to the level of the railway. At the top, a crowd of chaotic men was industriously moving rocks from the pit ahead of them to the tiny cast-iron rail carts.

As Carnarvon and his daughter reached the perimeter of the cavity where the excavation was presently concentrated, Carter turned to his patron. "Look at where the fellahs are working, sir. Tell me what you see."

This was an unfair and rather tactless question for Carter the expert to ask his patron. Carnarvon hadn't a clue what he was supposed to be looking for and Carter knew it, yet the Egyptologist continued unrelenting. "It is difficult for the lay eye, I know. Observe the change in character of the soil. What that means I shall explain... You remember that our purpose here was to remove all recent surface rubbish until we reached undisturbed bedrock - deposits that could be recognised to have lain here for millennia? That is what you are looking at now, sir. Look at it closely. See how the texture and colour of it differ from the material above. This is ancient flood debris - the very material, at much the same elevation, that covered the uncorrupted tomb of Yuya and Tuya - Davis's triumph."

The earl thought for a moment. "But that doesn't mean there is anything beneath - probably just bare, virgin rock, surely?"

"Probably," said Carter. "Possibly. But success is not born of doubt. Success comes from curiosity, observation, recognising the signs, and analysis." He did not allow Carnarvon another word. "Come, I have a small discovery to show you."

He took them over to the spot where he had placed the objects recently found close to the entrance of the tomb of Ramses IV.

"What do you say to these, sir?"

Carnarvon's eyes lit up. The earl was enchanted. Carter's minor theatrical had had its desired effect. As things were to turn out, it would not be long before the pleasure was repeated.

By midday Carnarvon and Lady Evelyn, and Carter himself for that matter, were quite fed up with watching labourers carry rubble from one place to another. The earl suggested lunch. As they walked over to the open tomb which had been prepared for them, the reis ran up to them from the pit.

"Mr Carter, sir. A find! Please come."

They forgot their hunger immediately and walked briskly over to the edge of the excavation. There below, protruding from the wall of the fresh diggings, was the distinct, smooth, convex shape of a large jar. Carter couldn't believe his good fortune. The find was embedded in the debris level he had been pointing out to the earl just a few moments earlier.

As the two men stood at the edge of the excavation looking down, Lady Evelyn surprised both of them by hoisting up her skirt and scrambling down the slope to where the object lay. Carter was quick to follow after her - he didn't want her to stumble; neither did he want her to disturb the find.

His lordship remained at the top. He was not that firm of foot, in recent years rarely seen without the support of a walking cane, and was not about to risk negotiating the unstable slope.

By the time Carter had reached Lady Evelyn's side, she was prising the caked silt from around the jar. "Miss Evelyn, please be careful," he implored. "It could be broken."

"But look, Howard," she said. "Look. The handle is in the form of an ibex head. See... the horns."

Carter stooped to look. She was absolutely right. The smooth calcite surface curved outwards to form the jar's lip and from the lip extended the twin horns of an ibex, sweeping in a fragile arc to a diminutive head attached at the neck to the body of the vessel. The carving was simple but exquisite and apparently undamaged.

As Carter flashed his expert eyes over the rubble mass that surrounded the pot he noticed, spread widely distant from one another, two other gaps between the stones. Barely visible within the shadows inside these tiny windows were other smooth surfaces unmistakably fashioned by the hand of man.

"There are more, Lady Evelyn," he said with some excitement. "See... here... and here."

"Oh, Howard. How exciting! Howard, may I excavate them myself? It would give me so much pleasure."

A very real step within Carter's private territory - this was asking a lot. The lady had absolutely no technical experience. She could easily damage what she was seeking to recover. Worse still, she was excited, and in the exuberance of the moment might be too intoxicated and impatient to take the care required.

Carter was not a tactfully political man. But over the past few years he had had plenty of time to reflect on which side his bread was buttered and on the manner in which he would contrive to keep this sustenance in good supply. After a thoughtful pause he conceded.

"As your ladyship pleases. I will record the positions and descriptions as you excavate. But take the greatest care, I implore you."

He drew out his notebook and watched her closely as she removed the dirt with her bare hands. He advised her now and then as to which piece of gravel to remove to ensure the best chance of the jar releasing itself from the soil in one piece. To his great relief she did take care. It took her over half an hour to clear the area, and when she had finished she had before her a pair of soiled hands and no less than thirteen complete jars, all calcite, all beautifully shaped, to varying degrees all damaged, but all complete and readily restorable.

"A true professional!" Carter congratulated Lady Evelyn. "I could not have done better myself. We must now carefully package the pieces. I will want to take some samples of the contents for analysis at Lucas's labs in Cairo. And, of course, unfortunately we shall have to show the hoard to Lacau. It is he who will decide who gets what."

He turned and looked up at Carnarvon who was still standing at the edge of the pit.

"Things have changed since you were here last, sir. You remember me telling you so? Changed for the worse, I am afraid. And Pierre Lacau is a part of it. You will find that in the matter of division of discoveries they are not as generous or as equable as they once were. Quite to the contrary. But you will see soon enough when we take this little lot to 'Le Directeur'."

The pieces were carefully wrapped in cotton wool and boxed. Each jar had its own separate box. Each was laid on a stretcher and carried back to Carter's house.

That night, as the three relaxed on the terrace of Carnarvon's hotel in Luxor, Carter mused at his good fortune and worried about what he might have to do next to maintain his patron's interest. For now, at least, this lucky event had bought him some time.

His elbows resting on the arms of his wicker chair, he held the gin tumbler in both hands and pressed his chin to the lip. He stared thoughtfully towards the sunset.

"A penny for them, Howard," piped up Lady Evelyn.

He smiled. "I was reflecting on our fortunes of the day. The find was a good one was it not, Lady Evelyn?"

"Oh, yes. And all the more pleasing to be there at the moment the jars were discovered - and so fortunate to take part in their recovery. It was most generous of you to allow me the breach of discipline." She nodded a knowing glance at Carter.

He took her meaning and smiled. "I must admit, my lady, you had me a little worried for a while. But, as I observed, you have a natural skill - a gentle touch - So I quickly became relaxed about it."

"Yes, Howard. She did damn well," chimed the earl. "But can we better this tomorrow?"

"Well, that's another thing I was dwelling on, sir," said Carter. "I should like to be quickly put out of the misery of worrying about how much of the find Monsieur le Directeur might allow your lordship to keep. If it fits in with your wishes, sir, I would like to travel with the pieces to Cairo tomorrow to get it over with. Besides, at the same time we can visit with Mr Lucas at his laboratory to see if he can shed some light on the nature of the jars' contents. What do you say?"

"Capital idea. Capital. Will y'come with us, m'dear?"

"If you don't mind, Father, I should like to stay here and rest a little. Today's excitement has quite worn me out. I could do with a day's relaxation. Do you mind?"

"Not at all, m' dear. Do you good, I'm sure. The trip's not exactly without its hardships. In fact, now I come to dwell on it, I think I could do with a day off m'self. We don't get much sleep if we're to rise early enough to get the through-train. Do you mind if we put the trip off for a day, Howard? I believe the reality of fatigue is being suppressed by all this excitement."

"Agreed, sir. I could usefully use the time back at the house. I have notes to catch up on. In any case, I shall have to telegraph Lacau to ensure we have an appointment."

As Carter sailed back to the west bank later that evening he felt relieved - he had fended off another few days of oversight by the earl. He didn't know why, but at the present time he didn't feel all that lucky, notwithstanding their successes earlier in the day.

On their day of rest Carter studied the inscriptions on the cache of jars. They turned out to be attributed to Pharaoh Merneptah. The location of this particular Pharaoh's tomb was situated at one of the points of Carter's triangle of investigation. Their discovery, therefore, led him no nearer to Tutankhamen. So far as his ultimate quarry was concerned, he felt more depressed than elated by the find. And he could hardly bear the thought of being watched by his patron for the remainder of a what he now felt assuredly would turn out to be a barren season. A few more days of diversion would be welcomed.

Carnarvon and Carter were at the station long before sunrise. The trip took all day. The train ride began uncomfortably enough, but later, in the heat of the day, it would become almost unbearable. As the carriages rattled and rocked over the well-used rails, the thickly warm draught would provide little comfort. Nevertheless, some breeze was better than no breeze at all.

Carnarvon's doctor travelled with them in case of emergency, plus the earl's man who laboured on board carrying a large picnic hamper. Carnarvon would never take the food and drink served on the train. Abdel and a colleague sat in the baggage car with the earl's and Carter's belongings and the antiquities.

Following a wash and brush up and a change of clothes, they were soon to be found seated comfortably on the sunset-lit veranda at the Continental Savoy. Their personal, red-fezzed waiter stood at attention at the door, broad-shouldered cut-lead-crystal tumblers of iced gin and tonic reclined securely in their hands, and cucumber sandwiches lay fanned out on crested porcelain centred within a silver tray. This cocktail of impressions went a long way to settling them peacefully back into the cosseted environment in which the earl had grown up and Carter had grown to enjoy. Tomorrow they would have to brave the streets on their way to Lucas's lab and thereafter to the Director's office, but for now they could relax and forget the noise and chaotic carry-on that existed just outside the hotel perimeter.

The following morning the team of two with their Arab carriers arrived at the lab with samples of the jars' contents. Lucas rushed down the corridor to meet them, his unbuttoned white lab coat flapping all about him. "Howard!" he shouted. "Overjoyed to see you, old boy!"

"Me, too," answered Carter, turning to the earl. "May I introduce his lordship, the Earl of Carnarvon. Doctor Alfred Lucas, sir."

"Sir, a great pleasure."

"All mine, Doctor Lucas. I have heard much good said about you. A detective - a sleuth no less - so I am told."

He even looks it, thought Carnarvon. He was a slight man, with oiled and combed-back black hair cropped extremely short on the sides, dark black eyebrows and a small moustache. The hair, although thin, had not gone from the top of his head but it had receded sufficiently to expose a lofty forehead which extended down to a large nose, on which rested a pair of wire spectacles. 'Quite the country Detective Inspector', thought the earl.

"You are too kind, sir. I..."

Carter cut in. "Don't be modest, Alfred. His lordship knows I only tell the truth about other men. Besides, you can prove yourself. Look here. We have something innocuous to test your analytical skills."

By now they had walked into the laboratory itself and Carter slowly unwrapped the substances and placed them on the tiled table.

"What say you?"

After a pause Lucas said, "Pretty innocuous." And they all laughed.

"When do you think you might have an opinion for me, Alfred?"

"Got rather a lot on right now, Howard. Could take a while - 'specially since it doesn't look that interesting." He watched for the downcast expression. "But for you, my friend - and for his lordship - I shall attend to it immediately. How about tomorrow?"

The visitors both smiled and shook Lucas by the hand.

"Have you time to join us for dinner tonight, Doctor Lucas," asked Carnarvon. "It would be our pleasure."

The prospect of a free four-course meal with the aristocracy at the best hotel in Cairo would be a welcome change to the pattern of Lucas's routine and rather singular life, even if he did have to dust off his black tie.

"I would be absolutely delighted, sir."

"How about eight o'clock at the Continental Savoy?"

"Eight o'clock it is, sir. I may even have some results for you by then."

Carter looked at his pocket watch. "We must be going, sir, or we shall be late for our appointment with Monsieur Lacau."

As they left, Lucas called after them, "Mind your Ps and Qs with that one, Howard. No sense of humour, even for a Frog. He takes life very seriously does Pierre."

The imposing figure of the Frenchman politely greeted the two at the front door to his office. "I am most honoured by this visit, Lord Carnarvon."

"The honour is ours, Monsieur le Directeur," followed Carnarvon. "It is always a great pleasure to be in the presence of one so distinguished as yourself."

Carter turned his head away and rolled his eyes.

"For me, too, but doubly, your lordship. To be in the presence of one who has given so much and so generously to this country's heritage and, at the same time, in the presence of one so accomplished at his work."

He turned to look directly at Carter, who acknowledged his attentions with a barely perceptible smile.

"Come, let us sit down and take some tea." He waved at his houseboy and the servant disappeared.

"Now. What may I do for you?"

"We have just two days since made a modest discovery in The Valley."

"As expected. I knew your methods would bear fruit. Modest discovery, you say?"

"Yes, modest. We have brought the cache with us for donation to the Cairo Museum..." Carter paused for a moment. "...and to obtain your judgement on the division." Carter summoned Abdel into the room with the stretcher.

"Well. Let us take a look."

Lacau pushed the objects and papers on his desk to one side.

"Nearly all of it requires restoration," Carter cautioned as he unwrapped one of the balls of cotton wool. "But I am happy to say that all the pieces are accounted for. It is a funerary cache of thirteen calcite jars of different sizes and styles, all of them attributed to the burial of Merneptah. See the inscription on this piece."

Lacau nodded in recognition.

"All found close to the tomb entrance - within the triangle of our investigation."

"Some beautiful carving," the director acknowledged as more and larger pieces were unwrapped, among them the ibex-headed handles. "Most exquisite." He examined the fragments closely. "Très beau. Magnifique!"

He replaced the piece he had been looking at and slapped his large hands down on the desk. "Lord Carnarvon! Mr Carter! This is truly a remarkable find. A great windfall for the Cairo Museum. Once more we are indebted to you."

Carter sat back. Listening to all this he was totally bemused. 'What is the man up to? 'Indebted' is a good word, but why so conciliatory? These are not the greatest finds Lacau has ever seen. He has already made it quite clear to me where he stands on the subject of so-called qualified archaeologists. And he's not normally this polite with aristocracy. The smarmy Frog's up to something!'

"Thirteen jars you say?" asked Lacau, looking directly at Carter once more.

"Yes... Yes, sir," answered Carter.

"Mmm. The board of directors will react badly if I do not recommend they receive the majority of the find."

He paused momentarily, apparently thinking, but he had had what he was going to say in his mind for some time already. "How about... seven for the museum; and six for you?"

Carter sat speechless.

Carnarvon was not. "That is most satisfactory, Monsieur le Directeur. A most satisfactory settlement."

Carter interceded. "What... what about Quibell?"

"What about Quibell? I'll fix Quibell. The curator does as I instruct him."

"I will have them restored first, so that we may see them complete, and then return the six to you, Lord Carnarvon." Lacau continued, "If your lordship is not in Egypt at that time, I shall have them placed in the safekeeping of Mr Carter who will return with them when he leaves for the summer."

"Thank you, Monsieur Lacau." Carnarvon rose to take Lacau's already extended hand. "I look forward to seeing these fine pieces complement my collection at Highclere. And I look forward to the moment when I may entertain your presence there, Monsieur Lacau."

Lacau made a polite half-bow in acknowledgement.

Carter was puzzled: 'The apparent generosity is out of character. He cannot be doing this with any sincerity. He's up to something.'

They emerged from the Director's office to Carnarvon's car which was awaiting them at the front door.

"Home, James," Carter quipped to the driver. "What a successful negotiation, sir. Quite remarkable."

"I must say," said Carnarvon somewhat surprised at Carter's obvious relief. "I do not see why you were so concerned. I thought you had indicated to me that the situation was changed in Egypt - that the Egyptians and those foreigners who worked in their interests had become tightly nationalistic. I remember your words. I must confess, up to this point I have seen none of which you spoke. In fact, quite to the contrary. I would say that Monsieur Lacau has, on this occasion at least, been more lenient than our long departed and much loved Monsieur Maspero. Am I wrong? Is there something so subtle in this that I do not observe?"

Carter for once was at a loss for words. He had not had time to analyse what the director's strategy might be. "Sir, believe me, what I have told you is true. I do not know why on this occasion Monsieur le Directeur is feeling so generous. But I fear he has something brewing in that deceitful Froggy mind of his."

"Carter!" scolded Carnarvon. "Give the man's charity some credit, for God's sake! You are always so critical of others. I do believe you have the greatest difficulty in seeing the best in men."

Carter could see that this was no time to argue. Besides, he was still uneasily sceptical of what Lacau's strategy was and needed time to think the situation through.

As the car bounced down the road, claxon blaring, dodging between the milling masses of preoccupied pedestrians, he turned to the earl. "Sir. You are quite right. I am uncharitable. I apologise. Never mind his reasons, let's take his offer and run!"

When Carnarvon came down to dinner that evening, Carter was already in the lounge with Lucas and the two were heavily into their second cocktails.

"My lord." Lucas got up and pulled a lounge chair forward for him. "We were just talking about the results of my analysis on the deposits you had brought me earlier today. I am afraid it's not too exciting. Interesting to the scientist, but I don't suspect my news will meet your lordship's expectations."

"You have already sparked my curiosity, Doctor Lucas, so don't hold back!"

"Well... merely a mixture of quartz and limestone fragments with some traces of a vegetable pitch and a little resin. A curious concoction. Not a substance associated with embalming but decidedly from a foundation deposit - by Mr Carter's account."

"Yes," Carter added. "From what I can make of the jars' inscriptions, sir, they refer to 'holy oils' of various manufacture. Clearly not what ended up in them. I cannot fathom for the life of me what the chemistry of these contents can mean."

Carnarvon predictably was quick to lose interest. He sipped at his drink and the subject moved on to hunting.

By now it was late May. Carnarvon had left for England some time earlier. Mercifully, the summer heat had held off this year. As he waited for Lacau to complete the restoration of the Merneptah jars, Carter found it not unduly uncomfortable to continue work in the field.

On the less tolerable days he stayed at home and made preparations for his eventual departure. He wanted a quick start-up when he returned the following winter. He had decided to break his normal routine and had authorised Ali to restart the dig on the first of October, more than two months before he intended to arrive back on the west bank. This decision reflected three things: he was anxious to accelerate the clearing of the entire area; he was prepared to relax his normal standards; and he held the greatest confidence in the discipline and ability of his principal reis. And in any case, in his present strangely unoptimistic mood, he felt there was virtually no risk of a discovery of any importance during his absence. He had left little to chance, however. The reis had been instructed to clear only to the base of the most obviously recent deposits.

On the first of June, just as Carter's patience was beginning to fade, Abdel brought in a telegram:

Carter STOP Partage des antiquités trouvées dans la Vallée des Rois STOP Campagne 1920 STOP Il est complet STOP Lacau.

About bloody time, thought Carter. "Abdel! Start packing. I am departing for Cairo tomorrow morning. I must telegraph the steamer company to ensure I have a berth. You will send it for me."

When he arrived at Lacau's door, Carter had but two hours' daylight left to get to the steamer company office and secure his ticket.

Lacau was as condescending as he had been at their last meeting. "Monsieur Carter," he greeted, holding Carter's outstretched hand. "it is so good to see you again. May I get you a drink?"

"Non, monsieur, merci. I must get to the steamer company before it closes to ensure my booking on the next passage."

"Ah," acknowledged Lacau. "Then here is the certificate for exportation. Please sign for receipt. I believe as we speak my men are placing the crate on your carriage. Bon voyage."

He shook Carter's hand vigorously. Too vigorously for Carter's taste. Not that it was all that strong, but Carter read deviousness into every one of

Lacau's gestures. He felt uncomfortable. Up to this point, he still could not fathom his own uneasy suspicions. He extracted his hand and took out his fountain pen to sign the certificate. He signed underneath Lacau's signature on the two copies, tore one off and pocketed it. Lacau escorted him to the front door. Carter touched his hat to the director as he left. Turning, he saw the crate stacked and securely bound on the rear platform of his carriage. He got in and the carriage drove away.

Lacau watched him disappear into the mêlée of dust and carts and animals and cars and people and turned back towards his office. There was a satisfied smile on his face. In this negotiation he had conceded little of value. If there were a next time, there was ample justification for the favour to be doubly repaid. And, with the Englishman's thorough approach to excavation, there was almost certain to be a next time. Carter, also, was convinced of that. But neither Lacau nor Carter had any conception just how much of an issue that could one day become for them.

That evening, back at the Continental, someone else's luck changed Carter's priorities. He received a telegram from a dealer friend of his in Luxor:

Sir there has been a great find STOP To the south of The Valley STOP By infidels STOP Know who they are STOP Have heard they already arrange sales with the French and other dealers STOP No time to be lost STOP Return immediately STOP Have room reserved for you at WP STOP Nadir

With the sailing still five days away he was on the six a.m. train.

Carter strode up to the earl, beaming from ear to ear.

"You've got it, haven't you?" said Carnarvon expectantly. "The princess's jewellery - it's in that bag of yours, isn't it?"

Carter couldn't contain his feelings. The achievement, after all said and done, was truly remarkable.

"Yes, sir. I have a good deal of it here. And I have negotiated first refusal on the remainder - subject to terms, of course. I do believe, ultimately, that we shall have the lot."

"Capital! Capital!" exclaimed his lordship, rubbing his hands together. "Let me see it. Here, on the desk."

Carnarvon removed the inkwells and blotter and a number of papers from the broad desk in his library and placed them on a nearby seat. Carter methodically unfastened the straps on his leather case and sank his hand into the interior up to his elbow. He pulled out an oblong mat of cotton wool and placed it on the desk.

"You open it, sir."

Carnarvon's fingers were trembling with excitement as he teased the wool apart. He pulled the upper layer back to reveal a necklace of small beads, carnelian, lapis lazuli and gold with, spaced exactly eleven beads apart, twelve diminutive caricatures of seated baboons, each of them cast in gold.

Carnarvon caught his breath. "It's exquisite, Howard. Absolutely exquisite." And after a pause, "How much did it cost me?"

"Less than you might expect, sir. Sufficiently less for you to make a fine profit from the sale of it, should you so wish. The Met is eager to obtain possession." He quickly added, "And all the other pieces, should you want to secure them."

"Marvellous, Howard. Absolutely marvellous! You have more?"

"I have, sir."

One by one, Carter carefully removed the objects he had in his bag until they were all displayed across the surface of the desk.

"I am all but speechless, Howard. With all those melancholy letters of yours, I must confess I was not looking forward too much to your report."

Carter lowered his eyes.

"But this... this... this trove! I know I have had to pay for it, but the very fact you may be able to capture the entire contents of a rifled tomb... Such compensation for the lactlustre results of our own efforts in your so-called 'triangle of opportunity'."

That was a low blow, unintentioned as such by the earl but deeply felt nonetheless by his colleague.

"I shall enjoy these pieces amongst my collection. Pride of place they will have. Perhaps I will sell them on... to the Met, or the British Museum. But not for a while yet, at any rate. You may, in time, make the arrangements. Keep them waiting a while first, though. Make 'em sweat, eh? Ha, ha, ha."

The earl was clearly stimulated by his new acquisitions. Carter's theatricals had altogether the desired effect. Better still, the lately unsuccessful archaeologist stood to make a substantial financial killing out of it through his own profit and, in addition, through his commission for arranging placement of the goods. Carter hadn't felt this gratified for some years, and the joy of it was, neither had his patron. Carnarvon's personal expectations now switched to the more tangible acquisition of antiquities that he knew already existed 'above ground', so to speak. Carter could see that his lordship had put the frustrations of the past year's relatively fruitless digging to one side, for the time being at least.

'If I can get a bit of digging done while I am making money on the purchases,' Carter reflected, 'I shall have the best of all worlds - keep Carnarvon's interest and make progress in the triangle - make money!' He drew long on his cigarette and let the smoke curl slowly from his nostrils.

Carter returned to Luxor in November. His gamble had paid off. The men had cleared a significant area during his absence and had found nothing. He immediately set about preparing for Carnarvon's next visit, assembling the facilities the earl would expect to be available the moment he arrived. In the depths of the tomb of Ramses XI Carter would prepare a space to store his lordship's wines. He would clean and level the upper reaches so that the party could take lunch in comfort.

Towards the end of the year, Carter had returned his men to working in the vicinity of the ancient workmen's huts. He could not spend too long in this spot but, on the off chance that something might turn up quickly in this, the area he had the greatest hopes for, he thought it worthwhile to devote just a little time to digging. Soon he would have to stop for the forthcoming state visit of the current ruler of Egypt, Sultan Hussein. Anyway, with the tourist season upon him, he would have to work elsewhere to avoid risking a fall by a clumsy tourist visiting the tomb of Ramses VI, the door to which stood immediately above the site of his steadily deepening excavation.

It was the end of another month. Time to put pen to paper and once again report progress to his patron. Carter sat at his desk that evening, his notebook in front of him, and chewed on the end of his fountain pen, searching for the right words. Somehow he wanted to make his own frustrations clear to the earl while at the same time indicating some cause for optimism. The words weren't coming, however.

Carter replaced the cap on his pen. Actions would speak better than words.

In his urgency to discover something of value to present to his patron, Carter temporarily lost faith in his clearance area and moved his men to a gully in the southern extremity of the valley lying just ahead of the entrance to the tomb of Tuthmosis III. There, eventually, he found another lacklustre assemblage of foundation deposits.

It wasn't good enough. He was feeling the pressure. He had been seriously attacking the 'triangle' for three seasons and was now in his fourth. All he had to show for it of any significance were the six jars that Carnarvon had received as his share from the excavation in which Lady Evelyn had participated a year ago.

Carter cut his losses and moved his men back to the centre of the valley. He placed them further north where there was evidence of other ancient workmen's dwellings. There the men toiled a further two weeks. And there something finally turned up.

"Master! Master! Come! There is something!"

As he had done every day this season, Carter was standing above the excavation watching and directing the men at their work, and looking for all purposes as fresh to the task as if he expected a discovery any moment. When he heard the man shouting, he immediately scrambled down the gravel bank towards him.

"What is it, Ali?" he shouted. "What have you found?"

"See, sir."

The man gestured towards a crevice in the bare rock face. There, in a dark recess, faintly twinkling in the sunshine, lay a set of dirty bronze studs. They were the like of those shown in many wall illustrations, sewn in an even pattern on a funeral pall, the type that would have been draped over the frame enclosing the funerary shrines which housed a mummy's sarcophagus and coffins.

Carter was cautiously encouraged by the discovery. While these studs could indicate that a tomb was nearby, they could also indicate that it was robbed, part of the debris trail of a hasty retreat. Judiciously he recorded the location of the find, the pieces numbered according to his system, and had them carefully packed.

But this excitement was short-lived. Another month passed with nothing to show for the effort. After years of toil, hundreds of tons of characterless rubble had been removed from the area. The tailings of the excavation now extended some considerable way towards the valley mouth, a testament to all the effort and dogged perseverance.

It was getting warm. It was time to bring another disappointing season to a close.

Carter left Egypt for England in April 1921 and, somewhat despondent at his melancholy progress, felt disinclined to return too soon. This time he had not prepared his men to begin work early the following season. He told them to await his return, saying he felt he was close and needed to be present at all stages of the dig from now on. The fact was that there was little of the area left to be cleared.

He felt depressed and did not know how he was going to go about confronting his patron with yet more of this fruitless news.

It was a glorious early May. At Highclere the rhododendrons were blooming in bursts of vibrant colour all over the estate. The contrast with the desert was so extreme that on his way along the drive to the house Carter felt compelled to stop the car and sit a while to take in the atmosphere. He pulled the car onto the grass verge, stopped the engine, rolled down the window and took a deep breath. There were rhododendrons all about him. The heavy, sweet scent of jasmine hung in the air. Carter got out of the car and walked into the shrubbery. Purples, reds, pinks, whites, yellows, blues, and oranges blazed all about him. He found a clearing, took off his jacket, laid it on the grass and sat down. Drawing his knees up under his chin and clasping his legs tightly in his arms, he gazed dreamily at the colourful spectacle. A breeze rolled through the trees and the massive clusters of blooms waved before him. As he stared with unfocused eyes into the panoply of colours, they slowly coalesced.

The colourful mixtures began to form into shapes. The features of the figures were indistinct, but there were many, all filing past him in serried ranks. The column had a slow, reverent, swaying motion. There appeared to be a funeral bier. He thought he could make out the shape of a coffin.

A sudden and brief gust of wind turned the flowers behind the leaves momentarily and the apparition disappeared into the shadows, like a body into its tomb.

Then the pain hit him - right in the pit of the stomach, it seemed. It forced him to fall on his side in the grass clutching at his waist. He moaned some expletives and wriggled around for a while in an effort to find a more comfortable position. As he did so, the pain gradually abated and presently he found he was able to get to his feet. Still bent almost double, he hobbled back to his car. He dragged himself into the driver's seat, pulled the starter and drove on to the house.

Carnarvon's butler had heard the car approaching and was at the bottom of the steps ready to open the car door. By now the pain was coming back again and Carter, his body arched over the steering wheel, whispered something unintelligible to the man.

"Mr Carter, sir!" the butler exclaimed in surprise.

He leant in, took Carter by the armpits and pulled him from his seat. Once he had managed to get him out, he could tell the man was in too much pain to make his own way up the steps. He crouched underneath him, took the weight of his body across his back and struggled into the house. One of the chambermaids rushed up to him.

"Get the doctor, Mary!" shouted the butler with a sense of urgency. "Tell him Mr Carter is taken poorly. I will put Mr Carter on the sofa in the library and alert his lordship."

The girl took off up the stairs and the butler, the dead weight of Carter now causing him considerable discomfort, pushed through the library doors and with some relief, rolled the incapacitated archaeologist off his back and onto the sofa cushions. He loosened Carter's collar and hurried off to get the earl. By the time they had returned, the doctor was already prodding at Carter's abdomen and receiving intermittent groans from his unfortunate patient.

"My God, Howard! What is the matter?"

Carter responded. "Sorry... Sorry about this, sir. The pain has passed - or at least it will if this butcher of yours will stop messing me about."

The earl's doctor, a surly man known for his morbid sense of humour, turned to address his employer. "Mr Carter, your lordship, is decidedly not at his best. I fancy he does not deal with pain too well. I believe he has gallstones. He will need to be hospitalised. Go under the knife, I fear."

As he said this, his face took on an inwardly pleasing but outwardly menacing grin. He turned back to the whining invalid. "The knife, Mr Carter."

Carter's words were punctuated by quick breaths as he winced at each stab of pain. "I've been experiencing... abdominal pains... For some time now, sir... but never this bad... Seems... seems I will have to... get it seen to."

The doctor chimed in merrily again. "Yes indeed. Messy operation, by all accounts. Got to go in deep. Blood all over the place. Nasty. I'll get him a bed at your lordship's hospital in Leeds. Sir Berkeley Moynihan, m' lord. You know him well. Poetry with knives. However, the Irish, y'know, not known for their accuracy." With this parting reflection he disappeared.

"Don't mind him, old boy. Sick sense of humour for a doctor - but a good man at his trade for all that."

Carnarvon turned to the chambermaid. "Better make him up a bed right here for the present, Mary."

"Yes, your lordship. At once, your lordship." And she trotted off upstairs again.

With the earl's doctor's help, Carter was found a hospital bed within twenty-four hours. His surgery was over before the day was out.

The healing period, however, was a lot longer. He did not leave the hospital until a month and a half had elapsed, and then he had to rest up in Carnarvon's London home until he was fit enough to travel.

Carter arrived in Cairo on 25 January 1922, still a bit sore. That did not stop him hurrying to reacquaint himself with the local dealers in search of any new material that might have turned up while he had been away. Nor did it stop him making forays into the markets. Practically three months of the winter season had been wasted.

His patron arrived early in February. Carter was resigned to this visit. He'd had a good run of relative solitude, and it was time to pay his dues.

As things turned out, it was just as well this was a short season. Carter was not fully fit and tired easily. The ever sensitive Carnarvon could see it. The earl would urge him to close his day's work and get to bed earlier than usual. After repeated encouragement from the earl to take things easy - more than he could take, really - and the season's lack of success having monotonously followed the pattern of the last few years, Carter was relieved to be able to return to England prematurely. He was happy to accept that he had no need to prolong his stay and had willingly taken his patron's advice. He left in April. The earl himself had gone by the end of March.

But in the parlour room of the steamer, on the trip back to England, as he nursed his aching abdomen with an ill-advised Scotch, Carter began to whine to himself. 'Damn this unfortunate malady,' he brooded. 'Bloody poor timing. Could have done with a full season's work. Might have found it by the time he'd turned up. Another bloody year up the spout.' He swallowed a large mouthful and spoke out loud, "Another bloody year up the spout!"

"Language!"

This retort came from a fat, ageing priest in full black habit and dog collar who had just entered the room. In his right hand he carried an empty champagne flute.

"Seamus!" shouted Carter in happy surprise. "What great good luck! Where have you been all these years?"

"Well, Oi was going t' ask you exactly d' same question, Howard. Actually Oi'm surprised you reco'noised me so quickly. Oi have grown a little, have

Oi not? An' not in all d' roit places. Lost a tad on top, an' all."

"The habit, the nose, the glass, Seamus. You are unmistakable. How the devil did you recognise me?"

The priest laughed. "You won't loike dis... D' serious expression. Saw it all d' toime on our one an' only previous trip. Never seen one loike it since. Doesn't matter what shape you're in dat expression gives you away every toime. Miserable old sod y' are!"

Carter didn't mind a bit - he was elated. It was exactly what he needed at exactly the right time.

"Seamus. I can't tell you how happy I am to see you again. So many years. So much has happened. Have you time to talk?"

"Dis boat is on d' water, is it not? Until Oi can get off dis tub on to droi land you have all me attention, Howard. Is it a confessional you'll be wanting?"

"Don't try me too hard in my present state, Seamus, please. I am, to say the least, a little fragile... mentally... at this point. Can I get you some more champagne?"

"T'ank you, Howard, no. Oi'd 'ave bin most grateful 'ad Oi bin wantin'."
He drew a half-full bottle from behind his back and placed it on the wine table. He sat down and eased back into the deck chair beside Carter.

"Well now. Where should I start?"

"How about from d' beginnin'? Oi do 'ave d' toime."

"Well now." Carter, in his relief at finding a friend in this moment of melancholy was at a loss for words again. "Well now. The beginning..."

It had been some time. He tried to recall the events in order. A draught would help oil his senses.

"Cheers!" He clinked glasses with the priest, drank it down in one and began.

"After I left you at Alex I was taken almost immediately into the desert. The early impressions were magnificent. Hard taskmasters but great sights. All off the beaten track. Things millions never have the good fortune to see. And I a mere boy. It was such a lucky time for me. I worked with several important Egyptologists - Petrie..."

"Petrie, indeed? Met him moiself. Ungodly man. Couldn't aboide 'im. Got no soul."

"Well, I agree with your impression. Not a man I could grow to love. But very inspired. Very clever. Very good at what he does. Good training for one such as I at that time."

"Typical English Oirish-hater!"

They laughed together. Carter refilled his glass and took another mouthful.

"Then it was Davis. American. Y' know him, too?"

The priest reflected for a moment. "No. Don't believe Oi've come across d' man."

"You haven't missed much." Carter chuckled and swallowed again. "Philistines, the Americans. Baptist I believe he was. Loadsa money. Arrogant. No bloody brains. No bloody class. You know the type."

"Never had no toime for dem Baptists - all foire an' brimstone - no fun. God loikes a happy flock."

"Then... Then..." Carter paused.

"Yes, Howard? Yes? Well? Well? Den what?"

"Well... I met an English gentleman. You Irish wouldn't understand, of course." Carter was quite serious but the priest only laughed the louder.

"Loiked 'im, did you? One of dem, was he?"

"Seamus! That's unkind. He's a good man. Besides, he pays the bills."

"Ah. Definitely one of dem. You're lucky, Howard, that you're not blessed with boyish good looks. In fact Oi would go so far as t' say... a pretty ugly boy..."

"Do you want me to tell you what has happened these past years or don't you?"

"Me apologies, Howard. Me apologies. Anoder drink would you be having?"

"Please... Scotch and water."

Seamus waved to a distant waiter.

Carter, placated, continued. "He was introduced to me by the Director of Antiquities in Cairo - Monsieur Maspero - a good and a fair man... not like the Froggy bastard who took his place." Carter took a breath. "Anyway this earl - old money and all that, you understand - needed someone who knew what he was doing. That's where I came in."

"Sounds loike a perfect union t' me."

"Fact is, this man was and is fascinated by Egyptian history and the acquisition of its artefacts, and I am the only man who can satisfy him..." Carter paused. "Er, poor choice of words..."

They both laughed.

Carter continued, "Finally got the right to dig in The Valley of the Kings. Been digging for four years. Know what has happened?"

Seamus was growing intrigued. "What?"

"Bugger all. Pardon me. Virtually 'b'-all anyway. Damned unfortunate." Carter went silent for a few moments. "It's there you see. I know it's there. Somewhere..." Carter was getting wrapped up in his emotions again. He looked down pensively.

Seamus broke the silence. "What is dere, Howard?"

"Tutankhamen, dammit! Tutankhamen! Why the hell...? Why ever do you think I'm in such a state?"

"An' who may dis 'Tutan-someone' be when 'e's at home?"

"I apologise, Seamus. I have been living with this thing for so long I totally forget it may be a mystery to others. Let me fill you in..."

"Before d'loight anuder drink," cut in the priest.

Carter began his lengthy monologue and the two descended slowly but innevitably into a state of peaceful inebriation.

The price was paid the following morning. Carter awoke to a high and slowly rolling sea. Within minutes of becoming conscious, he was running for the bathroom.

When Carter arrived back at his lodgings in London he found recent mail from Carnarvon.

My dear Howard,

Welcome home. I do hope your trip was a comfortable one and that you had the time to get some well-needed rest. When you feel strong enough, it would be my pleasure, as you well know, to entertain you here at Highclere. Perhaps you can come when Newbury next meets - the last week of June. We can have a grand old time and take in a few brace from the grounds. Do say you will come, but I will leave the timing up to yourself. I have few commitments that are expected to take me away from here, but none that I should not be able to reschedule around your own plans.

I want to show you how I have displayed our recent acquisitions from the dealerships in Cairo.

Also there is much else for us to discuss.

I hope you will feel up to it shortly and I look forward to your reply.

Your ever admiring friend,

Carnarvon.

'Much else for us to discuss.' This was less an invitation, and more a set of marching orders. It was time to be called to account for the long years of disappointing results and what had, as Carter was only too well aware, grown into a considerable capital outlay. He had rehearsed the coming meeting many times over in his mind. He took time to count his blessings. There was comfort in the fact that he had been allowed to go this far in his search. Without result, the earl had freely given him his confidence for longer than any normal philanthropist could be expected to tolerate. The impatient Davis would have withdrawn from the area long since and perhaps fired him to boot. It was almost a relief to Carter that the moment had arrived at last.

He was quite ready for it. There was no question that clearance of his 'triangle' in The Valley had to be completed, but he would not ask the earl for further funding. By now he had enough money saved to do it at his own cost. All he would wish from the earl was for him to agree to hold his concession for one more year so that the excavation could continue. He would go directly to his favoured spot, the workmen's huts lying beneath the entrance to the tomb of Ramses VI, and get it over with.

He enjoyed a good sleep that night - no more brooding.

At breakfast the next day, Carter pulled out his pen and paper and wrote back to his patron accepting his invitation and stating that he would be there no later than the first week of July.

When he arrived at the front steps of the great house, Carter was feeling remarkably fit. He was in the best of spirits. The adrenalin of excitement and anticipation that he truly should get this chance to dig where he had most wanted to these past few seasons buoyed him up. As he greeted Carnarvon in the library, his beaming smile was quite genuine.

For the first three days at the estate, they talked about anything but The Valley. Carter could tell that the earl was uneasy about how or when he could broach the subject. The Egyptologist decided it might even be to his advantage if he himself first broke the ice.

As they promenaded in the gardens, Carnarvon continued to eulogise his past season's pheasant shoot. "Five hundred and thirty brace in one day, Howard. What do you think of that? Had a bit of help, mind you. Actually, never had so many guests at the house at one time. Capital session though. Haven't enjoyed m'self so much in years."

Carter spotted the opportunity and took it. "No, sir. The years have been pretty lean elsewhere, have they not?"

"What?" The earl feigned a lack of understanding for a moment. "Oh... The Valley. Aye. We have had a run of bad luck there, Howard. A long run."

He paused. It was in his eyes. Carter could see him struggle for the right words. At last he drew a long breath and said what had been on his mind these last five months. "Fact is, my old friend, I just can't afford to fund another fruitless season."

Now that he'd said it, the earl became embarrassed at the hurt he had perpetrated against his friend. He was fearful of the response. He continued without stopping and spoke rapidly, running one sentence into another. "I think we should release the concession back to the Director of Antiquities. There must be other sites with more fruit to pick. Perhaps with not so much of an ambitious goal but nevertheless yielding real cherries. We have given this one our very best, have we not, Howard? Given it our best. Davis was right after all. Shame to be proven wrong by an American, don't y'know. But the world is changing. Our sun is setting. Theirs is on the rise. I know very well this will be a great disappointment to you, my friend. Please do not let it harm the relationship we have built over so many years. I reproach you nothing for what has transpired. Five years we have laboured hard. We can pat ourselves on the back - an achievement in itself. Believe me, this was not an easy decision. I have lain awake many nights dreading this moment. But if you do not wish to join me in a search for new ground, you know I will see you all right, old chap. I hope, of course, you will allow me to retain your services for future purchases on the internal market..."

He paused just long enough to allow Carter to break in. "Sir," Carter began politely, raising his hand as a gesture of acknowledgement and holding the moment, "I too have sat up nights wondering whether we were on a fatefully useless track. I am not a man who is used to failure, as you well know, and all that has not happened has been most distasteful to me, not least because it is your money I have been spending. But it has been put to judicious use every step of the way and you know that we have not yet finished this 'mission' of ours. That which we planned to do is not yet complete."

Carnarvon nodded recognition of each of Carter's statements, but it was clear he had spent sufficient time debating his decision and that his mind was firmly made up. There would be no going back on it.

Carter continued, "Sir, I know you have made up your mind, and not lightly, but please hear me out..."

The earl smiled. "When have I ever been able to shut you up when you have it in your mind to say something, Howard?"

The atmosphere became more relaxed. Carter pulled a map from his inside jacket pocket and unfolded it on the carpet between them.

"You have seen this map develop through the years, sir."

"Oh, yes. A finely accurate record of the positions and character of all finds by us and by others in the past. We must publish it in our next book."

"Perhaps, sir. But not before we have added the location of the tomb of Tutankhamen!"

"Him, again. Howard, as we have proven, it is tough enough to find a tomb at all, let alone that of a particular Pharaoh..."

Carter cut in. "...And by such little account in the histories written on the walls and ostraca all about Thebes, not a Pharaoh of much note. But there is so much physical evidence that he was indeed buried in the area. At least at one time he was. Maybe now he has been moved to some other place like so many others. But I do not believe this. Of all the missing Pharaohs the evidence points to Tutankhamen being there still. The one place we have not probed within our 'triangle' of investigation - the one place we already know has lain untouched since the time of Ramses VI - is the area beneath the workmen's huts situated at the very doorway to that tomb." Carter stabbed at the map with his finger. "The place we have found is difficult to touch thus far for the inconvenience it would have caused tourists visiting Ramses's tomb. This is the place we must now use one more season to uncover... One more season."

The words hung suspended in the pregnant pause that followed. Carter didn't expect his patron to yield and continued without waiting for a response. "I can get started before the tourist season really gets into full swing. It is not a big job and will not cost much. I can well afford it. All I need is your lordship's assurance that you will hold off on relinquishment of the concession until I have finished this last effort. One more season. In your name, of course."

This Carnarvon had not anticipated. It had never occurred to him that this man of considerably lesser means would even consider dipping into his own pocket. With an astonished look on his face, he fell back in his chair. He had literally no defence for this proposal. How could he stop him if he would pay for it himself? To continue with his intention to relinquish the licence would appear unfriendly and bloody-minded, especially after all they had been through together over the years. And then there was the great bounty of artefacts the earl had acquired, all entirely through Carter's doing.

"Goodness, Howard!" the earl exclaimed after a brief pause. "I can't let you do that. You know I can't let you do that."

Carter misunderstood what the earl intended by the remark. "Oh, but you must, sir. Do not deny me this last chance, I implore you..."

"No! That is my last word on the matter. I shall pay as I have always done. I am not about to change my ways now. One more season."

Carter's relief was self-evident. He stood up immediately, leaned forward beaming and took Carnarvon by the hand, shaking it vigorously.

"I cannot thank you enough for your continued support, sir. Together, sir, we shall bring this one home together."

The grandee's generosity and faith filled him with confidence. Carter had convinced himself he would be successful. His excitement, and knowing now that this was indeed to be the last season, did not permit him to give the chance of failure a second thought.

They stared at each other silently for a moment. At last the earl summoned the butler.

"Let us drink on it!"

Carter was really thirsty.

The Egyptologist was true to his word. He arrived back in Cairo the second week of October, at least two months before the tourist season really took off.

He made a brief run around the dealers in Cairo to see what may have cropped up while he had been away. The shopping trip was fruitful. He bought several pieces for Carnarvon and during his browsing around the bazaars found he could not resist buying something for himself - a canary - to provide him with some tuneful companionship during the long nights of solitude at Castle Carter. The whole lot accompanied him on the train back to Luxor.

The ever faithful Abdel met him at the station. "Master!" he exclaimed on seeing the canary. "A bird of gold accompanies you. Surely a sign of good luck!"

Carter smiled at the thought. Truly he hadn't felt this buoyant in years.

He lost no time getting started, and by the first of the following month he had his men situated immediately beneath and slightly 'downstream' of the entrance to the tomb of Ramses VI, busily digging at and through the south-westernmost corner of the floor of one of the ancient workmen's huts.

After three days' digging, as usual, nothing had been found. Carter arrived at the site each morning well before his men. He paced over every piece of newly revealed ground, head down, looking for the slightest suggestion of something out of the ordinary. But there was only featureless rubble at the bottom of a featureless pit.

On the fourth morning he was later than usual. He had dawdled at his house, poring over the details of his map.

Up at the excavation site, Ali had called on one of the boys to get another jar of water. He noticed the lad was having difficulty trying to get it to stand upright. He could not sink it into the sand deeply enough. Ali went over to help. When he took hold of the jar and attempted to grind the base into the loose debris, he felt hard rock just an inch or two beneath the surface. He passed the water jar back to the boy, got down on his hands and knees and scraped away at the rubble with his hands.

"Mr Carter! Mr Carter!" The reis came running through his open front door and flailed through the house, skidding on the tiled floor in his leather sandals as he dashed from room to room trying to find his master. He finally slid to a stop in Carter's study. The archaeologist slowly turned in his chair to see what all the commotion was about.

"Mr Carter, sir. Forgive my rudeness, please, but I have much of importance to tell you. May I speak, sir?"

"Ali. Whatever's the matter, man. You look most distressed. Sit. Have a drink... of water. Settle yourself. Then speak. Is it trouble?"

Carter handed him the carafe of water and the sweating Arab poured himself a full glass and immediately drank it down. He barely drew breath before speaking again. "We have found a flat rock, sir! A flat rock! Perhaps a step, sir! It is real! It is real!"

Carter did not dare believe the man: Not after four days... not after five full years... not just four days.

He was up from his chair, in his car and on his way to The Valley before the man got another sentence out.

The two hurried to the edge of the pit. Carter stopped and looked down. The labourers, assembled in a circle, were all standing silent and motionless, looking up at Carter expectantly. They had arranged themselves around a small and extremely shallow rectangle of excavated ground only a few inches deep.

Carter scrambled down the rubble slope and stepped into the centre of the shallow depression. He bent down and felt all around the contours of the single, visible step. The signs were unmistakable... Finally!

There was no question about it. At last he had found something. Carter could not disguise his pleasure any longer. Beaming at the reis, he yelled at the top of his voice, "Ali! Ali Hosein! Allah be praised!"

The reis grinned back at him through his blackened, broken teeth. Carter looked around at the group of faithful labourers standing all about him. Each shared some feeling for the excitement of the moment. Like an enormous collection of gargoyles, rows of blackened teeth were revealed in the smiles surrounding him.

"Praise be to Allah!" The shout from the chorus line of labourers echoed and re-echoed around the valley cliffs.

He beamed back.

"Continue!" he shouted to Ali as he jumped back up the slope. "We must expose the entrance way completely."

Carter's excited anticipation was to remain hanging. There was so much ancient debris around and above the small pit that even by nightfall the men had not succeeded in exposing the entire surface area of the stairwell. Carter posted a guard and reluctantly returned to the solitude of his house for the night.

He felt horribly alone. He had no one with whom he could share the eager anticipation of this moment; no one around to help console his longing for the one outcome that could change the pattern of his life for ever. Even the canary was silent. What he wouldn't give to have the dear Dorothy by his side.

His mind flooded with images. As he sorted through all the possible outcomes, he became desperately anxious. It was all too much for him. Overcome by sheer exhaustion, he fell into a fitful sleep.

By the end of the morning of the next day, the fellahs had at last cleared the upper portion of the surface cavity. At the opposite end from the originally exposed step, where the bedrock began to rise at the base of the valley flank, was now revealed the hand-cut facing that should overlie the lintel to a doorway. Carter controlled his impatience.

"Clear down some more - carefully now - there may be objects in the debris. Feel for the door gently. If it is still intact it will be faced with plaster - very fragile - we must be careful not to damage the surface. There may be seals."

Carter could hardly contain his excitement. He fidgeted, at one time holding his hands tightly together, at another folding his arms close to his chest. He paced about. He could feel himself tremble.

The labourers slowly cleared some more of the rubble. Another step was revealed, then another and another. More of the walls, cut cleanly shear either side of the gradually descending staircase, were steadily exposed. With the cavity cleared down to the twelfth step, the base of the door lintel appeared and beneath it a mud plaster wall. Carter called the men out and jumped back into the deepened pit to examine the first few inches. There were seals - royal cemetery seals. The tomb, to this point at least, appeared whole. But, so far as he could tell, the seals were generic - necropolis seals. None of them bore a name. There was no indication whose tomb this might be.

Carter kept his men digging until they had revealed the entire staircase and the doorway was exposed to its base. As more and more of the door had been revealed, he could see that the patterns in the seal impressions changed. Those in the upper left corner of the door facing looked different, their placement less orderly than those elsewhere.

With all the debris now removed, the men climbed out of the pit and stood expectantly around the lip of the staircase. Carter walked slowly down to the door, at each step feeling himself on a new threshold, untrod in millennia. As he reached the bottom, he could for the first time clearly see that the tomb had been resealed in antiquity. Robbed. That much he had expected. It mattered little. The evidence notwithstanding, this discovery was undeniably a tremendous stroke of good fortune.

Carter spent some time on the bottom step looking in detail at each of the seal impressions before him. As he read lower, the anonymous necropolis seals gave way to different, less distinct types of impressions. He couldn't see them too well. The entire cavity was in shadow. He touched the indentations with his fingers. Within the larger outline of one of the seals he sensed the arch of the top of a cartouche - the racetrack-shaped border that usually surrounded the name of a Pharaoh. His fingers trembled with anticipation as he drew them lightly down over the impression, trying to feel for the slightest change in contour. There was an orb. He moved his forefinger around it to be sure it was a circle. He felt below it. Another orb? He squinted at it in the darkness. Everything was black. He couldn't make out a thing. He felt around the lump and thought he could sense appendages emerging from at least three points. A scarab? Feeling slightly below this, he could make out three bars, a rough semicircle, then the base of the frame.

Carter's body seized up with a rush of excitement the like of which he had not experienced ever before. This was real. There was no mistake: sun disk, scarab... Nebkheperure! Tutankhamen! It truly is Tutankhamen!

He turned and looked up at his expectant tribe gathered about him at the surface. Ali could tell it before he spoke. He had never observed such a grin on the face of his master.

"We have him, Ali! Tutankhamen! We have him! Praise be to God!"

The Valley filled with noise as the Arabs repeated Carter's words.

The impulse now to dismantle the door and penetrate the depths of the tomb was almost too much. But before he took another step he knew he must call his patron to this place. Then he remembered the Tomb of the Horse.

He sighed. He called to Ali and asked him to bring his satchel. Carter undid the straps and withdrew a steel probing rod. Placing the rod against an unstamped part of the plastered doorway, he carefully excavated a small hole. He chipped his way through the gap between the mud bricks which lay behind until he felt the rod give. He withdrew it and introduced a small torch. Manouevring the torch within the confined space, all he could see was a slope of rubble rising to an inclined ceiling. The corridor which lay behind the door was filled - filled by the hand of man - that, at least, was quite clear.

The prospect of a great deal more hard labour before he came upon anything of significance confirmed his decision. He would indeed stop here. He would telegraph his patron with the news. The seals had confirmed it was well worth the risk.

He pulled himself up and turned to look at his men silhouetted above him. They all stared downwards expectantly. Carter squinted in the sunlight and drew his hat over his eyes. He addressed them in Arabic. "Men. We have discovered what may prove to be the burial of Pharaoh Tutankhamen. I have all of you to thank for that... Refill this place immediately. Mind you, now - take the greatest care not to damage the plaster at the bottom of the steps. Drop your loads gently. There is plenty of time... I must summon Lord Carnarvon to the opening. Repost the guards when you have finished. Ali - mark you now - the strictest security!"

Ali got the message all right. A word from him and the men began refilling their baskets with rubble. In an orderly and unhurried fashion, they filed down the steps to redeposit their loads.

"And Ali!" added Carter, "make sure you get your most trustworthy colleagues to guard this place."

Carter thought for a moment. He snapped his fingers. "Of course! Why didn't I think of it before? Sergeant Adamson! Ali! Never mind. Forget what I just said. Sergeant Adamson is in Luxor kicking his heels. Go to him at once. Tell him I have a most important assignment for him. Now, if you please!"

The reis took off down The Valley bound for the ferry. As he made his way across the river he pondered on what purpose the sergeant could have by kicking his heels, and in Luxor of all places.

Carter remained at the top of the pit supervising the men as they refilled the excavation. He watched the door and the steps disappear and, as the last basket load was tossed on the ground, he addressed the labourers once more.

"Thank you, men. Leave now and return only when the reis summons you. This will not be soon. We must await the arrival of his lordship from England. The reis will provide you with some additional reward for this day's work. Go home to your families and, once again, my thanks to you all... and thanks be to Allah!"

Carter sat cross-legged in the sand and watched the men disappear. While he waited for Ali to return with Adamson he dwelt on his achievement. Too good to believe! Vindication! But then he knew he had been right. The long wait had been worth it. Now he felt the boyish excitement of waiting to open a Christmas present. He pulled his notebook from his jacket pocket and took the pencil from behind his ear. His fingers were trembling as he recorded the moment.

He closed the book and sucked on the end of his pencil. Must cable Carnarvon tonight. Won't tell him about Tutankhamen just yet. Much better to save that for his arrival.

Carnarvon was having a restful breakfast in bed. The butler brought the telgram on a silver salver. The earl slit it open with a paper knife. The crisp, dry paper cracked as he opened it.

"It's from Carter. Dammit, it's in code. Get me my folio from the library desk drawer. The one I use on my trips to Egypt."

The minutes the butler was away on his errand seemed interminably long to Carnarvon. 'Must be important. Must have found something. No other reason for him to code it.'

He was unable to contain his anxiety. He pushed his breakfast tray to one side, got out of bed, put on his dressing gown, grabbed his walking stick and went towards the stairs. He was met by the butler on the landing.

"What took you so long, man?"

He grabbed the folder from him, sat down on a stair step and rifled through the pages. He found the sheet he was looking for and wrote the words on a scrap of paper as he decoded them.

Carnarvon scrunched the paper together in his fist and pressed it to his lips. He got up and called to the butler. "Make up my things - and the Lady Evelyn's - and book us two berths on the next steamer to Cairo. We'll go even if they don't have a suite!"

He hurried down to the hall and thence into the library. Grabbing the phone in his left hand, he took the earpiece off the hook and clicked the rest a couple of times. "Operator? Operator. Get me Mr Gardiner's number. Quickly, if you would be so kind."

There was a pause. While he waited for the connection, Carnarvon paced impatiently up and down in front of his desk. The phone rang.

"Gardiner? Alan, old chap. Just heard great news. Had to share it with someone before my head burst. Carter has found a tomb. Intact, man. Intact! Unbelievable! After all this time..."

Gardiner responded to the earl's euphoric words, but Carnarvon wasn't listening.

"It couldn't be... not Tutankhamen, surely?"

As the last limestone boulder was thrown on the filling in the stairway, a fissure moved ever so slightly within the body of rock beneath. A lace-like curtain of fine lime dust fell gently from the ceiling and lightly powdered the gilding on the roof of the shrine.

For a moment the absolute silence had been broken. Within the innermost coffin a body had been disturbed. Its waxy wrappings momentarily glowed bright orange in the enclosed darkness. As the last of the ancient oxygen was consumed, the smouldering corpse gave up its temporary light and faded once more into blackness.

Chapter Seventeen
A Warning

A nest of rats had made their home in a cavity high up within the mud-brick walls of Horemheb's chambers. Some thoughtless remodelling completed in preparation for the Pharaoh's formal coronation while the mother of the rat family was giving birth had sealed up their only means of access to the outside world. Cut off from any source of food and water, they had all expired some days later. The odour - sudden, obscene and totally unsociable in its heaviness - precipitated the evacuation of all the royal residents from the palace complex. The servants were left to manage the ordeal.

While the cleaning and redecorating of his rooms were under way Horemheb had chosen the vizier's palace for temporary quarters, and once in residence he took over virtually every aspect of the vizier's life. Of all the Pharaoh's interferences, there was one that irritated the vizier far above any other. If just that would go away, he could tolerate all the others. It began the first night.

The vizier had seen the same look in Horemheb's eye on many occasions. Prior to this it had involved others. But not this time. Now, it was clear, Horemheb coveted the youngest of the vizier's wives. He knew he could not refuse him - not Pharaoh - if he was to keep the privileged office he currently enjoyed. Nevertheless, he lay awake most of the nights that Horemheb was there imagining the ugly scenes taking place a few walls distant. Strain how he might to listen for signs of movement or a whisper, she never cried out, and each morning she would return to the harem apparently untroubled, saying nothing, almost serene. The thought that Horemheb might actually be pleasing her far outweighed any concerns he may have harboured for her personal discomfort. Sleeplessness would dog him for as long as the Pharaoh remained at his house. And Horemheb would happily relish every moment of anguish he generated within his host - total power over even the highest-ranking of his subjects - absolute control. The vizier would never again feel completely at ease when Pharaoh was resident at Thebes.

"My dear Royal Vizier," Horemeheb slapped him firmly on the back as he left to return to his restored palace. "Fantastic time. Best I've had in years. You are a loyal friend indeed. The gods will repay you."

'Not Pharaoh,' Nakht grumbled thoughtfully as he bowed.

The security of Horemheb's eternity was far more important than matters of state. In this, his priorities were much like any other. No sooner had the Pharaoh sobered up from the final night's celebrations of his coronation than he began his planning for a perfect departure to the afterlife. Nothing would take priority over the design and preparation for his safe spiritual transition. Once these plans had been set in motion, but for periodic progress reports, he could virtually forget about them and return to the daily business of administration of his empire.

'Matters of State' in large part embodied the broadcast of his ascendancy to the realm of the gods. He would accomplish this, as had those before him, in the form of great buildings, particularly temples, massive flattering likenesses of himself - most quite unlike himself, however - and prolific wall writings. His name would appear prominently everywhere, often overwritten on those of his predecessors. Most of all he would annihilate all vestiges of the memory of the cult of Aten and secure his personal acceptance through energetic promotion of the old order.

But, first and foremost, he must prepare the ark. The grave goods inventory was the easy bit: a fairly standard equipage of staples to sustain him, immaculately executed, of the finest materials and workmanship, and a plethora of ushabtis to serve him, including an ample number of females. He would make a special listing of the personal items he wished to accompany him on his great journey. And to cover the guilt of his life's misdemeanours he would have to ensure a sufficiency of amulets, far more than had been placed on the body of the youthful innocent he had dispatched just a few years since - more even than the recently departed Ay. To hide all his wrongs successfully the inventory would of necessity be substantial.

Neither was Pharaoh going to risk an unfinished sepulchre at the time of his passing. He would lose no time in commissioning the excavation - ultimately to become the grandest tomb of all time.

Starting from a clean slate...

"Torch it! Burn every bit of it! Every building; all of their belongings, especially those they returned with from Akhetaten. I want nothing that even smells of Aten," Horemheb sneered. "But protect the artisans - they must not be hurt. Pademi is to be rebuilt, enlarged, and resupplied. They will all remain whole - their families, everyone; no one must be harmed. But make sure you cleanse that place - nay, cauterise it! The gods will be watching you!"

Vizier Nakht carried out Pharaoh's command with almost clinical precision. Pademi, and most of what was material within it, died in a fiery holocaust on a day that every man was at work in The Valley and all the families, young and old alike, Hammad and the washer women included, had been directed to The Valley of the Queens to pay tribute to Ankhesenamun's passing, or disappearance - call it what you like. By the time they noticed the great pall of smoke hanging over the hills behind them it was too late.

The vizier was well prepared for their dismay - adequate temporary quarters were provided in the temples; adequate provisions from the temple stores; even some of their most personal things had been selectively saved. The work of rebuilding would begin as soon as the stones had cooled.

Some months later Ugele was summoned to Pharaoh's presence. He was escorted from his home by two palace guards. Although massive enough themselves, the tall Nubian standing between them in the entrance to Pharaoh's chambers practically dwarfed the two sentinels.

Horemheb pushed an attentive servant girl off his knee and addressed the master of the masons. "In The Valley of the Tombs of the Kings you will begin immediately on the construction of the greatest sepulchre ever fashioned by the hand of mere man."

Ugele knew exactly who it would be for.

"It will be the longest, the deepest, the most exquisitely decorated. A fitting new world for Pharaoh. You will see to it. I have marked out a place. You will bring me plans fit for Pharaoh. I know your artistry. It will be acceptable. Bring the plans to me tomorrow at this time."

Ugele bowed respectfully and backed out between the guards.

Horemheb's words hung like a capital threat in his mind. He could not conceive how big would be big enough; how long; how deep. He did not know, even by way of comparison, how large the largest of the older tombs was, or which it was.

But then, he thought, 'Pharaoh probably doesn't know either.' One thing he was certain of, however. Horemheb's tomb would have to be demonstrably larger than that of his predecessor, Ay, and Ugele was quite familiar with the size of that particular tomb.

The master of the masons did not finish the plans until sunset of the following day. Honouring Pharaoh's orders, he took the product of his draughtsmanship directly to the palace. The king opened the papyrus on his lap. Horemheb's face broke into a full smile. Aside from these physical signs, however, there were no thanks. Nevertheless, Ugele's sense of relief was immediate.

"I command you to begin at once. I will visit the place in seven days. By then the doorway to my ark must be complete."

The master mason was too pleased with Pharaoh's clear satisfaction with the plans of the tomb to feel any undue anxiety at the king's request. In any event, initial excavation of the doorway in preparation for tunnelling into the wall of the valley was usually a relatively simple and least exacting affair. The entrance portal would be easy to alter if Pharaoh complained - not so the corridors.

This had been a time of festival in the village - the last mud brick had been laid in the reconstruction; the plastering and painting had been finished; the last house to be completed was now occupied - but, the morning after, a still silence pervaded the streets.

The men were nursing their heads after days and nights of eating and drinking. Nearly all were asleep and in no fit state for work. The less overpowered lay with their wives who had been neglected these last few days. Others lay with women they had preferred to their wives at the time they had given themselves up to drunken sleep. Rounding the team up was not going to be easy.

Astride his donkey, Ugele rounded the hill which shielded Pademi from the eyes of Thebes and entered the village. He'd rarely experienced the place this silent. Only the cats, which were everywhere, were making any noise, mewing impatiently at the lack of food this far into the day. Even the children seemed to be sleeping in. All, that is, but for Perna and his younger brother. This day it was their responsibility to keep the village supplied with water. They had begun early so as to make as many trips to the well as they could before the sun got too high. Their two donkeys, led by the boys but owned by the community, plodded towards Ugele, their backs bowed by the burden, and stopped at a doorway just ahead of him. The boys together lifted an animal bladder from one of the donkeys and poured the water into the vessel on the doorstep.

Ugele dismounted and acknowledged the boys with a wave of his hand. He knocked at Parneb's door. Silence. He knocked more loudly and for longer. Silence. He tried to open the door but although it was not locked something was obstructing it. He pushed harder. With some difficulty he managed to edge the door inward a little, just enough to squeeze himself through the opening.

He stood inside the threshold for a moment, allowing his eyes to become accustomed to the darkness. An image gradually materialised from the gloom. It was not a pretty sight.

The scribe's feet had caused the obstruction. The still, naked body lay on its stomach on the stone floor, its face planted securely within the crotch of an unrecognisable and equally naked female lying spreadeagled on her back. They were both sound asleep. They must have passed out simultaneously. This indelicate composition presented itself to Ugele in all its uncompromising obscenity. But he wasn't about to give up on the man. All of his team could be in this kind of state. If he was unable to revive this one, what chance had he with the others?

The woman, of course, was not Parneb's wife. If Ugele moved fast he could be doing Parneb a favour, not that the scribe was unknown for his philandering, but quick action now could save his friend from another nasty tongue-lashing and perhaps something more physically painful. For a moment the Nubian contemplated how he might resurrect the man. He went outside once more and summoned the boys to hurry down the street with a water bag. He whisked it from them and returned to the bodies. In one movement he uncorked the bag and poured the contents liberally over Parneb's back and buttocks.

The previously motionless body drew breath suddenly and uttered a shout loud enough to awaken the entire village. The woman also had been shocked into consciousness. As Parneb struggled to pull himself upright, she brought her legs together so fast her knees connected sharply with the scribe's ears. This led to an involuntary scream of pain and a string of obscenities. As the woman sat up, she saw the dark shape of Ugele standing over her. She hurriedly covered her breasts with her arms and turned to scramble for her clothing. Parneb, in the meantime, had managed to stand up, his hands to his ears, and confronted his adversary.

Before the scribe could organise his thoughts sufficiently to raise a hand to him, Ugele spoke. "Parneb! Pull yourself together, man! Put on your clothes and get rid of this woman. We have been commanded by Pharaoh to begin work on his tomb today. He will inspect our progress by the week's end. There is no time to lose!"

Ugele's words were like a slap of cold iron upon Parneb's smarting head. He mumbled something unintelligible and turned to retrieve his smock.

"This is most unkind, mason. Would that I were not a scribe with the heavy responsibilities attached to that office. Would that I were a simpleton. Would that I was abed." Parneb rolled his eyes and subsided once again to the floor.

"Rise, Scribe! Take account of your blessings," ordered Ugele. It was time for another lecture.

"The profession of the scribe is the greatest of all professions; it has no equal on earth. Even when the scribe is a beginner in his career his opinion is consulted. He is sent on missions of state and does not come back to place himself under the direction of another.

"Now, take the worker in metals. Was a smith ever sent on a mission of state? The coppersmith has to work in front of his blazing furnace. His fingers are like the crocodile's legs and he stinks more than the insides of a fish. The metal engraver works like a ploughman. The mason is always overhauling blocks of stone and in the evening he is tired out, his arms are weary and the bones of his thighs and back feel as if they were coming asunder... Believe me, I know this!.. The barber scours the town in search of customers; at the end of the day he is worn out and he tortures his hands and arms to fill his belly. The waterman is stung to death by the gnats and mosquitoes and the stench of the canals chokes him. The ditcher in the fields works among the cattle and the pigs and must cook his food in the open. His garments are stiff with mud. The builder of walls is obliged to hang to them like a creeper. His garments are filled with mortar and dust and are in rags. The gardener must work every day and all he does is exhausting. His shoulders are bowed by the heavy loads he carries and his neck and arms are distorted. He watches onions all the morning and tends vines all the afternoon. The farm labourer never changes his garments and his voice is like that of a corncrake. His hands, arms and fingers are shrivelled and cracked and he smells like a corpse. The weaver is worse off than a woman. His thighs are drawn up to his body and he cannot breathe. The day he fails to do his work he is dragged from the hut, like a lotus from the pool, and cast aside. To be allowed to see the daylight he must give the overseer his dinner. The armourer is ruined by his expenses. The caravan man goes in terror of lions and nomads whilst on his journey and he returns to Egypt exhausted. The reed cutter's fingers stink like a fishmonger. His eyes are dull and lifeless and he works naked all the day long cutting reeds. The sandal-maker spends his life in begging for work. His health is like that of a fish with a hook in its mouth. He gnaws strips of leather. The washerman spends his whole day beating clothes. He is a neighbour of the crocodile. His whole body is filthy and his food is mixed up with his garments. If he delays in finishing his work he is beaten. The lot of the fowler is hard, for though he wishes for a net God does not give him one. The fisherman has the worst trade of all, for he has to work in the river among the crocodiles and there is nothing to warn him of the vicinity of a crocodile. His eyes are blinded by fear. There is no better occupation that can be found except the profession of the scribe, which is the best of all." *(Quotations of Tuarf to his son, Pepi; from papyri in the British Museum. See Budge, 1926.)*

Parneb was grateful - not so much for the improving lecture but more for the fact that the mason had finished. He sighed and, with no will left to speak let alone argue, he made a sign that shortly he would follow.

Ugele left his friend for the next house, passing the two sniggering water carriers at the door and sending them on their way. The other members of his team were not in quite the same incapacitated state as the scribe, but all had been asleep when he came upon them. All awoke in various stages of post-euphoric distress. All was forgotten as soon as they heard what it was they must do.

By the time the sun was fully overhead, the master of the mason's entire team had assembled at the spot in The Valley that Horemheb had chosen for access to his tomb. It was no surprise that the site was in the main valley and greatly removed from that of Ay's tomb, recently laid waste. But it was a little surprising that it was so close to where the entrance to the tomb of the boy king had been, long since buried beneath the debris of floods.

No matter. Ugele knew there was no possibility that excavation of the one could collide with and penetrate the other. They set to removing loose rubble from the rock face and the floor of the valley so that they could begin their excavation. The work went slowly - each man went about his labours with an unnecessary burden that day.

By the time of the sixth sunset, they had successfully completed a steeply stepped slot into the valley floor and left a rough-cut, sheer, vertical slab of rock that had the height and width of what would become the doorway to the first corridor. Happily, Pharaoh did not come to inspect their progress as previously threatened, so the entire team, much relieved, returned home to catch up on their rest.

More than a year passed before Pharaoh made his first visit to the site of his tomb. By then excavation was complete to the first chamber and the walls had been rendered smooth. Ugele, in the whitest of his robes, attended Horemheb in his inspection of the threshold to Pharaoh's ultimate accommodation.

The entourage descended the staircase and moved steadily deeper within the cavity. The sureness of line and the perspective provided by the extreme length of the first illuminated corridor pleased Horemheb greatly. He walked on, occasionally pausing to feel the walls. They were coarse to his touch, but to the eye they were true enough. The master of the masons and his men had done good work indeed, a considerably better performance than in the tomb of Amenhotep III and much improved over that of Ay. The Pharaoh gave no thought to comparison with that of Tutankhamun. To Horemheb that pathetic cavity was little more than a basement store room and was best forgotten.

Slowly he descended deeper beneath the valley floor until he entered what was to become the first of several enlarged chambers. This was as far as the excavation had penetrated. The cavernous vestibule lay just beyond the well which had been marked out but not yet dug. This first room was an oblong affair with two pillars in its centre. The masons were cutting a set of stairs in the floor to the left. This was the beginning of the second processional corridor which ultimately would lead to the burial chamber itself.

Horemheb looked down at the half-finished stairwell. Suddenly he felt chilled. He turned and looked back towards the light at the entrance. He trembled a little, shrugged his shoulders and marched briskly back towards the sunshine.

As the Pharaoh's entourage finally emerged into the sunlight, Horemheb stopped. He turned around slowly, sat down on the lower step of the entrance stairway and gazed back down into the throat of his tomb. The oil lamps were spread at intervals along the corridor and barely twinkled, a double row of faintly flickering flames coming to a pale point of light at the top of the second staircase.

The Pharaoh drew a long breath. The coldness about him became more acute. His trembling increased. A pressure built within his head. Colourful images began to fill his mind...

He lies deep within, sealed into his new world for ever, in total darkness, in total silence, in total sleep. He awaits his ka to deliver him from his slumber. And then, as he languishes in the secure silence, he hears faint noises at the doorway, far away in the blackness. The sounds grow louder. Suddenly a distant rumble as the first mud bricks in the doorway are smashed inward and fall to the stone floor of the corridor. The thud of a body dropping to the floor. Another. And another. And then voices. Echoing towards him as they grow louder. They are in the upper chamber now. Many loud crashes as they sort chaotically through the funerary equipment, tearing the gold plate from the furnishings, tossing the wood aside, rummaging through the boxes of toiletries, bagging the ushabtis, tearing the jewels from the clothing, stripping the gold from the royal weaponry, ripping the gold statues from their cases, emptying the boxes of their jewellery.

They come ever closer, scurrying down the final corridor. The cacophony of noise is all about him as they hunt through the piles of grave goods stacked box upon box in the storerooms adjoining his burial chamber. The sounds of destruction are everywhere.

Then, a sudden silence.

There are the voices once again. They are very close now; they are all around him; even above him. He senses their hands on the roof of his shrine. The pop of rivets as they begin to dismember it, prising away the sheet gold, ripping at the walls, tearing the one from the other, tossing the panels aside.

Another silence.

There is the sound of copper on stone and the great stone lid to his sarcophagus begins to shift. As it is levered up a little, at one corner the seal breaks and there is a rush of exchanged air. Then a loud grinding as it is slid over to one side. It tilts under its own weight and crashes to the ground, breaking into pieces.

They are now inside contaminating the sanctity of his holy burial. The sheets are pulled off. There is a frantic tugging at his coffin set. He rocks within as the lid of the first is torn from its dowels and thrown to the ground. Then the second. Gasps of excitement as the robbers look upon the third coffin. Here and there, where the holy unguents did not adhere, glimpses of gold flash in the flickering light of the oil lamps.

With far greater difficulty, the third lid is slowly raised, tipped and allowed to fall to the floor, rolling unceremoniously onto its face. The robbers cover their ears. The deafening, blunt echoes of solid bullion striking stone fill and refill the chamber - for minutes it seems.

And then he feels the frantic digging of fingers seeking for a purchase around the edges of the mask upon his head. His body rocks from side to side until the mask loosens and is ripped from his face, the bandages and some of his facial skin tearing off with it. His body falls back into the coffin. The clawing, grubby hands grab him by the feet and drag him out and over the lip of the stone sarcophagus. The oily, bandaged body in its crimson shroud, stiff as a log, falls to the floor and rolls onto its back.

The dark shadows of anonymous common criminals tower above him. He stares up into their faces - Pharaoh at the mercy of scum. He struggles to move but his arms, tightly bound within the mummy bandages, are fixed rigidly across his chest. As Pharaoh calls to the gods for help, one of the infidels raises a hatchet high above his head and, with all the strength he can muster the robber brings it sweeping downwards. The blade chops deep into the mummy's chest...

The entire valley repeated with Horemheb's long, agonised scream. As the last piercing echo faded and withdrew into the valley head, an awful silence fell on the group of onlookers. They stared in shock at the trembling figure crouched on the stairway.

Horemheb was sitting with his knees drawn up hard against his belly, his head bent low and hidden between them, his hands clenched tightly together over his wig, his whole body shaking in bursts as if he was in some kind of epileptic convulsion.

The maligned vizier, himself shocked by the violent spontaneity of Horemheb's outbursts but otherwise not inwardly displeased at Pharaoh's obvious discomfort, was the first to break the silence.

"Pharaoh. Oh, Great One. He who is father to our lands. He who applauds the gods and is himself applauded. He who..."

Horemheb broke in, speaking from between his knees, "Shut up, Vizier. Can't you see I am afflicted. Away with you all."

He squinted open one eye and saw that no one had moved. He raised his head and spoke between clenched teeth. "Leave me, I say! Out of my sight! All of you!"

"If that is your wish, lord."

The vizier directed the entourage to return to the royal barques awaiting them at the head of the canal.

Ugele walked at the rear of the party and looked anxiously back towards the tomb entrance. The king had come to the surface but had resumed his foetal position in the sand. There he remained, still and alone but for two of the royal palace guards either side of him.

Up to the point at which they had emerged from the unfinished tomb, Ugele had sensed nothing but Pharaoh's satisfaction at what he had inspected. 'What could this mean?' He feared a dreadful punishment for some unintentioned oversight.

He did not sleep that night. He lay on his bed on the roof of the house and stared up at the stars. But the following day no one came to take him away, and not the next day, or the next.

Finally, he felt brave enough to return to the tomb. He had related the story to Parneb and his friend was eager to view the scene of Pharaoh's 'possession'. When they arrived at the doorway, they peered in cautiously. As their eyes became accustomed to the light of the distant oil lamps, all they could see were a few painters and draughtsmen working on the wall decorations deep inside.

"It happened just as I told you, Parneb. Pharaoh inspected every part of the corridor and the first chamber. He examined each wall surface - even felt the floor for signs of imperfection. Then he came out here into the light - here, where I am standing - and turned once more to look inside. He sat down here on the step and remained quite still for some moments, staring into the corridor. I was watching his face. His eyes grew large as he stared. His fists clenched. His face took on an expression of great fear. His body began to shake. And then... After some moments in this habit he let out a terrible scream. Such a terrible scream. The whole valley seemed to scream. And he huddled himself into a ball - shaking in spasms - without control."

"He became afflicted with an evil humour, then," diagnosed Parneb with authority. "It was not displeasure with your work. The king has much to answer for. The gods took a moment to remind him."

"You must not say such things, Parneb. Pharaoh has done great things for the people. He has done great deeds on the battlefield. Without him we would have been overrun by invaders many times."

"You speak the truth, my friend. But do not let your loyalty blind you to other truths. Great men also have a dark side. Your memory is short, Ugele, if you do not recall how he came by the throne."

Ugele disliked the way the conversation was going. He knew exactly what his colleague was referring to, but, having found himself happily out of the woods in so far as any regal dissatisfaction with his workmanship was concerned, he preferred to let sleeping dogs lie. He ignored Parneb's last statement as if he had not heard a word of it and walked off back up the track that led to the village.

The Pharaoh attempted to exorcise his fear by wiping out the last visible traces of Tutankhamun and Ay. He gave instructions to raze the mortuary temple that Ay had usurped from the boy king and ordered the construction of a much more extravagant affair on the same site, dedicating it to himself.

But this did nothing to alleviate his insomnia. For the rest of his life, King Horemheb would retain this awful dream. Some nights would be worse than others, but pretty much every night he awoke and at some stage shook uncontrollably for a minute or two before sliding back into unconsciousness.

One night, during his longest sleep, the stuff of his nightmares would prevail.

"Watch your elbow, Kopchef! That's the third time my chisel has slipped. You are too close."

Ugele pushed at his colleague's shoulder. He was one of six, each of them on their knees frantically sculpting the lowest register of sketched figures. The conditions were so cramped that their bodies touched as they worked.

"I am sorry, master. I was pushed myself - by Bek of the third generation - he who is on my right. He is not yet skilled. He is slow. It is difficult. There are too many of us in this place."

"All I hear is excuses! Do it once more and I will pray the gods will punish you! Mark my words. And push the lamp closer. I can hardly see what I am doing. Like as not, I'll cut off my fingers as I try to follow the line."

Ugele, his years and experience not reflected in his impatience, was aching and fatigued from hours of painstaking chiselling in the dust-choked atmosphere of the great pillared hall.

The lower reaches of the tomb were crowded with artisans and labourers of one type or another. There were draughtsmen laying out the grids on the walls for the artists to draw by. Two priests, like orchestra conductors, stood in the centre of the room directing the work of the artists as they sketched line upon line of figures and texts. Behind them, rows of sculptors with copper chisels brought out the drawings in pale relief. The painters were completing the artwork in the well room. The excavators were still there, too, busily digging out new rooms beyond the burial chamber. The sounds of mallets, chisels and falling masonry echoed about the confining walls. It was almost unbearably hot. Lime dust filled the air and choked the lungs. The chambers echoed to everyone's coughing.

There had never been such activity. All because Pharaoh was ailing and likely to die. Time was running out to complete the largest, the greatest, the most beautiful and most noble sepulchre of all time.

'They have no business commanding me to do this at my age,' thought Ugele, 'and for such as he...'

The master mason's reflections were cut short by the voice of a man calling from the direction of the entrance corridor. The noise became louder as the messenger ran towards him, repeating the same words over and over. As he drew closer, everyone stopped work and strained to make sense of his shouting.

"Pharaoh is dead! Eternal life to Horemheb! Long live Ramses!"

The sweating messenger slid to a stop over the fine dust on the floor of the great hall. He looked about himself. In the faint light of the oil lamps a mass of grimy faces emerged from the settling dust.

Ugele addressed the messenger. "The news does not sadden me but for the fact that now we know exactly how much time we have to finish the job. But two months. We shall have to work all the harder. No rest for the people of Pademi!"

"No, Master Ugele. Hear me out," gasped the messenger. "You are all to cease work at once. This very moment. Ramses has ordered it so. You are to leave this place immediately."

"Down tools?" asked Kopchef, grinning expectantly.

"Yes. Stop work. Leave at once. Your work is finished here."

Ugele needed no further encouragement. He gestured to those about him, waving in the direction of the entrance. He stepped over to the stairs which led down to the burial chamber and beyond, and shouted at the top of his voice. "Men! The king is dead! Pharaoh Ramses has ordered our work to finish here! Gather up your things and leave! Now!"

"'The hell with Horemheb,' he thinks. No doubt Pharaoh Ramses has plans for us to begin work on enlarging his own sepulchre," moaned the wise Ugele under his breath. "No peace for the souls of Pademi!"

For once the tired, dirty crew straggled out of the mouth of the tomb before dark. They began their long walk back over the hill to the village - to welcome food, drink, and the comfort of their families.

Approaching dawn, a solitary bat found a comforting roost in the depths of the unfinished tomb. As it flew in, it would not have taken any notice of the curious condition of this magnificent, vacant, expectant place.

After the first stairway falls into the depths from the valley floor, there are two bare, inclined, arrow-straight corridors of about thirty cubits each, separated by a second flight of steps as long but steeper than the first. At the base of these, there is a deep well brilliantly decorated about its top with flattering paintings of Pharaoh and the gods in vivid colours. Beyond the well there is a large chamber with two pillars and a staircase which leads to a third inclined corridor of about twenty cubits in length. This ends at a fourth staircase which opens into an impressively painted vestibule of about ten cubits square. Another doorway leads to a large, six-pillared hall about eighteen cubits square with coloured decoration on one wall, the others unfinished in various stages of draughting and sculpture, two partially sculpted horizontal registers along one of the walls. This opens via two short flights of stairs which descend to the burial chamber of twelve by eighteen cubits, the walls again incompletely decorated. Several storerooms lead off both sides of each of these rooms and, at the rear, northern end of the burial chamber a single, small doorway leads to three further, incompletely excavated storerooms, the debris of excavation still filling the entrance. The whole tomb is driven some two hundred and thirty cubits into the depths of the limestone bedrock of the valley and over fifty cubits below the valley floor.

Come nightfall, the bat flew from its roost and left the tomb to forage. A spattering of excrement lay spread untidily across the burial chamber floor.

A gentle breeze from the east raised ripples on the surface of the lake. The golden light from the setting sun danced briefly from one to the other. The Hittite queen raised her hand to shade her wrinkled eyes. The endless sunshine, the trials of life and the sands of time had etched their signatures into the once smooth features of the face that in her youth had enchanted all who had been privileged to look on it. Her habitual evening meditations were taken in solitude upon the private terrace which overlooked these waters. As she had approached her fiftieth birthday, the time she chose to languish in this place had steadily lengthened.

The waters of the lake were deep. Its shores, the gaping mouth of a long dormant volcano, fell sheer to unknown depths. She gazed reminiscently across the huge body of water towards the hills beyond. The deepening shadows reminded her of the darkness which daily would bathe the west bank of the river of life.

Tia approached her and knelt.

"There is a messenger, my lady. A boy from your kingdom to the south. He asks for you by your previous name."

"Bring him to me. At once." A great thrill of anticipation flooded through her. She had waited so long for news. It had seemed that the infidel would live for ever.

The grimy, sweating messenger boy prostrated himself before the queen. He clutched an elongate wrapping of fresh mummy bandages. Ankhesenamun took the package from his outstretched hands and, one by one, slowly peeled the soiled linens from it. Her face glowed with anticipation. From the weight of the bundle she knew very well what it was she was about to uncover.

As the last of the bandages was removed, a roll of papyrus fell to the ground. It was Horemheb's 'Book of Gates'. She picked it up and summarily tore it to shreds, allowing the pieces to be scattered by the wind... 'He shall have to manage without it.'

She placed the golden statue on the table beside her. Two tiny forearms stretched vertically from its head, their hands open, the palms facing forward. Below this headdress was that familiar, grotesquely squat, round face, the fat lips, the oblate, rippling body, a golden tunic gathered about its stout waist. The likeness was uncompromisingly true and utterly repulsive. The artist who had fashioned this must have done so with some personal gratification, representing the king as he had appeared in life, not at all as he would have wished to have been remembered.

The royal widow felt a consuming sense of release. For years she had remained preoccupied with a single yearning. For years her new marriage had been troubled with her fixation. Her husband had understood at first but, as the years passed by, her continuing private obsession had driven him elsewhere for affection. She had let him play. She would not ask much of him. Just that he be there to talk with her when she needed the company. He played his part well.

As the sun touched the distant horizon, a flash reflected off a facet scratched into the gold. The queen brought the small statue closer to her eye and examined the script etched crudely into its buttocks: 'For Queen Ankhesenamun. Loving wife of Tutankhamun. For our eternity.'

It was signed with the nomen of 'Dashir'. She smiled in contentment. They had been true to her to the end.

Still holding the gold figure, she got up from her seat and knelt down on the stone floor to face the last glimmer of the evening sun. She whispered a prayer to her loyal servants to protect them from discovery and the possibility of awful punishment. As she uttered her last word, she clenched both her fists tightly about the legs of the statue, raised it at arm's length above her head and with all her strength brought it hard down on the stone floor. The pavings rang as the head broke at the neck. Turning over and over again in the air, it bounced down the steps before her, finally splashing into the water's edge and disappearing for ever. She stood up quickly and tossed the mutilated figure after it. The queen and the boy watched as the ripples grew outward and gradually died.

Ankhesenamun called to her maidservant and pointed to the boy. "See that he is washed, fed, rested and clothed. He may return to Thebes when he wishes. Until then, be sure you look after him well."

She turned her back on the lake and on her past. What she looked forward to now no man but Tutankhamun could share with her. She sat that night in her chambers, cradling the diminutive gold statuette in the likeness of her dead husband. Now, assuredly, the royal couple could live life eternal, together and in peace.

Ankhesenamun had returned from hunting with her Hittite husband. He had taken ill during the day and was escorted from his horse by his apothecaries and thence to his bedchamber. The evening was maturing swiftly into night and, as was her custom, the queen retired to the shrine of her departed consort to pray. She knelt in the quiet solitude of the small chapel and gazed up at the golden likeness of her boy king. The flames of the lamps which surrounded her brushed their pale orange light over the little statue and laid faintly wavering shadows on the walls of the tiny room.

She whispered, "Speak to me, Tutankhamun. He who holds my heart in his embrace."

The flames reflected off the burnished surface of the figure. In the rippling folds of light she felt sure the lips moved. The faint but coherent voice of her late husband responded to her call.

"Your words fall gently like drops of wine upon mine ears, my Queen. You have done exceedingly well. Horemheb and Ay are extinguished... for ever. The time has come for you and I once more to live together in peace."

The figure drew a deep, whispering breath.

"But I feel the coldness of fear, my love. My journey may yet be ended by those who seek to steal that which I need to sustain me. My sanctified tomb remains inviolate, yet I fear for its safety. Possession of that which you worship is not sufficient. My mortal remains must be left to rest in this place. A curse has been laid. Warnings will be given. More than this I cannot do alone... I miss you, my Queen. I need your good counsel, your support, your warmth. When will you come to me?"

The flames flickered momentarily and died. The statue stood inanimate.

Ankhesenamun fell speechless in front of the figure. She felt comfort and security in the company of her living husband, but she ached to be with her boy king once more.

She had kept the poison close by her person ever since Tutankhamun's bloodied body had been discovered all those years ago. At that time it was in fear of misconceived retribution. Apart from her childhood maidservant, she had not been able to trust anyone in the palace. Self-inflicted death would have been more charitable. Until now, though, she had had too much to do to contemplate suicide. In her anxious wait for news of Horemheb's death and his ultimate destruction she had given no thought - none at all - to her own.

Tia had been dead these past three years. Perhaps now was the right time after all. He waited for her. She wanted him. No one stood in their way. She had not been a good wife to her new husband. There were no offspring from their marriage. Perhaps he would not miss her. Doubtless he would find another. Better she did it now and be done. No farewells.

The poison, while deadly, was not quick, but neither was it painful. It would bring on sleep slowly. She turned and looked outside for signs of life. By now it was completely dark. There was no one about. A clear, moonless sky, resplendent with stars, sparkled limitless above her. It would take her only a few moments to reach the lake side. There seemed little risk of being spotted.

She turned back into the shrine. She took a long breath and drank the contents of the vial in a single swallow. The liquid warmed her from within. She picked up the statuette, placed it inside her cloak and wrapped the waist cord tightly about her. Grasping the papyrus tightly in her right fist, she walked purposefully towards the lake. As the queen neared the terrace from which she had pitched the dimembered figure of Horemheb, she felt a strange slothfulness coming upon her. She sat down on the bottom step, slung her feet out into the water and pushed herself off with her hands.

The water felt cold, but as she swam a pleasing numbness came over her. She found it difficult with the extra weight to keep herself buoyant, harder still with her growing sleepiness. She swam as far as her consciouness could carry her. Then, finally, consumed by an overwhelming desire to fall asleep, she slowly descended beneath the surface and into the depths, the image of her husband bound in with the bodice of her clothing, the roll of spells still held firmly in her hand. The ripples closed above her, extinguishing any trace of her disappearance. There were no bubbles, the waters now black, unreflective, featureless. She had disappeared without trace.

There had never been a funeral like it, not the least reason being that there was no body. He had loved her. He had loved her deeply, notwithstanding her perpetual distraction. There would be great celebration. She would be dispatched with precision according to their custom. He would watch her go: the flames consuming her funeral pyre, a symbolic package of her most personal belongings upon it; a raging fire taking her soul to the gods.

Her husband watched the fire grow. Within moments it was a furnace, the cauldron of heat pushing him back. He felt the skin on his cheeks begin to burn. He moved further away. Bright, glowing particles of ash flew everywhere, circled and bounced in the night air and, drifting upon the updraft above the inferno, ultimately lost their energy and fell on the circle of onlookers, dying in their head gear and on their shoulders. As the fire exhausted itself and the funeral pyre collapsed, one by one the group in attendance solemnly departed. For a time, the glow from the dying embers reflected on the surface of the lake, the flashing ripples seemingly maintaining its life on the water. And then nothing, coal black, with an occasional sparkle of reflected starlight.

It was over. She was gone. The door to this part of his life had closed for ever. He turned and followed the others.

The loyal tomb builders' destruction of Horemheb's tomb had totally cleared it of anything of value. They had not attempted to remove his sarcophagus but took everything else. The mummy, after being torn to pieces, had vanished without trace. Surely, like Ay, Horemheb would not pass through the doorway to the new world. Like Ay, he would find death absolute.

Ankhesenamun and Tutankhamun were at last reunited. And there were other familiar faces. Tia was there to serve the queen once more. Dashir, who had passed on after an orgy of drinking, was there to provide for them. Best and most treasured of all, their children were there, reincarnated with their parents.

They enjoyed each other. Their renewed blissful peace passed timeless before them.

Outside their world, time continued to pass. As it had been written, thousands later in time and space they found him. It would be he who would reach the place and have the means to touch the king's holy sepulchre. It would be he who would be the one wholly responsible. Without him the necessary coincidence of events could not occur. They knew at this time that all they could do was give a warning - create some way to divert him from his course by his own choice, as they may not physically stop him. The curse would do that, ultimately, but likely too late. Like the sting of a bee left within its victim, both would die. Both would pass into eternal oblivion.

Chapter Eighteen
Something Good

Carter had waited two hours at Luxor station. The train carrying Lord Carnarvon and Lady Evelyn was not unusually delayed. He didn't mind the wait. Two days earlier he'd greeted them on their arrival in Cairo but had travelled back to Luxor ahead of them to complete further preparations for reopening the stairwell to the tomb.

The last weeks had been agony. Holding back his urgent need to discover what lay beyond the rock-filled corridor had been almost unbearable. But now the wait was almost over. Soon they would all be able to see for themselves.

The morning sun was above the horizon as the train steamed slowly into the platform. The decorative Victorian wood picket wedges along the trailing edge of the roof threw sawtooth shadows against the white station walls. The three carriages drew to a stop and a horde of would-be porters hurried forward seeking business from the few first-class passengers. Through the sunlit steam issuing from beneath the carriages, Carter spied the silhouette of Lady Evelyn alighting and he signalled to Abdel to run forward and assist her with her bag. The earl followed almost immediately, passed a small leather attaché down to Abdel, and stepped down slowly, using his cane to steady himself. Carter came forward, doffed his hat and greeted them both. There was a vigorous shaking of hands. This time he was really pleased to see his patron.

Fatigued from his journey, the earl was not feeling all that energetic but he had the presence of mind to congratulate his colleague warmly. "Howard, m'boy..." he chuckled. "Good to see you again, even if it's the second time in two days! Looks like you've done it this time!"

"Thank you, sir. You look a little pale, sir, if you'll pardon me for saying so. I hope you didn't pick something foreign up on your trip."

"Fatigue. Not a bother. G'me a stiff drink and a good night's rest and tomorrow, bright and early, you can take me to our great discovery."

"That I will, sir... Lady Evelyn. That I will. But let's get you both settled in first. The tomb has waited a millennium or three. I believe it can wait a few more hours." Carter looked up and down the station. "Where's the doctor?"

"Left him in Cairo, Howard. Wanted to visit some of his professional friends in town. He'll follow within the week."

The three squeezed into Carter's car and drove to the Winter Palace Hotel. Abdel remained at the station to collect his lordship's trunks.

Before taking lunch, they assembled on the terrace and sipped cocktails.

After a moment's reflection, Lady Evelyn turned to Carter. "Howard, during our brief time together in Cairo you mentioned that before you took us to the site you would tell us the story of its discovery. Now would be a good time. Every detail, if you please."

Carter drew a deep breath. They both stared at him in anticipation. No diversionary small talk this time. He was going to enjoy telling this story.

The earl was not known for rising early and the following morning he even surprised himself - he was up at six. He ordered breakfast in his room, washed, shaved, showered and dressed, and was out on the terrace drinking coffee in the sunrise before his daughter had opened an eye. He paced about the balcony impatiently. Carter had arranged to have them picked up at nine, but the earl was far too anxious to wait that long. He walked back into the hotel and rapped hard on Lady Evelyn's door.

"Who... who is it?" an apprehensive voice sounded from the other side.

"Evelyn! Get up, daughter. We are ready to leave!"

"Just a minute, Papa."

For the next few minutes there was much commotion from inside. Then at last the door was unlocked and a fully dressed Evelyn stood before her father.

"Well? Where's Howard?"

"Change of plan, my dear. He's waiting for us on the other side. Come, there is no time to lose. We are already late."

"But I have had no breakfast, Papa."

"We'll get it at Carter's house. Now, come on!"

His excitement gave him new-found energy and Evelyn was not inclined to resist it. They descended the staircase that swept down in two long arcs from the entrance to the hotel and summoned a horse and carriage.

While all this was going on, an unaware Carter had been busily organising his men at the site. He had his old colleague Arthur Callender to assist him. Re-excavation of the pit and the stairway were already well under way.

When the earl and his daughter arrived at Castle Carter at 7.45 a.m., the Egyptologist was not there. Having left Callender in charge, he was on his way to prepare for his trip over to Luxor to pick up his patron. The two parties met each other at the entrance to The Valley.

"My God! Sir... Ma'am!" exclaimed an astonished Carter. "Touch of insomnia?"

"Very funny, Howard. Very droll," answered Lady Evelyn. "The fact is, my father got me here at this unearthly hour under false pretences."

"Couldn't wait, Howard. Couldn't wait. C'm on. Let's to't. This will be the day of all days."

The aristocrat was uncharacteristically euphoric. Carter hadn't seen him this chuffed since he'd found that mummified cat, all those years ago. He could hardly believe it had been so long. The earl had quite lost control of his feelings. He was out to relish every moment.

They took only a few minutes to get to the site. It had an established look about it. Anticipating much interest from passing tourists, and anxious to keep them at bay and safe from falling in, Carter had arranged for a stone wall to be built around the pit at the level of the valley floor.

Carnarvon and Evelyn looked eagerly over the edge. The fellahs had hardly removed sufficient rubble to re-expose the top of the doorway, but the earl was in such a state of excitement and anticipation that the glimpse of mud plaster beneath the rock-cut lintel was treasure in itself. Immediately he stepped down awkwardly into the pit, almost losing his footing as he probed with his cane to find a firm purchase within the loose rocks. The men stopped their labours for a moment and moved aside to give him room. He bent down to study the cavity more closely. It would have been too difficult and painful for him to attempt to crouch low enough to be able to feel the plaster surface with his fingers. He touched it lightly with his walking stick and turned back towards Carter who was standing at the edge of the pit.

"Solid as a rock, m' boy. Just like you said. We're the first. I feel it!" He looked around at the labourers who stood motionless, watching him. "Come on, then. Stop your gawking. Back to work. Much to do before we sleep tonight."

Carter repeated the earl's orders with a few softer words in Arabic and the reis signalled his men to resume.

Extending an arm to help Carnarvon back up the slope, Carter whispered in his ear, "Sir, please don't get your hopes up too high. I fear there is evidence that the tomb has been breached at least once in antiquity. If you look behind you..." They both turned. "There. The upper left corner. It is clearly patched and restamped. But that is the good news. They would not bother to reseal it if there were nothing there. At worst, we could be looking at a mummy cache."

The earl smiled and nodded in acknowledgement.

Once back at the top, they found Evelyn in conversation with an unwashed and unshaven Adamson.

"Ah, Sergeant, may I introduce his lordship the Lord Carnarvon, the sponsor of this dig and my very good friend."

"My pleasure, y' lordship," said the sergeant politely, clicking to attention and extending his hand.

The earl shook his hand warmly. "Carnarvon. You may address me as Carnarvon, Sergeant."

"Thank you, sir... er, Carnarvon. H'I'd be most h'onoured if you would likewise address me as h'Adamson, sir."

"Adamson it is. I see you have already acquainted yourself with my daughter, Lady Evelyn."

Adamson smiled. "Indeed, y' lordship... er, Carnarvon. H'I wish h'I'd known you wuz coming so h'early this morning. It 'asn't been my 'abit of late to h'attend to me toiletries h'until I've 'ad me breakfast. Caught me in the middle of it. Bit of a surprise! Be better prepared next time."

"No matter, Sergeant," chimed in Evelyn. "Truth is, this is a most unusual event for all of us. Driven out of bed early because we were unable to contain our anticipation. Doubt we will demonstrate such urgency heretofore."

'Ere-to-for?' thought Adamson. 'Wot the 'ell's 'ere-to-for?' He didn't dare ask. He excused himself and returned to his breakfast.

The three sat down next to one another in a line along the wall. Motionless they watched the activity below. Before too long, however, the sun had breached the cliff edge and beat down unhindered into the valley bottom. Both the earl and his daughter were quick to give up their vigil and seek the shade and coolness of the tomb that Carter had prepared for their comfort and fortification. He had cleaned out the entrance corridor to the tomb of Ramses XI, situated less than a hundred yards back towards the mouth of the valley. There he had prepared a long table and adequate seating. The provisions, including the earl's imported stock of wine, were stored deeper in the tomb where the temperature remained more equable.

They sat around the table, which was already set for lunch, and Carter outlined his plans for the next day. He had no means of knowing what he would find at the other end of the rubble-filled corridor and was unable to look any farther forward than that.

"The men will clear the stairwell by mid-afternoon. We shall then examine the door in detail. The impressions at the top are just anonymous necropolis seals. They tell us nothing of the owner. There will be more seals below. After examining all the seals, we shall dismantle the door. And tomorrow we can begin on what lies beyond."

Carter had decided to keep what he already knew a secret. He wanted the earl to discover the name of the tomb's inhabitant himself. The grandee well deserved the thrill and the honour of first discovery.

After personally devouring the best part of a bottle of claret at lunch, Carnarvon was compelled to take a snooze on the canvas campbed laid out for that very purpose in the tomb corridor. Lady Evelyn settled her father down and went out to join Carter who was back inside the pit ensuring that Ali did not allow his men to damage the surface of the door. It was by now two-thirds uncovered.

"Howard," she called. "Do you make anything of the seals there?"

"I'm sorry? Wh... what did you say, Lady Evelyn?"

"The seals, Howard. The seals. Can you make anything of them?"

"Ah... Necropolis seals, Lady Evelyn. Anonymous so far. Perhaps there will be no name on this door. Please go and check on his lordship, Lady Evelyn. I would not like him to miss the first complete uncovering of the doorway. If he should stir at all, please wake him and bring him here."

Evelyn disappeared and Carter settled back to sit on the stone stairway.

The men continued clearing the rubble. In the noise of industry, he didn't hear Adamson's hobnailed military boots clicking down the steps behind him.

"Mr Carter, sah!"

Carter turned, startled. "Mmm? What? What d'you want?" Irritation at this untimely interruption was quite evident in the tone of his response.

"Er... H'I f'ought I'd take advantage of this slack moment to h'ask you a faver, sir."

"Well?"

"Y'know when you sent for me to do this job - as we've spoken before, like - h'I 'adn't expected to be h'officiating 'ere h'every bloody day an' h'every bloody night, an'... An'..."

"Yes, man. Go on. Go on. I'm busy. I'm expecting his Lordship any moment. Be brief."

"Well, sir, since it is necessary for me t'be 'ere all the time - h'I do understand why, an' h'I am in your debt for the responsibility you 'ave placed h'upon me shoulders, an' all - h'I would appreciate a few 'ome comforts."

"Yes?" Carter was only half listening to the sergeant. "Home comforts. Such as?"

"Well... Some form of h'entertainment... To relieve the loneliness of th' place, like."

"Are you suggesting...?"

"Music, sir. Music. Gramophone. Some records. H'I like classical stuff. H'an' sergestive biscuits, if you please, sir. Crawfords. H'I likes Crawfords. Me Mum raised me on 'em."

"'Suggestive biscuits'? Ah. Digestive biscuits. I will see to it."

Carter had neither the time nor the inclination to negotiate. Adamson had got him at just the right moment. Besides, the earl's stores were excessively plentiful and close by.

By the time Carnarvon had returned to the wall above the pit, the stairwell was completely cleared and swept clean. Carter was on the bottom step pretending to examine what was impressed on the mud plaster close to the base of the sealed doorway.

"Howard!" the earl called to the archaeologist as he attempted to negotiate the first of the stone steps. "My boy. What have you found there?"

Carter beckoned the earl forward so that he could examine the impressions for himself. With the aid of his cane, the earl struggled down the uneven steps as fast as he dared. Carter received him with a steadying hand and guided him close to the wall of mud plaster. There was a pregnant pause as Carnarvon took the time to focus on the blurred impressions stamped higgledy-piggledy in front of him. Finally he turned, beaming to his colleague, his face the very picture of delight.

"Howard! My boy! This impression is complex but I believe within it I can make out the prenomen of the boy king Tutankhamen! And there is more than one. Pharaoh Nebkheperure! He is here! We have found him! I cannot believe our good luck! Come, look!"

"My God, sir! Let me see."

"It is dark," cautioned Carnarvon with authority. "Difficult to see in so little light and with so much brightness above. But once your eyes become accustomed to it, my boy, the relief comes forward to you. Look at this one," the earl indicated with a trembling finger.

"Evelyn! Evelyn! Give me your cosmetic mirror. Quickly, girl!"

Carnarvon's daughter, now at the bottom of the steps herself, pulled a small bag from her sleeve, found the mirror and passed it to him. He angled it to take advantage of the sunlight and reflected this across the relief of the seal.

"See?"

As if it was his first time, Carter dwelt on the impression for some moments. The king's name was located in the middle of the top portion of the seal. A simple disc above the head of a scarab; three vertical lines in a row at its base; below this, a semicircle. He turned, smiling and winked at his patron.

"Howard, m' boy! We've done it! At last, we've done it! I am speechlessly proud of you!"

Praise indeed and justly administered. Even if, in the event, there was nothing beyond the corridor, Carter felt vindicated. But he held no personal doubts. There just had to be something significant ahead.

Carter sat on a step and pulled an index card from his coat pocket. He wrote on the top 'Obj. No. 4' and, with the precision of an architect, began to sketch each of the different impressions he saw before him, carefully scaling them against the horizontal lines on each card. Carnarvon patiently watched over his shoulder. He was familiar with Carter's disciplined routine. Should there be more finds literally everything would be recorded with the same patient attention to detail. At the time, of course, they had no idea just how large this catalogue would become.

Carter finished his drawing and note-taking and pocketed the card. One last act before this first day was out.

"A moment, m' lord. Let us investigate what lies behind the door." Carter turned and looked up at the silhouettes of the men standing all about the wall above. "Ali! My probing rod, if you please."

The reis disappeared for a moment and then returned with Carter's iron probe. Carter took it, wet the tip with his tongue, and gingerly pushed it into the small hole that he had made some weeks previously. Feeling the anxiety of the moment, Carnarvon grabbed Carter's hand to ensure he did not push the probe in too violently in his haste to discover what may lie beyond and thereby risk damaging some priceless object.

"No matter, m' lord. I will be careful, I promise you."

312

He pushed the probe through the hole very slowly. It passed but two feet before it came upon an extremely solid obstruction. Carter withdrew it quickly to examine the end for signs of paint or other residue. There was nothing more than a few grains of white calcite adhering to the tip.

An anxious earl leaned over Carter's shoulder. "What do y'think, Howard?"

"I do believe we have a rock-filled corridor ahead of us, m' lord. Since we have no way of knowing how long it may be, how long it will take us to empty it I do not know. We shall get started first thing tomorrow. I must have the doorway impressions photographed first. Harry Burton, my old colleague from the Met, is here with his wife. He has been staying in Luxor these past weeks. I am sure he will help us. If the situation proves worthy I shall, of course, cable the Met to obtain official approval for our exclusive use of his services. But for now a simple request for his expertise on account, so to speak, will suffice. A favour, y' know."

Carter was right. Burton, although on a long-term assignment to photographically document the lavish and picturesque tomb of Seti I, was only too pleased to get involved, and it didn't need the proverbial gin and tonic that evening to persuade him.

At first light the following morning, he was at the site along with his entourage of carriers fully laden with the equipment of his trade. With the help of electric light wired in temporarily from an adjacent tomb, Burton was able to illuminate the door at an angle sufficient to bring out the detail in the seal impressions.

As the photographer finished his last plate, Carter's patience finally gave out. Already on the bottom step alongside his colleague, Carter began carefully chipping away at the plaster, taking it down in coherent pieces, one brick at a time. On this occasion, in his anxiety to establish whether he truly had something of significance, Carter did not wait to learn if Burton's photographs had been developed successfully - an act he would be careful not to repeat. He set about the brick wall energetically, but with consummate care.

With the door dismantled and nothing but the rubble fill exposed, Carter realised he probably had a long job of excavation ahead before anything of significance was revealed.

Carnarvon came by three or four times that day. At first early to ensure that Carter's original prognosis was correct and there indeed was a fill of rubble behind the door. Once he had seen for himself, he became less eager to stand around and watch the relatively boring process of removal of the rocks and the tomb chippings which filled the corridor completely to its ceiling and for much of its length. He retired to his campbed in the cool of the tomb of Ramses XI. He was resting there when he heard Carter call.

"Carnarvon... Carnarvon!" Carter appeared at the entrance, "Carnarvon! I have found something exquisite!"

Carter was brightly backlit by the midday sun. The silhouette was totally black, its surroundings glaringly brilliant. Carnarvon, temporarily dazzled, could barely make out the form of his approaching colleague.

"Need something to pack it in for the time being."

"What is it, my good man? What have you found?"

Carter, marching purposefully down the entrance corridor of the tomb towards his patron with his new discovery cradled in his arms, could see the earl perfectly and in the excitement gave little regard to the excruciatingly bright view in the opposite direction.

"Look at it, m' lord. Just feast your eyes on this piece." He thrust it before Carnarvon's squinting eyes.

The earl eased his legs off the bed and turned towards his colleague. As his numbed eyes accommodated to the light he could make out a head. "A bust. It's a wooden bust...", he started, "...of a boy. It seems to be the likeness of a boy. The shape of the cranium... elongate... most odd. Most attractive artistry, however. What do you think it depicts, Howard? The boy king himself?"

"The very thing, Carnarvon! The very thing! Marvellous, don't y' think? Absolutely bloody marvellous!"

"Well? Where did you find it man? Where did you find it? Is there more?" The earl was now putting on his shoes, eager to return to the site.

"Stay, m' lord. No hurry. We're still digging out the corridor. Found it in the refilled robbers' tunnel. Must have been left there in antiquity. In their haste to escape, perhaps."

He lifted the head up to catch a shaft of light beaming across the relative gloom of the corridor. The coloured pigments almost glittered in the sunshine. The features, particularly the fulsome, boyish cheeks, chipped a little by rough handling, were nevertheless beautifully structured.

"I need something to pack it in, m' lord. You have some wine boxes in here, do you not?"

Carnarvon turned and pointed deeper into the darkness. "Over there in the corner, Howard. You'll find the claret over there. Take the bottles out. We'll have one later tonight. Use the case."

Carter opened the case, took out a couple of bottles and rearranged the straw to prepare a bed for the head. He carefully rested the object inside, jammed a little more straw around and over it, and replaced the lid. He became pensive for a moment. "Engelbach isn't here, dammit. Not good form. He or the authorities really should be summoned lest, and before, we find anything of significance - should we be so bloody lucky!" He almost shouted the last words in his excitement.

"You are right. Engelbach's not here, Howard. So what do we do about it?"

They looked at each other. They both had the same thought.

"What they haven't been witness to...", Carter began.

"...They cannot choose to keep!" Carnarvon completed his sentence for him. In the absence of the authorities, the earl, particularly after so many lean years, was not about to share that which he might not have to share.

Carter smiled and made his decision. "We shall hide this one. For the time being at least. Where would be best do y' think?"

Carnarvon thought for a moment. "Behind those cases. No one will think of looking there. I'm the only one selecting the wine for the evening. Put it back over there, Howard. Just like it was."

Carter put the case back exactly where he had found it. He lifted the top open again for a moment to catch another glimpse of the face. The large, outlined eyes stared up at him through the strands of straw. He replaced the top of the crate and turned to Carnarvon. "Will y' join me back at the dig, m' lord?"

But there was no one there. The eager earl had already left.

When Carter got back to the steps, his lordship was issuing orders to Ali in a broken Arabic which the reis was struggling to understand, interpreting as best he could, and then doing what he thought his master was directing him to do.

Carter rushed to his patron's side.

"M' lord. Please leave the man be. Ali knows precisely what to do. Directing him otherwise will only confuse him and slow things up. Believe me, he and his men will find everything of value that there is to find in that corridor. They will bring it up to us with due haste. Have no fear."

The earl showed no offence at Carter's mild correction but, nevertheless, as the afternoon's digging wore on, and in the continued anxiety of his impatience, he was unable to resist issuing the odd cautionary word to the reis.

By evening, the corridor had been half-cleared to floor level. Carnarvon stayed until the shadows had grown across the pit and he was finding difficulty seeing anything in detail.

The darkening valley was a signal that it was time for the customary evening tipple, and the earl was well on his way back to his field wine cellar before Carter and Lady Evelyn had noticed he was absent.

Catching sight of him hobbling awkwardly down the valley track ahead of them, Carter turned to Lady Evelyn. "You go with him, Evelyn," he encouraged. "I'll be along presently."

Carter finally assessed that the light was now poor enough that small or dull objects might be overlooked. He dismissed the men and set the guards in place. Dusting himself off, he walked back to the tomb of Ramses XI.

Supper was already laid and Carnarvon was on his third glass of claret. Evelyn, Callender and Sergeant Adamson similarly had been enjoying refreshment for some little time.

"You have been working too hard, Howard. Have a drink."

Carnarvon greeted the tired archaeologist and drew up a chair. Carter turned to acknowledge the earl and, as he did so, a befezzed and white-robed waiter smothered Carter's face in his left armpit as he eagerly bent over him to pour the wine. Carter tweaked his moustache, squeezed his nose, and rolled his eyes. He pushed himself back in his chair to put some respectable space between himself and the armpit. All at the table chuckled and the echoes from within the confining stone walls awakened the dozing valley.

"An experience h'I wouldn't relish meself, sir," remarked the red-faced Sergeant Adamson with a wry grin. The sergeant had seated himself presumptuously next to Lady Evelyn. He was looking quite the part in his freshly laundered and crisply pressed uniform. He too was on his third glass of claret.

"Nearly finished, Sergeant?"

"Yes, sir. Don't mind if I do..." And he proffered his glass for a refill.

Carter's face took on an expression of authority. "Then you'd better go check on the guards. With the corridor partly excavated and Lord Carnarvon on the very threshold of discovery, I don't want to give any idle tomb robbers a head start. About your business, if you please."

"Sah!" Adamson hurriedly drained the bottom of his claret glass, pushed his chair back and snapped to attention. He took his leave of Evelyn, his boss and his lordship and disappeared into the twilight.

The following morning was the twenty-sixth of November, in the twelfth year of the reign of our sovereign, King George V, Nineteen Hundred and Twenty Two.

Carnarvon and his daughter were at the site just two hours after daybreak eagerly anticipating that the end of the corridor would be revealed some time during that morning. This time they were expected. Carter was standing at the edge of the pit watching Ali's men. He saw the two approaching along the valley track and greeted them with a wave of his Homburg.

"Top of the morning to you, m' lord; lady Evelyn. You are up betimes once more, I see."

"Anxious not to miss anything, Howard. This could be the day of days - I feel it in me waters!"

"I do wish you wouldn't keep saying that, Father," corrected Evelyn. "Wishing us such good luck will only assure us bad luck. And it will not improve the condition of your bladder either, I shouldn't wonder."

"Lady Evelyn," said Carter. "To ward off the evil spirits Abdel has brought along my canary. He is convinced it will bring us good fortune."

Evelyn giggled. "Perhaps Porchy and the bird will cancel each other out. We shall have neither good nor bad luck - just so-so."

"You may well be right, Lady Evelyn," returned Carter with a note of seriousness in his voice. "The work has been going slowly. We are taking great care to examine each load of rubble for signs of tomb debris. Odd fragments have been coming to light but, other than the wooden head of the boy king, nothing much of value - certainly nothing in one piece. The indications so far - small tomb debris in the corridor fill and obvious signs of robbery - suggest we may be on the threshold of another cache of re-interred Pharaohs - possibly not Tutankhamen himself. If so, a magnificent find in its own right, but not so much a prize as the burial of the boy king."

At this moment Carnarvon came back with a set of common-sense observations that quite stunned his colleague - all the more because they came from a relative layman. "With respect, Howard, I think you are quite wrong," began the earl. "You unnecessarily belittle this find. Observe. The resealed robbers' tunnel is too narrow to introduce one let alone several Pharaohs' coffins. Furthermore, that which can't go in, can't come out. While small articles may well have been taken, the larger stuff may well have survived; perhaps damaged by the robbers, perhaps stripped of sheet gold, but otherwise still there."

Carter just hadn't come to expect this kind of deductive reasoning from his patron. In addition he felt truly embarrassed that he had not really taken the time to think the clues through for himself. Rather, he had allowed himself to enjoy the emotion of at last finding something, and something that had much pleased his patron.

The earl continued. "Last night, turning these observations over in my head, I hardly slept. Always I came back to the same conclusion. It is so exciting! There will be wondrous things in there, Howard, mark my words!"

There was the smile of a conqueror on the earl's face. He had dared to invade the hallowed ground of Carter's technical territory and he had got it right.

Carter was duly impressed. Nevertheless, as the professional he felt a natural and uncharitable inclination to correct the layman, even if only in a small way. But as he opened his mouth to respond to his lordship's comments, his words were drowned out by Arthur Callender shouting from deep within the corridor.

"Carter! Your lordship! Come quickly! We see the top of another doorway!"

Callender was a big man, and when the other three had reached the bottom of the entrance staircase all they could see was the mass of a large, tweed-suited figure kneeling near the top of the remaining rubble fill at the far end of the corridor, his body crouched beneath the ceiling. Callender turned to look over his shoulder at them. "Come up here and look at this, Howard. More seal impressions. And more scars of entry."

Carter scrambled up the slope of limestone chippings to reach his colleague's side. About two feet of the top of a second mud-plastered door were visible. Several different types of seal impressions had been uncovered. Carter didn't waste time examining them. He had already made a quick mental calculation. They were halfway through the afternoon. If they continued clearing at the pace they had maintained thus far, the door should be cleared to its base by early evening. They should be able to make a preliminary investigation beyond the door before closing down for the night.

"Ali! I want this passageway completely cleared of debris today so that we can examine the door in detail. Be sure to continue taking care to look for small objects. I do not want to miss anything."

He descended the remaining rubble pile, pulling Callender after him by his lapel, and came face to face with his expectant patron. "A door it is, m' lord. We shall know what lies behind it before sunset. Have a little patience. Enjoy the wait!"

To be truthful, for all of them patience was a commodity in short supply, particularly at this juncture. However, the discipline of Petrie's training and his years of experience - success and failure alike - gave Carter the authority he needed to influence his colleagues. He was, when all said and done, the man in charge.

Carnarvon and Evelyn looked up at the lintel expectantly. The earl was hardly able to contain his anticipation. He was visibly trembling.

Evelyn took his arm and guided him gently back up the stone steps. "It will be some hours before we can address the door, Porchy. Why don't we all go back to the comfort of Ramses Eleven and sit awhile?"

Carnarvon could hardly bear the wait. He had to concentrate hard to stop himself fidgeting. While they sat around the table in the other tomb Carter, normally relaxed and himself much more disciplined and practised in these situations, became alarmed at his own nervousness and found it difficult to participate in the conversation. The atmosphere was electric, all of them fit to burst at any moment.

Following a late tea, the earl found that he could stand the waiting no longer. "Going back to check on progress, Howard. Anyone coming with me?"

"H'if you would permit me, sir." Adamson had awoken and was eager for some exercise. He handed the earl his panama. "H'if it's all right wiv you... Carnarvon, h'I would be most h'onoured to accompany you to the h'excavation."

"My pleasure, Adamson."

"Sir."

No one else seemed to be prepared to get up, and, without taking the time for a second request, the two left swiftly and disappeared into the brilliant sunlight of late afternoon.

His lordship hurried to the spot as fast as his dexterity with a walking stick would allow. Adamson helped him to the steps, fending off the labourers who, like so many beads on a moving rosary, were flitting in and out of the corridor with their baskets and loads in regular pulses. At the threshold, the infirm earl shrugged off his assistant, brought himself to aristocratic attention and stepped deliberately into the mouth of his discovery.

About an hour later, Adamson came running back to Ramses XI to tell Carter and his colleagues that the door was finally cleared and his lordship awaited them. The three left their seats together and followed the sergeant back to the tomb.

As he walked out into the sunlight, Carter shouted to his servant who was reclining in the shade of his robe. "Abdel! Go fetch Mr Burton at once. And get the electric light organised again. Hurry man!"

Abdel jumped to his feet and took off along the valley track for the tomb of Seti I.

As they descended the stone staircase, they quickly saw that the entrance corridor was not only cleared but, on Ali's fastidious instructions, it had been swept spotlessly clean. At the base of the inclined shaft, the freshly exposed, dark and mysterious doorway stood beckoning before them.

"The probing rod, Ali."

With a rapid swirl of his hand, Carter signalled urgently to his reis who, in anticipation of his master's request, and grinning that awful, blackened toothy grin of his, immediately produced the rod from behind his back.

Carter took the rod and examined the door for a spot that was without seal impressions and where the mud plaster contours appeared to indicate the join of two bricks. He carefully bored into the mud, alternately twisting clockwise and anticlockwise, feeling sensitively for the line of least resistance, until the rod broke through to the opposite side. As the rod jerked inward, those intently watching him drew a sharp breath.

In the silence of the moment, there was a very faint but plainly audible hiss as the pressure of the ancient gases from within equalised with those outside. Carter looked back at the row of anxious faces. Without a word, he turned back to the door and slowly pushed the rod further inward, feeling for signs of resistance. He introduced it slowly, further and further and still further. To its full length of three feet there was nothing. He turned once more to his colleagues.

"Nothing. Not a damn thing. Another corridor, I'll be bound. Fortunately for us, it seems there may be no more digging. We shall look into this next corridor this very evening. I am going to enlarge the hole so we can take a peek."

Carter withdrew the probe and gently chipped away at the wall until he had excavated a hole large enough for him to introduce his hand and a source of light and still have some view of what might lie before him.

Callender was quickly by his side with a lit candle. Carter took the candle and raised it to the hole so that it shone its pale light through to the other side. There was silence in the corridor as the three behind waited for him to describe what he was able to see. No one expected him to see much, just the blackness of another corridor extending ever deeper into the tomb - if they were lucky, perhaps some faint suggestion of wall paintings.

He was silent for some time, his eyes slowly accustoming themselves to the gloom. As he strained to make out what was before him his quickened breathing caused the candle flame to flicker. The limpid candle light fanned the walls of the room beyond with its faint energy. The flame threw dimly fluid, blurred shadows against the wall opposite. The pale light picked out shapes in the darkness. The images were indistinct but they were real.

Carter's view was restricted by the thickness of the mud-brick doorway. Nevertheless, what filled Carter's limited field of vision dumbfounded him: 'A jumble of objects. Most indistinguishable. But a lot, that much is certain. And a glint here and there. The glint of gold. Boxes. Piled high. On tables. No. Animals. Couches. Beds in the shape of animals. So much stuff. So much stuff!'

It was clear to all who were standing behind him that Carter was able to see something that lay the other side of the doorway.

Carnarvon couldn't wait any longer. "What do you see, man? Tell us what you can see!"

Carter didn't turn his head from the hole. Still peering intently into the dimness, he softly murmured, "It's wonderful. Wonderful things..."

For a moment, Carter relaxed his tension against the door and drew back, breathing heavily. This was enough for Carnarvon to grab his shoulder and pull him from the aperture. He pushed him to one side against the wall, and took the candle from Carter's hand so quickly that the flame extinguished.

"Quick, Callender, quick man. Light it for me." The earl's words were full of impatience.

Carter didn't move. He rested back against the wall of the corridor, gathering his thoughts.

Carnarvon turned to his colleague. "Callender! Callender! Help me, man!"

Callender pulled out a matchbox from his coat pocket, opened it and fumbled for a match.

"Come on! Come on, man! Strike the damn thing!"

After three attempts, Callender managed to relight the candle and he passed it carefully back to Carnarvon. The earl took it from him in a slow, more controlled manner this time. In his excitement, he neglected to thank the man.

Carter hadn't moved. He remained slumped against the wall with his head back, gazing thoughtfully at the ceiling.

Carnarvon put the candle to one side of the aperture in the doorway and stared intently inward. There was a lengthy, expectant silence as his eyes grew accustomed to the frail illumination. Then, after spending some moments absorbing the scene before him, "Oh, my God! Evelyn! Evelyn! Come look at this. Such wonders!"

The earl graciously pulled himself away from the door and pressed the candle into his daughter's hand. She had to stretch on tiptoe to see through the hole.

Carter, meanwhile, had returned to his senses and had gone outside. Evelyn was still peering through the hole when he ran back.

"Where's Burton? Where's Abdel? Where's Burton, dammit. We must get this door photographed at once!"

Carter had committed himself to his next move. He had to know what he was dealing with here. He had to know. A distinguished discovery or a find of a size beyond his wildest expectations - a fabulous treasure trove! What he had seen through the small hole in the doorway certainly suggested it. How much work lay ahead of him? A quick, superficial investigation before the authorities arrived. No more 'Tomb of the Horse' fiascos. He had to know sufficient about the contents and their layout to be confident of no embarrassment at the official opening and, more than this, enable himself to plan and prepare for the excavation effectively.

Notwithstanding the rules of protocol, to be honest with himself he was an explorer at the threshold and the explorer in him had to know now. There would be no way he could leave the place tonight without penetrating it, if only briefly, to its most remote and secret cavity.

Eventually Burton arrived. It was five-thirty. He set about his business rearranging the lighting, his tripod and reflecting sheets. Carter all the while impatiently paced about outside. The results of Burton's work were always exemplary, but for this Carter knew he had to pay the penalty of time. Right now, at this moment, he felt particularly anxious and, as he waited, wore his own path in the sand, stepping the same criss-cross course repeatedly. The remainder of the group had retired to the relative cool of Ramses XI to talk about what they had seen through that tiny hole.

At last a welcome bellow from the depths of the entrance corridor, "All done, Howard. All done."

Carter ran down the steps to help Burton dismantle and remove his equipment. This time, in a show of great discipline and willpower, Carter waited until Burton had confirmed that the plates had developed as intended. Then he called for the others.

There for a moment, in a pregnant silence, they stood still and quiet before the brick and plaster door. Carter drew a deep breath and started gently chiselling, removing the mud bricks one at a time and placing them carefully along the left edge of the corridor. It didn't take him long to excavate a hole large enough for even the portly Callender to clamber through.

"Before we go in," said Carter, "a few precautionary instructions. There will be little room to move without touching something. Keep extremely close to me in case we inadvertently break something. Follow my footing precisely."

They each stepped down through the opening and stood together on the lower threshold. The four of them huddled close, their shoulders touching, the one with the other, enabling each to obtain a somewhat separate view. Surrounded by the gloriously extravagant bric-a-brac they had recently glimpsed through the original small aperture in the plastered door, all four of them were now struck dumb with the abundance of exquisitely strange objects arranged all about them. There was absolute silence. Communication was unnecessary. For each of them it was an intensly personal moment. Individually they drank in the panorama.

Carter leaned forward and placed his candle on the floor, then turned and drew an electric light from the other side of the door. The room was immediately transformed from gloom to an eerie, pinkish brilliance. As he brought the lamp around himself to bear upon the wall to the left of them, it first flashed against what was clearly a jumble of golden chariot frames and their disassembled wheels, piled carelessly, it seemed, against the wall in the near corner. Then, as he continued his movement, great, black, oblong and spiked shadows swept across the wall in front of them like manifold hideous forces of the night riding urgently to their evil business.

Carter drew the bowl of light thrown by his electric lamp to the right illuminating the objects directly ahead of them. Three high beds, apparently gilded and each in the form of animals, were stacked head to tail along the wall. Beneath the one furthest to the left, a hole was clearly visible - an entrance to another chamber.

"Since this lamp will go no further, I will take the candle and have a quick gander through that hole - glimpse what might be in there."

Carter handed the lamp to Callender, picked up the candle gently and got down on his knees to inspect under the bed. His buttocks protruded from underneath as he pushed between its legs. His arms ahead of him, he thrust his head expectantly into the room beyond. He could see in the gloom that the room was small and filled to the brim with a jumble of objects chaotically piled one upon the other. Superficially at least, none was individually as impressive as those he was now crouching beneath, but nevertheless there was a mass of articles. He looked towards each side - up - down. There was no visible additional exit.

Carter backed out from under the bed and rejoined his expectant friends.

"A storeroom. It lies below the level of this one. Lots in there. Nothing apparently as breathtaking as what we have seen here. It appears mostly utilitarian, and in such a mess. Looks like someone threw it all in there - an absolute jumble of objects, and no apparent exit... Come, look for yourselves."

Three hands groped for the candle. Carter passed it to Evelyn. "Please, take care not to drop the candle under any circumstances!"

Evelyn nodded and scrambled into the small opening. The others did so in turn, each taking some considerable time to examine the faintly lit scene before them.

While Callender finished his inspection of the small room beneath the golden bed, Carter and the others examined the remainder of the first room. Below the second bed, which stood directly in front of him, this one a cow-like creature with a leopard's body, were boxes and oblate wooden cases. More boxes lay beneath the one to its right, this one more like two cats and, standing above and behind their heads in the far corner, a black sentinel holding a stave and scantily clothed in gold. There was another identical statue facing it in the last corner. Both were draped in faded cloth that had rotted so much it resembled thick cobwebs.

Carter directed the lamp at the area of the wall between the two sentries. There was a large, discoloured, oblong panel, the height of an average man, covered with seal impressions. The tomb so far had shown nothing of the lengthy corridors that normally preceded the burial place of a king but this clearly was another sealed door - to another corridor, to another room, or maybe to the burial chamber itself.

Carter noticed another discoloration at the base and near the centre of the blocked doorway. "Another breach. See? Resealed in antiquity!"

While the others remained silent, overawed by what they saw around them, Lady Evelyn said, "We... we are the first to intrude into this place for... for how long, Mr Carter?"

"Three thousand years..." Carter whispered respectfully in the stillness of the chamber.

"That is, of course, providing the plundering was accomplished and reparations completed almost immediately after the burial. From the looks of the place, I am pretty sure that was the case."

Intruders themselves? They felt nothing of the kind. Explorers? Adventurers? Entrepreneurs? Discoverers? Lucky? They were all these things.

Carnarvon grinned at Carter and then looked down at the resealed robbers' hole...

Chapter Nineteen
Conspiracy

So it was on that one remarkably sunny day in Bavaria, on his way to meet his wife at the little town of Schwabach, that George Edward Stanhope Molyneux Herbert, the Lord Porchester, erstwhile autophobe and speed-hound, purposefully aimed his open car down the long Roman road which, vacant of traffic, stretched straight as a die ahead of him. He pushed the accelerator firmly to the floor. As the roadster speeded up, Trotman, his chauffeur for over a quarter-century, sat rigidly upright in the passenger seat alongside his lordship, the expression on his face a picture of virtual apoplexy.

Before them, the sun was fairly low on the horizon, crisply highlighting the countryside ahead. The brightness of the illumination erased any sense of contrast in the contours and, before they realised it, they were on a rise that just as quickly fell away beneath. As the car crested the small hill, it briefly parted company with the ground. Carnarvon felt a momentary rush of excitement, then the wheels took hold of the road again. The driver flashed a broad grin at his terrified passenger.

An instant later, the thrill was erased. Two stationary ox carts completely blocked the roadway barely a hundred yards ahead. The earl reacted quickly and skilfully. Realising he would be unable to bring the car to a safe stop in time, he drove it deliberately onto the relatively flat grass verge, taking a line that would have negotiated around the obstruction. But Carnarvon was concentrating on the objects on the road before him and not on the verge itself. As he strained to manoeuvre the roadster, the left front wheel bounced over a large cobble on the side of the road. The brief impact was enough to pitch the speeding vehicle into the air in a sweeping arc, flipping it over to the right.

Trotman involuntarily parted company with the car as it began its roll, and landed on his shoulder in the grass. The heavy turf helped break his fall. Carnarvon was not so lucky. He held on tightly to the steering column until the car hit the ground, upended above him.

The chauffeur, dazed only a little by the shock of the event, found himself relatively unscathed and was on his feet within seconds. He scrambled to the overturned car and looked urgently for the earl. The vehicle straddled a ditch. Peering under the driver's door, Trotman could see the earl's contorted body, his head buried face down in the mud of the ditch.

'My God, he'll be drowning!' thought Trotman.

He got down on his hands and knees, reached under the car and grabbed Carnarvon by the shoulders of his leather coat. Summoning all the strength he had, he managed to drag his master from the wreckage and place him on his back in the grass. He quickly wiped the mud from the earl's face, clearing his nostrils first, and desperately looked for any signs of life.

Trotman looked all around for help. The men with the carts had gone. They were now so far away he could barely make them out in the distant field. It was almost as if they had never existed.

There were some farm workers not far away in the same field. They were seated incongruously in a group having their packed lunch and dispassionately observing the traumatic events at the roadside. Trotman called to them in English but got no response.

He got up and ran over to them, asking whether they had any water. They looked at him without comprehension. He noticed one of them had some water in a can and, in one swift movement, he grabbed it and ran back to his master.

He splashed all of the water over Carnarvon's face. Immediately the earl drew breath and coughed, and within seconds he was breathing regularly. Trotman sat back on his haunches in relief. The farm labourers dashed up behind him and began gesturing for the return of their can. Trotman chose not to understand the sign language.

As they observed the broken man lying immobile in the grass, one of them shouted, "Doktor!" Immediately he turned and dashed down the road, recovered his bicycle and quickly peddled off into the distance.

The earl breathed easier with every passing second. Help would shortly be on the way. Trotman settled himself to embarrassed smiles of acknowledgement as he and the remainder of the group conversed in expressions.

Carnarvon's recovery was slow. In fact, from the ordeal of this road accident he would never become fully restored to his former self. He had been permanently damaged, his way of life changed for ever - a disfigured palate that would hamper his elocution; a permanent limp and an unsteadiness of foot that would require the use of a cane; his resistance to infection a tenth of any normal man. Nevertheless, this incapacity was not sufficient to keep him from pursuit of his fondness for discovery. Ironically, through medical instructions to direct himself towards habitats with cleaner air and more clement winters, the accident had put him directly on a course for Egypt.

Rather than divert him, progress towards the inevitable encounter had become irreversible. Their early conspiracy had turned out to be considerably worse than total failure.

Together the royal couple had watched the relationship grow. Together they had witnessed the bond develop. Together their anxiety had steadily increased. And then, as if that were yesterday, the two explorers had reached beyond the threshold.

The queen whispered in the king's ear, "We must be more direct."

"Why?" asked Tutankhamun. "He who leads is to die by the curse. That will be warning enough."

"But more than a single event will have a better chance of getting their attention - make them think," Ankhesenamun continued. "The accident we contrived all those years ago did no more than strengthen that man's intent to come to Egypt. It seems to me that these people do not share our knowledge and perception of the unnatural world and, since they do not believe it exists, they do not fear its power. To bring them to comprehend this energy, we must act more often - develop situations that can not so easily be dismissed as mere coincidence."

"But what, my Queen?"

"Summon Dashir. He will know what to do."

Dashir, and all those who had been loyal in life, had joined the boy king in his heaven. All now enjoyed the fruits of their labours. All attended the royal couple in much the same ways that they had done all those millennia ago but this time absent of any preoccupation with survival.

Dashir, the king and the queen looked down on the scene below. They watched and listened to every facet of the daily operation - in the tomb, Burton, Gardiner and Callender and the two draughtsmen; in the laboratory, Mace and Lucas; Carter busily moving between them; Carnarvon's visits; the official showings; transport of the king's possessions to the riverside by way of the tiny, laboriously regenerated railway; and their discussions; and their evenings; and their nights; and their dreams. There was no aspect of their consciousness that the royal entourage did not share.

After a week of watching, the artisan turned to his king and queen.

"Your Majesties, the noble one is to die and soon. That is written. Queen Ankhesenamun is right. The event should be seen as just one of many catastrophes. It will not be easy to contrive these in their world but they are, as I understand, susceptible to suggestion by the unexplainable. I have a few ideas... I have noticed there is little affection or respect between those from the foreign land and those now in power in Egypt. There is, perhaps, room for some manipulation here. We can aggravate as easily as we can heal the rift: disturbances in the tomb itself as they work there; the death of someone close, even a pet; fanciful writings in their press; of curses and omens and dreadful consequences; nightmares to haunt them in their sleep. Should all this fail, we may have to contrive to kill. My good friend Meneg and I shall see to it presently. We shall do our best."

They began with the poltergeist.

Breasted, alone in the tomb, became the victim. The place was entirely silent - silent as the proverbial grave - so much so that every time he hesitated in his work he could feel the stifling claustrophobia of dark, noiseless, restricted confinement. But the third time he stopped to straighten his aching back he thought he heard it - a creaking. He sat motionless, waiting for the sound to repeat itself so he might locate its position - nothing. He began once more to address the object before him - again an audible creak. It appeared to come from inside the annex. It sounded as if someone or something was making its cautious way across the jumble of objects that littered the little room.

Cockroaches, he thought. Perhaps a scorpion. He returned to his work.

But the next sound caused him to stop. A distinct and, in the confines of the stony chamber, loud crack. For a moment it resonated about him. Again the echoes didn't permit him to locate the origin of the sound.

He waited for another, sitting silent and inert for minutes. There was nothing. He shook his head in frustration and returned to his labours. Almost immediately he did so, another resounding crack filled the room.

He sat bolt upright. The room fell into total silence once again. He decided he would listen for longer this time. He must have waited fifteen minutes without hearing anything of significance. He sat so rigidly motionless he could hear his heartbeat. He could make out the sounds of the voices of the crowds and labourers outside the tomb, but heard nothing more from within. Cursing under his breath, once more he turned back to his work.

Hardly had he touched the piece he was working on than the silence was broken by a noise which sounded like something wooden had become dislodged and fallen to the floor. Once again he could not locate the direction.

This was really frustrating. He got up and walked out of the tomb and into the sunshine. Stretching, he spied Carter who, with his usual purposeful step, was on his way back from the laboratory.

"Howard!" he called. "You won't believe this, but I have been hearing noises within the antechamber. Noises like there is something alive in there with me."

Carter smiled wryly. "Touch of the sun, old chap?"

"Don't be daft. Come and listen for yourself."

Carter was returning to the tomb in any case, so the only irritation was a few moments of silence to placate his colleague's anxiety. They stepped down onto the antechamber floor and Breasted signalled to Carter to be still.

They stood silent for a time. To Carter it seemed like an eternity.

'Nothing. Not a damn thing,' thought Breasted. 'Bloody typical.'

Then Carter spoke. "What's that?... Hear that?... There." Breasted couldn't hear a thing. "A thumping. Rhythmical. Bump-a, bump-a, bump-a. Can't you hear it? It's seems to be coming from over..." Carter moved towards his colleague, "...here." He rested an ear against Breasted's chest. "Yes. Definitely a case of the heebie-jeebies! 'Fraid I'll have to pronounce you unfit to work in confined spaces, Mr Breasted. A catacomb's definitely not your cup of tea!"

Breasted was not amused. "Dammit, Howard, I did hear it. Just don't know quite where it came from. Will y'not stay with me a while longer to see if it happens again?"

"Sorry, old man. No time to hold y' hand. Got to get back to the lab. Enjoy your hallucinations."

He carefully picked up a piece that Breasted had finished earlier and darted off.

The sounds of Carter's scuffling up the stone steps subsided and the dust settled. Then something in that room snapped. Breasted held his breath. He looked about him. Again he could not pinpoint the location of the sound. This was all becoming most disturbing. He sat back on his haunches and listened - nothing. He turned to the piece at hand as if to begin work once more - nothing. He picked up some heated paraffin and pretended to apply it - nothing. He applied it - Crack!

'Where did that come from?' he asked himself. He went over to the tiny entrance to the annex and looked in. There were no signs of movement, only silence.

He sat back in the centre of the antechamber and set himself to listening once more. He sat motionless for more than half an hour, long enough for Carter to have returned once more to retrieve the piece that his colleague had been working on earlier.

"Not finished. Sorry, old boy. Give me another hour."

Carter was not happy.

"James," he began, "y' know damn well we have a tight time schedule. Can't afford any slowdowns. If it wasn't for the damn visitors and press we'd have some flexibility. But as it is we have no margin for error - not if we are to break into the next room before we leave for the summer. And we will have to do that early in any case with all the damn royalty and officialdom that are already booked in February; all of them descending on us in expectation of that occasion. They won't delay. They will not tolerate the warmth of spring. Dammit, man, can't you hurry up?"

Carter's impatience was bluntly self-evident.

"Jeez, Howard, give me a break," pleaded Breasted, clearly irritated by his colleague's insensitivity.

Carter knew very well that preservation took time. But, at the same time, it appeared to him that Breasted was becoming preoccupied with fantasy, the occult or some such. He could not afford to be patient with the idiosyncrasies of his staff.

Breasted's face was a picture of frustration. "Howard, old chap. There really are sounds in here. But one has to be patient and wait for them. Will y' not sit with me a while in the silence?"

"James, I do not wish to unsteady our professional and personal relationship, but this much I have to say. We are falling behind. The antechamber must be emptied before the VIPs arrive in Luxor. The artefacts require our diligent attention. This takes time. This leaves no time to indulge our fantasies. Like as not, the noises you may indeed be experiencing - for I do not doubt your story, old chap, remember that - are generated by the artefacts themselves as they adjust to the modern atmosphere that now pervades this place and must infect them. Plus, there must by now be an abundance of life down here. This can only serve to underline the urgency of our work. Please get to it."

He left before Breasted could respond.

Breasted accepted Carter's logic, but his recent experiences within the tomb filled him with so much anxiety that, notwithstanding his colleague's common-sense analysis, he could not bring himself to continue the work at hand until he had taken some time to sit once more, unmoving and in silence, alone in the centre of the antechamber.

While he waited absolutely nothing happened. Breasted finally gave up his vigil and returned to the work.

The second his brush touched the object before him, a great cracking noise broke all about him. This time he did his best to ignore it and continued working. But now everything that remained in the room appeared to be creaking at the same time until he heard the steps of Carter once again within the corridor on his way back down to pick up another piece. As Carter appeared the tomb once more fell back into eerie silence.

Dashir looked at his king. The king looked at Ankhesenamun. They all agreed. This activity did not appear to be working.

"We must quickly move to the next, my lord. As they sit together tonight, today's events will become the subject of conversation. We must add another event to the stories they will tell."

"It is for me to play the part this time, is it not, Dashir?"

"It is, my lord."

And almost immediately, as his queen and the servants watched, the image of Tutankhamun dissolved before them and the gold uraeus at his forehead fell to the floor.

Carter left for Cairo that afternoon to purchase more supplies.

Breasted continued his work in the antechamber and tried to ignore the continuous creaking and movement of inanimate objects all around him.

The canary in its cage in his master's bedroom at Castle Carter heard the grains of sand and dust grind together between body and tiled floor like so many boulders tumbling in a torrent from the cliffs above.

"It was a cobra, I... I think," Callender told Carter with some embarrassment as he met him at Luxor station. Callender had seen a snake of some kind slithering out the back door before he discovered that the canary was missing. The golden creature that had brought gold to the explorers was dead.

Carter lamented that he had not given the canary one moment of his attention since the tomb had been discovered. He was not a superstitious man, and it was only an animal, but he would miss the company of its song and the knowledge that another warm body shared his bedroom. Sad, but that was an end to it.

Ali was more direct in his interpretation of the event. "The golden bird is dead, sir. It is a sign. Bad luck now walks within The Valley. There will be more deaths."

They did talk about these things while at dinner that night, and they did share their individual interpretations and concerns.

"What you said by way of explanation was quite sensible, Howard. But, with respect, you were not there when it happened. You have not experienced the feeling. You cannot then comment on it with any authority. All you can do is speculate." Breasted was quite emphatic and direct in his statement. "I believe - and I mean these words - I believe it really could be a poltergeist."

Evelyn giggled nervously.

As if he had some concern that any lack of negative response might implicitly recognise the possibility of some supernatural presence, Callender quickly cut in, "Rot. Absolute rot, James."

"Tommyrot," added Carter. He did not elaborate further, lowered his eyes and continued to sip his coffee. His mind was preoccupied with the monumental job ahead of him.

Carnarvon had been listening intently. Like most of the others he was intrigued by Breasted's story. He had always held a healthy respect for all things occult. He was interested in the possibility that something of a supernatural nature was actually present at and about their excavations. Even little things were of significance to him.

"Did you notice the lightning storms last night?" added Evelyn. "But there was no rain. And they stopped dead at daybreak. And then there were dust storms all day. Funny weather."

"The lights went off in the tomb when I entered it yesterday," said Mace. "After I got them working they went off again. Kept blowing a fuse. Couldn't work out where the short was. Left the place at closing time that night with the cause of the problem still unresolved and the damn things came back on by themselves! Then found I couldn't turn them off - until I pulled the plug."

Carnarvon was not impressed by these particular stories and found himself unable to resist... "When I was in Jamaica a few years ago I met a witch doctor who read my tealeaves. A brand of Fortnum's I believe they were. He told me then that the coincidence of a dead canary, storms, noises off, in, under or beneath, and inexplicable electrical happenings would be portents of disaster! I didn't think anything of it at the time, but now you come to mention it..."

Evelyn whispered to her father, "Your joke is in very poor taste, Porchy.

It's not fair to the others." She thought her father's sarcasm inappropriate in such scholarly company.

Carter momentarily grinned in approval, but continued to pretend he was ignoring the conversation.

Then Breasted added a comment. "All joking aside, I have told you chaps this before but up to now you have not taken the time to listen. I am absolutely sure that on most occasions when I visit the tomb, some of the objects have been moved from their original positions to some other. Not by much. Not that the casual observer might notice. But moved nevertheless. Even Howard has mentioned that he thought something appeared to be strangely situated. Do you recall, Howard?"

There was no response. Carter remained absorbed in his thoughts and refused to recognise the enquiry.

"That's an easy one to check," added Callender. "We can pull out Hall and Hauser's records."

Carter remained silent.

The story that finally did the trick was Alan Gardiner's. He hesitated before he spoke. "I... er... I wasn't going to mention this. Dismissed it as a figment of my imagination, or memory loss - more likely at my age, I confess - that is until the fellahs mentioned having the same experience."

He had everyone's attention but Carter's.

"The crates on the cars of the Decauville railway. They take a long time to move, do they not?"

"That's a gross understatement. Damn ridiculous state of affairs giving us only thirty metres of line to play with," groused Breasted.

"Not the only reason for delay, I fancy. If my recollection is correct, that is. Now bear in mind that I cannot prove what I am about to tell you. But that is the essence of the supernatural, is it not?.. Just two days ago, I was overseeing the transportation of three crates towards the river. We had just started and had got them to the end of the initial length of laid track and, in the usual fashion, we were about to disassemble the upstream portion and re-lay it ahead of the cars. It was the hottest part of the day. Wetting the rails so they were cool enough to handle was becoming an exhausting chore in itself and the fellahs reminded me of the hour and that we should take advantage of some shade and rest awhile. This we did and, leaving the cars where they were, we retired to Tomb Seven... Imagine my surprise when later I emerged from the tomb entrance to find that the cars were once more back at the beginning of the track! As if we had not moved them an inch. They had returned, or had been returned, to the beginning of the track - against the gradient!" Gardiner emphasised this last observation by stabbing at the air with his forefinger.

The group sitting around Gardiner were silent. But they all looked directly at him, even Carter.

After a brief pause, Gardiner continued, "I recall my thoughts at the time.

It was as if... as if someone was telling me these treasures should not be moved - not be removed, I should say - from their original resting place. A gentle message to us to replace that which we were taking. For just a moment I really felt I was being watched. Crazy, I know, but I truly did feel a presence about me, and not just one being - several. It was a most curious and somewhat disquieting experience. I am glad to say it has not occurred since."

Carter drew a long, slow, deep breath. "Alan, did anyone else experience this?"

"Actually, yes. As I said, some of the fellahs who were with me at the time. If it was imagination or forgetfulness, it was not only mine. At least three others recollect the same phenomenon. They are impressionable souls, I know, so it's not what I would call real proof. But ask them all the same, if you will."

Carter knew he didn't have to ask. Gardiner's word was sufficient. 'Damn difficult to believe,' he thought, 'but there has to be a rational explanation.' He shrugged his shoulders. "No time to dwell on these phenomena. A monumental task still lies before us. Back to work everybody."

Reality is a simple fact; superstition and conjecture are not.

On the night of April the third, over four months later, the Earl of Carnarvon lies sweating in a hotel bed in Cairo, suffering from a terminally debilitating case of pneumonia. His eyes are open. They are wet with tears. Tears of hopeless frustration that his frail body is unable to resist the disease. Frustration that he is to be prevented from seeing his great triumph through to its glorious conclusion.

As he stares at the ceiling, mixtures of gold, black, blue, red, green and white begin to sparkle in the haze of his fading eyesight. The fragments slowly coalesce into an image. It is a woman. She is slim; quite small. A great golden collar broadly encrusted with red, blue and green glass hangs over her shoulders and about her narrow neck. Her dress is white gossamer, pleated below the waist. Each of her bare arms is enclosed by golden and jewel-encrusted bangles; her feet with golden slippers. She wears a black wig. The plaited ropes uniformly drape her sweet face. Heavy gold earrings hang from each ear lobe. There is a perfume cone on her head. The wax appears to glow as it runs in tiny rivulets over her cheeks. Her eyes are heavily outlined in black.

Her arms move towards him. There is the merest suggestion of a beckoning...

Chapter Twenty
Something Bad

Carter, Carnarvon, Lady Evelyn and Callender had finished their soup. It had been a long and eventful day, truly the 'day of days', and much of the night to boot. A light supper was quite sufficient. Their minds were racing with the sights they had beheld, each with a different perspective, each with different memories.

"We must to bed," Carter ordered. "There is much to do. Much to prepare. We may not feel it at present because of all the adrenalin, but if we stay up any longer we will regret it in the morning. You will overnight here, of course, your lordship, m' lady, Pecky, old boy. Far too late to return to the east bank. A bit cramped, but I believe we'll all fit okay."

Each member of the party nodded and took it in turns to use the limited facilities.

Carter lay in bed staring at the ceiling. It was tinged a light shade of blue in the reflected moonlight. Damn all chance he was going to get any sleep for what remained of tonight and he knew it. His jacket hung on the chair next to his bed. He leaned over, took a pad and pencil from one of the pockets and began committing to paper the great list of tasks that presently tumbled through his sleepless mind.

The earl, in the spare room with his daughter, was also staring at the ceiling. He sat up and pulled his jacket from the end of the bed. He also withdrew something from the side pocket. He lay back into the pillow and slowly opened his fist in front of his face. The small ivory figure of a pony at full stretch rolled onto his palm. He felt the thrill of possession and, at the same time, the temerity of deception. But both were enjoyable. He studied it for a minute or two, then turned over and tucked it under his pillow. He felt the passive comfort of its gentle contours beneath his head and easily fell into a deep, contented sleep.

He was not the only one. Next to him the diminutive figure of an ivory gazelle was being examined. In the hall behind them, Callender's trousers hung by their braces from a hook on the wall. A tiny, seated bronze dog with a gilded collar, its smiling head looking over its shoulder, reclined snugly in the right-hand pocket.

That night each of them held their personal secret close, but by breakfast it had all become far too much to withhold. At the start, each of them was silent. Little more could be heard than the shuffling of the servant and the drinking of the coffee and of the tea and the crunching of the toast. Each held the group's guilty secret. Each held a personal guilty secret. With the sole exception of their host, each of them was bursting to tell a colleague.

Carter helped break the silence. "Lady Evelyn. Did you sleep all right? I am unused to so many guests, so I hope you will forgive these congested surroundings."

"Most soundly, Howard. A most restful night's sleep." She lied. But it was not the heat or the insects or for want of a comfortable bed. For her, like the others, it had been a night full of thoughts, full of pictures, full of memories, full of the most wonderful memories.

Abdel left the room to replenish the coffee.

Evelyn could stand it no longer.

"Gentlemen," she said. "I cannot contain my guilt for another moment."

The three men stared directly at her, wide-eyed.

"If I do, I shall not be able to concentrate for the rest of the day." She picked up her handbag and placed it on the table. Parting the clasp, she put her hand inside and, with some ceremony, drew out the tiny carving.

Evelyn looked at each of their faces, from one to the other around the table. She anticipated the most awful scolding, particularly from Carter. In the event, the response was totally unexpected. Carnarvon smiled... Callender smiled... Then, at last, Carter smiled. They all smiled at one another. Evelyn smiled back nervously in relief. And they all laughed.

They shared the three small objects and passed them around.

Examining the ivory pony thoughtfully Carter turned to the three with a stern expression on his face. He whispered above the noise of Abdel's returning footsteps, "This much - oh, I almost forgot, and the head - shall we take, but no more. These precious things are plenty enough to remind us of the thrill of our first moments inside the sepulchre. But there can be no more. Swear this to me, my good friends. Swear this to me."

"We swear, Howard!"

Carter's serious composure persisted. "Later, for my private records, you must tell me exactly - exactly now - where you found these objects."

By now Abdel had returned to the room to replenish their coffee cups. The conversation ceased.

Carter felt for the bulge in his jacket's outer pocket. He would keep that particular secret to himself.

"Your lordship, I am sure it has not escaped your attention that we have here the best of all possible worlds - particularly in view of the political situation current in Egypt at this time?"

"Don't follow your drift, Howard," said Carnarvon, puzzled.

"The new rules of your concession, sir. All discoveries from an 'unplundered' tomb are the indisputable property of the State. All discoveries from a 'plundered' tomb are to be shared equally between the concessionaire and the State. Now do y' follow?"

The earl smiled broadly. "Letter of Egyptian law, Howard. Don't forget that. Not the 'Laws of the Realm'. Not quite the same, I'm afraid."

"Well, all the same, a good basis for argument, wouldn't y' say?"

"Today, m' lady, gentlemen, is a planning day," he continued. "We must prepare for the recording, preserving and emptying of the tomb, and we must prepare for the people. All those people. All those people who will want to gaze at what we have found and what we are doing, while we are doing it... My good, good friends. This is a most crucial time. Before we set foot in that place again, we must be entirely prepared. Last night I jotted down some thoughts on these matters. Let me share them with you and get your comments.

"First, we must get a proper steel door made to secure the tomb whilst we are away. Within the next few days I will go to Cairo and organise its manufacture.

"Second, there is a team of experts to be assembled the like of which, I fancy, the world of archaeology will not have seen before. I have thought long on this and know exactly who we will need. Some of these men will be familiar to you - Percy Newberry for instance - others less so. We need an experienced chemist. While in Cairo I will try to enlist the services of Alfred. Inscription interpreters - Alan Gardiner and Jim Breasted. And from the Met - Mace, Arthur Mace. He is a great authority on conservation. We need accurists in draughtsmanship. I would like to get hold of Lindsey Hall and Walter Hauser. Charles Wilkinson I will need to assist me - and Burton, of course. It is essential he continue the photographic recording. I will cable the Met with these requests today."

Carter referred to his list again.

"Third, we need to select and obtain permission to use a tomb or two for stores. We need a darkroom on site and a workshop, laboratory or whatever. Somewhere where we can work on the preservation of the artefacts in the cool and out of the public's prying eyes."

He turned towards the earl. "Sir, your position and influence will best facilitate this provision."

Carnarvon indicated his acknowledgement with a nod.

"Fourth, the stores themselves. We need packing cases, packing materials, chemicals... I have assembled a long list here. More for me to attend to in Cairo."

He looked back at his patron. "This will all take quite some time. While these preparations are under way, we will need to reseal the tomb."

"But first you must have an official opening," observed Carnarvon. "How and when do you plan to do that, Howard?"

"Yes..." Carter sighed. "Just the first of many unhelpful digressions, I suppose." He pulled at his moustache thoughtfully. "Allenby?"

"Of course. And the local Egyptian officials and members of the Antiquities Service. Watch the protocol. I shall make a list first to ensure we don't miss anyone of importance. If we make any thoughtless omissions it could hurt us later. Get the invitations out. That had better be our first order of business today. I'll do that, Howard, with Evelyn's help. You deal with the stuff you're good at - the technical stuff and your technical pals."

"All right." Carter drained his coffee cup and pushed his chair back. "Let's to it."

Carter would never feel more fulfilled than he did that first fortnight following the initial penetration. Showing the place to the first few visitors and VIPs was a novelty and a consummate pleasure - a total fulfilment of his life's ambition. It would not be long before it became an almost unbearable chore, he knew that. But right now, this minute, it was immensely satisfying.

Harry Burton sat on a boulder on the flank of the valley that lay opposite the tomb entrance photographing the visitors with his cine-camera. Carter, passing by below, noticed Burton wave to attract his attention. Like a precocious child, without reservation or embarrassment, he willingly cavorted for the camera.

Things just could not get any better.

Arthur Mace arrived on Christmas Day. That evening, at the Metropolitan Museum house, the assembled team participated in traditional seasonal celebrations. Within two days Mace was hard at work in the laboratory tomb, painstakingly removing the decayed pieces of embroidery and leather articles from the first box to leave Tutankhamen's tomb in three thousand years.

Each man in Carter's team knew the limits of his own particular expertise and to whom to go for help when he needed it. The team worked extremely well together and, had they been left to themselves, perhaps a cross word might never have passed between any of them. As it was, however, their leader was not used to working alongside his peers - alongside anyone for that matter - and to varying degrees Carter found it at times most difficult, and sometimes downright impossible, to avoid interfering with their work. Unfortunately, this happened so often - and without Carter's recognition that at times he was taking a step too far - that two of the team, the draughtsmen, ultimately would reach the limit of their tolerance, down tools and walk off the job.

Adamson turned restlessly in his canvas bed. It was a clear night and the full moon filled his tent with a pale lilac light. He had had way too much brandy before turning in for the night but, as things were to turn out, this would serve him well.

Outside, unknown to the sergeant, the sentries had left their posts. They had been well paid. The inevitable loss of job would be inconsequential to them. Others, many others - for there was much to achieve in one night - fearful of their tasks but paid sufficient to overcome any feelings of insecurity, were about to busy themselves with the business of grand larceny.

They had watched the British soldier on previous nights. His schedule was regular; his movements predictable. He would always retire at eight o'clock. Music would soon be heard coming from his tent. The alien noise would go on for at least an hour. Any sound they would make would be inaudible above the scratching of his gramophone. Besides, they had nothing to fear, they had weapons and he was only one.

Holst's 'Mars' hit another crescendo and Adamson rolled over a little too far. The collapsible bed tipped over, spilled the sergeant to the ground and jarred the gramophone, causing the needle to score across the record to the spindle.

The robbers' lookout noticed that the music had suddenly stopped and gestured to his colleagues to be quiet for a moment.

The sergeant sat up and shook his head. He turned to look for another record. Unable to read any label in the darkness, he grabbed for the hurricane lamp hanging from the ridge pole. He lifted the glass, struck a match and lit the wick. Replacing the lamp on the hook, he resumed his examination of the record labels.

The tent now glowed - inside the silhouette of some grotesque creature began to move about. The lookout felt a little unsure of himself and summoned his colleagues to share his view of the curious light display below. The shape continued to change, flashing first from one panel of the tent and then another, growing, then becoming smaller, then growing large once more.

The Valley became filled with sound again. It was a low, lilting tone, dream-like, wailing almost, like a host of mourners, the pitch rising and falling with each movement of the dark creature in the tent. The sound carried into the canyon and repeated, echoing to and fro between the towering walls. They had heard nothing the like of it before. With each echo the gathering crowd of mourners seemed to grow larger and louder.

Inside the tent, Adamson was sitting on his bunk listening to the chanting of monks, one of his new records. Suddenly he felt the need to relieve himself and, forgetting for a moment his confined surroundings, pulled himself bolt upright. His head connected smartly with the stout ridge pole and he fell to the ground in a senseless heap. The hurricane lamp rocked wildly about its hook, throwing distorted shadows off the jagged rocks around the valley flanks. The record jumped a track or two but continued to play. To the apprehensive onlookers, it was as if Lucifer himself and his choir of black angels had come to ignite the very rocks themselves and punish them for their evil intent.

The ghostly wailing; the revolving shadows; the flashing light - it was all too much for the team of infidels. They took off pell-mell for the river, guns and all.

The sergeant had averted disaster but would remain blissfully unaware of his selfless actions. In the light of day, however, he discovered the sentries' betrayal and it was with an aching head that he reported his findings to his boss. "They must've scarpered while h'I was asleep, sir."

"You're sure nothing's been touched?"

"Nuthin', sir. Not a bleedin' pebble."

"We must count ourselves fortunate. And count yourself damn lucky, Sergeant. Be sure the police you select this time are well supported with affidavits from Monsieur le Directeur. I would even suggest that you get some police to watch the police... And..." Carter added after a short pause, "sleep, if you have to, but very, very lightly from now on. And I mean very lightly!"

"H'I won't fall asleep again, sir. H'I promise. H'I'll sleep in the day time. H'as Gawd is my witness...." After reflecting a moment, Adamson added, "H'and if I does drift orf - but h'I won't never, honest - h'even the steps of a creepin' dung beetle will wake me, let alone the stumblin' plates-a-meat h'of a bleedin' fuzzy-wuzzy!"

Carter gave the sergeant a suitably stern look and returned to his breakfast.

After his patron had left for England, Carter took a couple of days in Cairo busying himself with the purchase of a car, photographic materials, restorative and preservative chemicals, packing boxes, and huge volumes of calico, wadding, surgical bandages and the like. The local tradesmen soon found themselves cleaned out of their entire stocks and rushed to the telegraph to replenish their inventories by the next available steamer.

On his return to Luxor, to his delight his old friends from the Met - Herbert Winlock, his wife and his daughter, and James Breasted, his wife and son - had established themselves at the 'Palace'. All were eager to see the discovery as soon as Carter could accommodate them. He lost no time in getting ready for their first viewing.

He wanted the impact to be spectacularly rewarding, not unlike his own first fantastic glimpse, and he prepared accordingly. He had Burton's lights fully on, flooding the antechamber and its contents with their brilliance, and suspended a white sheet from the lintel at the tomb's entrance. The linen totally obscured what lay at the other end of the inclined entrance corridor.

When the group arrived at the tomb on the early morning of Christmas Eve, Carter, tweed suit, suede shoes and Homburg, was sitting on the spectators' wall waiting for them.

"Families Winlock and Breasted!" he greeted his friends, and leapt down. "Welcome to the tomb of Tutankhamen! You are all going to relish this moment for a lifetime. Follow me."

He gestured forward with his right hand and followed them down into the pit and down the steps until they stood before the threshold. A rectangular, pale reddish-gold glow filled the sheet. A light breeze caught it and the image eerily rippled.

After an appropriate pause to build his audience's anticipation, Carter continued. "Are you prepared for this?"

They all nodded eagerly.

Like a cavalier whisking his cloak to the side, he drew back the sheet in a single movement, permitting an instantly full view of the open doorway at the entrance to the antechamber some thirty feet ahead, and of all that lay beyond it against the opposite wall.

First there was absolute silence. Then Winlock's daughter broke ranks and scampered down to the steel gate at the end of the corridor. The rest quickly followed. They pressed themselves against the gate as each tried to get sight of the treasures at either end of the room. The view was only partial but the effect no less startling.

Carter stepped forward and dismantled the padlocks securing the steel gate. He pushed it open and stepped down into the antechamber, beckoning to Winlock and Brestead to follow. "Just the two for now - no room for more - we might step on something."

Carter stood quietly behind his colleagues with just the slightest suggestion of an expectant grin and, with the excitement of a child showing off his first two-wheeler, he waited for their initial impressions.

They were numb to the stifling heat. There was silence. At last Breasted, his mouth agape, turned and shook Carter vigorously by the hand. There were no suitable words.

Near midday in late December it was sharply cold. A crisp breeze cut the air. It was brilliantly sunny and the shadows of the leafless trees cut starkly black across The Mall and flashed against the windscreen of Carnarvon's Daimler as he was driven towards the rotunda in front of the palace gates.

As he neared the palace, the earl swelled with pride. Recognition of this ilk was truly a moment to be cherished - likely a once in a lifetime event. Nevertheless he felt totally relaxed. This paled in comparison to that moment of discovery. Nothing could eclipse it. The car drove through the gates and into the quadrangle and drew to a halt under the portico at the official entrance way. A brightly uniformed footman held the door for his lordship while another took his arm and helped him out and up the short flight of stairs. He bowed at the entrance to the reception room where the king awaited him.

"Carnarvon!" bellowed the king as he saw him enter. "I've been awaiting this moment ever since this time last month. Come and sit down, my good man. Take some tea with me. I wish to hear the full story from the man responsible for this great discovery. You have done your country a great service. A wonderful - a truly wonderful achievement!"

"You are too kind, your Majesty. But your praise is at the very least equally deserved by Mr Carter. I was all for calling a halt to our search. Had it not been for his tenacity and discipline, the tomb would still lie buried today."

"Ah... yes... Carter. He is a small person. Testy, too. Few manners. I'm sure it was a necessary match, the two of you, but I'll bet it's been a difficult one at times. Your forgiving nature is a credit to you. I seem to recall a lingering nasty taste when his name and that of the French come up in the same conversation. Just as well a man of means and breeding can lend his name to this discovery. Don't know that I could stomach an audience myself."

"Nonetheless, with your leave, sir, I will pass your words of gratitude to my colleague on my return to Egypt late next month."

"As y' please, Carnarvon. He's your cross. Now..." the king continued without taking a breath, "...I want the full story - not a word - not an observation left out."

He stared intently at Carnarvon, his face the very picture of anticipation.

While in London during the first week of the New Year, Carnarvon sat at his desk to review, glance at and possibly read some of the mountain of mail that was addressed to his attention each day. He took it upon himself to read one in three. One of the three he hit upon on that particular day got his attention immediately and stopped him reading any more. In a macabre fashion it appealed to his superstitious nature. At the same time, however, it disturbed him.

The letter read:

Dear Lord Carnarvon,

My wife and I have some degree of psychic power. We do not use this to commercial benefit you understand, but nevertheless we are so gifted. From time to time we are visited. That is, we sense from time to time an alien presence and sometimes even establish a dialogue.

Be this as it may, we are writing to you on this occasion through no other compunction than a wish to preserve you from what we believe to be a mortal danger.

Last night we had read with interest the latest bulletin on the great discovery that yourself and Mr Carter have made in The Valley of the Tombs of the Kings in Egypt. We were discussing the latest findings when, without warning, the lights in our room began to dim. As the light faded an image of a woman in ancient Egyptian dress began to materialise. She appeared royal and she pointed to the desk upon which lay a pad of paper, and beside it a pencil. I felt compelled to pick up the pencil and place the point on the paper. I did not feel any sensation in my fingers but it must have been within just a few seconds of my picking up the pencil that the image disappeared and the light was restored. Both of us were extremely disturbed by this event, but we became absolutely thunderstruck when we realised that in those few moments I had actually written something on the notepad. And this is the reason for my letter to you. The words, all in capitals, read:

'LORD CARNARVON NOT TO ENTER TOMB. DISOBEY AT PERIL.

*IF IGNORED WOULD SUFFER SICKNESS; NOT RECOVER; DEATH
WOULD CLAIM HIM IN EGYPT.'*
  *We feel it our responsibility to bring this event to your attention. We are telling
you this as fact. Make of it what you will.*
  Whatever you decide to do now, my wife and I wish you well, and God's speed.
                              Sincerely,

                           The Hamons

The earl crushed the paper in his fist. He believed so fervently in the
supernatural. But at the same time this discovery, after so many years of
defeat, was of such monumental proportions that it had become literally the
biggest news of the day. From shy and reserved, albeit rich beginnings, he
had become a worldwide celebrity. Everyone who was anyone wanted to
meet him and visit, or at least hear about, his encounter with the splendours
of Tutankhamen's treasure and experience the discovery of the body of the
boy king himself. To distance oneself from such public notoriety was
unthinkable.

With strength of will and not a little nervousness, he suppressed the fear
which the note had generated and focused himself on completing his
business in England and returning to the site as soon as practicable. But an
uneasiness remained with him and haunted his sleep.

Carnarvon's first and most important business of the New Year was lunch
at his club with the manager of *The Times*, William Lints Smith. An old friend
of the grandee's notwithstanding, Smith was totally focused on the
tremendous scoop he was about to secure for his newspaper. Similarly, the
earl was absolutely certain of the unique and uncountable value in the
exclusivity of this story, and of the stories he knew were yet to come. There
would be no bargaining.

Friends they may have been, but this was business and Carnarvon was not
about to elicit less than full value for the opportunity he would present to
the man on the other side of the claret bottle. He didn't have to worry. They
were both gentlemen and Smith was in any case prepared to obtain the sole
rights to the greatest story in newspaper publishing history at almost any
price. He had come armed with a draft of their forthcoming agreement with
everything complete but for a couple of gaps left for the final figures
regarding the Carnarvon family's compensation.

Having spent a little time reading all the provisions in the ten clauses, the
earl said, "Five thousand pounds and seventy-five per cent."

Smith nodded.

Perusal of the menu and the choice of a dessert wine had taken longer
than the negotiations. Without further ado, they set to enjoying their stuffed
quail.

Lord Carnarvon drained his brandy and blotted his lips with his serviette.

"A truly agreeable agreement, in all senses of the word, William. It's good for *The Times* - it's good for Carnarvon - it's good for Carter. He hates publicity. He hates the public! Since publicity and the notoriety that accompanies it are inevitable, this arrangement will permit him the least and the best organised interference. I can guarantee he won't be pleased with our arrangement, but he will be a lot less unhappy than he would have been had we permitted it to become a free-for-all. Trouble is, he probably won't appreciate it and I have no doubt he will be downright rude to Merton on occasion. I hope your man has the personality for it, and a tough hide - he'll need it!"

They both laughed.

The little biplane leapt over the rim of The Valley clearing the rocks by just a few feet and, like a dragonfly hitting a downdraught, immediately fell towards the people milling about above the entrance to the newly opened tomb. All of a sudden The Valley was filled with noise. The roar of its engine bounced off every cliff face. Several of the Arab labourers scattered willy-nilly in fear for their lives. It swung so low that it kicked up dust and then climbed back out to make another turn.

"Bloody hell!" shouted Carter over the din of yelling men and machine. "I'll bet that's Weigall, sir!" he shouted at the earl, lately back from the festive season in England. "I told him he was barred from The Valley for the time being. Absolutely fumed about it. Not to be outdone he finds another way in. How the hell did he manage that?"

Adamson chimed in above the row. "Give me a rifle, sir, and when 'e comes back for anuver run I'll 'ave 'im out the sky h'in the blinkin' of an eye. That'll fix 'im... for good an' all!"

"Isn't he now a reporter, Howard?" the earl shouted back over the din.

"*Daily Mail.*"

"Well, we needn't worry at all about that. They're not going to get the story. I've fixed it already."

The noise died momentarily as the aircraft disappeared over the ridge.

Carter looked puzzled. "Fixed it? What do you mean, 'fixed it', sir?"

"Negotiated an exclusive rights contract with *The Times* whilst I was away. A story such as this has to be fully reported in the best newspaper in the world. It is inconceivable to have it any other way. Besides, an exclusive contract will mean badly needed money in me pocket, Howard."

The financial aspects were of no concern to Carter. He estimated the number of non-constructive interviews and pestering he might become exposed to. The daily presence of reporters was more than he wished to contemplate at present.

"Believe me, Howard, this is for the best. All interviews will be under our control - at specific times and no other. You will be able to carry out your important work to a schedule which only you will control. I promise you the least hindrance... and no Mr Weigall."

Carter would be glad of that.

The earl gestured skyward as the biplane came in for another low pass. Everyone held their ears. As the plane swept past and opened up its throttle to make the climb over the cliff face, Carter noticed the camera lens flash in the sunlight.

"Damn man's taking pictures of us, your lordship."

"Can't stop him taking pictures, Howard. Tourists are taking pictures all the time."

"Yes, but he'll be publishing them, sir."

"Not the official ones, Howard. That's all that matters to us. Official pictures with official captions - the only correct ones."

"If you say so, sir. If you say so." The earl's personal complacency aside, Carter couldn't help his irritation.

As the noisy biplane disappeared over the ridge line, Carter saw an object fall to the ground about twenty yards in front of him. He trotted over and picked it up. It was a piece of paper wrapped tightly around a small pebble. He opened up the paper and read the few hurriedly scribbled letters inside: 'SAY CHEESE! W.'

He rolled it up once more in his fist and threw it to one side out of the earl's field of view.

The encounter in the Winter Palace bar that night was inevitable. There were only so many places with Western-style comforts that one could go to in Luxor and the press were in all of them.

"Hope we didn't blow your hats off today!"

Weigall slapped Carter on the back as he was leaning forward to place his Scotch on the coffee table. The drink spilled into the ashtray, extinguishing Carnarvon's cigar. The two turned to glare at the man who had so rudely interrupted their elite gathering.

"Oh. Sorry chaps, er... ladies, your lordship, Carter, Callender, Breasted, Burton."

He acknowledged each member of the seated group with a repetitive nodding of his head.

"Please, let me get you another."

He turned around quickly and called to the waiter at the bar.

"Effendi! A Scotch and...?"

"Water."

"...Water for Mr Carter - a double. And bring the box of cigars. My deepest apologies, your Lordship. Most clumsy of me."

"Quite all right, Mr Weigall. Couldn't be helped. Please, would you like to join us?"

"You are most kind, sir."

Carter and Callender made room for him and he pulled up a chair.

"I don't believe you have met the ladies. Some introductions are in order. Mr Weigall from the *Mail* - Lady Evelyn, my daughter..."

He leant forward to shake her hand. "Delighted, Lady Evelyn."

"...Miss Dalgliesh, visiting us from England for a fortnight..."

"Charmed."

"...Mrs Burton and Mrs Breasted, accompanying their husbands during their travails with us."

"Blessed, I'm sure."

He shook the hand of each of the ladies. Following his recent blundering embarrassment, his fingers were wet with perspiration and each of them in turn wiped their right hands on their hankies; all except Mrs Burton who was wearing silk gloves.

Weigall couldn't contain himself. The opportunity couldn't be wasted. The group resigned themselves to the inevitable interrogation.

"What a find, Carter! What a find!" He turned towards Carnarvon. "My congratulations, sir! My congratulations to you both! The world salutes you! The archaeological discovery of the century! No, the greatest ever!"

This was all a little too much for Carter who, as the returning waiter broke Weigall's flow, couldn't resist tempting fate. With a contemptuous grin beneath his moustache he said, "How many years was it you controlled The Valley, Weigall? Recall your comments of 'amateurism'? How many times did you tell us that after Davis we were wasting our time? Bandied about his words (God rest his soul) - 'No more tombs' - all over the place, as I recall. Bit ironic this, don't y' think?"

Carnarvon broke in, "Now, now, Howard. No room for sour grapes. He came to give us his good wishes. Take it in the spirit in which it is given. Let bygones be bygones."

Weigall, in any event, hadn't taken Carter's words seriously. He was concentrating on his next move in the golden opportunity now presented to him and stepped right in. "Your lordship," he continued, "may I avail myself of some of your time for an interview? The *Mail* will see it is printed - all over the world!"

"Ah..." The earl choked as he bit off the end of a new cigar. His response was clinically short. "Sorry, old boy. No. Absolutely not. Since you are so desirous of the facts, I suggest you refer to *The Times* as the authoritative source."

Weigall's condescending smile cleared from his face. He stared at the earl, speechless.

"Cat got your tongue, Weigall?" Carter provoked.

The silence continued for a moment or two more. Eventually, the astonished archaeologist-cum-reporter managed to pull himself together sufficiently to stammer out a few words. "An exclusive?"

Carnarvon nodded to him.

"You... you can't do that."

"Done, old boy."

"But... Never heard the like... Can't be legal..."

"It is. Better get used to it. Cause you less pain. Thanks for the cigar."

The earl joined Carter in a wry smile.

Weigall was becoming angry. He was just about to blurt out something he would no doubt later regret when a man wearing jodhpurs, high leather riding boots and a short-sleeved khaki shirt clapped him on the shoulder.

"Been looking for you everywhere, Wigger me old man! Going to introduce me to your lady friends?"

Between his embarrassment, disappointment, shock and anger, Weigall was now totally confused. But civility prevailed and he turned to introduce the tall stranger standing at his shoulder. "Er... Captain George Stanley. My pilot."

"Your servant, ladies, gentlemen." Stanley bowed. "My great honour to meet such a famous group. I hope I didn't frighten any of you today. Just trying to get a good picture for old Wigger here."

Minnie Burton turned to Dorothy Dalgliesh and whispered, "What stunning good looks, Dot. Lovely long blond hair. Such strong arms."

"Shhh! He'll hear you!" Dorothy cautioned back in a whisper, catching Stanley's eye as she did so. Her faced flushed with embarrassment. She felt so obvious that she was compelled to speak up.

"Captain Stanley, however do you manage one of those things? They look so terribly fragile. As if a breath of wind would break their wings."

"Very easy, Miss Dalgliesh. They're truly easy to fly and much tougher than they look, I assure you. Doesn't take much brains to fly one of those things, otherwise I wouldn't be a pilot! You must let me show you. It'd be me pleasure."

"Oh, Captain Stanley, I should love that!" Dorothy innocently beamed. She was genuinely excited by the thought. "May we all have a go?"

Carnarvon cut in before the captain could answer. "Now just a minute. Let's not get too hasty. These things are not that safe. Don't want to go losing anyone. I think it better we all keep our feet squarely on terra firma. Me for one, anyway, thank you."

"Me too," chimed in Carter. "Got more important things to do below ground. Thanks all the same."

"I understand your feelings, sirs, and respect 'em. If you'd rather not try it I'd be the last to push you." He turned to the ladies. "Really, though, the plane is very safe and very reliable - never had a problem with her."

'Always a first time,' thought Carter, maliciously.

But Dorothy wasn't to be dissuaded. "Well, I really would like to have a go. Even if I am to be the only one. White feathers the lot of you!"

There was some slightly embarrassed giggling from the other two ladies and fairly stern looks from the seated men.

"It will be my great pleasure, Miss Dalgliesh. You will be in the best of hands, I promise you. When would you like to try?"

"Would tomorrow be convenient?"

"Tomorrow it shall be. Let's say ten o'clock. I shall have my beauty all spruced up and ready to receive you. She has never carried a lady before."

Carter wasn't pleased. Worse, he was jealous. But he didn't show it. He'd not felt this kind of emotion before. It confused him and he was not at all good at dealing with feelings he did not understand.

Later, when Dorothy and he were alone, his tone was critical. "No, I don't approve," he told her. "Not the kind of thing for young ladies to be doing. Not right at all."

"Better than sitting under a parasol for hours waiting for you to emerge sweating and grimy from the depths with some new object in your arms," she responded cuttingly. Then, seeing the disappointment in his expression, she placed her hand on his and said, "Sometimes it's worth the wait, however." And she smiled.

He smiled back.

She knew where his thoughts lay now. Fact was, he had very little real time for her. There was just too much else to do. He couldn't afford the preoccupation. Their smiles reflected a mutual understanding.

He kissed her hand and she bade him goodnight. Tomorrow she'd see what he looked like from the air.

While this social banter was taking place Weigall, still recovering from the shocking news that exclusivity of the reporting rights was irrevocably committed, had noticed a man within the group to whom he didn't believe he had been previously introduced. The man was busily writing away on a notepad.

Carnarvon observed Weigall's attention and all at once realised he had been remiss during the original introductions. "Forgive me, Mr Weigall. I forgot Mr Merton of the *London Times*." He waved his arm. "Mr Weigall - Mr Merton."

"A pleasure," noted Merton, distracted from his note-taking.

"All mine," answered Weigall, hiding his distaste.

During this momentary interruption, Merton had noticed that his notebook was being overlooked from behind his chair by a ponderous lady who was extending herself for a better view. He pretended to ignore her and immediately resumed his writing. Within a few moments, the woman pulled herself upright and moved away across the room, fanning herself briskly.

Weigall picked up on this interaction and gestured quizzically at Merton. The reporter turned the face of his notepad towards Weigall. In plain, large and very legible capital letters he had written: 'IT IS UNLADYLIKE AND RUDE TO LOOK OVER A GENTLEMAN'S SHOULDER'.

Weigall laughed; Merton smiled, it was perhaps the only cordial exchange they would ever have, but the intensity of the situation had been softened.

The wind was so fierce in Dorothy's face that she squinted even though she was wearing goggles. As the fragile biplane dipped its wing steeply to the right, she dared herself to look down into The Valley. Like so many foraging ants, people were streaming around in columns along the narrow valley corridors beneath. It was easy to make out where the tomb was situated. There were so many people about the place. It was obviously the spot.

As the little plane wheeled above the dusty crags, she felt a tap on the shoulder and turned her head.

Stanley yelled at her, "Do you want a closer view, Miss Dalgliesh?"

The plane had been bumping from side to side as it flew over the tumbling thermals which rose in waves from the midday oven between the walls of the valley. She was beginning to feel a little queezy. She mouthed words declining the offer but he didn't hear them and, convinced he had read her lips correctly and believing her to be the adventurous kind, he turned the aircraft into a looping, precipitous dive towards the crowd below. Dorothy caught her breath. The yellow ground loomed up towards them and all feelings of sickness were at once extinguished by extreme and unadulterated fear. The engine screamed and she could see the shadow of their plane grow as it plummeted earthwards. As the little aircraft bore down on the crowd, the expressions of alarm in the eyes of the spectators beneath grew ever closer.

Stanley pulled back on the stick and the plane briefly levelled off. To Dorothy it was like a free-falling lift swinging to a sudden stop. The pressure was too much. Involuntarily, she was compelled to discharge her brunch into her lap. But the slipstream caught most of it and an astonished pilot became the unfortunate recipient as glutinous particles of partially digested eggs Benedict splattered across his face and goggles.

The obscenity, however, was secondary. In panic, he clawed at his goggles to clear his vision. They were low in The Valley and the cliffs were close about and above them. He instinctively pushed forward the throttle and pulled up on the stick to climb, not knowing if he was already too late to negotiate the cliffs which, through a slimy fog of congealed albumen and yoke and puréed ham, he now briefly glimpsed. A great wall of solid rock rose directly ahead of him.

The little plane pulled itself almost vertical as it struggled to gain altitude, finally breasting the cliff top and disappearing over the other side. But for the crowd's excited babble, The Valley was left in relative silence.

As Stanley pulled back on the throttle and allowed the biplane to flutter downwards to the first piece of flat land he could find that was sufficient in length for him to land safely, Dorothy threw up again. This time the issue remained with her and her fouled pilot was spared another pasting.

The plane skidded to a furiously dusty stop and Stanley killed the engine. He tore off his goggles and threw them to the ground. The odour all about him was revolting. For the moment, he restrained the urge to clean himself off and called to his passenger. "Miss Dalgliesh! Miss Dalgliesh! Are you all right?"

She was panting too hard to answer. The whole tumbling ride had been quite too much for her to handle. Exciting perhaps, but an ordeal notwith-standing.

Stanley pulled himself out of his seat, threw his leg over the side and placed his foot in the step below her position so that he could assist her. "Miss Dalgliesh! Are you all right?"

She slowly turned to face him and then burst into uncontrollable laughter. Surprised, but at the same time gratified that she was not overly distressed, Stanley lost his precarious purchase on the side of the plane and fell backwards to the ground. When he had gathered his senses and once more pulled himself up to her side, she was still laughing.

"Good God, woman, what in the name of Hades ails you?"

"What a ride, Mr Stanley! What a ride! And you look much the worse for it!"

She started giggling again. Dorothy reached down for her handbag and pulled out her powder compact. She opened it and faced the mirror towards him so that he could see himself. She giggled once more. "I am afraid, Mr Stanley, that I have soiled myself, your plane, and you. I am so sorry. Perhaps I am not so much the air traveller that I had wanted to be."

"You had me very worried there for a moment, Miss Dalgliesh. It was foolish of me to have played such tricks with the aeroplane. Can you ever forgive me?"

"Perhaps we should find somewhere where we can clean up a little. The smell is most unsociable!"

"Can you stand another short flight? It will be the quickest way to the hotel."

"I will give it a try. But mind you fly straight and level this time, Mr Stanley."

"I will indeed, Miss D. I will indeed. I have no wish to be soiled again by the fair hand of a lady."

Dorothy laughed momentarily, then quickly sobered herself as Stanley swung the prop and the engine chugged back to life.

The short flight back to a road close to the hotel was relatively painless. Stanley was doing his best to limit the chances of his receiving another faceful from the gentle maid up front. He had to make a couple of circuits while the fellahs cleared the traffic to allow him to land, but the turns were smooth and gradual and Dorothy felt no further discomfort. There was no bounce when the plane touched down and, within just a few yards, Stanley drew it to a halt. He leapt out and helped his passenger down.

She was a little wobbly in the knees when she first felt herself on terra firma but she soon found her feet. With a brief wave, she got into a horse and carriage that had drawn up in search of a fare and took off towards the hotel.

Stanley, disgusting flying helmet in hand, watched her disappear and then turned back towards his aircraft.

Dorothy was down to the bar first that evening. But, finding Stanley absent and seeing no one else she knew present at the time, she returned to her room to sit and read awhile.

Stanley was still at his toilet. He wanted to be sure he was absolutely purged of the dreadful concoction that had been liberally and indiscriminately sprayed on every part of him during their flight. He had totally immersed himself in fresh baths again and again until he was sure that the water remained clean. He was now at his mirror completing his shaving and oiling his blond hair, combing it straight back over his head without a parting. Finally, he balanced his black bow tie, pulled on his jacket, and departed his room for the bar. Even after such thorough preparation he could not resist stopping a moment and sniffing all about himself before committing himself to descend the stairs. As he turned the corner and took the handrail of the staircase, he heard his name called from behind.

"Mr Stanley! Wherever have you been all this time?"

"Miss Dalgliesh," he acknowledged in surprise "My, you look lovely tonight." He bowed.

"I know," she quipped, trying to prise a more relaxed reaction from him. "Not difficult after the way I appeared just a couple of hours ago."

Stanley, not used to such a show of temerity in a woman, was for a moment at a loss for words. "I, er... I did mean what I said, Miss Dalgliesh."

"I know. Dot. Please call me Dot."

"Dot it shall be. Likewise I would be most grateful if you could call me George."

"George, then, it shall be. And what shall we do this evening, George?"

This was most destabilising for Stanley. The pilot was quite unused to ladies of so forward a nature. He grappled with how he might regain the high ground in this conversation. He needn't have overly concerned himself. Dorothy was quite prepared to submit when the time was right. But he couldn't read the signs and, to be fair, she wasn't making them all that clear.

She had already thought through the consequences of leaving Carter to the splendid isolation of his work. She had no option. That course had been decided for them both the moment he had stepped into the antechamber. Whatever had been maturing before would be placed in suspended animation. There were no options. The task before him was so vast and so important that he could do nothing else. God only knew how many years it would be before they could visit one another again without his being entirely preoccupied with thoughts of what still lay beyond the threshold of that, or any other dark, stone doorway.

'So, that aside, let's see what this George Stanley is really like,' she thought.

"I have to know. Have you managed to excavate every fragment of my breakfast from every crease in your skin? Do you feel finally cleansed?"

"Thank you, yes, Dot. I must confess it was an ordeal I have no wish to repeat."

"Me neither," she giggled. "I don't know how I may make amends, George. Have you forgiven me?"

"Of course, Dot. It was my fault, after all, for being such an ass and flying with such lack of consideration. It is I who needs your forgiveness."

"Forgiven you most surely are, George. And tomorrow - if you have the time - I should like to try again. But not in The Valley this time. Perhaps a more sedate flight to oversee some other points of interest that do not require such airborne gymnastics to get a good eyeful."

"Well! You are the brave one. I don't believe I have ever met such an adventurous lady. And I will be only too pleased to take you up tomorrow. We shall fly down river to Abydos. Take a picnic. Spend the day there. Just tell me when you would like to leave. Any time. Your choice."

"Abydos... I have heard Howard speak of that place but he never took me there. I should love to see it! How about ten o'clock?"

"We shall meet for breakfast at nine."

"Remind me not to have eggs Benedict."

"Stop that scratching! It won't get any better if you keep picking at it like that." Lady Carnarvon had not had the greatest of evenings and the sight of her husband, in full evening dress, glass of brandy in one hand, a cigar clipped firmly between a couple of outstretched fingers, the other scratching away at a pimple on his chin, exacerbated her testy state of mind.

"The cursed thing itches, madam. Don't spoil my only comfort. It's the only way for me to turn pain into pleasure."

Carter mumbled something under his breath.

"What... what was that you said, Howard?"

"Mmm? Nothing, sir. Thinking out loud. Bad habit of mine."

"Something troubling you, Howard?"

Yes, there was something troubling him. There was a great deal troubling him. His early excitement had taken second place to the reality of the situation. He had become so troubled with the enormity of the work that lay ahead and the huge responsibility that went with his stewardship that sometimes, in the privacy of his own room, he would literally shake in panic.

"I, er... I confess, your lordship. I sometimes wonder whether I am equal to the task that lies ahead of me."

"Something you're forgeting, Howard, m' boy. It's not 'me', it's 'us'. You have a lot of the most authoritative, willing and able help - a veritable army of expertise at your beck and call. An archaeological force the like of which the world has not before beheld - and is never likely to again, I'll be bound. Not all in one place."

The earl's remarks notwithstanding, this evening Carter was convinced that the entire burden was his, and felt too sorry for himself to be receptive.

"Sir. I could do with an early night."

Carter got up to return to the west bank and get some sleep. He took his leave of Evelyn and smiled a condescending grin at the earl. His patron gave an affectionate but rather limp wave and Carter turned and left the room. Wrapped up in the multitude of worries that weighed heavily on his mind, Carter could have been forgiven for not noticing the outward signs.

Weigall's frustration was written all over his face. At breakfast that morning, spooning sugar into his coffee, he regarded the ceiling thoughtfully. At the tenth spoonful he looked down at the cup. The coffee had overflowed a little into the saucer. Cursing under his breath he stirred it slowly, wiped the bottom of the cup against the rim of the saucer and raised the cup to his lips. He grimaced in distaste and slapped the cup down noisily into the swimming saucer, splashing coffee onto the tablecloth. He called for the waiter to bring a clean cup and saucer.

The journalist fell back to thinking: 'What the hell am I going to do about this?' He had to find a way around Carnarvon's and Carter's stranglehold on current information, otherwise his presence at the site was almost a total waste of his time and the *Daily Mail*'s money.

The photos he had attempted during the infamous overflight with Stanley had turned out to be unusable. The speed and vibration of the biplane had together conspired to return only blurred images. Just about nothing was going right.

As he continued to indulge his personal feelings of melancholy, his nemesis walked into the restaurant and took a table in the far corner. It was enough to put him off the remainder of his breakfast. He pushed his plate to one side, gulped down his coffee, and rose to leave.

As he picked up his hat Carnarvon spotted him and beckoned him over. Angry though he was, it would have been most impolite to ignore the invitation.

"Mr Weigall! Good morning. And how are you today?"

"Good morning to you, your lordship. I am well, thank you." The reporter's reply was without emotion. "And yourself?"

"To tell you the truth, sir, a little out of sorts today. Not at all tip-top."

"I am sorry to hear that, your lordship." The response was quite genuine. Weigall had already observed that the earl looked somewhat sallow.

"Oh, I am sure it will pass. Something I ate. The water, probably. Should follow me own creed and stick to the wine, don't y' know!" he smiled.

Weigall softened and returned the smile. "How are things going at the clearance, your lordship?"

"Rather slowly, sir. Rather slowly. So much stuff. Much in a parlous state of preservation. Carter and his merry men are spending more time in the lab than in the tomb. Still, mustn't complain. All necessary work. Carter says he should be ready to open the burial chamber in a week or so." The earl quickly corrected himself. "At least, that's what he thinks the next sealed door might lead to."

"Indeed? Well, we all look forward to that."

The earl's eyes suddenly lit up as his daughter entered the restaurant and came over to join them.

"Lady Evelyn!" greeted Weigall. "Good morning. I trust you slept well."

"Mr Weigall," Evelyn acknowledged.

Weigall drew back the seat opposite Carnarvon and assisted Evelyn in taking her place at the table. "Lovely to see you both, but I must be off. The work of a journalist is ever current."

"Indeed, sir," said Carnarvon. "Hard and sometimes frustrating work it must be at times," he added knowingly.

Weigall didn't need to be reminded, least of all by the source of his frustration.

"By the way, sir," the earl continued, "Mace and Carter told me last night that they soon expect to have enough material to compile a volume on the progress this season. They plan to publish sometime later this year. It'll be crammed full of Burton's plates. You'll probably want to obtain an early copy. Thought you'd like to know."

"Of course, your lordship." Weigall, a little startled at this news, was at a loss for words.

"I'll ask him to send you one."

"Thank you, your lordship. Most kind." And the reporter quickly took his leave of father and daughter and walked briskly from the room.

As he got into the carriage to begin his journey to the west bank, it dawned on him. Why not publish his own popular work and take advantage of current public excitement? He had published before and was well known as a writer. Carter was not. Carter and Mace's book should nevertheless be an instant success. Why not publish a parallel commentary on the back of their success? No doubt theirs would be expensive. He could make his competitively priced.

A capital idea! He congratulated himself. And, when he arrived at the site, the prospect of another long day's wait outside in the heat for once did not seem quite so unbearable. *(Weigall published his work in November, 1923 the same month that Carter and Mace's first volume went on sale. It appears intentionally crafted to much the same size and thickness as the other, with about the same number of pages. Even the dust cover, at first glance, has a similar layout to the Carter-Mace volume. Although Weigall credited the tomb's find to Carter, reference to his adversary is decidedly understated in the text. The book was published competitively at fifteen shillings. The Carter-Mace volume went to the book stores priced at thirty-one shillings and six pence: see Weigall, 1923).*

Carter was busy and focused on his work as usual as he supervised the labourers carrying trays of objects from the depths of the tomb. He passed Weigall several times that day, but not once did he notice the reporter's uncharacteristic grin.

By February, the antechamber had been largely cleared and they were ready to confront the mud brick and plaster doorway that stood between them and the burial chamber. Carter and Mace had together constructed wooden shields to protect the black gesso and gilt statues, which to that point still remained in the antechamber, and a wooden platform at the threshold of the doorway itself. The step was just high enough to obscure evidence of the breech which the surreptitious four had made less than three months earlier. Once Carter had dismantled the doorway, the evidence would be destroyed for ever.

But that was the easy bit. The hard part was keeping knowledge of the big event from all the press. That voracious rabble thronged about the entrance to the tomb most of the day, and it was only after lunch, when the heat became unbearable and metabolisms slowed, that the crowds began to thin out.

It was such a time that Carter chose for the official opening. Those fortunate through their office to be selected arrived to the total surprise of the few remaining diehard reporters still at their posts on the wall above. Before a camera shutter had clicked, the party of invitees had assembled themselves in the specially arranged seating in the cleared antechamber beneath. Those left above could only wonder.

"Your Majesty, your Lordship, your Excellencies, ladies and gentlemen. Please excuse my informality but I am sure you will understand why I must strip for action."

Carter asked Carnarvon, who was sitting in front with the Queen of the Belgians, to hold his hat, then his jacket, then his waistcoat, then his tie, then his shirt. He pulled the tail of his long-sleeved vest out of his trousers and let it fall comfortably loose about his waist. Thus prepared, he mounted the step, took a crowbar from Mace and began to chisel away at the bricks in the upper left corner of the door. The plaster fell to the platform in many differently sized pieces. Mace would do his best to catch every one, but now and then pieces would crash to the wooden step and thence in smaller fragments to the floor. As each brick loosened, Mace quickly took hold of it to prevent it from falling inward and possibly damaging the shrine. He lifted each brick carefully from the wall and stacked them on the floor of the antechamber.

After most of the bricks had been removed but before the entrance was clear, Burton called to Carter to stop for a moment so that he might record the event in progress. Carter, now only too willing to act the showman and at the same time glad of a breather, complied. He stood motionless on the left side of the doorway, Arthur Mace to his right, until Burton signalled that he had finished the exposure.

The two turned back to their tasks. Within the next twenty minutes they had the door completely cleared. They stood back so that the illumination from Burton's floodlights shone into the burial chamber. The seated audience was silent; speechless at the sight that blazed back at them. Within a metre of the doorway and completely filling it stood a wall of engraved gold and inlaid blue glass. Everyone was awestruck, including Carter, who himself had squeezed by this wall just three months earlier.

Two large, golden utchat eyes stared back at the onlookers. The brilliance and the sternness of the stare held the audience's attention. No one spoke a word.

Carter broke the silence. "Your Majesty, your Lordship, excellencies, ladies and gentlemen - the burial chamber!" he announced, and swung his arm wide with ceremony. "Please retain your seats while I investigate. I will return to escort each one of you once I have ascertained the lie of the land, so to speak."

Carter stepped carefully down inside the chamber and disappeared to the right between the wall of the room and the enormous golden shrine. There was an expectant hush upon the crowd within the antechamber as each strained to hear Carter's scuffling footsteps disturbing the dust of ages. He wasn't long away and, reappearing at the doorway, he beckoned to Carnarvon and Lacau to advance.

"I am afraid it will have to be just two at a time. There is barely enough room to turn around in here and we don't want to damage anything with a careless step."

Carter kicked the remaining rubble from the wooden platform and helped the two over the step.

Lacau turned the corner and spotted the prone jackal on its bier, the decomposed shawl still about its neck. He tugged thoughtfully at his great, grey beard. He turned back towards the earl who was close behind, hoping to catch his reaction. For himself, having seen these sights some weeks earlier, Carnarvon was likewise intent on catching the reaction of the French inspector ahead of him. As their eyes met, the shy grandee looked away and nervously scratched at the scab on his chin.

Carter's canary died that night. Callender, who had been sleeping there alone, was saddened at his own stupidity in leaving it caged in what had clearly been an accessible place. But Carter, when he was told, dismissed the event as trivial. There was far too much else on his mind.

Callender, nevertheless, deeply regretted his carelessness and retained a sense of personal guilt which he could only extinguish by applying himself selflessly to hard work in the tomb.

Carter had committed himself to catalogue, preserve and clear the objects in the tomb with all the thoroughness that the technology of the day permitted. There were a myriad of things to do and keep track of. He didn't have to worry about Burton, other than the seemingly unending time the photographer took to get his pictorial record to the level of perfection he demanded. However, coordinating the activities of the others was an exacting and very necessary task. But far worse and totally wasteful of his time and talents was the energy he had to devote to scheduling visits by various VIPs, few of whom knew or really cared the foggiest for the research he was engaged in. This became an all too frequent and time-consuming occupation.

The nights in Luxor were so frenzied with visitors and reporters wishing to talk with him that after only a few days he kept himself closeted away on the west bank, unless it became necessary to take the train to Cairo for procurement of additional supplies.

More or less everyone intimately involved in the project was becoming an irritation to him, even his patron, and he no less to them. Carter, in his focused concentration, continued to be insensitive to the reactions of those around him. In particular, he was quite oblivious to the effect he was having on the earl. It was not about to get any better while they stayed in such close proximity to each other, day in and day out.

"If you don't mind my saying so, you were a bit unnecessarily vocal with the press yesterday." Carnarvon was compelled to correct his intolerant colleague whom he felt, quite justifiably from his point of view, lacked the social basis and skills to be accomplished in the generally accepted rules of etiquette, diplomacy and tact. Alien as it was to Carter, this code was at the same time a way of life to most of the VIPs with whom he was now forced to associate.

It was an unfortunate time for the earl to bring this to his colleague's attention. And on this occasion his lordship had chosen the wrong place, the wrong time *and* the wrong pitch. It was approaching the end of the working day. Carter was in the laboratory tomb. He had been delayed all morning by unexpected and unwanted additional visitors authorised, if not by the authorities themselves, by their individual station in society - in Carter's eyes a circumstantial and insignificant qualification. To add to his distress, the heat of the afternoon had reached a level that was almost unbearable. Due to the interruptions and the conditions he was having to endure, he was, therefore, hot, dirty, tired, frustrated and irritable.

He was anxious to complete clearance and renovation before the profusion of remaining artefacts became irreversibly degraded by the effects of intrusion. But it had dawned on him that, with the sheer volume of material, he could be doing this one thing in this one valley in this one small hole in the ground for the next few years - perhaps five, perhaps more. It was, at that jaded moment, more than he cared to contemplate.

And then this privileged aristocrat - luckily born to his fortune, with little to do but look for sources of amusement with which to lighten his otherwise pampered but melancholy existence - was arrogant and insensitive enough to suppose that to mention this correction at this particular time was more important than the work at hand. In Carter's mind the grandee couldn't have brought to his attention anything less trivial. So trivial, indeed, it might have remained ignored. But unfortunately the earl didn't stop there.

"...And while I'm on the subject," continued Carnarvon, "you need to watch the way you behave with Evelyn. There is an indelicacy in the manner in which you sometimes address her in the company of others - particularly the press. They would love to make a story out of it. In view of their frustration with my arrangement with *The Times* I'm surprised they haven't picked up on it already."

It became finally too much for Carter to contain his silence.

"I can't believe I'm hearing this from you, sir. Dammit, sir, you've a... you've a brass nerve! And I've no time for it. Take your self-indulgent concerns and leave this place before I do something we'll both be eternally sorry for."

He stabbed a forefinger in the direction of the way out and turned back to his work.

The loudness and aggressiveness of Carter's delivery, amplified as it was in the confining stone walls of the tomb corridor, took his well-meaning patron by surprise. Carnarvon was set back on his heels and quickly had to adjust the position of his walking stick to avoid losing his balance.

Carter's posture at the trestle table was a statement of finality. He turned his back on his patron and readdressed the piece before him. His arched back presented the earl with a defiant expression of dismissal.

Carnarvon stood where he was for a moment. Try as he could, there was no way for him to come up with the appropriate words. He was hurt. Not so much by Carter's outburst, but more so because he had somehow offended the colleague with whom he had suffered so many years of hard work and relative disappointment. He who had at last brought him excitement and fame beyond all expectation.

But, for the present, his strength wasn't up to dealing with the situation. He sputtered something unintelligible, turned, and slowly walked out into the darkening valley.

Alone once more, Carter paused his labours for a moment. He blew at the piece in front of him and picked up a brush to dust off the crevices between the glass inlay and the gold. The strokes were gentle and considerate, but the grip was tighter than necessary and the whites of his knuckles revealed his innermost feelings. He dropped the brush, gazed up at the ceiling, and sighed.

The incident weighed heavily on the sensitive earl. His heart was bursting with emotion. He felt a strong sense of urgency to bring this disagreeable moment to a peaceful end.

Out of the blue, and all the more strangely since his patron was staying just across the river from Carter's house, the following day Carter received a letter from the earl.

He read it quickly, then methodically replaced the letter in the envelope and stared ahead, unseeing, at the wall. His lordship's tone had been pleading, apologetic, full of hurt. It was difficult to move a person like Howard Carter, but on this occasion his eyes were glistening with tears. He pushed the envelope into his jacket pocket and walked outside to the car. This once, he had to go over to the east bank. This once, he had to reaffirm his attachment to the earl. He couldn't bear the thought that the grandee could be in any doubt about the enormous debt Carter felt he owed the man, and about the closeness of his undemonstrated attachment.

After exchanging brief pleasantries, and before the earl had time to gather breath, Carter launched into a humble monologue.

"Your lordship, I received your letter this evening and had to come over to you straight away." He took a breath as if to recharge his delivery, but the pause was still too little for Carnarvon to interject. "I realise I have been merciless in my quest for this tomb. I have been and continue to be wholly preoccupied with its preservation. I am sure you understand all this. But clearly, in my determination to see the job done, I have unknowingly ignored the feelings of those most dear to me and without whose support I could never - never in a thousand years - have come this far. In the weeks and months and years ahead - for I believe it will be years before this job is done to our satisfaction - I am sure I will continue to act in the same way I have to this point - a way that has clearly hurt you, even to the point that what you feel may damage our relationship. But you must understand me, sir. Whatever I may say, whatever I may do or forget to do - the lack of a 'thank you' for a favour bestowed, the absence of response to a question the answer to which is so obvious to myself - these are the traits of Howard Carter, a Norfolk artist's son, who made a quest of the scarce his life's work and has now, with your help, come upon the greatest find - by far - of all time. I am devoted to this work - my mind, my heart, my very soul. All of my energies I give to this work. It has to be done right. We cannot risk any carelessness that might rob future generations of this experience - the experience of witnessing what we are most privileged to see now. In another thousand years, to our succeeding generations, these objects must appear as fresh as they do today. Our great good fortune has brought us the heaviest of responsibilities. I am totally consumed by this urgent need to focus my energies, and because of myself I appear, perhaps on occasion, rude to those who love..." he paused, "and I love." He paused again. "...and support me. I cannot help it. I urge your understanding. I know I can and will not change my ways. Yet none of my actions belittles my strongest regard for you and my deepest gratitude for your support all these years... Please forgive me..." He paused again, slightly longer this time. "... and please let me be."

Carnarvon nodded his understanding with a gentle smile and touched Carter on the arm. The two knew they would have problems henceforward but, having cleared the air between them, each now would be internally sympathetic to the preoccupation of the other.

But not Dorothy. She had been seated at the adjoining table. She had overheard the conversation. She briskly gathered up her silk shawl and left the room.

Carter, still staring into his patron's eyes, hadn't noticed.

"Let's seal the tomb, close the lab, and take a few days off."

Carter's welcome words came as he reported for work the following morning.

"It's been wonderful but a bloody strain at the same time, and if we keep at it like this we shall all get sick and everything will suffer as a consequence. We all need a break... and perhaps a little solitude." In this regard he spoke for himself.

Mace and Lucas were already at their labours, but they eagerly accepted Carter's suggestion and both quickly finished what they were doing, and then assisted Carter with the 'lock up'.

Carnarvon had been feeling out of sorts for some days now. Each evening he went to bed he thought he would be feeling better by morning, but each morning he felt the same - some mornings a little worse.

A jumble of divergent thoughts were tumbling through his mind. He was perhaps coming down with something and he should see a doctor. He was still melancholy and overly reflective after what had so recently transpired between himself and his industrious colleague. A break in contact would be welcomed by both of them.

With so much wealth already uncovered in the tomb and riches many fold yet to come, he had some pressing unfinished business to settle in Cairo. Even though he hardly felt up to the trip, he must clarify with the Director of Antiquities, once and for all, a mutually satisfactory mechanism for the division.

To attend to these concerns, he decided to take the train that very evening. He welcomed Evelyn's company on the journey. He was feeling weak, tired and lonely, and she brought him comfort. She had insisted on coming in any case. The deterioration in his mood and pallor was entirely visible to her and she fully understood that with his inadequate physical resources he required much closer attention than most. His health could slip so easily to a stage beyond help. So it was that she ensured their first business in Cairo was with his physician.

It was clear to the doctor that the earl was unwell, but he could not yet confirm a diagnosis. While he took time to ponder the symptoms, the doctor provided the earl with a tonic and some stern advice to rest.

With a considerable degree of determination quite disproportionate to his weakness, and ignoring the silent, unseen, viral cocktail brewing in his blood, the following evening Carnarvon went to the moving picture theatre for some entertainment.

Carter hadn't even noticed the earl's absence from Luxor. But Evelyn's first letter brought him back to reality with a bang.

Porchy looks really awful. He is so much more pale than usual. He is really seedy, Howard. He won't obey the doctor. He insists on dining out each night and returns to his bed totally washed out. I fear it will not be too long before he cannot get out of his bed. Perhaps a forced rest will help him recover, but quite frankly I fear for him. Do come, Howard dear. Do come to help me put some sense into him. He will listen to you.

Carter read the letter a second time, then folded it up and stuffed it into his coat pocket.

"Abdel!" he shouted. "Pack my things. I take the morning train to Cairo."

The following morning, while Carter was crossing the river on his way to catch the train, Carnarvon was at his toilet, preparing himself for his important meeting with Lacau. This morning he felt still worse than the last. Nevertheless he was determined to confront Monsieur le Directeur and get this negotiation successfully behind him.

As Carnarvon arrived, Lacau's imposing figure filled the door to the Antiquities Service building. The director quickly stepped down to help the earl up the stairs. The general appearance of the man and the weight that Lacau felt on his arm were sign enough that the earl was not himself.

"Some water, your lordship?"

"Thank you, Monsieur le Directeur. I apologise. I feel somewhat out of sorts today."

Lacau led the earl to a soft leather chair and poured him a glass of water.

"I am very sorry to hear that, monsieur. It is no doubt the strain. In these circumstances it must have been an immense effort to come all this way. We could always meet another time, when you are more yourself."

"No." Carnarvon was quite direct in his reply. "No." He took a breath. "The season is all but over and I must return to England. But before I do so there is some business of great importance to us both which we must conclude."

"You are talking of 'the division', are you not, sir?"

"I am." Carnarvon took a longer breath. The effort was enormous. He could feel his strength draining by the minute.

"As you know, while it might appear clear in the concession document that for an undisturbed tomb the objects are to be reserved to the State of Egypt, this tomb, replete as it is with the most wonderful things, has been disturbed - at least twice - in antiquity. Some..."

Lacau could see that the earl was struggling for breath and broke in. "Your lordship. Please forgive my interruption but I am aware of what you are trying to say. I, myself, have given this much thought in recent weeks. I have discussed it at length with my superiors in government and we have already reached our decision. So, to save you the energy and the time let me say this:

Please be assured that the Carnarvon estate will be permitted a generous share of the artefacts."

The earl visibly relaxed back into his chair.

"This I can promise, but not in writing. You are appraised, I know, of the political upheavals which have become a part of everyday life in Egypt - in Cairo in particular. Like it or not, we are guests in their country, and while we - each of us - contribute greatly to its well-being, it is an unavoidable fact that we remain foreigners in a foreign land and can expect to be treated as such. So, any official word that relates to foreign possession of Egyptian artefacts - no, riches - will immediately ignite anger and repercussions which neither of us would wish to be a party to. This means that the Nationalist Party must not - must not - have proof of this arrangement. It must remain verbal and solely between ourselves. Do you agree, sir?"

Carnarvon nodded.

"Thank you, monsieur. I could not have wished for more."

"I, too. I am gratified that you are content with this informal arrangement."

The earl was exhausted. It seemed to him the more so for his relief at hearing Lacau's reassuring words. He struggled to get up to leave.

The director came to his aid once more and helped him back to his car. Lacau shook hands with the earl through the car window and bid him, "Bon chance." He waved as the vehicle moved slowly off into the mass of thronging pedestrians. As he turned back towards his office, he stopped for a moment. "Peut-être," he sighed under his breath and disappeared inside.

Carnarvon slept a deep sleep, the discomfort of pneumonia notwithstanding. The congestion caused him to cough now and again, but this night it didn't appear to bring him to consciousness. Yet his eyes were open, staring at the ceiling.

Carter was in the room next door and heard him move. He got up and headed for the bedroom door. By the time he had reached Carnarvon's side Evelyn was already there, holding her father's hand tightly. He didn't move his head, but his eyes, full of tears, flicked from one to the other. His lips quivered for a moment and he murmured something indistinct. Before either of them could speak, he fell back to sleep.

Back at the excavation, the doors were secured for the summer recess and the staircase had been filled with rubble and sand and tamped down with water. Below, the darkened cavity was silent once more. Over the coming months of peace, the dust which still remained buoyant in the atmosphere would be allowed time to settle softly on the objects beneath.

As Carter's party had left it, the antechamber was empty but for a couple of alabaster vases, a wooden figure of a black swan, the remains of a few rush baskets and the two life-size black and gold sentinels which still impassionately faced each other either side the opened doorway to the burial chamber and its golden shrine. But for the tiny pieces that the privileged party had secreted in their pockets on that first night of exploration and the treasures already removed to Cairo, all else that the tomb contained remained untouched and perched in rearranged stillness as it had been for centuries.

Thousands of miles away to the west, beneath an inclined marble tablet on a treeless hill overlooking Highclere House, the same darkness, the same silence enclosed the long oblong casket within. The final resting place of George Edward Stanhope Molyneux Herbert, Lord Porchester at least had this in common with Tutankhamen's resting place.

This had been an event of the greatest significance. To Carter, the loss of a vital ally. Quite apart from the money, the earl had been the only man in the team who matched experience with standing more than sufficient to deal with the politics of any situation - an area that Carter would never be able to handle effectively, much less want to. As for the money, he felt confident that it would still be there once Almina, the Lady Carnarvon, got over the shock.

To the world's newspaper-reading public, stories surrounding the circumstances of the grandee's death - the lights reportedly extinguishing in Cairo and at Highclere at the moment he expired; the coincidental death of Suzy, his fox terrier - became undeniable evidence that a curse existed upon the tomb. Continued activity, they avidly reported, would surely lead to more deaths.

The Egyptologist, intent on completing the immense task ahead of him, never gave it more of a thought than to decry it in the text of the first volume of his book on the discovery which, with considerable help from Arthur Mace, he completed during the succeeding summer in England.

Carter now had a heavy additional responsibility, discounting the other current extraneous complications, heavier even than his task in The Valley. Lady Carnarvon had written to ask him - no, it was more than that - order him to hasten to Highclere to act as executor of his lordship's collection of Egyptian antiquities.

He complied dutifully, notwithstanding the work of planning the forthcoming clearance of the tomb, and turned up at the elegant front door of that great place within a month of receiving her request.

"My lady," he started, "it is with great sadness and a very heavy heart that I visit this house today."

"I understand, Howard." She gestured to the butler. "Tea, Robert, if you please." She turned back to Carter.

"After tea, Howard, I wish you to begin the cataloguing and valuation of our entire collection. Then you must arrange to remove it to some safe holding place. The Bank of England, perhaps. I must sell it - sell it all - in its entirety. I cannot bear to have it about me. The constant reminder. You understand, of course?"

No, Carter could not wholly grasp her ladyship's situation. His first love was and always would be for the objects. They were permanent, trustworthy, unpretentious; there to be appreciated for what they were, unlike people who, on balance, were quite otherwise. Besides, he had more than an academic attraction to the collection. He had helped Carnarvon build much of it over the many years of their close association. He felt he had almost as much right to possess it as his benefactor.

He had been thrown off balance. It was as if, quite out of his control, a great asset of his was to be taken from him. His initial reaction was to take his leave on some pretence, but for the life of him he could not think up a sufficiently plausible reason. In any event, if he would not help, her ladyship would get someone else to fulfil her wishes; better him than any other.

He bumbled a response, "I... I understand, your ladyship. But... may I be so bold as to ask... why... why at this particular moment? Why now? We have not yet completed the work his lordship began."

"Howard, you must understand. I have thought long and hard on this. While this stuff is about me, I see him. I see him wandering about, looking at it, touching it. He fondles it. He kisses it. He even talks to it. Howard, I cannot stand these thoughts any more. I just cannot stand to see him when he is not in reality with us any more. You do understand me, do you not?"

Carter was slow to reply. "I... I do think I understand, your ladyship. I think I understand your feelings. The hard part for me - to be bluntly honest - is... is to contemplate the break-up of this great collection. The years of sheer hard labour..."

Carter paused. He knew he was beginning to overstep the mark. Lady Carnarvon said nothing. At last he capitulated. "I will sell it. As you wish. It will be done. It will be done," Carter repeated, as if to confirm he had indeed made the decision himself.

"Thank you, Howard. Porchy will be most grateful. I know he will."

She turned her head away from Carter's and quietly whimpered into her handkerchief.

Carter, with everything else that was on his mind, became more embarrassed than he could stand. "I will begin at once, your ladyship."

He removed himself from the drawing room and, pocketbook already in hand, advanced towards the rooms containing the great collection. He did not look back.

Carter quickly became engrossed in the task. Within minutes he was oblivious to anything but the articles displayed before him. He walked over to a glass-covered tray. Inside were small pieces, none of them as grand as the larger articles already retrieved from the tomb, but several in themselves individually magnificent.

"He would have wanted you to have that." Lady Carnarvon was standing behind him.

"Your ladyship?"

"That one. I don't know where he got it from but I know he wanted you to have it, Howard."

She pointed to a tiny, carved ivory horse lying on its side on the floor of the cabinet.

That melancholy summer in England he received a second gift. When he returned to his lodgings in London, a small brown-paper parcel, cross-bound with string, the knots secured with ceiling wax, awaited him on his hall table. It was a copy of the privately printed edition of *Seven Pillars of Wisdom*. *(see Lawrence, 1935)*.

Chapter Twenty One
Bandits

The death of Lord Carnarvon was attracting a good deal of alarmist publicity. In the royal party's celestial home this was cause for a good deal of celebration. Successfully fuelled by a plethera of frustrated journalists, there was developing amongst the news-hungry public a steadily maturing craving for the supernatural. The stories, amounting to no more than speculative conjecture, had been communicated virtually worldwide. Tutankhamun had become witness to many conversations concerning the various stories written by newspaper reporters in the United States, Great Britain, and in several European countries. There had been headline articles in India, Hong Kong, Australia and New Zealand. Most chose to conclude that there must be some truth in the curse. Clearly this new public had an insatiable appetite for the occult. To the king, the nature of the response was most gratifying.

Unlike the reading public, however, his scholarly victims, busily planning their next season's evil work in The Valley, did not appear to be so quick to make any connection with the supernatural. And the king knew it would not be long before Carter would return to attack the shrines. If the royal couple were to succeed in their endeavours to block further violation of the tomb, there was still a great deal to do.

The efforts of his entourage extended far and wide. Meneg and his colleagues were attempting to influence the authorities in Cairo. Ankhesenamun spent her time repetitively entering the dreams of the more impressionable on the team, although now that it was summer the team was separated, each member attending to his own personal business in England. Her hauntings had little effect. Each insomniac put the occurrences down to stress or the emotional eagerness to return the following season, and thought no more of it. Tutankhamun spent most of his time closely observing Carter. He wanted to learn more about the man who was so hell-bent on breaking into the shrines and exposing the king's earthly remains. This small foreigner was not at all like the robbers of Tutankhamun's own era; unlike, even, those other alien plunderers of just one hundred years ago. Both he and his colleagues had, to a fault, been gentle and respectful in their handling of the grave goods. There had been no hurry to their work. He had witnessed no wilful damage. Each object taken from the holy sepulchre had been painstakingly preserved and carried with the greatest care to exhibition in Cairo. In the museum halls, the common people were now permitted to look upon but not to touch the possessions of a royal.

It was not a little puzzling to him. Why did they not sell what they stole? Why not strip the gold for profit? There was appreciation, admiration, even respect in the way they addressed each object. They appeared intent on preserving everything, even the desiccated bouquets. Those earthly blooms had drooped and fallen just a few days after the ceremonies had finished. Now shrunken and dried to a crisp, they could crumble to powder at a touch. Tutankhamun would watch fascinated as Lucas and Mace spent hours treating the fragile stems where they lay until they were sufficiently held together to be moved without damage. All this just for the common people to share?

Notwithstanding the violators' apparent good intentions, careful and reverent as they were, their ultimate course was self-evident - they were driven towards exposure of the king's remains. Of that he was certain. That the king's naked body should become paraded before the general public was absolutely unthinkable; that it be removed from its place of rest unacceptable. The thought made him tremble. He looked down again.

Carter was in England visiting Mace in his lodgings. The two sat at either side of a broad partners' desk, the top liberally spread with papers. They were busily comparing notes on the first volume of their book.

"I can't get over how much you've been able to complete in such a short time, Arthur. Don't know what I'd have done without your help. After all said and done, it looks like we'll get this thing published before we take off back to Egypt."

Mace turned to face his colleague. He smiled for a moment in acknowledgement of Carter's appreciative remarks, but then his expression hardened. "Howard," he began deliberately. "There is no easy way to say this. This coming season will be the last for me. After 1925 I doubt if I'll see The Valley again."

Carter drew back from the desk but said nothing. He stared incredulously at his friend. "But... but there's more than a year's work, man. You can't be serious!"

"Doctor's orders, I'm afraid. Hadn't been feeling too good during the last few weeks in Luxor. Decided to consult my physician when I got back. His conclusions were difficult to take - need to keep out of harm's way... not supposed to return to the Middle East... possibly not too much time left." Mace's last words faded to a whisper.

For a few moments neither man spoke. Carter was in shock. After a seemingly interminable pause he said, "My God, Arthur, what am I going to do without you? In my most desperate hours of need, first his lordship, then you? I will be unable to cope. I feel deserted, man. How am I to carry on without you?" he repeated as if to himself.

"Howard, old boy. Y' know damn well you have the best team of experts ever assembled for the task. You won't need my help as much as you did in the early days. You and I took on the initial work almost single-handedly. Now you have a well-organised, well-equipped team of professionals to take you through to the end. That is," Mace mused, as if to put a lighter complexion on the conversation, "as long as you don't bollocks it up by pissing any of them off through the single-bloody-mindedness you know you are prone to, and force any more of them to walk off the job! You won't miss me that much, but I'd agree with you on one thing, I don't think you can afford to lose anyone else."

There was a decided finality in Mace's statement. Carter knew there would be no way he could persuade him otherwise and it would be cruelly uncharitable of him to attempt to do so.

Mace smiled. "But I wouldn't miss the opening - doctor or no doctor. I'll be there this coming season, make no mistake."

They raised their glasses together and wished each other good health. Their glasses touched. Just out of their field of view there was a movement. For a split second a sequined mixture of gold, azure and red ochre sparkled on the facets of their cut-glass tumblers. Mace noticed it. Much like one of the many visions he had had of late. But, seeing no spark of recognition in the face of his colleague, he thought the better of mentioning it.

"What have they done for us that is to our advantage? Nothing! What have they done to us that is repressive? Much!"

There were nods of assention and considerable thumping on the tables in the smoke-filled bar. The speaker was a tall black man. As he emphasised his point, his white teeth and the whites of his eyes flashed eerily from the shadows .

"They don't have our culture - they don't believe in our God - even less do they understand."

Murmurs of agreement.

"They take, our men for labour; our women for housemaids; our works of art, ancient and modern, back to their own country, but they give nothing back. The rape must be stopped!"

"Vote Nationalist!"

A shout from an unrecognised source at the back of the small bar-room was all that was needed to bring everyone to their feet. The entire group spilled out into the street chanting the name of the new political party.

This was not quite what the proprietor had wanted. Up to that point, business had been remarkably good. All at once the place was deserted, and several bills remained unpaid.

Ugele and his friends had spent many fruitful days about the markets and official hallways of government in Cairo inciting disquiet amongst all kinds of Egyptians in all walks of life. Just as he was beginning to enjoy the carousing in the street, he felt a familiar touch from behind. He was compelled to leave.

366

"You have done well, Ugele," said the queen quietly. "It is time for us to sit back and observe the seeds you have sown and so carefully fertilised. Let us watch them germinate and flourish. We look forward to an angry harvest!"

Over the following few weeks, as the elections approached, and to the great satisfaction of the spiritual onlookers, there was much ado in Cairo - clashes between the crowds and the police, the looting of some shops, the burning of some vehicles, a few killings even. It was all great publicity for the Nationalist opposition. The people were clearly unhappy. The current administration had to go. And go they did.

With the investiture ceremonies over and a new cabinet in place the royal party focused its attention on the newly appointed Minister for Public Works. This particular governmental position had authority over the antiquities of Egypt, the country's manifestly bountiful heritage, and was charged with a responsibility almost as great as that of the Ministry of Defence. As it happened, however, the new Minister cared little for the value of his country's great historical treasure trove. Rather, he looked upon his position as a wonderfully public opportunity to harass and hopefully eject the foreign element in his country, particularly the British, and he was determined to exercise that authority to maximum effect. That the Minister's cause was different mattered not to the boy king and his entourage - the outcome would be the same.

To help execute the Minister's wishes it was his exceeding good fortune to have at his side as Director of the Antiquities Service a Frenchman who felt loyalty to Egypt first, and to his country of citizenship second. He was, better still, a Frenchman who had an internally broadcast distaste for the English - in particular that certain Englishman who stood presently in the spotlight of the world's press.

It became Meneg's job to ensure that the chemistry between the two men became an inflammable cocktail. The master carpenter would ignite the unstable mixture at the appropriate time.

Through dreams and private thoughts, Meneg had to engineer a conspiracy which would once and for all take the tomb away from the Englishman and restore it under the absolute control of the authorities. They would decide for themselves, in their patriotic wisdom, to cease work on the tomb and leave it as it currently was - in suspended excavation. It would become an Egyptian shrine to be reserved wholly for Egyptians, visited by them only during annual celebrations, as if in remembrance of the young Pharaoh, leaving the regal body in place and in peace as had been sanctified so many centuries earlier. Only then would the royal couple and their followers be preserved for eternity.

Meneg's efforts to educate the principal players in this unfolding drama were showing some success. The two were indeed suitably on course towards a crisis that should ensure that the tomb became sealed, to all intents and purposes, for ever. The trouble was, however, his delicate manoeuvring had taken time, and in that time the Englishman and his colleagues had made considerable progress towards their ultimate goal.

The golden sepulchral shrine had been dismantled. The fragile linen pall, profusely sown with golden rosettes, lay on the floor of tomb fifteen awaiting stabilisation. The team of excavators had assembled lifting equipment over the sarcophagus. Ultimate violation was imminent.

Through the thick walls of the sarcophagus and the enclosing caskets, he could hear the muffled voices of those at work above him. Then the scraping sounds; the brief hiss of foul air from an alien age as the cold, ancient atmosphere within sucked at the warmth without. Then the light - a blinding flash filling the space above him. It was like opening his long-closed eyes to the brilliance of a dozen suns. Then the first defiling touch, their fingers clawing at the outer shrouds.

Then, quite suddenly, all above him became still. The voices receded. With an echoing crash, the great steel door closed on the tomb. The echoes gradually faded away and he felt silence descend with the darkness. They were gone again. Within the crucible of his afterlife, the king lay once more in an uneasy peace.

Meneg must see to it that the violators did not return.

That first day the line-up in the visitors' gallery of Court No. 1 in the Mixed Courts of Cairo was impressive, but the high and mighty of Egypt greatly out-numbered those from Europe.

Following the opening of the tomb and the worldwide publicity which had accompanied the great discovery, Carter had come to terms with himself. He felt more confident than ever. He had recovered fully from the shock of having forcibly lost the right to access his tomb. On a wave of self-confidence he was convinced that the Egyptians had at last made a monumental tactical blunder by going so far; they had set the stage for him - a very public stage - to once and for all clear the muddy waters of negotiation over distribution of the treasures within the tomb through force of law. He was sure he would obtain an absolute ruling that not only should the team's rights to excavate be reinstated but that they should become entitled, by law, to a fifty per cent share of what would be discovered, or at worst the monetary equivalent.

He entered the courtroom well prepared. He had an almost jubilant smile on his face. It was as if by some off-stage bartering he had already secured the ruling he had been seeking. As he walked down the centre isle of the gallery he was acknowledged by a number of his British and American colleagues with a nod and a knowing grin and, from those who were close enough, a pat on the shoulder.

Pierre Lacau, whose enormous form was already seated just behind the Defendants' table, turned his head to look. He sensed some personal discomfort, less in the confidence of his adversary's stride, and more so in his distaste for the entire wasteful affair.

Carter had cause for optimism, not just in his own blind conviction that the rights of the team holding Almina Countess of Carnarvon's concession were inviolable and had been unjustly usurped and therefore justly contested, but also in the knowledge that the Defendants in his case had attempted to negotiate a settlement out of court and could only have wished to do so because they felt unsure of their position in the affair. He was supremely confident of victory. Now it was just a question of how much he could publicly besmirch his enemies. And he knew that in Maxwell he had the right man to expose their true colours.

However, at another time and in other surroundings, Breasted had counselled him once again to be less ambitious in his goals and perhaps more cautious than his present overconfidence would permit. Carter had thanked him for his sound advice. He reminded him with a smile, "We have by law an American chief judge and the panel is split evenly between locals and those from the countries that have a vested interest in the outcome of this affair. Nothing to fear, old boy. They'll see us all right. It'll be quite a sight! Be sure you're there to witness it."

The team of judges entered the courtroom and all those present dutifully stood up as the legal triumvirate took their seats. The ordered ceremonial was acceptably British.

The Chief Judge declared the court in session.

Without a moment's pause, the Government's Counsel leapt to his feet and addressed the panel eloquently and briefly. "Your lordships, I move that this trial be declared a mistrial and the case against my clients be dismissed!"

The Chief Judge leaned towards Counsel for the Defense and stared directly into his eyes. "Kindly explain under what circumstances you make such a claim, Counsellor."

With no hesitation he responded, "On two counts, your Honour. First, the plaintiff, the Carnarvon Estate, has no lawful representation in this court. Its agent, Mr Carter, is present, but in the eyes of the law he does not represent the Estate.

"And second," he paused a moment, "it is not the function of the Mixed Courts to deal with administrative matters such as the cancellation of this concession."

The Chief Judge did not bother to consult with the rest of his panel but renewed his fixed gaze on the Counsel for the Defence.

"Mr Rosetti," he began. "First, there is no earthly reason why this trial may not be conducted without the plaintiff being present - unless, of course, he or she is called as a witness. Mr Carter acting as agent, as you have been at pains to point out, is the plaintiff's representative. He has been so for many years now in his close association with the late earl, and he is certainly the most qualified to bring evidence in this case. Second, I would point out to you..." From the higher vantage point of the bench he leaned forward a little more to emphasise his delivery. "...that, within the clear guidelines that have been laid down, it is their Lordships' discretion as to what nature of case may be tried in this courtroom and not at the judgement of Counsel. Motion denied!"

The judge rested back in his chair and folded his arms.

Rosetti was not for a moment taken aback by these comments. He continued politely, as if nothing had been said, "Mr Carter claims he has a right to conduct the excavation of the tomb of Tutankhamun. His rights pertain to the language of a revokable concession. That concession has been revoked. Now he has no more rights than myself to enter that place, much less 'own' it, as his manner and attitude certainly suggest is his intent."

"Mr Rosetti!" The Chief Judge raised his voice to interrupt. "Please confine your argument to fact, not speculative interpretation."

Carter couldn't resist a subdued grin.

"Sir," acknowledged Rosetti in deference to the authority before him. "I will proceed with the facts...

"The concession has been revoked. Fact. It has been revoked because Mr Carter and his team of archaeologists walked off the job. Fact. This irresponsible gesture has endangered the integrity of the fine historical objects still remaining within the tomb and those awaiting restoration within Tomb Fifteen. Fact. In the name of the Carnarvon Estate Mr Carter claims a right to possession of selected objects. Fact. Mr Carter signed a paper in 1918. Fact. In part the intention of that paper was to clarify under which circumstances a share of the discoveries would not accrue to the concession holder. The circumstances in question would be on the discovery of an intact, or very nearly intact, tomb. Fact. The tomb of Tutankhamun can be described as such. Fact. Mr Carter is not entitled to any share of the objects in the tomb. Fact. And..." He paused to sense the anticipation of the audience about him. "...Anyway, the holder of the concession is regrettably no longer with us and in reality no concession actually exists in The Valley. That is, this case is groundless."

Carter jerked forward to interject but Maxwell grabbed him firmly by the shoulder and pulled him back whispering. "No. Not now. Not before we have thought this through a little. We will have time. The judge is sure to call a recess."

Chief Judge Crabites caught the movement out of the corner of his eye and raised his eyebrows at Carter in a gesture of expectation. For once Carter took the advice of his Counsel and did not respond to the invitation. Seeing no response, Crabites returned to the court.

"I need to reflect with the panel upon the statements of Mr Rosetti. There will be an adjournment until tomorrow."

Carter looked at his watch. It had been a long and, for him, difficult private session with his colleagues and his solicitor. It seemed indeed that finally they were all of the same mind. It was time he heeded the advice he was being given. Rosetti was right on his technical point. They had no representative of the Carnarvon Estate available at the trial. In the opinion of Maxwell, in the event of a representative being called as witness, it truly could be ruled a mistrial and the Estate would lose - everything.

What had been unthinkable just a day or two ago, Carter now was finally resigned to. The letter that the Egyptologist now signed had been drafted by his solicitor. In unsaid acknowledgement of the existence, intent and interpretation of the infamous paper he had set his hand to six years earlier, Carter, on behalf of the Carnarvon Estate, finally and undeniably signed away any rights to any object found in the tomb of Tutankhamun.

As he replaced the pen in his coat pocket, a feeling of personal betrayal fell upon him. His patron had not been one year dead and Carter was abdicating, on the earl's behalf, everything he had always assumed a right to. His desperate need to see the work completed fought his resolution never to give way on what was just reward for what they had achieved. 'The whole damn issue,' he thought to himself, 'is so incredibly unfair. The world deserves the heritage with which these people had been so luckily bestowed - the entire world. And were it not for the fortunate mixture of a few dedicated, talented and extremely rich people all coming together at one time with one goal in mind this pathetically backward country would never have seen much of the fortune that has lain for so many years beneath its dry and unyielding soil.'

Carter leaned forward, his arm outstretched, to grasp the piece of paper he had just signed. Breasted pulled it out of reach as the fingers approached.

"It is done, Howard. It's for the best. Without it you would not see the tomb again. I guarantee it. It is unthinkable that anyone else should be selected to complete the work you have begun. For that we must make some sacrifice. Besides, once things have cooled down - tempers on a more even keel - they may be more receptive to permitting some treasures to come our way."

Just at that moment, like a guilty boy close to being found out, Carter felt a sudden icy cold course through his veins. He recalled the tiny statuette of the boy king's head that he and Carnarvon had hidden in Tomb Four during those heady days of initial discovery. 'God, if they ever find that, there'll be hell to pay. No going back and no mistake. Breasted's right, damn his eyes. Got to cure this issue now and get back to work. The place is in dire risk of damage with every tour Lacau organises. Besides, even if they are intransigent and retain everything for Egypt, I still have that head!'

Carter slept much better that night.

The following day, as he alighted from his taxi to go up the steps to the courthouse, he felt recharged and at the same time relieved. In his own mind he had found the solution to what could have been a potentially disastrous future problem and, as his solicitor greeted him, he once again felt positive about the forthcoming proceedings. Maxwell had news to reinforce his feelings.

"Great news! Sir John has turned up. Quite out of the blue! It's marvellous. Just marvellous!"

Carter's eyes lit up. "No mistrial?"

"No mistrial," Maxwell confirmed. "Now that Sir John is here, they can have no legal grounds. And as added insurance, he has countersigned your renunciation. The endorsement will surely turn their heads to reinstatement."

"Capital," remarked Carter smugly. "That should seal it, then."

"Well, we've not yet got them exactly where we want them, but a good deal closer, I'd say. I will ensure we retain dignity in our abdication. After Rosetti's tainted litany at the outset of this contest, I am determined that we should not leave this place without setting the record straight."

There was more than a note of professional competitiveness in Maxwell's voice. Carter felt some foreboding in it. Nevertheless, the two marched together into the courtroom with straight backs and took their places at the table in front of the bench. They did not know it, nor did they sense it, but they were not alone.

Maxwell was one hour into relating the course of events as the Carter camp saw them when Crabites felt compelled to ask a question. He raised his hand to stop Maxwell in mid-sentence.

"Why, Mr Maxwell, did Mr Carter close up and abandon the tomb before he issued the writ which you are now presenting? It seems the wrong way about to me. Do y' follow?"

As the cigarette smoke in the courtroom drifted up into the beams of sunlight cutting down from the open windows, Carter thought he noticed the faintest suggestion of a sparkle of colour just above Maxwell's head.

"Your Honour," Maxwell answered, quite taken aback and irritated by his lordship's apparent lack of attention to the argument he had been so eloquently presenting. "Your Honour, that was not the case. Perhaps you misunderstand the situation. Mr Carter still retained possession when he issued his writ, but since then, and prior to this hearing, the government has come like a horde of bandits and forced him out of possession by nothing short of violence!"

As if a great hand had closed about the mouths of all those present, a muted silence fell upon the place. Suddenly the courtroom doors banged shut as three Egyptian journalists who had been taking notes rushed out to make their report.

Merton didn't move, however. He was wondering how he was going to put this scene into words suitable for the British public.

The courtroom gradually came back to life. There were loud murmurings all about the public gallery.

Carter, still seated at the table, had his head in his hands. With just one word and a little accompanying anger, Maxwell had dismantled Carter's confidence and replaced all his anxieties. Worse, he had earlier successfully persuaded his client to give away everything, only now to get absolutely nothing back in return. After just one word - 'Bandits' - there would be no way now for the government to concede a re-establishment of the concession.

Carter left the court without even so much as a farewell to Maxwell. Further discussion was pointless. There was nothing to do but book the very next passage home, leave this distasteful scene and, in different and more clement surroundings, try to put it out of one's mind; purge the system of its miseries. A deck chair, a double whisky, and a fresh sea breeze would be a good start.

In Tutankhamun's court that night, however, there was much to celebrate.

Chapter Twenty Two
Ambush

The telephone rang. Carter lifted the earpiece. The voice at the other end said, "This is a trunk call for a Mr Howard Carter."

"My name is Howard Carter."

"Caller, you are connected."

"Howard? This is William."

"Wil! How are you, old chap?"

"As well as can be expected. But not half as well as you, to be sure! I have had a devil of a time getting your number. I wanted to congratulate you personally on your magnificent achievement. What I should have given to have been there with you. Even Vernet tells me he'd promise not to whine about the heat if you'd return the favour by showing him around!"

Carter laughed out loud. "He lies, William!"

They both laughed.

"Howard. Seriously though... Reason for my telephoning you was to ask a favour."

Carter sighed. "Anything, William, in my power..."

"Well, you are a famous man now. I have never been called forward to the presence of anyone famous before. No one of any great importance has ever commissioned my work. I would be greatly honoured, Howard, if you would do so. Do you have the time to sit for me during this summer's holidays?"

Carter visibly flushed with embarrassment. The thought had not remotely occurred to him and he was deeply touched by the thoughtfulness of his brother's request. "Oh, Wil. What can I say?"

"Yes would be acceptable, Howard."

There was a moment's silence.

Then Carter said, "But of course, Wil. And whatever my schedule I will make the time."

"Smashing! Absolutely smashing! I'll come up to visit you. Do it in your lodgings. Just name the day. At last I am going to paint the portrait of a famous man!"

"Not famous, Wil. At least, not yet. Lucky, that's me. When I have my portrait, then I will be famous! How about a fortnight Monday?"

"It's a date. See you then. Can't tell you how happy this makes me. Toodle-oo." And he rang off before his brother could respond.

It was a foregone conclusion that Howard Carter would be pleased with the product. The finished painting was every bit the likeness he had expected. The quality of the brothers' art was so consistently matchless that satisfaction had never been in question. It was indeed a finely painted, accurate portrait, neither flattering nor unflattering, a plain picture of a plain, ordinary, famous man.

Carter propped the unframed canvas against the desk and sat back in his easy chair. He regarded it from a distance.

'Unassuming', he thought, 'and understated'. It was just the way he wanted it. He'd leave his fame to *The Times*. He relaxed back in the heavily upholstered cushions and for a moment put aside thoughts of the incredible complexity and prodigious quantity of the work and the politics that lay ahead of him.

'I was lucky,' he reflected, 'but I was also damn right!' He smiled to himself. "Got it right! Bang on!" he shouted out loud in the privacy of his empty study. 'Lucky dear Tut, is still there. Very lucky.'

Then his eyes set upon the tiny ivory horse lying on the desktop and the realism of the situation came flooding back. The grandee was gone, secure within his own private tomb on the summit of a modest hill on a not so modest estate in Wiltshire. The grandee was gone and along with him the irreplaceable power of status and ability to communicate and negotiate with the policy makers. What remained would be an up hill climb from a position of permanent subordination. Carter's personal fame, no matter what public heights it attained, would never compensate his social position, much less the loss of his patron.

The following day, Carter visited his niece's school. He had promised her, in a brief letter hurriedly scratched during the previous heady season, that he would come to her school and give a short lecture describing the early days of discovery. The thought of speaking to a hall full of girls sounded like fun - no one who could influence the future course of events in Egypt, no threatening personalities, just eager, fantasy-hungry listeners - and he had come well supplied with illustrations to excite their immature minds. He looked forward to it.

She ran to him as he emerged from his taxi. "Uncle Howard! Uncle Howard!"

"Phyllis, my dear! How lovely to see you after all this time! And how lovely you are! My goodness, you look quite the lady."

She kissed him on the cheek and whispered in his ear, "And now you are so famous! Everyone is asking me about you. I am so lucky to have you as my uncle!"

She paused a moment. "Oh, I am forgetting my manners. I am so sorry. I should like to introduce you to my very best friend, Miss Kellaway. She has been most anxious to meet you."

She turned to her friend who had been standing to one side and presented her to her uncle.

Carter took the girl's hand and gently shook it.

"I am honoured, Miss Kellaway. Are you two great friends?"

"Oh, we are, Mr Carter," she replied. "Phyllis has told me so much about you. It is such an honour for me to shake the hand of so famous a man!"

Carter was quite softened by the young lady's admiring comments. Previously hard won, he had not experienced such freely given appreciation before. The feeling was warming to him and he smiled broadly. Without thinking, he instantly proposed to the two that following his lecture they should skip the school supper that evening and permit him to take them out for a bite to eat in a nearby hotel. They jumped at the opportunity.

Carter's hour-long lecture took place late in the day. Phyllis was becoming impatient for a square meal and fidgeted all the way through the talk, but not her friend. The young lady was quite star-struck. Attentive to his every word, she studied each of his lantern slides with obvious intensity. When he had finished and the audience, excepting Phyllis who was by now standing at the speaker's side, had dispersed, she remained in her seat, solitary, staring at the podium.

"Miss Kellaway?" said Carter, still on stage. "Is that you?"

She did not answer.

"Yes it is," confirmed his niece. "Can we go now?" Phyllis tugged at his sleeve.

"Just a minute, my dear... Miss Kellaway, are you all right?"

Carter walked down from the stage and approached the single figure sitting alone in the hall.

Her eyes followed him as he walked up the isle to her chair. "Oh, I am just fine, Mr Carter... just fine. Your lecture... it's all just so fascinating. I quite forgot myself. Please forgive me. I did not mean to be rude."

"Good Lord! Think no such thing. I am pleased my talk sparked your curiosity. Did it not spark your appetite like it did my niece's?"

The two girls giggled. Phyllis took Carter's arm and pulled him in the direction of the door. "Supper, Uncle?"

He looked down at her.

"Supper, Uncle." The determination in his niece's expression made a clear statement.

"Supper it is then, my dears."

They accompanied him in his taxi to the hotel. Carter had had a table reserved and his hungry guests settled themselves to studying the menu.

Phyllis noticed Carter observing their concentration and commented with some embarrassment, "It is so exciting to be treated to some real food for a change, Uncle Howard!"

They were not about to underplay the opportunity.

Having ordered their first course, Carter clinked glasses with the two girls. "A toast, ladies, before we embark on our feast. In great respect, great appreciation and fond memories... to his lordship, the Earl of Carnarvon. May he rest in peace."

"The Earl of Carnarvon," the two repeated and together took a sip of their orange squashes.

"Mr Carter," Phyllis's friend began, "your talk this afternoon was most interesting, about the finding of the tomb and all, but you didn't say much about Tutankhamen himself. Could you tell us a little about his life and times?"

Carter smiled. The diversion was refreshing.

"Well, to tell you the truth, Miss Kellaway, I don't know that much about him! Nobody does. Other than the grave goods - none of which, I may add, so far includes anything written about the king and his exploits - little remains that might help in constructing the story of his life. He came to power at a time of great instability in Egypt, as the country struggled to re-establish order between the reigns of the heretic Pharaoh Akhenaten and the army general who became Pharaoh, Horemheb. King Tut was one of three short-lived Pharaohs of the time - his brother before him reigned perhaps only three years, he himself for no more than nine, and his uncle after him for perhaps just another three years. His much longer-lived general saw to it that everything he could find that related to King Tut's reign and that of Akhenaten and the other two Pharaohs was destroyed or erased. Consequently, we know quite a lot about Horemheb and very little about the others." Carter smiled. "But we may speculate to our hearts' content!"

And then he launched into a lengthy personal interpretation of what the boy may have been like, his marriage, what he himself might have accomplished in his short life, what might have been accomplished during his reign and how he might have met his end.

Throughout it all, the girl was most attentive, throwing a question at him now and then, and not taking her eyes off him for a moment. By the time he had finished, with interruptions to take the odd mouthful of food and drink, the meal was over and the bill was paid.

He had come prepared to leave a small gift with his niece, but it was quite clear to Carter that Phyllis's friend had been far more attentive to his storytelling. He felt compelled to make an additional gesture before he left.

"Before we part, Phyllis, I have a little something for you."

He pushed a small, bow-tied package across the table towards his niece. She took it, drew the bow, unfolded the wrapping and opened the box. On a bed of cotton wool lay what appeared to be a dried flower. It was a rather dull olive-grey colour. She looked a little puzzled.

Carter leaned across and whispered directly into her ear, "Promise to keep a secret... forever... between you and I... A-B-S-O-L-U-T-E-L-Y no one else?"

Without hesitation she nodded again.

He continued to whisper so her friend could not hear. "A fragment which I found on the floor of the antechamber to Tut's tomb. It had fallen from a bouquet presumably left by the departing mourners over three thousand years ago. The oldest flower you will ever receive from a gentleman."

She smiled.

"Remember. No one - ever - should hear of this. OUR secret. MOST important!"

She nodded once more.

He rested back in his chair and returned her smile. Then he turned to her friend. "And for you also, Miss Kellaway..."

He reached into his jacket pocket, pulled out a ball of newspaper and unwrapped it carefully in front of her. Inside was an undecorated, tiny calcite oil lamp, so small it could be completely enclosed within his fist.

"Just a little trifle I plonked in my pocket while I was inside some pyramid," he said. "Not really large enough to have been intended as a working oil lamp. More a facsimile for the use of the dead, I fancy."

"Oh, it is charming, Mr Carter!" Her face beamed with delight.

"Please keep it... to remind you of this pleasant evening we have shared together. I hope it will help to cultivate your clear interest in the subject. Treat it with care. It is extremely fragile."

"Oh, Mr Carter, I don't know what to say."

"Your smile, your company, and your curiosity are thanks enough.

"And now, Misses Walker and Kellaway, this tired old archaeologist must take his leave of you. It has been much fun for me, but I fear I will miss my train if I linger to enjoy your company longer."

The two thanked him with vigorous shakes of both his hands. He touched his hat as he got into the taxi and was driven off.

"He is such a famous man," Phyllis whispered to her friend as the car disappeared from view. "It's in all the papers."

"It is time to take an in-depth look at the character behind the mask," said Breasted. "Pierre Lacau, Howard, is far more than a stodgy, Arab-friendly, French bureaucrat. There are two aspects of his make-up which mean that, in any difference of views with him, if you do not bring yourself around to understanding or even caring about them, you will never be able to take the political high ground."

On this particular subject Carter's mind remained closed. "Obdurate Frenchman... Grudge against the British... Uses *The Times* agreement as an excuse to go out of his way to make our lives difficult..." Carter scowled into the drink he cradled in his lap. "...Needs to be put in his place."

"Howard, that is not the way to move things forward. You must not try to run over the man. He has the sympathy and support of the Egyptian authorities. He can stop you working here if he has a mind to do so. It is a battle you cannot win. And you will get no personal satisfaction out of berating him. All that will do is drive him to a decision that I do not think he actually wants to make. However, should you press the approach you now consider, he might find avenues more acceptable to us closed off to him and the tougher course inevitable."

"But he is wrong. We have right on our side. Of course we will win. It'll be an unwelcome diversion from our labours, take a little time, but in the end it will all have been worthwhile. I'll not stand by and let it happen their way."

"But Howard..."

Carter was visibly irritated by his friend's continued entreaties and, already personally committed to his position, he wished to put a stop to what he considered further fruitless dialogue. He cut Breasted off. "Look, old chap. You have one opinion. I respect that. I have another - which I choose to honour. Please let that be an end to our pointless bantering."

But Breasted was utterly convinced that any continuation in Carter's stance could seriously jeopardise the team's chances of ever completing their work. Worse still, they could be forced to abandon it to far less expert hands. Much stood to be lost to the world at large should they do so. It was imperative that he steered his determined colleague towards the middle ground.

In Carter's present mood, now would clearly not be the time. He must be vigilant and find the right moment to press his case. The anxiety he felt for the future of the project was paradoxically as overwhelming as Carter's, notwithstanding the fact that their positions were entirely opposite.

'There are stormy days ahead and no mistake,' thought Breasted, resigning himself to silence. 'This time next year God only knows where all of us will be.'

He felt a foreboding sadness as strong as his frustration. In complete contrast to the recent exuberant excitement of discovery, it was in a curious atmosphere of desperate melancholy that Breasted excused himself to retire to bed that night.

As if attempting to drown his mounting anger by filling his lungs with pungent smog, Carter rammed another cigarette into his ebony cigarette holder, bent down to strike a match on the stone floor, took a long pull and inhaled deeply. He snorted the smoke out through his nostrils quickly and pointed at the piece of paper in Lacau's hand.

"That, sir... that is totally unacceptable. Not long ago I thought we might be getting somewhere, but now there are elections on the horizon and it is becoming quite clear that you wish to consolidate your position such that whomever your new master might be you will be seen in a favourable light and retain your exalted situation. You have changed all the rules. This could end up in the courts. Do you really want that?"

Lacau ignored Carter's accusation. "Mr Carter, please be reasonable. All the Minister wants is a list of your collaborators."

"Dammit, man, you make it sound like I am conspiring with a group of infidels! The very thought that you could conceive of finding it within your purview to vet the qualifications of the team of worldwide accredited experts

I have chosen... This... this angers me beyond all description! You would be well advised to leave this place before..."

"MR CARTER!" Pierre Lacau raised his voice. Standing up straight he used his intimidating size to ensure that he had Carter's attention. "Mr Carter! As the recognised authority over The Valley of the Kings it is myself and my colleagues who must dispatch our duty judiciously and without cause for inciting criticism. As the controlling authority, we must police this excavation to ensure that no unauthorised persons visit the site. We do not seek to exclude any whom you approve as being needed for the execution of the scientific work at hand. But, to confirm that we have not been delinquent in our duties, we must have a list of those so authorised."

Carter counter-attacked. "I view this as an insidious plot to wrest control from those whose right of ownership of this project is inviolable. If the authorities do not withdraw their demands, you will leave me with no choice but to cease work, seal the tomb and take this matter to the courts for a just decision."

"Is this a threat?"

"Take it any way you damn well please. My position should be clear to you. That's an end to the dialogue. My work has been interrupted for far too long. I'd be obliged if you would leave."

Lacau felt like a man caught astride a tumbling river with one foot on each bank. Whichever foot he chose to move, he would surely fall in and drown. If he was to keep Carter secure as the only man talented and tenacious enough to see the project through to a successful conclusion, and at the same time administer the directives of the Egyptian authorities, in particular the Ministry, somehow he would have to maintain this painfully precarious position.

Carter in no way comprehended Lacau's situation and, had he been made aware of it, would have cared less. 'Please God bring back Maspero!' he screamed inside himself.

Yet, to quite some degree Lacau enjoyed piquing Carter. The man's arrogance often bordered on rudeness. He needed to be taught a lesson. However, the job was there to be done. There was no going back now. Carter was, despite his irascible nature, the lesser evil - indeed, the better man for the job. 'But how evil the nasty little Englishman really is!' thought the inspector as he was driven back to the ferry in Carter's car. 'He tries my patience to the very edge of reason.'

Working in the tomb, and there had been precious little this season due to the time-consuming banter between the authorities and the excavating team, was therapeutic rather than exhausting to Carter, and he returned to set about removing the golden shrines and reveal the sarcophagus.

But in the evenings, after the team had finished recording their day's efforts, the conversation would once more revert to sorting out how, in the eyes of the Western world, they were to vindicate themselves while at the same time shaming the Ministry and the Antiquities Service.

After several long evenings of drafting they completed the letter. It was not signed by Carter but by four of his colleagues - Breasted, Gardiner, Lythgoe and Newberry - and delivered by runner to Monsieur le Directeur in Cairo.

The letter praised the efforts of their leader and bore a litany of obstructions perpetrated by the Director. It concluded with a lambasting of Lacau's failure to execute the responsibilities of his office.

The excavation team returned to work.

After some time, it dawned on Breasted that there had been no response from Lacau.

"How could there be?" pouted Carter. "You can't answer a good telling off when your position is indefensible. You watch. He'll soften. We shall continue as if all was as before. He won't follow up."

"Wouldn't be so sure, Howard," cautioned Breasted. "The man takes his orders from the Minister. He has little control over the Minister's mind and no knowledge of the politics in..."

Breasted ceased talking in mid-sentence as a panting Newberry emerged from the entrance corridor. "Heard the news?" he gasped.

"What news?" the three in the burial chamber all said at once.

"Yehia and his government are out - the Zaghuls are in!"

"Oh, Christ!" exclaimed Breasted. "That *is* bad news."

"There's worse," continued Newberry after he'd caught his breath. "The new Minister will be Hanna." He looked at each of them expectantly.

"Morcos Hanna? The one we imprisoned for treason? The one that Maxwell tried to get executed?" asked Carter.

"Morcos Hanna. The very same."

"Oh, my God! Now we're for it."

"No wonder Lacau's been quiet," observed Breasted. "He's been waiting on the outcome of the elections. Now he knows who his new boss is, and one so enthusiastically nationalistic, he'll be after us again."

They all looked expectantly at Carter. Carter absorbed the news quietly. Finally he broke the silence. His words were cold and deliberate. "I admit that in my anger over this situation I had not considered that things could actually get worse." He paused for a moment. "But, that doesn't mean our case is any the weaker - it's just the hill we have to climb's a little steeper... Make no mistake, gentlemen. This concession is held in the name of the Carnarvon Estate. I have told Monsieur le Directeur many times before that our rights to complete the clearing of this tomb are inviolable. No change of government leadership can alter that. But, to be on the safe side, I'd better go and pay my respects to the new Minister before his opinion is tainted by the dozy Frenchman. He needs to hear the other side of the story - the true side - from the horse's mouth. I shall start by discussing details of the official opening." Carter patted the dusty lid of the sarcophagus. "That'll get his attention, and hopefully break any barriers that Lacau may have attempted to construct between us... Arthur! Go and find Abdel, will you, there's a good chap? Tell him to telegraph for an appointment with the Minister as soon as possible and report back to me before nightfall."

It was early evening as Carter walked into the vestibule of the Minister's offices in Cairo for his first audience with the new incumbent. He announced himself and was directed to a seat in the corridor outside the Minister's rooms. He glanced at his watch and sat down. He was on time.

Once again, he reflected, he was somewhere other than at work. The lengthening list of delays was wearing. He knew he would be lucky now if he could achieve his target of getting to and unwrapping the king's mummy before he had to close up and leave for the summer. There would be that much less to talk about in his forthcoming lecture appointments in the United States of America.

He looked about him. The place hadn't changed much from his last visit. It seemed a little noisier than usual. Perhaps the commotion was due to no more than the new appointees getting used to the place, running hither and thither trying to find things.

Presently, the Minister's secretary emerged from his office and spoke to Carter in Arabic. "Mr Carter. His Excellency is not here at present but I expect him momentarily. Would you like some coffee?"

"Please," answered Carter, dutifully. It was not good form to decline.

About ten minutes passed by and then Paul Tottenham, Lacau's aide, emerged from his own office just along the corridor. Tottenham spotted Carter and walked briskly over to him.

"Mr Carter, sir. Glad I found you. Please come into my office for a moment. There's something I must relate to you before you see the new Minister."

Carter reluctantly followed him into his office. Tottenham ushered him in and then took two furtive glances either way down the corridor as if to ensure that he had not been observed. He closed the door behind him and stood in front of it with his hands behind his back.

"Mr Carter, sir. It's like this, see. You must not discuss anything with the Minister that is not strictly to do with the arrangements for the official opening ceremonies. Nothing at all." He stared intently into Carter's cold eyes.

Carter sighed. "Mr Tottenham. That is exactly what I intended. However, sir, there will be more to the conversation. It's like this. I am going to relate the history of these last few preposterous weeks. He is going to hear my side of the story. Factual, truthful and clear. I shall refer him to the lengthy file of correspondence between us. I will not stand by while you and your boss paint your corrupt and biased picture of our proceedings at the tomb."

Tottenham twitched nervously. "That's unwise, sir, if you don't mind my saying so. Because... because of this, sir."

From behind his back he drew a piece of paper and handed it to Carter to read.

Carter recognised it almost immediately. It was the agreement Carnarvon had signed concerning their previous concession outside The Valley of the Kings; a concession in which his lordship had agreed to no division should a discovery be found robbed but almost complete.

Carter felt a warmth in his cheeks and feared the flushing would display his emotions. 'Surely they can't be drawing an analogy between Tutankhamen and this?' He spoke out. "Surely not!"

"What, sir?" The words out of context confused Tottenham.

"I said, surely you cannot be suggesting the two situations are analogous?"

"No. No, sir. Not analogous. On the contrary, the Inspector judges them identical. A precedent has been set."

Carter started shouting. Tottenham tried to quieten him down but he wasn't about to stop until he'd said his piece. He had hardly got a word out when there was a knock at the door and the Minister's secretary poked his head in to say that the Minister had returned and was now ready to receive his visitor.

Carter felt completely off balance. As he walked to the Minister's office he tried to gather himself. This first meeting was important. It was important for both men. The Minister had been well briefed. He was also well aware of Tottenham's diversion.

Morcos Bey Hanna was a generously proportioned man. He relaxed in his chair wearing what appeared to be the same dark grey suit, Carter observed, as he had worn on the occasion of his trial. The jacket fell unbuttoned at the front to expose a white, green and blue tartan waistcoat, a white, high-collared shirt, and a red tie. Complementing this ensemble, on his head he wore the familiar bright red fez, on his feet black socks and shoes. Notwithstanding his strong beliefs, he remained a typical product of Westernised Arab officialdom. His carefully manicured moustache twitched as he drew breath to speak.

The Minister began by greeting him warmly. "Mr Carter! This is a great pleasure for me. You are a very famous man and I do not have the opportunity to meet many so notorious as yourself." He had chosen the word intentionally.

"Please sit down. I have many questions for you as, I am sure, you have many for me."

The coffee was set on a small table between the low couch in which Carter was now uncomfortably embedded and the padded, green leather chair in which the Minister languished.

"You have quite a team of experts in The Valley, do you not? Quite a team. Tell me, this Gardiner fellow, is he one of your better men?"

"Of world renoun, Excellency," responded Carter. "As every one of them."

"Hmm. He didn't impress me too much when he visited a couple of days ago."

Carter was destabilised again. He was still trying to regain his composure from the Tottenham manouevre. "What visit is this that you are referring to, sir?"

"Dr Alan Gardiner, right?"

"Yes, Excellency."

"He asked to see me two days ago and naturally I did my best to fit him into my busy schedule. It's not easy starting a new job, you'll appreciate. Much to learn. Particularly your predecessor's mistakes." He leaned forward in his chair to emphasise the point.

"Anyway, I fitted him in. But then he had the effrontery to dispatch a fusillade of complaints pertaining to my Department of Antiquities. Complaints, I must say, that in the absence of Monsieur le Directeur, could not be defended. He knew that and took advantage. I dislike tactics. I respond poorly to them. I am not receptive." He leaned forward once again. "You understand?"

As he broke his monologue, Carter thought briefly on the strategic display he was witnessing. He took the time to think through his answer before responding.

"Excellency. I knew nothing of this visit until now but let me say that I am sure Dr Gardiner took it upon himself to have an audience with you with only the best of intentions... in order to relate to you how this most important of projects - to the State of Egypt and the world at large - is jeopardised by the constant interruptions and bureaucratic boulders thrown by the Antiquities Service, none of which is in the better interests of science or the good of your country. Do you comprehend the fragility of these three-thousand-year-old masterpieces? Now the seal has been broken they will decay, just like an opened can of food. These interruptions - delays - cause criminal damage!"

The last statement was unnecessary, especially since Carter lacked any personal sensitivity to the fact that he was talking down to the Minister.

But the Minister politely listened. Lacau had been accurate in his description of the man. Morcos Bey Hanna gave no outward sign of his distaste for this arrogant, tweed-suited Englishman with the bow tie and the Homburg. He politely allowed Carter to finish and then moved directly on to the next item on his agenda.

"Tell me, Mr Carter, how are your relationships with the members of my Antiquities Service?"

"I would describe them as cold, verging on the icy, Excellency." Blunt, unfeeling frankness. He was good at it. Had any of his colleagues been present, however, they would not have been impressed. Carter continued without pausing, "There appears to be little that they do that is of a practical nature. It was run a good deal differently when I was in the employ of the

Service."

That did it.

"Then you clearly need to write these problems down and submit them to me," the Minister coldly returned. "But I would rather suggest that with the onset of this new administration you forget the past and we all start afresh. I think little fruit will come from harbouring old differences. Do you not agree, Mr Carter?" The Minister leant forward as if to demand an affirmative answer.

Carter begrudgingly responded, "That can be done, sir. If we all set our minds to it." He didn't believe it for a minute.

The Minister moved directly on to the next subject. "And *The Times* newspaper - the arrangement between Lord Carnarvon and *The Times* - what is to come of it?"

At last it dawned on him. The Ministry's request to review a list of Carter's colleagues was born of the intense frustration of the local press over *The Times* agreement. They sought the opportunity to expel Merton.

Carter quickly changed course. "Oh, that will be history by the end of this season's work."

"Ah." The Minister nodded with an expression of approval and moved on again.

"And America. I am told you are to desert us to make a lecture tour in the United States early this summer. Do you not think your time would be better spent at your duties in The Valley?" He paused only briefly. "Forgive me if I misunderstand, but I seem to remember you saying that 'delay' would be a criminal act. I think you used the word 'criminal'. Is that not what you said?"

Carter was by now firmly on the defensive. He was not getting the breathing space to organise his thoughts and he was making no headway at all with the new Minister. It seemed he wasn't being allowed to. Perhaps it was all by design. He was still remembering the paper Tottenham had shown him. There seemed no way to win this man over. It was all so hopeless. Another wasted trip. But he was not about to leave without making his point.

"With respect, sir. We are not talking about quite the same thing. It is common practice to close down operations during the spring. No one, not even the fellaheen, can tolerate the summer temperatures. I meant we are currently wasting valuable winter season time."

The Minister did not acknowledge Carter's reply. As soon as Carter paused he turned to his secretary. "Ask Monsieur le Directeur to join us, if you will."

'That's all I need,' thought the beleaguered Egyptologist, 'Monsieur l'Obstacle.'

Pierre Lacau's massive figure filled the doorway to the Minister's office. He was at once friendly but not overly so. He stooped and shook Carter's hand firmly.

"Now we wish to talk about the visitors to the tomb, Mr Carter," said the Minister. "Professor Lacau has a number of names he wishes to discuss with you."

Lacau placed a slip of paper in Carter's hand.

"These people you have admitted to the tomb at one time or another, have you not?"

Carter perused the list for a moment. "Yes. I know all of these people."

"None of these people was authorised by us to visit the tomb."

Lacau and the Minister stared at the Egyptologist as if he were expected immediately to admit his infraction and apologise. Carter, of course, did neither.

"Excellency. Monsieur le Directeur. That is not a requirement. I am the one most qualified to judge who may and who may not and when they may visit the tomb - no one else. You know that only too well, Monsieur le Directeur."

The leather squeaked as the Minister moved in his chair. "Frankly, I am at a loss for words. You honestly believe that it is you who has the authority to select and grant passage into this discovery? You actually believe this?"

"Excellency." Carter's anger was welling. Everything else - anxiety, analysis, strategic thinking, diplomacy, construction - was overwhelmed by the natural rage that was building within him. Unlike before, the words came easily. "Excellency. You must understand what your employee does not. That is, that this discovery is so rare, so rich and so immense that it is too great for Egypt to hold to its own. That is, that I am employed by the holder of the concession for this excavation. That is, that I am he who is qualified to perform this work with diligence. That is, that I am he who performs this work for Egypt and the world at large. That is, that without my team's expertise most of what you have already received in the museum in this great city would have been damaged irreparably or lost altogether."

He looked for a glimmer of acknowledgement in the Minister's black eyes. There was not a flicker of it.

"I am not asking for thanks," he went on. "I am asking to be left alone to complete the work efficiently and satisfactorily, with the absolute minimum of harm to those wondrous pieces that still lie within. Please leave me to do my best. And that includes the selection of those who may enter the tomb. You will not be disappointed at the result, I promise you."

For a moment there was silence. An angry Howard Carter had addressed his counterpart at his own level. For once the delivery was almost without emotion. For now he thought he'd caught up.

He was wrong. As if nothing had been said thus far, the Minister launched immediately into a dispassionate monologue concerning his proposals for the opening ceremony. After presenting a longish list of selected VIPs and requesting that Carter arrange all the seating and refreshments for the appointed day, the Minister asked at what point and in what manner the mummy would be revealed to him.

"No, sir. Not at this ceremony," answered Carter patiently. "I am almost certain there will be at least three coffins - one within the other within the other - and the opening of these in sequence will be a most delicate and time-consuming process. I am afraid there will have to be a second ceremony - perhaps in the next season - for the revealing of the king. However, allowing the anticipation to build can only make the final event more exciting and satisfying don't you think, Excellency?"

The Minister was not amused. With an expression of frustration on his face he said, "Well, that being the case I do not feel it necessary or appropriate for me to be at the opening of the sarcophagus. I am a busy man and it promises to be far too mundane an event. You will advise me when you are ready to reveal the king. If I am available at that time I will come..."

Carter did not allow the Minister to continue. He broke in, "And if you are not I will close the tomb and hold things until you can come, sir."

He wasn't trying to be polite. He knew damn well the Minister was about to instruct him to do just this. All he wanted was to appear more generous and accommodating than the Minister cared to let him.

It was to Carter's satisfaction that his interjection had been timed so well. Lacau noted it, too. But it was lost on the Minister. "Now, if you will excuse me, I have work to attend to."

Carter was very disappointed with the way the meeting had gone and very angry at the earlier conspiratorial tactics of Lacau and Tottenham. Nevertheless, he maintained his outward civility and thanked the Minister for his time.

He was quickly ushered out by the secretary.

On the journey back to Luxor, he turned his mind to thoughts of the tomb and tried to shut out the feelings of remorse that had been eating at him. He had achieved nothing at the meeting but for a better feel for who and what he was dealing with.

It was over, and the excitement and anticipation of what lay ahead of him in the tomb returned to fill his mind to overflowing.

Two dozen persons attended the opening. That was about as many as could stand in the area immediately adjacent to the sarcophagus and still be assured of some view of the proceedings. At Carter's invitation, James Breasted, at the time a very sick man, was among the group. Driven by the adrenalin of excitement coursing through his system he had left his bed against the orders of his doctor. After all, no sickbed could keep any man from an experience with a once-in-a-lifetime opportunity that held this magnitude of promise. The images fresh in his mind, Breasted would record his vivid experience two days later as he lay once more in his bed in Luxor, exhausted but immensely satisfied. *(See Breasted, 1943).*

Standing on a low wooden platform to give himself some leverage advantage Carter manoeuvred a crowbar between the granite lid and the top of the quartzite casket and attempted to raise up one corner. He pressed down with all his weight until the lid eased. Immediately the base of the lid cleared the top of the casket, Mace jammed a couple of metal angle-irons into the gap. The two continued to work around the sarcophagus in this way, bringing up the two halves of the broken lid separately until they were both sitting level about one inch above the lip. To ensure that the two broken halves stayed together, Carter and three of his colleagues slid in timbers lengthwise along each long edge and, with the aid of slender sticks, passed ropes from one to the other under the timbers and secured them to the pulley system above the lid.

The time had come to take the strain. As the weight was taken at either end, the ropes stretched and audibly creaked and then, slowly, the lid began to rise.

"Enough!" whispered Carter urgently.

The lid hung swaying slightly just twenty or so inches above the stone casket. Everyone leaned forward to squint inside. The lights that flooded the burial chamber were standing too high to illuminate the interior of the sarcophagus. Inside was virtually impenetrable blackness.

Carter, standing at one end, pulled a torch from the pocket of his trousers and shone it between the two great slabs of stone. Everyone leaned forward, pressing closer to the gap between the lid and the lip. Within their field of view lay a large mummiform shape tightly wrapped in a dull black shroud bespattered with a tawny dust and some tiny fragments from the granite lid. Carter's torch picked up flashes of gold from deep inside the casket. "I can see the funeral bier," he announced. Murmurs of acknowledgement issued from his spectators.

Carter put his hand inside the casket until he could feel the texture of the shroud. The sense of touching the unviolated coffin of a king for the first time gave him a strangely apprehensive feeling.

He withdrew. "Burton. Where's Burton?"

The whirring of the movie camera stopped. "Here, Howard." A soft voice came from the darkness behind the pressing audience.

"Harry, we will leave for a moment while you take some plates. Gentlemen, if you would be so kind..."

He gestured to the straining eyes to his left and everyone dutifully pulled back to give Burton the room to shuffle by with his equipment.

There was a considerable buzz of excitement in the chatter of the privileged onlookers, Arab and English alike, as they waited for Burton to complete his photographic record. To give the photographer the room he required Carter himself sat back on his haunches against the wall between the burial chamber and the treasury. He wiped his forehead with his handkerchief. He looked at it. It was filthy. He was covered in the dust of ages.

When Burton had finally cleared his stuff and confirmed that his plates were all right, Carter and Mace positioned themselves at the head of the sarcophagus.

Burton's lights blazed into the cavity. The heat was oppressive but not a single person present that day had any thought of discomfort.

'Illumination sufficient to awaken the dead,' thought Carter. He prepared to peel away the ancient cloth. "It's tight on this side. What's it like on yours, Mace? What do you think?"

Mace leaned in and gripped the head end of the shroud gently. To his horror he could feel the threads begin to tear.

"Dammit, Howard!" he whispered in an urgent tone, "It's damn brittle. I can feel it giving way. For God's sake don't pull too hard!"

Carter had maintained his grip on the shroud. He didn't feel any yielding in the fibre of the cloth itself and, although he was pulling pretty hard, the shroud held together. It appeared stuck fast. He considered how the ancients might have succeeded in tucking the shroud in so tightly around so obviously a heavy and immovable object. Then, all of a sudden, without tearing, the material gave way and he found himself holding the ends of two shrouds free in his hands, several inches above the coffin.

"It's come free, Mace," he whispered. "There are two of them."

The audience to his left leaned close to the rim of the casket to get a better look.

"Gentlemen. A moment, please. If you would move back just a little. As we unroll the shrouds Mr Mace and I will have to move along either side of the sarcophagus. You will be able to look closer presently."

The observers moved away as instructed. Given more room, Carter and Mace slowly began to roll back the dusty upper cloth.

"Arthur," cautioned Carter. "Be careful to contain the stone fragments in the linen if you can. If they slip down the sides they may wedge between the coffin and the wall of the sarcophagus and we'll have a devil of a job getting it out."

Like a pair of solemn undertakers, Carter and Mace steadily rolled the shroud to the foot end. They then took hold of the second shroud and rolled this in the opposite direction. This revealed a third sheet beneath, or so they thought until they had reached the head end once more and discovered this shroud was a single piece folded back on itself.

As they rolled this longer shroud back towards the foot, Carter and Mace stared hungrily downward. The brilliance of gold shone up at them. A perfectly balanced, brilliantly golden, young face stared at them through deeply black eyes. The effigy wore the nemes headdress. The gold veneer was torn a little where the wood, desiccated by eons, had cracked beneath, but the vulture and serpent insignia of regal office stood proudly out, the two encircled by a tiny, delicately threaded bouquet of what appeared to be dried flower petals - a tiny, final, fond goodbye set upon the ornament at the forehead.

Carter and Mace looked at one another. Mace smiled. Carter smiled. It was a magical moment.

They proceeded on to the foot and the richness of the entire body of the coffin was revealed. It looked as clean and fresh as if it had just been laid to rest. Every part of it glittered in the brilliance of Burton's lamps - except for the foot. This clearly had been wilfully damaged. There were some brilliant flashes of gold from the side of the foot, but the toe had been roughly cut, virtually hacked off.

Finally they drew the shrouds from the coffin. Realising in the tension of the moment that they still held the soiled, ancient linen rolled up firmly in their fists, they placed it to the side on some packing materials and then turned back to lean over the head end of the sarcophagus.

The guests pressed forward to look. No one spoke.

Carter was face to face with the likeness of the dead king, the monarch he had been searching for all these years. This, then, was what the boy king had looked like. It was all a little too much to absorb fully in a few minutes, even an hour - it could take days, perhaps weeks. Carter felt more overawed than the moment he had first set eyes on the objects in the antechamber. This was personal. This king, in history virtually unknown, Carter now felt strangely closer to than any person in the living world. The eyes seemed alive. They spoke to him through the blackness of the obsidian of which they were made.

Carter was so totally absorbed in what he was looking at that he lost all sense of time. When he finally recalled that he had an audience and raised his head to take their questions, there was no one there. One by one the guests, profoundly struck, had quietly left to contemplate what they had witnessed in their own private way.

Carter and Mace stepped off the wooden platform and walked out into the auburn light of early evening. Burton set up his camera equipment once more.

The entire audience had assembled at the top of the stone staircase. They greeted Carter warmly as he exited the tomb. He received a vigorous, grateful handshake from every one of them. He thanked them all in turn, ending with Pierre Lacau. Holding the Director's hand a little longer than the others, and for the moment suppressing his disdain for the man, Carter took the opportunity to give Lacau the courtesy of hearing his immediate plans.

"We are to have the press conference tomorrow, as agreed, then four days of official visitations, again as agreed, and then I can get back to work."

Lacau nodded and smiled, knowing only too well Carter's dislike for the formalities.

"Before the press, however, I should like to escort the wives of the excavators into the tomb for a viewing. They have sacrificed much by being here with their husbands dedicated to their tasks and I would like to give them some reward for their tolerance. The Minister isn't likely to have a problem with that now, is he?"

"I'll check with him, Mr Carter, to be on the safe side."

The statement was clinical. There was something in Lacau's expression that Carter didn't like. Carter, the euphoria of the moment still coursing through his veins, shrugged his shoulders and bade a cordial "au revoir" to the Director.

He turned back down the steps to his colleagues. "We'll get the wives over here tomorrow before he has a chance to respond," he murmured confidentially. "Give them a full view of the place before the smelly ones arrive in an orgy of local publicity and self-importance."

The others quickly nodded in agreement.

Reassured by the unhesitating support of his colleagues Carter set about closing up for the evening.

The party of visitors left The Valley busily relating one another's most recent impressions. As the noise of their chatter died away Carter was once again within the tomb inspecting the lifting tackle that was straining under the suspended weight of the great granite lid - perhaps one ton or more. In the strong light of Burton's arc lamps, Mace and he closely examined the ropes and pulleys for any signs of impending failure.

The cavity for once was soundless and everything looked secure. The excavators returned to the outside and Carter instructed Adamson to get the guards to lock the gates and take their positions for the night.

Abdel came in the car to fetch him back to Castle Carter for supper. He said goodnight to his colleagues and in little more than five minutes he was at his front door. He walked inside, across the hall and into his bedroom, spreadeagled himself on the bed and fell almost immediately into a dreamful sleep, still fully clothed.

At once he found himself reclining with Dorothy Dalgliesh on the cool, sunlit lawns of Didlington Hall recounting his experiences of the last few hours to her intent delight and riveted attention.

Abdel knocked on his door to tell him dinner was ready. There was no response. His master's mind could not have been further removed from thoughts of dinner in the Egyptian dust.

The food did not go to waste.

The precisely pressed-dressed, never-mind-the-heat Egyptian emissary arrived at Castle Carter at eight in the morning with a white envelope secured with a blob of crimson sealing wax. Abdel took it in to Carter who had just risen from his bed and was in the process of stripping off. In his vest and underpants he sat back on the edge of the bed and took the envelope.

The wax was tacky and stuck to Carter's thumb as he opened the letter. He unfolded the single sheet of paper with the crudely printed Ministry letterhead and read it. In a few short lines of impeccable English, the Under Secretary of State for the Ministry of Public Affairs clearly stated that the Minister of Public Works was prohibiting Carter from admitting the wives of his colleagues to the tomb.

Carter flicked the sealing wax across the room. His fist tightened around the paper. He stared at the floor for a moment and then looked up at Abdel.

"No breakfast. Coffee! Now! I go to meet with Zaghlool as soon as I have dressed."

Angry as he was and tense with a feeling of urgency, he nevertheless took the time to complete his normal morning routine. The man who emerged from his bedroom that morning looked the same as he had always done - the white shirt; the bow tie; the tweed waistcoat and trousers; the beige suede shoes; the grey socks. There was no visible indication of the inner torment - just the square, stubborn jaw and that expression of dogged determination.

He picked up his jacket and Homburg, stuffed the letter into a trouser pocket, and walked purposefully outside to his car. Before he reached the ferry he met a policeman coming the other way. The policeman had another communication for Carter. This one was accompanied by a cover letter from Lacau which attempted to soften the tone of the order from the Under Secretary of State forbidding, until further notice, any access to the tomb to anyone who had not the express approval of the Ministry.

This second salvo following immediately after the first hit well below the waterline. Carter's mind was verging on a state of rage but his sensibilities told him that any attempt to reverse these orders was futile and he abandoned his Zaghlool mission. Instead he would go to confer with his team and develop a strategy.

As he walked down to the ferry, the District Governor, whom he had not noticed in the crowd of people standing around the slipway, called after him. His timing couldn't have been worse. "Mr Carter, sir! Mr Carter! While you are away may I make use of your car and driver to get to The Valley? We would be appreciative of a lift."

The policeman who had served Carter with the order was with the Governor. Carter glared at the man. "As a friend I would be only too glad to assist you, sir. But if your business is connected with this policeman, I am unable to. You will have to find some other means."

He briskly walked away.

He found his friends eating breakfast at a private table on the veranda of the hotel. Burton wasn't there but Lucas and Winlock were.

"Drop what you're doing and come with me at once! We must secure the tomb. The Minister's refusing to allow the wives to enter before any Egyptians! Damned outrage! Time to teach him and that lackey Lacau a lesson! Time they realised just who they are dealing with here!"

Carter threw the screwed-up letter on the table in front of them. The two men, expecting a more normal working day for a change and to that point happily absorbed in their bacon and eggs, were absolutely astonished by Carter's outburst.

Before either of them could react, Carter continued. "We must lock it up! We're downing tools! Give them a bellyful of a great British tradition!" He grinned. "Come on! No time to waste! We've got work to do! We'll lock up Fifteen first. Clear your stuff up. Make sure everything is stabilised. Then the tomb... After this morning's press party."

By now the two had read the piece of paper Carter had tossed at them.

Winlock looked up. "This is not right. We must write a rejection to this order, Howard. Make a public statement. Let's do it now, before we leave."

Carter looked at his friend. His eyes were afire. "Yes! Good idea. Something of the sort. But we have business on the west bank first. I'll get with poor old Breasted later and between us we'll draft it. Get it posted on the 'Palace' noticeboard. Capital!"

After twelve attempts, each succeeding version a little less vitriolic than its predecessor, the finished public notice would announce that, due to the vagaries of the Public Works Department, Carter and his team would be ceasing work on the tomb and its contents and the tomb would be closed from midday of 13th February 1924.

Apart from the puzzled guards who remained at the site, The Valley was deserted, unmoving, silent. Sand began to settle on the stairway to Tutankhamen's tomb. The materials in Burton's darkroom gathered dust. The faded funerary pall, still awaiting conservation, lay forgotten on the floor of the laboratory. A faint whiff of breeze lifted a corner. In the pitch darkness of the tomb the dead king lay in nervous peace within his opened sarcophagus.

The Minister tucked a rolled-up Egyptian pound note into the belly dancer's waistband and rested back in his armchair to watch the remainder of the evening's performance. His face held an expression of utter contentment. It had been, after all, a most satisfying day. He had been able to take the initiative and gain the public high ground over the arrogant Englishman - a publicly political statement of the power he held over all that the English represented in Egypt.

He despised the West and all it stood for. In his younger years, he had been militant, one of the bolder ones, and had suffered time in the British Army penitentiary for it. But that was all behind him now. Now it was his turn to write the protocol, make the laws, force compliance. And just today he had succeeded in pulling off a most satisfying public coup. He had cancelled the Carnarvon concession and barred Carter and his colleagues from entering the Tomb of Tutankhamen. On his orders the padlocks Carter's team had put in place had been forcibly removed and replaced with new ones - with different keys.

As he reflected on his day's achievements, a sinister smile broadened across his face. He took a sip of coffee and refocused his attention on the rhythmically swaying, perspiration-oiled torso barely an arm's length away from him.

"Ibrahim!" Carter shouted.

He knew the little man from his previous life with Theodore Davis. He had been the reis in charge of their labour force. The diminutive Arab was sitting upon the low wall which surrounded the pit above the entrance to the tomb.

"Ibrahim! What in the name of Allah are you doing, man? And what are these militiamen doing here?"

The Arab at once jumped down and bowed apologetically.

"I am commanded by the Inspector of the Antiquities Service to..." He took a deep breath and then blurted out quickly, "to stop anyone from entering this place... in... including you, sir!"

"Ibrahim, you scoundrel, you should know damn well there is work in progress here."

Carter stopped a moment to gather himself and attempt to reason rather than harass the man. He began again in a softer tone.

"Ibrahim, you need to understand the situation. As we speak and dawdle at this entrance a huge slab of stone hangs precariously above the coffin. A coffin of unsurpassed beauty and magnificence, Ibrahim. Had you set eyes on it you would not so stupidly keep me from my work. What will happen to that priceless work of art should the stone fall? In all the time we worked together I never took you for a foolish man."

The reis felt decidedly uncomfortable. After a long pause he finally gathered sufficient strength to whisper back. "These are my orders, sir." He pulled a folded piece of paper from under his sweaty headband and nervously stretched his hand towards Carter.

Carter snatched it from him. It was another Service Order issued by Lacau. He only had to read the first paragraph banning all entry to the tomb and specifically mentioning Carter himself.

Carter couldn't believe this was happening to him. To him of all people. Lacau surely had not the intelligence to use Carter's strategy against him - call his bluff? It was unthinkable.

The unthinkable then occurred to him. Perhaps that had been his mistake all along. He had never given a second's thought to a carefully constructed conspiracy by those whom Carter considered so inept. But now, in seriously underestimating Morcos Bey Hanna's tactics, it appeared that the Egyptologist's arrogance had been skilfully exploited by the Egyptian.

The angry Carter turned back to Ibrahim, his face an expression of abject disgust. "Just you remember, Allah watches this place. He sees that which you do. He sees it is unworthy of you to betray an earlier loyalty."

To any Arab of conscience such scolding from his past master, whom he had always respected, would have fallen heavily upon him. But to this man the duty in hand and its forthcoming financial compensation were easily the more important. The eyes of Allah were upon him, yes, but so they were at all times, and there was money in his hand besides.

Once more, Carter lost the fragile control he had over his temper. "Unlock the bloody gate, Ibrahim! At once!" he shouted. His face flushed. The entire valley roared back. It was as if a crowd of Carters was shouting at the reis.

The Arab tilted his head to one side, shrugged his shoulders and made an 'it's-out-of-my-control' gesture with his hands. "The militia guards the entrance, sir. I have no power over them."

Carter became yet more agitated. He thought for a moment. 'Thank God the earl was spared this experience. Prevented from accessing that which is rightfully his - an insult of diabolic international proportions.'

The infuriated Egyptologist threw an obscenity at the Arab and stormed back to his car. The reis knew that he had been cursed but had no idea in what manner and cared less. He sat back on the rock wall and contemplated his next meal.

As he rode back in the open rear seat of his car, Carter thought through his next action. 'In the interests of upholding the dignity of my departed patron, there can be only one rational course. For true Englishmen, rudely wronged, in a backward foreign land populated with powerful unsophisti-cates - sue. After all, the justice system is British-based. Bring the fellaheen to their knees, in public, for all the world to see. Publicly embarrass the Egyptian government. A less aggressive approach is inconceivable.'

Within hours of arriving in Cairo, Carter had retained the services of one F. M. Maxwell, the irascible lawyer who some years earlier had convinced a jury to convict Morcos Bey Hanna of treason and who at the same time had argued, unsuccessfully at the time, for the death penalty.

To Howard Carter, the strategy seemed perfect, and the situation that this mixture of characters would create, a kind of poetic justice. In his command of Egyptian law Maxwell was undeniably the most accomplished of all Englishmen. He would make mincemeat of the opposition. To ensure that his forthcoming success was effectively communicated to the world's press, Carter had Merton, the *Times* reporter, in attendance. The stage was set for a very public showdown. British post-Victorian arrogance was dressed and ready to carry the day.

Chapter Twenty Three
Turn For The Worse

Tutankhamun and his people had much to be pleased about. Their engineering of the trial had been a great success. Carter was gone from Egypt - hopefully for good. There were still visitors to the tomb, but the tours were formal and closely supervised, disturbance was minimal, everything was left in its place and the king's body itself remained in relative peace. It looked at last as if the royal party and its group of loyal friends could once more resume a peaceful coexistence. But, before they could release themselves to the pleasures that accompany eternal afterlife, they had first to consolidate their position.

"Before we can establish what still needs to be done here, we must first of all inventory everything in its current place in the tomb of Tutankhamen, and likewise every other tomb that the Carter party had requisitioned."

Pierre Lacau was surrounded by a group of white-coated and red-fezzed Egyptian attendants who had eagerly made themselves available for conscription by the Cairo Museum in order to accompany him to The Valley. While his first inclination was to go to the tomb of Tutankhamen, he somehow felt compelled to begin with the laboratory tomb and, following his direction, like a well-trained detatchment of soldiers, his loyal platoon sallied forth.

They stopped at the open doorway and looked inside. One of them observed the general situation of the interior and noted it down in his journal. All was as it had been that fateful day when Carter had been so unceremoniously barred from re-entry - preparation trestles against either wall in the entrance corridor; underneath and against the walls, purpose-built crates, readied for their contents, the protective padding remaining carefully positioned within them and overlapping their rims; open trays of objects awaiting attention; and six cases of wines, each boldly labelled:

FORTNUM & MASON LTD.
181, PICCADILLY,
LONDON, W.

Although behind his party of helpers, the Director General of the Antiquities Service towered head and shoulders above them and thereby commanded a very adequate view of what was in the chamber corridor.

Without question, the objects on the tables still awaiting the conservators' attention were lovely but there, a little more distant, was the cache of wine. Lacau's inner senses were French after all, and he was naturally drawn in that direction first - the innanimate treasures from an ancient past could wait for the time being. He authoritatively pushed his way between the men in front of him, walked over to the closest crate and removed the already loosened lid. There were three individual wine boxes remaining inside. He reached in and pulled one out, sliding the wooden cover off to look at the bottle. He became absorbed by its blood-rich colour and for a few moments quite forgot himself, what he had come for, and who accompanied him. He took the bottle out and examined it closely, turning it gently. He held it up to the light which blazed in from the doorway. The sun's rays sprayed a rippling magenta backwash across the white limestone walls behind him. Reverently he drew his hand over the wine bottle before carefully replacing it in its box.

As he slid the cover closed once more, he couldn't help but wonder. If he could secrete it away in the carpet bag he had with him, what chances were there that anyone would miss it? For a man of his position, such a thought was reprehensible and, with a reverence only a Frenchman could bestow (and only another Frenchman could recognise), he put the box back in its case.

His helpers remained standing at the entrance, patiently awaiting their instructions. He was about to turn back to them when something made him feel he should look further. There was another layer of wine cases below the first. He removed the top case and looked at the one beneath. The romance of the label warmed his heart: 'Chateau Margeaux 1888'. This was irresistible. Trying not to disturb the contents, he picked it up carefully and stood it on another crate. Expectantly, he lifted off the lid.

As if awakened by the brilliance of light filling the doorway to the tomb, two wide-open eyes stared back at him from the small, chocolate coloured, carved head of a boy enclosed all about by a generous padding of straw.

For a moment the Director stood stock still, his mouth agape but quite speechless. There were murmurings from behind him. By now, all had caught a glimpse of what he was looking at. His surprise at making this discovery and the placid exquisiteness of the piece itself had quite taken his breath away.

He lifted it out gently by the base and examined it more closely. A few flakes of auburn paint which had fallen from the peeling cheeks lay behind in amongst the straw. He turned it over, then stood it on a nearby table. He examined the case more thoroughly for evidence of any identifying note. Carter had methodically catalogued every piece he had unearthed and this one surely would be no exception. But Lacau found no label; nothing at all.

He ordered his men to get about their business of inventorying while he himself set about opening every case of wine in the corridor. In the event, all he encountered was more wine.

Lacau had the Carnarvon party's catalogue papers with him, and a cursory study confirmed that this piece had not been accounted for. The Director's emotions moved from wonderment to conjecture and thence to suspicion. He shook his head. It was unthinkable. He had sufficient respect for Carter's professionalism not to think him culpable. But he would not have so easy a time explaining the discovery to the Minister. He would need some convincing words from the man himself.

Having assured that the piece now was clearly identified and described on the inventory being prepared by his assistants, Lacau took himself off to the Winter Palace to send a telegram.

He had previously won a battle of principle with Carter. So far as the Director was concerned this was now behind them. In his own mind, common sense had prevailed. There was no one else that he had access to who could manage the continued clearance of the tomb so well as the arrogant little Englishman whom he had ejected and excluded from the place in an atmosphere of some considerable public disgrace. But the deed was over and done with and that was an end to it. There would be no question now that Carter could elicit any agreement for a share in the past discoveries and those yet to come. Lacau and the Egyptian government were in complete control. All Lacau needed now was to get Carter safely back on the job by the next season. But it would be hard to persuade the Minister and, if this incident became public and went unexplained, well nigh impossible. Ironically, the country would suffer at the hand that had sought so skilfully to protect it. He therefore decided not to inform the Minister of his findings until he had allowed Carter himself to explain.

Lacau had always been a realist. Carter's eminent qualifications made him the only choice to continue clearance of the tomb. He was therefore anxious to give Carter the room to provide a full and credible explanation. He called for Herbert Winlock who, in Carter's absence from Egypt, was acting as his proxy. He asked him to draft a cable describing the find and the circumstances in which it was discovered and politely request an explanation. In the event that no explanation was forthcoming, Lacau suggested that Carter might say it had been purchased. That would be a risky story but probably untraceable.

Both spent many wakeful nights while they awaited a response. They need not have worried.

Carter had received the cable when he registered at a hotel in Chicago on the third leg of his lecture tour in the United States of America. The gruelling schedule was taking a toll on his limited stamina. He took the envelope up to his room without opening it and did not settle down to read it until he had laid out his things, received a large gin and tonic from the room service waiter, and made himself comfortable on the sofa.

Upon opening the small yellow envelope, he could thank his fatigue for the mildness of his shock. It had been a fear he had harboured subconsciously for too many months. At last he could come to terms with it.

He worried that if he could not find the right words for a response, or if they were taken vindictively in the wrong way, as he fervently believed Lacau might already have planned, the last thread of his connection to Tutankhamen could be severed for ever.

His response was coolly factual. Notwithstanding his calculated story, Carter could not resist placing a diversionary sting in the tail. He expressed dismay at the knowledge that the piece had been shipped to Cairo in haste and without restoration, preservation, or even stabilisation prior to dispatch. To Carter this was yet another shining example of the incompetence of the Antiquities Service.

By the time he'd scribbled his measured and critical reply, there were three empty tumblers on his desk and he was well into the fourth.

The boy king was not at all happy with Carter's lucidity with words. The return cable, despite its being a blatant lie, looked every bit credible. And, as the king had feared, it was just what Lacau had wanted - to all appearances a clinically factual explanation of events.

Monsieur le Directeur could not have wished for a more acceptable answer. He could now relate the story of the discovery to the Minister without fear of inciting his anger. Morcos Bey Hanna might become somewhat disgruntled after first being presented an opportunity to further cement his country's dislike of the insidious British, and then losing it to a piece of prose so skilfully eloquent that it would easily repudiate any accusation he might attempt to construct, but in this regard Lacau felt he could contain the Minister's sense of loss.

He was quite correct. The Minister gave no outward sign of irritation. Neither did he ask to see the piece in question. The timing was fortunate. He was preoccupied with more pressing political matters.

Nevertheless, Lacau's report reminded the Minister that the business with the tomb was not finished and he took the time to enquire what was to happen next. "Monsieur le Directeur." His chair squeaked as he shifted position. "Monsieur Lacau. Now that the British archaeologists are gone from The Valley, what are your plans for the tomb that has become such a spectacle of worldwide interest? I am aware you have organised many official visits to the place. How do we intend to orchestrate its exposure to the public?"

"Ah," Lacau paused. He should go along with the Minister on this one. Give him what he wanted to hear. It was not the time to raise radical issues. He could manufacture a temporary response and await the right moment to tell Hanna what his real intentions were. Besides, the way things were going between the government and the British at that moment, this particular Minister could be out of a job within weeks. It made eminent good sense for him to bide his time.

"For now, your Excellency, we shall leave the tomb as it is. No further clearance. Let the visitors benefit from viewing the remaining artefacts, the most important ones, in their place. But limit the attendance, of course. It is a little place and, if filled to capacity, difficult to police effectively. Admission will be charged for non-official visits. I think it only right that the general public contribute in some small way to a fund which will support the efforts of the Service. As you are only too painfully aware, there is no money for the kind of operation that Carnarvon so ably led."

He stopped talking and swallowed hard. It was an unnecessary reminder. The Minister's temperament was still sorely aggressive towards the earl's men and it would be suicidal to remind him of the inadequacies of the Service relative to the proven capabilities of the English.

But, for the present, Hanna's mind was otherwise preoccupied. So, noticing the Minister's eyes turn briefly to some papers on his desk, Lacau took the opportunity to quickly excuse himself. The door to the office of the Minister of Public Works was closed behind him before the Minister could acknowledge Lacau's departing salute.

Carter's tour in the United States continued to follow a rigorous schedule. Were he to fall behind in his timing, there was no room in the programme to pick up speed. It had been extremely well planned. Every moment had been accounted for.

But his spirits were high. Lacau had telegraphed a most consoling message back to him. Finally, he no longer dreamed that restless dream. He rose to every podium full of energy and pride, standing with his back rigidly straight, his right hand gripping the lapel of his jacket, his left resting on the papers in front of him. He was in the habit of taking them with him to every lecture, but he didn't need to refer to them any more. All the nerves were gone. All the visions in their glorious sequence were there, crystal clear in his mind. Solemnly he would tell his attentive audience of his feelings as he first laid eyes on the contents of the antechamber.

The Americans lapped it up. They had welcomed him with such generosity. He began to feel like a member of the royal family. After all, they were treating him straightforwardly and honestly, like the unique celebrity that in truth he was. He was becoming relaxed enough to lap it up himself.

Then, Winlock, now returned from Egypt for the remainder of the summer, topped it all off with more news.

Carter was resting in the glittering bar of the Waldorf Astoria in New York. His friend from the Met came charging in with a broad grin on his face.

"Hi, Howard! How'ya doin'?"

Carter took a deep breath. "Just fine, Herbert."

Winlock, to that point bubbling with his news, stopped dead. It showed. Carter had been enjoying a quiet moment with his gin and tonic. He was winding down after another busy day. He sat on the bar stool with his foot on the rung and his 'gin arm' supported on his knee. He was not feeling receptive to company.

But his friend had great news to tell him and by God he was going to hear it. Winlock's expression became sombre. "Howard, old chap. I have something tremendous to tell ya," he said, almost apologetically.

Carter immediately sat to attention, expecting that the news would be that he had finally received an invitation by Lacau to return to Egypt to complete clearance of the tomb and, in addition perhaps, Lacau had agreed to concede a share of the finds to the Carnarvon Estate. These thoughts and more raced through the reawakened mind of the mildly inebriated Egyptologist. He gazed expectantly at his colleague.

Winlock could see the change in mood and smiled once more. "Howard, guess what?"

Such teasing was extremely vexing. The matter at hand was far too important for this kind of frivolous behaviour. "Spit it out, man! The concession is to be restored?"

Carter's rhetorical question temporarily stopped Winlock in his tracks. In the euphoria of the news he was bearing, he had forgotten the most important item on his colleague's agenda. He felt a sudden surge of remorse, but quickly put it aside. After all, what he had to convey to his colleague was a true honour.

"No, Howard. No. At least, not yet. But I am sure that affair will be resolved in due course. The tone of Lacau's last telegram was most conciliatory. And, as I hear it, Hanna is gone!" he chuckled. "No. But the news that I bear is, in its own way, almost as great."

Carter's expression withdrew once more to one of melancholy.

Winlock was himself too excited to notice. He announced with some formality, "In recognition of your achievements in Egypt and in enriching the historical knowledge of the Western world, you are to be bestowed a great honour. Yale University, our premier academic institution, is to confer an honorary doctorate upon you: Doctor of Science."

He raised his tumbler and clinked it against the glass which hung casually from its fragile purchase between Carter's forefinger and thumb.

For a moment the Egyptologist looked directly at Winlock without expression.

Winlock clinked glasses again. "Dr Carter, I presume?"

Carter's impassive face finally softened into a grin and the two swiftly broke into uninhibited laughter.

The nouveaux riche languishing about at various tables within the lounge turned their heads to look. Lita Chaplin pulled her dark glasses down her nose and looked over the top of them. She thought she recognised the less well dressed of the two men. 'In the newspapers, wasn't it?' But the name escaped her. She pushed her glasses back up her nose once more and returned to the attentions of her husband.

Carter, quite wrapped up in himself, did not look at, let alone recognise, anyone else in the bar.

Howard Carter returned to New York in the middle of July. It was asphyxiatingly hot. Good old east coast humidity had set in with a vengeance and, back in his Waldorf hotel suite, he found himself stripping down to his underwear. He dragged a chair up to the open window, sat down and looked out at the traffic and the people milling about below. He dwelt on memories of Swaffham, of Didlington Hall, and of Dorothy Dalgliesh. Two of these were lost. If he could find Dorothy again, what would she think of him now? Disgraced in Egypt. Garlanded with the accolades of capacity American audiences. The degree they were about to bestow on him. It was an incongruous mix.

When he raised his glass to take another draught of his gin, the ice had melted and the tepid cocktail, now diluted with water, tasted weak and decidedly unrefreshing. He looked reflectively at the bottom of the tumbler.

'Dr Carter'. Would people, colleagues, and friends call him that? If he were truthful with himself he wouldn't want them to anyway. The fact that he had attained the title was inward satisfaction for him and quite enough in itself. He would have it always. No one would be able to take it away from him. Recognition at the highest academic levels in the United States was enormously satisfying. (*However, on the two volumes of 'The Tomb of Tut.Ankh.Amen' that were yet to come, he would make sure he had the right letters after his name - for all to see. See Carter, 1927; 1932*).

As he sweated restlessly in bed that night, unable to watch the setting sun for the buildings all about him, he felt a hot blast of wind from the open window. Sand grains brushed against his face. Behind the cold steel gate stood a small teenager in a golden mask, a regally dressed girl at his side. The two had their arms defiantly folded before them.

There was the challenge and there he must return.

The royal pair were beside themselves with frustration. Despite the well-publicised reports in the press and the buzz of rumour in Luxor and amongst the onlookers in The Valley, they had barely ever heard it discussed between the members of the excavation team, and then only in the most disparaging of terms. They could not conceive why. The deaths were factual. The victims' associations with the tomb were real. The story of 'the curse' was well known and consistently reported. Why had the team not made the clear connection?

Tutankhamun had concluded that it was because they were blinded by their tenacious desire to seek out and clear every corner of his sepulchre. Clearly avarice, expectation and anticipation were far more powerful emotions than fear. To stop them now, it seemed, they had little choice but to attempt the systematic extinction of the team itself.

Tutankhamun looked at Ankhesenamun. Ankhesenamun looked at Meneg. Meneg looked at Ugele. Ugele couldn't find anyone to look at.

"I... I believe I know what you are thinking, lord. But it has been my feeling all along that killing is too radical a means to achieve your ends. In any case, it is difficult and with uncertain outcome. The consequences, also, are hard to read. Your ark now being exposed, there will always be others who will gladly follow, no matter what the risk. See how these men ignore it. For them the prize is far too great a temptation.

"It is my firm belief that we should continue to aggravate the already strained political relationships between Egypt and the foreigners who seek to control it. If we can cause unrest sufficient to delay any agreement to continue the excavation and if we can do this for long enough - until a great storm comes to bury the tomb once more - your Majesty may once again rest in peace."

"You are a good and peaceful man, Ugele," said the king. "And we admire your respect for human life. You may try your way. Should you fail, however, I fear that we shall have to resort to more physical means. Even this, as you say, may fail. Then the outcome for ourselves will be inevitable."

Ugele bowed. He turned to contemplate The Valley below.

First he must slow Carter down. He knew that Carter retained a fondness for the Dalgliesh girl. But so far as emotional attachment and the tomb were concerned, the man had long since made his choice. The Nubian could see that the girl still felt her unrequited affection for Howard was, well, unrequited. She, too, had come to terms with the realisation that this Egyptologist with his life's ambition before him and within his grasp, felt a huge responsibility for the care and preservation of all that he discovered. She was very much in second place - not even a close second at that. There could be no balance between these two realities.

He had watched her with some vigour purposefully expose herself to a considerable number of social occasions involving the opposite sex ever since the last encounter with the Egyptologist. Neither the pilot nor any of the others had managed to capture her attentions for any length of time. But she was not discouraged and keenly continued an active social life.

Somehow he had to get them back together again, and not just to meet but in such circumstances that would ignite some deeply passionate chemistry between them. Ugele would have to create a far greater passion if he was to cause Carter voluntarily to give up any notion of returning to the tomb.

The Nubian had one great advantage. Lovemaking was a particular skill with his kind and he felt supremely confident of his persuasive abilities. He decided to begin by working on the prize.

He found her at home, sitting by the fire in her living room, reading a letter. It was from Carter. It had been posted in the United States.

Good timing, thought Ugele. She will be receptive. But when he got within her mind and read the letter for himself, he realised that the task before him was a heavy one. The words clinically recounted Carter's adventures. First the mundane - the stumbled lectures, the better ones, the applause, the press (there were several cuttings accompanying the letter), the quality of the hotels, their food, their service, their guests, their rooms, his itinerary, the trips, the long nights on the trains, the cabs, the cab drivers, being late, getting to bed late, sleeping late, the American breakfasts, the coffee shops, the cars, the people in the streets, and the museums. Then the high notes - the private lecture session with the President, the White House, his questions and comments, the honour bestowed at Yale and, finally...

...However, the best news I can relate to you, Dot, is that the government has once again changed - this time to our advantage - and I have received from my colleague in Cairo news that Prof. Lacau has accepted my explanation for the overlooked bust of T. and I am once more held in good favour by the authorities. There is, therefore, a strong chance I will be able to return shortly to continue my work!

You can imagine my current state of excitement. Hopefully, by the time I see you next a date for my return will have been confirmed and I shall be able to prepare for resumption of the work. In the time I have had to think on it I am now convinced that to do a proper job will take my team at least another five years. I dearly hope and pray nothing has been hurt in this unfortunate interim.

Until Southampton.

My love,

Howard.

Dorothy threw the letter and the unopened cuttings on the fire. She watched the pages briefly glow, curl, char and crumble to soot.

Bad news indeed. There would be no turning this worm. Ugele's timing had been impeccably bad.

In the foggy cosmos of the afterlife, in those dense and swirling mists of time, there were two other spirits, other energies abroad. Invisible and unknown to each other, they acted independently, each one pursuing its desperate charge, each one intent on its own goal, each able to control aspects of the present, each capable of influencing the future, each able to touch the lives of mortals.

There was no way that these forces could meet. They existed on separate, individual planes, each a perfect representation of their own world as they had known it from birth to death. They looked down on the modern world. They saw all that happened there. But they could not see each other. They were both there at the same time and neither ever knew of the other's existence.

One of these forces was doing its utmost to preserve the sanctity of its wordly tomb. The other was intent on assuring its total violation. Because of the separation of their planes, the boy king himself had no sense of any other conspiracy. Likewise, neither was Horemheb aware of the activities of

Tutankhamun.

Horemheb, for his sins, was almost alone. But for a few ephemeral servants, no one in his previous life had accompanied him to his personal plane in the afterlife. Most had perished.

Sitting in a street side cafe in the sukh in Cairo, his body wrapped in a dirty white robe and his fat head in a black and white burnous, the scheming, oblate spirit's ragged posture looked every part the infidel. He had had little success in his attempts to get the rabble to support some local insurrection, so he decided to take on the job himself. He was, after all, eternal now and he could afford to take risks.

It was early evening and the Commander-in-Chief of the protecting British forces was shortly to ride by on the way to his residence. Horemheb had drunk several cups of coffee while he waited. He was becoming impatient to get the job over with so that he could return to his own little piece of paradise, be it ever so lonely.

Following twenty or so outriders in several regimented lines, mounted on a finely dressed, white Arab stallion, the brilliantly white, erect and imperial figure of Sir Lee Stack finally appeared from a side street.

Horemheb got up from his table and walked briskly into the road. It was over in a moment. Closing within a yard or two of the great man, he drew a gun from under his robe, aimed it at the man's head and fired. Stack fell to the ground stone dead. The gun lay in the dust. The man who had fired it was gone.

The police quickly wrestled an unfortunate suspect to the ground. That, but for the mechanical formalities of lawful process, was an end to the matter.

What this single act of assassination had achieved, however, was a grave turn for the worse for the designs of the boy king. Within weeks, the scandal had forced the old government to stand down. The new government was far less unsympathetic to the British. It would demonstrate a willingness to be receptive to the Carnarvon Estate's wishes to return Carter to his job of clearance. This being the case, completion of the excavation and ultimate violation of the mummy became a virtual certainty.

Horemheb had much cause for self-congratulation. With a complacent smile on his face, he lay back on his couch and reached for the goblet of wine offered by a servant girl. He winked at her lustfully. She leant closer, the bulging top of her bosom blossoming from her tight dress. He pulled at the neckline with one finger. The sensuous image slowly dissolved before his eyes.

"To Seth with this afterlife!" he swore. "Is nothing real? Am I condemned to a life of eternal frustration?"

He was right about one thing.

They could not believe their misfortune. Everything had been going so well. What forces of evil were at work against them? Could it really have been the singular act of a madman, or was there some more sinister foe out there amongst the ordinary people in the streets? The royal couple had discussed the possibility with their followers and dismissed it - both Ay and Horemheb had been irrevocably eliminated; there was no way their spirits could have survived to the time they now inhabited. Akhenaten, then, or Smenhkhare, because Tutankhamun had been moved to return the religious order to the old ways? No, it was unthinkable they could have turned against their own blood.

"There is one way to be sure, my lord," said Ugele. "One way we might know the true nature of this evil force or whether this is just a most unfortunate coincidence."

They all looked at him.

"We can lay a trap."

"A trap?"

"A trap, yes. If there is someone, something out there conspiring against the king's spirit, it surely would be attracted to assisting in the execution of a plan that, if successfully completed, would seal the fate of our king's mortal remains. The infidel, if he in fact exists at all, would be exposed."

"We would be taking considerable risk," cautioned Meneg. "The plan must ultimately fail. Out lord's eternal future depends upon it."

"Your words are wise, old man," said Tutankhamun. "This is a most dangerous direction for us to take. We risk oblivion."

"And what do you think this current situation is relentlessly developing into?" asked the queen. "In order for us to have a chance to turn the tide of evil, we have no alternative but to take risks. I would like to hear what nature of trap it is that the master mason might suggest. We must wrest control of forward events from those who act against us. We can only do this through our own actions. We cannot sit and watch, hoping by chance that things will take a turn for the better. Ugele, what plan have you in mind?"

"My lady, I have not fashioned a plan. This is something we should work on together. I have an idea, though..."

"This is madness," said Tutankhamun.

"Hear him out, my king, I implore you. Proceed, Master Mason."

Ugele paused and looked at the king. After a moment or two Tutankhamun nodded his assent.

"This man Carter will be returned to work in The Royal Valley. If not, your Majesties need not worry. But it is likely, as you say, that he will be permitted to return. He has already begun to expose the holy of holies. It is therefore correct to assume that he will continue this process. If we can succeed in physically stopping this man before he reaches the portal, it could force the evil adversary, should he in fact exist, to act. He may become careless in his urgency, thereby exposing himself to us."

"But how do you propose laying the trap?" Meneg asked.

"That is where I need your help."

There was a long silence. Every mind was at work. There was a lot at stake. The outcome could mean their survival or their annihilation.

Tia was the first to speak. "My lady; my lord; good friends; this we could do: influence the Director of the Antiquities Service to preserve the tomb in its current form. We have successfully influenced him in the recent past."

"Impossible!" exclaimed the king. "They take everything for public display in the new city in the north land. They will not do otherwise. Besides, they would open and inspect everything first. Their desire to see all overcomes everything else."

"I do not believe so, my lord," Tia returned bravely. "There could be some real attraction for these people to seeing things in their untouched state. That will be gone for ever once the man Carter has exposed the coffins. In any case, to expose our quarry, all we have to do is to make it appear that the Director is about to do this."

"Tia is right, lord," said the queen. "We can do this."

The king thought for some moments and then said, "Very well. There is little choice. We shall try. My queen will compel the Director to move towards this objective. Dashir and Ugele will watch for the appearance of the infidel. If it does not work and we find no such evil force... kill them - kill them all. That, at least, will ensure that they meet an equable fate."

Horemheb was beside himself with rage. The Director was in the act of proposing to the new Minister of Public Works that, while Carter should be returned to the concession, it should be but to complete preservation and shipment of the articles already removed from the tomb and still awaiting his attention in the laboratory. He should then be directed to prepare the tomb in its current state - minus the lifting tackle - for permanent display.

The general took a deep breath to calm himself and began to think how this turn of events could have come about. Try as he could he was unable to explain such a change of direction. There was no logic to it - Carter, no doubt, would become insensed at the news and another court case would ensue; equally there could be no doubt he would lose again, this time probably for good and all. And Lacau - why the change of heart?

"He must be here, now. He must know. Why did I not think of this before? Stupid! All the time he has been watching me. All the time one step ahead. How could I have been so complacent? It is time to bring the curtain down on this regretful episode once and for eternity."

Tutankhamun's loyal followers roamed the streets in search of any sign of mischief - in The Valley, in the bars, the cafés, the smoking houses in the sukh, the brothels, even the city jail. Their principal problem was that they had no idea who it was they were looking for. They would have to recognise suspicious signs, activity, talk, and follow these up. All appeared to go nowhere - just dead ends. And they couldn't be everywhere at once. The task was much harder than they had thought.

Horemheb, on the other hand, believed he did know who he was looking for and was on the lookout everywhere he went.

The slight figure was vaguely familiar. Somewhere in the mists of time he felt he had seen the man before. The two at the table were deep in conversation.

"You will meet him," said the robber, "and the others. We gather here every day at noon and prepare for the job."

The general was uncertain. He did not like to have doubts. Loyalty was never a quality of fiends, and 'trust' a word not in his vocabulary. But, linked together with a prize beyond price and the avarice to go for it to the exclusion of all else, a band of infidels had a common, solid bond and would look out for one another, at least until the job was completed. But this man - there was something about him. Remaining in the shadows he racked his memory for a name.

Dashir was sure he was onto something. The 'job', although he had not been told anything difinitive as yet, had to be big. The man clearly anticipated enormous booty. Dashir did a little more risky fishing. "If you need someone with experience you have him - here before you. I have robbed tombs - there in The Valley." He gestured over his shoulder.

The robber was surprised at so direct a statement and it raised his suspicions. "That so? And what makes you think, my fine friend, that it is a tomb robbery that we have in mind?"

"Ah, well, I just assumed. A big job. What else could it be. And I am sure I know which tomb!"

Dashir's overconfidence and directness were about to get him into a whole lot of trouble. Then he felt the king summon him. He excused himself to get another drink and disappeared into the crowd.

While the robber waited for the stranger to return, the general came out of the shadows and stood over him. "Who was that man?" he asked.

"I know not, master. I had put the word about that we were looking for men and he was one who came to see me. He worries me, though. I told him nothing more than we were preparing for a job and straight away he tells me he knows it's a tomb and he knows which tomb - bold as brass! I do not trust him. Since he has guessed right what do you think we should do?"

"He will not come back today - your words frightened him away. Find him. Dispose of him."

But Horemheb was almost certain the man would not be found. Could he really be a spirit such as he and not a king?

The general and his co-conspirator had been unaware that they were being overheard.

"Who do you think he is?" asked the queen.

"We know it can't be Horemheb, right? You destroyed everything -

absolutely everything?" asked Tutankhamun.

"Oh, yes, my lord - everything - to the last piece." Ugele, Dashir, Meneg and Parneb all nodded together. "No doubts."

"Then who is this infidel that seeks to destroy me?"

There was silence for a few moments, then Meneg said, "Perhaps no more than a common criminal."

"We can stop him - if he is mortal," said Parneb, but with no note of conviction in his voice.

"You'll have to find him first," said Dashir, who had continued to watch the goings on in the bar below. "He has disappeared! Just vanished before my eyes."

"We will find him - fear not, my lord," reassured Parneb. "We found him once, and now we know what we are looking for."

"IF he is mortal," Dashir repeated to Meneg.

As things turned out, however, neither the robber nor his leader were ever seen again. And Monsieur le Directeur did not succeed in convincing the Minister of his proposal. It was not a viable proposition. Egypt and the world needed to see and study everything that still lay buried in that tomb - it all had to come out.

Carter was waiting.

Chapter Twenty Four
Turn for the Better

Carter dunked his Peak Freans water biscuit in his tea and sucked it down noisily. The breeze off the Atlantic was comfortably cool. As the ponderous engines of the steamer throbbed beneath him, he sat back in his deck chair and contemplated the vast, tossing seascape before him. His mind drifted first to Egypt, then to thoughts of lush summer pastures in the countryside of England, and finally to preparation for his forthcoming lecture tour in the United States of America. He approached the task with some trepidation, especially the invitation he had received to meet with the President - a parallel honour so far not bestowed by his countrymen - but he did not dwell on it.

He was happy to be getting away. Hard and unfamiliar work it may turn out to be, but it was different, sufficiently different to improve the likelihood of his forgetting the distasteful moments of this past season and hopefully form a basis for carving out a new future.

But two concerns remained.

So convinced was he of the righteousness of his position throughout the great fight he had just lost that he felt compelled to commit its history to paper; this to vindicate himself and his colleagues and expose the unjust ruling before his peers. He had brought copies of all the relevant correspondence with him and would get the facts onto paper quickly before the memory became tainted with time.

And then there was that beautiful head. It might be discovered. If not, some day he would have to risk going back to claim it. Every time he reflected on it, clouds of guilt would quickly form and close in around him.

He pulled his notebook from his inside jacket pocket, rolled off the rubber band that secured it and turned to a clean page. He patted all about his jacket in search of his pencil, eventually finding it neatly secured in the hatband of his Homburg. He sighed, placed the hat back on his head, and began to write.

The blue, foaming waters roared all around him, occasionally flinging salty droplets onto his face. As he wrote, he tasted the water with his tongue. The words flowed freely. For once he felt unpreoccupied, released from all diversions. He scribbled with considerable energy, barely pausing for thought.

The boat violently lurched on a high wave, causing him to break his pencil point. The steamer crashed down onto its other side, belching a great wall of sea spray all over him. As the deck pitched, Carter's chair skidded alarmingly sideways towards the handrail. His teacup and saucer fell from the armrest, bounced on the decking and rolled over the side.

Enough, he thought. He stood up and shook the water from his notebook. He brushed at his damp clothes, gathered up his things and unsteadily descended the steps to the deck where his cabin was located.

Safely inside the security of his cabin, and comfortably stripped to his stockinged feet and underwear, he relaxed on his bunk. His mind drifted back to thoughts of America. He could see himself standing at the podium, making his first lecture to a packed hall of distinguished academics. He saw a hand raised at the back of the room. He was glad of the opportunity to break his one-way monologue and was about to take the imaginary question when his thoughts were interrupted by a soft knock at the door.

"Who is it?"

"One guess," came the whispered reply.

Carter sighed. He didn't want company. He certainly didn't wish to play games. He would have dismissed the caller without so much as an enquiry as to his identity, but there was something familiar in that accent.

After a moment's pause, Carter whispered back through the louvres, "A clue?"

"Dis toime tis Oi who feels d' sickness."

"SEAMUS!" Carter quickly pulled on his dressing gown and threw open the door. He stood in the doorway for a moment grinning from ear to ear, then moved aside.

"Come in! Come in, Father. Oh, I can't tell you how much this happenstance meeting pleases me!"

Carter was absolutely genuine. They embraced.

"Please. Please sit down. God. Ah. Oh. Forgive me. It must be thirty years, surely, if it's a day."

"No, t'ree to be exact, sir. Just t'ree. D' last toime we met was t'ree years ago, an' just before y' became famous. One tends t' count more accurate when one's in one's sixties, on account of d'ere isn't d'at much left, y' see. An' th' meetin' always on a boat an' in a storm, so it seems... Well. Let me look at y' - a famous man an' all, is it?" The corpulent priest looked Carter up and down. "Oi couldn't believe it moiself, so Oi couldn't. Oi was readin' d'is manifest, y' see, an' me eyes came upon d'at famous name an' Oi 'ad t' come an' foind you. An' roight glad I am d'at Oi 'ave. Roight glad."

Carter looked soulfully at his hands.

"To be honest about it, Seamus, I had no wish to see anyone this afternoon." He paused and then smiled. "But the sight of you has changed all that. Will you have a drink? No champagne, I'm afraid, but probably just as well. Your 'cure' certainly took my mind off the nausea, but I paid for it on the train from Alexandria! I occupied the first-class toilet almost the entire journey to Cairo!" Carter laughed.

The priest chuckled. "Yes. Y' told me about it d'last toime we met. Tis a moite early but Oi t'ink Oi'll 'ave just a little of y' gin. Would y' be havin' it in d' cabin?"

"Indeed! What self-respecting Englishman would be without a bottle of 'mother's ruin' close by his person?... And tonic?"

"Oi t'ink not. Oi've to give a sermon in d' first-class lounge at t'ree dis afternoon and Oi needs to keep a clear head. A little neat gin will sharpen me senses - permit me to do God's work wid a little sparkle, so t' speak." The priest grinned.

"Oh, Seamus, it's so good to see you," Carter repeated, clearly relieved. "But what takes you to New York?"

"Dey tell me dere's a loada Oirish awaitin' me blessing. An' you? What brings you to the States?"

"I have been invited to give a number of lectures. Oh, Seamus, there is so much to talk about..."

"Dat dere must be... for you, dat is. For me? Not dat much. When you're engaged in d' work of d' Lord, tis only d' confession dat brings de odd moment of excoitment. To tell you d' truth... An', God don't hear me now, for moi sake..." He raised his eyes to the ceiling in a momentary gesture of communion. "...Oi know'd Oi had d' callin' - virtually any religion would 'ave done - but twas only d' Cat'olic faith dat could provoide dat necessary interlude - dat brief, enjoyable respoite from d' day-t'-day repetitive, almost boring, routine of d' laying on of hands - dat brief moment when y' hears about someone's dreadful indiscretion. Oh, just t' t'ink on dem glorious indiscretions!"

He paused for a moment. A broad grin developed across his face as he reflected on some of the more racy adventures he had previously forgiven in the Lord's name. "After Oi 'ave taken a few more of dese," he brandished the empty tumbler at his friend, "p'raps y' will get t' hear a few! Anonymous a' course."

Carter laughed, refilled the glass and said, "Seamus, I look forward to a few tales. But first a few of my own. Much has happened since I saw you last. There is much that has been troubling me of late and there has been no one to talk to. Your good counsel may help me."

As if recently released from a penetintiary filled with mutes, Carter launched into a long diatribe on the history of his search for, the discovery of, and the clearing of the tomb of Tutankhamen. Every major detail. Every personal feeling of injustice. Every fear for the future. For him this was the best kind of exorcism.

There was much toing and froing in the conversation - Carter waiting to hear the priest's reactions, the priest fascinated with the complexity and variety of the adventures. Finally Carter reached the point in his story where had received an invitation to give a lecture tour in North America and here he stopped.

"We 'ave talked about a good deal, Howard. Many stories. Many croises. But y' know dey need you. Dey will have y' back."

Seamus reflected for a moment.

"Amongst it all Oi noticed d' mention of one lady. From what y' said and d' way y' said it, seems dere was more dan a passin' relationship betwixt d' two of you. Tell me, what has become of her?"

"You are referring to Miss Dorothy Dalgliesh?"

"Dat's d' name!"

"We correspond. Infrequently, I must admit, but we do converse. She lives in England still but does not venture to Egypt any more. Little wonder; I could never spare but the odd evening hour to socialise. The demands have been great. It sounds callous, I know, but I literally had - have - no time for her, much as I would have liked."

Carter was sincerely apologetic. He regretted his total commitment to the work. At the same time he was realistic - he knew he had been willingly consumed by it. "I am very fond of her, y' know... but one has to face facts," he continued defensively.

There was a short break in their conversation as the two paused for refills.

"Oi've noticed, 'owever," continued the priest, "dat dis lady appears more often in y' conversation dan y' p'raps realoise. P'raps now dat you are temporarily suspended from work on d' tomb y' should try to seek her out. If she'll still 'ave you, dat is."

The priest sighed and took a moment to reflect. "Dere was a lady in moi loife once. When d' juices were flowin', as dey say. P'raps if Oi 'adn't taken up d' faith Oi would have matured d' at relationship. P'raps not. Who knows? Oi felt d' stirring in me loins from time to time. Have you felt d' stirring in y' loins, Howard? Y' must 'ave. A tough little terrier like y'self. T'tell y' d'truth, Oi've had to relieve meself a toime or two - if y' see m'meanin'."

Carter looked at his friend, incredulity written all over his face. 'This is a priest, for God's sake! Whatever next!' But it was fun. He was truly enjoying the accident of their rendezvous. It was completely pleasing. So much had been stored up inside him. Until this moment he had not realised just how considerable a load he had been carrying.

"Seamus," he began after a long pause, "you are very frank!" They both laughed out loud. "Very frank. I do not believe I can be so. But I will try my best."

The priest gestured with his tumbler as if to urge his colleague on.

"The discovery, you will appreciate, has changed my whole life. Before, I was an archaeologist, an excavator, an artist-cum-buyer-seller-trader-keeper of antiquities. This was not so unlike any other job in its balance between work and leisure - other than living for at least six months of every year in a foreign and relatively inhospitable land... Then my life fundamentally changed - in every way. After..." He paused to restructure the sentence. "I am a modest man, you understand, Seamus. But let us be realistic." Another pause. "Forgive me if this sounds like self-praise." Another, shorter pause. "Which it is - justifiably, you understand!" He winked. "...After the greatest, richest, most undamaged archaeological discovery of all time - let's bandy no words here - we must not underestimate the achievement, discovered only through dogged personal commitment and systematic digging in pursuit of this prize, along with his lordship's undying, vital and persistent backing, of course - God rest his soul. Once the discovery was made, I had no choice but to become committed to its rapid, considered and effective clearance, restoration and preservation. I was - I am - the right man in the right place at the right time. There can have been no better occasion to coin the phrase. This is something about which I feel no humility."

"Y' always were d' modest toipe, Howard."

They smiled at each other.

"Oi'm proud of you, Howard. Who could 'ave suspected d'at sick strippling on d' Mediterranean in '91 was destined to become d' most famous man d' twentieth century moight ever see?"

He needed that. The praise was most welcome. Carter felt a rush of pride. He took another drink. "Over the past years, Seamus, I have developed my archaeological expertise but, additionally, I have become accomplished as a writer, a politician, a tour organiser, an entertainer of VIPs - wogs and real ones. I now have a considerable number of names to drop - even royalty. I have also become a banqueteer - if there is such a word - and, worst of all, lately a barrister..."

"Nobody's perfect, Howard. Don't distress y'self. But let's get back t' Miss Dorot'y..."

"...And now I am about to become an orator."

"...Oi said what about Miss Dorot'y? A comely lady Oi would not be surproised t' hear?"

"Oh, yes, Seamus. She is lovely, to be sure." Carter looked at the ceiling. "More lovely than the likes of I deserve."

"Dat y' certainly have no roight t' say," said the priest. "Dat is up t' her t' judge."

Carter thought for a moment. This was the first time he could remember that he had taken private time to talk about someone who meant something to him. He had never talked about his feelings regarding his father to anyone; never talked about his mother or his brothers; occasionally about Carnarvon, even though he found it painful; certainly never about Dot. It was not going to be easy now. But he liked Seamus and was comfortable in the priest's company. And Seamus, so far as Carter knew, knew none of Carter's acquaintances. So there was nothing potentially to be lost by his confiding in this man. He was, after all, almost a virtual stranger, albeit a close stranger, and he would keep the secrets they shared close. Anyway, Carter's own stories surely could never hold a candle to the confidences that the priest had experienced during his years of confessionals.

"There might have been something when I knew her in the heady days at Didlington. Then I may have had some room for commitment. But we are both much older now. Much older. And I have had all the commitment I can manage these past few years."

Carter swallowed another mouthful of gin.

"No room for anudder? Dis is one sad confessional. It is an' all."

The priest crossed himself symbolically and waved his empty tumbler at Carter again. Carter leaned over to his friend with the gin bottle and poured another two inches. Seamus took a sip.

"Ah! Oi feel a sermon comin' on, t' be sure! Dis'll put me to roights, an' dat's a fact!"

He took a longer pull at his gin and turned back to Carter with a perceptible tic in his left eye.

"Are y' disposed t' a little advoice, Howard?"

Carter glared at his guest. It showed clearly in his steely eyes. The answer was 'No', but he knew he was going to get it anyway. He relaxed back into his chair and submitted himself to the inevitable.

The priest took this as a receptive posture and launched himself into his solitary sermon, not a little gilded by the alcohol. "Advoice comes from one's own experiences - largely unhappy experiences - d' failures in one's loife, d' t'ings one wishes one 'ad never done - d' t'ings y'd give y' roight arm to get d' chance to do over again - an' Oi've 'ad a few."

To emphasise this statement Seamus nodded at at his host, gazed reflectively into his tumbler and explicitly wiped the dry bottom out with his finger.

Carter obediently reached for the bottle again.

"Well now. Let's get started. First of all, when you're wid her, when you're t'inking of her - do y' get dis sense of urgency in y' loins? Answer me dat, now." The priest ordered Carter to respond.

'God, he's talking loins again!' Carter stuttered back, "I... I have a fondness for her... an affection... if that's what you mean."

"What y' mean is..." asserted the Irish cleric, "y' have felt a growth in y' trousers! Now be straightforward wid me. No nonsense, now. Y' did feel some excoitment widin yer underwear, now didn't y'?"

The priest looked expectantly into Carter's eyes. But he had stepped inside Carter's limits. The Egyptologist was not amused.

"What possible reason can you have for this line of questioning?"

"What possible reason? What possible reason? Am Oi talking wid a unuch, is it? D' y' 'ave no balls, man? Is dere nuttin' angin' dere between y' legs? Oi can tell y' now... priest Oi may be... took d' faith an' all d' at... But Oi 'ave sumthin'... An' many a man would be proud t' supplement 'is own wid just a few ounces of what Oi've got, an' no mistake!"

Carter was shocked and visibly offended by his friend's vulgar immodesty, not to mention his line of interrogation. He tried to shut it out but Father Seamus was unrelenting.

"Ah... An' many a woman Oi could've put to roights wi'd me own equipment. But me takin' up d'religious orders denied d'world of d'at, t'be sure. Sad... Sad." He reflected into his glass for a moment.

"But 'fear not', Oi sez, we 'ave a foine, fit gen'l'man of intellect 'ere 'oo is ready an' willin' t' satisfy d' hunger dat 'as been left by moie abstentions. Good luck to 'im. An' good luck to d' lucky female dat gets 'im. 'Ere's to Miss Dalgliesh! May she bear fruit for y'!"

He drained the last of his gin.

Carter was dumbstruck. The tic was still in the priest's eye, as if urging Carter to do things he had never really taken the time to think about. But as he stared into his own empty glass, he pictured her sweet face in the thick, opalescent frame of the tumbler.

The priest read Carter's change of expression. He could be getting to him at last. With a wry grin, he leaned back in his chair.

Carter's anger had calmed down somewhat and it was he who broke the silence. "You may be right, Seamus, in some of the things you say. When I return to England we may see each other. At least she said that had been her intent in her last letter. But I have no way of knowing for certain if she will be there." He looked deep into his glass again.

The priest smiled. "She'll be there, Howard. Mark my words." He pulled out his pocket watch and regarded it for a moment. "Must go, Howard. The Lord's work, y' know. Oi'm sure dere are many sinners waitin' out dere for absolution. Should be some good stories on a boat, don't y' t'ink? Oi'm kinda lookin' forward to it."

"Thanks, Seamus," said Carter, shaking the priest's hand as he prepared to leave. "Enjoyed it... Most of it. Dinner?"

"Deloighted, sir. Deloighted. See y' at seven in d' saloon."

As the door closed between them, Carter stuffed his hand inside his jacket and pulled out his wallet. He withdrew a number of scraps of paper from one of the pockets and fingered through them. A tiny, dog-eared photograph fell to the floor. He picked it up and studied it closely. The picture had been taken in Thebes over ten years ago. They had posed together with Maspero and his wife. It all seemed so distant now. Carter looked out of the porthole wistfully. Was there really a chance she would be there when he returned? It was so far away.

At dinner, Carter contemplated the vacant space between the cutlery neatly laid out on the table before him. It was all a bit too much. This was not the right time. He felt an urgent preoccupation with preparing for his forthcoming lectures. Besides, the very process of so personal an analysis was alien to him, particularly from another man, even if he was a friend. He had spent a lifetime sorting out his own problems. This was no different. He would sort it out for himself, given time.

The waiter placed the main course between them.

Carter picked up his knife and fork, uttered a faint, "Bon appetit", and began stripping the sole from the bone.

His guest scooped up a virtual mountain of mustard from the pot in the middle of the table and spread it along the edge of his plate. He picked up his knife and fork and attacked his steak as if to extinguish any remaining life. Having cut a largish piece off, he stabbed it with his fork, turned it in the mustard until the entire piece was yellow, raised it to his mouth, and pulled the meat off the fork with his teeth. He chewed for a few moments and then swallowed audibly. This was followed by a barely perceptible gasp and at least thirty seconds of absolute silence. Seamus touched his napkin to his eyes.

"English mustard!" he croaked. "Nothing loike it for cleaning the passages dat is hard t' reach! Fair brings tears to d' eyes, it does!"

Carter returned a polite smile that was so subtle it stayed hidden beneath his moustache. He willed the conversation to turn to non-personal matters.

After his throat had recovered from the purging effects of the mustard, the priest helped him out. "About dis lecture tour of yours, Howard. Oi was wonderin' whether you 'ad t'ought of including some references to d' scriptures in ye text?"

"Scriptures?" responded the Egyptologist, quizzically. "Include scriptures?"

"Scriptures, m' boy. Indeed. 'Ave y' not t'ought how dey could add a spiritual element what would otherwise be a wholly factual accountin' of what y've been doin' in dat valley?"

"To what purpose? And, assuming you can define a purpose, in what way?" Carter was relieved at the change of subject.

"Glad y' asked dat question, m' boy. Glad y' asked." The priest put his knife and fork down for a moment, sat forward in his chair and regarded his host at close quarters. "Was not King David of d' Good Book a contemporary of y' boy king? Why don't y' pick an example from dat chapter? Oi'm sure dere's one dat's appropriate. Don't y' t'ink dat could add a little flavour to y' story? Oi can look it up for you if y' want..."

"No thanks," Carter cut in. He was not impressed at the priest's apparent inability to recall scriptures at will. "Am I to believe that you do not know the Bible from cover to cover?"

"Well... not exactly cover to cover, Howard. Dere are a few passages dat come easily to moind. 'Specially dem about all dat 'begattin' dat was bein' done during King David's toime. Oi knows several of dose - learned 'em at school - 'specially dose Oi 'ad t' write out foive 'undred toimes after bein' caught wroitin' naughty rhoimes in d' girls' toilet!"

Carter laughed.

"Well, dere was no toilet roll in d' boys'. Would y' believe Oi 'ad no choice? 'Twas a revelation 'twas." He leaned forward in confidence. "D' rhoimes in d' girls' loos, now dem was sometin' to behold. Dey was far dirtier an' more 'maginative dan dose in d' boys'. Oi tell y', men can't hold a candle to d' creative filth dat breeds widin dat female head. T' say not'in' of what may beat between dem female breasts!" The priest looked up at the ceiling. "Lord forgive me!"

He crossed himself, pulled on another forkful of mustard-coated steak, swallowed, belched, and clenched his teeth.

Carter felt obliged to come back into the conversation. "Seamus, I do believe you have got worse in your old age. I had never placed vulgarity as an attribute of a priest."

"Vulgarity? Vulgarity is it? Well Oi begs t' differ. One of d' attributes of d' English language, moi friend, is dat it is so resplendent in vocabulary dat a man such as Oi, skilful wid words, so t' speak, can craft expression a t'ousand ways. You 'ave just been fortunate enough t' hear one of d' ways. If Oi say so meself, spoken loike a true linguist."

Carter's mind began to wander. Every mouthful of food and each additional glass of champagne allowed him to hear less and less of his partner's rhetoric. Thoughts of Dorothy blanked out everything else. He looked into the middle distance.

A moment or two passed.

The priest swallowed another mouthful of meat and mustard, gasped and waited for the pain in his nostrils to subside.

Carter noticed his discomfort and pulled the bottle of Lanson from the ice bucket.

"My apologies. A refill, perhaps?"

"Oi t'ought y'd never ask," said the priest, clearing his throat and pushing his glass forward.

By the time the two were into their second brandies and coffees Carter's head was far too muddled to pull any coherent thoughts together. Neither did he want to. All he desired now was a good night's sleep. And he would pray that he would not rise with any legacy from the evening's indulgence.

But Seamus, whose metabolism permitted him to be well able to hold his liquor, was now at the peak of his performance - at the nadir of his sensibilities - the very condition in which, he recalled with a complacent smile, he had produced the very best of his sermons. And he felt one growing within him now.

Carter got it both barrels and, being defenceless, received it without a whimper. All the time the priest was talking, Carter's elbows remained firmly planted on the table, his head in his hands. Carter had fallen suddenly and solidly into a deep sleep.

Father Seamus finished his monologue and awaited Carter's reaction.

"Howard?... Howard... Howard!" Still nothing. "HOWARD!"

The dreaming Egyptologist raised his head a little and opened one eye. "Mmm?"

"Dammit, Howard - forgive me dear Lord - Oi do believe y've not heard a word of what Oi've been sayin'."

"Mmm."

That was statement enough.

"Well, so be it. Your loss. Better words of advoice y' wouldn't get from anyone. Just t' rown away upon ignorant, stony ground. Your loss."

Carter's head subsided back onto his palms. When the waiter placed the bill face down on the table, the priest pushed it closer to Carter, got up and quietly left.

By the time their journey was over, Carter had had quite enough of his ecclesiastical friend. When they finally arrived at their destination, the parting ceremonies were brief and perfunctory. Carter's mind was now firmly refocused on his lecture schedule.

As the tugs nudged the ship slowly alongside Southampton dock, Carter's eyes searched the crowds below for some sign that Dorothy was there.

The gangplank was down and the passengers were beginning to disembark. He looked at his watch. The boat wasn't that late, maybe an hour or so, but he couldn't see her anywhere. He took one last long look along the rows of waiting people, sighed, turned and went back to his cabin to pick up his things.

Carter emerged onto dry land in a state of anxiety. He hadn't been able to pick her out in the waiting crowd, but with so many people why should he expect to? It would have been easier for her to find him. Perhaps she was making her way through the throngs towards the exit from Customs this minute.

During the hectic period of his lecture tour, he had had little time to reflect on the encouragement he had received from his conversations with the priest. And, on the boat back, his mind had been filled with the list of things he had to do to prepare for the new season in Egypt. The realism of his preoccupation was abundantly clear to him. Practically speaking, had she been there to meet him, what would he, what could he, have done next?

Perhaps their moment had passed after all.

After spending a restful early autumn in England, Carter returned to Cairo fully recharged.

An eminently professional lecture tour had been completed. Columns of newsprint testified to his public recognition. And, to boot, he had returned freshly equipped with his diploma - 'Doctor of Science'. Potentially permanent disaster had been averted and converted once more to prospects for success - in part helpfully engineered through the unpredictable and volatile politics of Egypt.

On the ship over, he had planned the protocol of meetings and purchase of supplies and had developed a timescale of activities for the season's clearing. Tying in with this he had telegraphed his colleagues to ensure their presence at the site by specific dates.

Once back in Cairo, he administered the necessary courtesy visits with characteristic poor diplomacy and commensurate lacklustre enthusiasm, collected a sufficiency of provisions with his usual efficiency, thrift and attention to every detail, and re-established himself in the Continental Hotel.

In a considerate gesture of welcome, the hotel manager had assigned him the room that Lord Carnarvon had always had. Carter was touched by the manager's thoughtfulness and would always remember the honour.

Anxious to return to The Valley as soon as possible, he applied himself with energy to the three short weeks of preparations in Cairo.

In no time at all, it seemed, that was all behind him and he was driving up the mouth of The Valley in the early dawn light. It was almost as if he were discovering the place afresh.

Lucas greeted him warmly as he alighted from his car. "Jeez it's good to have you back, Howard. Beginning to wonder if we'd be the first to see the king after all."

"You were not alone with that concern," Carter returned. "And I'm damn glad to see you, too."

Ali and his men ran forward to show their relief at the return of their master. Carter greeted them all in turn and by name and then looked around.

"Where's the rest of 'em, Alfred?"

"Winter Palace, Howard. But I don't think Harry's in the area yet. You didn't see him when you came through, did you?"

"Didn't stay there last night. Came straight to the 'Castle'. Couldn't wait to get a night's sleep in me own bed. Nothing quite like a scratchy horsehair mattress to ease the long-travelled bones. Amazing therapy!" He clapped his hands and rubbed them hard together. "Well, let's not wait for those who breakfast late. Let's see if the young lad has missed us."

Carter disguised his inner fears with his enthusiasm to get on with the job, but he had been truly troubled with thoughts of what sights awaited him as he entered the tomb for the first time since he had been so ignominiously prevented from doing so.

The steps had been dug out for him and all that remained was to unbolt the succession of doors. Standing in the corridor at the threshold to the antechamber he leant in and peered all about anxiously. The stale atmosphere made him catch his breath. In the silence, the almost reverent stillness once again took possession of him.

His eyes didn't miss a detail. It was very different from the first time. It was bare but for a few insects scattering for cover in the bright electric light. Carefully, he eased himself down onto the floor of the antechamber and down again into the burial chamber. He walked over to the open stone sarcophagus and removed the dust sheet which covered the plate-glass panel now protecting it.

He looked down once more upon the gilded outer coffin of the boy king. At the head, the large black eyes stared fixedly skyward. The tiny, dried-out floral wreath still encircled the uraeus at the forehead. Nothing appeared to have been touched. All was as it had been for three thousand, two hundred and fifty-five years. All soon would be revealed to him.

There was an uneasy stirring within.

Chapter Twenty Five
The Sickness

Horemheb lay back on his couch and regarded his balloon-like belly, rising as it did above the horizon of his chest like a great polished planet. He stroked it with his plump, stubby hands. He grinned. He had been witness to a great many pleasures in his time, but there were few so personally gratifying as the events of the past few weeks. He had watched with satisfaction as the plunderers had made their way ever closer to the king's body, finally reaching the corpse itself, denuding it of its wrappings and its finery, systematically dismembering it in their avarice to obtain every piece of jewellery that surrounded each limb, taking samples of the charred flesh for analysis, posing about the blackened corpse for the photographer, and placing it, reassembled, tiny, naked and without dignity into a sand tray so that it could be photographed as if it were complete and unharmed.

Perhaps his greatest comfort came from seeing the body itself for the first time. That pathetic, dried and shrunken, charred skeleton, almost fleshless - the noseless face, the purplish cheeks. And there was more. When backs had been turned, the reis had plucked off the shrivelled penis.

He regarded his navel once again - a most satisfactory final gesture of insulting disrespect - such complacent comfort for Horemheb. 'And what additional mischief shall I design to alleviate the boredom of my eternal existence? What more can I do to confirm his painful return to mortality?'

He remembered the pathetic fragments remaining from the destruction of his own tomb, the dismembered and faceless skeletons of the guardian statues that had protected the doorway to his burial chamber, stripped of their gold and gilding to the bare wood. Though now preserved in their parlous state and currently on display in the Cairo museum they would shortly be removed to a darkened storeroom to make space for the far grander, perfect specimens from the tomb of Tutankhamun. Total destruction of the grave goods was required, he decided, more so than his, if that were possible.

He thought long and hard on how he might engineer some untimely accident. 'No matter that I shall be denied the pleasure of seeing him in his agony. Agony he will surely have. Agony in the extreme'.

He patted the globe of his belly contentedly and gazed upwards into the limitless blackness of space.

Tutankhamun and his queen sat on cushions on their royal balcony and looked down on Tomb Fifteen and the scene unfolding within it. They held hands. Obscene though it was, the couple couldn't stop themselves watching every movement. Tutankhamun felt the queen's grip tighten.

In a bed of cotton wool, the photographer gently positioned the mummy's dismembered head. He made first one adjustment, then another. Each time he took a picture, the photographer would climb up one side of a wooden trestle specially constructed for the purpose. The camera was positioned at the top, facing downwards. He would spend some time with his head under a black cloth before reappearing. He would slide a small panel from the back of the camera and stack it with some others in a box. He would then take another from a second box and replace it in the camera.

This was a most curious procedure. The queen watched fascinated as he repeated it over and over again. She knew that when he was inside this instrument he recorded like an artist, but far more realistically, and apparently without the help of his hands. She had wondered what he could be doing with his face underneath that black cloth. Whatever it was, he was surely most skilled with his tongue.

The king, however, was preoccupied with the mutilation of his corpse. He turned to his queen, his eyes aflame. "Enough! All our efforts to prevent this from happening have been in vain. They tear my body apart like robbers. They dismember me, as in the murder of Osiris. They expose and penetrate every part of me. It is systematic desecration. They discover everything. They remove everything. I am no longer whole. They shall pay for this - they shall die, all of them; die without prospect of an afterlife - eternal damnation!"

He looked behind him. "Ugele! You have served us well, great Nubian. You have toiled long and hard to avoid our having to watch these awful events. Nevertheless, you and our other friends have failed - not through incompetence, not through negligence. There are powers at work here that defy our control, powers that have grown through the ages since we ruled Egypt, powers that we have not been able to grow along with, much less learn their ways, powers we are unable to influence."

He stood up and addressed all those gathered around him. "I want them all dead - everyone remotely associated with this desecration. A massacre so large and so quick that those who observe it will know, not speculate, KNOW that there is a power out there that they do not, cannot, and will not understand until they themselves, those of them, that is, who retain some measure of goodness, touch Osiris."

He glared at his group of loyal followers. Meneg gestured nervously that he wished to speak.

"Speak, Meneg. We wait upon your words. Address us - all of us here."

"Great Regent. Great Queen. Friends. What we have experienced over the past years - what we are experiencing today - none of these things can go unpunished. It is our solemn duty to wreak revenge amongst the perpetrators of these heinous crimes. But one thing is clear." He paused. "We need help."

"And who or what do you suggest?" asked Ugele.

"Lord." Meneg turned back to his king, "I have a suggestion - the centurion; he who searches eternally for his life's love; he who searches for Pharaoh Cleopatra."

Egypt is an unusual place - to the non-Egyptian, that is. The Egyptian himself has survived within this incredible environment all his life and sees nothing untoward, nothing out of place. There is no yardstick for comparison. Boundless barrenness - hugely boundless, reaching as far as the eye can see - nothing but desert sand and bare rocks, dry as a bone and hot as hell. Within it, running right through it, a solitary artery of sustaining water. Throughout its entire course, the Nile carves a corridor of abundance, greenness and thriving life. Like a benevolent knife it divides the country.

Alongside this fruitful fountain grew a civilisation, a great power, second to none - but eventually, as all powers, second to one. Tutankhamun had watched from above as they had come in their multitudes - powerful, ruthless armies; fearlessly disciplined; well supplied; sustained by well-trained support; tactically experienced; war born; strategic in their warmongering; arrogant in their victories; bent upon broadening and enriching their empire with the wealth and culture of new frontiers. Yet, through practicality, they were merciful. They came fully prepared to dominate through integration and absorption - a policy of limited but nevertheless generous acceptance and redistribution of wealth to those of the conquered who showed talent beneficial to the empire, and above all those who demonstrated loyalty and a clear ability and willingness to conform.

So it was that the boy king had laid his eyes on Antony, observed him through his tumultuous youth, his burgeoning career, his personal agony and the agony of his death. Like the king himself, his life had ended prematurely, but in Antony's case by his own hand.

He had been mummified and entombed, in Egyptian fashion, in the Faiyum. His likeness had been painted on the head end of a single, wooden coffin. Unlike Pharaoh, these Romans were not gods. Their burials were poor by comparison, but appropriate to their position in the order of things. After all, following the passing of pharaonic culture, there were no gods, at least none the like of Pharaoh himself.

The king knew Antony for a goodly man and a talented tactician. In the centurion's continuing search of the heavens, he had visited their plane on several occasions and come to know them equally well. He would be an appropriate addition to their subversive team.

"See that man there?" Tutankhamun pointed out Harry Burton. The photographer was steadying himself on the top of his ladder and preparing to take a picture of the naked mummy's legs.

Marc Antony nodded.

"I want him dead. And I want him dead before their day is out."

Without a second thought Antony said, "With respect, no, my lord. Murder is a human sin and will not achieve your ends. If you wish to engender a realisation, at the very least a suspicion, of the power of the paranormal, you cannot use any method that could be attributed to human hand. They will seek and find a human solution, right or wrong - believe me. What we must cause to come to pass are processes that are impossible to interpret within their natural law - that is, events that are compellingly supernatural. That way we can conjure some mischief and plant the virus of anxiety amongst these mortals. Why not many viruses? Let them prosper and multiply. They will worry themselves to death!" Marc Antony smiled.

The king nodded in agreement. There was eminent sense in what the centurion said.

"However, my lord," he continued. "We must be honest with ourselves in our appraisal of this situation. One thing we cannot influence is the strength of their individual capacity for rational thought. If, in the event, they choose to dismiss any evidence of the occult, there will be little we can do to redirect their attention. We will fail."

Tutankhamun raised his right fist at the Roman. "There will be no failures. NO failures! You will see to it."

"Well. What will be, my lord, will be. I can do this with the help of your Majesty's occult powers. Bestow these upon me and I can do this."

"You are thus enlightened, centurion. Fail me not."

Antony shrugged his shoulders, mumbled something, and turned to leave. Tutankhamun called after him.

"What was that? What did you say just then, Roman?"

"Nothing, my lord. Merely acknowledging your wishes. That is all. I will go about my business forthwith."

"See that you do. Succeed and you will always find comfortable harbour here. We understand your odyssey and wish you success. But, should you not succeed, you may seek no welcome back here. No welcome."

The king would never have spoken such words to Meneg or Ugele or any of the others in his court. Much as he had endeared himself to the royal couple and their entourage, the Roman was not one of them. He had his part to play, nothing more. The benefits of success would be his. The penalties of failure also would be his.

The centurion disappeared.

He had been feeling out of sorts for some time now. Having to travel on a steamer during a particularly stormy crossing of the Mediterranean only made him feel worse. With his wife as his travelling companion, he was at least well cared for and this additionally provided him with some feeling of security. Her support took his mind off what had been preoccupying him these last few weeks. By nature a hypochondriac, he had a profound fear that his heart was about to give out.

But today he had a more immediate concern. The seasickness made him feel absolutely dreadful and, as the boat smashed into another great wave and yawed alarmingly to starboard, he was once again compelled to empty what was already a very vacant stomach. The sweat ran freely from his scalp. His face glistened in the dim light of the cabin. Involuntarily straining to evacuate what was not there took every ounce of strength in his aching body.

His wife dabbed his forehead with a damp cloth. "Hold on, my darling, this won't last for ever. We will be in Alexandria by morning." She turned the light down lower. "You try and get some sleep. I'm going up on deck for a breath of air."

He rested back, appearing to relax a little, and closed his eyes. She pressed the flannel, warm from his own perspiration, into his hand, got up from the bed and left.

The howling wind was cool on her face, but she felt chilled by the sea spray that spattered her with every roll of the ship. She had to hold on to the guide rail tightly to ensure she did not lose her footing. The dark clouds rolled and the white, foaming wave tops pitched around her. For a moment she forgot her ailing husband and drew the fresh air deep into her lungs. Frightening as the storm's fury appeared, it nevertheless invigorated her, and she rubbed her hands hard over her wet face, tasting the salt in the water.

A brilliant flash of light wiped out the view for a moment and a physically shaking clap of thunder immediately followed. She decided to return to the safety of her cabin. Temporarily blinded, she stumbled along the deck towards the stairs, guiding herself by the handrail. With partial vision, she made out the number on the cabin door, turned the brass knob and, as the ship rolled once again, stumbled in. The wind slammed the door shut behind her.

"Sorry, darling. Didn't mean to wake you but I was frightened by the lightning and had to get back quickly. I am afraid. If anything the storm appears to be worsening. How do you feel?"

There was no answer.

"God, it's good to see you again, Howard! Fair raises the spirits." Arthur Mace was ecstatic at seeing his colleague back from the 1925/26 season. "You have seen much this season. I know it. You must tell me everything. Leave nothing out. Please sit."

Carter was uplifted himself. Mace, his principal colleague after all this time and all this history, the man who had written most of his first volume on the discovery for him, had in many ways replaced the guardianship that Carter had felt with Carnarvon. He had missed the man enormously this past season.

"Arthur! If you only knew what this means to me. And what it has meant not to have you by my side. If you only knew."

"Before we talk, a drink?"

"A drink."

Mace did the honours.

Carter downed his in a mouthful.

"Another?"

"Please."

The two men settled into an incongruous silence for well over a minute.

Mace, who had been reflecting on their past association and his present personal physical weakness, felt he had to say something. For some unidentifiable reason he felt apologetic. He had let his respected colleague down and must explain. However, what came out of his mouth was far from sincere.

"Howard. Seems like decades since we worked together. Decades. So much has happened, has changed, in the time that has passed. You know damn well, don't you, that if it weren't for this blasted sickness I'm perpetually cursed with, I'd be with you every season?"

Carter himself had been taking a moment to reflect, too. He had been thinking about how he could be helped with the second volume of his book and wondered how he would work around to the subject. He had not heard every word that Mace had spoken but, pulled from his introspective silence, he answered as best he could.

"Nonsense, Arthur, you always could see the funny side of things. I am likely to take everything very seriously and I need to hear your irreverent slant. It does me good. I wish to God you were with me now, though. Not to belittle the efforts of our current colleagues - Burton and Lucas, so competent, dedicated - but we need you, too. Not so many months ago we had the perfect team."

"This is not helping me, Howard. I'd be a helluva lot happier if you stopped at the compliments, accepted my situation, and forgot your desires."

Carter, elbows on his knees, contemplated the gin tumbler cradled in his hands. He looked up and stared directly into Mace's eyes. "What 'situation', Arthur? What is this 'situation' you speak of? The truth now, please."

Mace hadn't wanted to deal with this. What difference did it make, anyway? He was too sick to return to Egypt, to travel anywhere outside Britain for that matter. Carter had been told this. Why didn't he accept it? Did he believe there was some ulterior motive?

"Frankly, Howard, and truthfully, I am at a loss to understand this line of questioning. Believe me, I'd change places with you any day." That was the truth. His fingers visibly tightened about his glass. "Believe me."

Carter placed his glass to one side and regarded his friend more closely.

The man had lost weight since they had last met. That much was obvious. His complexion was sallow in comparison to the ruddy cheeks he had developed during his efforts in the desert. His chest noticeably heaved each time he got up from his seat to replenish their glasses. The man was run down, quite clearly - but sick? Was he really sick?

Mace could read Carter's expression. He drew a deep breath. "I had hoped to spare you this, my friend. So you want the truth?" He looked directly back into Carter's eyes. "Started with pleurisy. You remember? Why I had to leave. Then trouble with the tummy. Can't take food any more. No hankering for it. Gives me the bellyache. Now, to cap it all, the bloody heart's on the blink. Doctors say I have months. If lucky, and with care, a couple of years." He paused. "Egypt? No, old boy. Out of the question. Quite out of the question."

There was little more to be said.

The compassionate side of Carter's emotions rose to a height he had not previously experienced. Without giving it a second thought, he reached across to take Mace by the hands. He pressed them to his chest.

"I am sorry, Howard. I'm so sorry."

"I am the one who's sorry, old boy. Tell me how I might help."

Mace smiled. "Don't bloody make me feel guilty no more! That's how you can help."

"Don't die on me, Mace. The list is growing alarmingly. I've already lost another of the team."

"Who's that?"

"Our radiographer. You never met him. He died on the bloody boat on his way down this last season. Wife found him dead in bed. Never known anyone to die of seasickness before. Poor bugger. And two of the Arabs who were present at the dissection - they died the same year."

"Blimey. I'd not heard about that. Heard about Gould, though."

"Oh, yes, Gould! Now that was damn peculiar. Dropped dead the day after I showed him round the tomb. Can't say I blame the papers for picking up on the story. Bloody tommyrot!"

Mace, regardless of how he felt in himself, and always one to reflect on the funny side of things, looked up at the ceiling and cleared his throat. "Heard the one about the surgeon, the radiographer, and the gynaecologist?"

It was now 1928, and Carter was glad to leave England. The year had started poorly. Arthur Mace's death, this sad finality occurring in the spring, had removed yet another great piece of his life. The emptiness he felt could never be refilled. His two greatest allies were now buried in British soil - with all those memories he could not remain in England another moment. He was back in Luxor by September.

It was difficult for Carter to comprehend that he had been working in this place, on this single, magnificent project, for close to six years, and still there were masses of material in the laboratory awaiting restoration and package for the journey to Cairo. The king once more lay at peace, reassembled within his outer coffin and sarcophagus, with a protective glass plate above. The tomb itself was otherwise pretty much cleared but for the shrine which, in pieces, still lay within the burial chamber.

The excavation team returned this season in blissful ignorance of what awaited them. Plots had been hatched, designed to follow closely on the heels of Mace's passing. A virtual viral soup had been brewed and liberally distributed amongst them.

"There's a bit of everything in this," Marc Antony had revealed to the king.

The first to come down with it was Alfred Lucas. He was diagnosed with typhoid.

Carter was in no shape to manage in Lucas's absence, not to mention the possibility that he might never see him again. He was still trying to cope with the death of Mace. Abdel observed him as a crouched figure in the laboratory, his head in his hands, motionless for many minutes at a time. Carter attempted to console himself by acknowledging that things could be a whole lot worse... They got worse.

Harry Burton arrived late as usual. Almost immediately he began complaining of pains in his limbs.

"I am not surprised," commented Carter with authority. "It's those awkward positions you have to get yourself into in order to take those shots. Take some aspirin, old man, and get a good night's sleep." He was trying hard to be upbeat and helpful.

Burton did as Carter had instructed and got a good deal worse very quickly. It was dengue fever.

And then Carter himself began to feel out of sorts. In the absence of professional help, he took to his bed at Castle Carter. This was unusual for him. Had he had anyone fit enough to work with him, he would have attempted to shrug off his illness. But now there was no one. Both of his principal colleagues were sick - really very sick - so he might as well take the time to rest. By the time he recovered, perhaps they would be well on the mend and the team could get back to work together, adequately refreshed.

He had thought he could relax on his bed at Castle Carter, catching up on his notes, perhaps doing a little work towards the last volume. But he found himself becoming progressively more feverish and listless. Soon he subsided into a fitful sleep.

The three of them tossed about in their individual distress.

Lucas was delirious most of the time. His consciousness was in another time and place. He was the lucky one of the three.

Poor Burton felt everything. He had never felt so awful in his life. He tried to keep up his spirits by telling himself that if he disciplined himself to keep taking the tablets, following the next dawn he would begin to feel a little better. Every dawn, it seemed, he felt more and more wretched.

Carter, languishing in his bed at home and uncomfortably damp on sweat-soaked sheets, tossed around in dream-interrupted slumber.

'What is that damn dog doing in the room?' Carter couldn't believe his eyes. There was a dog in the room. It was tall, lean, with a pronounced ribcage and narrow waist. It was black. It also had pointed ears and an even longer, bushy tail.

As he watched, the dog looked about itself and, apparently satisfied that there was little of a threatening nature in the immediate vicinity, gradually settled down with its skinny front legs stretched out before it. Its head alert, it stared straight ahead, directly into Carter's eyes.

Carter squinted at the beast. The gaunt, black silhouette gradually dissolved in front of him. He rubbed his eyes vigorously, muttered something under his breath and, the weakness returning, fell back, his head once more on the dank pillow.

'What the hell is happening to me?' he thought. 'Must be delirium.'

He shivered with cold and rose to get his dressing gown. The moment he pulled the heavy sheets away from his body, the black dog reappeared at the end of the bed. It lay outstretched as before, poised precariously on the footboard. In the flicker of the hurricane lamp, its cold, dark eyes glinted with life.

The dog barked.

Carter caught his breath. Taken by surprise he instinctively reached for his revolver. The gun, unfortunately for him, was on his desk, and to get it he had to get up and take at least four steps across the room. But, as soon as his legs took the weight of his body, he realised how little strength he had and, allowing his own weight to tip him backwards, he managed to steer his tottering body back onto the bed for a soft landing. He lay still for a moment, inhaling deeply. Then he raised his head to see if the dog was still there.

'The damn creature's smiling, I do declare!' thought Carter.

To be sure, there was a definite upward curl to the join of its lips.

Carter stared directly into the dog's eyes and raised his finger. "Go... Go away, damn you."

The animal continued to stare at him dispassionately.

Carter's finger slowly dropped. He could not muster enough strength to keep his arm up. But he kept watching. And, as he watched, behind the staring dog something else began to form.

It was all out of focus at first. Above him, beyond the end of the bed, a golden orb took shape. Then, within the orb, a face began to form. Something brightly coloured began to frame the face. Now beneath, piecemeal, the features of a torso materialised. The chest was naked. The arms were encircled with glittering bangles, the fingers with many heavy gold rings and golden thimbles on each fingertip. The waist was hung with a circlet of gold and beads of coloured glass, a decorated leather belt with a dagger and sheath of embossed gold, and a skirt of fine, white, pleated linen. Below this were firmly muscular brown legs, the feet set in thonged, golden sandals, with golden covers on each toe.

As the apparition came into focus, Carter swallowed hard. 'Nothing more than a dream,' he told himself. 'Nothing more.'

Then it spoke. "You violate my sepulchre. You, your colleagues, you shall all die for this."

Carter shook his aching head. 'There is no curse. This is a dream. An hallucination precipitated by my sickness. It shall pass.'

Despite his conviction, he felt irrationally compelled to respond in his defence and spoke out loud. The words that emerged demonstrated a coherency that belied his woeful condition.

"What we do is not for avarice. What we do, with reverence and great care, is so that our generations may learn of yours, from yours, and thereby enrich their knowledge. We are not reckless and greedy as the peoples of your own generation. We do not tear your tomb apart for profit. We preserve it. The profit is in learning. Learning about your ancient ways. Knowledge for many generations to come. I promise that your mortal remains will reside there for eternity."

The image began to dim.

"No! Don't go! Don't go! You must understand me!"

Carter's subconscious, in the haze of his fever, was totally absorbed in the paranormal.

As the apparition faded into the blackness, and with it the dark figure of the dog, the frightful conclusion dawned on him. He had never thought; he had dismissed all thoughts of the possibility that Carnarvon's loss could have been anything more than a tragic, albeit most untimely accident. But then Mace; and then the radiographer; the others; and now, perhaps, all of them? It had been unthinkable, preposterous, sensationalist newspaper fodder; but now...?

In the discomfort of his fever, the litany of tragic coincidences, and the insecurity of his loneliness, a cold fear crept over the Egyptologist. Along with it came a great feeling of weakness. Finally, overcome by fatigue, he fell back into a deep and blessedly restful sleep.

The king returned to his queen's side. His mood was subdued. Hers, too.

"What ails you, my queen? Why do you mope so?"

There was a long pause. She turned and looked him in the eyes. "You are feeling the same emotions as myself, my king. I have observed what you have observed. We have been touched alike. He speaks much logic. He speaks from the heart. He speaks the truth. There is nothing avaricious about this man. He genuinely believes in your preservation so that future generations may become enriched, not for possession of our gold, but for the knowledge of our culture." The queen paused again. "What unjust and terrible thing have we set in motion? Is there to be no going back?"

Tutankhamun looked down at Carter's prone body, once more given up to unconsciousness.

The king smiled. "I can turn them all for the better, my queen. I can do this." He looked back at his wife. "Forgive my hate. It was great. I shall make amends. For those who remain alive at this point, no real harm has been done. And those who are already passed we shall welcome to the precincts of our celestial palace. They shall be rewarded with personal enrichment in our culture."

"That would be reward indeed!" said the queen.

Marc Antony appeared at the doorway to the royal couple's room.

"My lord, I am happy to report that my engagement has been wholly successful. I am sure that your Majesties have observed that they are dropping like flies, one after the other."

"Ah... Yes." The king looked at his wife. "There has been a change of plan, centurion."

"A change of plan?"

"Aye. The dying is to stop. At once. We have changed our minds."

"Changed your minds? May I be so bold as to ask what has caused this redirection?"

The king ignored the Roman's question.

"What I have done may not be undone."

"You have done as we had asked. You have done well. Perhaps, for our current purposes, a little too well. But we have the powers to lift the evil you have implanted in these mortals. We have nothing but praise for your untiring devotion and loyalty and, in reward, offer you solace here for as long as you wish."

"That is most generous. However, if it is all the same to your Majesties I will continue my quest for Pharaoh Ptolemy's daughter."

He politely took his leave.

There was much to do and very little time. The royal couple descended to Carter's bedside. He was still asleep. Perspiration continued to trickle from every part of his body and into his soaking mattress.

With a gentle wave of his hand, Tutankhamun turned the tide of the fever.

That morning, after a fitful sleep brought upon him by his ugly sickness and his eventful dream, Carter awoke glad to be alive.

That was not all. There was an awareness. "It all fits. They killed his lordship. They killed Arthur. They killed what's-his-name, the X-ray specialist. They probably killed George Gould and the two from the Service. Perhaps they are killing us all."

At the same time, however, he felt remarkably energetic - considerably better than he had been overnight. He pulled his legs out of the bed and drew himself up - not the slightest dizziness; no feeling of instability. His strength was back. He felt completely recovered.

He washed and dressed as quickly as he could, took a hearty breakfast and left in pursuit of the welfare of his colleagues.

Neither Lucas nor Burton were to be found in their hotel rooms, nor in any part of the hotel. Concerned that they may have been removed to the military hospital, Carter enquired at the reception desk. He was told they had left for the west bank that very morning and at the usual time. Much relieved, he took off back across the river and drove up into The Valley.

As he arrived, the sun was still low on the horizon and The Valley lay in a subdued, almost melancholy orange light. Carter drove faster than usual, eventually skidding to a stop at the mouth of KV15. He switched off the engine, pulled on the handbrake and stepped out. The cloud of dust that he had created in his haste to catch up with his colleagues quickly overcame car and driver, temporarily obliterating Carter from view. He emerged from the yellow pall coughing and dusting himself off.

Lucas and Burton had heard the motor coming. Immediately they stopped what they were doing and came out to greet him.

"Feeling better, old boy?" said Burton.

"Much. (Cough). Much. And you chaps?"

"Fully recovered. Skunk of a thing while I had it, but feel like I've pulled through without a sense of ever being under the weather." Burton seemed ecstatic.

"Me, too," followed Lucas. "One minute I was wishing for the last rites; the next I was up, washed, shaved, freshly pooped, dressed, and away to work. Feel bloody marvellous, too! You...?"

"Not bad at all." Carter cleared his throat again. "Not bad at all."

It was as if each of them had just returned from a long and restful holiday. They needed to feel that way. They were not counting, but they had four more years of hard labour ahead of them before the tomb would finally be declared cleared.

It was Lacau himself, on one of his duty visits to the museum, who noticed the odour first. To a shooting man it was unmistakable. He felt the chill of fear. "Cordite! Gun powder! From somewhere through there, I think. Quickly everyone!"

He called to the museum guards standing in the mummy room. "Follow me!"

The group dashed to the door at the rear of the hall and disappeared into the room beyond. Lacau stopped and sniffed about him. He could still smell it but the odour was fading and he couldn't detect where it was coming from.

Then one of the guards excitedly shouted, "There, sir! Smoke! From under the storeroom door."

They dashed to the double doors and threw them open. A great ball of acrid smoke belched over them and almost immediately there was a brilliant flash of red as the smouldering rags, refreshed with the breeze from outside, burst into flame. Within seconds the flames were on the sides of the packing cases stacked two high all over the floor. Fanned by the draught, they quickly took hold, clawing at the dry wood, the glowing embers leaping from case to case until the entire room became an impenetrable inferno.

Lacau and his men, pulling off their jackets, attempted to beat down the flames, but soon they were beaten back themselves. The heat was unbearable. As the temperature built inside one of the wooden crates, and before the flames tearing at their outer sides had seared through the heavy planking, the piece of golden furniture inside that had patiently tolerated the drying process of three thousand years literally exploded into fire, the gold plate and gilding quickly breaking away and turning swiftly to the consistency of treacle. The gold dribbled to the ground. The inlaid faience floated in the liquid gold and dropped, as if in slow motion, drop by drop, piece by piece onto the ashes beneath.

As the woods crackled and split all about them, Lacau thought he heard a scream, then laughter. In the excitement and panic of the moment he must have been mistaken.

The Cairo fire department managed to safeguard the public part of the museum, but the stores, where the fire had been started, were almost totally destroyed, their contents rendered unsalvageable.

That afternoon, the Director sat in his office composing a telegram to Howard Carter. He had no idea how he was going to break this news. The responsibility for the accident was deeply personal. But, regardless of his embarrassment, if he did not get on with it quickly the news, already heating up the wires to Europe and Luxor, would reach Carter before Lacau's telegram. That would be quite unacceptable and the consequences unthinkable.

For H Carter STOP Most urgent STOP Regret to inform you T articles so far received in Cairo destroyed today by fire STOP Holocaust STOP Nothing survived STOP Deeply sorry..."

Lacau put his pencil down for a moment. Such a cold message for so crippling an event. But why search for sensitivity in a telegram? He fumbled for the pencil again and continued...

...for all our sakes STOP Me to Luxor tomorrow STOP Much to discuss STOP Lacau

He hastily rubbed out 'Lacau' and wrote, 'Pierre'.

"Mustafah! Take this to the telegraph office immediately - and hurry!"

No sooner had his fellah gone than there was a rapid knock at the door to his office.

"What is it?" Lacau shouted with irritation. He desperately needed some time to himself.

It was a messenger with a telegram.

Lacau visibly blanched as he took the envelope. 'He couldn't know already, surely not?'

He tore it open, pulled out the yellow paper and unfolded it. The telegram read:

For Director Lacau STOP Luxor-Cairo train derailed in desert west bank between Asyut and Manfalut STOP Some loss of life STOP Explosion and fire STOP Tutankhamun antiquities losses unestimated but significant STOP Please come STOP

It was unsigned.

Lacau screwed the paper up in his fist and fell back into his chair. He stared at the ceiling. 'This can't be happening to me. If Carter sent this, what is he going to feel when he receives my news?'

The thought was too obscene to contemplate. He turned in his chair and looked out of his window at the teeming populace in the busy street below. Would he were one of them right now.

Chapter Twenty Six
Mummy

The old irritations were still there. Monsieur le Directeur - he who must be obeyed and must be present at the opening of the mummy or this climactic event could not take place - was holidaying in Europe and would not return until November. It had been Carter's plan to clear the burial chamber and the treasury this season. To be held up by having to wait on the pleasure of his old adversary, Lacau, was a frustration likely yet again to bring him to boiling point.

"Bloody French have no sense of immediacy!" he grumbled.

With the help of Lucas's conscientious counselling, and several whiskies, for the time being Carter put his concerns aside and directed his attentions to busying himself with the work immediately in front of him. He assumed there would be three coffins before he would reach the mummy itself. He bubbled with immeasurable excitement and anticipation. He felt rejuvenated. The thrill of it all. He loved every minute. Each new discovery held the promise of the first.

With little difficulty, but with consummate care, he removed the pins from the tenons which attached the outer coffin lid to its base. Together they lifted the coffin lid clear of the sarcophagus. A dark, partially perished linen shroud was revealed, closely covering the second coffin lid. On the shroud lay dried garlands strung profusely about the head and crossed arms. At the forehead a circlet of tiny, desiccated flowers surrounded the lump in the shroud caused by the uraeus underneath.

Harry Burton photographed each stage of the proceedings. He knew only too well the importance of this work. It was a one-time opportunity and he felt greatly privileged to be a part of it. What he was recording was unique. It would never look like this again. Once the collection of objects was complete, his photographic record would place them in context. The pictures, therefore, had to be perfect. That not only meant precision in preparation for each plate, but also immediate processing before any further clearance work took place to ensure that there was nothing amiss with the film itself and that the prints were perfect.

Carter addressed his team. "Here is the plan. We must raise the coffin base and its contents whole and place it on a table we shall prepare over the top of the sarcophagus. That way we will be able to view it complete and get at it more easily.

Carter handed a couple of heavy metal screw-eyes to Lucas.

"Twist these deep into the wooden rim... about here... and here... and, as we attempt to haul the coffin set upwards, pray hard that the wood is strong enough to hold on to the threads!"

The 'eyes' proved difficult to screw into the wood but this was good news. The wooden body of the three-thousand-year-old casket was still firm. The labourers attached the ropes and took the strain. The immense effort showed in their faces. Far more muscle power than had been expected was required to raise the coffin set. The sweating labourers finally succeeded in getting it up high enough for Carter and Lucas hurriedly to lay five stout wooden planks between the body of the coffin and the top of the great quartzite sarcophagus. Quickly they placed some padding on them and the men eased the massive, golden mummiform coffin base slowly back down onto the platform.

The reis and his men took down the block and tackle.

Carter sensitively removed the fragile garlands, placed them on a tray to one side, and turned to address the faded shroud. Starting at the head, he took the cloth in his hands. He could feel the brittle fibres cracking as he gently began to roll the shroud back.

A stunningly beautiful, gilded coffin, far more colourful than the first, appeared before him.

Burton took his photographs and left to get them developed.

Carter quickly repositioned himself over the two massive coffins. They literally glittered in the floodlights. He soon realised that the next stage presented a problem. The seam of the second coffin lay well below the lip of the first and the gap between their walls was too small to permit complete withdrawal of the pins securing its lid.

"Bugger!" Carter shouted, and he threw up his hands in a gesture of hopelessness.

"What's the problem?" asked Lucas.

"Can't get the lid off this one, Alfred," said Carter sticking his fingers down the space between the two coffins as if to confirm his disappointment. "There's no room to pull the pins out. Just our luck. First of all I'm angry that bloody Lacau is swanning around the Mediterranean when he should be here; but now, rather than sat on our arses waiting for him, I'm worried we won't even be ready by the time he's due back."

His colleague clambered onto the planks beside him and leaned over to look.

After a brief inspection he said, "But there's space enough to pull them out a little, Howard, enough to allow us to attach wires. If the pins can stand it, we could suspend it at this point, then lower the outer coffin back into the sarcophagus. This one would then be out, sitting on the planks. We could open it easily then."

The solution was so simple. Carter was not known to applaud the efforts of others, but on this occasion he felt such an extreme sense of relief at the simplicity of Lucas's idea that his response was spontaneous and most complimentary. "Brilliant, Alfred! Bloody brilliant! Funny how, in the undying effort to appear clever, one tries so hard to find a complex remedy when a simple one is starin' you right in the face. Bloody brilliant, Alfred... Well now, let's get after it. Mohammed! Go get some stout wire. About fifty feet should do. Make sure it's relatively easy to twist. Copper would be ideal, providing you make sure it's thick enough. This thing's damned heavy."

As soon as Burton had returned from his darkroom to confirm that the last plates he had taken had turned out as expected Carter's sense of urgency resurfaced and he and Alfred Lucas, now positioned either side of the coffin set, each set to easing out the pins holding the coffin lid in place.

The reis returned with the copper wire and his team reassembled the block and tackle. Carter and Lucas secured the copper wire to the beams and to the extended pins, making the intervening length as taut as they could manage. The labourers increased the tension on the block and tackle and raised the complete coffin set above the wooden planks just sufficient for Carter and his colleagues to pull each one of them clear. Then, on Carter's order, they gently released the tension on the ropes supporting the outer coffin. As the lower portion of the first coffin was slowly lowered back onto its bed lying within the sarcophagus, the copper wires attached to the complete second coffin took the weight and twanged noisily as they stretched. There was a disturbing cracking sound as the two coffins separated from each other. Slowly but steadily, the outer shell of the first disappeared into the dark sarcophagus beneath. As it fell from sight, the colourful lower half of the second coffin became fully revealed.

With the lower shell of the first coffin resting safely on its ancient bier within the sarcophagus, Carter and Lucas helped each other once again to slide the eight planks across the top of the stone casket and, stretching beneath the suspended second coffin, stuffed a number of strategically placed bundles of cotton wool into the one-inch gap between the base of the coffin and the planks.

"Alfred, we are at a sensitive juncture. Take these pliers and, watching me all the time, untwist the wire at the foot end until you begin to feel it give. Then go to the next on your side at the same time as I as on mine and so on. In this way, it should ease itself down into the wadding pretty gently. With a bit of luck."

As the two worked, the creaking and twanging of the wires caused each on occasion to jerk his pliers away and hold his breath in fear that some great and irreversible accident should occur. In fact the still suspended coffins made no urgent movement and, by the time Lucas and Carter had loosened the last wires, under its own tremendous weight the suspended coffin set caused the remainder to untwist themselves slowly. In slow motion, the massive package settled itself into the cotton wool on the planks.

As the timbers creaked under the load, Lucas's and Carter's heavy breathing became loudly audible.

"My God, Carter!" exclaimed Lucas after all movement had ceased. "Could have dropped. Could have broken through the wood. Could have damaged both coffins."

"Didn't, Alfred. Didn't. Burton! Quick man. Take your pictures."

Carter's impatience and excitement had got the better of him. He knew he couldn't hurry Harry Burton, but no sooner had Burton cleared his equipment, with no less care than he had shown throughout the clearance but with a whole lot more urgency, Carter set to pulling the pins out, one by one. He placed each carefully on a strip of muslin in the order it was removed, passed it to Mohammed, and then turned back to his waiting colleague.

"You take the head end, Alfred. Mo, put some padding in that tray and bring it over here."

"But before we proceed we should wait for Burton to come back, Howard. Check the photos were okay."

Carter stopped. Like an impetuous student chastised by his teacher for shortcutting his homework, Carter put his hands in his pockets and sat back on some boxes.

"You're right, Alfred. I'm letting my excitement get the better of me. Go and check on how he's doing, will you? There's a good chap. I'm anxious to finish this bit tonight if I can. I'll wait here."

Lucas dutifully left to visit with Burton in his tomb darkroom which lay immediately opposite on the other side of The Valley. For Carter it was an agonising fifteen minutes before his colleague returned.

"All perfect, Howard."

Carter said nothing. He quickly signalled Lucas to the head end of the coffin set. The two felt for the lip of the coffin lid with their fingers and began to take the strain. For a moment nothing happened, no movement at all, then a 'crack!' as the tenons, seated firmly within the desiccated wood for the last three thousand years, relented.

The lid began to rise. Carter looked underneath to ensure that it had cleared the top of whatever lay underneath, and then gestured to Lucas with a nod of his head to lower the lid onto the tray beside them.

Inside the lower half of the second coffin, a dark-red ochre shroud lay neatly draped over the body of the third. With the precision of a mother cosying her young son up for the night, it had been tucked in tightly all around and up under the chin. A broad and intricate collarette of flowers had been placed around the neck. The scalp was cushioned from contact with the frame of the second coffin by a folded linen napkin.

Carter noted some curious black stains on the inside lip. It looked like some liquid had been spilt on it.

"Burton!" Carter called again. "At once, please."

No response.

"Burton, old chap! More photographs, if you please."

Still no response.

The fact was, Burton had left for the day. By the time he had emerged from the tomb with the last batch of plates, the evening shadows were already long, and, since it had not been Carter's habit to work in the tomb after dark, he had decided to leave for Luxor as soon as he had finished processing the film. This he subsequently did and, by the time Carter called for him again, he was nowhere to be found. He was soon to be seen languishing on the hotel balcony accompanied by a stiff martini. The cocktail would not give him orders, much less show impatience and irritability.

Carter fumed. He was deeply wrapped up in the task of discovery and was most desperately anxious to get to the body itself that very evening. His sense of impatience was almost overpowering. It took him and Lucas over thirty minutes of running around in the dark and questioning various hangers-on before they finally ascertained that Burton had indeed left The Valley. In the end, Carter threw up his hands and stormed off like a spoilt boy who had found he could not have his own way, leaving Lucas to clear up and secure the tomb for the night.

He was so frustrated that he did not return to join Lucas and Burton at the hotel later that evening but retired straight to his bed at Castle Carter. He spent a miserable night. He hardly dozed. The suspense of what lay before him in that third casket filled his mind with hallucinations. He had to learn the truth as soon as possible. Thank God the sun was rising!

However, fatigue from the loss of sleep had done much to calm Carter's anger of the night before. By the time Burton arrived at the tomb that morning, punctual as ever, Carter greeted him warmly as if nothing had happened.

While Carter appreciated that the process of photographic recording was of necessity a slow one, he nevertheless wanted Burton to be as quick as the quality of his work would allow. Burton, therefore, had crossed paths with Carter's abrasive nature on many occasions. But these confrontations were infrequent and the strong mutual bond of respect that existed between the two, each acknowledged experts in their own distinct field, always prevailed. It was more frequently Carter who found himself having to simmer down lest his zeal for discovery should overpower him. This was one of those occasions.

Burton emerged from his darkroom and pronounced his work 'acceptable'.

Carter and Lucas, now accompanied by the recently arrived pathologist, Doctor Douglas Derry, took off back to the tomb to advance the next stage. The two walked briskly into the burial chamber and were soon intently stooped over the still enshrouded third coffin. Carter gently lifted out the linen padding at the head and removed the floral collarette. On either side

440

of the casket, Lucas and he, with carefully coordinated movements, gradually rolled back the red shroud until the entire form of the third coffin had been revealed.

At this first sight of the third coffin, in the midst of his euphoria, Carter felt an extreme sense of disappointment. It was horribly stained with a thick, black substance which, below the crossed arms of the mummiform figure, appeared to cover most of the casket. It filled much of the space between the casket and the shell of the second coffin. But the foot of the coffin, which had no doubt been too steep for the black substance to adhere to, was relatively clean.

Disappointment turned to elation. Carter smiled to Lucas. Lucas smiled back. Their conclusion was mutual.

"Gold!" they each exclaimed at the same time.

"It is gold, Alfred! Solid gold! No wonder the bloody thing was so heavy! God in Heaven, what have we found?"

"Yes, Howard," Lucas acknowledged with a broad grin.

"Call for Burton while I take a small chip of this black stuff. It's a ceremonial oil of some kind but I haven't a clue what."

Carter couldn't take his eyes off the colossal object before him. How did they make such a thing? If they did this for an insignificant king, one who barely made the history books, what would they have done for the likes of Ramses? Carter could not bear to think of the scale, the immensity of the riches previously plundered from this great necropolis. It was at once elating and at the same time deeply depressing.

Lucas looked across at Carter. The Egyptologist was staring downwards, transfixed by the object before him. The chemist understood his colleague's preoccupation. "Don't worry yourself, old man. I'll get him."

He manoeuvred himself around the coffin, clambered down from the scaffolding and left the tomb to summon Burton.

To complete their work on the remaining coffin and ultimately the body itself, Carter had the third coffin and the bottom shell of the second in which it sat removed to the antechamber. The gold coffin was fixed solidly within the base of the second by the black substance which Lucas had now identified as a ceremonial unguent, and Carter had decided to leave the two cemented together for the time being until he could find a way of separating them without damaging either. In the meantime, in his urgent desire to get to the source, he would continue to work on removing the lid of the third coffin.

Again they had found that the seam of the third coffin was well below the lip of the second and there was insufficient room between the two caskets' walls for them to fully remove the pins that locked the lid shut.

Because the two were cemented together so tightly, Carter and Lucas decided that damage to the gold pins that secured the lid to its base was, in this case, inevitable. They removed the pins a little at a time, prising them out as far as they would come before further movement was restricted by the inner wall of the second coffin, and then sawed off most of the protruding pin. This left just enough to grasp with pliers and pull out a little more until the entirety of each pin had been extracted. In this way, the complete set was successfully removed and the lid was raised.

"Finally..." whispered Carter as he first set eyes on the contents of the third coffin, "...I have him!"

There, staring straight up, was the funeral mask crafted in the form of the boy king's face. The face itself shone in the electric light that bathed the antechamber, its serene expression veiled by the small, particulate debris of three thousand years of steady corrosion. Carter felt a welling urge to touch it but held back.

"Lucas. Lucas! Come and look at this."

The entire mummy looked almost exactly like those pictured in innumerable funerary texts - a lifelike mask at the head of a body, tightly wrapped in linen, the arms crossed at the chest, false fists of gold holding the remains of the almost totally decomposed crook and flail of kingly office. Positioned immediately beneath the crossed wrists, a humanoid bird - the ba bird - its coloured glass-encrusted gold wings lying outstretched across almost the entire breadth of the chest. Four heavily decorated gold bands, evenly spaced from the chest to just above the ankles, bound the body and secured the wrappings. This regal 'necro-cocoon' fitted the contours of the golden coffin perfectly, as if welded to it - so indeed it was, by the unctuous material that had been, in antiquity, so generously applied.

By the time Derry and Carter were ready to begin unwrapping the mummy the Director of Antiquities had returned from his holidays. Carter summoned Lacey to make haste to the site. He and his entourage appeared the following day.

Howard Carter bent down over the open coffin, a magnifying glass in his hand, and watched his colleague address the mummy wrappings.

Dr Derry lightly scored the wax-hardened fabric of the mummy with his scalpel. As he drew his knife along the length of the body, but for the barely audible popping of the threads, the corridor of the laboratory tomb was in complete silence.

"Slowly... Douglas... Please," Carter whispered.

"Shh, Carter. You are disturbing my concentration."

Derry, a serious and most precise fellow at the easiest of times, was not at all receptive to interference from others. He gave Carter a cold look and then resumed drawing the scalpel along the surface of the linen, continuing all the way to the feet.

As he bent over the coffin next to Carter, Lacau felt an irresistible impulse to touch someone and his huge left hand closed over Carter's. The Egyptologist, concentrating hard as he was on the job before him, naturally was alarmed by this but only for a moment. He turned his head upward quickly to acknowledge the gesture with a brief smile and then, politely withdrawing his hand, returned his attention to the developing autopsy below.

Derry finished his incision.

Carter said, "Right, gentlemen. Let us begin."

He pocketed his magnifying glass and stood up to address his audience. "Doctor Derry and I are going to - very gently and carefully - peel back the outer layers. Please give us a little room."

The linen, burned it seemed to a crisp, came away in handfuls, tearing or disintegrating into a black, sooty dust at each attempt.

As the unwrapping progressed, they appeared one by one - the unmistakable glint of tarnished golden objects placed about the body and within each layer. As soon as Carter felt he had completed removal of one layer, he stopped, quickly pencilled a neat sketch of the layout, placed numbered cards on the objects and asked Burton to take his pictures.

For each of the onlookers the succeeding hours became perhaps the most memorable of their lives. As the layers were removed one by one, immeasurable riches revealed themselves before their eyes. Each article, though stained by the copious black substances that had been liberally applied during the burial ceremonies, looked unbelievably extravagant. If not as pristine as they had been when placed in position so many millennia before, they were, nevertheless, literally out of this world. Despite his expectations, which by now were not modest, Carter was no less impressed with the grandeur of what now appeared before him.

A day later they reached the body.

What he saw now, Carter had not been expecting. It was little more than a blackened skeleton. For an unviolated mummy it was one of the most pathetic examples he had ever laid eyes on. The thorax and the feet had some flesh on them, but over the thousands of years those parts that had been more liberally soaked in the ceremonial fluids had smouldered slowly away and little but the bone had survived. Chemistry, time and the mummy's inviolate security had consorted against the discoverers.

Carter looked up at the expressions on the faces of the onlookers. Derry and Lucas, analysts through and through, showed no sign of emotion, but the faces of Lacau, the Egyptian authorities present, and Harry Burton were each a picture of shock and disappointment.

"A sad sight, gentlemen," said Carter solemnly. "It appears that all the care taken during his preservation was in vain. Destruction was perpetrated through the ignorant hands of the devout and the mourners themselves. Tutankhamen himself, having been liberally 'marinated' with holy oils, has been effectively cremated, sealed within the oven of his gold coffin."

"A three-thousand-year-old pot roast," Burton irreverently whispered.

Carter was not amused.

It had taken them five days to clear the body to the head. By this time, with the exception of the Director himself, the 'hangers-on', as Carter disrespect-fully referred to them, had returned to Cairo. It was just as well. The final stages of clearance were best left to the few witnesses that remained. With so much jewellery attached to the body itself, Carter had been forced to separate many of the limbs at the joints. The operations had been distasteful but necessary if the complete funerary equipment was to be recovered and, once he had come to terms with making the first break, the subsequent dis-articulations came all the easier. The worst was the last.

"The mask is firmly cemented to the bandaging about the back of the head. Ideas, gentlemen?"

"Heat," responded Lucas. "Let's try using heated knife blades. See if we can gradually melt a cavity between the two. But we'll have to lift the whole thing out to do it. Break the neck."

Carter accepted the proposal without question. He was anxious to look upon the king's face,

With due care and patience, the method worked admirably and the mask finally came free of the black, tarry glue which had, when a liquid three thousand years earlier, insinuated itself into the space between the gold sheet and the mummy wrappings. Once the mask and the linen wrappings had been completely removed, the face of the dead king was revealed to his onlookers for the first time since his mummification. It also was charred by years of slow combustion. Nevertheless, it retained a better state of preservation than the rest of the body. The skin, although cracked and parted in places, was still present. There was a semblance of a youth's face. Also there was a peculiar irridescence in his cheeks.

They unwrapped the cranium layer by layer, allowing Burton to take his photographs at each stage. The head, finally naked but for the beaded skull cap which was so tightly bonded with the skin on the roof of the cranium that it could not be removed but bead by bead, was photographed by Burton in all manner of postures and at all angles.

"Decidedly young - noble features, and the shape of the cranium - does it remind you of the family of Akhenaten?" Carter observed, turning the head over in his hands.

"Indeed, there is a strong likeness," acknowledged Lucas.

Burton's final picture was of the entire disarticulated body reassembled piece by piece in a wooden tray on a bed of sand. It would be the last time anyone would see the body entirely whole.

Burton having completed his work and removed his equipment, the team prepared to rewrap the body and replace it in the second coffin.

"Ironic," said Lucas, for a moment allowing his mind to drift from the job at hand, "that in this one case it is the richness of the grave goods that survives and the body that does not - and not by the hand of the plunderer but by the hand of those who sought so reverently to preserve him."

"Ashes to ashes, dust to dust." Carter felt compelled to add his epitaph.

"In this case, just ashes," added Burton coldly.

As they turned to collect up the bandages, Carter noticed the reis of the day, Mohammed, who had been staring fixedly at the skeletal remains for some time, bend down over the body in what appeared to be a final gesture of farewell. 'Touching,' he thought.

Carter, Lucas and Burton were taking an evening cocktail. Each sat in an upright canvas collapsible chair set on the sand outside the front porch of Castle Carter. As the sun set behind them, they watched the waters of the distant Nile gradually darken.

They all felt a sense of closure to the project. The ultimate object had been discovered. There was a huge amount of work yet to do, and many more treasures yet to be uncovered, but from here on the adrenalin would not be flowing at quite the same rate.

As if to dismiss his feelings of anticlimax, Carter shook his head and got right back to discussing the work ahead of them. "Lucas. The gold coffin is held fast by this solidified unguent. How are we going to go about separating them, do you think? Any ideas?"

"Well..." started Lucas after a pause, "...without taking the time to research an appropriate solvent, and I don't think I've ever heard you say we have plenty of time, Howard..." Carter nodded. "...There is only one realistic alternative. And you're not going to like it."

"Try me."

"Done so in the past. Never done me any good!"

"Try me again, all the same. Promise to keep my temper this time!" Carter smiled back.

"Well... heat."

"Heat?"

"Yes... heat... flame... blow torch... portable paraffin stove... that sort of thing."

"You're crazy. It'll damage the metals. Crazy."

"You don't like it. Told you so. But hear me out. We don't apply the heat directly. We use zinc plate between the coffin and the heat source. Zinc melts at a much, much higher temperature than gold and will distribute the heat relatively evenly over the body of the coffin and its contents."

Carter was listening.

"However," added Lucas, "watching the process is going to scare the living daylights out of you! Got a pencil and paper?"

Burton pulled his pencil from behind his ear, tore a sheet of paper from his notebook and passed them to Lucas. Lucas placed the paper on Carter's knee and drew two 'Vs' upside down and a crude rendition of an upturned coffin resting on them. He sketched a couple of flames underneath to depict the lamps that would be used to apply the heat.

Carter regarded the sketch for a moment.

"What if the bloody gold coffin just falls out of the second? It's as heavy as hell."

"Won't, Howard. It won't. This black stuff is solid - like Bakelite. Count yourself lucky if it moves at all. The process, when it begins, will be an extremely slow one. No fear of that happening."

"Let me get this straight. We line the inside of the gold coffin with zinc. We turn it upside down, and support the outer wooden coffin on two trestles, one at each end. We drape the upper surface of it with wet blankets. We place two smaller trestles between the others to catch the third coffin. We place paraffin lamps beneath the whole thing... and blaze away?"

Lucas nodded. "Simple as that."

"Tommyrot!"

"If it doesn't work... you can hold my pay for this month."

"Hmm," Carter shrugged his shoulders contemptuously.

"Trust me, Howard. Have I ever let you down?"

"Well... no. But then this kind of problem is not your expertise." Carter was never one to mince words.

"That is true, Howard. But I am here to analyse, deduce and solve problems. I am sure this is a viable solution. So let's do it. First thing tomorrow. Now, how about another Scotch?"

Carter called Abdel. While they waited, Carter became pensive once more. After a pause, he straightened up in his chair.

"No. I don't like it. Why don't we try something gentler first? See if it works. Same basic procedure but using the sun. Gets bloody hot in the afternoon. Natural heat. The process feels more comforting to me. Let's try natural heat."

Abdel came out of the house with a tray upon which was a bottle of Gordon's Gin, two bottles of tonic water, a bottle of Dewar's and a small bowl of ice. The three of them in turn replenished their glasses.

"Have it your own way," said Lucas after a quick sip. "Won't work, but have it your own way. You'll have to be careful the sun does not damage the outer shell of the second coffin. We'll give it a try."

The next day, Carter emerged from the laboraory tomb at around four in the afternoon. It was his turn to relieve Burton who, under the shade of a large umbrella, had been watching for signs of movement. The coffins had been sitting outside, upturned on trestles through the heat of the day.

"Nothing, Howard. Not a damn thing. I've touched the stuff with my fingers. Feels warm, but just as solid as ever."

"Hmm. Lucas may be right. Cannot abide the thought of applying flame to it, however. Goes against my better judgement. Really worrying."

"I think you must accept, Howard, that there may be no other way short of taking the entire thing to England or the United States for treatment -

and we know that will be impossible, let alone timely."

"I'd better go in there and admit my defeat with honour, then."

Carter turned back towards the entrance to the laboratory and called to Lucas, "You win, Alfred! Finish up and come on out. Time for a drink. We'll try your method in the morning."

Carter watched in tense horror as the flames of the Primus lamps burned beneath the zinc-clad gold coffin. After two hours of staring, tension mounting all the while lest he miss the first signs of movement, Carter snorted, got up from his canvas chair, and walked back towards the tomb.

"Where are you going, Howard?" asked Lucas.

"Fed up watching, Alfred. Damn process isn't working."

"But it will, Howard. Just have to give it time."

"Something we haven't got."

"Well, if you don't mind, I'm going to wait here a while. Waited all bloody day for the bloody sun. Might as well give the flames a similar go."

Carter didn't answer, and when Lucas turned to see where he was he had disappeared. Lucas turned back to the coffin set and called for more water to be poured over the blankets. He took a glass of water for himself and manoeuvred his umbrella a little to make sure he had the maximum shade. Slipping off his seat, he dragged himself on his back until he had a full upward view of the open coffins. He re-fixed his gaze on the open seam between the two, hoping against hope for just a tiny suggestion of movement.

He lay there prone for what seemed to be an age. Not a sign. He blinked and as he did so he thought he saw the inner coffin ease towards him. He stared hard at the rim. There was movement! Very, very slow, but definite movement. He turned over immediately, shut down the lamps, and pulled himself out.

"Abdel! Get Master Carter at once!"

By the time the panting Carter had returned to the spot, the inner coffin had already settled down onto the second set of trestles lying just an inch below.

"It's still warm enough, Howard. We must raise the outer shell before the damn stuff hardens again."

Positioned at either end, the two of them struggled to lift. Gradually each sensed the outer shell easing away from the gold coffin beneath it. As they strained, the lifting became easier. Abdel and another helper moved the trestles on which the outer coffin had been resting to the side so that it could be replaced on them away from the base of the third coffin.

Once revealed, the back of the solid gold coffin was not a pretty sight. Globs of the black treacle-like substance lay all over it and, like long black icicles, the substance hung in straggling ribbons below it.

But Carter was far less than dismayed.

"Well done, Lucas!" he applauded as they laid down their load, positioning it securely on the trestles. "You were right. I promise never to question your judgement again."

"Fat chance, Howard." Lucas held no illusions.

A season almost as exciting, certainly more grand than the first, was over. Carter was glad. It had been emotionally taxing, particularly the earliest stages, and the work itself had been almost overpowering at times. Oftentimes he had fallen into bed in complete exhaustion, barely able to take his clothes off, let alone wash, overwhelmed by the responsibility, the problem solving, the immensity of the physical labour, the painstaking discipline of sequenced clearance, the long hours of restoration, the ever-present visitors of importance, the endemic politics. He should have been well used and equal to it all by this time but he wasn't. His innate inability to deal with the whole picture with equanimity had been his problem all along, particularly in the absence of his sophisticated patron. That and the confined, subterranean labour, the very atmosphere of the tomb, had combined to make him feel positively ill at times.

And then there had been the dreams. So many of them. So real. But now, happily, it seemed that he was free of them, for the time being at least. Rising that morning, he had slept a good long night's sleep and recalled nothing. For once he felt fully rested.

And so it was, following a brief period of highly visual and horrifyingly credible nightmares, that Lacau himself returned to the real world. He was a good deal more humbled than before; a good deal more watchful, besides. On its journey to Cairo not a single packing case had been lost. In the subsequent storage, unpacking, further conservation and display, not a single artefact had been damaged.

He accepted the experience as a warning. He would reinforce his efforts and see to it that the security of the treasures was without equal.

Chapter Twenty Seven
Osiris

Mo sat on his haunches in his toilet cradling the blackened, desiccated, shrunken phallus in his hands. He'd had the thing three years now and still had not been able to get his wife, or any of his other liaisons for that matter, pregnant. The cursed thing didn't work. How he had wanted a boy all these years. How he had prayed. Now he had by his own good fortune, not to mention the craftiness of his deceit, obtained what should have proved to have been the most potent fertility symbol of all. Nor had it done anything for his libido - it had been one huge disappointment.

Unlike him, however, his wife was considerably less disappointed. Nine girls were a sufficiency, even though four, as it had been written, died in infancy. Since the latest, she had not become pregnant these last five years. The thought of producing another child after all this, whatever the gender, was unthinkable. She calmed his ravings with words of affection, and occasionally, when he appeared pretty bad, manipulated him with her hands and her mouth. Only then, it seemed, would he forget his most personal of failures.

A bead curtain was all that protected the toilet and her husband from the outside world.

"Mohammed el Hashash! Stop playing with it!" she shouted from the other side. "It's not going to get any better. You and I, we are past it. Accept it. You should never have taken the godforsaken thing in the first place. God knows what curse has been laid upon you for the deed. Your impotency may be the least of your worries. And should your master find out - he still returns from time to time, remember - I could lose a husband to the rat-ridden cells of the Luxor prison." She paused to reflect a moment and her expression lightened to a wry grin.

Mo drew the curtain aside. "What are you smiling at, woman?"

"Me?... Oh, nothing." She became serious again. "Give up your worries and count yourself lucky to be walking free after such an obscene crime."

'One final prayer?' thought Mo, gazing down at the pathetic object. He thought again. 'No, pointless.'

He got up from his toilet, went out into the street, and tossed the talisman irreverently into the open drain that ran beneath the front wall of his house. Almost immediately, and literally out of nowhere, a black jackal scrambled from the shadows, closed its jaws over the discarded artefact and ran off.

The dog disappeared into a pall of dust thrown up by a passing donkey cart. Unnoticed by Mo or any passer-by, the stray never emerged from the other side.

Carter sat on the veranda of the Winter Palace Hotel, rocking gently in his wicker armchair. He contemplated his whisky. The manager of the hotel, a good friend for some years now, saw he was alone and went out to join him. Carter's face lit up when he saw the man approach.

"Anton, you old rogue! What brings you to idle your time away commiserating with a temporary guest? Surely there is work to be done?"

"It has been a while since I have seen you, Mr Carter, and I would like to have the pleasure of your company for a moment or two so that I may catch up on your activities these past months." He dragged up a chair and sat down. "So. What is it these days that you have been doing with yourself?"

This was an unfortunate question, since the answer that Carter felt almost compelled to give was 'nothing much'. But he resisted this conversation-stopper with another response. "Busying myself with..." He stopped in midstream. "Oh, do forgive me. Will y' join me in a drink?"

"Thank you, no, Mr Carter. Too early for me. Besides, on duty, you appreciate."

"As y' wish. Don't much like drinking on my own, however." Carter swallowed a draught and continued where he had left off. "Busy with tours. Everyone seems to want 'Doctor' Howard Carter to give them a personal guide to the antiquities. Y' know how I love tourists!"

Both men smiled.

"It is good to see you smile," the manager confided. "For a moment there, seeing you by yourself, I thought you might be moping."

"Moping? About what, may I ask?" Carter had no intention of indicating his real mood.

"Oh, you know... I guess nothing much, just finding and clearing the greatest and richest archaeological discovery of all time. It is a hard act to follow. Surely things must feel a trifle anticlimactic at present?"

Carter had not expected his friend to be quite so direct. He brushed it off quickly. "Alexander."

"Alexander?"

"Alexander. His tomb. Know where it is."

"No!"

"I do. At least, I've got a pretty good idea. I'm planning the excavation as we speak."

This was a most unexpected turn of events. The hotel manager immediately pursued him for more information. "How 'pretty'?"

"About as 'pretty' as the idea I had going into my search for Tutankhamen."

"Down in the delta somewhere?"

"Exactly. 'Down in the delta somewhere'. But don't press me any further on this. Has to be hush-hush, you understand. Don't want the damn tourists, or the French, following me everywhere I go in expectation of being on the spot when I make my next great discovery - or trying to pre-empt me when I get close."

"I understand fully, Mr Carter. You can rest assured I shall keep our conversation confidential."

"I always had the greatest respect for your integrity, Anton. Now..." Carter looked down at his empty glass.

The manager clapped his hands to get the attention of the waiter. "I'll join you with one after all. Since you have faith in my integrity, have you got anything more to say on the subject?" He stared at Carter expectantly.

"I'm sorry, Anton. It wouldn't be fair to give you any more details. Too much of a responsibility. You understand, of course."

His friend nodded seriously. It was clear to him that Carter was uncomfortable. Anton felt happy enough with what he thought to be a unique confidence. Tonight he would have something different to tell his wife. With a little embellishment the story might take on some of the trappings of an adventure - the unknown, the excitement, in any case something a world apart from the general humdrum, day-to-day business of the hotel.

Six in the morning found Carter sitting in the porch outside his bedroom in Castle Carter. He had been wakeful all through the night. Thinking this perhaps would be his last Luxor sunrise, he wanted to miss not one moment of it - drink in the atmosphere, memorise the very odour of the place, listen to the waking waterfowl stirring in the marshes below him, hear the fishermen beating the Nile waters, and watch the sun bathe the Theban hills one more time.

He kept his eyes on the river. The broad indigo artery threaded its way soundlessly across his field of view. With no wind this morning, the river appeared flat as a mirror. Its stillness belied the power of the currents at work beneath. Within a few moments, the sun's amber disc embarked from the east bank and began its daily crossing to the opposite side.

Carter kept his eyes fixed on the water until the sun's reflection began to break up and sparkle in amongst the reeds and crops rimming the west bank. He breathed in deeply and stretched. He smelt the smoke from the kitchen. Abdel was already about the business of breakfast. Carter smiled. This would be a special breakfast. He would have enough chairs placed around the table to accommodate the spirits of Carnarvon, Evelyn and Pecky Callender. They would discuss, together, privately, intimately, that infamous night's excitement one more time.

Abdel noticed the extra chairs but thought nothing of it. He placed the plate of mixed grill at his master's place and returned to the kitchen.

Carter sat himself down at the head of the table and began his fried eggs.

After consuming a few mouthfuls, he laid his knife and fork on the plate and reached into a leather satchel which he had previously placed under his seat.

"Take a look at this," he whispered. "Any of you recognise it?"

It was the large, blue glass headrest that Burton and Lucas had come across at the time they were closing their work in The Valley. He put it on the table in front of the place where Carnarvon used to sit.

"Well?... Sir, I find you speechless. Why ever is that? Is it because this is the piece you surreptitiously removed from the tomb and told none of us? Or is it because this is the piece that Evelyn took from the tomb and, to protect her from suspicion of guilt, you took it from her and hid it? With which of these explanations do you concur?"

The earl remained silent.

"Lucas found it - jammed into the wall around the tomb entrance. We built the wall so it had to have been hidden recently. I am curious to know not who did it, but why they hid it. Why, once successful in removing a piece that had not previously been recorded, did you not run off with it? I do not understand why it came to be so purposefully hidden."

The earl turned his head to look at his daughter. Evelyn turned her head to stare at Callender. Callender turned to Carter.

"Why is everyone looking at you, Pecky?"

He shook his head.

"This is most aggravating. This is an unrecorded piece. For my own professional reasons I need to know who found it, where they found it, precisely, and why they secreted it in such a, I must say, stupid place."

All three stared back at Carter in silence.

"All right. Let me start again...."

At this point Abdel walked back onto the porch with the coffee. Carter assumed his usual position. Abdel poured him some more coffee and left.

"Abdel! Come back here, man! Leave the pot and go about your business. Go feed the animals. I'll call for you if I need you."

Alone once more, Carter renewed his conversation with the empty chairs.

"You assume much responsibility, your lordship. I think in this case too much - too weighty. Me too, for that matter. To tell you the truth, Lucas found this, Burton and I wagered for it, and Burton won. Two years later, on my sixtieth birthday, Burton presents it to me as a gift. No better gift, yes?"

He observed nods of agreement from all at the table.

"Now. All I want to know is, where did it come from?"

After a moment or two, Carnarvon's mouth moved but Carter couldn't make out the faintest word.

"I'm sorry, your lordship. Could you say that again, please?"

Carnarvon's lips were forming words, but Carter couldn't hear a single one of them.

"This is most frustrating, your lordship. I have not comprehended a word you have said."

Carter stopped his questioning. Pictures began to form in his mind. He saw Carnarvon in the antechamber. He saw him watching Carter disappear into the cavity that provided access to the annex. He saw him look at one of the golden beds and turn as if to take something that was standing on it. Before Carter had extricated himself from the opening, the earl had placed the object carefully in a corner, in the darkness, on the other side of the partially dismantled doorway separating them from the entrance corridor.

Carter gave the earl a knowing look. The grandee smiled in recognition.

Abdel returned unannounced and the entire suite of guests disappeared.

"Dammit, Abdel! I told you not to come back until I called you."

"I am sorry, sir. You had been here for some time and I thought you might be in need of some more coffee. I am sorry."

"Get out at once! I am busy."

His confused servant departed.

Carter realised the stupidity of his statement. He shrugged his shoulders and turned back to address his guests. But the moment had passed. The seats lay vacant once more.

As he disembarked from his taxi at the front steps to the Winter Palace, Anton was there to greet him. "Oh. I am honoured," said Carter.

"No honour, sir. I'm just here to make sure you actually do leave."

The two smiled together. Anton took his friend by the arm. "Particularly brilliant starlight tonight, Mr Carter. Looks like Osiris has come out in his best attire to wish you 'bon voyage'. It seems all are pleased you are, finally, departing this place."

Carter could take the sarcasm. They had quipped cruelly to each other on many occasions in front of company - sometimes mercilessly - so he ignored it. He looked up at the night sky. There was no moon. The backdrop was as deeply inert as patent leather. Across it the stars stood out like gemstones. The great constellation of Orion reached over him like a protective arch, the bright stars in its belt like the distant pyramids at Gizeh.

He became conscious of a presence the like of which he had only experienced once before, while he was in the tomb. He felt sure he was being watched. As the two of them made their way into the hotel, he looked around.

"What are you looking for, Mr Carter?" asked the manager.

"Mmm? Oh, nothing... Nothing, Anton. Just thought I recognised someone. These old eyes, wrong again."

"I hope not the infamous Mrs A-O!" quipped the manager.

"Ooh, no! Long forgotten and never repeated, thank God," smiled Carter.

"I have reserved a special suite for you tonight, Mr Carter. I hope you approve. Special night. Special room. The suite Lord Carnarvon used to use. No extra charge!" The manager's eyes gleamed, anticipating Carter's reaction.

"I am truly honoured!" He really felt it. The gesture could not have been more appropriate.

Anton entered the room first, held the door open for Carter, and went over to the window to draw back the shutters. The evening breeze played with the curtains. Carter turned to Anton and smiled. It was enough.

Anton saw he was about to speak and interrupted, "Sir. Please. No thanks. It is not for *you* to thank us. It is *our* position to thank you. You cannot know how much you have done for us. Egypt of course, as well, but for this hotel... So much... So many visitors... So many generously rich clients... I cannot count the names. So much money!" He raised his arms with his palms outstretched, gesturing as if he were holding a giant sack.

"You have been a blessing to this place. All I ask of you is that you come back one day. Make a great new discovery. We will be waiting for you with the red carpet! There will be no bill. Thank you. Thank you, that is, from all of us."

So saying, Anton bowed and ceremoniously backed out through the door. As he grasped the handle he said, "See you for dinner at his lordship's table... at eight?"

Carter nodded and the door was pulled shut.

Nothing less than black tie and tails were in order that night and, as he was shown to his table, Carter looked every bit the part he had come to play. Anton had prepared a special menu for the evening. Two of the creations had been his lordship's favourites. As it happened, Carter had never been all that partial to either dish, but tonight he was not going to disappoint his host who had been to so much trouble to get things just as they were all those years ago. The very same claret was on the table, too, and Carter immersed himself in it with relish, turning down the offer of his usual Scotch.

Anton poured the drinks and sat down opposite him.

They took up their glasses, clinked the crystal over the centre of the table, and together said, "To absent friends."

The Egyptologist drained his glass and his friend reached across the table with the bottle and replenished it.

"Anton. Thank you from the bottom of my heart. There could not have been a more appropriate 'goodbye'. How can I ever repay your hospitality?"

"As I have said before... *That* you have done so many times already... over and over again. It is I who is, and will remain, in your debt."

The two smiled. Carter took another long draught and smacked his lips.

"While my intent is not to get myself soused on such an occasion as this, I may yet find, as the evening wears on, that this admirable claret will overtake my senses and cause some loss of control."

His host laughed out loud. "A moment to be enjoyed. A moment to be treasured. A moment to be remembered. Have another."

By the time the main course had arrived, Carter *had* lost control. He was telling jokes and laughing at Anton's long list of stories of funny incidents during his many years at the hotel. He had completely forgotten his earlier 'last-night-in-Luxor' melancholy. Free of his usual inhibitions, he was having a whale of a time; the hotel manager, too. The two of them became a considerable disturbance to the other guests in the dining room that night.

Carter drained the bottom of his coffee cup and wiped the residue from his moustache. "Anton. My compliments to you and the chef. A meal that his lordship would have relished. Let us dedicate it to him once more."

They raised their brandy glasses and took a long sip. Carter placed his napkin on the table in front of him and brought his fist up to his mouth. There was a moment's pause and then a subdued belch. "Pardon me! Fun... great fun, Anton. I fear... I fear I shall need some assistance in finding my room tonight! I feel just a touch seedy, and once I stand up I will find that my mechanism for balance is somewhat at odds with the ability of my eyes to identify an horizon!"

As he pushed back his chair, Anton called to the head waiter to help.

The hotel manager got up, shook Carter's hand warmly, and watched the two of them as the head waiter manouevred Carter carefully around the tables and the seated guests. As he left, and without looking back, Carter gave a final wave of the hand he had placed over his assistant's shoulder.

Then he was gone.

That night, in the deep sleep that quickly overcame him, the gods and Pharaohs of the ancient Egyptians had visited him, one by one. It was a truly regal farewell; after all was said and done, he could have expected nothing less. He had welcomed them into his bedroom, colours sparkling about every one of them as they drifted through from wall to wall. He had recognised some of them and there were a few notable absentees. Tutankhamen was among these. That he found most curious.

With the advent of the pale light of dawn, the eternally energetic and lustful cocks of Luxor town awakened Carter without mercy. He had got to bed past twelve that night after a truly sumptuous dinner and, after falling asleep, had not contemplated waking.

Moaning just a little, he rolled himself out of bed and pulled on his dressing gown. He walked over to the window, placed his hands on the sill and leaned out. Outside, rich clusters of maroon and amber dates hung from great umbrellas of palm fronds. The broad, arching, herringbone leaves fluttered in the breeze, giving momentary glimpses of the Nile below. Beyond the river, the unmistakable skyline of the wall of rocks that protected The Valley of the Kings shone brilliantly in the horizontal light of early morning. The great bowl of rock which cradled the lavish temples of Hatshepsut, of Mentuhotep, and of Tuthmosis - they gleamed together like many ivory teeth embedded within the jawbone of the limestone escarpment.

He soaked in the view. In his heart he knew he could not, would not, touch those rocks again. There was no energy any more. From now on, it would all be memories; nothing but memories.

There was a knock at the door. His host awaited him at breakfast.

The stark nakedness of the tomb disturbed him deeply. There were no servants present to tend to the king's needs; there were no supplies to sustain him; no boats to take him on his journey; no weapons, no animals to protect him; no clothes for him to wear; no cosmetics for the greater good of his body; no jewellery to embellish it; no chariots to take him hunting; no music and no games for entertainment; no furniture for his comfort; his children had gone. But for the singular presence of his body, one of his coffins, his sarcophagus, and the remaining pictographs on the walls, there was nothing. It was, indeed, most depressing. All those things had had a purpose. Until ten years ago, they had appeared to serve him well.

The fact was, however, they still were. His servants tended him every day. The architects of his grave goods, they were all there. He had his wife and his children. Indeed, he had everything he needed for a life of happiness in perpetuity. Maat had returned. The absence of the physical objects of his previous life - stacked row upon row, layer upon layer within the claustrophobic limestone cells adjoining his burial chamber, gathering the dust of ages, gradually degrading with time - had had no effect. Safely hidden and resealed they may have once been, but ultimately, of their own accord, they were destined to break down into dust. There is no permanence in the earthly world.

The king thoughtfully ran his fingers over the wings of one of the guardian angels carved into one corner of his sarcophagus. Then he turned and walked back up the sloping entrance corridor, climbed the sixteen stone steps and emerged into the cold night air. Exiting the walled enclosure which surrounded the entrance to his tomb, Tutankhamun turned to his right and walked around the bend and up the closest arm of The Valley. He stopped at the first tomb entrance. He contemplated the doorway for a moment. The cavity before him fell away into the ground. The murderer's - the usurper's grand edifice! He walked down the steps and into the first corridor.

It was no surprise to him that the general had seen to it that his own final resting place was far richer and more decorative than that of his victim - richer, perhaps, than any other contemporary dead Pharaoh entombed in The Valley of the time. One hundred and fifty cubits into the tomb, and still he had not reached the burial chamber. The boy king felt a good deal dismayed at the grandeur of this place. Compared with the futile smallness of his own sepulchre, this was a palace indeed.

Tutankhamun hesitated. The tomb was as grand as any Pharoah's should be. It had been cleared. As all had been. But in the burial chamber... Did the body of the infidel still lie there?

He walked down some steps and stood on the floor of the largest room of all. Now he was at the threshold. This was the important one. This was the room he had to see. The sarcophagus, in design not unlike his own, lay open just like his own. It stood parallel with the far wall. The decoration on the walls which surrounded it was vastly more elaborate than that in his own tomb but it was incomplete. That the general had expired with his grand design still in the process of execution was a most satisfying discovery, and Tutankhamun relished the thought of a vile life foreshortened. He pictured the artisans scampering out, happily leaving their artwork unfinished - partly painted reliefs; partially sculpted reliefs; drawings awaiting the sculptors' chisels; drawings in progress; the architects' guidelines awaiting the draughtsmen; totally blank areas awaiting the architects.

All most satisfying. At least in his own sepulchre, small and unambitious though it was, his faithful artisans had fully and reverently completed the decorations before the doorways had finally been sealed.

He walked over to the sarcophagus and peered inside. Nothing... Nothing but the dust of ages. He breathed a sigh of relief and turned to leave.

It was then that he spied it. Through a doorway to an otherwise empty side-chamber, alone on the far west wall, a life-size figure of Osiris painted within the outline of a shrine. The picture of the god pointed the way to the afterlife.

The boy king instinctively made a low bow of respect and prayed that the tomb's violators had destroyed Horemheb's mummy before its ka had had a chance to follow the god's signal.

He turned and walked back out of the tomb. As he emerged at the top, The Valley and its tributaries were bathed in the darkness of the moonless night. Tutankhamun could see all as if it were as bright as day. He ran from tomb to tomb, investigating each to the burial chamber itself. But for that of Pharaoh Amenophis II, there were no bodies anywhere. His, violated but rewrapped, was one of only two still to be contained within their original arks.

And this man they called Howard Carter, it was he who was responsible for the preservation of both!

Satisfied that he had exhausted all the sepulchres in the royal necropolis, the boy king climbed the hill which lay to the east and above his own tomb and sat down on a boulder. Before him, plateaux of limestone separated by slopes of scree were spread out like the layers of an enormous cake. Below lay the open throats of cavities of earlier and later pharaohs than himself.

He contemplated the heavens. He had never once seen or heard of any Pharaoh outside of his own time walking the heavens along with him. All he had were his own people, those he had trusted, just as it was during his life on earth.

Where had all the others gone? Could it have been that ultimate preservation of the body in its original place of rest was the only prescription for survival of the king's soul, that of his wife, and that of every one of his loyal subjects? Could it be so? But if this were the case, where then is Pharaoh Amenophis?

He looked towards the The Valley entrance. The open mouths of the tombs of Ramses II, his sons and daughters, of Ramses IV, and of many others lay there - now all exposed; empty of every thing and every body.

He looked up the valley arm behind him. The kings, Ramses I and X had once slumbered there. Father Seti I also. None of them had slept unhindered for long.

He looked south.

So many kings had lain in so many crypts, all now removed; if not destroyed in antiquity by the vandals of the time, now placed irreverently on show in the museums of the world.

There was no question in his mind. Of all Pharaohs he, and he alone, through his body's continued presence in The Valley and the preservation of his grave goods - albeit removed from his tomb to another place but preserved all the same - had survived. He would continue to be the only one to live in eternity.

The central portion of her husband's mortal remains now a gold-encased amulet about her neck, Ankhesenamun felt in possession of new powers. She sat cross-legged beside her husband and happily reflected on the final outcome of their hard work in influencing the course of events at the site of the tomb.

That Horemheb had made some efforts of his own to cause their plans to fail; of this they continued to be blissfully unaware and would remain so for ever.

For Horemheb, he would never know that the outcomes he had observed were the product of their labours. He for ever retained the belief that he had caused eternal anguish in the mind of the boy king. He may not have deserved to have been left with thoughts so personally pleasurable as these, but the fact that he was mistaken in this belief was blessing enough. Being personally convinced that Tutankhamun was now in eternal hell meant that he had no cause to trouble him further.

So it is that Tutankhamun remains convinced of Horemheb's destruction, and also of his own survival. To this day, the two remain blissfully ignorant of each other's eternal existence.

Chapter Twenty Eight
Decline

"One last time." Carter signalled his colleagues to wait for him as he turned to descend the steps of the tomb. Everything had been evacuated but for the quartzite sarcophagus with the second coffin and the body within it. These remained, these last, never to be removed. He walked down the sloping passageway and stopped at the threshold. Standing for a moment at the entrance to the antechamber he peered in, sweeping the room with his eyes. It was so clean, almost anonymous.

He tried to recall that first sight once more. It was there, as clear as a bell, just as if it had occurred that very morning - his first breath; the rancid taste of stale air; an overpowering vision of gold shimmering in the faint light of the flickering candle flame; that weird pink glow from the fungus *(One of the bacilli which inhabit the walls of the tomb is known to be responsible for the consumptive deaths of a number of visitors who also suffered from some degree of immune deficiency)* which had attached itself to every wall; Carnarvon pulling at his sleeve like an impatient schoolboy.

Carter made the step down onto the floor of the antechamber and looked to his right. Where the plastered wall had once stood, there was now a large square opening. Beyond, lay the lonely sarcophagus. It looked strangely lost down there in the well of the large room, once so crowded with the sheer walls of the great, enclosing golden shrines and a literal multitude of precious objects clustered in the rooms all around it.

The rock dust crunched loudly beneath his feet as he walked over to the side of the great stone sarcophagus and peered down. Within the colourful coffin, the boy king lay at peace. But he was without his treasures. There were no boats for him to sail the cosmic waters; no servants to tend to his every need; no food; no clothes or jewellery to wear; no goddesses or jackals to protect him on his eternal journey; no games to pass away the long hours; no music to entertain him; nothing to hunt with; no chariots to ride on; no ornaments to decorate his celestial palaces; no furnishings to relax on or beds on which to slumber; even his children had been taken from him.

Carter felt remorseful. But there could be no going back. Of the thousands of individual articles removed from this tiny, crowded mausoleum, very, very little had been lost or damaged in its passage from tomb to museum. The record of how it had been when first discovered was perfect and complete, almost. He would find comfort in his near exemplary professionalism. He could be proud of the achievement.

In the symbolism of a fond farewell, he touched his hand to his forehead and saluted the coffin.

Lucas called from the mouth of the tomb. "Carter! Carter, old chap! Come up here... Quickly! Carter!"

Carter gently touched the sarcophagus one last time and turned to leave. As he hurried back to the entrance corridor he put his hand to his cheek - it was warm. He wanted to turn back to check the temperature of the stone casket but Lucas's calling grew all the more urgent.

He ran up the stone stairway. Lucas and Burton were standing close together at the top of the stairs and within the pit surrounded by its protective dry-stone walls.

"What... what is it, man?" Carter panted.

"Look what I have found."

Lucas, who had maintained his back to Carter for greater effect, at once turned and thrust his cupped hands under Carter's nose. It was a blue glass headrest complete and undamaged. It had a single inscription on the base of the stem. The inscription included the cartouche and prenomen of Tutankhamen.

"Where... where'd you get this?"

"Found it here... There..." Lucas gestured at the base of the wall. "...Behind that rock. Must've fallen from one of the trays when we were carrying the stuff out and got kicked in there. Can't imagine how it's avoided being missed all this time."

"Not possible," said Carter emphatically. "Everything's been accounted for at Cairo. Nothing missing. Besides, can't have been dropped, let alone kicked. No damage. It's perfect."

His eyes were alight with pleasure. He thought for a moment. "This ground has been refilled. The damn thing must... it must have been placed here."

The Egyptologist faltered as he felt the temperature in his cheeks rise. Then it dawned on him. Carnarvon's cache! He never did show everything to me. He looked at his colleagues. "Oh my gosh, how do we get out of this one?"

"Howard, old chap," Burton started after a moment's silence. "I... I think it best we keep it to ourselves, don't you? I mean, if we bring it to the attention of the wogs at this stage we could really start something, don't y' think?"

"'Fraid you're right, Harry. Big, unnecessary trouble. To be avoided at all costs. Would be a less than fitting end to almost ten years of abject slavery. Let's toss for it!"

"No thanks, old man," said Lucas. "Not a betting man, myself. You and Burton play for it. Go ahead." His sentiment was not gratuitous, rather more akin to superstition.

Carter looked at Burton. The photographer reached in his trouser pocket and pulled out an American nickel. "Heads or tails?" He flicked it, sending it spinning into the air.

"Heads!" yelled Carter, unable to contain his excitement.

The coin fell into the dust, tails up. Carter handed the piece to his friend. "Congratulations, old man."

Burton couldn't disguise his pleasure. His face beamed from side to side. He took his camera out of its substantial leather box and replaced it with his new acquisition.

"Something a little more precious than the tools of my trade!" he quipped. He bent down and picked up the nickel, dusted it off and handed it to Carter.

"Here. Take it. A lucky nickel. It'll remind you of our last day."

Carter took the coin happily, kissed it and stuffed it into his waistcoat pocket. "It'll never move from there unless I have it cleaned. Nobody else will see it. This is one story I can tell no one."

The three laughed and walked off towards KV15 to finish their tidying up.

The knock at the door to his London apartment was expected.

Carter himself at last was able to epitomise the great Francis Griffith, the man who had, many years since, stood in judgement of the teenage Carter's abilities and subsequently provided him the opportunity to launch a career. Now Carter could or could not, at his discretion, do the same.

The young candidate's name was Cyril Aldred. He was eighteen years old and infatuated with Egyptology, just as Carter had been. He was ambitious. He had a most deliberate nature and was confident he had the ability to excel in the profession.

As Carter opened the door, the young man smiled and removed his cap. He presented himself well. He was dressed respectably and cleanly manicured, his immature moustache like to mimic that of Carter. He was quite terrified.

Carter welcomed his visitor warmly. "Please take a seat, Mr Aldred. Would you like a drink of something? It is my fancy to have a whisky at this time of day. Will you join me?"

"Thank you, sir, no. I do not drink."

"How about some tea, then?"

"Thank you, sir, no. I am not in need of refreshment."

"As you wish. But I hope you will not think it remiss of me to partake while you do not."

"Of course not, sir!"

Carter poured himself a Scotch and soda and swung into the seat immediately opposite the young man. "Well. Let's get to it. You've a hankering for Egyptology, I understand."

"Yes, sir. Most definitely." It showed in the boy's eyes.

"Well then... Well up on your studies are you?"

"I... I believe so, sir. Yes." He knew a test was coming and he dreaded it.

"Indeed." To increase the stress of the moment, Carter paused. He remembered all those agonising hours with Petrie - the one-way monologue; taking orders; having his every move watched. He wasn't going to make it any the easier for Aldred.

"Indeed. Well... What period do you think this piece comes from?"

Carter drew out a small ushabti from his desk drawer and handed it to the young man.

Aldred examined it for a few moments, turning it over in his hands. Carter noticed the boy's fingers were trembling.

"Er..." The young man's expression appeared confused.

Carter smiled with contentment.

"Umm..." He turned his face towards Carter. "Er... New Kingdom?... Circa 1350BC... Amenhotep III... Valley of the Kings."

Carter was astonished, but he did not show it in his expression. He calmly handed the man another piece - a small alabaster jar with a hieroglyphic inscription on it.

Once again the young man turned the object over and over in his hands, examining closely every facet of the piece. After a few moments, the same puzzled look. "Er..." He paused a moment. "I... Er..."

"Yes... Yes. Come on, my boy... Speak up."

"Er... 11th Dynasty. Mentuhotep I. About 2010BC."

Carter couldn't contain his pleasure and surprise one moment longer. "Mr Aldred! Two absolutely fine, precise, and most impressive identifications! Tell me, sir, how did you do it?"

The young man looked confused.

"Well? Come on. I know you have not seen the pieces before. Tell me, how did you deduce their age and even their provenance?"

After a moment, Aldred took a deep breath and looked Carter directly in the eyes. "Well, sir... You see, sir... Er... Well it is written on the labels underneath them, sir. See?" He turned the last object upside down.

Aldred had thought it a trick but Carter had totally forgotten that the pieces were labelled. He laughed out loud. "Oh, my boy! While your Egyptological expertise has not yet been severely tested, your integrity certainly has!"

To Carter, the boy's honesty was as strong an attribute as any academic knowledge. Carter decided this had been test enough and chose to turn the entire interview around.

"Mr Aldred. Is there something - anything - you would like to ask me about my experiences in Egypt these past forty-one years?"

The young man's eyes lit up. There most certainly was.

By the time he'd downed his second Scotch, Carter was in full cry. He was in his element. The stories were rolling out one after the other and in explicit detail. Not all were technical. He talked about the troubles in Egypt;

dealing with officialdom; dealing with visitors; pandering to dignitaries; balancing the archaeological work with administrative responsibilities; organising the fellahs; their pay; the equipment; the supplies; the lunches; the parties; the tours; the security; the concession agreements; the laboratories; the photography; the lifting tackle; the problems; their solutions. Not like a lecture this time, just stories, blow by blow, just as if they were really there. It was all so fresh in his mind. Once more, he felt the excitement of the planning, the anticipation, the discoveries - new and wonderful things, one after the other.

The nature of Aldred's perceptive enquiries was all Carter needed to make a most favourable assessment of the young man. He was really most agreeably impressed with his grasp of the subject and the depth of his knowledge. The boy had schooled himself most judiciously.

"And now, sir," said Aldred, after Carter had concluded another story, "what next?"

"Ah!" responded Carter. "After Tutankhamen? Good question, my boy. Tough act to follow, as they say." He looked wistfully out the window. Now nothing was real any more. Now he had to lie. It came easily.

"After I've completed the scientific work - Tutankhamen's not finished until that's been done - after that... Alexander. I fancy having a crack at finding 'Alex'. Got some ideas, y' know. Need to follow them up. I return next season. Would you like to accompany me? You'd be admirable help, I am sure, and you will learn a great deal."

Aldred smiled. He had passed! "Sir, I am truly flattered by your kind offer. I know I would gain much from the experience. But I am currently set upon a course of education and would like to complete this before I apply myself in the field. I am fully committed, I am afraid."

"Oh? And where would that be, Mr Aldred?"

"King's College, sir... London, sir. I hope you understand, sir. Terribly sorry to miss the opportunity, but thanks all the same. Perhaps in a few years when I have completed my studies - if you have not made the discovery by then, of course!"

Carter was not disappointed and fully comprehended the young man's direction. 'Well balanced. Makes his plans. Sticks to them,' he thought.

He sighed. "Well, if I don't find Alexander the Great within a couple of years or so I think I'll be for hanging up my trowel and watching the antics of the likes of you, my boy. Damn good luck to you." He smiled warmly at the young man.

They shook hands firmly and Aldred took his leave. There would not be a second meeting. Carter wrote his official recommendation on Aldred that very evening.

During his winters in Luxor, Carter was not accustomed to receiving letters, so this one came as a bit of a surprise. He took it from the silver-plated salver balanced on the waiter's fingers and looked at the address on the envelope. He was pleased to note that it was not a telegram, so surely it would not be urgently unwelcome news. It was written in an educated hand, but not one he recognised. He slid his finger beneath the flap and eased the paper out. It was a single sheet inscribed on both sides.

Clouds Hill,
Nr. Bovington Camp,
Dorset

1st. Feb., 1935

My Dear Carter,
Forgive this impulsive note. Out of the blue, I know, but I am sure a gentleman with your capacity for observation will remember our meeting, lamentably all those years ago.

I brought to you a miscellany of artefacts which I had been fortunate to come by in the deserts of my recent travels of the time. I am sure you will recall.

The reason for my letter is that I have just finished reading the third and final volume of your 'magnamopus' in three parts - 'The Tomb of Tut.Ankh.Amen' - and am so impressed with the achievement that I felt myself compelled to communicate with you at once.

By a stroke of damnable luck, I departed Cairo just three months prior to your magnificent discovery. This irks me deeply.

So, sir, I am writing belatedly to congratulate you on your work. But I know that this is only the 'trailer', as they say in the moving picture theatres. You have great plans, I am sure and, no doubt, you are already hard at work upon it, and at great pains to complete the scientific study that should accompany such a find of this magnitude. I look forward to the publication of this future work and humbly request that you reserve a first pressing for this brief acquaintance of yours. A bit of a nerve, I know, but I can recall from our first meeting more than a passing commonality in our interests. Besides, you owe me, do you not?

Meantime this current series is a work of art that I will keep protected within my library for ever. I look forward to the next. I and the entire Western world will be indebted to you for your scholarship, your intuition, your discipline, and your execution.

With kind regards,

T. E. L.

PS - Should you do me the honour of replying to this letter I would be most grateful if henceforward you would address any communications to me as 'Mr

Shaw'. You see, in order to keep one step ahead of the news media and live in relative peace, I have been forced to assume an alias.

Carter looked over the letter once again, then carefully refolded it and placed it back in the envelope. He took a drink and looked up at the starlit sky. The Milky Way, the Nile of the cosmos, streamed sparkling over the blackness above him. He drained his glass and summoned another.

The waiter placed Carter's refreshed gin and tonic on the table beside him. He drank it down in one and, with some effort pulled himself up. He walked across the bar and through the lobby towards the staircase which led to his room, steadying himself on the pillars as he left. He fumbled for his key, unlocked his door and went in. He pulled the door closed behind him, tossed the letter onto the sofa and let himself fall back onto the bed. He rested his head on the pillow and gazed up at the ceiling. Proud as he was at being honoured so by a man of such wordly fame, the responsibility was overpowering. 'Love to but I haven't got the energy.' He closed his eyes and fell asleep.

Carter awoke with a start at three in the morning. The entire notion had come to him in his sleep. 'Lawrence himself. Why not? He's a scholar of archaeology. A proven literate. Publicly famous. Expertise. Good publicity. Great mix. Use my notes. Those of Lucas, Mace, the rest. He would need to visit the museum. Spend some time there on the details of the objects. I could pay for that.'

Carter got out of bed and lit the lamps in his study. He sat down at the desk in his pyjamas and immediately began to write:

Winter Palace Hotel
Luxor, Egypt.

24th. Mar., 1935

Dear Colonel Lawrence,

I was most gratified to receive your letter of 1st Feb. It was most timely.
It would lift my spirits greatly should we have the opportunity to meet at least once more. And I have a proposition to make to you.
You are yourself a scholar of archaeology, as am I. The work you speak of in your letter is indeed necessary but, quite frankly, while it festers within me it is too much for my meagre inner resources to manage alone. I ail. From a cancer, so I am told by my doctor. I am not so bad that I cannot think, but I am bad enough that I have little energy - little enough yet to write but far too little to delve into the depths of analysis that will be required to bring out the true value of the objects and their history in the late Lord Carnarvon's discovery - and, on top of all this, probably not that much time. But that's the hypochondriac in me talking!

In any event, it occurred to me that, although this could be considered the deepest of impositions after so brief an encounter as ours, this work being so important, and your clear interest in seeing its conclusion, you might consider obliging me by joining in on this endeavour and helping me in its conception, execution, and its eventual completion. You are, after all, most handsomely qualified to take on such a task.

I must be frank. In this, I will expect of you the majority of the labour, any travel, the writing. I will act as the technical and historical referee, of course, and provide illustration where that is necessary. My hands, I am glad to say, remain steady. I fear I can do little more than this but, from my experience, I will closely advise you in the course of your work all the way to closure.

Having given this considerable thought, I am convinced this may be the only way I will be able to see my achievement completed. I await your reaction with the greatest expectations.

I am shortly to leave for home. Once I am re-established back in London I will attempt to make contact with you in Dorset.
I very much look forward to seeing you again.
Your most obedient servant,

Howard Carter

Carter folded the page and slipped it into an envelope dutifully addressed to a 'Mr Shaw'. He called for Abdel to take the letter to the post office. The following silence brought him back to his senses. He was in a hotel. He was alone. It was four in the morning. He laid the envelope on the desk, walked back to his bedroom and fell into bed.

Carter returned to England in May. He had not received a response to his letter but this had not discouraged him. The mail system to and from Egypt was a good deal less than reliable and the period of transition lengthy. However, receiving no response to a telegram despatched while in transit, he decided to go directly to Dorset and seek Lawrence out for himself, unannounced.

He arrived at Wareham at 12p.m. on Thursday the 30th. As he emerged from the extravagantly Victorian station, there was a solitary taxicab parked at the threshold. Carter opened the door and threw his bag inside. "Bovington Camp, cabby. I understand the home of a Mr Shaw's is located nearby there. The address is 'Clouds Hill'. Do y' know the place?"

"Oh yes, sir. Ev'ryone round these parts knows 'is place. Real gen'l'man, sir, but not one f' socialising wiv the locals. Kept to 'imself. Bit of an 'ermit, y' might say."

The past tense comment was lost on Carter. His mind was filled with expectation and hope.

"Will y' be wantin' lodgins for the night, sir? There's 'The Bear' in the 'Igh

Street. Should be comfortable enough for a gen'l'man of your standin', sir."

"Mmmm?" Carter was preoccupied with anticipation. "Not right now. Worry about that later. 'Clouds Hill' first, if you please, cabby."

They drove off.

Within a few miles they turned off the main road and were alone driving down long, narrow country lanes.

The cabby regarded his passenger in the mirror. "May I ask why you wishes to see 'is place, sir?"

"You may not," answered Carter rudely.

The cabby, summarily put off, remained silent for the remainder of the journey. After a few miles they turned left at a signpost for Bovington Camp. Almost immediately the taxi drew up at a gate on the left.

"This is it?" asked Carter.

"The very place, sir."

The cottage lay just a few feet from the road. It was largely hidden from view by a tall hedge. Carter got out of the taxi and looked about him. There was not another sign of human habitation anywhere to be seen.

Truly a lonely cottage in the country. Carter felt strangely comforted by the thought.

"Please wait for me, cabby. I shall return presently and let you know how long I expect to be. Should you leave I'd be lost out here. I doubt many taxis come by this way looking for fares."

"Right you are, sir."

He unlatched the gate and walked onto the gravel fronting the area between the house and a small, shed-like garage opposite. The cottage was tiny - little more than a two-storey box with a single pitched roof and four small windows at the front. Its only remarkable feature was a tall, central brick chimney with a tiled spark cover at its top. The structure was quite out of scale with the rest of the building. It portended that a veritable furnace might lurk below.

Carter approached the front door and rapped briskly on it with his knuckles. He waited a while, listening for signs of movement within, but there was nothing. He walked over to one of the tiny windows and peered inside. The lace at the window made it almost impossible to see anything. He could make out a camel saddle and a sofa spread with a colourful blanket. But there was no light inside and, stepping back from the cottage and looking up, no smoke from the incongruous chimney either. It did not look at all lived in.

Perhaps Lawrence was abroad again. No wonder he had not received a reply to his letter.

Carter returned to the taxi with a heavy heart. "Let's find a place to rest my tired head, cabby. Is there somewhere closer than driving all the way back to Wareham?"

"Bere Regis, sir, on the Dorchester road. Drax Arms should see you awright, sir. In the main street at the top of the 'ill. Nice people. Me an' me team plays skittles there. Better beer than in Wareham."

Carter was not interested in the cabby's observations and, as the taxi made its way north, he gazed absent-mindedly at the countryside. He would have to enquire if anyone in the town knew of Lawrence's whereabouts. Pointless going all the way back to London if the man was expected to return within the week.

Arriving at the Drax Arms, Carter paid off the cab driver and knocked at the door to the lounge bar. Presently there was a turning of keys and a sliding of bolts. The door was flung open to reveal a rather large, red-faced lady in a floral-print cotton dress covered by a stained, blue and white-striped apron.

"Yes?"

"My name is Carter. Do you have lodgings for the night?"

The lady regarded the plump gentleman standing before her. The weather was unseasonably cool for late May and he wore a long, dark overcoat that reached almost to his ankles, black shoes, black leather gloves, a grey scarf at his neck and a black Homburg, and he carried a moderately sized, leather travelling case. Looking, therefore, relatively well-to-do, if a trifle moribund, he passed inspection.

"Well, you'd better come in then."

Carter removed his hat and followed the woman inside. She took him through the bar to the back and up the stairs.

"This'll be your room then. Barfroom's at the end of the landing. 'Ot water's from a gas boiler above the barf. You'll need to call me to get it working. Got a temp'rement 'as that boiler. Won't work for just anyone. Clean towels is in your room. If you'll be wanting dinner, I'll need to know no later than five o'clock. Rarver you didn't really since I 'as to 'elp wiv the bars. There's a fish-and-chippy jus' down the road."

"I'll take care of myself tonight, thank you." Carter was weary of the instructions.

"Please yerself. Brekfust is downstairs in the parlour 'tween eight and nine. If you're late I can't promise you'll get any."

"Thank you," said Carter trying to close the bedroom door on her. "I will not be late. Good afternoon."

Finally left to himself, Carter removed his coat and jacket and hung them in the tallboy. He threw his suitcase on the bed and opened it. From pockets around the inside, he withdrew a matching set of tortoiseshell hairbrushes, a comb, a shaving brush, a cut-throat razor and a sharpening strap. These he arranged neatly on either side of the water stand. From a sleeve in the lid, he drew out a small journal. He left his clothes in the case, closed it up and slid it under the bed. The metal studs in the base of the bag made a dinging sound as they made contact with the jerry, pushing it out of reach.

He sat down at the small dressing table and began to draft a letter to his niece, Phyllis Walker. Having been thus far unsuccessful in taking this first positive step towards beginning the scientific work on the tomb, he felt pregnant with anxiety. He had to unload on someone.

Some time later, but only two pages completed, he became conscious of voices below. The bars had opened and, it seemed, people around these parts lost no time in filling them up. He felt in need of a drink himself. It was an easy decision. He put the cap back on his fountain pen and closed his journal. He looked in the mirror and slicked back his hair, put a comb through his moustache, pulled on his jacket and went downstairs.

The fact that Carter had not bothered to change but had gone down to the bar in the same clothes he had been wearing all day was out of character. After the many years of his associations with the rich and famous, he had matured the habit to wash regularly and change for dinner. This time, however, his mind was preoccupied with his objective. All he thought about was meeting the man he had not seen for who knows how many years and getting his next - his final - great project started.

"Travelin', sir?" asked the proprietor as he placed the gin on the bar.

"Mmm...?"

"Just passin' through, sir? On yer way to sumplace else?"

"No." Carter wasn't in the mood to talk. "No. Here to see an acquaintance of mine."

"Well then, sir. Welcome to our little part of the world. I 'opes yer enjoys yerself here, sir. If yer needs any directions, just ask. Only too glad to 'elp."

The man left to serve the noisier clientele in the public bar.

Carter sighed and rested back in his chair. He tasted his drink. Not as strong as those to which he had become accustomed over the years. But that's the way they do them in the provinces, he thought.

He turned to observe the proprietor as he served drinks to the others in the lounge. It was clear that the man knew these people well. Carter could hear them talking about their families - mostly gossip; a mixed babble; little of substance. Then, all of a sudden, someone, Carter couldn't detect who, mentioned the name, 'Lawrence'.

Carter stood up. He wasn't sure what to do next, or in which direction he might move but, now standing prominently in the middle of the bar room, with his glass in hand, he had made himself obvious enough to shut down the local chatter.

A deep, expectant silence descended on the small bar. Carter stood rigidly in the centre of the room. He quickly realised he was being observed intently by nearly every person in the lounge. For a moment he felt an extreme sense of embarrassment. But then he thought about all the dignitaries he had dealt with in the past - the meetings, the dinners, the society parties, the tours. Dealing with the general public had been a chore, but it had become second nature. He spoke up. "I am new to these parts. Came to look for Colonel... er... Mr Shaw. Believe he lives near here. Any of you know him?"

The recognition in the faces about him signalled immediately that he was in the right place. But there was something else. The publican came out from behind the bar and approached him. "Mr Carter, isn't it?"

"Yes."

"Thought as much. Stayin' upstairs, right?"

"Yes."

Carter sat back down in his chair.

"Owner told me."

He leaned over to look Carter in the eyes. "You knew Colonel Lawrence, then?"

"Er... Yes." Carter was unsure whether he should admit knowing the name but it was too late now.

"And where would that be, sir?"

"Egypt."

"Egypt? Egypt!" The man looked about at everyone in the bar. There were murmurings from the crowd about him. He looked back at Carter. Like an expectant policeman at an interrogation, he wiped his hand across his lips. "By any chance, sir... are you... could you be that Mr Carter, sir?"

Carter was flattered with the recognition - and in such a parochial place.

"Well, I don't know about 'that Mr Carter,' but I am Howard Carter, yes."

The room went into an uproar of shouting. All at once the door to the public bar was flung open and a multitude of people came forward en masse, each eager and intent on grasping him by the hand and, after gripping it firmly with strong farmers' muscles, shaking it vigorously. Carter found himself at a loss for words, and in considerable pain.

In some discomfort he might have been, but his new-found acquaintances, in their gratitude for having someone of such notoriety within their midst, embraced him enthusiastically. They drew the line at offering him a drink, however. Welcome he was, but this did not mandate accompanying generosity. Rather, they were expecting the famous visitor to declare the bar open for their pleasure. To their forthcoming disappointment, Carter did nothing of the kind.

A red-faced stranger recently arrived from the other bar looked closely into his eyes, at the same time pushing an empty beer mug suggestively across the table before him. There was a moment's silence before the man spoke. "Tell me, sir. How did y' stop the curse from getting to yer?"

Carter did not show his irritation at the question. In his response he was quite matter of fact. "There was no curse..." Then he resumed his line of enquiry. "...Tell me, my good man, where may I find Colonel Lawrence?"

Carter's correspondent of the moment was set back on his heels. "Lawrence? Who?"

"T. E. Lawrence. Colonel Lawrence. Do you know of him? Where I can find him? It is of the utmost importance."

"Ah."

There was some indication of understanding in this expletive, Carter thought.

"Ah?"

The man rattled his empty beer mug on the table but there was no reaction from the visitor. Silence descended on the room once more.

The publican spoke up. "Colonel Lawrence. Otherwise known in these parts as 'Mr Shaw', right?"

"Yes." Carter lit up. "Yes... Shaw. I believe he has assumed that name."

The beer mug began to chatter on the table again. Carter was close on the brink of one of his patience precipices. He took a deep breath. "Where may I find him?"

"Well, sir. Don't rightly know how to say this, you 'avin' come all this way to see 'im an', an' all..." The publican began to stammer.

"Well? Well? Come on, man. What's troubling you?"

The publican waved to the onlookers to disperse. He took a seat opposite. "Well... It's like this, sir... 'E's dead, sir... Fell off 'is motorcycle - accident some say, some say not - about two weeks ago... Died in 'ospital... Funeral was Tuesday before last, at Saint Nick's, very near 'is 'ouse. 'Twas in all the papers. Thought you'd 've seen it."

Carter was stunned. "I... I was travelling."

"Sorry, sir."

"You are sure we are talking about the same man?"

"Oh yes, sir. 'Fraid so, sir. Colonel Lawrence. Late of the Arab Bureau... and the 'Raf'."

There was no doubt. Carter felt crestfallen. He had had such hopes for his grand solution. He had identified able help and embarked on securing the assistance he required. It would have been absolutely the right chemistry. All for nought.

"Anuver drink, sir?"

"No... thank you. How much do I owe you?"

"One and six, sir, if you please."

Carter placed a florin in the man's hand.

"Keep the change."

He got up from his seat and walked out into the evening sunshine. He took a deep breath of the country air and sat himself down on a bench at the side of the road.

All seemed stacked against him. Another of his associates dead. The list had already become too long to contemplate. But he would read nothing into the event. His earlier expectations had filled his head with a sense of light euphoria. Now he felt the weight of hopelessness. He had not been so low since Arthur Mace had confided his condition. All of a sudden it seemed there was nothing left but to fade into old age and obscurity.

A tractor drove by, towing a four-wheeled wooden cart bearing a healthily mature pile of sileage. The reeking assemblage was besieged by a cloud of flying insects. Caught in the act of breathing a deep sigh, the acidic stench tore through Carter's nostrils, seared his senses, and brought him back to reality.

The driver acknowledged him with a wave of his hand and a toothless grin and drove off in the direction of the setting sun. His expression reminded Carter of the hundreds of fellahs with whom he had become acquainted over the years. After a day's labour, many of them, along with their flies, had smelt worse.

Managing to release a mild smile, he half-heartedly gestured back to the farmhand, turned and went back into the inn.

Carter rested back into the cushions of the wicker easy chair. There was a comforting breeze to help chill the day's heat. He looked up at the sunlight sparkling between the rippling palm leaves. He brought the glass tumbler to his lips. The gin drew a line of comforting alcoholic warmth down the centre of his chest. He pressed the cold glass to his forehead and closed his eyes.

There really was nothing for him here any more. It was time to close the chapter on Egypt for ever. Although, after all these years, the country was as familiar to him as England, he could feel himself ailing and realised that his health was at last becoming too vulnerable to endure the daily commonplace hardships of the place - the periodic diarrhoea; the more common vomiting; the occasional violent sicknesses - all these discomforts he had trivialised during his earlier years. But they would keep occurring. There would be no peace from them. And they would get him in the end. They had taken dear old Breasted a couple of Christmases ago - another fruitful chapter closed. 'Yes. It is time to get out of harm's way.' He had made up his mind. He would leave, finally, and for ever, this coming April. But before he made the final break, one last exploration.

On this particular journey he would take no one; no professional contemporaries, that is. He had no authority to excavate, nor did he wish any. All he wanted to do was find enough clues to satisfy himself that his theory had a strong chance of closing in on the location; no more than he had had at the time he and Carnarvon embarked on their great project to clear that triangle of ground in The Valley; no more than three or four points of reference.

To accompany him on his last journey, he called on Ibraheem and Abdel. It would be a great honour to those who had served him so faithfully all these years. He told them this expedition would be his last; that what they might find and where they might go they should keep to themselves to their graves, as he would. Whatever they found would become their secret, their possession for eternity. For once, he felt he could trust them to keep their secret close. Perhaps some members of the family might, on some merry evening when alcohol loosens the tongue, hear some snippets of information that would raise their curiosity to probe further. But he felt confident that the two would ultimately honour their promise, especially if he died first. Should they compromise their pledge, he would be there waiting for them, ready to exact retribution. They knew that.

The three arrived in Alexandria on 31st March. Carter had already booked his passage to England on the third steamer from that date. They had made a reservation at a drab hotel on the outskirts of town. No one knew him there and he went about his business unobserved. After two days of provisioning, they left their hotel and drove west in a taxicab, away from the town, in the direction of Abusir.

Carter signalled the cabby to stop. The road was already bad and they could not have proceeded much further without danger of becoming bogged down in the soft sand. In Arabic he told the taxi driver that they would walk the rest of the way. He was to come back for them at this same spot, at this same time, every day for six days, whether he found them there or not, otherwise there would be no payment. This security now assured, his two faithful followers, with their loads on their backs, fell in close behind him, and the lonely party plodded steadily westward.

The taxi turned around and soon disappeared in a cloud of following yellow dust.

As the sun began to redden before them, Carter stopped and turned to face his colleagues. "Abdel. Set up the tents over there. That flat spot. Make sure it's firm before you drive in the spikes... Ibraheem! What are you doing?"

Ibraheem turned to face him. He had the Primus stove and a pot in his hands.

"Ah! Good man. What food did you bring?"

"For tonight, fresh lamb and fresh vegetables, sir. From tomorrow, however, we shall have to make do with tinned food. Enjoy while we can, sir. Enjoy while we can."

It was not long after dinner that Ibraheem and Abdel fell asleep.

Carter's mind was too full of images to succumb to tiredness. With a warm gin in his right hand, he reclined on his sleeping bag and looked up at the clear night sky. The stars and the constellations shone crisply from the heavens. He stared at Orion until the stars themselves appeared to move before him.

He rubbed his eyes.

"Are you really all up there? Show yourselves... I can see Osiris... But where are the rest of you? Ra. Shu. Tefnut. Geb. Nut. Isis. Seth. Nephthys."

He took a sip.

"Ptah. Khnum. Heh. Heket. Sokar. Soped. Neith. Seshat. Sobek. Selket. Amun. Horus. Toth. Nekhbet. Renenutet. Reshef. Hapy. Hathor. Wadjyt. Mut."

Another sip.

"Khons. Maat. Anubis. Min. Montu. Satet. Sekhmet. Bes. Khepri.

Nefertem. Nun."

And another.

"Bastet..." He held his breath.

Appearing quite suddenly on the crest of the dune just ahead of him, back-lit by a full, platinum moon, was the unmistakable silhouette of a cat. It sat down, assuming the elegant posture so characteristic of the ancient Egyptian figurines. The animal turned its head to look in Carter's direction. As it did so, there was a momentary flash of moonlight about its head.

Carter struggled to his feet. "Can't be." he whispered. Then he shouted, "It has earrings! It's got gold earrings!"

Startled by the stranger's outburst, the cat took off and disappeared into the darkness.

The bodies of Carter's assistants did not stir. They were stone dead asleep, their eyes tight shut against the twinkling firmament above.

Carter walked over to the dune. He reached the spot where the cat had been sitting and looked at the sand. There was not a paw print to be seen. The sand all about the area was undisturbed. He must have been dreaming. He looked around for evidence of some movement. He saw a flash again, some distance to the left, in the direction of Alexandria. He stared hard into the blackness, hoping for some sign that what he had seen earlier was real. As he turned slowly around, examining every detail of the moonlit horizon, two large silver eyes moved into his field of view. They could not have been more than ten feet away. He strained to see the face before him. The eyes stared directly back.

Unable to contain himself any longer, he took a step towards it. The eyes immediately disappeared. Carter sat down. The creature, by now at the top of the dune and on the skyline, stopped and looked back at him. Its body lit up by the moonlight, he could now clearly see this was not the cat he had previously encountered but a dog, a desert jackal - scarce in body, long in muzzle, thin in tail, stiletto ears, as black as night. The animal cocked its head and the ears glinted in the pale light of the moon.

"Not possible!" Carter whispered to himself. "No. Don't believe it. Can't be. Hallucinating again!"

The creature settled down on the sand, undisturbed by his observer's excitement. Its front legs stretched out long and slender in front of it. It turned its head. In the light of the moon the eyes glowed pearl white. Carter reached for his notebook. As he pulled it from his jacket pocket, the dog got up and disappeared behind the dune.

Carter got up. As quickly as he could, he climbed to the ridge of the dune on which the dog had been reclining. He looked over the other side. The pale blue light, once he had become accustomed to it, was sufficient to spot the slightest movement. And there it was. There were two of them, trotting back towards the scent of Carter's earlier meal. He stood absolutely motionless and watched them walk up the flank of the dune. They trotted by him within twenty feet or so and down the other side towards the small encampment. As they disappeared behind the tents, Carter followed.

He could hear the noise as he approached the camp. Amongst the debris of his supper, the dogs were busy eating everything they could find. All he wanted to do was get a good view of the larger dog, nothing more.

He crept as quietly as he could towards the noise. As the dogs' wagging tails came into view, he eased himself back onto the sand and regarded them from a distance. Almost immediately, the black dog turned to look in Carter's direction. Surprised by the almost personal attention, Carter nevertheless kept himself absolutely still. For some time the animal looked directly at him.

'It's the dog in my bedroom! It is Anubis!' He made no attempt to stop himself crying out. "Anubis!" he cried at the top of his voice. "Anubis!"

The grey dog ran off immediately, but the animal of his attention did not appear at all startled by his outburst. Rather, it turned slowly and walked off to the west a few steps and sat down again, beside another creature. It was the cat Carter had spotted earlier. The pair of them stared directly back at him.

He turned to look at the tents of Abdel and Ibraheem. His two assistants remained still. 'The Arabs always sleep well', he thought. He envied the profound capacity of a vacant mind and turned back to look at the animals. They had gone.

He walked over to the spot where they had been sitting. Once again, there were no paw prints, just a small depression. He gazed into the interior of the desert. There was nothing.

After searching the horizon for about thirty minutes, he gave up and walked back to his sleeping bag. He slid deep within it and abandoned himself to its warmth and what was left of the night.

Before the sun was quite up, Carter had dragged a disgruntled Abdel and Ibraheem out of their beds to show them the small pit he had found at the foot of the dune. After a quick breakfast, he pressed them to work with their spades. He seated himself comfortably in a folding canvas chair, rested back under a parasol and regarded their labours from the top of the dune.

The two dug for at least four hours.

In the impenetrable silence of the desert, the ring of metal on solid bedrock was unmistakable. Carter pulled himself to his feet and tumbled down the flank of the dune, sliding to a halt at his fellahs' feet. The broad grin framing Abdel's blackened and stunted teeth was enough. He bent down and brushed the sand away to reveal a clean flat surface clearly dressed by the hand of man.

Carter felt the same rush of feeling he had experienced over a decade ago. 'Could it be here? Could I have been right once again? Could it really be here? Surely this is too good to be true?'

By evening, his exhausted helpers had cleared to the fifth step.

That night the three enjoyed their meal and savoured their coffee. Abdel and Ibraheem, both exhausted, were asleep within minutes of sundown.

Alone in his tent, Carter swallowed one more warm gin. Excited though he was, his maturity and the experience of years now permitted him the control to rest and conserve his strength. He lay back on his pillow and subsided into a deep and restful sleep.

Meanwhile, within the close confines of the crypt, metal on stone had rung like a cathedral bell. The great general had maintained a peaceful coexistence with his gods for so many millennia. What could it be now that would break up this blessed normality?

It was a day created in Hades. Carter had never seen the like before. The wind had got up at dawn and since then had considerably worsened. They could not see their hands in front of their faces, let alone one another. They held hands to make sure they stayed together, huddling down with only their blankets at their backs to protect them from the ravages of the driving sand.

By ten o'clock, the storm had blown through and the three of them were up to their chests in sand. Carter pulled himself up, took off his Homburg and thrashed away at his dusty clothing. He looked in the direction his men had been digging the day before. The entire landscape was unrecognisable. The dunes had moved their positions. The shapes had changed. So far as he could ascertain, the spot they had been concentrating on was now buried beneath the centre of an enormous pile of sand. Methodically, he looked about for some landmark which he could use at some future date to relocate himself.

"Abdel. Ibraheem. I am tired. We must leave this place. Return to Alexandria. If we leave now we should be back in time for the taxi."

His two servants dug out their belongings and packaged them up into portable lots. The three plodded off back towards their rendezvous with the cabby.

The story of the place where he had taken his men during those last few days would remain untold. He was indeed not so much intent on taking the knowledge to his grave, but more on keeping it close in the faint hope that his condition one day would improve sufficient that he could try again for himself.

Three days later he made his final farewells with his two faithful Arab helpers and left Alexandria to return to Britain.

As he descended the gangplank at Southampton, the cold rain lashed into his face. He felt a chill the like of which he could not recall and began to consider whether he had made the right decision in returning to England.

He closed the door to his apartment and sealed himself off from the weather outside.

It was 1938. For Howard Carter, the door to life itself was preparing to slam shut.

The early morning light of one of those special, smogless and cloudless summer days cut the silhouette of Carter's diamond-paned study window into the wall opposite. The man himself was reclining in his sofa, a cup of tea within easy reach.

He had been feeling out of sorts of late, the nausea following his recent X-ray treatments had been almost intolerable, but today his stomach was settled and the cheery light raised his spirits. For once, he felt the day might show some promise.

He picked up the newspaper and opened it at the editorial. It was a diatribe on the nature and futility of Chamberlain's negotiations with Hitler. Carter turned the pages to look for something more uplifting. He was hard enough at war with his own affliction and was not prepared to contemplate any other.

'It is barely twenty years since they were beaten into submission', he thought. He shook his head in disbelief and turned to the theatre pages. He hadn't felt the urge to go for ages, but Charlie Chaplin was playing at the Odeon and he was in the mood for a good laugh.

The air was warm on his face as he left the building. It was so warm he had to remove his overcoat before crossing the road. There was the usual line of hackney cabs waiting at the plaza in front of the Albert Hall, so he did not have to walk far.

"Saville Club, if you please," he shouted to the cabby. He fancied a little luncheon before the matinée.

It was a good show, but by the time he had returned home he was experiencing some considerable discomfort. He felt bloated and very tired. He lay back on his bed, fully clothed, and gazed up at the ceiling. The lights were on in the living room and threw a faint, prismatic glow into his bedroom. Perhaps there was something there, but his eyes were not at their best any more.

The Last Chapter
Atenset

He ran his eyes around the room. That Bretby brick still sat incongruously in the centre of the mantlepiece. Burton's nickel lay close by. Carter managed a quivering grin. He looked down into his lap and leafed through the pages of the first volume. It had been handled so many times the book was quite worn out. The spine had separated from the binding. The front cover had become detached when he had dropped it one day. The cloth binding was frayed and stained. The pages and the plates had become crinkled and rubbed by the repetitive probing of his old fingers. All of the disengaged pieces now were secured with sticky tape.

What had he done with his life since the last chapter of the third volume had been completed? Lecture tours, speaking at society dinners - 'for his supper', some of the least charitable had quipped - trading on the London antiquities market - hardly achievements. But what more could he have done having completed his life's work these six years since?

He had thought about it many times. The scientific work, the monographs, lavishly illustrated, translated into many languages, read, reread, studied and admired by scholars of Egyptology the world over. The pinnacle of his achievement. A work of truly giant proportions. *(The individual volumes in the Tutankhamun's Tomb Series, with multiple authorships, were begun in 1963 and are still in progress. Collectively, the first eleven volumes measure over six inches thick; see Tutankhamun's Tomb Series).* If anything like as comprehensive as his efforts within the tomb itself, this would have become a massive undertaking indeed. But the work had not been done. Much less, it had not even begun - a few notes, nothing more. Through what would have been many years of painstaking research, measurement, analysis, speculation, precisely scaled drafting, illustration and compilation, there would have been none of the sheer excitement of discovery.

He was realistic enough with himself to know that he never had the will to set about it alone. Help, by an unfortunate accident, had eluded him. Now he came to think of it, even the relatively simple task of writing his popular work he had left in large part to his colleagues.

On his side of the Atlantic, there was no professional recognition. With the passing of time this had ceased to irritate him. In the way of things in England, he could not hope to achieve scholarly applause without official acceptance into the exclusive circles of the learned. He had failed that test. Completion of the scientific work in itself would never have been enough.

478

His failure had begun over thirty years ago through his stubbornness with those flippant, well-connected French delinquents at Saqqara. In the sanctified halls of this gentlemen's profession memories were long-lived and prejudices unshakeable - they satisfied envy.

But not in the United States of America. There they honoured men for what they achieved without regard for their roots, the institution of their education, the depth of their pockets, or their professional indiscretions. And the Americans had proved it, bless them, by recognising him accordingly. They had done well by him, too - the British Museum watched helpless as much of Carnarvon's collection had found its way to the Metropolitan in New York.

He grinned. His eyes watered, glistening in the faint light entering through the bedroom windows.

And then there was Alexander. Had he really said that to Anton? Fatuous. In his dreams. He had come close but it was clearly not meant to be. Alexander would become someone else's challenge.

Once again, that familiar feeling of anticlimax was overcoming him. He let the book slide from his hands, lay back into his pillows and stared up at the ceiling. There was nothing more he could do and no energy for it anyway.

It had been three thousand two hundred and sixty one years, close to the day, since Pharaoh Nebkheperure had died.

His niece had come to stay with him as soon as she became aware that his illness was severe enough to keep him in bed. When he awakened the following morning, she made him comfortable, fluffing up his pillows and easing his shoulders into them.

So far as he could recall, he had rested well and deeply that night. Nevertheless, even though he had slept late, this morning he felt heavy with fatigue. Asleep or not, his body continued its relentless but futile attack on the cancer inside him.

Phyllis offered him some tea. He curled his lips into a faint smile of appreciation, but with a roll of his head he declined the beverage and closed his eyes. A pulse of pain coursed through his limbs. She noticed him wince slightly. It did not last long and all at once he appeared to be lying peacefully again.

His niece pressed a small object into the palm of his hand, gently closed his fingers over it, adjusted the bedclothes, and left him to rest.

He was comfortable once more, his body almost weightless in the mattress. He felt the object in his hand. The texture and the shape were familiar. The piece fit comfortably within his calloused fingers. With some difficulty he pulled his arm from under the eiderdown, raised his hand to his face, opened his eyes, and slowly uncurled his fingers.

As if it were yesterday, he could see the tiny horse in amongst the reeds on the floor of the antechamber. Illuminated in the light of Burton's flood lamps, the brilliance of the gilding on the larger pieces of furniture dominated the room and almost rendered the object invisible.

Carnarvon, in a single movement, had plucked it up and secreted it away in his jacket pocket.

Suddenly there were voices...

I looked around the room. Evelyn was there. The excitement of the moment shone in her young, petite features. Callender was there, an unemotional man by nature, rather like myself, I fancy, but it was clear he was visibly moved by the event. And there was Carnarvon. The smile of satisfaction on the grandee's face told the whole story, standing in the midst of our ultimate achievement, his expression a picture of outright astonishment.

I thought on the daunting task that now lay ahead of me.

"Please! Please remain still and close," I cautioned. I was terrified one of them would inadvertently step on something.

Carnarvon took me by surprise by wresting the torch from my hand. He stood before us and shined the light on the floor so that we could all see his face.

"Thus far we have come, my friends. Are we not up for a little more this night?"

"Of course! Where to now, Porchy?" Lady Evelyn almost yelled in her eagerness.

The earl turned the torch to illuminate the small, square patch of darker plaster that lay at the base of the wall to our right. The two dusty, black sentinels at either side of the walled-up doorway remained unmoved, staring into each other's eyes.

"The burial chamber lies beyond that. Why not enter through the robbers' hole? See what they found. See what is left!"

It was tempting. That it was. But I was resolute. "No, your lordship." I ordered emphatically. "Out of the question. In due course, of course. But not now."

"But Howard, old chap, we have to know what lies before us. The scale of the task. The Egyptian authorities, Lacau in particular, they would not abide it, but there is no need for them to know. We can cover our tracks adequately enough to deceive the Antiquities Service. You yourself were one of them. You know their ways... Come on, man!" The earl squeezed my arm. "We have waited many years for this, our day of days. Let us taste it. Let us relish it to the full!"

My patron was trying to persuade me through force of authority. The arrogance in his tone was repugnant to me. I would have nothing of it but, when one considers the moment, I was uncharacteristically diplomatic and controlled in my response. "I do not think this is necessary, sir. There is plenty of time. We should not disturb anything we cannot document or record properly first. And we are far too far gone... I mean, far too tired tonight to do any such thing."

But the earl wasn't listening to me. "Well. Get Burton in to record it in its pristine condition now, there's a good fellow. Then we'll break through."

"But what then, your lordship? What if there are more doorways?"

"Very well. I understand. Just one further penetration just to see if we really have something. Please, Howard. Please!"

The childishness of his pleading was tremendously irritating to me. "Of course 'we have something', sir."

The lack of discipline shown by my patron at this exceptional moment - and I concede that this moment was indeed exceptional - was quite beyond my comprehension.

The earl persisted. "Howard, you would agree that thus far we have come across something beyond our wildest dreams, a project of enormous magnitude, even in this first room?"

I struggled for the right words but could do nought but nod my head.

"Surely you need now, right now, to comprehend the size of the task ahead of you? You need to have enough information to plan your excavation, the supplies you will need, the time it will take, the scientific team. Right?"

He was reading my mind. I nodded again.

"And remember, old chap, there is a significant risk that all this will go to Egypt. This may be our one chance to assure ourselves of at least some meagre compensation, don't y' think - 'on account', as it were."

It did not surprise me that the earl was eager for some early trophies. I had to nip that one in the bud. At last I had found the words. "Your lordship. With respect, please hear me out. I implore you to take pause. We shall get our just rewards by and by."

"Y' know my confidence in that is weak, Howard. Permit us to take a modicum, sir. A mere, undetectable modicum."

"Absolutely not, your lordship. Absolutely not." I shook my head. My expression may have appeared resolute but I confess that my spirit was weak and eager to be turned.

Carnarvon looked me straight in the eyes. In the torchlight I tried to keep a stern expression, but the earl, it seems, could sense the anticipation which burned alike within me, perhaps more even than his own. I had the strongest of desires to discover what lay beyond that sealed door.

"In the name of England we shall enter, Howard. In England's name we shall discover what lies within. The wogs will have to wait."

The thought had tremendous appeal. I recalled the 'Tomb of the Horse'. I smiled. In the heat of this incredible moment I found myself incapable of thinking completely straight.

I drew a deep breath in the thick, ancient air, coughed as the dust of ages caught the back of my throat, and handed my hat to Evelyn. In that single movement, my mind was made up. There would be no going back this night.

"Evelyn, please call for Burton and ask him to bring his tackle... You must agree, your lordship, that during the course of this clandestine exploration you will do nothing but observe, and return with nothing but memories. It is on this understanding that we shall penetrate the sealed door - no other."

The earl smiled at me, but I could tell what was going on in that determined mind of his. He would have some compensation on account tonight and to hell with it. Already his pocket held something snatched up from the floor of the antechamber. And, I am ashamed to admit, my own intentions were leaning in that same direction.

A few moments later the dutiful Burton arrived.

"Harry. Do you think you can get a picture of that without moving anything?" I said, and waved my hand around the circumference of the discoloured plaster at the

base of the sealed doorway.

Burton regarded it for a moment and then began setting up his equipment, carefully placing the legs of his tripod on bare patches of the stone floor. One exposure; a fresh plate; one more exposure; then he dismantled his paraphernalia and prepared to leave. It must have taken him just fifteen minutes. All the while I observed Carnarvon in the shadows, pacing impatiently from one foot to the other.

"Thanks, Harry," I said. "You can photograph the rest of the stuff tomorrow. You go and get yourself a well-earned cocktail. We'll join you by and by."

I was anxious to get Burton to leave. In the cold light of day, the gesture may have seemed unnecessarily mean, but it was important to me to limit the number of persons with any knowledge of our forthcoming indiscretion. As those of us who are experienced in these matters well know, everyone has a very best friend with whom he may share a close secret, and that best friend will tell no one but another best friend who himself will tell no one and so on and so forth. The four of us presented a sufficient risk.

Burton did not linger. He had to make his way back to Luxor that evening in any case and was glad to be relieved of any further work. On his way, he left the exposed plates in tomb fifty-five. He was tired enough to trust to luck and leave developing them until the morning.

Within seconds of Burton's departure, I armed myself with a chisel and quickly positioned myself close to the base of the sealed doorway. Crouching down between the two dusty sentinels, I began chipping away carefully at the bottom of the wall. I was conscious of at least five sets of eyes watching me at my work - those of my colleagues and those of the two wooden gilded black guards of death.

I reopened the robbers' hole only sufficient in height to admit myself. Pushing the mud bricks and debris behind me, I prepared to enter.

"Keep an eye on that. Don't forget any of it when we leave this place tonight. Every scrap must be replaced before we go. No one must ever know we have reopened this aperture. We can disguise the breach. It will not be difficult."

Carnarvon grinned broadly like the veritable Cheshire Cat. He was used to getting his way.

I felt a pressing need to lay down the law again. "Now... Before we investigate, some rules. Look before you take a step. We have only the one lamp. If the light be insufficient to show that the way is clear, do not take the step. Ask me to illuminate the area for you. Step only in areas where you can clearly see that the floor is clean - even of debris. Touch nothing. Last, and most important - take nothing. I must be allowed the time to accurately record everything we see in its original position." Pointless my saying it, I know, but it had to be said.

I got down on my side and dragged myself through the low opening. Fragments of dried mud brushed onto my tweed clothing as I pulled myself through. I pushed the torch ahead of me.

As I looked ahead, the reflection from my torch temporarily blinded me. To my utter astonishment and delight, the illumination from the torchlight glared back from what appeared to be nothing less than a massive wall of beaten and engraved gold *immediately in front of my face. I looked from side to side and up and down. The magnificent golden mural extended beyond my field of view in all directions. It was without question one of the outer walls of the shrine which should enclose the king's sarcophagus and, hopefully still within it, his coffin set.*

I was already in the burial chamber! I had Tutankhamen! The boy king lay within a foot or so of me! Can you imagine my excitement?

It suddenly dawned on me that I was forgetting my expectant colleagues. I pulled myself onward and inward only to discover I was about to fall. The floor of the burial chamber was deeper than that of the room I was entering from. I allowed myself to slide downward until I felt my outstretched fingers touch the chamber floor, and then walked along on my hands until the rest of my body was fully inside. This done, I sat upright and looked about myself to get my bearings.

There was a vessel just ahead on the floor and other objects beyond, but the area where I had settled was fortunately clear. I drew back a little and summoned the others to follow.

I could hear Carnarvon talking to Evelyn. "Never mind the dust, my dear. Frankly you are already pretty grubby. I will follow you directly."

Evelyn was way beyond caring about her general appearance, never mind the state of her clothing. She prostrated herself, her hands grasping at the edges of the aperture, and began to drag herself through.

As her head appeared, I whispered to her, "We have already found the burial chamber. Mind the drop when you enter. There is precious little space between the wall and the shrine, and the floor of the room is about a yard below you."

Since I had the torch pointed ahead of me, there was precious little light thrown behind my body, so on entering she must have found herself in almost total darkness. I moved on to the corner of the shrine and drew myself up to a standing position. With the torch held high above my head, I was able to illuminate the narrow passage Evelyn had been trying to negotiate in the darkness. While her skirt restricted her ability to manoeuvre, her more diminutive size permitted her much easier access than myself, and she was presently standing right beside me in the confined space.

Carnarvon's head appeared at the aperture. "This is damned difficult for an infirm man, Howard. Give me a hand, will you?"

I must additionally confess that, in my state of euphoria at the time, I for once felt uncharitably disinclined to go to my patron's aid. But I am glad to say that my inherent goodness triumphed over my bad side. I sidled along the wall until I was close to the earl and able to assist his lordship into the narrow gap between the flank of the golden shrine and the unyielding stone of the chamber wall. I helped Carnarvon to his feet.

"Where's Callender?" said the earl, once he was vertical.

"Here! Stuck! Damnation!" The words came from the man himself, positioned about one quarter into the opening and with nowhere to go.

"Too damn fat! Sorry to have to admit it, old boy, but there it is. Can't beat nature. Sins of gluttony have caught up with me at last, dammit. Too much beer and fish and chips!"

"Are you able to withdraw?" I called. It would have been more than embarrassing to

have been discovered here corked up, as it were, by my stuck-fast colleague!

"Of course, Howard. Don't worry. I'll keep watch with Adamson while you lot investigate. If I howl, you'd better come a-scurrying."

I think it was then that it finally dawned on Carnarvon. In his excitement, he hadn't heeded the possibilities. What if we had been discovered in the act of opening the holy sepulchre? I, however, had already considered the consequences and discounted the risks. No one in authority was likely to venture into The Valley that evening. And Adamson would make sure that any casual passers-by did just that, pass by.

"You shouldn't concern yourself, m'lord," I comforted. "I wouldn't have made any attempt at this were there any risk of discovery. You need not worry... I am making my way toward the east end of the shrine. That is where the doors should be. We shall be able to see whether they remain sealed. Take the greatest care. I implore you... Do not to touch anything," I repeated.

My two followers squeezed around the southeast corner, taking care not to brush against the painted wall and the side of the shrine, and to avoid some objects stacked against the wall. They were obliged to keep as close to me as they could. I held all the light they had to see by.

I could see another opening. "There is another low doorway around this corner, ahead and to our right. This one's totally open. High enough to walk through as long as y' stoop. Can't quite see what might be in there yet but..." Just then I saw it. "Damn! Damn and blast!"

I knelt down and placed the torch upright on the floor. Hyperboles of light reflected brightly off the embossed gold sheeting covering the doors to the outer shrine. As I turned to my expectant colleagues, the golden light threw eerie, rippling shadows across their faces.

"Possibly bad news. No seals! There are no seals! Someone has opened the shrine in antiquity."

"Why don't you withdraw the bolts and take a look inside, Howard?" Lady Evelyn, also crouching, was peering around her father's flank.

"No, Lady Evelyn. We are taking sufficient risk as it is. I do not want to leave indelible marks that could betray our early entry. Let us just leave everything as we find it. We shall know these answers soon enough."

I was more cross that things might be disturbed inside the shrine. But the body had to be there, unless the shrine had been built over an empty space. I recalled the empty coffin in the 'Tomb of the Horse'. I shook my head in disbelief. This just could not happen to me again!

"Besides, whoever it was can't have taken anything of any size through that small opening. Even we had trouble squeezing through it. Tutankhamen will be whole. I am certain of it. Providing he was put here in the first place!"

I began to find the old, stale atmosphere in the chamber uncomfortable to breathe and started coughing again. The noise echoed, it seemed to me, from everywhere. It startled my colleagues so much that Carnarvon jumped and Evelyn fell back onto her bottom, luckily onto nothing more than the dusty stone floor. I picked up the torch which Carnarvon had just kicked over and, bending down so I could see better, turned to look behind him into the additional room.

It was my turn to be startled. Right in front of me, no more than a yard from my face, and confronting me directly, was a somewhat larger than life-size black Anubis jackal covered in a dull, dusty and insect-eaten shawl. Its head was in the style of the period - erect and alert with enormous, gold-tinted ears pointing vertically upward. The torchlight picked out the dark, obsidian eyes. They seemed to flash sternly back at me. I must have stood there transfixed for some seconds.

My impatient friends had to tap me on the shoulder to get my attention.

"Whatever is it, Howard?" Evelyn, heavily intoxicated with excitement, giggled in the darkness behind me.

"Come and look, Lady Evelyn, your lordship. We are confronted by the king's guardian, Anubis. What a magnificent beast. His like I have only seen in a damaged and parlous state before - that recovered from the tomb of Horemheb."

Our eyes were by now well accustomed to the pale light thrown by the single torch, and we all could see quite plainly that in the room ahead of us the dog, lying prone on a shrine of its own, sat in guard on a host of objects of all shapes and sizes placed in orderly, serried ranks about the room. The most commanding object lay behind the dog - the most beautiful creation I had ever set eyes on - a large golden box framed within a gilded portico which rose almost to the ceiling. On its roof was a frieze of brightly coloured cobras, and facing each of the visible walls the slight, golden figure of a goddess with her arms outstretched in a gesture of protection. In front of this shrine stood the golden head of a bull with tall, upright, ebonised horns. Boxes and boats were stacked everywhere in profusion.

A truly fabulous treasure trove! We adventurous three stood in silent amazement.

As I carefully observed the entire room, I remained speechless. Eventually I drew breath to steady myself and gestured with my finger. "The canopic chest... A true treasury... Everything looks complete, if not a little rearranged... And no exit... I believe... Yes... This could be all there is."

Carnarvon interjected curtly, "Just listen to yourself, Howard. That last comment of yours must go down in the history books as the greatest understatement of all time!"

"Bless my soul, sir! Well. Yes. That it probably is!" I quickly responded smiling.

Then, after a brief pause, I said, "My friends. Take the time to drink in this moment. You will never experience its like again."

I was deadly serious. Surely they must have shared the sheer intensity of it - discovery of this sacred place, its violation, the silent, illicit entry, sharing the stale air of millennia, the enormity of intimate contact with so distant and uncorrupted a past - in recent times at least.

"Have a good, long look," I continued, "at what it is you are seeing, your lordship, Lady Evelyn. Commit it to indelible memory. Remember for ever this first view. We shall not see this repeated within our lifetime... perhaps anybody's lifetime." I truly believed that, and still do.

So saying, with all the drama that this moment so excellently afforded, I raised the torch above my shoulder and behind my two craning companions so that its jaundiced light brushed the interior of the room before us.

485

There we surreptitious explorers stood, in absolute silence, viewing and reviewing the inventory of objects laid out before us. While Evelyn and her father individually picked out a few pieces of special interest and examined them in detail from a distance, I methodically registered each piece presented within my field of view.

There on the left, behind the figure of Anubis, stood rows of boxes probably containing jewellery and personal items of clothing and toilet. Many of the boxes appeared to have been opened at one time and hurriedly repacked - the contents partially spilling from beneath the lids. Some lay open, their lids missing.

In the corner was a large model boat and, on the right of the canopic chest, multiple rows of wooden shrine caskets. There had to be figures inside. And stacked above them I could count eight, maybe nine more model boats. Then my eyes fell back on the chest and the gentle golden figures holding it in the protective embrace of their slender, extended arms. There were two figures visible, each facing inwards on the two visible walls of the shrine, each looking towards one corner. From where I was standing, they looked like they were both about three or four feet high. By the insignia on their heads, I could tell they represented the goddesses of the south and of the west. Their counterparts would stand likewise against the sides which were as yet hidden from us.

Our silence was broken by a distant, anxious voice. "Carter! Carnarvon! Lady Evelyn! Can anybody hear me?"

It was Callender.

"Of course, Pecky!" I yelled back with some irritation. I found the interruption irreverent. "What is it?"

"Oh... nothing... Just wondered where the hell you'd all got to. It has been so quiet for so long. Thought you could have fallen down a well or something."

I turned to my colleagues smiling. They all laughed. It was a blessed release to the tension that had gripped us all since we had first scrambled through that tiny opening into the king's chamber. Callender's concern was understandable.

"The tomb is small, Pecky. But the wonderful bounty continues! We're on our way back. Be with you and relate what we have seen in a moment."

I turned to his lordship. "We must not overstay our trespass, your lordship - for trespass it surely is. I believe we have seen enough to be able to plan our investigation with some degree of accuracy. That is something which we should now set our minds to diligently and with some urgency these next few days. I can already see that our good fortune is to become an enormous duty. We are charged with the responsibility to complete our excavations here correctly, as befits the bounty so fortunately bestowed on us... If you both now would be good enough to return the way we came, I shall try to negotiate my way around the other side of the king's shrine to see if there is another chamber. I'd rather you did not come with me, if you don't mind. There are a lot of objects on the floor and more feet will only increase the risk of damage or dislodgement. I will meet you on the other side."

Carnarvon and Evelyn reluctantly left me to rejoin Callender. I shone the way for them with my torch until both had disappeared through the robbers' hole.

In picking my way carefully around the walls of the shrine, I found no evidence of further openings. For a moment I felt disappointment, but soon pulled myself together in rationalising my extreme good fortune. My lack of perspective was almost comical.

I returned to my colleagues by way of the small opening in the burial chamber wall.
"Nothing else. Just the one room.

"Come, help me, I have to replace the bricks. Gather up some straw, Lady Evelyn.
We must cover up evidence of the breach. The place has to appear undisturbed. Pecky,
pass me that raffia basket lid, please."

I placed the raffia lid over the hole and piled some dried reeds around it. After
making a quick note of their position, I pushed some small alabaster vessels in amongst
the straw to give the illusion of original chaos. We removed all traces of our footprints
by brushing the floor of the chamber with our hands and, one by one, we clambered
through the hole in the antechamber doorway and back into the entrance corridor.

I felt much like a naughty boy exiting the apple orchard with my hoard. I daresay
the others felt much the same. The illicit intrusion had been wonderful but, I confess,
emotionally exhausting. There was the added physical fatigue. The sense of relief at
being once more outside... It was overwhelming.

He tightend his grip on the little horse and raised his eyes to stare up at the ceiling. The room had darkened about him. It had become almost ebony black. He felt heavy, as heavy as that brick on the mantlepiece, but at the same time warm, comfortably warm. A sense of peaceful satisfaction descended on him. His eyelids fluttered for a moment and then closed.

Then, in the darkness, like diamonds, a few bright stars began to sparkle. There was a pattern to them. He recognised it immediately. It was the constellation of Orion. As he watched, the envelope of the seven stars loomed above him... ever larger... ever brighter. As they grew nearer, he began to make out a figure standing within the central star. The figure was dressed in brilliant white linen which tightly conformed to the shape of its body. On its head it wore a tall, white crown. In its clasped hands, crossed against its chest, it held the emblems of kingship. Gradually it grew closer, finally enclosing him in its comforting celestial embrace...

Putney Vale Cemetery, 19th April, 1939...

It is a fresh, sun-bathed April day. New growth pushes up through the ground everywhere. Blossoms fill the trees. Flowers of all colours line the cultivated borders of the parks. The air is filled with birdsong. It is one of those days when, no matter what your troubles, it feels good to be a part of the boundless energy all about you.

She had returned to plant some more permanent blossoms on his grave. The remains of the bouquets, limp and curled in on themselves by a late frost, lie in tatters over the low mound. She clears away the dead material and, using a trowel she had brought in a carrier bag, she makes a number of holes in the earth. She plants the bulbs, carefully pressing them into the soft soil and thinly covering them. She weeds the remainder of the area and stands back to regard her accomplishment. 'Next year, it will look much nicer,' she thought.

"Miss Dalgliesh!"

The call is from her left, within the walls of the graveyard. Startled to hear her name called out, she turns in the direction of the sound.

Two gentlemen emerge from beneath the low-hanging branches of a mature copper beech.

"H'it is Miss Dalgliesh, is it not?"

She is a little apprehensive at first but her face soon lights up with a broad smile of recognition. "Bless my soul, Sergeant Adamson! It is so good to see you. What a most pleasant surprise. He will be so happy you are here." She looks in the direction of the grave.

The two walk up to her.

"Miss Dalgliesh, may h'I introduce Father Seamus. A h'old acquaintance of poor Mr Carter."

"Father Seamus," she acknowledges. "I don't believe I've had the pleasure..."

"Oi'm most pleased t' meet you after all this toime, Miss Dalgliesh. Howard spoke of you so often. Oi 'ave come to know y' well Oi t'ink."

Dorothy expresses her embarrassment with a nervous nod.

"Happy he may be to see us, Miss Dalgliesh, t' be sure, but Oi'm unhappy in meself for not being d' one t' administer his last roights, as 'twere."

"Frankly, Father, I don't think he needed them. I hope I don't offend by saying so but perhaps, knowing him as you did, you will understand my meaning."

488

"Oi t'ink so, an' roight enough, Miss," agrees the priest. "Oh. Are y' still 'Miss' Dalgliesh?"

That embarrassed nod again. "Yes. For a while I did take another name but now I am 'Miss Dalgliesh' once again."

Adamson clicks to attention and chimes in. "H'it's a real h'onour t' be 'ere, Miss. World won't see the like of 'im again, an' that's a fact."

All three look down at the grave and nod appreciatively.

"Tell me, Father, Sergeant, why did you not come to the service?"

"Out of d' country. Anyway, not invited, Miss."

"Me neither," says Dorothy. "Didn't stop me, however."

"Well, moi dear, when all's said an' done, y' can't 'ave two priests at a funeral. T'other would feel d' pressure of me presence, if y' know what Oi means - competition." The priest winks.

"H'at least we're 'ere t' see where 'e's safely put away," adds Adamson. "For 'is achievements 'e deserved a fifty-one gun salute, an' no mistake. Grumpy old bastard - forgive me language, Miss - 'e may 'ave been at times, but h'I respects 'im more van any h'uver."

Seamus ignores the sergeant and continues, "Dere's anoder reason why Oi'm glad Oi came across you, Miss Dorot'y. Oi've recently returned from Egypt and Oi am d' bearer of a letter which Oi believe should be delivered to Howard's niece - a Miss Walker, isn't it?"

"Yes. Phyllis. She took care of him during his final illness."

"Could y' give this to 'er, please? Oi'm gettin' too old for foindin' me way around big cities loike dis. Oi'm told she lives around dese parts."

"Marble Arch. But, to tell you the truth, although I have met her on one occasion, we are not even so close as to be called acquaintances. I'll be glad to do it but, if it's all the same to you, I will just pass it through her letter box."

"Dat's just foin. T'ank you Miss."

Seamus hands her the letter.

"Now, can Oi tempt y' to a wee drinkie, Miss Dorot'y, before we part company? Sergeant Adamson an' me, we feels a wee bit of a t'irst comin' upon us. De atmosphere in cemeteries fair drois d' trote."

Dorothy smiles. "Oh, that is very sweet of you, Father, but I must be getting back. I am presently living out of town and have a train to catch, and before that... a letter to deliver." She waves the envelope at them. "I'd best be on my way."

Adamson calls after her, "Take care, Miss Dorofy. Don't speak to no Germans!"

The two men wave to her as she leaves the graveyard and then turn and walk over to the freshly turned grave. Standing on opposite sides of the low mound, they look down. The priest points to the grave with his walking stick.

"Not much of a 'tomb', Sergeant."

"No, Father. Not much at all. All 'e would 'ave expected, though, I'll be bound."

"Oi'm not so sure, Sergeant. Oi t'ink 'e would 'ave loiked to 'ave been buried in d' bowels of d' earth loike all dose 'e did 'is best to remove from deir place of eternal sleep. Oi t'ink 'e would 'ave wanted 'is own food, 'is Scotch an' soda, 'is gin an' tonic, 'is champagne, 'is smokes, 'is 'omburg, 'is tweeds, 'is suede shoes, 'is bow ties, 'is furniture, 'is car, 'is 'orse, 'is pets, 'is books and 'is notebooks, 'is memories and 'is artefacts about 'im."

"Per'aps. Per'aps not. Don't forget, h'I spent dozens of days an' nights cooped up in that 'ole in the ground. Bloody spooky it was. Bloody glad t' get away. 'E spent nigh on 'arf a year in h'every one of nine effin' years in that 'ole in the ground. I don't fink 'e wants t' go back. No effin' way... Yer reverent." Adamson lowers his eyes apologetically.

Father Seamus smiles in acknowledgement and tips his hat to the grave. Adamson crosses himself.

The priest regards him for a moment. "Don't look so forlorn. It's not far. Oi noticed one on d' way in - about a hundret yards from d' gate."

Adamson's florid face lights up and the two set off for the nearest public house.

Dorothy takes a cab to Phyllis Walker's address. Drawing up outside the house, she asks the cabbie to wait. She steps up to the front door, quickly pops the letter through the letter box, returns to the cab, and takes off for the station. There will be no second meeting.

On her way to Carter's niece's house she noticed that the envelope was not sealed. She did not resist the temptation to read it. *(The text of the letter is quoted in James, 1992).*

Flinders Petrie leans over the table in the reading room of the University College library and folds the first page of *The Times* back on itself. There is too much talk of warmongering for his tired eyes. He turns the pages one by one until he comes to the obituaries. The print is small and he pushes his reading glasses further down his nose so that he can focus a little better.

He rests back in his chair. There it is - a suitably brief paragraph.

He reflects on the well-publicised man he had trained all those years ago. He is proud of his younger colleague's archaeological achievements - exceptionally proud. For an individual from a working-class background, lacking in scholarly training, breeding, and every quality of etiquette and tact, he had, after all said and done, acquitted himself remarkably well in his work.

The great Egyptologist smiles contentedly to himself. The grounding he had provided had been firm and suitably employed. Yes, he had done well by him.

He replaces the paper in its rack, picks up his walking cane and, with some difficulty, eases himself to his feet and walks slowly towards the exit. Helped into his taxi by the cabby, he is driven off into the teeming rain of a grey March day.

On the way home, he relaxes back into the leather rear seat and gazes unseeing through the misty window. The passing of his protégé is already a distant memory.

Petrie's mind turns to the sorry state of affairs in the world at large. He had weathered one world war. The thought of another is more than he cares to contemplate, let alone wish to live through.

Thankfully, there are more pleasant things to look forward to - a return to his beloved Jerusalem. But first, a neat malt whisky, followed by a hearty supper, followed by slippers, his usual armchair, a roaring hearth, another malt, and bed - the seven wonders of the world!

It does not occur to the old scholar to pay his respects at Carter's funeral, nor will he visit the gravesite. For the lesser man, that kind of acknowledgement remains outside acceptable convention. It is wholly unimportant.

And meantime, in his otherwise spartan afterlife, Horemheb, for his own amusement, has some time since turned his mind to the encouragement and support of one rather short and severe looking man from Austria.

GLOSSARY

Ab The heart. Closely associated with the soul. Essential it was kept within the body. In amulet form represented as a scarab beetle.

Akh The resurrected body in a parallel existence; not a part of the earth of the living.

Amulet Talisman - decorative object of protection, possessing magical powers. The ancient Egyptians had no conception of repentance; rather they would in death cover their sins with as many of these objects as they felt necessary to eliminate all visible evidence.

Amun (Amun-Re) King of the Gods. Several forms. Usually represented in the form of a human male with a ram's head and wearing a double-plumed crown. Often described as 'mysterious of form', implying that the god's true identity could never be revealed.

Ankh Amulet representing 'long' life. Symbol most commonly associated with the Pharaoh and the Gods.

Anubis God of the dead. Form of a black jackal. Most often associated with the embalming ritual and there depicted as a human male with a dog's head.

Aperu Peasant, slave (lower) class.

Aten God of the sun. Form of a disc. In the time of Akhenaten, the 'sole God'. Thereafter removed and replaced by Amun.

Ba One of the body's five distinct parts. Its soul. Form of a bird with human head. Able to bear the deceased from the tomb and return each night.

Bastet Daughter of the sun god. Form of a cat. Sometimes represented as a human female with the head of a cat, particularly later; from the first millenium BC
Bes Demonic protector God. Form of a dwarf with a protruding tongue.

Burnous Long circular hooded cloak.

Canopic jar/chest Vessels/containers for the viscera removed during mummification.

Cartouche Pharaoh's name. Hieroglyphs contained within a pseudo-elliptical boundary representing a rope tied at one end.

Chapters of coming forth by Day (Book of Gates/Book of the Dead) Funerary texts. Spells to help the deceased on his journey through the afterlife.

Cubit About 0.5 metres, or 0.45 yards.

Decauville railway Narrow gauge portable track on which the rolling stock is manhandled.

Djed pillar Amulet representing stability. The backbone of Osiris.

Faience Ceramic material composed of crushed quartz or quartz sand with small amounts of lime and plant ash or natron. Mixed with water before moulding and fired with glazing material to form a blue glaze.

Faiyum Lake province on the west side and fed by the Nile, situated about fifty miles southwest of Cairo.

False door Literally that. A part of the architecture of many tombs and mortuary temples. A place to lay offerings to the dead.

Fellah An Arab peasant/labourer.

Foundation deposits Buried caches of ritual objects placed in the vicinity of corners, axes or gateways of tombs and mortuary temples.

Geb God of the earth. Form of a human male; sometimes ithyphallic. Responsible for vegetation. His sister and wife was Nut. Their offspring was Osiris.

Hapy God of inundation. Form of a fat human male with headdress of aquatic plants.

Hathor God mother of each reigning king. Form of a bovine, or of a human female with headdress of a wig with horns and a disc held between them. Usually associated with the pleasurable aspects of life. Each evening she received the setting sun and protected it until morning.

Heh God of infinity. Form of a human male kneeling with a palm rib in each hand. Represented longevity.

Heket Goddess of childbirth. Form of a frog. Assisted the dead in their journey to the sky, and in the latter stages of labour.

Henmemet Gentry, aristocratic (upper) class.

Hieroglyph Ancient Egyptian pictographic writing

Horus God of the sky. Form of a hawk or human male with falcon head. Protector of the Pharaoh.

Isis Goddess of motherhood. Form of a human female with crown of cow horns surrounding a disc, identical to Hathor. Symbolic mother of the Pharaoh. She had medical powers. One of the protectors of the dead king's coffin and viscera.

Ithyphallic A modern term normally used to describe dieties with an erect penis; in particular Amun and Min.

Ka One of the body's five distinct parts. The double of the dead person. Form of a male with two raised arms on his head. Could move about independently and inhabit any statuesque likeness of the king, remaining earthbound.

Khaibit The shadow. Closely associated with the soul. Could move about independently.

Khat The physical body.

Khedive Premier of the turn of the nineteenth century in Egypt.

Khepri God of creation. Form of a scarab beetle. Closely associated with resurrection.

Khnum. God of pottery (creation). Form of a human male with a ram's head.

Khons. God of the moon. Form of human mummy wearing the sidelock of youth. Associated with childbirth.

Khu The spirit. Closely associated with the soul.

Maat Goddess of truth. Form of a seated human female wearing an ostrich feather. Believed to regulate the seasons, the movement of the stars, and the relations between men and gods. Also a term used for the 'ideal' state for which the Pharaoh was the responsible keeper.

Magic bricks. Four mud bricks placed on four sides of the tomb to protect the deceased from evil.

Mahdi 'The chosen one' in Islamic belief.

Min God of fertility. Form of an ithyphallic human male. Symbol of male potency.

Montu God of war. Form of human male with head of a falcon with a headdress of a sun disc and two plumes.

Moudir Regional chief.

Mut God mother of each reigning king (like Hathor). Form of a human female wearing a vulture headdress surmounted by the double crown of Upper and Lower Egypt.

Natron Natural evaporitic salts mined locally and used for dessicating the cadaver.

Nefertem God of the lotus blossom. Form of a human male with lotus flower headdress.

Neith Goddess of creation. Form of a human female with the red crown of Lower Egypt. One of the protectors of the dead king's coffin and viscera.

Nekhbet Goddess of kingship. Form of a vulture. Appeared on royal headdress next to the Uraeus.

Nemes Royal.

Nephthys Goddess of protection. Form of a human female with hieroglyph headdress. One of the protectors of the dead king's coffin and viscera.

Nomen The birth name of the Pharaoh. As used for the subject of this book: Tutankhamun, or Tutankhamen.

Nun God of the primeval waters. Form of a bearded human male holding up the solar barque.

Nut Goddess of the sky; the vault of heaven. Form of a naked human female. Every evening she swallowed the setting sun and every morning gave birth to the rising sun.

Opening of the mouth Ritual by which the deceased and the funerary statuary were brought to life. Usually carried out by the dead king's heir, ritually touching all the sensory parts of the mummy with an adze-like instrument. Transforms the mummy into a vessel for the Ka.

Osiris (Osiride) God of death, resurrection and fertility. Form of a human male mummy with hands projecting through the wrappings holding the royal crook and flail. Unlike Ptah, the mummy wears the tall white crown of Upper Egypt flanked by two large feather plumes on its head. One of the most important deities of ancient Egypt. The Osiris legend is perhaps the most bizarre of all Egyptian stories - of murder, dismemberment and dispersal, collection and reconstruction of the remains, ultimately returning the body to life.

Ostraca Limestone chips used for recording notes.

Perfume cone Coloured cone of incense mixed with fat worn by ladies on top of their wigs to improve their odour and keep insects at bay. During the heat of the day these would gradually melt down and mat the entire wig.

Prenomen The throne name of the Pharaoh. As used for the subject of this book: Nebkheperure.

Ptah God of creation. Form of a human male mummy with the hands protruding through the wrappings holding a staff. Unlike Osiris, the head is shaven and covered with a skullcap.

Ra God of the sun. Form of a human male with the head of a hawk wearing a sun disc headdress.

Reis Workers' supervisor.

Rekhit Artisan, learned (middle) class.

Ren The name of the king. If not preserved he would cease to exist.

Renenutet Goddess of protection and fertility. Form of a cobra, or human female with a cobra head.

Reshef God of war. Form of a bearded human male wearing the white crown of Upper Egypt with the head of a gazelle on the front and a ribbon hanging down the back.

Sahu The spiritual body. The habitation of the soul.

Satet Goddess of southern Egypt. Form of a human female wearing the white crown of Upper Egypt with antelope horns on either side. Wife of Khnum.

Scarab Dung beetle. Since the beetle's young were observed to emerge from the ball of dung - nothing more than body refuse - the beetle was believed to have the power of creation.

Sed festival Usually held on completion of the first thirty years of the Pharaoh's reign to renew the ageing Pharaoh. Celebrated at least every three years thereafter to continue the Pharaoh's revivification.

Sekhem The vital force of the king. Closely associated with the soul and the spirit.

Sekhmet Goddess of feminine power. Form of a human female with the head of a lioness.

Selket Goddess of magic. Form of a human female with scorpion headdress. One of the protectors of the dead king's coffin and viscera.

Seshat Goddess of writing and measurement. Form of a human female clad in a long panther-skin dress and wearing a headdress of a seven-pointed star and a bow.

Seth God of chaos and confusion. Form of a human male with the head of a mythical animal, long-nosed, with square ears and bared canine teeth, or as a hippopotamus, pig or donkey. He was the son of Nut, brother of Osiris, and the evil side of the Osiris legend. Physically manifested in storms and bad weather.

Shu Son of Re. God of the air and sunlight. Form of a human male wearing a plume or sun disc headdress.

Sistrum Hand-held musical instrument similar to a rattle.

Sobek God of the sun. Form of a crocodile or human male with crocodile's head wearing a headdress of the horned sun disc and upright feathers.

Sokar God of the necropolis at Memphis. Form of a mummy with the head of a hawk.

Solar barque The deceased was carried on this on his journey through the netherworld.

Soped God of eastern Egypt. Form of a crouching falcon.

Sukh Market.
Taweret God of protection. Form of a female hippopotamus. Protected women during childbirth.

Tefnut Goddess of moisture. Form of a human female with the head of a lioness.

Toth God of writing and knowledge. Form of either a baboon or an ibis or a human male with the head of an ibis.

Unguent Ointment.

Uraeus Rearing cobra. Symbol of kingship. Normally adorning the headdress.

Ushabti Mummiform figurine, usually small. Placed in tomb as servants to the dead. There were 413 found in the tomb of Tutankhamun - a worker for every day of the year, a supervisor for every ten workers, plus one senior supervisor for every month of the year.

Utchat Eyes of Horus; the sun and the moon.

Vizier Governmental official with responsibilities and powers similar to those of a modern-day Prime Minister as he relates to the Queen but under the orders of the Pharaoh and without any military power.

Wadjyt Goddess of kingship. Form of a cobra. Appeared on royal headdress next to the Nekhbet. Sometimes appeared as a human female with the head of a lioness surmounted by a cobra and sun disc.

Was sceptre Slender cane with a head similar in form to that of an ibex, at the other end a bifurcated base. As common an accompaniment of the Pharaoh and the gods as the ankh. In association with the ankh and djed pillar, a symbol of life, stability and power. Recently interpreted to be a representation of an extracted bull's penis and may, on occasion, have been made from such.

Window of Appearances A specially prepared 'balcony' where the Pharaoh, with or without the royal family, would present himself to the public.

Bibliography

Aldred, Cyril, *Akhenaten King of Egypt* Thames & Hudson (London, 1988).

Allenby, General Sir Edmund H. H., *A Brief Record of The Advance of the Egyptian Expeditionary Force*, Government Press and Survey of Egypt, (Cairo, 1919).

Aufrere, S. and Golvin, J.-Cl., *L'Egypte Restitutee*, Tomes 1, 2 & 3 Editions, Errance, (Paris, 1997).

Baines, John and Malek, Jaromir, *Atlas of Ancient Egypt*, Andromeda, (Oxford, 1980).

Belzoni, Giovani, *Fruits of Enterprise exhibited in the Adventures of Belzoni in Egypt and Nubia; with an Account of his discoveries in the Pyramids, among the Ruins of Cities, and in the Ancient Tombs*, rev. ed. NY, Charles S. Francis, Boston, Joseph H. Francis, (New York, 1842).

Bierbrier, Morris, *The Tomb-Builders of the Pharaohs*, Charles Scribner's Sons, (New York, 1984).

Breasted, Charles, *Pioneer to the Past* Charles Scribner's Sons, (New York, 1943).

Breasted, James Henry, *A History of Egypt*, Charles Scribner's Sons, (New York, 1937).

Budge, E. A. Wallis, *The Dwellers on the Nile: Chapters on the Life, History, Religion and Literature of the Ancient Egyptians,* The Religious Tract Society, (London, 1926).

Budge, E. A. Wallis and King, L. W., "The Book of the Dead" in *Books on Egypt and Chaldaea, Vols. VI - VIII,* Kegan Paul, Trench, Trubner & Co, (London, 1901).

Capel, Anne K. and Markoe, Glenn E., (eds.) *Mistress of the House, Mistress of Heaven: Women in Ancient Egypt,* Hudson Hills Press, (New York, 1997).

Carnarvon, The Earl of, and Howard Carter, *Five Years' Exploration at Thebes*, Henry Frowde, Oxford University Press, (Oxford, 1912).

Carter, Howard, *The Tomb of Tut.Ankh.Amen: Statement - With Documents, as to the events which occurred in Egypt in the winter of 1923 - 24, leading to the ultimate break with the Egyptian Government* (for private circulation only), Cassell & Company 1924, in *Tut.Ankh.Amen - The Politics of Discovery* with an introduction by Nicholas Reeves, Libri Publications, (London, 1998).

Carter, Howard, *The Tomb of Tut.Ankh.Amen Volume Two*, Cassell & Company, (London, 1927).

Carter, Howard, *The Tomb of Tut.Ankh.Amen Volume Three*, Cassell & Company, (London, 1932).

Carter, Howard and Mace, A. C., *The Tomb of Tut.Ankh.Amen Volume One*, Cassell & Company, (London, 1923).

Clayton, Peter A., *Chronicle of the Pharaohs. The Reign-by-Reign Record of the Rulers and Dynasties of Ancient Egypt*, Thames & Hudson, (London, 1994).

Cromer, Earl of, *Modern Egypt*, MacMillan & Co., (London, 1911).

Davis, Theodore M., *The Tomb of Hatshopsitu*, Archibald Constable and Company, (London, 1906).

Davis, Theodore M., *The Tomb of Iouiya and Touiyou*, Archibald Constable and Company, (London, 1907).

Davis, Theodore M., *The Tomb of Queen Tiyi*, Archibald Constable and Company, (London, 1910).

Davis, Theodore M., *The Tombs of Harmhabi and Touatankhamanou*, Constable and Company, (London, 1912).

Desroches-Noblecourt, Christiane, *Tutankhamen. Life and Death of a Pharaoh*, Penguin Books, (London, 1989).

Edwards, I. E. S., *Tutankhamun: His Tomb and its Treasures*, The Metropolitan Museum of Art, (New York, 1976).

Fletcher, Joann, *The Intimate Life of Amenhotep III*, Oxford University Press, (Oxford, 2000).

Forbes, Dennis C., *Tombs Treasures Mummies. Seven Great Discoveries of Egyptian Archaeology* KMT Communications, (Sebestopol, 1998).

Frayling, Christopher, *The Face of Tutankhamun*, Faber & Faber, (London, 1992).

Freed, Rita E., Markowitz, Yvonne J. and D'Auria Sue H., (eds.)., *Pharaohs of the Sun: Akhenaten, Nefertiti, Tutankhamen*, Bulfinch Press/Little, Brown and Company, (Boston, 1999).

Gardiner, Wilkinson. *The Ancient Egyptians - Their Life and Customs Volumes One and Two*, Random House, (London, 1996).

Gohary, Jocelyn, *Akhenaten's Sed-festival at Karnak*, Kegan Paul International, (London, 1992).

Hornung, Erik, *Akhenaten and the Religion of Light*, trans. David Lorton, Cornell University Press, (Ithica, 1999).

Hornung, Erik, *The Tomb of Pharaoh Seti I photographed by Harry Burton*, Artemis Verlag, Zurich und Munchen, (Zurich, 1991), (Burton photographs by The Metropolitan Museum of Art, New York).

Hoving, Thomas, *Tutankhamun. The Untold Story*, Hoving Associates, (New York, 1978).

James, T. G. H. (ed.), *Excavating in Egypt. The Egypt Exploration Society 1882-1982*, The University of Chicago Press, (Chicago, 1982).

James, T. G. H., 'Cyril Aldred 1914 - 1991', *The Times* (obituary), (London, 1991).

James, T. G. H., *Howard Carter. The Path to Tutankhamun*, Kegan Paul International (London, 1992).

James, T. G. H., *Egypt Revealed. Artist-Travellers in an Antique Land*, The Folio Society, (London, 1997).

KMT, *A Modern Journal of Ancient Egypt*, KMT Communications, (Sebastopol, 1999 - 2000).

Lawrence, T. E., *Seven Pillars of Wisdom: a Triumph,* Doubleday, Doran & Company,. (New York, 1935).

McDowall, A.G., *Village Life in Ancient Egypt*, Oxford University Press (Oxford, 1999).

Mahdy, Christine el, *Tutankhmen: The Life and Death of a Boy King,* Headline Book Publishing, (London, 1999).

Moran, William L., *The Amarna Letters*, The Johns Hopkins University Press, (Baltimore, 1992).

Naville, Edouard, *The Temple of Deir el Bahari*, introductory memoir and 6 vols. (London 1894-1908).

Newberry, Percy E. and Griffith, F. L., *El Bersheh Parts I & II,* The Egypt Exploration Fund, (London, 1892).

Ordnance Survey, *Thetford Forest in The Brecks*, Ordnance Survey, (Southampton, 1999).

Petrie, Sir William Flinders, *Seventy Years in Archaeology*, Sampson Low, Marston & Co, (London, 1935).

Redford, Donald B., (ed.) *The Oxford Encyclopedia of Ancient Egypt*, Oxford University Press, (Oxford, 2001).

Reeves, Nicholas, *The Complete Tutankhamun*, Thames & Hudson, (London, 1990).

Reeves, Nicholas and Taylor, John H., *Howard Carter before Tutankhamun*, British Museum, (London, 1992).

Reeves, Nicholas and Wilkinson, Richard H., *The Complete Valley of the Kings*, Thames & Hudson, (London, 1996).

Romer, John, *Ancient Lives*, Weidenfeld & Nicolson (London, 1984).

Romer, John, *Valley of the Kings: Exploring the Tombs of the Pharaohs*, Henry Holt & Co., (London, 1989).

Shaw, Ian and Nicholson, Paul, in association with The British Museum, *The Dictionary of Ancient Egypt*, Harry N. Abrams, Inc., (London, 1995).

Strudwick, Nigel and Strudwik, Helen, *Thebes in Egypt*, Cornell University Press, (Ithica,1999).

Tutankhamun's Tomb Series, Griffith Institute, Oxford University Press (Chronological order):
I - *A handlist to Howard Carter's Catalogue of Objects in Tutankhamun's Tomb*, compiled by Helen Murray and Mary Nuttall, (Oxford, 1963).
II - *Hieratic Inscriptions from the Tomb of Tutankhamun*, by Jaroslav Cerny, (Oxford, 1965).
III - *Composite Bows from the Tomb of Tutankhamun*, by W. McLeod, (Oxford, 1970).
V - *The Human Remains from the Tomb of Tutankhamun*, by F. Filce Leek, (Oxford, 1972).
VI - *Musical Instruments from the Tomb of Tutankhamun* by Lise Manniche, (Oxford, 1976).
IV - *Self Bows and other Archery Tackle from the Tomb of Tutankhamun*, by W. McLeod, (Oxford, 1982).
VII - *Game-Boxes and Accessories from the Tomb of Tutankhamun*, by W. J. Tait, (Oxford, 1982).
VIII - *Chariots and Related Equipment from the Tomb of Tutankhamun*, by M. A. Littauer and J. H. Crouwel, (Oxford, 1985).
- *The Small Golden Shrine from the Tomb of Tutankhamun*, by M. Eaton-Krauss and E. Graefe, (Oxford, 1985).
IX - *Model Boats from the Tomb of Tutankhamun*, by Dilwyn Jones, (Oxford, 1990).
- *The Sarcophagus in the Tomb of Tutankhamun*, by M. Eaton-Krauss, (Oxford, 1993).
- *Stone Vessels, Pottery and Sealings from the Tomb of Tutankhamun*, by Ali Abdel Rahman, Hassanain el-Khouli, Rostislav Holthoer, Colin A. Hope, Olaf E. Kaper, Edited by John Baines, (Oxford, 1993).

Tyldesley, Joyce, *Hatchepsut, The Female Pharaoh*, Penguin Books,. (London, 1998).

Tyldesley, Joyce, *Nefertiti, Egypt's Sun Queen*, Penguin Books, (New York, 1999).

van den Boorn, GPF, *The Duties of the Vizier - Civil Administration in the Early New Kingdom*, Kegan Paul International, (London, 1988).

Watterson, Barbara, *Gods of Ancient Egypt*, Sutton Publishing, (London, 1996).

Weigall, Arthur, *Tutankhamen and other Essays*, Thornton Butterworth, (London, 1923).

Weeks, Kent R. (ed.) *Atlas of the Valley of the Kings*, The American University in Cairo Press, (Cairo, 2000).

Winlock, H. E., *Excavations at Deir el Bahri: 1911 - 1931*, Macmillan, (New York, 1935).

Wynne, Barry, *Behind the Mask of Tutankhamen*, Taplinger Publishing, (New York, 1973).

www.apexpublishing.co.uk